F   Andersen, Kurt,
Andersen   1954-

            Heyday.

ALSO BY KURT ANDERSEN

The Real Thing
Turn of the Century

HEYDAY

RANDOM HOUSE

NEW YORK

HEYDAY

a novel

—→•←—

KURT ANDERSEN

Heyday is a work of historical fiction. Apart from the well-known actual people, events, and locales that figure in the narrative, all names, characters, places, and incidents are the products of the author's imagination or are used fictitiously. Any resemblance to current events or locales, or to living persons, is entirely coincidental.

Published in the United States by Random House, an imprint of The Random House Publishing Group, a division of Random House, Inc., New York.

RANDOM HOUSE and colophon are registered trademarks of Random House, Inc.

ISBN 978-0-375-50473-0

Library of Congress Cataloging-in-Publication Data

Andersen, Kurt.
Heyday : a novel / Kurt Andersen.
p. cm.
ISBN-13: 978-0-375-50473-0
ISBN-10: 0-375-50473-7
1. United States—History—1815–1861—Fiction. 2. California—History—
1846–1850—Fiction. I. Title.

PS3551.N3455W66 2006

813'.54—dc22   2006045165

Printed in the United States of America on acid-free paper

www.atrandom.com

4 6 8 9 7 5

Designed by Stephanie Huntwork

Fic.

FOR KATE AND LUCY

America is a land of wonders, in which everything is in constant motion and every change seems an improvement. . . . No natural boundary seems to be set to the efforts of man; and in his eyes what is not yet done is only what he has not yet attempted to do.

—ALEXIS DE TOCQUEVILLE, *Democracy in America,* 1835

. . .

If I venture to displace, by even the billionth part of an inch, the microscopical speck of dust which lies now upon the point of my finger, what is the character of that act upon which I have adventured? I have done a deed which shakes the Moon in her path, which causes the Sun to be no longer the Sun, and which alters forever the destiny of the multitudinous myriads of stars that roll and glow in the majestic presence of their Creator.

—EDGAR ALLAN POE, *Eureka,* 1848

Part

ONE

1

April 27, 1848
. . .
New York City

BENJAMIN KNOWLES WOBBLED into the New World. He hadn't stood on solid ground for nearly two weeks, and as he stepped from the gangway onto the Cunard pier he felt shaky. The adventure continued! Albeit for the moment in a place called New Jersey. Until an hour before, he had never heard of New Jersey.

But after a few moments he found his feet and spoke to his first American on American soil, the ship's assistant bursar, a man with a swollen red nose standing at a portable blue cabinet. He took one of Ben's £5 coins and counted out American money in exchange—a ten-dollar gold piece, two five-dollar gold pieces, and a silver dollar.

"Trade you *four* good Lady Libertys for just *one* of *your* girl," the man said as he clicked and rubbed his dirty thumbnail across Victoria's face, winked, then placed the four coins one at a time in Ben's palm.

Ben stared at his new money. Each of the coins carried a portrait of Liberty, and all were extremely shiny.

"Plus your three cents for the ferry and another besides." As the man dribbled the pennies onto the gold, he glanced behind Ben at some commotion near the gangway. "That foreign fella seems to be wanting *you* pretty bad, sir . . ."

What?

Ben spun around, suddenly in a freak, his heart in his throat, imagining the worst—

But it was only Mr. Memmo, his fellow passenger, held up by an immigration agent skeptical of his true nationality.

"Mr. *Knowles*," Memmo shouted, "because I am delayed here, I must say the fondest farewell to you just *now*—so off to our Gotham on your own, eh?"

Ben took a deep breath and waved goodbye. "Gotham"! It was a word he had read only in books.

The day seemed sunnier than any in London ever, and the river smelled sweet in comparison with the Thames. As his ferry, the *Davy Crockett*, chugged from New Jersey toward Manhattan, it passed through a flotilla of market boats sailing in every direction, dozens of sloops and schooners piled with sturgeon and lettuce and peaches and husked corn, the *Coxsackie* packed to the decks with snow-white lime and the *Doctor Faustus* with ten-gallon cans of milk, the *Favorite* full of dead ducks and the *Revenge* carrying live spring lambs. The river was so wide that each of the smaller craft   other ferries, a longboat here, a flat bottomed launch there, cutters and yawls and even a few little punts—was apparently free to plot its own course at any angle it wished, channels and charts be damned. One big side-wheel steamer called the *Novelty* was pulling away from a pier straight ahead as another, the *Intelligence*, steamed in for a landing from the north, its puffy tails of black smoke and white steam extending almost the whole width of the river like some heavenly bridge.

The *Davy Crockett*'s engine slowed. Ben was at the bow, bags in hand. At the next pier over, cotton was being unloaded from a Charleston steamer. He wondered if these very bales might now be shipped across the Atlantic to his father's mills in Lancashire. The year Ben had worked there, the arriving American cotton bales had always reminded him of coffins—coffins in a dream, white and soft and impossibly heavy. This morning they looked only like cotton.

Ben stepped off and wandered into the confusion.

He looked and listened and smelled more acutely than he ever had before. His preconceptions were already sloughing away as the actual America, bit by vivid bit, began to replace accreted years of wishful speculation. His last look at the Old World had been Liverpool's orderly stone wharves; this first glimpse of the New World was all rotting wood and ramshackle sheds, a jumble of painted signs and paper billboards and chalked words and prices on blackboards. Everything and everyone seemed to shout and hawk.

A few yards away a respectable-looking older woman was addressing a pair of respectable-looking younger men, one of whom was not just laughing aloud but *guffawing* in the street so madly that he seemed about to tumble over. The bustle of people and carts and animals seemed greater than in London, wilder and even slightly desperate, but also somehow *happier*. And strangers looked at him as intently as he looked at each of them—looked him straight in the eye, as no Londoner who wasn't a whore or a lunatic would think of doing.

In this place of which he had only read and dreamed, he had the odd sense of arriving home. A "cosmopolite," the friendly American newspaperman he met on the ship this morning had called him. Ben savored the phrase, hoped that it might become true. It was a word that his brother Philip used as a polite disparagement for artists and feckless Europeans and Jews.

In the footpath on the far side of the street he spotted two Negroes, a man and a boy, maybe father and son, starting to sing at the tops of their lungs and clap in time to their tune. *"He got the whole danged world, he got the whole world in his hands."* Ben's mouth dropped open at the sight. He had stepped off the boat only a minute ago, and here was minstrelsy, no cocoa butter and burnt cork on white men, no West End stage parody, but the real thing, in the American street. Their associate, a white boy, held a tin bowl he shook for coins from onlookers. Ben handed over his remaining penny and lifted his bags to go. *He's got the whole world in his hands.*

As he walked toward a cluster of hackney cabs, he happened to glance at the smallest sign among the scores that surrounded him. He was walking down a street called Liberty.

His cabdriver was friendly and talkative in just the brassy way Americans were reputed to be. In their first minute together, he had asked Ben his age (twenty-six) and if he was planning to stay in New York for a while (yes).

"That there is the superb Trinity Church," the driver said as he turned north, pointing like a hired guide at a brand-new fake-Gothic spire.

"Anglican?" Ben asked.

"Aristocratic," the driver said without a smile, "and the tallest doggone thing on the continent."

"And that fine place," Ben asked of a building across Broadway, "is an army headquarters?" Two black men in regimental uniforms stood guard at either side of the main entrance.

"Because of the darkies at the door? *Ha!* You are a comical one, if I can say so, sir." It was the Lafayette Bazaar, an arcade of shops, reading rooms, and photographers' studios. The two men in blue costumes, the driver explained, "are just, well, hired *showmen,* I expect you could say."

Ben's first impressions of his hotel were disheartening. White and new and fine, the Astor House was the very picture of ten-shilling-a-night respectability. Except for its great size, it was in no way vulgar or strange, and Ben had come to America craving vulgarity and strangeness. His room, on the sixth floor, was outfitted with a feather bed, a steam radiator, water from a tap, even a water closet with plumbing. He did not feel that he was at the center of a rough new democratic dynamo. Indeed, he might as well have been in the most luxurious hotel in Rome or Paris or Berlin. With its marble and mahogany and miles of drapery, and a score of liveried men and footboys carrying parcels and platters and answering bells, this establishment would suit his father, or—good God—his brother Philip.

Yes, Ben said to himself, *and what else should one* expect *of the* Astor *House, a hotel built by the famous millionaire himself?* He had taken his father's suggestion and used the firm's travel clerk to arrange lodgings, and now he wondered if the Astor House was part of an Archie Knowles stratagem to pamper and disillusion him from the moment he arrived, to persuade Ben that he was indeed (as his father had said) "an overromantic carpet knight" who had sailed three thousand miles only to encounter the familiar. Ben vowed to find a permanent place to live in a more suitably . . . *American* way. Whatever that meant.

But as he walked downstairs for dinner, wondering why the public rooms of such a hotel featured so many large and empty brass flowerpots, the man walking just in front of him turned his head and, hardly pausing at all, spat a large bolus of syrupy tobacco juice several feet into the nearest pot. Aha: *spittoons.* Ben smiled. He was pleased. No such thing had ever happened in Berkeley Square.

THE TWO YOUNG New Yorkers were seated in a corner of the largest of the dining saloons at the Astor House. Duff Lucking wore a brown serge frock coat, his first new one since before he left for Mexico. Polly Lucking wore her favorite dress, a brocaded yellow silk with a lace bodice, and her high-heeled kid boots. Until they'd arrived, their destination had been a secret to her. For this week's dinner Duff had announced he would "fête her royally" to celebrate the happy, happy news.

Duff had never tasted champagne, let alone Heidsieck at two dollars a glass. "A toast . . ."

Polly smiled as if embarrassed, but the show of humility was rote. She was as pleased as she had ever been. She had learned the day before that she was cast to play the young heroine Florence Dombey in the stage production based on Charles Dickens's new novel. It would be the most significant role so far in her somewhat whiffling theatrical career.

"Now come on, Polly—raise your glass!"

She smiled and lifted her ginger fizz an inch or two off the table.

"To New York's—no, to the *nation's*—truest and finest young female player, *Mary Ann Lucking*!"

She wondered if she ought to drop her nickname professionally and begin to call herself Mary Ann.

"Prepare, New York," Duff continued, a little loudly, "for the up-and-coming star of 1848!"

She smiled and sipped. She would now be a true actress, exclusively an actress. And how pleased she was that she had made the choice to leave Mrs. Stanhope's employ *before* this stroke of good fortune. She was tempted to thank God for rewarding her right actions so promptly, even though her mother's funeral Mass in '46 was the last time she had even stepped into a church.

"Thank you, Duff. You are too generous."

"Does this news mean you are finished with the lesser endeavors, Polly, the, the . . . other performances?"

"Queen Gertrude, do you mean?" she asked, feeling a little hurt. Polly would debut the next night in a brief run of *Hamlet*—not in the role of young Ophelia, the part for which she had tried out, but as Hamlet's mother. She and King Claudius and the ghost of Hamlet's father were the only adults in the production, since the manager had decided to cast infant wonders in every other role—children no older than twelve, the girl playing Ophelia barely eight. "It *is* Shakespeare . . ."

"*No*, of course, indeed. No, I mean . . ." The scar on his cheek started to sting. "The other job. You . . ." He could not bring himself to utter the words. And he said so. "I am flummoxed, Polly."

"At Heilperin's?" Heilperin's Studios was one of the places in the Bowery where men, amateur "artists," paid fifty cents to sketch female models arranged in tableaux vivants and dressed (or, rather, all but undressed) as figures of antiquity and myth—Venus Rising from the Sea, Lady Godiva, a Greek Slave Girl. "Oh, *that* travesty," she said. "I quit Heilperin's weeks ago. Have I not told you?"

Duff smiled and sighed. "Well," he asked, "do you know when you are off to Philadelphia with Burton's company?" *Dombey and Son* would play its first performances there.

"At the beginning of July, they say. By steamer." She would be a member of a *troupe of players,* on the road with *fellow actors*! "And then return at the end of the month to debut at his new theater in Chambers Street."

A waiter arrived with their plates.

"No," Duff corrected, "the Calf's Head in Brain Sauce is for my sister." Polly had not yet made herself over into a vegetarian, as she intended. Duff was having Small Birds, Italian Style.

Across the room, a pianist was playing a Schumann song.

Duff and Polly did not notice the arrival of a young gentleman seated alone four tables apart from them.

And Ben Knowles's eyes were darting like a boy's, alert to every foreign detail—more spittoons scattered across the floor, diners gulping water, a fat man at the next table saying, "That's the guy's moniker, or what?"

"Dinner at the Astor House, Polly," Duff said rather grandly. "I hope it is all that you imagined."

She no longer wished to lie to Duff. But nor was she prepared to burden him with the entire truth. She had, in fact, dined here before, twice, once with Samuel Prime and once with a timber dealer she had met at 101 Mercer Street.

"It is," she said, "*precisely* as I knew it would be. Every bit as splendid." He smiled and took her hand.

"And you are indistinguishable from the whole company of fashionables around us." He raised his champagne again. "To our evening as *snobs.*"

Ten yards away, Ben pored over the blue-and-gold Menu of Cocktails. He wore a dazed smile and moved his lips as he read the names of the American drinks he knew (Mint Julep, Sherry Cobbler) and wondered about the ingredients of the ones he didn't—the Timberdoodles, Syracuse Smashers, Flip-Flaps, Drizzles, and Great Big Boys. He considered ordering a glass of "the finest Pennsylvania rye whiskey ('Monongahela')" but decided instead on "the finest Kentucky corn whiskey ('Bourbon')."

He glanced around to find a waiter . . . and spotted a young woman just as a smile broke across her face. She was illuminated by a pool of gaslight.

He wanted to stare. Instead he ogled her for three or four seconds at a time, again and again, interrupting his gaze by pretending to read his menu. Her hair, the color of hay, was braided in a sleek chignon but hung a little loosely in front over the sides of her face and ears. In London she would be counted as a Mayfair flirt, no doubt—as carefully powdered and probably as high-strung as Lydia Winslow, Ben's former fiancée, but with none of Lydia's careful curls, and an easy smile of which Lydia was incapable. This girl moved her hands in the air as she spoke, like a European. She might be twenty, Ben thought, or perhaps closer to thirty; her eyes and smile seemed too womanly and sly for a girl's, but her tomboy laughter was too natural for an experienced minx. He returned to his menu.

He was charmed by her, a young woman anyone would find pretty (although a little sharp-featured, and almost mannishly tall), but whom Ben found beautiful. Indeed, he was smitten as he had not been smitten in . . . months, certainly, or maybe years; no, to tell the truth, as he had never been smitten before.

And now he looked over again, this time eyeing the man holding her hand. He found it hard to credit this tanned, muscular young fellow as her beau, not because he looked unintelligent or uncongenial or (the scar on his face notwithstanding) ugly, but because he seemed so entirely *boyish*.

Duff stood and walked past Ben's table to a side hallway across the room.

Ben's glances at Polly grew longer. He watched her use her napkin to dab the corners of her mouth and then, so quickly that no one else in the place noticed, pluck a bread crumb from her bodice. He watched the tendons in her neck as she turned to look out the window at an old man walking a terrier on a leash down a turf path in the hotel's interior garden. He watched her absentmindedly stroke the edge of the white damask tablecloth in her lap like a toddler rubbing the hem of her baby blanket.

When the pianist started playing a Chopin *Fantaisie Impromptu*, she suddenly turned toward the piano and happened to meet Ben's glance for the briefest instant before they both turned away—she to greet her returning tablemate, he to inspect a random, grinning American whose side-whiskers were as broad and woolly as an unshorn sheep's hock. Polly was accustomed to strange men stealing glances. Ben seldom eyed women so attentively, let alone wolfishly.

A half minute later, Ben looked over again and saw that she was now in animated conversation with her scarred, eager boy-man. Ben imagined, bitterly, that they were rhapsodizing about their married life, pledging eternal affection, sharing secrets, making love.

"You've turned gay as a cricket," Polly said to her brother when he'd returned from the lavatory.

He began to explain, then stopped himself. "This is not proper table conversation."

"What is it, Duff?"

Duff let his eyes widen and leaned in toward his sister to whisper. "The *water closet*. The *seat* is *vulcanized*. And when you pull the lever the stream comes out fast, like a millrace, as fast as a pump at a well. It absolutely *blasts*, Polly, and in an instant"—he started to blush—"everything . . . simply *disappears* down an iron drain."

It was his first encounter with a privy hooked to a Croton water pipe. He had to restrain himself from actually recommending that she leave the table now to visit the ladies' facility. And Polly had to restrain herself from confessing to him that she already had, months before.

"It absolutely takes the cake," he said.

His slang amused her. "I am sure it does, if one has eaten cake."

Duff was embarrassed by her little joke, as she had intended. His ears and cheeks turned as red as his scar.

Ben turned away from the couple to attack his roast duck and buttered corn and aubergines ("egg plants"). The waiter brought him a serving dish filled with two pounds of fried chipped potatoes. He ate as much as he could manage, but enough food for a second and probably a third dinner remained. After his dishes were taken away, a senior waiter in more elaborate livery approached. He had a worried expression.

"Did you find the Suprême de Canard Montmorency in some way unsatisfactory, sir?" the man asked, pronouncing the name of the duck dish as if it were *supreme to Canada mount moron sea*. "And your *palms freet?*"

"I beg your pardon?"

"Your duck and your fried puh-*tay*-toes. Were they not tasty to you?"

"Very tasty indeed, thank you. But I am unaccustomed to your extremely generous portions."

The man relaxed, and seemed eager to pursue a different line of questioning. "A*ha*. English, eh, sir?"

"I beg your pardon?"

"You're from Great Britain, sir, are you?"

"Yes indeed."

"May I inquire, then—your first time in America?"

"Yes."

"And how do you find it?" the man asked, assuming the odd tone of fretful tenderness and faintly simmering rage that Lydia Winslow had used whenever she would ask if Ben really and *truly* loved her. Ben was considering what honest reply to give when the man answered for him.

"I expect the liberty and equality you find here may come as a shock. I expect you are also surprised, too, to find this city as sophisticated as London or Paris or any in the world—yet far more congenial and sincere. Am I correct, sir?"

"Well, I have only just arrived, actually . . ." Ben expected Americans to be impertinent—he welcomed it—but he was startled by this man's self-regard and appetite for praise.

"Our food at the Astor House is renowned for its excellence. The equal of any European table, they say."

"I am simply . . . full. And as for your city and country, I expect to find that it is indeed the best of all possible worlds."

Ben couldn't have been more sincere. The restaurant captain, however, certain that an arrogant John Bull was mocking him, nodded and strode away.

Polly glanced once, quickly, at the long-haired stranger as the waiter set down her dish of ice cream and strawberries; he was no longer ogling.

Ben did not dare to look at her again until she and her companion walked past his table to leave. He inhaled her lavender breeze. The back of her dress was cut with a slight dip at the neck. And so as she made her exit from the saloon and Ben Knowles's life, he turned and stared—helplessly, hopelessly—at those naked few inches at the summit of her long back.

He had dared in the last few minutes to imagine that he might somehow contrive to meet her, that she would fall in love with him, that she would become his American wife. But now—he returned to his meal and sighed—he knew he would never see her again.

But he would not mope. He took a deep breath. He finished his glass of bourbon whiskey and ordered another.

As he drank he considered once again the extraordinary turns his life had taken since February. And he decided that Lloyd Ashby would approve of everything he had done since the night in Paris they were last together. He dearly hoped so.

2

two months earlier—February 23, 1848
. . .
Paris

W<small>AITING</small> <small>MADE</small> Ben Knowles impatient. That is, he lacked the patience to wait contentedly. The impatience was always there, simmering just beneath his gentleman's pose—beneath the calm and polite and impervious marble-white English mask. Ben's impatience exasperated his parents, and it had puzzled poor Lydia during the year of their betrothal, but he refused to consider it a weakness, which puzzled and exasperated everyone all the more. *Waiting*—for a new suit of clothes to be finished or a sense of life's purpose to be revealed or an old friend to appear on a street corner—simply made him feel that underlying sense of foiled desire.

Was he standing on the wrong corner of Montmartre? The gas street lanterns were lit, twinkling up the boulevard in the gray winter dusk like two rows of very orderly planets and stars. He had discovered—smelled—that he was standing not far downwind of a hydrogen gasworks and a huge butchery. Perhaps Ashby had said to meet him at five o'clock *not* "where the Rue des Martyrs hits the Boulevard des Martyrs," as Ben recalled, but, rather, *across* the square where the Boulevard des Martyrs becomes the Boulevard Montmartre. On the other hand, it would be in character for Ashby to choose the vicinity of a gas factory and an abattoir for a rendezvous.

They had impulsively decided on this meeting in London at Christmas—an odd arrangement, as arrangements involving Ashby tended to be. Ben's railway train had arrived in Paris at half three. He should have asked his friend to meet him at the Gare Saint-Lazare. Instead, he had dropped his luggage at the Hôtel Diderot, walked to a taxidermist's, and then, as Ashby had instructed, made his way here. As he had stopped on various corners attempting to find his way with one of the cunning but awkward folding maps bound into the *Galignani's New Paris Guide* his hotel clerk had given him, Ben felt like a perfect caricature of an English tourist.

He was always a little rattlebrained in foreign cities. (As a child he had once spent two days in Glasgow under the impression he was in Edinburgh.) On the other hand, Lloyd Ashby was habitually tardy—his schoolboy nickname had been "Lord Later," awarded one day when he arrived an hour late for a cricket match. And while Ben's father approved of his intimacy with Ashby for the obvious reasons (Lloyd's father was a peer—a viscount, Lord Brightstone), Archibald Knowles regularly cautioned him to beware the "infectiousness" of Lloyd's "lazy and reckless approach to life." And living in Paris these last eighteen months, Ben reckoned, had surely turned his chum even more unsettled and exotic. For young Englishmen, a kind of exotic unsettledness was the point of Paris, even for those on a business trip, like Ben.

The sun had almost set. He checked his watch again: nearly quarter till five in London, so . . . half past five here . . .

But what of it? Ben inhaled a deep, cool breath and relaxed. He was in Paris. He was warm in his overcoat. The rain had stopped. He was exhilarated, as always, by travel—by leaving London, yes, but even more by having traveled *fast*, sitting inside a *machine* moving at *fifty miles an hour*, striking straight over the landscape like a bullet or a god. He was in the thrall of speed, the new speed of steam but also of clipper ships, of the telegraph's instant mail and the instant portraits of the daguerreotype. It was this that distinguished him in his own mind from most people he knew. When he had traveled from London to Paris ten years earlier as a student bound for Bonn, the journey took five days; today's trip had required not even one. Considering, then, this bonus of time that modern engineering had granted him, what was an extra hour of waiting?

He put the penguin down. Wrapped in damp gray pasteboard and string, it stood upright on the stone, two and a half feet tall. Only the tip of its bright orange beak poked out of the wrapping, looking like a wedge of old cheddar. The bird was one of sixty-seven shot by Sir Henry Pottinger off the Cape of Good Hope last year, shipped from Africa to the taxidermist on the Rue du Bac to be stuffed and distributed as gifts to Sir Henry's friends. One of those designated penguin recipients was Ben's father, who had asked Ben to make himself useful, as long as he was going to be in Paris on Knowles, Merdle, Newcome & Shufflebotham business, and pick up his *Spheniscus demersus*. Mr. Knowles wanted the penguin as soon as possible in order to show it off. *Spheniscus demersus* wasn't rare, like some of the specimens in his collection, but its provenance made it a penguin worth coveting.

"*Monsieur.*"

Suddenly, on the walk just to Ben's left, like a sprite darting from a forest hollow in a fairy tale, a woman appeared. She was no more than twenty.

"Aidez-moi, s'il vous plaît!"

"Uhhhmm—bonsoir, mademoiselle," Ben replied, groping for the right words. "Je parle français."

She breathed quickly, each puff visible in the cold, and crouched, as if ready to spring into the air. Her pretty face was flushed and damp, contorted by fear, exertion . . . and by a sort of abandon that struck Ben as faintly carnal. Was she some odd French species of prostitute? She wore a twilled silk dress that exposed her shoulders, but no coat and nothing on her head. The bottom of her skirt was flecked with mud, and her palms and wrists were smutty with soot or blacking. In her left hand she held a heavy piece of pottery, and in her right a yard-long pole, a kind of rough cane with a large scrap of leather tied to one end by string. She looked less like a whore, in fact, than an actress performing the part of a vagabond in a play.

She glanced over her shoulder down the alley from which she had popped.

"Prends ça!" She shook her stick. The leather fluttered. "Tout de suite, s'il vous plaît! *S'il vous plaît,* monsieur!"

He recalled his father's declaration, a decade ago, that Ben's time at Universität Bonn was a waste of time, a folly, since a smattering of French, not German, was the only foreign language one required—and a *smattering,* he added, is *absolutely* all one required to argue bills with dressmakers and taxidermists. Here on a street in Paris at dusk, it was clear that Ben's French did not qualify even as a smattering.

"Mademoiselle," he tried again, "I'm afraid I really do not understand— that is: Je *ne* parle pas le français."

Each stared at the other for a long moment.

"Vous êtes *anglais!*" she said. "Parfait. English. Perfect."

He smiled. "Yes, just arrived." What was she after? "Perfect . . . ?"

"*Oui,*" she said, thrusting her clay pottery and pole into Ben's hands. She pulled her damp hair from her eyes with one blackened hand and leaned in close to him. "*S'il vous plaît?*" she whispered with an urgency Ben had never before heard in a whisper.

What his sniggering club friends loved to say after their trips to Paris was actually true, Ben thought: any young Frenchwoman, no matter how shaggy or charwomanish, is apt to be more entrancing than ten tittering girls at a London party.

This one certainly qualified as shaggy.

"Sir, I cannot have these things. Thank you! Je reviendrai—I return in a short time." She leapt back to the alley, grabbed something wrapped in a heavy cloth, and then ran off—literally *ran!*—down the Rue Pigalle, behind a coach, into a crowd and out of sight.

He propped the pole against the lamppost, next to his father's penguin, and hefted the girl's strange piece of pottery. It was the weight of a melon, and comprised a pair of small conical pots cemented together at their mouths and smeared yellow and black and white. From one end a piece of stiff twine dangled. He touched a yellow smear, then sniffed his gloved finger. He recognized the smell from his father's rubber factory. Sulfur?

"Why, *Ben Jonson!*" From the middle of the street, Lloyd Ashby strode toward him across the cobblestones. Ben Jonson was one of several nicknames by which Ashby called him. "I *saw* that! What did you *say* to that poor *gamin* to make her flee? Rascal! Dirty lewdster!"

Ashby had grown a beard. He was grinning, as usual, and wore a scarf and a waistcoat with broad yellow and white stripes but no coat, hat, or gloves. He held a cigarette in one hand. Ben had never seen an Englishman smoke a cigarette. "I am notifying a gendarme immediately."

"I believe she is crazy," Ben shouted back. "But perhaps I misunderstood her."

" 'Never go to France/Unless you know the lingo;/If you do, like me,/You will repent, by jingo.' " The lines were from a poem by a recently deceased acquaintance of theirs.

Ben prepared for the embarrassing Lloyd Ashby *hug.*

But as Ashby reached the gutter he stopped short, the smile gone. He threw aside his cigarette. Ben had seldom seen him with such a serious look—he must be playing some new joke.

"Lay that thing down, Ben."

"But it was my gift from the girl—who, by the way, was not *fleeing*, she—"

"Put it down. This instant. I am quite serious." He glanced both ways, then whispered, "It's a republican stinkpot."

"A *what?*" Ben said, glancing at the pots and twisting his face skeptically. "That's good—'republican stinkpot'! I believe my father called me that one night after his sixth brandy and water."

Ashby grabbed the contraption from Ben's hands and gently laid it on the pavement.

"Come." He linked his arm with Ben's, tugging at him. "Quickly."

"Oh, but a souvenir, at least . . ." Ben picked up his penguin and the girl's pole, with its fluttering piece of leather. Ashby snatched the pole away from him, threw it into the gutter, and pulled Ben along.

"You are *serious*." So queer: all their lives, Ashby had been the devil-may-care mischief-maker and Ben the more prudent good boy.

"Damned right I am," Ashby said as he led them across the street. He lowered his voice to a whisper. "That is a grenade. The stick is her staff-sling. The rioters are using them to throw bombs. They pack the stinkpot with quicklime, light the fuse, hurl them at guard posts. Makes a foul smell and a big sputtering show—"

"It wasn't lime, it smelled to me of . . . brimstone? Sulfur."

"Christ! *Gunpowder*."

"Ah. Right." Partly to confound his father, Ben had from boyhood declined to shoot, and taken up archery instead. "Of course."

"She handed you a *bomb*. Why, in God's name?"

"Because I'm English. She was very pleased to discover that. 'Parfait,' she said."

Ashby looked at him as if he were simple.

"I told you I thought she was crazy," Ben said.

"You don't know what happened yesterday, do you? Look around you, man!" He pointed to the stumps of freshly cut trees.

Ashby was relishing this opportunity. As they walked the smaller streets toward the Seine—more alleys than streets—he spoke very rapidly, in a kind of slang hybrid of French and English, and practically danced as he talked. To Ben the gullyhole stink was worse than anything in London, but Ashby claimed to enjoy the fumes. He leapt over one fecal delta just as he finished an anecdote about the king's "syphilitic sodomite" minister. He swerved and hopped to bypass cesspools and rivulets as he told Ben about the government's ban of the liberals' protest the evening before last, about the crowd of students and workers and loafers milling and goading one another on in the Place de la Madeleine yesterday morning, a couple of thousand by lunchtime, their march across the river toward "the crappo Parliament," joined by thousands of sympathetic onlookers, including Ashby himself. He described the police attack, the man next to Ashby struck by a cudgel, a few people shot, fragments of the mob running all over the Left Bank and the Right, "your girlfriend from the alley probably among them," sawing down trees and smashing things, looting gun shops, building barricades to block the streets.

"Overnight the army made camp around the Parliament, and at some insane hour this morning, some cavalry began blowing fanfares, on trumpets and *saxophones.*"

Ben looked at Ashby. "Saxophones?"

"An hilarious new horn," Ashby explained, "invented by a Monsieur *Sax.* The military bands use them now in place of *French horns,* if you can believe it. Anyway, I was just across the way in the Rue de Bourbon, asleep, and I thought, 'My God, *war!*' and scrambled outside in my nightshirt to look. The musicians were merely amusing themselves."

"But I thought you lived in——"

"The lady's rooms, Juliet, where I now spend most of my midnights and dawns. She calls herself an insurgent. Ben, these people are simply lusting for a revolution. They reach a point . . . *bam.*" Ashby made a gesture with his hands like a clap in reverse. "They can't help themselves, God love them, and every twenty years the cork blows and half the country climbs aboard a runaway locomotive for sport. Like thirteen-year-old boys. It's quite magnificent, actually. On my way to meet you earlier, I saw a crowd carrying clubs and knives, singing a song called 'Mourir pour la patrie'—'To Die for the Fatherland.' Do you know it? No? From a new work by our man Dumas, his play in the theater here last season. This *revolution* is inspired by a *story* and *actors* singing *songs!*"

"So you think they will not manage it."

"Will not manage . . . ?"

"To have a revolution."

"Despite your girl and her bomb, no. Certainly not. People are saying today that the old imbecile king has been persuaded to toss out the premier, shuffle some ministers around. Declare that the people have spoken, *le public a parlé,* remind the people that he is called Philippe-*Egalité,* then get on with the royal tragicomedy. As usual."

Ben nodded, thinking of his subscription at age fifteen to the radical *Northern Star,* the lectures in Cambridge and rallies in London, the pound notes he'd sent to help Engels's organization in Manchester (one textile heir's donations to another to liberate the workers of the world), the endless arguments with his father and brother, all the riled-up progressive impatience that in the end amounted to nothing at all. Ah no, no, *no,* not nothing: the government had repealed, finally, the Corn Laws. A loaf of bread was now a halfpenny cheaper. Hurrah.

They stopped. Ben felt the crunch of glass shards underfoot. He looked up: a smashed streetlamp, and down the boulevard a dozen more.

Twenty yards to their left they saw the burned hull of an omnibus on its side and next to it a horse, dead and still in its yoke, the head twisted nearly all the way around, its hindquarters black and blistery. Its mane was still smoldering.

"Good God," Ben said. "What happened?"

Again Ashby gave him his incredulous look.

"Of course," Ben realized. "The rioting."

"They have a cute name for their buses here." Ashby lowered his voice to a whisper again. "They call it *le four banal*—'the village oven.' There's a *French* revolution for you—they make their figures of speech literal."

A platoon of the Garde Nationale, having disentangled the limbs and trunks of plane trees from the windows and wheels of the charred bus, began to shove it, a few inches with each collective "Un . . . deux . . . trois . . . *poussez,*" to the side of the street.

A man wearing a real bear's head and a red woolen liberty cap (stretched tight over the late bear's ears) danced to a polka played by a woman on a clarinet. The tune fell into time with the soldiers' grunting *poussées.* A little boy crouched next to the woman, holding out a basket for coins.

Ashby spoke to the clarinetist's child, who leapt up, pulled the *bonnet rouge* from the bear's head, and handed it over. Ashby gave the boy two francs, which he waved in front of his mother. The mother smiled at Ashby with her lips still tight around the clarinet and, as Ashby rejoined Ben, started playing a new tune.

"Now, what do you suppose *that's* meant to signify?" Ashby said, shaking his head and smiling. "I told you they're all children, didn't I?" He started to sing along: " 'Lucy Locket lost her pocket/Kitty Fisher found it . . .' " Then he began clapping along. People stared. One man holding a drink raised it to Ashby in a toast.

"No, Lloyd," Ben said, shaking his head, "it's 'Yankee Doodle.' " In a whisper, he sang the words. " 'Yankee Doodle, keep it up,/Yankee Doodle dandy . . .' And so on. She takes you for an American."

Ashby stopped singing but he kept on clapping. "You know, that happens frequently. 'L'Américain.' At the start I thought it was because of the things I say against King Louis-Philippe and his ridiculous family. But Juliet told me that it is not politics at all—it's because I'm so *jolly* and *loud* they never believe I'm English. They ask me about the Indians and 'les Montagnes Rocky.' They wonder if I know 'le Colonel John Charles Frémont.' They sincerely imagine that I am from . . . *Cincinnati*, or *Alabama*."

"Lucky man," Ben said.

"Jealous, eh, Natty Bumppo?" This was another of Ashby's nicknames for Ben. He grinned and grimaced as he pulled his new cap low on his head like some backwoods idiot, then saluted.

Ben asked about the gray dust covering his friend's hands.

"Marble dust and rabbit-skin glue," he replied, rubbing his fingers with his thumbs. "Gesso, from painting." They continued their long walk in the direction of Ashby's studio on the Ile Saint-Louis.

He was jealous of Ashby now. America had been Ben's hobby for years. It started the summer he turned fourteen. The Knowleses were throwing a dinner in London in honor of his cousin Mary Motley and her fiancé, a Frenchman named Monsieur Clérel, and Archie Knowles had given Ben a copy of the fiancé's book about America. From its first pages it struck Ben with the power of Scripture, which Scripture itself had never done. *"It is evident to all alike that a great democratic revolution is going on amongst us . . ."*

He could barely believe he had received such a manifesto from his father—the son of a South Yorkshire wheelwright now eagerly doling out bits of his broadcloth and Malay rubber and mining fortune in return for the pretense of social respect. "Yes," his father had said to his son's smart remark at the time, "he *is* a Frenchman, but he is a French *count*. And you like books." (Archibald Knowles believed himself to be descended from a famous knight. His paternal great-great-great-grandfather, Archie's mother had told him on her deathbed, was the illegitimate child of Sir Isaac Newton.

One night years ago he had made a great show of revealing this family secret to his own sons, a secret Ben believed to be a fiction.)

"*There is a country in the world,*" the introduction to *Democracy in
America* declared, "*where the great revolution which I am speaking of seems
nearly to have reached its natural limits; it has been effected with ease and
simplicity . . .*" Ben had never been so excited by words in his life, and during the dinner with the author he concentrated so hard on every one that
came out of Charles Alexis Clérel de Tocqueville's mouth, he could barely
follow what he was saying. From that moment forward, Ben was in love.

His love for America amused his mother but rankled his father, which
only increased Ben's passion. When he practiced shooting his longbow he
no longer imagined himself one of Henry V's archers at Agincourt, but
James Fenimore Cooper's Natty Bumppo hunting game in some wild, infinite American forest. He had decorated his student rooms in Bonn with
aquatints of the American frontier. When the American painter George
Catlin opened his Indian Gallery exhibition in Piccadilly, Ben bought an annual ticket so he could return again and again to stare at Catlin's pictures, at
the wigwam and live grizzly bears and the imported Indians in full costume
miming their hunts and scalpings for the crowds of bewitched and appalled
Londoners.

He read Washington Irving's *A Tour on the Prairies* and *A History of
New York*. He read everything by Cooper—not just *The Pathfinder* and
The Deerslayer and *The Last of the Mohicans* but novels he could not buy
in London and had to order from America. He had just finished *The Oregon
Trail*, an excitingly matter-of-fact account of a transcontinental journey
just two summers ago by a young Boston gentleman.

The walls of his house in London were covered with framed lithographs
of American buildings and American scenes. Whenever his brother, father,
and other Londoners frothed with anti-American sentiment, Ben privately
cheered: *the old and stingy and meager and stale,* he thought, *envious and
hateful as ever toward the young and bold.*

During the year he had lived in Manchester he attended three performances by the black American actor Ira Aldridge, and when he returned to
London got caught up immediately in the Nigger Minstrel vogue. He attended shows by the Ethiopian Serenaders at the St. James's Theatre, saving
his most enthusiastic applause for their one actual Negro, a dancer called
Thomas Dilward. At a big party celebrating Ben's twenty-fifth birthday at
Ashby's parents' house on Cadogan Place, Ashby and their friend Frank

Haydon had hired Dilward to appear, along with the celebrated eight-year-old American dwarf Charles Stratton—P. T. Barnum's General Tom Thumb, who was performing at the Egyptian Hall.

As it happened, Frank's father, the painter Benjamin Haydon, had rented a gallery at the Egyptian at the same time to exhibit his two huge new canvases depicting Rome's decline and fall, with the intention of attracting some of the Barnum mob. But Mr. Haydon's scheme was a failure: from among the tens of thousands who came to watch the antics of the American dwarf, no more than twenty a day stopped to look at the big, serious pictures.

The morning after Ben's birthday party, Benjamin Haydon, aged sixty, bought a pair of pistols in Oxford Street, returned home, slit his own throat, and then shot himself. Ashby had for years studied painting under Mr. Haydon, dropping by for one-guinea lessons whenever he understood from Frank that the old man was broke. Two days after the suicide, Ashby announced that he was moving to Paris to paint.

"I AM REALLY amazingly pleased with this new picture of mine," he said to Ben as they entered a street so ancient and narrow that the ridge beams of the half-timbered houses on opposite sides appeared almost to kiss. "I took the idea from one of the Hans Christian Andersen stories I used to read to my youngest sister—'Kejserens Nye Klæder.' Do you know Andersen? The Dane?"

"I do." And Ben did, but only because Lydia Winslow had insisted he read the translation of Andersen's sappy novel *The Improviser*. The famous children's stories had been published when Ben was too old for nursery tales. Moreover, Ben was immune to the fashion for fairies and the magical Dark Ages.

"Well, it is a political painting," Ashby said. "A political allegory."

Ashby had always been resolutely above, or beneath, politics.

Ben smiled, shaking his head.

"Wait," Ashby said, "you shall see. A year ago, I had decided this was all a ridiculous spree. Paris! Art! Did you realize that one of every eighty Parisians calls himself an 'artist'? One in eighty! More *artists* than"—he scanned the street to finish his sentence—"than *street sweepers*. The morning I read that fact in the *Messenger*—a year ago, when you were in Rome breaking poor Miss Winslow's heart—I decided that my plan to be a painter was a sham, a *common* sham, that I was an impostor."

" 'We are all of us impostors.' That's what you said the day Mr. Haydon died."

"I was speaking meta*phor*ically at that moment," he said. "Romantic bosh. My blue spell. But now, here, finally, these last few months, I do my best for hours to turn bits of cadmium yellow and dragon's-blood red into a painting, and I—Ben, it is giving me moments now and then of, of . . . *satisfaction*. Dare I say? Of 'happiness.' I mean it, Knowles. I adore my musty studio. I adore my filthy painter's frock. I adore the girl from downstairs, my concierge, whom I pay a half crown to model for me."

Now Ben had a new reason to be jealous of his friend. A model living downstairs. A passion for work. *Happiness.*

"Although, to be frank with you, I may have had enough of Paris for my own good," Ashby continued. "It is a delight, of course, but perhaps *too* delightful. I think now that I need to travel awhile to some rougher place—and to some place where there are not so many *superior* artists."

"Where will you go?" Ben asked.

"A country where I know no one and nothing, where I can be a kind of . . . phantom. Where life itself is an empty white canvas. Like Alabama, or Canada."

"*You* are emigrating? To *America?*"

"No, Juliet is insisting that we run away to the *East*. I'm quite sure that you, Natty, shall reach the frontier shores long before me."

From close by came the sound of continuous, rapid drumbeats, and Ashby's thoughts skittered to a new subject.

"Will you visit your cousin l'comtesse while you're here?" he asked teasingly. He touched the package Ben carried. "A gift for them?"

"My father's African penguin . . ."

"Ah! Of course. You have brought daddy's penguin to Paris as your companion. Naturally."

". . . and Mary is not a countess, as you know. But I am to dine with them Friday."

"Well, I expect that this business," Ashby said, waving a hand, meaning the smashed streetlights and burned buses and liberty caps, "may require the Count de Tocqueville to cancel dinner and remain at the Palais Bourbon. In order to crush the uprising."

They heard a large bass sound, like thunder set to a rhythm. Both looked hard right and listened, craning their necks, trying to see through the twilight commotion of little cabs and big coaches, horses and people. Then at once they made sense of the noise—the chanting of a large crowd.

"Sounds as if it's over in the Capucines," Ashby said with excitement, as if he had suddenly recalled some ultrafashionable new cabaret. "Probably the Foreign Ministry." He was already walking briskly toward the sound, half trotting. " 'Bliss was it in that dawn to be alive,' he shouted, " 'But to be young was very heaven!' Did I not tell you Paris is like a dream? *Come, Aramis! Tous pour un,* one for all!" Ben, right beside him, nodded, failing to suppress a smile.

the same moment on the same day—
February 23, 1848
· · ·
New York City

"C-c-c-c-*CLAMS*! AND CA-CA-CA-*CAT*FISH!" the fellow cried as he loped up the Fourth Avenue.

He had a stutter. Duff Lucking looked out from his seat in the New York and Harlem Railroad coach, traveling north under horsepower. He regarded the man with sympathy and a little horror, thinking of his own lisp, which he had trained himself to lose as a boy by dabbing alum on the tip of his tongue. New York was full of stutterers, it seemed to Duff. He believed that the pace of the city triggered the affliction, just as the foul air of the slums produced cholera.

"Ca-ca-ca-ca-*cat*fish and c-c-c-*clams*!" the peddler shouted again.

Wisps of steam drifted up from the folds of burlap covering the tin pans of cooked fish rattling in his cart. A large terrier, trotting at top speed in a harness, pulled the little wagon along at precisely the pace of his master, who was dark-eyed and olive-skinned. The train moved at twice the speed of the fishmonger and his dog. *Fast for the big dog is slow for the little man,* Duff thought. He was pleased with himself whenever his idle thoughts assumed the form of aphorisms, and this occasional pleasure had become even greater since Skaggs had taught him the word "aphorism."

He took a cake of tobacco from his coat pocket and with his pocketknife pared a nut-sized plug which he tucked into his right cheek. Timothy Skaggs, sitting knee to knee with his young friend, gave the tobacco packet a glancing dirty look. He had a big box resting on his lap—a fine lacquered rosewood case with brass and ivory fittings. On top of it was another, smaller box with a hinged lid.

Skaggs poked his head out the open coach window and barked like a dog. The terrier looked over but refused to bark back at the man wearing octagonal blue spectacles—blue glass inside blue steel frames—and a bushy beard full of cake crumbs.

"C-c-c-*clams!*" the peddler cried again as the train rolled across Thirtieth Street and started the climb up Murray Hill. Not for another half mile could the horses be exchanged for steam. Steam locomotives were outlawed south of Forty-second, a frontier the city fathers pushed north every few years, every time an engine exploded.

"Ca-catfish!"

"I*cta*lurus punc*ta*tus!" Timothy Skaggs cried out.

"Ca-ca-ca-*cat*fish!

"I*cta*lurus punc*ta*tus!"

The coach was jammed, and all the other passengers glanced hard at Skaggs. He smiled at his audience, touching the brim of his hat in wholesale greeting. They thought he had a screw loose.

"How do you know that little Italian's name?" Duff whispered.

"You mean *Signore* Punctatus? No—I'm *translating* for him, back into the ancient language of his people. *Ictalurus punctatus* is 'catfish' in Latin, and vice versa. Hey, look—Thirty-third Street. We have arrived."

Skaggs hefted his precious wooden boxes by their handles. He swung the larger one in front of him, and stepped off the car first.

They walked east into a thickening crowd. Duff carried a tripod on his right shoulder, like a rifle, and enjoyed the glances of curious passersby.

"Come out of the street, you ninny," Skaggs commanded from the sidewalk, which had been shoveled clean of yesterday's snow.

But Duff continued on his way. He took some pleasure in publicly slogging through slush and muck. He was wearing new India rubber overshoes, and as a veteran of a year in Mexico, he imagined that his undaunted marches through sloppy New York streets gave him a noble, martial demeanor. He wore his glazed leather cap in the same proud, vain spirit, although he generally declined to talk about Mexico, to Skaggs or Polly or anyone else.

As they came upon a wheeled dram shop near the Third Avenue, Skaggs stopped to post himself at the end of the line of waiting customers.

"You're liable to get set up too late again," Duff warned.

"Hold on, bub, just a touch of irrigation before the matinee," Skaggs replied, waving a hand.

By the time he got his cup of hot brandy and ginger cracker, Duff had crossed the street and returned with a baked pear that he held by its stem, daintily, a foot in front of his face, so that the syrup would not drip onto his waistcoat. He had become something of a dandy since his return from the war. He did not go for the full Bowery b'hoy outfit—no loud checks, no red flannel firehouse undershirt worn in the street, no flared trousers, no greased sidelocks—but he was, for his age and station, fashionable. His sandy hair was long in front and short in back. His dress hat was a silk stovepipe, and he kept his short collar turned down over his necktie. And of course he always wore his silver-nickel breastpin, the number 15, pinned to his peacoat.

This far up into the Sixteenth Ward, the streets were usually quiet. The new telegraph poles, stretching in a line north toward Boston, were more numerous than townhouses. As it happened, Duff had visited this neighborhood a couple of times in the last day, but he rarely came this far north. There was little paying work above Twenty-third Street. And the suburban serenity made him nervous. He was excitable, and jostling through city crowds allowed him to discharge his pent-up energies. Among people it was easier to maintain good cheer. When he was alone in the quiet fringes of the city, however, his thoughts returned too much to himself. Winter on the empty rivers reminded him of the country, of his youth, of the endless watching and waiting for his father to return home from business trips.

Ever since his mother moved the family to Long Island and then into the city at the end of 1837, Duff had never traveled even as far up the island as Yorkville. Indeed, until he sailed for Mexico from Governors Island, he had left the city exactly once, when he was seventeen, to spend the day across the river in New Jersey with thirty thousand others watching a staged buffalo hunt. (The show took on an unintended verisimilitude when the animals broke free and stampeded through the streets of Hoboken.)

In a city, people somehow always find any new spectacle—like the maggots, Duff thought, that appear on an animal's carcass as soon as it dies. A good fraction of those gathering this afternoon were neighbors from the shanties around Dutch Hill, dirty Germans and dirtier Irish who slept and ate (and milked their sorry goats and whittled their piles of splinters for the match makers) inside rough cabins built from scavenged tree limbs and billboards. Another score of the spectators—those wearing self-satisfied smirks and snarls, the ones with cherry-handled whips tucked under their arms—were sporting men who every afternoon raced their two-wheeled gigs and chunky landaus up and down the Third Avenue dirt to 125th Street and back. Little boys and girls darted among the crowd, giggling and crying and pointing toward a crashing joist here or the sound of a screaming animal there.

The rest were curious citizens of every station, white-smocked medical students from the Bellevue Hospital, Kips Bay fishermen carrying baskets vibrating with bass and eels, bookbinders and lawyers and cigar makers and the usual New York quota of no-accounts, all of them predisposed to ride or walk a mile every now and then to watch a great fire.

A big blaze in the afternoon, like the one roaring today through the barns and sheds of the Granville & Sons Distillery and Dairy, always drew a big crowd. They watched the men of Engine Company 25 and Hose Company 39 as they ran to and fro, sweating and hollering, looking in vain for a Croton water stopcock this far east, then struggling to punch a hole in one of the underground pinewood water lines, then to keep their fifty-foot lengths of leather hose coupled, and finally to aim their geysers at the spreading hell across the First Avenue. It was a good show, and it was warm on a chilly day.

Timothy Skaggs's and Duff Lucking's interests in the fire, however, were professional.

Duff was a gas fitter and billsticker by trade, but down in the Tenth Ward he was known as a fireman. Beginning ten years ago this very month, just after Mrs. Lucking and her children took their apartment in the top floor of the house on Chrystie Street, Duff was spending all his free time down the block at the firehouse of Engine 15, volunteering to do whatever chores needed doing. And the chores were always plentiful. New York was perpetually ablaze, particularly Engine 15's piece of it. Just around the corner and across Canal, within a few weeks of Duff's arrival, the Bowery Theatre burned down. Before he turned thirteen he had become a signal-lamp boy, carrying the lantern to fires.

Even as a greenhorn he had had a knack for hearing the alarm bell before any of the experienced men, nearly before it started ringing. He knew by some instinct, sometimes as soon as they heard the first bells, whether the carriage ought to run north or south out of the shed. Did his country nose have a special sensitivity to smoke? Could his young eyes detect in the distance some faint corona invisible to grown men? The company also came to rely on young Duff to divine the speed and direction of the flames as they spread. After he turned fifteen and became the oldest boy in school, he stopped attending classes and devoted those recaptured hours not to additional paid labor plastering posters in the streets off Broadway, but to running with the machine, a fully fledged fireman.

This Granville & Sons fire was way beyond his bailiwick, of course. But some of the most spectacular blazes broke out up here, where nearly every building was wood. Duff knew a few of these boys from No. 25 and No. 39, and he could have told them, here and now, where he reckoned the thing had started and in which directions the flames were moving the fastest. But etiquette required that Duff offer no unsolicited advice. It was not his fire to fight; he had come to watch, and to help Skaggs take photographs.

Whenever a new acquaintance asked his occupation, Timothy Skaggs replied "unfinished physician," "ex-westerner," "retired newspaper libeler and slangmonger," or "undercompensated writer-for-hire of screamers and second-rate sensation novels." All of which were accurate.

Around Christmas 1839, some complicated business (involving a jar of chloroform, an alleged marriage proposal in Hoboken, and the auction of a stolen Assyrian bronze) had led to his very sudden emigration from the city. His friend Tom Nichols—like Skaggs a New Hampshire refugee, medical college failure, and New York journalist—had gone out to Buffalo to launch a funny, scurrilous newspaper called *The Buffalonian*. Skaggs spent half of 1840 in that city helping to publish it while Nichols was in the county jail, having been convicted of libeling some local leaders by calling them "hypocrites" and "Christian fiends." After Buffalo, Skaggs had continued west, taking a job with the *Illinois State Register* in the city of Springfield, where he remained until 1844.

Since his return to New York he'd held a number of different jobs. While working as a reporter and critic for the *Evening Mirror,* he persuaded the editor, a deaf and terribly nearsighted man, to join him for a private evening tour of the "shocking" concert saloons and "immoral" gaming houses tucked along Manhattan's far west side. Unfortunately, Skaggs arrived at their rendezvous thirty minutes late, by which time the editor had wandered off alone in the dark, stepped from a pier, and drowned. He now preferred contributing to new publications, unburdened by conventions or corruption—papers like Mad Mike Walsh's *Subterranean* and satirical magazines like the new weekly *John-Donkey*. For money, under a pseudonym, he wrote pamphlet novels, such as *Passions Down South, or, The Secret Adventures of a Famous Bluestocking Lady*.

Only days ago he was asked to discuss becoming editor of the *Brooklyn Daily Eagle*, but he declined. Walter Whitman, the recently sacked editor of the paper, was a friend, and Whitman's dismissal over the Negro question was a small cause célèbre among New York newspapermen. Neither did Skaggs wish to ride the ferry to work and back every day—nor, God forbid, to live in Brooklyn.

Besides, Skaggs's abiding new enthusiasm was photography. He had easily resisted all the other modern fevers—for canals, for railways, for the telegraph, for extreme physical fitness—but daguerreotypomania hit Skaggs hard. At the age of thirty-three, he had decided to become a daguerreian. With the eighty dollars he earned last year to write *Ruined by a Nunnery*, he had acquired a large camera for portraits and his portable rosewood model to use in the streets. He even kept a studio in a building owned by the publisher of his little novels, Ninian Bobo. Skaggs had begun recruiting New York celebrities of the second and third ranks to sit for portraits ("the folks *too interesting* to interest the grand Mathew Brady"), which he would present to them without charge—and then make a few dollars selling salt-print paper copies to the Bowery printshops. So far he had resisted Bobo's suggestions that he become a regular Portrait-in-Ten-Minutes huckster, open to the public. He lacked the spare time, for he also spent endless hours making daguerreotypes with no prospect of profit—street scenes in knife-sharp detail, blurry pictures of acquaintances in "natural" poses (laughing, eating a mutton cutlet, buttoning an undershirt), unromantic still-life assemblages of postage stamps and broken wine bottles and antivermin tweezers.

And, since Duff's return from Mexico, pictures of fires. Of these there were plenty.

Duff and Skaggs had met in 1844 during a theater fire. Skaggs had been trapped in a backstage closet with a half-dressed English actress, and it was eighteen-year-old Duff, as a member of Engine 15, who had chopped open the door and saved the two of them. The night of his rescue Skaggs insisted on taking his savior to Delmonico's to celebrate. It was the first time Duff had ever been to a real restaurant, and the two became chums. The friendship was unlikely—"the bohemian and the boy," people called them—but

Skaggs enjoyed his protégé's earnest curiosity, and Duff regarded Skaggs as a worldly, mischievous uncle.

One evening not long ago, Duff had suddenly announced, "I've got a *brainstorm!*"

"My goodness, really?" Skaggs teased, as he often did when Duff contrived to utter whatever bit of new slang he had collected. "Have you spoken to a physician? I would recommend an hourly dose of laudanum until it passes."

Duff's brainstorm envisioned Skaggs becoming "the Daguerreian of Fire." Duff could use the city's new telegraphic alarm system to get his friend to the best blazes quickly. All the watchtowers around the city were being connected by wires to the central station, and all eighty fire companies would be wired up as well.

So Duff had recruited a couple of the boys he knew at a firehouse near Skaggs's studio to shout the telegraphic reports of any big fire up to Skaggs. Duff had rushed today down to Ann Street himself, however, with the news of this Granville & Sons fire so that he could gather up Timothy and his gear personally. He knew it would be a regular holocaust.

And so it was. "You might get another twenty minutes of *intense* burning before she begins to snuff out," Duff explained. "No more than thirty. You can't see from here, but that last big shed back in the rear is full of fire, I'm sure of it."

Skaggs took a long look over the flaming distillery and dairy buildings, the hundred firemen in their dirty yellow costumes, the crowd, and, in the distance, steeples and roofs on Long Island. "Just a few rods further uphill," he told Duff, who had already planted the tripod and was tightening its iron screws. "If we go higher, we can have the river as the background. I would like the river in the picture." He winked at Duff, who started loosening the screws. "A great Stygian tableau at six and a half by eight and a half inches!"

A moment later one of the Granville stills exploded, blasting a cloud of smoke and metal flinders and flaming whiskey-soaked chunks of wood straight up through a roof into the afternoon sky, like a shot fired from some enormous artillery piece. Almost every spectator gasped and jerked or cowered or even scurried a few paces back.

Duff, however, stood his ground, and stroked the numb, puckered oval of skin high on his right cheek. It was his Mexican wound, the battle scar he'd received at the very end of the war, as big as a second nose. Although five months had passed since the piece of red-hot iron struck his face that morning outside Mexico City, and the bright purple had dimmed to a grayish pink, strangers in New York still looked at it. He pretended to regard those glances with patriotic pride.

The explosion of the still was the high point of the afternoon for Duff, and he made no effort to hide his pleasure. "According to one of the 25 Engine boys," he told Skaggs excitedly, "this all began with a blast at lunchtime."

"Ah," Skaggs replied. He was concentrating on setting up his camera.

"Might have been one of the mash cookers that blew. You know, I was an apprentice on the job rigging up their gas jets in there in '46."

"So you said."

"We could've laid the pipe out further from the jet, but the owners refused to pay the extra cost of a bypass."

" 'Bypass'? Did you make that up?"

"It's a word, in the gas trade."

"Poetry, nearly."

"If the fire caught in one of the mash cookers, that'd explain why the stillhouse went to cinders so quick. Or the bone-boiling room over up there. Might have been that. There's gas there, too."

"Hmm."

Skaggs enjoyed deciding on his picture—staring long and hard at some person or thing until he could no longer resist opening the shutter and counting one . . . two . . . *three*. Just now he was staring down into the rear of the camera at the ground glass, adjusting the lens knob to bring the roof peak of the burning cow barn into the sharpest possible focus. He could not take a clear picture of the flames themselves, though, not even by slathering the plates with extra bromine, which let him make exposures, in perfect light, of one second or less.

He did capture bits of the scene. A motionless fireman, grimacing, his mouth open, pointing his nozzle with both hands. A little girl's face dazzled by the flames. A shiny brass hose fitting in a puddle on the dirt. A half-burned distillery sign. And two blackened calves' carcasses laid out on the ground, next to the proud posing foreman of Hose 39.

The flames continued to rage, and the howls of dying animals were audible over the gush of hoses and the thunder and pop of the fire, the glass breaking, and the timpani beats of the engines' pumps. But by four o'clock the light had started to dim. The photograph of the dead cattle would be his final picture of the day.

The sight of buildings ablaze had nearly always struck Duff as beautiful, particularly when the companies' streams first hit the fire and the clouds of steam arose with a great hiss and swaddled the flames. And what looked chaotic and terrifying to ordinary people was to him an orderly process. At a fire he had the feeling he was witness in some privileged, magical fashion to the soul of the city, urban life whipped into a frenzy, slow, unremarkable weeks and months distilled into a brief, radiant pandemonium. Fires were a price cities paid for being alive; the only cities without fires (or the cholera, or stutterers) were dead ones, the cold stone ruins of antiquity. Humanity burned. People had built the warehouses and theaters and stables and factories, and filled them with timber and cloth and hay and oil and alcohol and stoves and gas pipes; and, but for the odd lightning strike, people were responsible for starting the fires; people were responsible for putting them out; and people would rebuild.

Before Mexico, even bad fires had been entertainments. But in Mexico the flames he saw consuming warships and forts and wailing men were not just more awful than an accidental conflagration at some Pearl Street book publisher's—they were more *significant,* because they were driven by quests for justice and honor as much as by tinder and spark. In Mexico, the fires ignited by both sides had intent.

They had meaning.

And so did the destruction that afternoon of Granville & Sons. The firm produced bad whiskey and worse milk. Duff's father, a suicide, had become a drunkard at the end of his life, but Duff blamed bankers and capitalists for Zeno Lucking's fatal misery, not the grog makers. Granville's great sin, in his mind, was its entry into the milk trade.

Out of the mash cookers each day they shoveled a ton of draff, corn and barley slop squeezed dry of whiskey and good for nothing but livestock feed. The big distillers had had a brainstorm of their own. Instead of selling the spent mash to dairymen, they had expanded into the milk business themselves. On this bright February afternoon, some hundreds of the several thousand dairy cattle in New York City were Granville cows in the burning barn on East Thirty-third. The beasts had lived their whole miserable lives eating the swill piped into their troughs from the distillery.

It had been a stroke of true American genius: Granville fed its dime-a-gallon whiskey to the drunkards, the sludge of the whiskey to the cows, the milk of the cows to the babies of the drunks—who, if they survived childhood, had a good chance of growing into whiskey-buying drunkards themselves. And if the children died, it now occurred to Duff as he watched the flames flicker against the darkening sky, *the surviving parents buy more whiskey to numb their grief*. A perfect, vicious circle.

Duff had first seen the Granville still-slop cows when he fit the gas pipes. They were hideous animals, ravaged by perpetual epidemics of tuberculosis, pneumonia, and fevers. Most were missing most of their teeth. Many had lost their tails. Their hides were ulcerated and oozing. But the distillers' milk cost only four cents a quart all year round, whereas the good milk shipped in by rail from the country was a nickel in winter. And so for the savings of a penny or two a day, most families in New York bought swill milk.

Duff remembered the first time he had encountered the stuff, another February morning—in the doorway of Chrystie Street, surrounded by other curious Luckings (the twins Grace and William, his mother), poking his face down into the big can as the Granville milkman stirred it with his dipper. In comparison with the milk Duff had known until then in Dutchess County, it looked watery and bluish, despite the secret ingredients (chalk, plaster) added at the dairy to improve its appearance. At ten and thirteen, Duff and his older sister were no longer drinking milk, but the twins, just shy of two that winter, sucked down a quart a day.

And, of course, he remembered the hot dawn seven months later that they found William dead, his bedclothes a marsh of bloody vomit and shit. Grace awoke spewing from both ends, and was gone the next evening. Duff had been angered by the cloud of vagueness that surrounded the twins' deaths. He was not content with the explanation that "diarrhea" had killed them. In the examining room of the clinic in Grand Street where Grace finally expired, he had insisted on a more precise cause. "Infantile atrophy," a nurse had replied, but the tautology of that phrase, after it was explained, only fired him up more. "Athrepsia, then," the attending physician had finally said. The arcane word satisfied Duff. And he didn't need to be told what had caused the athrepsia. Although his mother would never permit any discussion of causes and blame—babies *die*—he knew it was the swill milk that killed William and Grace.

And so now, a decade later, the fire consuming Granville & Sons Distillers and Dairy did not strike Duff Lucking as a very terrible tragedy. The blast had started the fire well away from where any men were working. And the diseased, decrepit animals were being put out of their misery.

Duff's left hand was in his coat pocket, touching his gold medal bearing a likeness of Saint Barbara, the patron of firemen (and miners). With his right he made the sign of the cross. He was smiling slightly.

"I've never seen a man more pleased by burning buildings," Skaggs said.

"Destruction and creation," Duff replied, "are the cycle of life." It was the explanation Duff's father had delivered after almost any awful event. *Destruction and creation, the cycle of life,* Zeno Lucking would say with an angelic expression—not pleased, exactly, but more hopeful than resigned. To Duff it seemed as true in New York City as in the Clove Valley of his boyhood. Life required death. Renewal depended upon devastation.

Skaggs winked. "Good for business as well, eh? The more this city burns, the more it builds, and the more it builds back up, the more they need, oh, say . . . *gas fitters.*"

"I don't want for work," Duff replied, and that was certainly true. Most weeks he was paid eight dollars for gas work and another two or three dollars for sticking up advertising bills, and most months two dollars more providing a money-exchange service for saloon acquaintances. On top of those jobs he fought fires fifteen or twenty hours each week—for free, for the crazy manly joy of it.

Duff was ready to head south now. The work here was done. He was off to his weekly dinner with his sister, and he had a gross of posters for a new play to paste around town later. He swung Skaggs's tripod up onto his shoulder and lifted the box of plates by its handle. "OK?" he asked.

"Why, yes, sir, Mr. Lucking," Skaggs said, smiling at his friend's bit of slang. He finished wiping the soot from an eyeglass lens, lifted the camera, and raised his free hand in a fist, punching the air as he started to walk west. "*OK!*"

the same moment, the same day
. . .
Paris

"To the wars, my boy, to the wars!" Ashby practically sang as he walked and occasionally skipped down the wet cobblestones toward the sound of the crowd and the drums. " 'He wears his honour in a box unseen,/That hugs his kicky-wicky here at home—' "

Ben knew it was Shakespeare. "*Henry V?*" he asked.

"*All's Well*, act two, scene . . . near the beginning, in Paris, the French count and his friend. 'To other regions/France is a stable . . . /Therefore' "—Ashby sped up, almost running—" 'Therefore, to the *war*!' "

The chanting in the distance grew louder, and both men could begin to make out the words. "Vive la *réforme*! . . . Vive la *réforme*! . . . Vive la *réforme*!"

As they came down the Rue du Helder, Ben got a look at the crowd through the darkness dead ahead.

People filled both sides of the enormous Boulevard des Capucines, shaking the trees as they passed, many walking arm in arm. Most were workingmen, judging by their blouses, but sprinkled among the multitude were young people of a different class, university students in shirtsleeves, some women, journalists and clerks, bearded idlers who wrote or painted when they weren't loafing and chatting in cafés. Three young men carried a painting on a bedsheet that was half as wide as the street, a picture of a bare-breasted woman wearing a red cap—a *bonnet rouge*—and carrying a musket at the front of a mob of men . . . a not-bad copy of Delacroix's *Liberty Leading the People at the Barricades.*

These people, so many hundreds, or thousands, were moving like the water in the rapids of a river, jammed into a channel and in their containment growing all the more turbulent and excited.

Half of them carried props—a barrel stave, a red flag, a broken broomstick, a torch. All of them roared "Vive la *réforme*!" On "reform," the marchers thrust their sticks and torches higher.

"It's . . . bedlam!" Ben said. The sight electrified him. His adolescence had coincided with the early days of the agitation in England for a universal right to vote. He had spent many daydream moments in Bonn and then at Cambridge imagining himself as part of the workers' insurrections in Birmingham and Sheffield. But all of the Chartists' rallies he had attended were orderly and dull. In England, he had never seen an unruly mob.

"Mm-hmm. Extraordinary people." Ashby, hands on his hips, had stopped. He was looking up, scrutinizing the building on their left. "This is number 7. Number 7 Rue du *Helder*! Do you recall who lives at this address?"

Ben set his stuffed penguin on the sidewalk. "There is a *revolution* taking place fifty yards in front of us."

"I doubt it," Ashby said, finally turning to Ben. "Louis de *Franchi* lives at number 7. I've never walked this block before."

Even Ben, at a certain point, refused to indulge Ashby's capering. "I've no idea who Monsieur de Franchi is, and this is no time for us to—honestly, Lloyd, I think you—"

"*Là-bas!*" a woman shouted from the top of the block. "*Là-bas!*" she shouted again.

It was the girl from Montmartre—the stinkpot girl—her face illuminated by a torch. She was kneeling in the back of a four-wheeled cart at the top of the street. Her wrists were bound together with a leather strap but she had raised them to point at Ben and yell, *Over there, over there.* Three soldiers accompanied her.

"Il est *là-bas!*" the girl shouted. "C'est mon ami anglais!"

The very young soldier standing next to her gripped her neck with his hand. The taller of the two soldiers sitting in the driver's box shrugged and nodded in a single motion, and as the cart turned down the Rue du Helder, he unclasped his repeating pistol from a steel hook on his belt so that it hung loosely in its leather sling.

"Arrêtez," the man in charge shouted without much urgency, "au nom de la loi." *Stop, in the name of the law.*

Now Ashby was paying attention. "Good Lord," he said quietly. "It's your girl, the *grisette.*" Remembering the wool liberty cap he had bought twenty minutes earlier, he wiped it off his head.

"Did she actually call me her *lover?*"

"*Mon ami,* 'my *friend.*' She is in serious trouble. These fellows are Garde Municipale. The rough lot. No making light with these thugs, Ben, understand? No calling him 'John Dam,' no humming 'La Marseillaise,' no jokes about Waterloo."

"*Me?*" Ben whispered.

"*Shhh.*"

The dray stopped very close, close enough for the horse to sniff at Ashby.

As the leader, a sergeant, stepped down from the box, the boy in back handed him a torch. With it he walked toward Ashby and Ben, yanking down hard on the horse's forelock and jabbing his elbow into its nostrils with his elbow, all in one move. The horse jerked back a half step, understanding its best course was to remain still.

Once again, from not far away, beating drums, unmistakably a call to arms.

"Bonsoir, Sergeant," Ashby said, nodding, hands clasped behind his back.

The tall, hard-looking sergeant stood in front of them, staring at Ben as Ashby spoke. His right hand rested on the pistol's wooden stock, and with his thumb he rubbed its cock and hammer. He pushed the torch flame close to Ashby's face to get a better look. Ashby smiled.

Just down the block, the mob now filled the boulevard entirely. Their chant was faster and more urgent.

"Michel!" the sergeant shouted, turning his head a few degrees left but looking squarely at Ashby.

"Oui!" replied the soldier guarding the stinkpot girl. Michel, a boy in his teens, helped her climb out—gently, even politely, taking both of her bound hands in one of his, with his other just touching her elbow as she stepped down. Once she was in the street, he took up his musket, gritted his teeth, and put a hand around her neck more roughly than before.

"Apportez notre *Mademoiselle Révolutionnaire* ici," the sergeant said, "à ses . . . *amis anglais*." His sarcastic pronunciation of *revolutionary girl* and *English friends* notwithstanding, he didn't crack a smile.

"Ashby," Ben said, "explain to the sergeant that I first encountered her not one hour ago."

At the corner, the crowd was fiercer than ever, still jostling but now almost stationary. And just around the corner, out of sight, the front ranks had come up hard against the infantry companies and cavalry squadrons of the regular army called out to guard the Ministry of Foreign Affairs. The hundreds of troops formed a dam; the mob could not suddenly reverse its course as it pushed into the rank of bayonets. Ashby's attention was riveted by the scene, each body full of agitation, each pushing and squeezing forward, but no one advancing.

"Ashby! *Speak* to the man, please."

Ashby approached the sergeant with his hands still clasped behind his back. They spoke for a minute, and the sergeant pointed at Ben's parcel.

"Un . . . pingouin?" Ashby answered. The sergeant grew angry.

"Caporal," the sergeant said, "l'épée." The driver turned around and reached down into the cart.

"Excusez-moi, monsieur," Ashby said to the sergeant, and stepped back toward Ben. He translated what he'd heard for his friend. "Marie here was wielding some sort of . . . ancient . . . explosive . . . dagger."

"*What?*"

"My French is not perfect. The girl is called Marie, they caught her smashing shopwindows with some kind of sword or gun, and she's covered with black powder—so they suspect her of planting a bomb that exploded near a royal coach earlier this afternoon. And she's blabbed to them, to prove her alibi, that she *had* had a bomb, but handed it off to *you*, and therefore couldn't have planted it anywhere."

"Good God."

"Yes. I told him we know nothing."

"Rather than the truth."

"Ben, the truth in this instance is entirely too odd and implausible."

The corporal, a stout man in his thirties, was holding up an enormous hunting dagger. It had an old-fashioned flintlock pistol built into the hilt and handguard, the gun's shiny brass barrel fastened snug against the engraved steel blade.

"Le P-P," the corporal said, shorthand for *pistolet-poignard,* pistol-dagger.

"Cela appartient à mon grand-père," the girl said, "simplement une antiquité."

"*Silence,*" the sergeant ordered.

"Her grandfather's," Ashby said, looking at the curious weapon, "an antique."

"Une antiquité mortelle," said the soldier Michel portentously, *a deadly antique.*

"*Silence,* Michel," said the sergeant, who had circled around behind Ashby. Ben and Ashby turned to face him.

"Pourquoi cachez-vous votre *bonnet rouge?*" the sergeant asked, pointing his nose toward Ashby's hands. "Le cadeau de votre petite amie révolutionnaire." *Where has the red hat gone, the gift from your little revolutionist friend?*

Ashby brought his hands to the front and affected an expression of casualness, as if surprised to find the *bonnet rouge* between his two fingers. *This girl is no friend of ours.* "No, elle n'est pas mon amie, et . . . et le cadeau . . ." *As for the hat, we . . .* "Nous . . . nous . . . nous—oh, dammit."

Then Ashby remembered: "Nous l'avons achetée. Pour deux francs."

Marie gasped. The corporal smiled. Michel said, "Ha!"

"Ferme-la, mon petit frère," said the unsmiling sergeant to Michel, *Shut up, little brother.*

"Vous savez?" Ashby explained. "Comme . . . une petite *plaisanterie?* Pour mon ami ici, Monsieur Knowles."

The corporal snorted, and even the girl shook her head and smiled now.

Trying to explain—that he had bought the red cap of the militants as a mere souvenir, that it signified nothing—Ashby had told the soldiers that he had *bought* the *girl,* paid two francs for her, as a *little joke* for his chum Mr. Knowles.

With a smile and a shrug, Ashby stuffed the cap into his pocket. He was encouraged by the gaiety he had accidentally provoked.

But the sergeant showed no sign of amusement. He grabbed the fingers of Ashby's left hand and bent them back. He swung the flame of his torch to within an inch of Ashby's open palm.

"*Poudre.*"

The sergeant grabbed his other hand, twisting the wrist and bending open his fingers with more dramatic violence.

"Et *poudre.* De sa boule—sa *bombe.*"

And indeed, black powder from Marie's stinkpot was smeared on Ashby's naked palms.

The sergeant let go of his hands, threw them down.

He handed the torch to his corporal and drew his pistol from its sling. He aimed it at Ashby's chest.

Startled and confused, the private, Michel, let go of the girl and took a step back so that he could hoist his musket. With its bayonet it was a good hand longer than he was tall.

"*Suivez-nous,*" the sergeant growled at Ashby.

"They want to arrest me," he told Ben, "because of the powder on my hands from her filthy damned stinkpot."

"*Caporal,*" the sergeant said.

The corporal, carrying a leather strap, hopped down from the wagon to bind Ashby's wrists.

The private kneeled and cocked his gun. "Par ordre du roi," he said, "vous êtes en état d'arrestation."

"By the *order* of the *king?*" Ashby repeated with a smile. "Is that so? The king! And one of the king's horses and three of the king's men. This country really is so awfully French."

His jovial attitude confused the corporal, who looked back at his sergeant for clarification.

"Looks like the pinch of the game, Aramis," Ashby said to Ben, keeping his eyes on the soldiers. "I hope you are still the racer you were at Westminster."

"What?" At Westminster School half their lives ago, Ben had been a champion runner. *"What?"*

"Time to scuttle—I to my hoyden, you to my Winsor & Newtons."

"What? Lloyd, no . . ."

"Two Bridges Street," Ashby said. "At number your-age-plus-one-half, the girl there is your sister. Ready?"

"Ashby, I—"

The sergeant was now angrier than ever. *"Silence,* Anglais!"

"Once more unto the breach, dear friend—"

"Ashby, I really do *not* . . ."

But Lloyd Ashby had already turned and started his sprint for the Boulevard des Capucines.

"Au nom du *roi,*" shouted Michel, *"halte!"*

The sergeant closed one eye and aimed his pistol at Ashby's back.

Ashby glanced over his shoulder—was that a *smile?*—but he never stopped running toward the mob.

Without thinking, Ben dropped his *Galignani's* on the pavement, hoisted his package by the twine noosed around it, grabbed the penguin's feet tight with both hands, and swung it like a cricket bat, hard as he could.

The beak pierced deep into the flesh of the sergeant's right hand the instant he fired his pistol, or perhaps the instant just before, and then the bird's neck slammed down on the kneeling private's long barrel.

The crack of the pistol shot; the sergeant's whinny of pain; the blast of the musket; the noise from the private like a cough resolving into a sigh. That was the sequence of noises, although later, as Ben reconstructed the moment—a review he would undertake a thousand times—the separate sounds merged into a single sound, a kind of awful chord.

The sergeant had chased after Ashby, toward the mob in the boulevard, his pistol raised and his corporal close behind.

Ben took the opportunity to run in the opposite direction, back up the street. Marie followed, but her cuffed hands made her gait a little slower and awkward, like . . . a penguin's.

And in the middle of the Rue du Helder lay the real penguin, a few feet from Private Michel Drumont, who was also supine, staring up at the painted blue number 7 over the door of the neoclassical building across the street. Blood squirted from a hole behind Michel's ear. "Gabriel?" he said, alone and confused in his last living moment—for Sergeant Gabriel Drumont was by then at the far end of the block, running, preparing to fire a second ball from his repeating pistol . . . and a third and fourth, as many as it might take to stop the fleeing Englishman.

Once again Ben failed to hear those individual shots, this time because their noise was subsumed by that of a great fusillade on the Boulevard des Capucines, the sound of twelvescore muskets and rifles firing at once. To Ben the fusillade sounded unlike guns at all, nothing like the *pop-pop, pop-pop* of his father and brother and their friends shooting at woodcocks and grouse in the woods.

Thieves aside, it occurred to him as he ran, did adults ever run?

The crowd's roar had grown both louder and higher-pitched, more of an ululation than a chant, more like a pack of dogs than people.

the same moment

. . .

New York City

AFTER PERFORMING OR even reading for a role, Polly needed to walk to clear her mind and flush the electricity from her body. And this afternoon she had already walked a mile. By the time she turned right down Broadway, she had jettisoned the last dreamy figments of Ophelia she had feigned so well (she hoped) for the manager of the Greenwich Theatre.

Without stopping, she glanced in the big window of the sewing machine shop. She heard the faint hum and syncopated *chukka-chukka-chukka* drumming. There was a new girl seated at the table in the window, like an animal in a cage. Polly had despised almost every day of her own time as a seamstress—working by hand, with only needles and thread—and wondered if the women in the window actually finished their shirts and handkerchiefs, or simply stitched and stitched, endlessly and pointlessly, ten times faster than anyone could sew without a machine.

Approaching Chambers Street, she felt, as always, a rising anticipation. Momentarily she would be recognized in just the way she longed to be recognized, to be treated with fondness and even, she imagined, respect. Elsewhere she was, at the very best, another unattached young woman at large in the city, one of the new horde of nannies and maids and shop clerks and publishing girls. From the moment A. T. Stewart's opened two years ago, just after her twenty-first birthday, Polly had been a habitué. She visited at least once a week, sometimes more often, and usually left with some new possession—a ribbon, a piece of sheet music, perfume, a pen, usually something perfectly inessential. Today, at least, she was on a particular errand—she needed to buy a costume for an upcoming performance, a chemise that could do duty as the Venus de Milo's toga.

Stewart's was a new kind of store—gigantic and comprehensive, a dry-goods emporium as grand as a palace but also unashamedly popular. And Polly Lucking was devoted to it, inspired by the hired salesmen standing behind their tables and display cases, smiling silently, encouraging her to stroll at will among all the merchandise, awaiting her choice, as if they were her own servants; and by the platoon of matrons in gray gabardines fluttering around the dressing rooms, ready to hold smocks or tie corsets or fetch a cup of Croton. Fresh running Croton water, free and unlimited!

As she paused to scrape the porridge of mud and shit and slush and lime from the sole of each boot, she looked up at No. 280 and felt something like pride—for the five stories of white marble as rich as a meringue and the plate-glass windows, each fifteen feet wide and nine feet tall, more windows than wall.

Her love of Stewart's derived most of all from the fact that it was entirely *new*. There were no foul-smelling oil lamps, no sooty streaks on the walls, no creaky floors, no chipped wainscoting, no cracked panes, no mysterious and capricious prices, no starchy crone or pinchpenny storekeeper giving her the eye. It was headquarters for the fellowship of the new, the most modern and democratic club on earth.

Yes, precisely, Polly imagined as she approached the entrance, the left corner of her mouth just curling into a smile, *I've arrived at my club.* She amused herself with this whimsy of a club that admitted women—let alone an actress, let alone a Mercer Street strumpet. *An actress,* Polly amended, *who did appear last year in* The School for Scandal *and* The Hunchback and the Dumb Belle, *and was only a* part-of-the-time harlot, *a ten-dollar parlor-house whore attired in a beaver-fur coat trimmed with swansdown and an excellent dragonfly-green cashmere dress . . . and carrying a sketchbook and pencils and* The Knickerbocker *magazine in her satinet handbag . . .*

"Welcome back to Stewart's, Miss Lucking."

Bliss.

As the doorman touched his hat and heaved open one of the eleven-foot doors, she touched a fluted column with one hand to steady herself and then inhaled deeply, the way she always did upon entering: clean dry stone, expensive varnish, Oriental rugs, cut flowers, linen writing papers, lavender water, the latest crinolines fluffy as French pastries, hundreds of pristine calicoes, damasks, and ginghams—the tonic aroma of so many good things *all brand new.* And that invisible cloud of warm air, luxurious and heavenly, so unlike the harsh heat of mere stoves. She shivered with pleasure. The store's two dozen clocks, with two dozen slightly different bells and rhythms, began striking three. The cheerful and nervous discord of the chimes pleased her.

Down the whole Broadway side of the store, big buttery shafts of afternoon sun poured through the windows. Polly walked along the western aisle, leaning over a glass cabinet to examine a Chinese ivory comb, then an India rubber umbrella, then muffs (of mink and ermine and monkey) and gloves (of cow and doe and rat). She waded in and out of the sun. She wanted to bask in this light, to let it warm her face and hands and make her hair even more perfectly golden.

She found the chemise she needed and paid for it, but decided to climb the stairs to the mezzanine. She lingered in the mourning department, where she had made a purchase a couple of years earlier—the fifteen pairs of black gloves for her mother's funeral—and more than once had pictured herself in the metal casket with the plate-glass window at the head end, like the maiden in "The Glass Coffin" by the Brothers Grimm. Today there was a new model on display, a Mr. Trump's Patent Corpse Refrigerator, with a false bottom that was to be filled with ice for the funeral—but filled now with hundreds of beautiful, clear glass marbles.

Finally pausing, both hands gripping the brazilwood railing, and looking out on the selling floor twenty feet below, at the acre of colored boxes and bottles and blankets and gowns and shawls, Polly assumed the air of the lady of this immense and up-to-date house. The things were not like ordinary merchandise for sale, stacked thoughtlessly on shelves or hidden in drawers, but arranged artfully, in the open, as if to suggest lives lived, as on a theater stage. Coming to Stewart's was for her a little like stepping into a play in which new characters and objects appeared each time she returned; a play in which she was the wealthy but fair and charming but strong-willed heroine. "You haven't the sense God gave a goose," her mother would say if she were able right now to divine her daughter's thoughts.

The clocks chimed again, the higher-pitched shattering-icicle sound of half past. It was time to go. She had a busy afternoon and evening ahead— one of her occasional meetings with Timothy Skaggs at his studio in Ann

Street (what he called her "pro bono episodes") and her regular weekly dinner with her dear Duff. Now that she could afford restaurants, she seldom
ate anywhere else. Her stubborn refusal as a child to study cooking, so maddening to her mother, had been vindicated.

But first she would take a minute to glance at the baubles on display in the
windows of Tiffany's new store across Broadway. Even from a hundred feet
away, she could see the glitter of gold. She was not one of those women mad
for jewelry—indeed, she imagined that she could disavow fine living after
she had enjoyed it a while longer—but she did enjoy looking at gold.

Paris

AS BEN RAN, his handkerchief slipped from his pocket and fluttered to the
street. His hat flew from his head. He had no idea that a street sweeper's
helpful cry—"Votre *chapeau!*"—was directed at him. He made turns up and
down entirely unfamiliar streets and stinking, misty alleys, not for an instant
considering why he was going one way or another.

He had never run so fast, even when he was young and had raced around
Hyde Park for sport.

The main sport he and his brother had shared was ferreting, which Ben
grew to hate as he got older. In the gardens in Kent they would release a ferret underground into a rabbit warren. As each terrified rabbit leapt toward
the light at the end of a tunnel, imagining it was about to escape, it would be
trapped in netting arranged over every hole and then shot. Here was justice:
Ben was an English hare scrambling madly to flee the French ferrets.

Were the soldiers behind him, ahead of him, to his left, his right? He had
no idea.

He became aware as he ran that he had never in his life made so many
choices of such consequence so hastily and arbitrarily. Until this moment,
his adult life had consisted of making a few, mostly trivial decisions with
elaborate deliberation. Now he was flying along, terrified and excited, feeling powerful in his powerlessness, as in one of his aeronautical dreams.

He could not recall the last time he had panted. *I am running for my life.
I am embarked on a real adventure.*

In front of a large deserted public building he stopped to catch his
breath—he watched the little steam-engine clouds of his own exhalations

appear and disappear in the cold air—and to form some plan. Tiny letters cut into the façade of the building spelled *Théâtre de l'Académie Royale de Musique,* the Paris Opera. A poster advertised *Jérusalem* by Giuseppe Verdi—*L'opéra,* it explained, *des Croisades, notre guerre pour la Palestine.* A small metal placard hanging from an iron stanchion beneath a gas lamp announced: *à l'intérieur* la lumière électrique *la plus fantastique et plus nouvelle.* And a hand-painted paper sign tacked to the door announced the cancellation of the opera—*Performance finale ce soir, notre grande* CRISE! Our Crusades, our fantastic new electrical lighting, our grand crisis. A country throbbing with operatic pride.

Ben was encouraged by his new ability to make out the basics of French: perhaps the prospect of dying had concentrated his mind. He wished Ashby were with him to share the moment. By now, he imagined, Ashby was already snug in his studio with a hot French cognac and warm French girl.

He peered into the bright lobby through the glass in the door, through his own harum-scarum reflection (hair wild, necktie askew, collar separating from shirt), and spotted only a porter picking up discarded papers. He turned away.

He heard another chanting crowd, as if the last hour had looped back upon itself.

The chant was growing louder. It sounded like a monster chorus singing *Ben Jonson, Ben Jonson* . . . His thoughts raced crazily. Had the Garde Municipale men heard Ashby call him by that nickname?

And then down a street to the right he saw several men heading in his direction. Behind them was a cloud of smoke and dust, illuminated by the flickering of torchlight.

No, not *Ben Jonson*—"Ven-*geance!*" he realized the crowd was shouting, "Ven-*geance!*" The sounds of wheels and horses' shoes filled the beats between the words, growing louder each time. "Ven-*geance!*"

Surely, Ben told himself, this crowd was not seeking vengeance against him, the stray Englishman, for stabbing the sergeant in the hand with the beak of a stuffed penguin and causing the young soldier to be shot by his commander. But that one act of recklessness tonight had been enough. He darted into the shadows, back to the theater. Ben Knowles knew he was too ignorant of too much to remain in the open.

He did not know about the massacre, even though he had heard it.

From where he and Ashby had stood they'd had no view of the stumbling, frightened front rows of the crowd as they had tried and failed to turn away from the nervous soldiers surrounding the ministry; Ben had seen only the mob's implacable grunting rear as it pushed forward, *forward,* angrily, blindly, inexorably, tragically forward.

And Ben did not know that it was the sound of those two errant gunshots in the Rue du Helder which had sparked the fusillade a hundred yards away.

Everyone in the Boulevard des Capucines, soldiers and rioters and spectators alike, had heard the shocking crack of the sergeant's pistol and blast of his private's musket, had been momentarily quieted by the shots, and then had waited . . . waited only a moment for the inevitable . . . for an infantryman in the line of regulars outside the ministry to tap the trigger of *his* musket, followed immediately by another, then half the troop, 237 shots in all. None of the victims had been more than a few yards from the muzzles, and most were only a foot or two away. And so, of the eighty-one struck down, forty-seven had died in the street, their blood covering their powder burns.

As Ben stole into the theater, he was ignorant of all this—of the mass killing minutes before, of his accidental part in it, of the fact that his brave, mad assault on the two soldiers aiming at Ashby had caused Sergeant Gabriel Drumont of the Municipal Guard to kill Private Michel Drumont, his younger brother.

Ben stepped into the theater and held his breath for a long moment. The porter was nowhere in sight. And from outside the crowd's cry of Ven*geance*! grew louder, now threading through a song for which it provided a beat, like drums. Ben bounded up the broad carpeted stairs into the darkness, two risers at a time.

He sat on a marble windowsill and examined his hands in the moonlight. On his left palm were four shallow punctures in the shape of a diamond, each prick surrounded by a tiny smear of his own dried blood. He had wounded himself with the penguin's claws.

From his corner of the opera house he looked down on the procession as it moved past. Many carried axes and pikes, and some had guns. He now recognized their tune as "La Marseillaise." Once, at Cambridge, Ashby had accompanied Ben to a Chartist rally and begun to sing it spontaneously, with astounding gusto, attempting in vain to get other students to join in. How he would relish this scene. It occurred to Ben that Ashby might even be down there among them now, singing along . . .

"*Contre nous, de la tyrannie/L'étendard sanglant est levé . . .*" Against us stands tyranny/The bloody flag is raised . . .

"Ven-*geance* . . . Ven-*geance* . . .*"

In the middle of the procession, Ben could see now, were five big open wagons, each pulled by two horses and laden with cargo. They rolled into the little square in front of the Opera. Each had a torch stuck in the whip-socket near the driver, with another six burning torches nailed and strapped around the sides.

"*Mugir ces féroces soldats/Ils viennent jusque dans vos bras/Egorger vos fils . . .*" The roar of these savage soldiers/They come right into your arms/To cut the throats of your sons . . .

"Ven-*geance* . . . Ven-*geance* . . .*"

The cargo in the wagons was people, all lying prone, washed in torchlight.

"*Aux armes, citoyens!/Formez vos bataillons/Marchons!*" To arms, citizens!/Form up your battalions/Let us march!

"Ven-*geance* . . . Ven-*geance* . . .*"

The singers led the march. The people walking nearest the wagons, it appeared, were the ones chanting.

In the back of each wagon were nine or ten corpses, of the forty-seven massacred in the Boulevard des Capucines.

Ben, staring down, saw only piles of strangers rolling slowly past. Arms and legs poked out the sides of the wagons. The huge stains and glistening trickles and drips covering the hands and faces and soaking the shirts in each wagon appeared, from his view, as one great random splatter. The distinctions among individuals were confused by the darkness, by the overlay of blood, by the torchlight, by the collective tremble of the bodies as the wagons rolled over the paving stones. The unity of these citizens was finally complete, unquestionable.

In the back corner of the last wagon Ben spotted his father's parcel, wedged between two bodies. The twine was untied, and the pasteboard had been torn from around the beak to expose the whole head. Unlike the human passengers, the penguin lay on its back, eyes pointed to the sky. To its right lay a woman.

Then, beneath the penguin, Ben saw the back of a waistcoat with broad, pale stripes, soaked through with blood. The head of the man wearing the waistcoat was buried beneath a woman's skirts. His feet and ankles hung out of the open end of the wagon.

Ashby. The sergeant had shot him after all.

Ben strode across the mezzanine. At the top of the stairs, the porter emerged from a storage pantry, his arms filled with stacks of playbills, a dozen of which slid to the floor as he suddenly stopped.

"*Monsieur*—il n'ya pas d'opéra ce soir." *No opera tonight.*

"Oui," Ben said, moving as if he were being dragged downstairs by a lodestone.

Out on the street he broke into a trot and caught up to the last wagon. LES MARTYRS had been scrawled in white foot-high letters on the side. A little stream of blood dribbled onto the rim of the rear right wheel.

The stripes on the waistcoat of the man lying face down beneath the penguin were gold and white. Ben hadn't noticed the silver piping earlier. Ashby, ever the fop.

Ben cried to no one and everyone, "Where are you going? Where are you taking them?"

A few marchers nodded sympathetically and continued chanting Ven-*geance,* Ven-*geance.*

He grabbed onto the corner of the wagon as he walked along beside it. "This is my friend!"

One of the marchers, a man wearing a proper coat and cravat, came over and put his hand on Ben's shoulder.

"*Oui, camarade,*" he said as they walked along, shouting to be heard over the chant and the song. "The friends of everyone. We show and now take the dead to l'Hôtel de Ville."

"But *this* man," Ben said, turning to point at the dead man in the striped waistcoat, "is *my* friend. He is English. He is . . . *mon ami.*"

"Ahhh," the fellow said, looking Ben in the eye. He reached over and gently rubbed his cheek with a rough thumb. Among the nightmare events of the last hours, a strange man touching his face seemed a normal thing.

From a big pocket the man took a thick red crayon and as he walked made a small *x* on the bottom of the dead man's right boot. Then he offered the crayon to Ben. "Le nom? And the place of his home?"

The wagon continued rolling, and Ben walked in a half trot just behind it, crouching down and propping his left elbow against the side, trying to hold the boot steady with his left hand as he wrote ASHBY, CADOGAN PL. LON-DON on the sole from heel to toe. He stood, gently lowered the foot, and handed the crayon back to the Frenchman. The Frenchman lifted the corpse's other foot and scribbled ANGLAIS.

Ben glanced at the penguin. He pointed at it. "That is mine. The bird."

"Ah! C'est à vous?" The man grabbed the penguin with one hand and presented it to Ben.

"Merci," he said, taking it in both his hands, more gently than necessary.

A few minutes earlier Ben had been infused with a sense of unambiguous purpose and high stakes—to escape, to survive. But what was he supposed to do now? Take up the chant on behalf of his dead friend, stagger along with these hundreds of zealous strangers, enlist in the struggle, storm a palace? And then?

He grasped at the first alloy of sentiment and logic that came floating to mind. He would obey his friend's final instruction. He had worked out the code Ashby had invented on the spur of the moment—Winsor & Newton was the maker of his oil paints, so Lloyd had meant for Ben to go to his studio, on the Ile Saint-Louis. He could get a few hours' sleep there. He might have something to drink and eat. He could wash himself, and gather his wits.

"Monsieur?" he said to the man with the crayon. "Où est la Ile Saint-Louis?"

The man turned halfway round and pointed. "Cette direction, to there, one kilometer, more, comprenez-vous"—he made a sharp turning motion with his hand—"un kilomètre more to la Seine."

Ben watched his friend rumble away. At least Ashby was near the top of this hayrick of bodies—and snuggled between a woman's legs, a fact that would have pleased him immensely.

As the wagon made its turn onto the boulevard, Ben looked away, took a deep breath, and set out. He couldn't recall if a kilometer was more or less than a mile. The hour was late. The sound of the crowd's chant grew faint.

His only moment of terror came as he turned down one narrow street and spotted, at the far end of the block, three soldiers. He jumped back, and when he peered round the corner saw that one of them was squatting and sobbing, and wore only his boots. The naked man's confederates shoveled up water from a puddle with their hands and splashed it on his face and back. Ben could imagine no explanation; he could not have known that a minute earlier from an upper window some anonymous defender of freedom had emptied a boiling laundry pot onto the soldiers.

He walked on, toward the east. The only pedestrians he passed were a few prostitutes, and small groups of young men and boys chattering excitedly, the men and boys all striding in the opposite direction, toward the action.

New York City

GOING UPTOWN, they had been in a rush to get to the Granville fire, but for their trip back downtown Skaggs had hailed a Yellow Bird, overruling Duff's ritual protestations that the railway was faster than a bus. "But speed is superfluous," Skaggs said, and Duff was mollified slightly by learning the word "superfluous," which he wrote down in his vocabulary journal.

As the bus stopped near Gramercy Park, a well-dressed young mother boarded, carrying her infant. This was one of the fashionable New York babies, his hair dyed bright red and braided with coral beads and blue ribbons and tiny bells. He sucked milk from a glass bottle shaped like a breast. Duff was embarrassed and looked away. But Skaggs stared at the child all the way downtown, entranced by the flash of the silver nipple in the lamplight with each rhythmic suck and release. No bitter black India rubber for this lucky lad! And surely no swill milk in his glass tit. He looked at the baby—and pursed his lips, bared his teeth, and opened his eyes wide, then wrinkled his nose like a snuffling pig. The baby stared back, unamused, but the mother glanced over and smiled.

"How did you commemorate the Father of Our Country?" Skaggs asked Duff. The day before was George Washington's birthday.

Duff shook his head. "Some of the fire companies held a Birthnight Ball, but I was, I was"—his scar stung—"busy. I was working."

"Ah well, there will be more celebrations before long for *you*, I am sure."

"How do you mean?"

"Have you not seen the *Herald*? President Polk's man in Mexico City has agreed to a treaty."

Duff nodded, said nothing, and continued looking out the window.

Skaggs changed the subject. "I understand your sister was reading today for a part in a *Hamlet*. She may be back on the stage soon."

Now Duff looked at him and shrugged.

"Duff Lucking, you are still in a bad humor over your boys' success with *A Glance*, aren't you? Envy is a *sin*, my son, one of the seven deadlies."

"*No,* I am glad that Frank and Ben have a hit." Last week a new play called *A Glance at New York* had opened, about a firefighting Bowery b'hoy. It was written by Ben Baker, from Duff's fire company, and Frank Chanfrau, another man from 15 Engine, played the hero, Mose. Skaggs had seen the play (he'd cadged free seats as a member of the press) and told Duff that the arriving carriages outside the Olympic had extended for half a mile, and that the audience had stopped the show several times with applause.

"Here you are, then," Skaggs said, pulling the strap. "Thanks again and off you go at *Hewwwston,*" he said, deliberately mispronouncing Houston Street to make it sound like the name of one of Duff's heroes, the Texas politician Sam Houston. Duff nodded goodbye.

Below Houston, the progress of the bus over to Broadway was slow. Half the road was blocked to traffic. Two Negroes were heaving dislodged cobblestones—chunks of the erstwhile Chatham Street, each stone half shiny gray and half filthy black—into a large wagon. A gang of Irishmen meanwhile raked gravel over the exposed and sunken roadbed. This was one of the celebrated new Napoleon-pastry pavements—gravel, planks, a layer of concrete, a thick layer of sand, finally a layer of flat, square-cut stone. These slick streets cost a million dollars a mile. But the new pavements would be (promised the politicians and engineers) so much quieter under the daily pounding and rolling of the city's hundred thousand hooves and ten thousand wheels. The men of progress did everything in their power to increase the racket of the city, then noisily spent and sweat some more to mitigate the racket they had created.

Why did the grandees in swallowtails and top hats not simply say: *We've gotten rich, boys, so we want to* look *rich, and also get a little richer in the bargain.* Skaggs appreciated that money burned holes in the pockets of New Yorkers. And a thousand new millions had been conjured in Wall Street these last few years. He begrudged no one's extravagance. But refrain, please, from pretending that *your* useless extravagance is virtuous because it happens to be *yours.*

Dusk had come and the bus was moving again, past City Hall. Since last he noticed, a new transparency had been installed in the big illuminated frame just below the Park, and a knot of pedestrians stood there now, staring, spellbound by the hidden gaslights, the sheet of glass, the giant lithograph, and "the healthful, modern MIRACLE of Brandreth's Pills." At the very moment of Skaggs's glance, a darkness enveloped and startled the spectators, and as a group they turned to gape: the huge Drummond Light on the roof of Barnum's Museum had been fired up for the night, and Skaggs's bus cast a moving shadow across the street, like a phantom leviathan swimming through the city.

Visiting bumpkins, Skaggs thought. With the rail lines already running halfway to Poughkeepsie and the whole length of Connecticut, country people seemed now to flow into New York City like water through the Croton pipe. All the chatter these days concerned the dumbfounding daily invasion of foreigners by sea—so many Irish! and Germans! and Jews!—but Skaggs generally welcomed that horde. *The more the merrier.* He was a democrat. But he wondered lately if New York might be losing its special tang, if his city might be getting a little *too* American.

Not that Skaggs was unsympathetic to yokels' interest in New York City, given his own yokel origins. He had grown up in New Hampshire, the youngest child of the mayor of Hillsborough. He had been sent down in 1832 to board with his Uncle Gaster on Barrow Street and become a physician. But while Columbia's College of Physicians and Surgeons failed to make a doctor out of him (he was asked to withdraw in 1833), the city quickly transformed him into an urbanite. Except for his four-year exile in the West and his two months in Europe last winter, Skaggs had lived and worked and gallivanted in these same few miles of Manhattan for fifteen years.

At Ann Street he grabbed the signal strap. His customary technique—two gentle tugs—was a courtesy to the drivers, whose leather-shackled ankles were pulled by a thousand strangers a day. He dropped his six cents in the fare box and stepped off the bus—directly into a deep puddle of half-melted snow and blood that just covered a submerged mound of dung.

As the bearded, blue-spectacled, open-collared, sooty-faced, soggy-footed Skaggs shambled down Ann cradling twenty pounds of ungainly apparatus in his arms, and with each step dragging his soles along the stones to scrape off muck, he realized the impression he was making on passersby, who zigzagged to grant him wide berth. He was walking like some old syphilitic, slow and spraddling . . . *Tabes dorsalis,* he recalled now from his one year of medical training. If he were suffering from a venereal disease, it had not yet affected his memory, at least not that part of his memory devoted to the Latin names for venereal diseases.

Suddenly he had the sense of having watched this scene before—as if his own image, right now, had been laid over an earlier image, like a camera plate exposed twice. As Skaggs reached the door of his studio building, he recalled the scene from the past he was confusing with the present: he looked like a clown—a particular English clown, "Percival the Intelligent Penguin," whom he had seen last year in Munich performing on the Max-Josephsplatz. He had been there to research a biography of Lola Montez, the Bavarian king's notorious Irish hurdy-gurdy dancer and mistress. And Lola, in turn, made Skaggs think of Polly Lucking, whose visit he expected in less than an hour.

Paris

BEN'S ROUTE WAS serpentine: the barricades, thrown up by the insurgents to slow the deployment of troops, became more numerous as he headed east into the dark, hard, poor arrondissements. He tried to walk along one wide road, but mounds of rubble and trash had been erected at every block, and when he turned down a smaller street his way was blocked by still more barricades. Each was a mess of broken ladders and hundreds of pulled-up paving stones, washtubs and lampposts, two-legged chairs and broken benches. At the center of one was a splintered piano, and stretching to each corner were piles of manure a yard high. Glass shards were sprinkled over the massive shit berms like sugar on a pudding, and two half-buried rat carcasses—the rats of Paris were much blacker than London's—passed for raisins.

Ben saw a pair of children and a drunkard gathered around the remains of a burning carriage to keep warm. A boy no older than ten sat on an overturned chamber pot looking at pictures torn from a newspaper while he grilled some miserable bit of meat over the red-hot end of an axle. Ben found himself transfixed by a patch of heat-rippled air above the flames. And then, as he was about to walk on, he shook off his daze and realized that through the heat shimmer he was looking at the tops of Notre-Dame's towers.

Dawn was breaking. The tile roofs around him were changing from black to red. Not twenty-four hours ago he had left London Bridge Station.

He walked and walked, and finally reached the river.

In a punt bobbing at the water's edge, a young woman lay asleep. Just above the boat, on the post to which it was lashed, he noticed a bronze sign: *Pont Marie*. Marie had been the stinkpot girl's name. Crossing the empty bridge to the Ile Saint-Louis, stepping into the open air and the pinkish light raking the river, Ben felt exposed and vulnerable, and once on the island he feared he might be trapped. He was startled by the sound of men's voices and the splash of oars, but it was only a laundry boat.

He saw a street sign, the *Rue des Deux Ponts,* and a blue tin number on a house, 39. *Two Bridges Street,* Ashby had said, *your age plus half.* Ben was twenty-six years old.

He found the concierge as soon as he stepped inside—or, rather, she found him, stepping from a shadowy corridor to block his way. She was younger than he. Her arms were folded.

"Bonjour," she said, radiating suspicion and unfriendliness.

The girl there is your sister. "Bonjour, mademoiselle . . . Isabel?"

She thawed. Her arms dropped and her jutting chin receded.

"Oui, je m'appelle Isabelle. Etes-vous l'ami de Monsieur Ashby— Monsieur *Knowles?*" She glanced behind Ben toward the street. "Et où est-il? Ashby?"

"Mort," Ben said.

"Non."

"Oui."

"Non, non, non, *non,*" she said, quick and confident.

For an uncomfortable minute she insisted that Ben was making himself badly misunderstood, that he did not mean to use the French word for "dead." Then she said that Ashby must be with his mistress: "Il est à l'appartement de Mademoiselle Juliet, certainement . . ."

Finally, in exasperation, Ben pointed at his eyes—"I *saw* him, dead, *mort.*" And then formed a pistol with his right hand, pointing the extended forefinger at his temple. "La Garde Municipale," he said, and made the gunshot sound of boys playing soldier. His own pantomime of Ashby's murder shocked Ben, and tears spilled onto his cheeks. He reached for his handkerchief but it was gone.

"Non, *non,*" the concierge said, and put her hands on the sides of her neck as she started to weep.

The studio was a loft, a large single room at the top of the house. It was dark, and neither spoke as they stepped in. She directed Ben toward a long pile of Oriental cushions stuffed into an inglenook, and poured a scoop of coal crumbs over the embers in the fireplace. She picked a newspaper off the floor and laid it on the fire too.

As he sat, sinking toward the floor with his knees in front of his face, he began surrendering to his fatigue, looking not at the fire but into the shadows, at nothing, with the rapt attention of a cretin or a saint.

Near him sat a green sharkskin-covered trunk serving as a table. The concierge struck fire, and he smelled the phosphorus as she brought her match near to light the candle. In the sudden bloom of illumination he found particular objects on which to fix his gaze. Placed around the candle on the trunk was a ceremonial Chinese knife, a couple of books, a rubber-covered tin matchbox, a red paper packet of Turkish cigarettes, a little dish covered with some crumbs of fried sage and salt. He remembered how shocked he had been in Glasgow twenty winters ago, at the first and last wake he had attended, when someone had placed a dish of salt on his dead grandfather's chest.

Isabelle returned with a glass and a bottle of sweet Italian vermouth that she set on the trunk. "Merci," Ben mumbled, and picked up the closest book. It was *Introduction à l'histoire du Buddhisme indien*. The other book was a Dumas story, *Les Frères corses*, in French—*The Corsican Brothers*. Ben had read it (in an American translation) at Ashby's insistence; according to Ashby, when they stopped reading Dumas, they would stop being young. "I know I am *supposed* to read Balzac and Flaubert," he had told Ben, "but I still crave the impossible coincidence. Give me Dumas, or Dickens."

Ben opened the novella to a page at random, and his eyes alighted on a familiar name: *Louis de Franchi.*

Across the room Isabelle jerked open the heavy draperies covering the tall windows, filling the studio with bright gray morning light.

Louis de Franchi, Ben now remembered, was the young Corsican who dies in a duel in Paris, and whose twin brother travels to the city to avenge his sibling in a second duel at the same spot with the same pistol. Louis de Franchi was the name Ashby had mentioned last night, the reason they had stopped to look at the building at 7 Rue du Helder, the reason the girl Marie and the municipal guardsmen had happened to spot them. Lloyd Ashby had died because of their chance discovery of the address of a fictional character from a stupid story. Ben sighed deeply, then poured himself a glass of the red vermouth and sniffed it. It smelled like candy and tobacco, bittersweet.

The concierge finally left him alone in the studio. He saw now that he was surrounded by a dozen of Ashby's finished paintings, all unframed, all but one sitting on the floor and leaning against the walls. Some were small, like the still life to Ben's immediate left (a candle, a rubber-covered tin matchbox, a packet of cigarettes, a dish of nuts, two books, a bottle of red Cinzano vermouth), but a few were huge, five feet by eight. Most were portraits, and in most of those the people appeared much larger than life, big as monsters, all with slightly sinister smiles.

The largest painting was across the room suspended on an easel, facing away from him, the stretcher on the back of the canvas an eight-foot-tall wooden cross. It must be the new picture Ashby mentioned last evening, his political allegory inspired by Hans Christian Andersen. *Last evening:* That seemed impossible.

Ben loosened his bootlaces and sank back deeper into the cushions.

He stared at several of the paintings in turn.

As he sipped the red liquor, he noticed that the right cuff of his shirt was red nearly all the way round; it was blood from the floor of the wagon—Ashby's or someone else's.

Bells chimed continuously, from far away and nearby. He listened to the February wind rattling the windows, and to the coos and pecks of pigeons on the ledge outside. He listened to his own slow breathing.

Never in his life had Ben sat so long doing nothing. His mental state, he realized after a time, was not stupor but rather . . . equilibrium. Until this moment, his life had felt like a dull piece of theater, as if he were a player on a stage reciting lines and performing scripted motions. But now he no longer knew how his story would end, and this filled him with a terrible and joyful new understanding that one's time on earth passed too fast to live life stintingly, to mope instead of plunging ahead.

It was impossibly romantic but indisputably true: fate had provided the chance to start anew. Not merely the chance, he amended, thinking of his dear dead friend—the *duty*. Ben Knowles had been a dutiful son. He had traveled to Paris as a dutiful junior banker and fetcher of stuffed penguins. One day he was expected to become, dutifully, the living Knowles in the firm of Knowles, Merdle, Newcome & Shufflebotham. But for the first time in his life, Ben felt a sense of obligation and honor in his heart, as a fierce desire rather than a dull weight. He had a duty now to throw off the old fetters of filial and social duty.

Perhaps he was delirious. Perhaps all courage was a species of delirium, and all happiness a kind of stupefaction.

He arose, groaning as he made his way up from the sprawl of cushions. Approaching Ashby's work area, he saw that his friend had vandalized a Chippendale tea table for his palette. Its ivory top was covered by a mess of streaks and dabs, most of the colors dry but the tiny puddles of white and dragon's blood and chrome orange still glistening. In a small clearing at the edge of the ivory he had signed his name, ASHBY, in tiny, careful cobalt black letters, as if the random scramble of colors were a picture. Nearby were Ashby's dozens of Winsor & Newton paints, the collapsible metal tubes laid out in two long, neat rows on a battered craftsman's bench.

As Ben came around the easel and saw the work in progress, he gasped.

It was unfinished—the sky and the buildings lining the Rue de Rivoli were white, primed but unpainted. The Luxor obelisk, however, was fully rendered, as were the human figures in the foreground. Six people stood on a balcony at the rear of the Tuileries Palace, with the gardens stretching toward the great granite pole behind them. It was the royal Orléans family, accompanied on the left by the female figure of French Liberty that Ben had watched pass by last night on the Boulevard des Capucines. In Ashby's painting, however, the mythical Marianne carried the flag but no gun, and not just she but *all* of the figures were *entirely* unclothed—except for the seated Duke of Nemours, who wore his naval officer's triangular hat, which covered the genitals of his elderly father Louis-Philippe, the king, standing behind him. A book held by the queen, Marie-Amélie, just managed to obscure her pudendum, but those of her young German daughters-in-law, the Duchess of Orléans and the Duke of Nemours's wife Viktoria, were partly exposed.

Ben felt his cheeks flush as he realized that the naked bodies of the younger women were versions of the same body—that of Isabelle, the concierge. Only Louis-Philippe's little grandson appeared even a bit uncertain about this curious scene in which he appeared; he was painted in profile, hands clasped behind his back, eyes cast down.

The picture shocked Ben. He was not offended by the monumental indecency. He had been to Holywell Street to browse the shelves of smut in the book and print shops. Nor was he surprised that his friend had produced such a lampoon. Lloyd Ashby was practically defined by his predilection for untoward jokes. One gift to Ben for his twenty-fifth birthday had been a private edition of Thomas Rowlandson's illustrated poem, *Pretty Little Games for Young Ladies & Gentlemen, With Pictures of Good English Sports & Pastimes*—which Ashby insisted that Ben read aloud, to the delight of most of those at the party. When he uttered the phrase "flying fuck," however, Lydia Winslow had started to sob, and had to be led from the room.

Rather, Ben was now flabbergast to behold such a rude fantasia executed so grandly and with such care. No work of art had ever produced such an effect on him. The Holywell Street pictures of anonymous whores and libertines were small, quick, embarrassed things. But this! This was perversity on a heroic scale. It was at least as scurrilous as any of Rowlandson's dirty caricatures, but it lacked every convention of comedy—no sketchy line, no ridiculous leers and grimaces and winks, no patent fools and greasy, stumbling drunkards. The painting looked as grave and reverent as a portrait by Ingres. The king and his family (and Liberty) wore expressions of nonchalance and imperious self-regard. They were simply naked.

When Ben leaned in close for a look, he saw that the queen's book was Tocqueville's *La Démocratie en Amérique*. Stepping back to the precise spot where his friend must have stood working the day before, he shut his eyes, sniffling and squeezing out tears. He chuckled. The chuckle became a giggle, and the giggle exploded into a sound like a cawing crow. He let himself crumple to the floor, and there he sat and began to bawl, his left hand touching Ashby's palette, his legs splayed like a child's. After a minute or two he pulled himself to his feet, stumbled back to the cushions, and cried until he slept.

the evening of February 23, 1848
. . .
New York City

UFF HEARD AND felt a rumbling from the front of the room and
looked up from his book. One of his clients had just entered the
tavern, and stood in the doorway stamping slush from his boots.
"Hey, Fatty," he said. "I've got your buck if you've got your coins."

Fatty Freeborn smiled around the cigar stub stuck in the corner of his
mouth, wiped his sticky hands on his pants (molasses scum from his job at a
bakery), and pulled a bundle from the pocket of his peacoat. Like forty other
men Duff knew, once every month or two he brought the pennies he'd
scringed and saved to Duff Lucking's regular stool at Shakespeare's. Duff
would give a brand-new dollar for every dirty hundred pennies they
brought him. Because of the lingering difference in value between *cents* (a
hundredth of an American dollar) and old *pennies* (just less than one-twelfth
of an American shilling), a hundred pennies were, in fact, worth $1.04. So
Duff made four cents on each transaction, a profit for which he had only to
sit in his favorite tavern for a couple of hours each week. The German who
ran Shakespeare's sometimes teased Duff about his little tabletop banking
business, but Duff insisted it was entirely consistent with his hatred of capitalists—he was sparing blacksmiths and masons and butchers the indignity
of slinking, hats in hand, into the prim-and-starch castles of the Bank of
New York and the Chemical Bank to exchange their own coins. Duff suffered in his fellows' stead, making a regular visit down to Wall Street with a

cart to exchange a hundredweight of pennies, fifty dollars' worth, for a three-pound packet of new Philadelphia dollars.

Duff emptied Fatty's pennies into his satchel and handed over a silver dollar.

"Is *Miss* Lucking not here at the crib yet, Duff?" Fatty Freeborn said, with what Duff took to be a leer. "I'm wanting to hear some gossip of the theatrical world from our favorite *actress.*" Freeborn all but snickered as he uttered the last word.

A fury rose in Duff, as it always did when he felt his honor or sense of justice under attack, but he was accustomed to Freeborn's smirking, and managed to temper his rage into a kind of cool menace. He forced a faint smile. "You know, Fatty, I have killed men."

Freeborn grinned back. "Come on there, hoss—am I not a first-rate customer of the Bank of Duff? A true businessman don't threaten his good customers." He spotted a group of his chums standing at the bar, which emboldened him. "And you ain't killed men, Lucking," he said loudly, "you only killed *Mexicans.*" The other boys chuckled, and Fatty turned to address them in an even louder voice. "He didn't kill men, fellas—the damned straight truth is he only killed Mexican *greasers.*"

Duff's face flushed and he felt the sting of blood in his scar.

Staring hard at Freeborn, he plunged his right hand into the open satchel of pennies next to him on the bench, found his enormous Colt's revolver at the bottom, wedged between his books, and made a fist around the walnut grip. Freeborn rocked back and forth on his heels, grinning. Duff imagined his satisfaction at watching the look on that fat face as the .44 ball flew toward it. And with that his anger was slaked.

He let go of the revolver, grabbed as many pennies as he could hold, and scattered them on the floor in front of Fatty. Then he tossed a second and third handful, like chicken feed.

"Take your pennies back. We're finished."

"Well, I am blowed! What a cracked one you are, Duff Lucking," Freeborn said. The clatter of coins had attracted the attention of every man in the front of the saloon, and now, as Fatty laboriously squatted, grunting and red-faced, to retrieve them from among the gobs of tobacco juice, there were guffaws and hoots from the onlookers.

"And besides, I'd trade three of *you,*" Duff said, "for any one of Santa Anna's men, I swear to God."

Freeborn retreated to the smoky back cove of Shakespeare's to play draughts and talk the cocky, artificial Bowery b'hoy talk with his bubs. Most were, like him, members of 25 Hose, what they called the United States Company, their firehouse only a few blocks away.

"Duff Lucking made a muss of you, Freeborn," one said.

"Oh, *gas*," he replied.

"We figured on seeing a real knock-down and drag-out," said another.

"*Gas*," Fatty said again. "I'll knock down and drag you, Toby Warfield."

"That was a prime show," said a third.

But Fatty used his new silver dollar to buy gin-and-cherry cocktails for his whole crew, and the teasing subsided with each round.

Polly Lucking arrived at half past seven. They each turned and looked at her, saying nothing, expressionless, clip-clopping their clay draught pieces across the checkerboard tabletops, then glancing up front again. Their shared silence sharpened their lust and made them uncomfortable.

"*That* is a *prime* peach," said Fatty Freeborn finally. "*That* is ninepence I'd be goin' to the floor for anytime."

At last the boys could smile and snigger instead of pining.

Duff jumped up as Polly arrived. He adored his older sister, felt proud of her smart manner and good looks. He wasn't altogether pleased that she had entered the show business, given the inevitable innuendo of wolves and rats like Freeborn. Yet what Polly said was true: "A dollar is a dollar, and better an actress three hours a night than a four-cent-a-shirt seamstress twelve hours a day, or a house servant for all twenty-four." He fretted that she had always been a bit too bright for her own good, and also too rash and too trusting. (It was her easy girlish trust of Mr. Nathaniel Prime—the *late* Mr. Prime, Duff was pleased to note—that had allowed the old scoundrel to defile her.) But she had also, during Duff's absence last year, grown into a genuine "quick woman," brimming with new ideas about the water cure and phrenology and marriage and the female sex that she seldom hesitated to express. He watched Polly set her pasteboard box of baubles from Stewart's on the deep windowsill near their table and hang her coat on a hook.

"Are you quite all right, Duff?" she asked as she sat. "You seem . . . what's your funny word?—*discombobricated.*"

She could see his moods too well. It made him imagine that one day she might divine all of his secrets. Indeed, he ached to confide in her each of his anonymous manly deeds. The ache to confess in turn made him feel unmanned.

At their dinner together each week he demanded a look at the new pages of Polly's picture album. She sketched graphite-pencil scenes of buildings and portraits of acquaintances, and sometimes pasted in flowers, twigs, bits of lace, ticket ends, newspaper headlines, all sorts of curious bits and pieces.

As a child, she had had a precocious talent for drawing, which is why her father took her to Washington the summer she was eleven. Zeno and Polly Lucking had spent their entire visit in and around the Patent Office. He would find a patent model in the exhibit hall for her to draw, retire across F Street for a glass of sparkling hock, return to the exhibit hall, assign her another model to draw, drink some more hock, and so on. After a few days they'd returned home to the Clove Valley with a portfolio of eight excellent pictures, each slightly altered, of eight newly patented inventions, including a galvanometer, an induction coil, and a dog-powered butter churn. He'd dated each one 1833, three years previous. His scheme entailed sending a drawing and an indignant letter to the respective inventors claiming that he, Mr. Zeno Lucking of Union Vale, New York, had constructed an earlier, nearly identical device—and threatening a lawsuit unless he was granted a share of royalties. Because the government had employed no patent examiners back in the thirties, and issued patents more or less automatically, the plan might have succeeded. Before he took his own life in 1837, his flam seemed to be working: a lawyer for the galvanometer man had offered to pay Zeno Lucking $160 to quit his claim.

"Who is *this*, then?" her brother asked, turning the book to show her a blue-and-red colored-pencil drawing of a reclining girl of thirteen or so.

"Priscilla—Priscilla Christmas. A good girl. An intelligent girl."

"The picture is very lovely, Polly. And so is she, by her looks."

"I found her selling doughnuts at night outside the Bowery Theatre." And submitting for miserably tiny bribes to degrading familiarities.

"She's a project of yours now, is she?"

"Priscilla is a half orphan—her dad is a terrible drunkard who's lost his job at a slaughterhouse." Polly exchanged a look with Duff that acknowledged their own father's awful, unemployed, gin-soaked end. "She was desperately circumstanced. I've got her going to public school is all. And helped her get a bit of regular, indoor work."

Fortunately Duff did not ask his sister to elaborate and thereby make Polly tell him a fib. The regular work she had arranged was at Mrs. Stanhope's house in Mercer Street. It consisted of an assignation once a week with Mr. Samuel Prime. Priscilla earned four dollars for her two hours every

Friday afternoon, more than she had previously earned all week long in the streets selling stale cakes and her filthy person. And the new arrangement allowed her time for school. To Polly, it seemed a reasonable trade, all in all.

Their dinners arrived—boiled pullets for her, beef cutlets for Duff.

"And what of you, Polly Lucking? Regular work, I mean. You have appeared onstage only the one time since I've been back in the States."

She looked at him askance. "You know as well as I that half the first-class theaters in town are rubble and cinders . . ."

This was an exaggeration, although he took her point: the Park Theatre was closed for renovations, and yet another new Bowery Theatre (destroyed in a blaze, for the fifth time) was under construction. For a moment his thoughts circled like a hawk, or a vulture, around an image of this latest Bowery blaze, which he had not actually witnessed. It occurred during his terrible final weeks in Mexico. And now his memories from his whole year of war . . . the scream and blast of batteries of howitzers and mortars, the bombs turning towns into dust and men into pulp, the musket balls whistling past, the hot iron approaching his face just beneath his eye, the smell of his own burning flesh . . . commingled with his eyewitness memories of those earlier Bowery Theatre fires to form a single cosmorama in his mind . . . *Destruction and creation, the cycle of life.*

His sister was still addressing him, still explaining the vicissitudes of a life in the theater.

". . . and it is winter besides," she added, retreating into the seasonal creephole of New Yorkers in every trade, an old annual habit of excuse-making that not even five straight boom years had checked.

"That's my very point, Polly—for work *between* theatrical engagements, you might could sign on with one of the intelligence offices." Duff had only lately discovered these agencies, which specialized in arranging employment for women at publishers and countinghouses and the larger shops.

Polly was having none of it. "Acting is my profession, Duff."

"Of course, I know that, and a fine—"

"Why should I steal the job of some poor girl who *wishes* to scribble numbers on ledger pages . . . or stitch sheepskin and fold books for Harper Brothers?"

"I only meant to suggest—"

"One must persevere. Just today, I applied to play Ophelia in a spring production. And the manager, who is a stranger to me, said he admired my style of acting. He said it was 'unvarnished' and 'singular.' "

In fact, her commitment to perseverance was growing a bit shaky. Most managers and critics were not enthusiastic about her peculiar, understated stage manner. Her career had never gotten back on course, she reckoned, after her debut in 1844 as the rich Miss Tiffany in the comedy *Fashion*. The critic in the *Evening Mirror* had described her as "somewhat fetching but *fidgety*" and having "a quiet voice more like that of an actual society girl than an actress." (The critic, who had signed himself "Boon Companion," was in fact Timothy Skaggs—a pseudonym Skaggs had chosen not to disclose to either Lucking.)

"That's excellent news! You know I fancy Shakespeare." Which was true enough, as long as Bibbo the Patagonian Ape or some amusing fiddler took the stage between acts of the play. "But gosh, another *Hamlet*?" Since December, Duff had pasted up posters for three different stagings of *Hamlet*.

Polly said nothing. Their dessert came, cheesecake for him and a greenhouse orange for her.

"Don't be angry," Duff said softly.

She picked with her fingers at the plate of peeled orange slices flecked with powdered sugar. Then she looked up at her brother, straight on. "'What a piece of work is man.'"

He was encouraged. Polly's teasing was preferable to her silences. He reached into his satchel. He dug down past a thousand pennies and brought out a book. She rolled her eyes.

"It's a new one, Polly," he said. "Based," he added, pleased with the word he was about to utter, "on *psychology*." He showed her the spine—*Hints to Young Ladies Who Are Dependent on Their Own Exertions*. Last month the readings were from *Hints on Etiquette, and the Usages of Society: Containing the Most Approved Rules for Correct Deportment in Fashionable Life.*

"I require no *improvement*," she said as he turned the pages quickly, searching for some edifying passage. "Why do you waste your money?"

Polly knew she was his project. *This* was the reason she called her appointments at the house in Mercer Street "rehearsals" and "readings." (Her *occasional* Mercer Street appointments: thrice weekly, four times at the uppermost.) This, she thought, looking at the carefully combed top of Duff's head, was why she sometimes considered abandoning Mrs. Stanhope's parlor house . . . not to relieve her shame, which she felt only slightly, and which was assuaged by the several gold eagles she earned each week. Rather, she wearied of the dissembling required to protect her brother from a truth he would find unbearable.

"Here!" Duff said. " 'A lady's conduct is never so entirely at the mercy of critics as when she is in the street. Her dress, carriage, walk, will all be exposed to notice; every passerby will look at her; every un-ladylike action will be marked; and in no position will a dignified, ladylike deportment be more certain to command respect.' "

"I believe I am more than sufficiently 'ladylike,' Duff."

"But there are *rules*. A thousand. More!" He turned a few pages and resumed reading. " 'Upon entering a room, she should not rush in head-foremost; an elegant bend to common acquaintance; a cordial pressure, *not shaking*, of the hand extended to her, are all requisite to a lady. Her feet should scarcely be shown, and not crossed.' "

Unseen by anyone, Polly crossed her right ankle over her left.

The front door opened. It was their friend.

"Hallo, Skaggs!" Duff said. "Your new hero was here earlier. Edward Alfred Poe."

For a moment Skaggs wore an expression altogether unlike himself, serious and unsure. As a contributor to last year's new, short-lived satirical weekly, *Yankee Doodle*, Skaggs had taken part in the magazine's regular bemocking of Poe's morbid poems and spooky tales and prickly self-importance. Three weeks ago at the Society Library, he had attended a lecture by Poe, "On the Cosmology of the Universe," intending to write a lampoon. But he had left at the end of three hours a changed man. Although he had not entirely comprehended what he'd heard, he could not stop thinking about Poe's scientific facts (the earth flies around the sun at *66,000 miles per hour!* the light from the nearest star takes three years to reach us!) or his hodgepodge of poetry and philosophy. Skaggs's friends accused him of falling for one of Poe's hoaxes. But he knew that he had witnessed some kind of incandescent genius.

"*Edgar Allan* Poe," he corrected. Skaggs shut the door behind him. The gust from the street doused the lard lamp on their table.

From his pocket Duff pulled a match safe—a tin box in the shape of a tiny pistol—and struck a lucifer to relight the lamp.

"My dear Miss Lucking," Skaggs said as he approached, touching his hat and nodding. "How good to see you again."

"Sir," she said, pleased for the pretext to end Duff's evening tutorial—and pleased, too, to be engaging in this charade with Skaggs, whose arms and creaky studio couch she had left hardly more than an hour ago. Was she not an *actress*, after all?

4

the next afternoon—*February 24, 1848*
. . .
Paris

WHEN BEN AWOKE in Ashby's studio, a blanket covered him. He had had the dream of flying, of being a balloonist without a balloon, swooping as usual over green hills, but the euphoria mingled with panic because in the dream his vision had been magnified, as if both eyes were telescopes, making navigation precarious. He wiped the crusts of dried tears from his eyes and cheeks.

On the little chest next to him he saw that Isabelle had set out a glass of wine and a plate with some smoked duck and a piece of cake. He yawned. He listened. He heard animated chatter and a friendly shout or two in the street, but no chanting mob. A few gunshots in the distance, but no more cannon fire or drummers beating nervous tattoos. Ben assumed the insurgents had been put down, and order restored. He picked up a scrap of purplish duck meat with his fingers. It tasted fatty and delicious.

IN FACT, DURING the last few hours a kind of order had been restored. While Ben slept, King Louis-Philippe, shocked by his army's massacre of forty-seven of his subjects the night before, and no less by his troops' refusal to cheer when he appeared before them, had announced his abdication. He fled Paris in a hired one-horse carriage, using the alias "Mr. Smith." The palace guards, each man wearing an enormous white *X* strapped across his chest, like a gunner's target, scattered. The mob arrived and, as the story required, ransacked the palace. From the windows came showers of satin undergarments and silver cutlery and porcelain trinkets. The throne was hauled outside and, with wads of gilded lace drenched in tallow for kindling, set afire.

Some of the mob had marched across the river to the Palais Bourbon, where they smashed open the great oaken doors to the Chamber of Deputies and there beheld an unimaginably arousing scene: the nine-year-old Louis-Philippe, whose grandfather the king had named to be his successor, stood with his mother, awaiting ratification by Parliament. The insurgents swept into the chamber, where they waved flags and bellowed slogans.

They crowded in close around the little princeling and his mother, actually *jostling* them—a tanner's sooty woolen shirtsleeves rubbed the duchess's organza, a hem of flawless Tuileries velvet wicked the sweat from a wheelwright's forearm—finally forcing this last remnant of the dethroned royal family to run, literally, for their lives.

No Parisian was not astounded by what had occurred, and how suddenly. It was like a dream; it was like a nightmare. During the last several hours, the monarchy had ended, the military capitulated, a republic was proclaimed, the revolution won. History had lurched in Paris.

BUT OF ALL this Ben Knowles knew nothing. His tongue flicked at a strand of duck wedged between two molars, and he poured a dram of the bittersweet Italian liquor into his water glass, watching the cloud of pink slowly roil and sink.

Ashby's death was so entirely pointless.

Further, Ben thought, it had been stripped even of its particularity, the irreducible dignity attending almost any death, by its freakish proximity to the massacre.

He started, like the jerk between consciousness and sleep, at the sound of a knock.

"*Sir?*"

It was a man. His accent was French.

Ben grabbed the Chinese knife from the trunk and crawled to the vestibule as fast as a rodent. If it was the sergeant from last night, Ben intended to avenge Ashby's murder, or die in the attempt. He slipped the weapon from its leather wrapper. He squatted near the door.

"C'est Mademoiselle Levy!" It was the voice of the concierge. Had she betrayed him? "*Isabelle* Levy. Nous avons des *nouvelles!*"

He had no idea what she was saying. He stood. He gripped the knife tight in his hand and held it near his head, like a red Indian laying an ambush in the Leather-Stocking Tales. With his free hand he threw open the door and made a low, guttural animal cry.

Before him were the concierge, dressed in a heavy cloak, and a flush-faced stranger about Ben's age. His eyes had a kind of lunatic brightness. He was dressed entirely in black, including his wool scarf. Ben's wild-man pose and yell had made the man smile fondly, as if he were accustomed to such greetings.

Ben lowered the knife and nodded politely to the man with whom he had, a moment before, expected to engage in mortal combat.

"I am Théodore Surville, the friend of Lloyd Ashby," the Frenchman said. "Mamselle Levy told to me he has become one of our heroes—one of our many martyrs."

"You are not with the army, or the Municipal Guard? Not an agent of the government?"

He laughed. "*No,* no, no, *no.* A fool. A lazy poet. And as well," the Frenchman added, "a man of the barricades. 'The government,' now it is ours. The king has run away." He made a silly running motion with two fingers of his free hand. "The Garde Municipale is already—*congédiée,* terminated, disbanded. It is a revolution. We are now all of us citoyens."

"Oui," Isabelle said. "Oui."

Ben stared. Standing there in the doorway looking at two strange French citizens, he was, for the second or third time in the past twenty-four hours, revising completely his picture of the world. He felt his spirits lift.

"You saw the corpse of Lloyd?" the Frenchman asked.

"I wrote his name on the sole of his boot," Ben replied.

Theodore frowned and then smiled again, apparently savoring this fact. "Good. Good, my friend. We will see to him now." He motioned to Ben to follow him out. "You shall come with us in the streets now."

Ben breathed deeply. "He did not die in vain. Did he?"

"Lloyd? *No!*" Théodore said. "No."

"Qu'a-t-il dit?" asked Ashby's concierge and model.

The Frenchman translated. "Si Lloyd est mort en *vain.*"

"Non!" she exclaimed. "Il est mort pour la *patrie.*"

"She says he died for our fatherland. So to speak. Except, of course, we all of us die always in vain, do we not, eh? Come with the two of us. Witness the new world."

What a queer man. "I need my boots and to gather my things," Ben said, glancing at the penguin as he walked away in his stockings to finish dressing.

"You seem not very English, Mr. Knowles. I believe you are the forgery of an American, like Lloyd."

Ben smiled.

The weather had turned mild and the drizzle had stopped. The streets were filled with people, every one of them gay. Stranger greeted stranger, delighted to call each other *citoyen* again and again, like boys repeating an obscene word they had just learned. Ben saw no soldiers or police. The eyes of nearly every person were red, whether from crying or sleeplessness or drink or all three, he could not be sure.

One gang of old drunkards marched past arm in arm behind a young drummer, all of them shouting "Vive la République!" at the tops of their voices. When one of the old men vomited on himself, one of his companions shouted "Vive le vomi!" Which Théodore repeated without smiling, raising his fist in the air as he did. "One must be drunk *always*," he said a moment later to Ben, "drunk in all meanings. This revolution is metaphysical also. Lloyd knew this."

A young woman strolled along waving a calf's leg in the air like a club.

A brown-and-white spaniel wearing a straw bonnet appeared from an alley and joined the marchers, darting back and forth between their legs like a shuttle in a handloom.

Wine was being poured for free by the *patron* of the Café Cuisinier.

An unharnessed coach horse wandered past, without a driver in sight, followed by a gaggle of honking geese. The feathers of one goose, apparently uninjured, were splattered in blood.

As a sprinkling of white dust cascaded onto Ben's hair and shoulders, he looked up and spotted a little girl on her balcony, half hidden behind a red flag, grabbing handfuls of flour from a tin and tossing them gaily into the air. He thought of Wordsworth's famous lines, about the revolution of 1789—"Bliss was it in that dawn to be alive,/But to be young was very heaven! Oh! times,/In which the meager, stale, forbidding ways/Of custom, law, and statute, took at once/The attraction of a country in romance!" Never had the sentiments of any poem seemed quite so true to Ben. His own nature seemed to him born again.

The red banners, the riderless horse, crowds, ferocious high spirits, white powder drifting down like snow . . . the scene was oddly familiar. Then he recalled: a year earlier almost to the day, he had been a tourist in a different smug and exquisite Catholic metropolis gone temporarily mad, during Carnival in Rome . . .

HE REMEMBERED RIDING out of St. Peter's Square in a huge carriage with his fiancée and her parents. They had watched a delegation of Jews kneel before the pope and present him with a bag of gold ducats—the 480th and final annual Carnival degradation of Rome's Jewish population. "I thought we would see them wear their red Jew cloaks, and ride donkeys backwards," Lydia's mother had complained. "Not in the present century, Mrs. Winslow," Ben had replied.

When they turned down the Via del Corso, he had been happily agog. Nearly every window and door and balcony had been draped with red and gold fabric. From upper stories householders had poured bags of plaster dust onto the crowd, or aimed lime-powdered papier-mâché balls at particular vehicles and pedestrians. Ben had never seen so many candles outside a church, candles set on the sills of every window and in almost every promenader's fist, dancing reflections of candles in windows, reflections of those reflections in windows across the way.

Just when Ben had attempted to direct their driver toward a spot in the Piazza del Popolo from which they might watch the evening Carnival race—riderless horses galloping down the corso—one of the little balls flew through the carriage window, struck Lydia Winslow's cashmered breast, and fell onto her besatined thighs, marking each with a sparkling white spot of lime. Ben had picked it up from her lap with two fingers, careful not to touch Lydia herself, and tossed it from the carriage. An instant later, Satan thrust his face through the window, and then his redpainted hand, holding the discarded ball, followed by Jesus, whose wig of long hair whisked Lydia's cheek. Without a word, she slammed the palms of both hands against the faces of Christ and Lucifer, crumpling the papier-mâché forehead of the former, breaking a papier-mâché horn of the latter, and provoking the masker who wore both faces, one on each side of his head, to threaten to set the carriage afire with his candle. Then Lydia felt a stinging speck of lime in her eye—"some deadly Italian *poison*," she cried.

Later that evening, Lydia Winslow had taken his hand in hers and mewled, "Benjamin Knowles—I wish never to leave Great Britain again. *Promise* me!" He declined to make the promise. In fact, it was that evening during Carnival in Rome that he had decided to end their betrothal.

. . .

"MONSIEUR KNOWLES!" ISABELLE Levy shouted. Ben had, in his reverie, walked several paces past them. He was watching a group of Parisians wedging loose cobblestones beneath a surrendered artillery piece in order to tilt the barrel downward toward the Seine, as if they planned to fire it into the water for sport.

"You are still sleeping, Mr. Knowles," Théodore said, a little teasingly, then pointed to his right. "We have arrived. L'Hôtel de Ville. The town hall. And now our morgue. You understand? The deadhouse for the martyrs."

Hundreds of people milled about the building, inside and out, meeting, strolling, arguing, speechifying, laughing, crying.

Ben and his companions entered a sort of ballroom as big as a railway station. It smelled like a Catholic church. Two men, each grasping the chains of an incense burner, paced the floor randomly, like altar boys adrift among the martyrs. The censers' smoke masked the smell of putrefying flesh. The hall was filled, end to end, with three neat long rows of camp bedsteads, two hundred in all. In each bed lay a corpse. The orderly lines of absolutely still cots reminded Ben of the rows of paint tubes on the bench in Ashby's studio.

Ben waited while Théodore and Isabelle went off to speak with a functionary about retrieving Ashby's body and shipping it back to England. They seemed to be arguing. Théodore had told Ben he was friendly with an embalmer at the medical school, but Ben said he thought embalming was unnecessary, given that London was only twelve hours away by rail and steam ferry. "*Ah,*" the Frenchman had replied, "now *hearses* by steam"—and then embarked on a rant about "the contest between modern machine and modern chemistry to serve Death," and how Paris was being "murdered by all of the new iron tracks and steam monsters at *five* railway stations now!" Ben had ceased to find this man amusing. The truth was, Ben could not bear the prospect of allowing a surgeon to cut open Ashby's belly, scoop out his intestines like a taxidermist, and stuff his empty gut full of spices and turpentine.

"It seems Ashby is nowhere," Théodore said when they returned from the attendant's desk. "He is not in this place."

The nightmare had become farce. The French murdered Ashby, and now they had misplaced his remains. What was it he had said yesterday about how the insurrections would end? As tragicomedy.

"They have some confusion," Théodore said. "It is the revolution." He shrugged. "A few of the dead were put out for the north already this morning, by coach, with ice, to Normandy. Lloyd is perhaps among them, I think."

"Vers l'Angleterre," Isabelle said.

"Yes, toward England. You named him, you wrote on the shoe, yes?" Ben nodded.

"Therefore," Théodore shrugged, "we shall wish for the body to arrive home." He seemed almost to enjoy the fact of Ashby's disappearance. "Perhaps he shall arrive even before you on the train."

It had come time for Ben to continue his own journey.

Outside in the square they found him a cab. At the Hôtel Diderot he would bathe and dress before going to Mary and the Count de Tocqueville's for dinner. Next morning he would try to attend to his Knowles, Merdle, Newcome & Shufflebotham business with the sewing machine manufacturer, as planned, and then head back to England.

He sighed. He looked at his father's penguin standing on the seat opposite. The bird was vibrating in a lifelike fashion as the carriage rolled along. Its glass eyes stared directly at him. Now that he was face-to-face with it, he noticed that its mouth was fixed in a kind of smile, and a smudge of blood remained on the underside of the beak. The wrapping around its body looked like a little straitjacket.

He had spent less than an hour yesterday at his hotel, but it now looked to him like the one familiar place in this alien city, a refuge. The door was blocked by a servant girl outside on her knees, her back to Ben, intently polishing the brass with a rag. He stepped close. She continued polishing. He cleared his throat. She did not notice.

As he mentally rehearsed the word and his accent—*Mademoiselle? Mademoiselle?*—a man on the pavement behind him said, "Bonjour, mon citoyen anglais."

Ben glanced back and saw the fellow, tall and unsmiling. He was evidently a workman come to make repairs at the hotel. But he was holding a book in his left hand, and the cover was open.

"Votre livre," he said, reading from the endpaper, "Monsieur Ka-nole."

"I am afraid, sir, that I am not Monsieur Ka-nole . . ."

But then Ben realized that the book was the guidebook he had dropped in the street, that "Kanole" was a French mispronunciation of "Knowles," that the man's right hand was bandaged. At first Ben had not recognized him, dressed in ordinary clothing. But it was the sergeant from last night.

Ben reached into his coat, unsure if he had pocketed—*yes*—Ashby's little Chinese knife. In a single motion he drew it out and stabbed into the bandaged hand, and hurled the penguin at his face, then shoved past the girl into the hotel, slammed the door, and twisted the latch shut.

Just ahead he spotted a darkened cloak closet and leapt inside. He stood very still, gripping the knife close against his chest. He heard two violent knocks on the front door of the hotel, wood against wood. He heard the sergeant shouting at the girl. He heard the clicks of a key working its way into the lock, and the door open. He felt the heavy thump and shuffle of boots just a few feet away. He imagined he could feel the heat of the sergeant's breath. Then he heard raised voices inside the hotel, and the clatter of wheels from the street.

A moment and an extra moment later, he tiptoed from his hiding place—and encountered the servant girl, looking shocked. Ben held his forefinger to his lips. She held his penguin in her arms like an infant, its neck now broken and head bobbling, and offered it to him. He shook his head and placed the knife back in his coat pocket. The front door was open.

He dashed out, and away, to the west.

He ran with all his might for five minutes, ten minutes, on the pavements and in the gutters, toward the sun. He had no hat to wear, no penguin to lug, no companion to abide, nothing but the stuff in his pockets; he was sweaty, uncombed, and nearly squalid; he was free. He moved so fiercely that the dogs and celebrating drunks and barrow boys dodged from his path.

As he approached a modest barricade, he did not turn away, or stop for a reckoning: he leapt up onto the rubble heap, and before his first stepstone slipped away he leapt left onto an overturned barrel, and then back into the street ahead, making straight for the Gare Saint-Lazare.

"Un billet, s'il vous plaît," Ben said to the agent, "pour Dieppe."

The agent looked him over. "Vous êtes un *Américain,* monsieur?"

Ben supposed that "Yes" was the right answer. His Foreign Office passport was in his pocketbook, but on the journey to Paris no official anywhere had asked to check it.

"Oui," he said.

The man's manner was unusually friendly and enthusiastic for such a factotum. Instead of writing out a ticket and asking for a fare, however, the man embarked on a cascade of explanation, long and complicated but evidently good-humored. Ben understood practically nothing. Finally, smiling, the agent finished with a question that contained the word "*expérimental.*"

Yes. That struck Ben as precisely the right course. He would proceed experimentally in all things. "Oui," he replied again, agreeing to do whatever the agent had proposed, and slid a twenty-franc piece across the counter. At this the agent's smile turned more typically French. He held the coin up and tapped its edge with one finger—pointing to the profile of King Louis-Philippe. " 'Le roi des Français,' " he said, quoting the inscription. He shook his head. "Il est *fini.* C'est la fin de *tout* cela."

"Oui," Ben replied. *He is finished. All that is finished.* This he understood.

Good luck, as it turned out, was flowing his way. The agent had said that the new track from Paris to Rouen was barely completed, and would carry no regular passengers for weeks. However, on each Friday until then a two-car train was making an experimental run to test the new track, departing at five o'clock. Although no paying passengers were officially permitted to ride, the ticket agent would make an exception for Ben, *un cadeau,* as a gift, because he was an American and now France was a free republic, like America. In Rouen he could catch the regular train to Dieppe, on the Channel. "C'est parfait, non?" the Frenchman said.

And perfect it turned out to be. For more than two hours, until one minute before five, Ben skulked cautiously in a corner of the station, touching the knife in his pocket whenever he felt a pulse of anxiety.

As the locomotive got its full head of steam at the edge of the city, near Batignolles cemetery, the driver pulled the whistle. Ben took a deep breath, exhaling along with the engine, and pressed his face against the window of the coach as it hurtled at a mile a minute toward the sea.

THE SUDDEN MONSTROUS lowing of the train whistle 150 yards away caused the sergeant and the priest to glance up from their two-meter hole in the earth of Batignolles. Sergeant Drumont would have preferred a grave for his brother among the lemon and juniper breezes in the hills above Ajaccio, on Corsica, but there was no family tomb and no money to ship the body. Anyway, Michel had grown up here. Thanks to his older brother Gabriel, who had brought the boy north when their mother died, Paris was Michel's home, now and forever, the poor dear boy.

BEN ARRIVED AT the dock forty minutes after the overnight Channel steamer was scheduled to leave, but the boat had been delayed to take on a skittish, odd-looking Frenchman wearing orange spectacles who arrived by coach in Dieppe with five trunks at the same moment as Ben.

Unbeknownst to Ben, the man was wearing a wig and false eyeglasses—a disguise for his escape from France. Until yesterday he was the deputy minister in charge of Sainte-Pélagie, the prison where insurrectionists and radical journalists had been jailed. During their hours at sea Ben repeatedly sneaked glances at the fellow, wondering if he was connected to the Municipal Guard; Ben's furtive attentions caused the deputy minister to imagine that Ben was a spy tracking him to England. At the Brighton Chain Pier they scuttled off in opposite directions as quickly as each could manage.

February 25, 1848

. . .

London

THE LOCOMOTIVE *JENNY LIND* had Ben in Victoria Station before one the next day, and he stepped up to his own red front door in Bruton Street only a minute after the baker's boy had left the afternoon bread. Ben picked up the wrapped loaf and brought the bag close to his face to breathe in the yeasty warmth . . . then remembered his resolve to resist the familiar and comfortable.

He stepped inside, glancing down at the letters and magazines (*The Graphic,* containing the penultimate installment of Dickens's *Dombey and Son,* and *Punch,* with the latest chapter of Thackeray's *Vanity Fair*) that his man Dennis had laid out in neat stacks on the silver tray in the entrance hall.

He paused. Among the letters was a small parcel, delivered by a messenger and printed with the return address of Ermen & Engels, the cotton cloth company. It contained an anonymous new twenty-four-page pamphlet with a green cover, printed in Liverpool Street. Its coauthor, according to the attached note, was his German friend Frederick, who had managed his own father's mill at Manchester during the year Ben spent there overseeing the installation of new power looms in the Knowles mill. When they first met, Frederick Engels had called Ben his doppelgänger, but during that year, in fact, Ben had realized he could summon no authentic hatred of capitalism or its technologies, only of the dreary paternal drudgery of counting money and managing laborers. Engels was the very opposite of Ben, an anticapitalist who nevertheless reveled in overseeing his own capitalist enterprise. When Ben told his father that his friend called himself "a huckstering beast," Sir Archibald had nodded approvingly and told his son that he "could stand to work up some spirit of the huckstering beast" himself.

Exhausted and frowsy, standing in the vestibule of his house off Berkeley Square, Ben examined Engels's new booklet. *Manifest der Kommunistischen Partei,* it was called, *The Manifesto of the Communist Party.* He tore the first pages apart with his finger and read the first sentence. *"Ein Gespenst geht um in Europa—das Gespenst des Kommunismus."* His German was rusty, but his favorite tavern in Bonn ten years ago had been Das Kleine Gespenst, "The Little Ghost," so he understood: "A ghost goes over into Europe—the ghost of communism."

"Ghost" was an odd choice of metaphor, he thought, very German. And then he thought of the late Lloyd Ashby, an accidental revolutionary, now an accidental ghost. Ordinarily Ben would not consider wading through such a work in English, let alone in German. Ordinarily the pamphlet would go directly to some out-of-the-way shelf, uncut and unread. But times were no longer ordinary. He would ask Dennis to cut the pages for him.

the same day—February 25, 1848
. . .
New York City

M RS. STANHOPE CALLED the fourth floor her "dormitory
suites," but to everyone else who worked in the house it was
"the barracks," for it contained the actual sleeping quarters
of the four women who boarded at 101 Mercer. A privy closet had been
rigged up as well, because Mrs. Stanhope considered it charmless for women
to step outside to the backyard to use the jakes (a phrase Mrs. Stanhope despised) when gentlemen were present.

But the largest of the snug rooms on the top floor was the upstairs pantry.
There each evening Mrs. Stanhope set out plates of chocolate-covered wal-
nuts and hard candies, and there was a shelf devoted to baking soda and
vinegar. But this pantry was not mainly a place for keeping food. It was,
rather, the largest, most specialized medical supply cabinet any of the girls
had ever seen. There was a shelf of instructional books and pamphlets, including *The Married Woman's Private Medical Companion* and *Mysteries
of Females, or, The Secrets of Nature* and *Every Woman's Book, or, What
Is Love?* There were pewter syringes and lengths of hose hanging from
pegs. There was a box of plum-sized sponges from which long pink and purple ribbons dangled. There were, lately, several spring-loaded India rubber
"circular dams" that Mrs. Stanhope had bought by mail from their inventor
(and which none of the girls wished to use). There were tins and bottles of
practically every powdered astringent in existence, strychnine, chloride of

soda, bromide of potassium, and all the acids—prussic, carbolic, tannic, boric. And on the occasions when those sluices and baths failed to neutralize every stray animacule and zoosperm deposited by the hundred weekly patrons of 101 Mercer Street, the pantry also had its shelf of poisonous compounds intended to undo accidental conceptions: Dr. Van Hambert's Female Renovating Pills, Madame Arnaud's Modern French Regulating Medicine, Grigsby's Infallible Antidote Tablet #2. The only patent medicines in the pantry with no proud maker's name attached were the Scientific Mercury Ointment and the Unfortunate's Friend, treatments for "blood poison," as Mrs. Stanhope insisted that syphilis be called.

The most reliable preventatives of disease filled a whole drawer of the pantry. Two gross of condoms arrived every month. And they were not the cheap fish-membrane or oiled-silk versions, or skimpy caps, but true "baudruches" (as the proprietress was pleased to call them), full-length French safes. And at 101 Mercer, each baudruche was used only once. Even in bulk they cost Mrs. Stanhope fifty-two dollars a month, but she knew that her patrons appreciated this gratuity. She had calculated that this fifty-two-dollar expenditure enabled her to charge two bits more per assignation. It was a similar calculus by which she had justified spending fifty cents a day for the "free" wine punch she served, and another fifty cents for ice in the summertime, and forty cents a day for her Croton water. Hospitality made sense if you could profit by it.

Conversely, she preferred not to pay cash money for goods and services. She had worked out a barter arrangement with the physician who visited 101 Mercer every two weeks to examine the girls. (This "Dr. Jones" was, in fact, Dr. Simon Solis, introduced to Mrs. Stanhope by his old pal and Columbia College classmate Timothy Skaggs.)

The recent proliferation of lust-houses up and down Mercer and Greene from Canal to Houston Street had weakened the counting-room will of most of the other brothelkeepers in the neighborhood and pushed prices down. The formerly superb place around the corner on Spring was now, late on some warm nights, attracting a small crowd of clerks and even mechanics smoking and spitting and laughing in the street outside; they paid no more than a dollar, and came and went in less than an hour.

Lately too there was talk of the rich widow Gibbs in Greene Street selling her house, which was just behind 101 Mercer, and of the prospective owner planning to rig up the place as an *eight*-bedroom parlor house with polka music and free oysters. But Mrs. Stanhope was resolute. In her opinion the difference between a Mercer Street parlor house and a Squeeze Gut Alley public house was clear. Her women were not *sluts*. Discreet pandering and public lewdness, she told them, were two quite different things, each with a distinct clientele and different dynamic of supply and demand. Do the hot-coal eaters in Paradise Square or the little dogs leaping through flaming wood hoops on the stage of some Bowery free-and-easy compete with Junius Brutus Booth onstage at the Park Theatre? By no means. If tons of rough hemp cloth are in the shops for six cents a yard, does the price of silk brocade fall? It does not.

Nevertheless, when Polly read in the *Sun* the estimate by some rector that one in ten young women in New York now "pursued the life of a prostitute at least a part of the time," she was slightly alarmed. Nearly all New York men with money paid women for sexual companionship; the demand would continue to meet the supply. What disconcerted her was not the prospect of a legion of new girls drawn into the occupation, but rather the phrase "a part of the time." Polly Lucking needed to consider herself *unique*. Except for the publishing assistant who had worked at 101 Mercer for a brief time last year, she was acquainted with no one else who worked as a prostitute a *part* of the time. Among the women of 101 Mercer, only Polly seriously pursued another line of work, and while her theatrical wages alone could not possibly allow her to live in the manner she maintained, she appeared onstage often enough that she could regard whoring as her sideline, a kind of lucrative hobby. (Not unlike her father's Sunday afternoon outings up East Mountain when she was a girl, only *successful:* Zeno Lucking had spent hundreds of hours digging a crisscross of ditches deep in the woods, searching for a legendary cache of gold Dutch guilders.)

She had enjoyed her enormous income this last year, but she also relished her visits to the house itself, its piped water, its cheerful colors, clean cushions, practical rules, and apple-pie order. She doted on its domestic comforts so much, in fact, that she'd decided from the first she should not live there, for she knew she would never want to leave. So Polly paid twelve dollars a month to live in two pleasant, respectable rooms in a building south of Washington Square. Yet even after expenses, she had put away $411 in the last fifteen months—managed to *save*, in other words, much more than she'd *earned* sewing slop shirts for two years in that dim, mildewy cellar on Centre Street.

But what of the ruining act itself? Giving every private inch of herself over to the slobbering kisses and rough caresses and animal squirts of any anonymous brute with a few bucks? For a start, the price at 101 Mercer was five and (for Polly) ten dollars: the tariff kept out most of the roughest and stupidest and stinkiest slobberers. Polly found her assignations tiresome, sometimes pathetic, occasionally amusing, but seldom awful. Virtue and sin aside, it seemed to her like a chore, not so different from caring for the family's sheep as a girl in the country—milking the seven ewes every morning, mucking out their pens once a week. What's more, her chores at 101 Mercer were freely chosen. And the "parlor work," as the girls called the talk and flirtation that preceded the hour or two of "bedchambering," Polly positively enjoyed. As a seamstress she certainly never had the chance to exchange pleasantries with bankers and lawyers and dancing masters.

"*Ah!* My Good *God!*" cried Mr. Skyring, the dancing master. He and the bed shuddered. "*Oh . . . oh . . . oh,*" he mewed. "My my my *my,* yes . . ."

Did husbands bellow out to wives in this fashion, or were speaking and moaning in bed among the unruly privileges for which men felt obliged to pay? And did married women *reply* to men's ejaculatory exultations? As a rule, Polly did not respond in kind, although sometimes she punctuated the void with a sportive coo or sigh, as if to say: *Well done, sir,* and *Let's move along.* But by his enthusiastic manner, Prosper Skyring—a man of sixty who visited the last Friday or Saturday afternoon of a month and always mounted her from behind—practically begged for a reply. And in this, as with his unorthodox physical practice, Polly indulged him. He was a sweet old boy, her favorite customer.

"*Yes,*" she whispered back. "*Yes.*"

She was, after all, an actress.

"*Elizabeth,*" he shouted as he plunged himself into her triumphantly.

After two or three softer thrusts, he pulled himself off and she felt his member graze the back of her thigh. She turned over to face him and pulled the blanket to her neck. She stared at his nakedness, examined it analytically— the way the "artists" at Heilperin's Studios pretended to do, seated in their semicircle around the unclothed models, each holding his rented sketchbook and pencil.

The euphemism among the women of 101 Mercer was "sausage." At this moment, just after the act but with the spent organ still wrapped tightly in the thin skin of a baudruche, the nickname seemed especially apt—but it looked to Polly like a sausage in a funny dream where time runs both backward and extremely fast, the meat turning in a few seconds from hot and plump and juicy to soft and raw.

When Skyring finally opened his eyes, Polly was fortunately looking not at his shrinking manhood but at his long white mane of hair, which had become wildly disheveled. The glimpses of tidy, well-furnished men in private disarray always pleased her.

"Many thanks, as ever, Miss Bennet," he said, giving his head a little dip as he pushed his hair back with one hand. "I am restored."

"My pleasure," she said.

"Ah, you are far too kind, my dear Miss . . . *may* I call you Elizabeth, Miss Bennet?"

"Of course you may, Mr. Skyring."

Polly Lucking used several false names with the clients at 101 Mercer. With the first man she had entertained, on the night of All Hallows' Eve 1846, she had decided to introduce herself, on the spur of the moment, as "Elizabeth Bennet," and the next evening, with the next client, she was "Catherine Morland." Later, with other men, she was "Betsy Bowditch," "Emma Woodhouse" and—her favorite, cobbled together from the names of her two most pious childhood acquaintances—"Presence Goodnight." She kept a little index of her fibs in order to keep the identities consistent. In fact, she knew that some of the men used aliases as well, although certainly not Prosper Skyring, as fanciful as his name seemed. It was painted in nine-inch green cursive letters on the window of his dancing studio in Bleecker Street.

Skyring retrieved his clothing from the armoire, and Polly pulled on her drawers and chemise. They were hand-stitched linen; she actually preferred the feel of soft muslin against her skin, but Mrs. Stanhope called factory-made undergarments "inexcusable inexpressibles," and required the girls at 101 Mercer to wear linen. Corsets were required for the parlor hours too, of course, although Polly now left hers on the peg. She was thin, and her dislike of tight lacing—the whalebone busk felt like a dagger between her breasts—had a scientific rationale these days. Skaggs's acquaintance Mary Gove, who was a medical lecturer and water-cure therapist, had told Polly that wearing a corset was actually unhealthy.

Opening the draperies, she looked out and saw that a dusting of snow covered the intersection. The filthy gray cobblestones and piles of dung and bones and wet ashes were, for a few precious minutes, disguised under a new coat of virginal white.

"Snow," she said. "The last of the season, if we're lucky."

Skyring sat on a stool, struggling a little with his boots. "The last of the season indeed," he said, winking an eye, "for I won't see you again until April." He stood. "Misery!" he shouted, then stepped toward her and placed a hand lightly on each of her arms. " 'From you have I been absent in the spring,' I forget the next, et cetera, and the next, 'when daisies pied and violets blue, and lady-smocks all silver-white, and cuckoo-buds of yellow hue do paint the meadows with delight, the cuckoo then, on every tree, *mocks* married men, for thus sings he' "—he raised his voice a ridiculous couple of octaves—" '*Cuckoo! Cuckoo!*' " He leaned forward stiffly from the waist and kissed her on the forehead. " '*Cuckoo!*' "

Polly giggled. He took a little parcel from his coat pocket and presented it to her in cupped hands, his head slightly bowed. It was her fee, ten silver dollars wrapped in brown paper. She took it in a fist and curtsied.

Two floors below, Priscilla Christmas sat in the front parlor, luxuriating in her own rosy aroma and well-scrubbed glow; in *Phantasmion,* the big fairy book Polly had loaned her; and in the warm macaroons and cold milk the housemaid had set out on the table for her. She rubbed her fingers over the plaits of her thick, freshly braided and beribboned black hair. Even the sounds of the room were sumptuous—the faint hiss of steam in the cast-iron heater, the whoosh and tinkle as Mary the housemaid (using one of the pewter syringes from the upstairs pantry) watered the pots of aspidistra and maidenhair ferns, the songs of the caged canaries, the pendulum swing and ticking gears of the ship's clock on the mantel.

Priscilla had just descended to await her appointment. Each Friday by four she arrived wearing a gray gingham smock that she stripped off as quickly as she could and left in a hamper with her underclothes for the laundry. And by quarter past five she was transformed—bathed, braided, perfumed, powdered, and attired in the costume kept in the closet next to the upstairs pantry, a periwinkle-blue velveteen dress with a brocaded bodice and enormous skirts that made her feel like a woman. Thanks entirely to Polly's generosity and this little job of work at 101 Mercer, she felt that she was enjoying much of the best of both worlds: the pleasures of a respectable childhood (sweet snacks, clothes washed every week, time to attend school and read adventure tales) as well as those of adulthood (a splendid dress, polite conversation, a decent income). And because her father was guaranteed to be dead drunk by the time she returned home at seven, she had no fear that he would start wondering why she came home so clean and sweet-smelling every Friday evening. Her secret was safe.

Although her name at 101 Mercer was Minerva Spooner, Priscilla let Mr. Prime call her by several silly nicknames of his own devising, such as "my nastypuss." But despite his kindness and recent, rather shocking professions of love, she had no doubt that whoring was sinful. She was unconvinced by the argument, advanced by a boy she knew, that the long limbo between the statutory age of consent (ten) and the statutory age for marrying (sixteen) amounted to a ratification of licentiousness for New Yorkers of their age. But surely God himself would prefer that she sin only once a week in a clean, well-heated house, rather than giving two-minute yankums for a quarter dollar in some foul back alley, or letting newsboys pay five cents to rub and squeeze her bubbies at night in the Park. Anyhow, *she* preferred it.

Not long before the parlor clock struck five-thirty, Priscilla shivered and looked up suddenly from her reading. The room was still warm. She was having one of her inklings. Once a week, sometimes less often, she experienced an odd prognostic intuition—seldom specific enough, alas, to help her dad with his gambling, but a second sight reliable enough to know whether her own luck was about to take a turn for good or ill. The shiver just now had not been a happy one.

POLLY HAD TAKEN a shower bath before dressing. She was still upstairs in the third-floor bedchamber, looking down at Spring Street. She leaned against the window, staring at the snow, already striped with the tracks of carts and coaches and sleighs. She moved her face close enough to smell the glass and feel the cold on her nose and cheeks. With each warm exhalation she turned the pane cloudy. She lifted her forefinger and drew a star in the steam. As she finished she dipped her head to look out through the star and spotted a man walking down Spring from Broadway, toward the house. It was Samuel Prime, here for his Friday afternoon appointment.

She harbored no hard feelings toward *this* Mr. Prime. In the summer of 1837, after her father's bankruptcy and suicide, her mother had moved with Polly and her three siblings to a drafty little three-room house leased for them by her brother-in-law in a suburb of New York. In fact, it was in a suburb of a suburb on Long Island, just north of the new town of Astoria, and

on the southern edge of Hurlgate, the Prime family's country seat overlooking Manhattan. Nathaniel Prime, Samuel's father, had been one of the city's
great moneymen, a banker and stockbroker and founder of Prime, Ward &
King in Wall Street. Samuel was in his thirties when the Luckings appeared
at Hurlgate, and from the start had behaved warmly toward his unfortunate
new tenants. He sat for one of Polly's pencil portraits. He even allowed the
Lucking children to play with his own three young children, and had
arranged for twelve-year-old Polly and ten-year-old Duff to work a few
hours a week in his family's icehouse (Duff) and hothouse (Polly).

It was in the hothouse late on a golden September afternoon, as she
paused from sweeping up bits of soil and yellowed leaves to look at the
splendid view (the sky, the water, the gardens of Rikers Island), that the elderly Mr. Prime had appeared behind her. He had a big, toothy smile, a dish
of vanilla ice cream, praise for her sketches, an insistence that she call him
"Nat," and—as it turned out—designs on Polly's virtue. As she lay beneath
him she had fixed her gaze on the words *Nil Invita Minerva* etched in the
rectangle of glass over the door. It was the Prime family motto—"Nothing
contrary to one's genius."

As he'd dusted himself off afterward, he half convinced her that she had
suggested or anyway provoked the lovemaking. She had done no such thing,
Polly knew now—although she had not very strenuously resisted his ad-
vances either, despite the story she told her mother. Why had she capitulated without much of a fuss? The greenhouse fragrance and humidity were
always intoxicating; the ice cream tasted wonderful; he was no taller than
she, which made him unthreatening; he was rich, famously rich, ten times
richer than her father had dreamed of becoming; she was flattered and curious; and she knew that she was still too young to become pregnant.

Thus was Polly Lucking "devirginated," as her mother described it some
weeks later to the lawyer at the Primes' offices—"sprawled in broad daylight on the filthy floor of a garden shed." Polly still recalled that visit to
Wall Street with exceptional clarity—indeed, more clearly than the incident
that brought her there. It was her first ride on a ferry and her first visit to
New York City. She thrilled at the huge new buildings—the Custom House,
the Merchants' Exchange. When she and her mother arrived at the appointed address, six men with muskets were standing in front of the building. For a moment Polly imagined they were there for her, but then she saw
they were guarding a pair of vans filled with tiny kegs, each one marked "B
of E." Later that week Polly's uncle read in the newspaper that the Bank of

England had loaned Prime, Ward & King $5 million—the two hundred little kegs, $25,000 worth of gold in each one, shipped from London to New York.

When Polly told Timothy Skaggs this whole story late one night last year, not long after they had become playmates, he had laughed and laughed, and accused her of fabricating the tale. "You were *deflowered* on the *last day of summer* lying beneath hundreds of *daffodils* and *petunias?*" he said when he was finally able to catch his breath. "At *Hurlgate*—the gate of *hell?* By Nathaniel 'Slice' Prime himself?" She hadn't known about the elder Mr. Prime's posthumous sporting-paper nickname, "Slice."

Even after she had come close to crying and finally convinced Skaggs she was telling the truth, he continued to joke about it. "Do you suppose," he had asked her, "it was some feeling of guilt concerning you that finally provoked the old man's suicide? I ask because I invented that very twist for a villain in one of my stories." Polly had considered and rejected this possibility. Three years after her greenhouse encounter with Nathaniel Prime, the old man was found dead in his house at the bottom of Broadway, his throat cut from ear to ear. She remembered learning of his suicide from Duff, who had run into the Luckings' apartment excitedly, practically gleeful, holding in each hand the articles he had ripped from the *Sun* and the *Herald*. "*No,*" Polly had replied to Skaggs. "When the Primes gave my mother the three hundred dollars, it was more than enough to atone on my account. It was some different demon," she said, "that killed Mr. Prime."

Charlotte Lucking had used most of that money to pay her late husband's business debts, and the remainder to move her family into Manhattan. Polly had hardly thought of the Primes again until last year, when Samuel happened to attend *The Hunchback and the Dumb Belle* and made his way backstage after the show to praise her performance. Polly wondered at that moment if she was about to be seduced once again by a Prime. But Samuel showed no interest—and when they next met, many months later for supper, he dismayed her by asking if she knew "of any financially needy *young* woman as attractive and intelligent as yourself." Yet Prime's wildly impertinent suggestion—she was only twenty-two at the time, and an actress, not a procurer—struck Polly as auspicious. She had just met Priscilla Christmas.

The arrangement had worked out well for everyone. Each Friday evening Priscilla went home to the Five Points with four dollars hidden among the school chapbooks in her satchel. Mrs. Stanhope spent an extra few cents a week on laundry and cookies, and earned a dollar for her trouble. Samuel Prime remained clueless that Polly herself had any professional involvement with 101 Mercer. He knew only that Mrs. Stanhope was a former actress Polly had met in the theater, and that Polly had sincere sisterly feelings for the destitute young Miss Christmas. According to Priscilla, Samuel Prime was exceptionally gentle during her weekly hour with him. "Well, it was more like a hug in the nude than a fuck," the girl had confided after the first time, managing at once to reassure and shock Polly. "He asked that I never call him 'Mr. Prime,' but 'Sammy Boy.' And the strangest thing of all? He *apologized* after he had finished."

Outside, a heavier snow was falling, hiding Samuel Prime's tracks twenty yards behind him as he walked up Spring. Polly knew he must be in his mid-forties, but he walked briskly. She watched him stop at the corner and lean slightly forward to glance up and down Mercer. It was a neighborhood—a mile north of Prime, Ward & King, a mile south of his Fifth Avenue house—in which Samuel Prime had no good excuse for loitering on the afternoon of an ordinary business day. *Exercise!* was the alibi he always kept on the tip of his tongue. *Sent the driver on, walking home for the exercise, sensible at my age!* But right now the coast was clear, and Samuel Prime crossed the street.

Staring out at the snow, Polly asked herself for the hundredth time: Had she improved Priscilla's lot? Yes, unquestionably. Had she also given Priscilla, at thirteen, a smart push onto a very slippery path that might end in misery as well? Yes, alas. Polly sighed deeply, trying to exhale this small agony—what in this life was *not* a choice between lesser evils?—and headed down the back stairs to the kitchen.

She opened Mrs. Stanhope's new patent refrigerator and laid her hand inside on the metal for the sheer magic of the sensation—to feel the artificial chill in this warm room, a trick of shelves filled with circulating water. She took a few pickles from a jar, cut a slice of ham, buttered a roll, and ate her meal standing up, using not even a plate or utensils. As she was finishing, licking butter from a finger, the proprietress appeared.

"Polly Lucking! What in Sam Hill are you *doing*, gobbling on your feet like an *urchin*?"

Polly smiled as she chewed the last of her bun. She wiped her hands on the cook's towel and reached for her coat. "Running late for a performance."

Mrs. Stanhope lowered her voice to a whisper. "Polly, we must speak before long about—" She cocked her head toward the upstairs.

Polly sighed and said nothing. Mrs. Stanhope helped her on with her coat.

"You *know,*" the proprietress said, still whispering, "that my *main* consideration is what is most sensible and advantageous for *her.*"

A few days earlier, Mrs. Stanhope had proposed to Polly that Priscilla take on another client, perhaps two, perhaps more. *She is not the prettiest girl in the city,* Mrs. Stanhope had said, *but with certain gentlemen I believe we could make an attractive fuss about her . . . her special powers.* The idea, more or less, was to advertise Priscilla Christmas as some kind of young trance medium, a "magnetic whore," and charge eight or ten dollars instead of five.

"I am very late," Polly said as Mrs. Stanhope tied Polly's bonnet.

IF POLLY HAD dawdled another minute inside the house, or if Fatty Freeborn had not stopped on Spring Street, he would have spotted her, and his suspicions would've been confirmed once and for all. He knew her by sight from Shakespeare's, and he had once spotted her on this block of Mercer, early in the morning in front of No. 101, talking with the conceited old mackerel bitch who owned the place. But Fatty had to relieve himself *right now.*

He turned away from the street, pulled out his knob roughly into the cold air, and only then looked both ways to see if any pedestrians were near. An elderly gentleman in old-fashioned breeches, arm in arm with his little grandson, was waiting to cross Spring a few yards behind him. As Fatty's stream gushed hot and noisily against some snow-covered paper trash, Fatty was pleased to imagine the gentleman's displeasure—he'd like to squirt right *on* the old bastard and his little whelp, send them home to Washington Square soaked in piss. He was famous among his friends for having a doodle as thick as the nozzle on a fire hose.

Although Fatty sweated six days a week mixing and punching dough (from noon to half past five) and minding ovens (from midnight until dawn), he did not call himself a baker. He was one of seven men employed by Mr. Enggas, the owner of the big Greene Street bakery. But Fatty had never defined himself by the way he earned his dollar a day. He was no apprentice hatter when they paid him to lug piles of beaver pelts up and down stairs in Water Street and smear them with dye—"a shit job for shit wages," he'd told the boss the day he was sacked. Nor was he really a hackney when he drove a carriage—"*nigger* work," he called it after he'd quit. Nor was he even a sledgeman for the four years he worked at the ironworks, hammering pieces of metal as thick as his own legs. The only job he'd ever enjoyed had had no proper name at all: every Saturday for six months a soap factory in the block where he grew up had paid him thirty cents to sit on a big iron dish of its scale while barrels were hoisted onto the opposite dish, since by law a barrel of soap was required to weigh 256 pounds, and at thirteen Fatty Freeborn weighed exactly 256 pounds. Alas, well before his fourteenth birthday he had grown too fat to keep the job, and it had spoiled him for anything more rigorous. The only easy work he knew about was copying lists of voters' names for the Democratic Party, but Fatty could not read very well nor write at all.

So he was now paid to mix dough and bake, but he was not a baker; he was a *b'hoy*, a Bowery b'hoy, meaning that the salient aspects of his life were what he did at leisure. Night after night he roamed in an unending loop among the same saloons and porterhouses on the same few blocks of the Bowery and Broadway, gadding down the street with his pals, all of them swinging their arms and shoulders like giant marionettes.

Their peculiar jargon started with their very name for themselves—*boy* pronounced with a little cough in the middle, *b'hoy*, stretched out into a syllable and a half. But Fatty and his b'hoys didn't just speak in slang, they were themselves human slang, and like new words had sprouted mysteriously and suddenly in the less respectable city streets and cellars. Every second young man in the lower wards started, all at once three summers ago, to wear his hair long on the sides and slicked down, to keep a cigar jammed in the corner of his mouth, and to wear a checkered coat and flared trousers and heavy boots. They were foulmouthed and theatrical, scruffy as well as foppish, working-class dandies. No one had ever seen anything quite like them, which was part of the point. They were the first generation of ordinary young men (and *women*—the cocky, overdressed g'hals) for whom the pursuit of happiness meant only the organized pursuit of *fun*, the first who had decided to remain unmarried as long as possible and prance and sport like brats at twenty and twenty-five and (in a few cases, like Fatty) nearly thirty years of age.

The snow had stopped. Finished with his piss, Fatty buttoned up and reached with his dick hand into his knapsack to take a long pull from one of the two quarts he had bought at the grocery in Houston Street. It was his turn to provide the whiskey and the lamb for the Friday Night Jamboree, as he and his four oldest pals called their monthly romp and barbecue dinner.

As the liquor warmed his gut he watched the old fellow in the fancy oldfangled costume shuffle across the street with his grandson. Fatty felt disgust for all the upper-tens, as appalled by the richies as they were by him. He'd have put up his fists if anyone had said that he and the other b'hoys were like minstrel renderings of the sons of Astors and Schermerhorns, living spoofs of young aristocrats. But it was true. Fatty and his chums had all the foppery and fecklessness and sniggering gaiety; all they lacked were the educations and five-figure incomes. He corked the whiskey bottle, hitched his trousers up over the lower half of his belly, and swaggered, in his oxlike fashion, down Spring.

But he stopped again at the corner of Mercer, lowered his bag to the pavement, and got the bottle back out. It was his dime that paid for the booze, wasn't it? He didn't want to get *too* loose beforehand, since he'd have to walk the last blocks from the butcher's to Avenue D carrying the little ewe. Sally would have her legs tied, but they always squirmed and kicked. He needed to fortify himself. The second drink was always his favorite.

As he stood, feeling it begin to stir his soul, he turned to glance up Mercer. He spotted someone coming out of No. 101. One of the maids, could be? *Leaving* the place at this time of day, she wouldn't be one of the whores . . . the whores all too fine and spiffy for the likes of a native working boy like Fatty Freeborn. One night Fatty had gone with his friend Charlie Strausbaugh to the door bathed and combed and wearing a clean shirt, ready to spend half a week's wage for one night of pleasure. But old lady Stanhope had turned them away, would not take their good money—wouldn't even tell them directly to clear off, had her black maid say they lacked "the required introductions." Waved away by a whore's pimp's nigger!

The girl was walking down Mercer toward him. He could see from her plain bonnet and ragged coat that she was only a scrubbing woman—no, a scrubbing *girl*, a kid, she was so young.

Kid—that's funny. Like a *lamb*. A little whiskey always made Fatty more humorous.

She's a pretty one, he thought. And then he had the idea that he recognized her. And so he did—it was that girl from last year, the black-haired girl in the alley behind the theater. The girl who'd disappeared around New Year's, whose pale face and slender body he had imagined many times since. *I'm there*, he thought.

The moment he swung into the street, aimed directly for Priscilla, she noticed him—and remembered. He had begun paying her nickels for a feel in the Bowery last summer, and then offered her two bits in November for a yankum, her first. He had been rough, and during their fourth or fifth encounter he'd started grunting terrible things in her ear as he handled and squeezed her—until she'd pulled away and said she wasn't being paid for *that*, and threatened to stop taking his nickels or even his dimes. It was the freedom from nasty oafs like Freeborn that made her arrangement at 101 Mercer seem to Priscilla like salvation.

She figured it was this looming encounter that had been the subject of her premonition in the parlor.

If I hurry, I can make it up to Prince before he cuts me off . . .

If I step quick, I can meet her before she passes the little alley that runs over to Greene . . .

He bounded directly into her path, but because he had no waist, his laborious attempt at a bow looked like a sack of oats slowly tipping over.

"*Hallo*, miss," he said finally.

Priscilla said nothing and walked past him.

"But I *know* you," he said, walking along beside her, still holding the whiskey bottle. "You know me. We can have our fun again! Besides that, it's late for a pretty girl like yourself to be out in the street all by her own self."

Priscilla did not acknowledge him, or stop. Fatty swung in front of her so quickly she bumped against him. She remembered his sour smell—cigar and liquor and sweat and yeast.

"I *seen* where you're earning your coins now, miss. I *seen* you leaving that house at 101 just now." He dug his free hand into his coat pocket.

She had to stop herself from blurting out, *Not two bits anymore, bub— four dollars!* "I do not wish to know you any further, sir," she said, affecting the chilly manner of an adult.

Fatty pulled out a quarter and held the coin between his dirty thumb and forefinger right in front of her nose. He grinned, and she saw that he had lost an incisor since last year.

"A yankum's twenty-five cents, ain't it, *punk*?" he said. "Two bits . . . and I don't even need your little ninepence in the bargain." He was *such* a funny fellow—two bits, no ninepence! He snorted.

Priscilla had once overheard her father's friends muttering "ninepence" when they were drunk, from which she inferred that it was a word for the female sexual organ. And she had overheard men on the streets calling prostitutes "punks." But no one had ever said either word to her face.

She started to walk on, jerking her shoulder away from his as she passed.

"Whoa," he said, stepping into her path again, "don't make a *muss*. You wouldn't want me to tell Duff Lucking the straight truth that his blessed sister Polly's nothing but a damned whore at Stanhope's."

He was bluffing. He did not know if the gossip about Polly Lucking was true, or if this little cunt was acquainted with her. But now he would find out the truth.

He saw fear in Priscilla's eyes. Such a *sharp* fellow as well! "You don't want that. Do you?"

"I do not know a Miss Lucking," she answered.

"I will tell. I will, you can bet on it. And *you'd* be the one to blame for all the terrible, terrible trouble and sorrow."

She looked down.

"But I can keep secrets," he said. "I can keep 'em good."

With not even a glance at him, she opened her school bag and pulled her handkerchief from beneath the book Mr. Prime had given her as a gift. She walked briskly left, ahead of Fatty, into Amity Alley.

And two minutes later he cried out, groaned, squeaked, gasped as if he were choking. Now she remembered the noise of him as well as the stink. It was like a sound at the slaughterhouse where her dad had worked. At his instant of ecstasy, Fatty Freeborn sounded exactly like one of the animals in the slaughtering pen.

As he buttoned up and she carefully cleaned her fingers with her square of linen, she accidentally let a drop of his spunk fall onto his trousers.

"You clumsy little"—with the back of his hand he struck the side of her face between eye and ear—"*bitch*." The blow sent her stumbling back against the wall. "You just *lost* your two bits."

She did not flinch. She would not cry. She stood her ground. She let her eyes meet his for the first time.

"*What?*" he asked.

She didn't reply, but for a disconcerting two seconds more looked straight at him, let her wadded linen napkin drop to the ground, and in a single motion, like a dancer, spun around and walked off.

"A little flash-house whore's life ain't all satin and cocktails, now, is it?"

She would not look back, she would not touch her throbbing temple until she was out of his sight, and she would not cry.

"And no *Christian God*," Fatty shouted, "would *want* it to be like that, neither, would he?"

He squatted to snatch up her handkerchief—perfectly good but for his effusions—and stuffed it into his knapsack. And as long as he was down, he decided to uncork the opened Granville whiskey bottle for one final drink, to replenish himself for the long evening of sport ahead. *Twice in one night,* he thought. *Such a virile b'hoy!* He would volunteer to build the fire, and let each of the four other boys have his go with Sally in the penthouse before him—make himself look like a good hoss and also give his own manhood extra time to rejuvenate.

As he started his hike east, he calculated. If he picked up Sally at the market in Pitt Street by half past six and built the fire by seven, they could all be finished with her by half past, then have her slit and cleaned and dressed and up on the stick by eight. Which meant they wouldn't eat until midnight. He dug into his knapsack for one of his swiped sugar buns.

Fatty was the one who had decreed that they should use just one name for all of the Jamboree ewes, and that it should be Sally, after the night a year ago when Toby Warfield, the dumb little chuff, brought a *ram* into their penthouse shack in the vacant lot on Avenue D. Everyone except Toby had refused to do the Jamboree deed with it. "We ain't about to turn into a crew of *buggerers,* Toby," Fatty had announced as he stepped into the open shed, toward his friend and the male lamb, and promptly cut the animal's throat with his knife—while Toby, eyes shut and trousers around his ankles, was still fervently engaged with the animal's hind end. That scene was, all the b'hoys except Toby agreed, the funniest thing they had ever watched in their lives. And they all agreed too (even Toby) that the ram's meat somehow didn't *taste* nearly as good and sweet as the Sallys', either.

March 1, 1848

. . .

London

*H*OLY *CHRIST!*" BEN's father shouted, loudly enough that a kitchen girl peeked out into the rear garden, wondering if one of Sir Archibald's American opossums had escaped again from the vivarium. "Leave it to the frogs to *lose* an Englishman they've murdered."

"I plan to write to Tocqueville today on the Ashbys' behalf," Ben said. "I thought perhaps he might assist—"

"*Count* de Tocqueville? In your new democratic republic of France, Monsieur le *Comte* will be lucky to escape the guillotine, let alone discover the whereabouts of your deceased friend. Have the frogs given Lord and Lady Brightstone any inkling as to precisely how or where they mislaid him?"

"They say they are 'making an investigation.' But, Father, honestly, Paris was in such disorder, and if you had seen the morgue . . . they must have had a hundred bodies in the place. And the people in charge were . . . volunteers, I suppose. Certainly not true undertakers."

Sir Archibald Knowles—disgusted, outraged, *excited*—threw a handful of dead crickets into the wire-mesh fencing that surrounded his new menagerie. Sitting atop a miniature mountain constructed of shiny blue iron slag, one of his pair of monitor lizards sped toward the shower of manna, making thirty feet in three seconds.

The seventh-richest man in Grafton Street (according to Sir Archibald) now turned to face his youngest child. "Well, *there's* your *revolutionists* for you! The softheaded king surrenders after a single volley, and your victorious fools immediately start bungling things." He raised his right hand and shouted: "*Egalité, fraternité,* callous bloody stu-*pid*-i-tay!" One of the toucans in the vivarium cawed, inspired by its master's cry. "Mark my words," Sir Archibald said to Ben, "the French will have an emperor again by next year."

Ben's father welcomed any opportunity to grouse about troublemakers, incompetents, or the French. The instant revolution in Paris, and now this bizarre news of Lloyd Ashby's misplaced corpse, piqued his indignation to full fire in just the way he enjoyed. Ben had not seen his father so happily perturbed since the celebrated Oxford priest John Henry Newman had converted to Roman Catholicism three years before, and Sir Archie personally lobbied the government to deport Newman to Rome.

"Has anyone any idea at all," he asked, "whose body it is they *do* have?"

This morning, five days after Ben had returned to London and informed Lord and Lady Brightstone of Lloyd's murder, a coffin from France had arrived by coach in Cadogan Place. The rough walnut box contained a hundred pounds of half-melted ice and the cold, naked body of a bearded young man who had been shot dead. The head was well buried in ice, so when the casket was opened Lloyd's parents had seen the penis before they saw the face. They knew it was not their son because this corpse lacked a foreskin.

"A Jew, according to Lord Brightstone," Ben said to his father.

"A *Jew?*" Mr. Knowles was surprised and genuinely curious. His regard for Jewish canniness was outsized, bordering on respect.

"A poor Jew was careless enough to be shoved by some French coward in front of a musket? What a mess." He stared at his feasting lizard. "You do know, Ben, you really ought to have brought the boy home yourself."

Ben had forgiven himself for leaving Ashby's remains in the wagon, given that his own life was in jeopardy at the time. But his father had a knack for expressing any shred of self-doubt Ben was privately feeling. "Along with Sir Henry's *Spheniscus demersus,* of course." The disappearance of the precious African penguin had deeply disappointed Sir Archibald. He looked Ben up and down. "But I suppose," he said finally, "that we should count ourselves fortunate. You are lucky to be alive."

He meant, of course, that his son was fortunate to have escaped death. Ben heard the meaning differently, however, as a general truism: One is *lucky* to be alive.

"Indeed I am, sir," Ben replied.

His father had already started back toward the house. Ben saw that his rheumatic shuffle now combined with the ancient limp in his left leg to make it appear as if he were dancing a very slow jig.

"I am off to Kent this afternoon. On what day and at what hour," he said with his customary tone of mild bewilderment and irritation, "may I tell the boys that your *train* is scheduled to arrive?" It was odd that a man who owned factories would profess such disdain for the railway. But finally one night, after several sherries, he had explained to Ben his reluctance to travel by rail: the experience of surrendering his physical person to a machine, actually entering the thing and letting it fly him through space at ten times normal speed, made him feel as if he were *intimate* with . . . an *apparatus*. Furthermore, the first time he had seen a small steam engine operate, when he was a boy, the action of the engine—the in-and-out thrusting, the hot sputtering, the explosive, barely controlled apoplexy—struck him as a parody of carnal passion. The Knowles mills and mines now depended upon steam engines, but Sir Archibald did not care to see them work.

"I arrive at the station at Sevenoaks Friday next, at half three," Ben told him. He was tempted to add . . . *barely half an hour after I leave London Bridge.* By coach the trip took almost three hours.

"Well, fine, then *you* can greet Monsieur Thimonnier on Thursday in King William Street—he wrote that he's fleeing Paris, fleeing your drunken French heroes who invaded his factory and wrecked his sewing machines." Sir Archibald stopped and turned to address Ben directly. "Given the havoc of your revolution, I should think Thimonnier shall be predisposed to do business with us on highly favorable terms." In other words, the chaos in France might bode well for the business interests of the firm. The firm!

Leaving his father's house and strolling, Ben found himself humming a tune as he crossed Pall Mall. Then, in Regent Street, as a wedge of sunlight appeared on the pavement just ahead of him, he was inspired to sing the words of the song, out loud.

" 'I jumped aboard the telegraph,/And traveled down the river,/The electric fluid magnified,' la di dah di dah."

How pleased Ashby would have been to see the commotion Ben was making. Two ladies in St. James's Square turned to stare as he passed.

" '*O*, Susanna! *O*, don't you cry for me,/I've come from Alabama, with my banjo on my knee!' "

He delighted in saying *Alabama,* as he did all the mongrel Americanisms jammed full of syllables and vowels, like nonsense words invented by children—*Appalachia, Allegheny, Kalamazoo, Mississippi, Mononga-hela.*

" 'I'm goin' to Louisiana, my true love for to see . . .' "

He stopped. Looming before him was the St. James's Theatre. It was here that he had first heard "O, Susanna" performed—by a minstrel group last Christmas, accompanied by Ashby.

—→>·•·<←—

7

March 10, 1848

· · ·

Kent, England

NTIL HE JOINED in partnership with Messrs. Merdle, Newcome, and Shufflebotham, Ben's father had been a manufacturer of muslin and importer of Malay rubber. But then he became a merchant banker, engaged in the far more respectable enterprise of investing money in other men's grubby manufacturing and trading businesses. Until Queen Victoria named him a baronet last year (in return for various benefactions, including the £3,000 he donated to the university at Cambridge in honor of her husband's appointment as chancellor), Sir Archibald Knowles had been merely Archie Knowles, pettifogger. And until the day, years ago, he had paid £14,000 for his country seat in Kent, Great Chislington Manor had been known as Little Titsey Lodge. A great fiction—*Sir Archibald Knowles of Mayfair, London, and Great Chislington Manor, Kent*—had been willed into being.

Through the Kentish countryside, all the way from the station at Sevenoaks, Ben sat on the driver's box next to his father's steward. "Joseph," he asked as they turned off the muddy lane down the Knowleses' long causeway, speaking in a loud voice to be heard over the sound of wheels on gravel, "has Mrs. Warfield arrived?"

"Yes, sir, early this morning," replied the old man.

This pleased Ben. Since his mother's death three years ago, his sister, Isabel, was the one member of his family with whom he could talk with complete candor and affection.

"She *and* Mr. Warfield. He's come down early."

Ben's cheerfulness shriveled a little. Roger Warfield was by all appearances a decent husband to Isabel, but he was perhaps the most tedious man Ben had ever met, and not only because he was a barrister who operated under the delusion that the world was fascinated by barristers.

"And Master Philip as well," Joseph said, pointing somewhere beyond the grove of silver birches and the old priory—a ruin rebuilt and reconstituted as Sir Archibald's "museum of natural history."

Ben sighed. His brother worked for the government, in the Foreign Office, so he had assumed hopefully that Philip would need to remain in London to monitor the situation in France—and the reports, increasing daily, of insurrection in Vienna and Milan and Bavaria. But Philip was here in Kent, no doubt accompanied by his sweet, glazed wife Tryphena. Their first daughter, Victoria, had died. Their second child, baby Helena—christened, not coincidentally, with the same name as the queen and Prince Albert's latest infant—would be in London with its nurse.

In the distance, Ben heard the brief thunder of gunfire, two shots, then a third, and the baying of dogs.

"Sir Archibald and your brother," Joseph explained. "Out with a leash of hounds for partridge and dove." Leave it to them to shoot only the very prettiest birds. "But your brother waited on the ferreting for *you* to arrive, sir. And the rat-lamping."

"How thoughtful," he said. As a boy, Philip had required Ben to carry the lamp into the barns at night so that he, Philip, could blast away at the scurrying rats. Gunning for rodents with his brother had been one of Ben's inspirations to become an archer.

He saw Joseph's son, the gamekeeper, walking toward the back of the house carrying four slaughtered geese.

"Your dinner party is early tonight, sir," Joseph said. "Guests due at seven."

And guests as well? Ben had looked forward to spending some days in the country with his father and sister, explaining his plans. *Joseph*, Ben wished he had the brass and bad manners to say right now, *you must turn the carriage around this instant—I have just remembered some urgent business back in London.*

The horses came to a halt and Joseph unfastened their check reins, a tiny ritual of liberation that often gave Ben a sympathetic sensation of relief. As he walked up the front step he heard another volley of shots from the hill—closer, louder, sharper—which caused Ben to form a mischievous thought: he would finally take possession of the double-barreled ten-gauge, no doubt still in its Groocock & Company wrapping paper, that his father had given him on his eighteenth birthday. He might actually have use for a gun now—or so, anyhow, Ben would enjoy saying to Sir Archie.

New York City

HIS THICK SPECS and beard notwithstanding, Skaggs certainly did not look like an old man. His freckles gave his face a youngish aspect, as did his quick smile.

Yet the world he'd known as a youth was gone. Skaggs had been born during a war against the *British*, which now seemed impossibly quaint, back when the flag carried half as many stars. What's more, he remembered Founding Fathers—when Skaggs was a boy, Monroe had been president and Jefferson was still alive. When he first smoked, friction matches did not exist. It was only in the previous decade that he had arrived in New York City, but it might as well have been another century. Photography was a fantasy. There were no one-penny newspapers, no private shops selling meats and fruits, no baseball, and precious few theaters or foreigners.

For all that, and even though he was this very day turning thirty-five, Timothy Skaggs did not feel old. He still had all but three of his teeth, and his "social anatomy," as he called it, remained in good working order, except on those nights when he consumed very large amounts of brandy or opium. He could still roister until dawn, and, as his father had put it in a birthday letter Skaggs received a few hours ago, he still filled his days and nights with "the pointless, puerile amusements of a conceited sluggard or first-class wastrel."

The elder Mr. Skaggs professed distaste for most new things and practically all new words, but last year he had discovered "wastrel" and could not resist using it as often as possible in his letters to his son. He had assumed that after failing to become a physician, Timothy would take up some respectable clerkish employment in Wall Street. For to Jacob Skaggs, writing satirical articles and trashy novels was puerile. Making daguerreo-type pictures—a task engaging his youngest child at this very moment—was pointless.

Timothy was most assuredly not, in his own estimation, a "sluggard." He worked at several different jobs. None of his occupations, however, was likely to produce much in the way of wealth or reputation. It was unlikely but not impossible that he might yet blossom into the American Dickens or Thackeray. But both of those men, Skaggs knew with dispiriting precision, were only a year older than he, and they had become *Dickens* and *Thackeray* already.

Skaggs had informed no one that today was his birthday. This particular March 10 struck him as too important to turn into one more excuse for an evening of sloppy toasts and rude jokes. He felt strangely sober, his mind atwitter with thoughts about unfulfilled promise, unknown destiny, undis-covered calling. Timothy Skaggs always wished to be and to appear blithe, so his present mood was highly uncharacteristic.

It was not that he wanted for money, or envied the rich. Oh, he har-bored a few small professional grudges against successful peers. He felt competitive, for instance, with Mathew Brady, whom he called "our ass-kissing, celebrity-worshiping, moneygrubbing camera boy." Brady was only twenty-five. Among the stray fragments of information teeming in Skaggs's brain were the birth dates not just of everyone he knew but—and this embarrassed him a little—of almost every well-known person near his own age.

He really didn't feel much jealousy toward the Great Men, however. He had known a few such personages.

Such as Frank Pierce (aged forty-three). When Skaggs was growing up, Frank had been the most promising boy in Hillsborough, the most admired student at school, the most respected young lawyer in the state. After Frank resigned his U.S. Senate seat because his wife believed that life in Washing-ton forced her husband to drink too much whiskey, Skaggs realized that men like Pierce and he were different creatures fundamentally. When Frank had enlisted as a private soldier to fight in the war, Skaggs wrote an article com-mending his boyhood acquaintance for his courage—his courage to admit that sweltering heat, disease, and carnage in Mexico was preferable to the same time alone with Jane Pierce in frigid New Hampshire. Timothy's brother Jonah, a junior partner with Pierce's law firm, pleaded with Timothy to send a letter of apology to Mrs. Pierce, which he finally wrote last summer after Frank fell off his horse in Mexico and broke a leg.

Horace Greeley (aged thirty-seven) was the other Great Man whom Skaggs had known before Greatness was visited upon him. They had been young newspaper hacks together, fellow New Hampshire émigrés. Even then Greeley had held more serious opinions, of which he was more certain, than any young person Skaggs ever knew. Soon after they met, Greeley began referring to Skaggs as "Brat." Most of the *Tribune*'s liberal ideas Timothy more or less shared (an end to the new business monopolies, freedom for the slaves), but Greeley's fanatical rectitude (against alcohol, against tobacco, against prostitution) he could not tolerate. Hadn't the both of them rushed from New Hampshire as boys in order to *escape* all that crabbed satrappery, not to carry the Moral War to Manhattan? During the winter of 1844, he became so weary of the virtuousness that for a while he stopped reading the *Tribune* on principle.

No, Skaggs was not a big bug like Pierce or Greeley—no big bug would be found on a chilly Friday afternoon on the sidewalk at the intersection of Nassau and Fulton streets squinting into a camera with a yard of brown cloth draped over his head.

Skaggs twisted the brass focus knob a final jot, forward and back, making the image on the glass a hair sharper. He adored focusing—it provided him the momentary happy godlike sensation of controlling one small spot in the universe. And, of course, he adored the opportunity (godlike as well) that photography afforded him to stare at people, to examine every detail of their eyes and lips, their bellies and bosoms, their fingernails and skin.

The Blue Man lay on his side in the gutter a few feet in front of the tripod, illuminated by a column of sunlight, undoubtedly the day's last. As Skaggs looked into his ground glass, studying the image (upside down, but so much more vivid than any unaided view through air), he wished it were possible to take a photograph depicting this poor riffraff's shade of blue. Not by exposing the plate to extra sunlight or hand-tinting the picture with paint, practices that Skaggs considered vulgar, but by some chemical means to capture the actual blue color on the plate. He had read in *Scientific American* about a Frenchman who had made such a picture, but the color image could not be fixed, and so disappeared; such evanescence struck Skaggs as worse than no color at all.

All the while he was setting up his camera, which took a good ten minutes, the Blue Man had been humming the tune to "King Alcohol," the

Hutchinson Family's hit about the evils of drink. When the fellow suddenly began to sing the words as well—

"For there's rum, and gin, and beer, and wine
And brandy of logwood hue . . ."

—it was too much for Skaggs. He pulled the little curtain of tow cloth from his head and replaced the cap over the lens. The song was increasing in volume as well. Passersby had been stopping to watch Skaggs and the Blue Man, and the song was attracting more spectators.

". . . And hock, and port, and flip combine
To make a man look bluuuuuue*!"*

"All right, sir," Skaggs said to the Blue Man, "our moment has come. I am about to make your portrait. No jiggling for the next while."

"Whoopee!" the Blue Man replied. "I'm in the *show* business, the *show* business, the *show* business!"

"If this were 'the show business,' " Skaggs told him, "the wage would be more than the shilling I'm paying you." He carefully pulled the viewing glass from the slot in the camera and replaced it with the plateholder.

"But you are making me the star of Journalismville for an hour!" The Blue Man pointed at the small crowd behind Skaggs who had stopped to watch.

"The *star* of *Journalismville?*" Skaggs said. "Is that what you said, sir?" He was startled now beyond mere amusement. Among these several blocks, an L-shaped district just east of City Hall and the Park, at least half of New York's dailies and magazines and book publishers and lithographers had their offices. "Journalismville" was a coinage new to Skaggs, perhaps new to the world. As for "star," he had never heard anyone outside the theater use the term. "Now then, sir—entirely *still*. Please."

"Is it sunshiny enough to make the picture?"

"For the moment, yes. Are you quite ready?"

"May I keep my mouth open? I go frightened if I breathe through only my nose for very long."

"By all means, do what you must to breathe," Skaggs said, "but you must not move. Do you understand? I'll count to ten, and when I'm finished you may sing and shout and jump all you wish."

He lifted the handle up to uncover the plate. In this position, the plate-holder reminded him of a cocked guillotine, ready to snatch a tiny head.

The Blue Man arranged himself in the gutter, resting his chin on one hand and opening his mouth wide.

"Eh ah oh hay?" he asked, his lips two inches apart. *Am I OK?*

"*Very* still, now." Skaggs reached out and in one swift motion pulled off the lens cap. "*One* California . . . two California, three . . ." One of the fellow's eyes twitched. ". . . eight California, nine California . . . *ten.*" He replaced the cap tight and shoved the dark slide down. "Excellent. Thank you, sir."

The Blue Man stood and took Skaggs's two half dimes.

BEFORE THE WAR, Duff Lucking had spent all his free time wandering New York City, by himself or with his young friends from the fire company. But now, if on a particular day he had no gas-pipe or postering job and the fire bells hadn't rung, he tended to keep to himself in the rooms where he lodged, particularly during daylight. It felt safer.

The sun had barely set but he lit his three lamps. He burned only coal oil; he blamed whale oil for his father's bankruptcy, and therefore his death. The light cheered up the place and illuminated the pictures—the painting on velvet of No. 15's firehouse, the engraved portraits of Jesus and the singer Abby Hutchinson, the colored-pencil drawings by his sister of his departed mother and father and siblings.

He returned to his bed, the folded woolen child's blanket tucked between his head and the wall, to read his new book. And he was so enraptured by *Old Hicks, the Guide, or, Adventures in the Camanche Country in Search of a Gold Mine* that he scarcely noticed the clamor of voices and wheels and horses outside in Orchard Street, rising the way it always did as afternoon turned to evening.

He imagined himself riding west with the pure and heroic Texas Rangers along the Trinity River, entering the Peaceful Valley of Indians—"a new Eden of unsophisticated life" whose "graceful creatures had been shut out, by their steep hills in this enchanting recess, from any knowledge of the gloomy and bloody strife which man has been waging with himself and all God's creatures since sin and death came into the world." He imagined a pretty Camanche girl healing him with the steam of hot stones and cold baths. He imagined his duel with the evil French Count Albert. At a particularly brilliant passage he nodded and murmured assent.

The great geniuses are and have been essentially savages in all but the breech cloth. They arrive at truth by much the same processes; they equally scorn all shackles but those of the God-imposed senses, whether corporeal or spiritual . . .

With the pencil he kept on his lampstand he drew three quick lines in the margin.

He looked up from the book. When he'd crossed the Rio Grande last fall, leaving the gloomy and bloody strife of Mexico, perhaps he should have ridden west and found his own Peaceful Valley, instead of returning east to the city.

Kent, England

BEN'S PASSAGE INTO his father's library was blocked by the backsides of Sir Archie and an A.N.N.—one of the "awful nincompoop neighbors," as he and Isabel called their father's country acquaintances. He stopped two paces behind them.

"It is an absolutely striking resemblance, sir," Ben heard fat Squire Somebody-or-Other say to his host as he reached for a fresh Smoking Bishop. Sir Archie and his guest were looking toward the fireplace, alternating their glance up and down between Isabel Knowles Warfield and the oil portrait of her late mother. Both were in profile. Isabel was in some animated discussion with a man, another A.N.N.

On Isabel's other side stood her husband, Roger Warfield, and Philip's wife Tryphena, who smiled dimly and faced the flames directly, heedless of the risk that the cosmetic wax on her face might melt, and ignoring the nuances of admiralty law that her brother-in-law Roger was explaining.

And farther to their left, near the door to the print room, stood the Irish owner of the neighborhood's new steam-powered flour mill. Philip was bragging to the miller and his wife about how he, Philip, had just persuaded the Lord Chamberlain to invoke the law against any fictional depiction of living royalty in order to prohibit a theatrical farce about King Ludwig of Bavaria and his mistress—*Lola Montez, or, A Countess for an Hour*—from opening in London.

"It is a fine likeness," Squire Whomever-It-Was said again to Sir Archie about Isabel, nodding as he sipped his sweet steaming drink.

"Beautiful specimens both," his host said. "Although the *Lady* Knowles," he added, "had a self-assurance and a kind of natural"—Ben, overhearing, silently formed the word he knew was coming—"*grandeur* that my dear daughter cannot hope to possess. For that matter, which no young person possesses these days."

"Neither possesses nor wishes to affect," Ben said, giving both men a start as they turned to greet him. The neighbor bobbled his fresh drink.

"The lurking commentator," Sir Archie said, "is my younger son. Benjamin—Mr. Reginald Fishbourne."

"Alas, I never had the pleasure of meeting Lady Knowles," said Fishbourne.

Nor did I, sir, since my mother, Ada Mactier Knowles, the daughter of a Glaswegian loan jobber, died of consumption in the summer of 1845, two years before the queen was persuaded to award my father his baronetcy—and therefore "the Lady Knowles," a posthumous imaginary creation, never existed.

"A pity, sir," Ben said, extending his hand to the man in greeting. "She was a remarkable woman," *not least because she was the only member of this family compatible with all of its members.*

Behind them came the bustle of guests arriving and handing coats to one of the maids.

"Ah, it is our esteemed barnacle expert!" Archibald Knowles nearly shouted as he turned and saw who had entered. "Come and warm yourselves, Professor, before dinner."

Ben assumed his father was being jocular, that the man was some minor shipping magnate and that his father called him "Professor" because the fellow quoted Greek verse, or because of his vaguely donnish appearance—tall, thin, shambling. Archibald Knowles had quit school at twelve, and would no sooner invite a scholar to a dinner party, Ben knew, than he would bring a parson with him to bargain for cotton at the Royal Exchange.

"This, sir, is our would-be *renegado*," Sir Archie announced to the new man, gesturing toward Ben, "who managed to lose Sir Henry's *Spheniscus demersus* in some filthy Paris alley. I'm only grateful I didn't give him the *Pinguinus impennis* for safekeeping, eh?"

When Archie was beginning his wildlife collection several years ago, with the plan of specializing in flightless birds, he had engaged an Icelandic hunter to find a great auk, *Pinguinus impennis,* on a rock in the

North Atlantic near Iceland. He was exorbitantly pleased with that particular trophy—which he claimed to have acquired from "a Danish collector," since killing the birds was illegal in Britain. As it turned out, Archie Knowles's *Pinguinus impennis* had been the last living great auk on earth. If he had known that the species was now extinct, his pride of ownership would have been uncontainable.

The new man's tired-looking wife smiled politely. Her husband, however, arched his eyebrows and practically grinned, and as he did so issued a fart so shockingly loud and long that Ben first thought he was hearing the sound of a piece of heavy furniture being dragged across the floor overhead.

Then, even more shockingly, it turned out the man really was a professor.

"This is my *younger* son," his father said. "Benjamin—Professor and Mrs. Darwin."

"We are eager to hear of your adventures in Paris," Darwin said as he extended his hand. He was at least a decade Ben's senior, but his manner and look—bald head and thick, broad eyebrows—made him seem even older.

"*Misadventures,*" Sir Archie Knowles said.

"My wife lived in Paris for a time as a girl, studying piano." Another fart boomed from Darwin, this one brief but much deeper and even louder than the first.

Ben's father had once or twice mentioned his neighbor, who lived in Downe, a few miles away. This was no mere "diddler with books and boys and foreign ideas," as Sir Archie described the archetypal scholar when Ben had considered becoming a fellow at Cambridge, but a celebrated professor whose book *The Voyage of H.M.S. Beagle* was a popular success, a well-to-do professor married to a granddaughter of the millionaire potter Josiah Wedgwood. And a professor who would fully appreciate the creatures on display in the building down behind the birch grove. Now Ben believed he understood Darwin's presence.

But he did not. Knowles, Merdle, Newcome & Shufflebotham had made a recent investment in a fleet of vessels for carrying guano, so it was actually Darwin's firsthand knowledge of Peruvian guano that intrigued Archibald Knowles. Sir Archibald had plenty of social ambition but he was still, at bottom, a practical man who never forgot that he was in trade. It was the fertilizer business that had made him befriend Charles Darwin, the prospect of buying the shit of cormorants and boobies for £3 a ton and selling it for £10 that had led him to solicit the company of a book-diddler. Ben knew none of this, nor that his father wanted his youngest child in the country on this particular day in order to provide suitably intellectual conversation for West Kent's resident expert in South American bird droppings, and for his artistic wife.

On the other hand, neither Ben nor his father knew that Darwin was a dabbler in investments, who figured that cultivating Sir Archibald Knowles might somehow, someday, prove useful to his own purposes.

As soon as they were all seated for dinner, Emma Darwin asked Ben to tell what he had seen in Paris, which he proceeded to do for the sixth time this week. His summary of his extraordinary forty-eight hours was now so well practiced he realized he could dine out for the rest of the season on his tales of riot and cannon and death. Tonight, he spoke for an entire course of whitebait, describing the barricades and burning omnibuses and mobs and musket fire as the guests washed down piles of fried baby herring with champagne.

". . . and after I arrived at Saint-Lazare Station," he finished, "I did not see the French sergeant again. I made my escape thanks only to the railway and the generosity of the French ticket agent who mistook me for an American." Never before had people considered Ben Knowles an adventurer. He was enjoying his new role.

"Nor, of course, did he see poor Mr. *Ashby* again," his father said. Sir Archibald had already explained to the table that the story now making the rounds in London—that Lord and Lady Brightstone "had been sent in their late son's stead some poor naked frozen French Jew"—was true.

"Simply dreadful, that," Philip said. "Lord Palmerston has requested an official inquiry."

Ben noticed that Philip's wife Tryphena was looking into a middle distance and pursing her lips repeatedly, as if impersonating a fish. Everyone knew that she was fainty, and tended to pay her no attention.

"Do you imagine, sir," Emma Darwin asked Ben, "that it is possible this mania you witnessed in Paris might soon explode in the streets of Manchester or Birmingham? Just this afternoon I received a letter from a French friend—she writes that everyone there is shocked."

"Well, I—" Ben started to answer, but his older brother cut him off.

"I can assure you, Mrs. Darwin, that Lord Palmerston and I were by no means surprised at what occurred in Paris. Although we rather thought *more* would die on the government side. Only eighty soldiers and police, according to our best reports. And in any event, I can assure you as well that Her Royal Highness Victoria is not the abdicating sort."

"But if it were to come to war in the streets here," Emma Darwin asked, "do you believe our troops would behave so differently?"

" 'War'?" Sir Archibald said. "This 'February Revolution' in Paris was no war at all. It was a tantrum run amok."

"It is the *French*, Mrs. Darwin," Philip said.

"Who are, in the main, ridiculous, melodramatic monkeys," Sir Archie said. "Monkey" was a favorite trope of Sir Archie's. On the table in front of him were salt bowls on the heads of silver apes and Ceylonese napkin rings carved from ivory in monkey figures. "Thirty-five million silly, jabbering *monkeys*, most of the people as well as the troops—whom I know all too well to be cowardly ambushers."

As a young man, Archie Knowles had fought the French under Wellington, and still called the limp in his left leg his "frog wound," even though it had been the result of one of the British General Shrapnel's fragmentation shells that had fallen short and killed half of Corporal Knowles's platoon. A shard of Shrapnel's iron struck Archie just below his left knee.

"Given the opportunity," Archie Knowles said, "the French simply fire without reason or run away—including their kings. *Former* king, I should say."

Philip raised his forefinger as his eyes darted up and down the table. "Who—*I* ought *not* to say—is at the present moment living not far from here with his family and precisely *one* servant."

Nearly the whole company smiled and—one servant!—shook their heads in wonderment.

"As befits the 'Citizen King,' " Sir Archibald said. "Queen Victoria has stuck the old white-flagger over in Claremont House, has she, Philip?"

"I certainly cannot say, Father," his eldest son replied with a proud smirk that made his brother want to grab the nearest candlestick and whip it across his face. "State secret," he said.

Ben wondered now, as he often had before, how Philip's poor, queer wife could bear life with him. As a girl in London a decade ago, Tryphena Matheson was intelligent and fetching. Glancing at her now, Ben saw that she was oblivious to her husband's performance, and continued to purse her lips every second or two. He wondered if she had a herring bone wedged between her teeth. In fact, she was silently and repeatedly mouthing the words *poor naked frozen French Jew.*

"Are we to assume," Darwin asked Philip, "that the new rulers of France are not to be allies of Britain?" At that moment a wind rattled the widows, and Darwin simultaneously emitted a long, soft, breezy fart. Ben wondered if he deliberately timed his flatulence to coincide with other sounds.

"No, sir, we applaud the popular aspirations in France—and across Europe. We have no perpetual allies and no eternal enemies. Our British interests are perpetual and eternal."

"Ah—*flexibility*," Ben said rather loudly, as if he were raising a toast. "It was flexibility that allowed my nimble brother to begin the 1840s a Tory and finish them now as a Liberal."

Philip smiled warily.

"Yet in addition to its interests," Ben said, still loudly. "I have supposed that this country is meant to stand for certain *principles* in the modern world as well. I had also supposed that *Viscount* Palmerston might see that history is now moving rather emphatically against the viscounts of the world. Not to mention," he added with a small smile, "against the baronets."

Sir Archibald, thunderstruck by this cri de coeur, both frowned and smiled at Ben.

"Benjamin," Philip said, "our government is sympathetic to—"

But the new Ben Knowles would brook no interruption. "As *monkeyish* as their revolution may have been, as spontaneous and disorganized as it certainly was, it was indeed a revolution. And that fever is bound to roll west, to England and Ireland, even as it is apparently now rolling east over Europe."

"Minor outbreaks, Benjamin, I—"

"Our *interest*, Philip, it seems to me, is in stepping out of its way and permitting the democratic spirit—the spirit of this century—to transmute this dull old nation as it will."

Ben could hardly believe the words that had come from his own mouth with such vehemence, as if he were a firebrand, or . . . an American.

Philip was unprepared to grant his brother the moral high ground. "Do you mean the democratic spirit as it is arising in Bavaria? The peasants beating and murdering Jewish moneylenders? Or the drunken, stupid Luddites bursting into factories to break looms and kilns?"

"No," Ben replied, "for as you well know I, unlike you, am fond of engines and the jangle of trade. Unlike you, I oversaw a mill that employed one hundred forty-two workers and shipped two hundred thousand yards of poplin and cotton drill each week. And unlike you, Philip, I am friendly with Jews. All I suggest is that what rages now in France and in the German states and who knows where else is simply . . . an uncorked flow, an irresistible tide. A tide that no dikes will hold back, and which just might prevent you, brother, from *ever* becoming *Sir* Philip Knowles."

"My red republican little brother," Philip said as he glanced around with a tight smile at the guests. "My brother the artificial American."

"As a student," Sir Archibald informed the table, "young Ben fancied himself a Chartist. And he joined up with . . . what was it, your socialist cabal, at Cambridge? The Brotherhood of the Virtuous?"

"No," Philip said, "the Confederacy of the Noble."

"The Federation of the Just," Ben told them. "Which is now the Communist League."

"Lady Knowles," her widower noted, "was a member of the Society for the Extinction of the Slave Trade and for the Civilization of Africa— endeavors I strongly support."

Ben did not mention, as he had once before when his father bragged about his late wife's abolitionism, that half their wealth depended upon the labor of enslaved, cotton-picking American Negroes.

"Father," said Philip, "is it true the Manchester mill has lately *increased* its profit since the old order was restored?" This was a goad at his brother. Ben's modest reforms at the mill—raising the minimum age for employees to twelve and reducing children's workdays to ten hours—had been reversed after he left for London last year.

Sir Archie nodded sheepishly.

Ben lifted his goblet. "To the hardworking toddlers of Manchester, by whose sweat and nipped fingers we profit so handsomely."

The fat squire mumbled "Hear, hear" and held his glass in the air for a long moment until he realized that the younger Mr. Knowles's toast had been a joke.

Roger Warfield, alarmed by any display of passions, tried to steer the conversation toward the balmier vale of the law. "I am given to understand," he chirped, "that the new French Assembly has passed a statute abolishing the death penalty for political crimes, even those involving violence."

A few of the dinner guests nodded but no one replied. Instead, they sipped wine or cut at their pieces of goose meat and mutton, waiting to see if the Knowles brothers' row would continue. Ben, however, was struck by

Roger's remark: it was the only time he had ever heard his brother-in-law utter an interesting new fact. During the few seconds' pause, he lost the fire for any more fight with Philip.

"But who *is* this poor frozen French Jew?" Tryphena Knowles abruptly asked. "And will they return him now to his family in France?"

Philip broke the silence with a practiced laugh, as if his wife had intended to be amusing, and others chuckled along. Several innocuous new conversations sprouted. Ben reported in detail for Darwin how he had used the penguin as a weapon in Paris, and Darwin told him in turn how intrigued he had been, a dozen years earlier in Tierra del Fuego, the first time he'd seen the little birds called sheathbills eating the excrement of penguins directly from the penguins' anal sphincters. Sir Archie told the squire and the miller's wife his theory that all successful colonial ventures were based on the commercialization of stimulants—coffee, cocoa, tobacco, opium, rum. Tryphena thought of fairies and hailstorms as she pretended to listen to Roger Warfield explain to the miller ancient laws concerning the weights of white versus black bread.

Up the table, Mrs. Darwin asked Philip if business in China was prospering more or less than expected since the Opium Wars. Tryphena Matheson Knowles's family opium business had employed Philip for several years in Hong Kong and still provided them with an income of £2,000. And were it not for her family's business, Mrs. Philip Knowles would not now be an opium gourmand—for Tryphena indulged not merely in the ordinary matron's occasional sip of laudanum, but ate Jardine Matheson opium like a candy, five or six secret, fragrant, luscious spoonfuls a day.

Philip, however, tended nowadays to affect a certain obliviousness to the China trade.

"Yes," he replied to Mrs. Darwin's question, "I understand that business is robust, up at Shanghai as well as Hong Kong. Although, as you might expect, my concerns now are rather focused more on affairs of *state* than on"—he shrugged, and reduced his voice almost to a whisper—"some Chinamen's chests of opium."

Philip's last word and disparaging tone snatched his wife's attention as if she had been tugged by the ear.

"*Philip,*" she said sharply, "are you speaking of *me?*"

"No, no, certainly not, my dear," he replied. "I was explaining to Mrs. Darwin that we have not much news of China."

Between the considerable wine Ben had consumed and the pleasure he was now taking in his brother's embarrassment, he only now noticed that Darwin was directing a question at him.

"Sir? Which college?"

"Which college?"

His sister interceded. "At Cambridge, Ben."

"Ah—Trinity," Ben replied. "Trinity College. Isaac Newton's Trinity." He was a little drunk. "The *family* college."

Darwin looked surprised, and Isabel apprehensive. "Your father is also an old member of Trinity?"

A rude laugh boomed from Ben, and immediately Darwin farted, like a bassoon answering a trumpet.

"Forgive me, sir," Ben said quietly. "Sir Archibald's higher education consisted of back numbers of *The Library of Entertaining Knowledge*. I was simply making a poor joke about Trinity, for one of my father's great-grandfathers reputedly . . . it is all a bit complicated."

Isabel touched her brother's sleeve.

Ben put his hand over hers and breathed deeply in and out—not a sigh, but rather as if he had just stepped outside on a sunny June morning.

"You see, one of our ancestors is said to be Isaac Newton, who, as you know, was a fellow at Trinity, so . . . that is all. I am sincerely sorry." He sipped some more claret.

"Heavens! So we are dining tonight," Darwin said to the table, "with descendants of Sir Isaac Newton!" He raised his goblet. "We are honored even more than we knew."

The other guests, slightly bewildered but compliant, lifted their glasses and murmured assent. Philip glared at Ben as if he were a barn rat in a beam of lamplight. At the head of the table, Sir Archibald's expression seemed to flicker between anxiety and delight, delight and anxiety.

"Well," Ben said, "at the time he fathered our ancestor Seth Knowles, if indeed he did, he was merely *Mr.* Isaac Newton."

Tryphena knew nothing of this alleged history, and she was struggling now to make sense of what Ben was saying. "Ben? I am confused. Why would Mr. Newton's son be called Seth *Knowles*? I am afraid I am quite confused."

"Forgive me, sister-in-law. The child was not called Newton because this particular great-grandmother happened not to be married to our hypothetical great-grandfather. Mr. Seth Knowles, I am afraid, was a bastard."

Philip made a sound like a cat's hiss.

As the guests looked to their host, who was now grinning, the big clock in the library began striking nine. "My younger son is an evil-minded, mischief-making telltale," Sir Archibald said, "but I cannot in good conscience call the boy a liar." He arose, and the rest of the company stood as well. Darwin's fart was masked by the sound of scraping chair legs and rustling dresses. "I ask the gentlemen to join me for some very old brandy in the museum."

On the gravel outside, Ben accompanied Darwin on the long walk to the priory. Two boys carried lanterns.

"You do know, Mr. Knowles," the older man said, "that there is no biographical evidence that Sir Isaac engaged in intimate relations with any woman during his whole life."

"Oh, I know that all too well, sir. My father was correct about my mischief-making mood tonight. Let me apologize for subjecting you and your wife to our quarrels and scandals."

"I know the nettles that pass between siblings. Nettles." He waved down toward the birches, only the tops of which were visible above a moonlit mist. "Or perhaps rather a *fog*. In families I think we stumble forever, searching for one another in a kind of permanent fog. Mrs. Darwin and her brother have a hard time of it—Mr. Wedgwood holds their family purse tightly."

Ben shivered, perhaps from the cold, or perhaps from imagining his own financial future after his father's death, when Philip—*Sir* Philip Knowles, Baronet—would be managing the Knowles fortune.

Happily, Darwin changed the subject. "Tell me, sir, precisely how *you* believe we ought to respond to this latest spasm of revolution? My family and I quit London in '42 during the labor riots."

"And quitting is one means of adapting to new circumstances. Perhaps the best means of adaptation."

Darwin smiled. "*Adaptation,* is it? To flee the problematical conditions? Scoot away?"

"Is it not? Despite my talk at table tonight," Ben said, "I am no true revolutionist, as I discovered in Paris. I may welcome the revolutions, but as for actually taking—"

Darwin tripped, and Ben took his arm.

"*Careful!* Hedgehog divot. But revolution or not, I shan't be taking up the fight myself."

"You are not an agent of . . . the national 'transmutation'?"

"Did I misuse the word earlier? Again, my apologies, I have drunk too much."

"No, not at all—transmutation happens to be an idea much on my mind . . . water becoming steam . . . a girl of the streets gradually turned into a respectable woman." He looked at Ben carefully. "Or certain types of creatures—barnacles, for instance—over many dozens of centuries, turning into different types." From a paddock they heard the whinny of one of Sir Archie's Arabians. "Perhaps even the ancestor of our horse was a tapir. And millennia before that, possibly, a rhinoceros.

"Or take your escape from the soldier in Paris. You mentioned that you raced as a boy. Your skill at running proved useful—indeed, essential—only *now*, years later. It may be the same with a bird's feathers, that he sprouts them *eons* before he finally uses them to fly."

"I *see*," Ben said. "So if a person can be transformed, and improved, like your whore, then whole societies may be changed, transmuted, adapted to new conditions. And so perhaps England shall not change as France is changing, *need* not change, because it has already reproduced itself in superior form elsewhere." His brain was afizz. "England spat out America like, like a seed, a . . ."

"A hybrid spore."

"Yes, *exactly*, America is England made new and improved—heartier, healthier."

They were approaching the priory, which was ablaze with candlelight.

"Mr. Knowles," Darwin continued, "may I ask how old you are?"

"I am twenty-six for a few more months."

"When I was younger than you, I was dead set on leaving England, on wayfaring through terra incognita, on having adventures. And while indulging that impulse seemed rash at the time, in retrospect, from my fortieth year, it appears to have been the wisest decision of my life."

Ben was feeling very fond of Darwin. He pointed to the birch grove. "Look—the fog has lifted in just these few minutes."

They arrived at the priory. As he stepped inside, Ben saw the great auk, as tall as a child, standing alone between two sconces in the vestibule, reflections of the fluttering candle flames twinkling in its glass eyes. He stopped and stared as Darwin walked ahead of him. The bird was turned to face the front door, its mouth set in a permanent welcoming smile, as if it—he?

she?—were the runty master of the house greeting all visitors, happy to have migrated for eternity to the south of England, now safe forever from hungry sharks and nasty Icelandic weather.

Have you come from Paris with my African cousin? the auk squeaked, with heartbreaking cheerfulness, in Ben's wine-fueled imagination. *And Mr. Ashby—where is Mr. Ashby?*

New York City

DUFF HAD DECIDED to stay in his rooms the rest of the evening to finish *Old Hicks, the Guide.* He could feel the book changing his life as he read. But to exactly which unspoiled tract should he decamp? How should he remake himself? Would that he could become a Texas Ranger like the heroes of the novel. But after all that had happened in Mexico, that was certainly not in the cards.

When New York's police department was organized the summer before he enlisted, Duff considered its military charge and demeanor—*deliverers of justice*—as honorable and alluring. But the b'hoys and sometimes even respectable people jeered the police and the copper stars they wore. And Skaggs had persuaded him that he would find the rules of the new department burdensome—officers were prohibited from chatting with one another in the street, and from leaving the city without permission of the chief. "Why not *commit* a crime and let them board you at Sing-Sing instead?" Skaggs had said. "It sounds about the same to me."

But all of that discussion and banter had happened before the war. His experience in Mexico had narrowed Duff's prospects. He returned to *Old Hicks* and its fabulous, sunny Peaceful Valley.

SKAGGS HAD PUT away the exposed plate and was dismantling his tripod. The Blue Man plucked at the crumbs of dirt and muck covering his trousers.

"Hey, look," somebody shouted from up Nassau Street, "it's the famous *Skaggs!*"

Timothy's eyes glanced up the street eagerly, looking for his fan. He was not Dickens or Thackeray, perhaps, not even Mathew Brady, but evidently his own name was known to some bit of the public . . .

But then he saw it was only young Dudley Thone, a *Herald* reporter who had worked at the *Evening Mirror* with him. Thone was leaving

T. W. Strong's bookshop with an even younger man, heading back toward the *Herald*.

"Hallo, Mr. Mercury," Thone said as he approached, and added, as if to his young companion: "Until he drowned our poor dear editor, Mr. Mercury here was a real top-drawer newspaperman."

The nickname "Mr. Mercury," which Thone invented, was a triple-edged jibe—a reference to the mercury Skaggs used to develop daguerreo-types; to mercury poisoning, the symptoms of which were premature aging and madness; and to mercury's more common connotation, as a medicine for syphilitic sores. "Your proprietor Bobo has you making portraits of freaks on the pavement now, does he?" Thone teased. "Leave all the true celebrities to Brady, is that his idea?"

"Dry up and blow away."

The boy with Thone held up a parcel wrapped in brown paper. "We're out collecting scenes of Mexico—research for Mr. *Bennett*, for the Sunday takeout, our victory souvenir edition." James Bennett was the owner and editor of the *Herald*.

Skaggs looked up from his work.

"We've won, officially," Thone said. " 'Firm and universal peace be-tween the United States of America and the Mexican Republic.' The war's all over."

The Blue Man, hearing this, saluted Skaggs and started marching away, gaily singing another familiar tune as he bounced off. " 'And shouting free-dom's holy songs, / Strike for your rights, avenge your wrongs, / Upon the Rio Gran-dee!"

Thone nodded toward the *Herald* building. "Senate ratified the secret treaty not an hour ago—got the news on our telegraph. And our fellow in Washington got a *copy* of the treaty we'll publish." The *Herald* had been pro-war from the start.

"Hip hip hooray for our universal Yankee Nation," Skaggs said in a tone of pointedly fake enthusiasm. He had not been much opposed to the war against Mexico. But patriotic hoopla annoyed him, as did the spurious argu-ment that Polk was obliged to attack Mexico before Mexico turned its weapons against the United States.

"Today, California," Skaggs continued, adopting an oratorical tone, "and tomorrow the South Sea Islands, as we fulfill 'our divine mission to'— what was it?—'to own for ourselves that spicy little nation and bully its mil-lions of starving Catholic half niggers' . . . ?"

"No, no," said the boy with Thone, "it was *this*." He paused earnestly, as if he were about to swear some solemn oath.

"Dickie . . ." Thone growled softly.

"Ah," Skaggs said, "so this is Dickie *Shepherd,* our famous 'professional peer.' "

Cockeyed, patriotic, and apparently now famous as well, Dickie would not be deterred, and slowly declaimed the line in question from a *Herald* editorial. " 'We believe it is a part of our destiny to civilize that beautiful country.' "

"Why, thank you, Tiny Tim," Skaggs said. Twenty-year-old Dickie Shepherd had recently published a manifesto announcing his determination to "reform, single-handedly if necessary, the slovenly and misleading ways in which the journalistic arts of this city and nation are often practiced." He refused to invent or even embellish scenes and quotations for his articles in the *Herald,* habits he had declared were exacerbated by "the taste for liquor among my professional peers."

Skaggs stood, lifting the camera by its handle. "I cannot imagine how I mangled Mr. Bennett's immortal and glorious words. Slovenly *and* misleading of me." He wrapped his other arm around the tripod. "A good evening to you both."

Twilight was descending. As he walked past the *Express,* the *Post,* the *Commercial Advertiser,* the *Journal of Commerce,* the *Courier and Enquirer*— down one of the principal newspaper lanes in . . . Journalismville—the wind whipping from the east felt like the beginning of a winter blow. The equipment had become a burden by the time he turned toward his studio. He reminded himself to end the casual self-deception: not *his* studio, Ninian Bobo's studio, where Skaggs worked as a kind of tenant farmer, required to sell half his monthly crop of portraits for the owner.

It was not the gathering darkness and cold disheartening him, nor even his annoying arrangement with Bobo. Rather, it was the letter from New Hampshire in his pocket. What rankled most were the final lines:

Your mother and I understand that you are unsuited to a prosperous, productive, and respectable life like that of your brother Jonah. You write your squibs and stories. So be it.

However, we both pray fervently that from the vantage point of your thirty-sixth year you might finally begin to sight land in the distance, and make for it with all due haste. Do you understand? I will no longer chastise you for your blasphemer's wastrel life, nor repeat that New York is too much of a good thing. But none of our journeys is endless, Timothy—death takes us when it wishes, whether or not we have reached our chosen destinations. Choose!

As ever, your loving father

Have a happy birthday, son—and don't forget for a moment that death lurks. "Blasphemer"? Yes. But "wastrel"? Bunk! His bank account never exceeded fifty dollars, but he was not, as his father seemed determined to believe, a lounger, a player, a New York City sporting man—he did not frolic during the day, did not play bowls and billiards or attend shooting galleries and poker dens and cockfight pits, seldom idled away afternoons in taverns complaining about the scrofulous, dirty, stinking, stupid, thieving, willful, drunken Irish. He had spent a morning last winter, on one of his final days as a reporter, watching all the passengers of the HMS *Sir Henry Pottinger,* one of the first Famine Ships from Belfast, creep and stumble onto Pier 27— the whole scrofulous, dirty, stinking, weeping, freezing, wheezing, skinny, dazed, pale, half-naked lot of them. Like every other New Yorker, he was accustomed to ignoring everyday misery, but his hour spent studying and counting those 423 Irish men, women, and children had shocked him into a kind of reverent despair.

But, alas, the reproofs in his father's letter were only a magnified version of Timothy's own accumulating doubts. His life was indeed something of a pleasant waste, diverting but pointless, like a puzzle or game of cards. His wit and his knowledge of a great many subjects—such a plentitude of *facts,* as if (his father would say) to compensate for his paucity of faith—made him skillful at games of all kinds. But the games of writing for newspapers and cheap book publishers had become too easy and comfortable. Photography was still novel and strange, to Skaggs and to the rest of the world. No one was fluent with chemical picture-making the way they were with pens and paintbrushes; for the moment, everyone was an amateur. Photography was a science and craft consisting entirely of immense *possibility.* Skaggs's strange pictures of firemen and tramps and harlots seemed oblique and mysterious to him, as if something profound and unknowable was being suggested by the images' very exactitude.

Two newsboys, their arms full of papers, ran past him, interrupting his thoughts, the first one slowing down to shout in his face: "*Herald,* sir? Latest news from Washington!" "Mexico is ours!" squealed the other.

"Already know that news, boys," he said, sending them on their way. *Mexico may be* ours, *but what on earth is* mine, *precisely?*

Perhaps his bit of dejection about turning thirty-five was no epiphany, just a whiff of the blues on a late-winter breeze. But it was also, he knew, a definite foretaste of something more bitter and poisonous. As he pushed open the front door with his shoulder and stepped into the darkness, he formed a clear-eyed thought: *If my life remains unchanged when I turn forty, or forty-five— and why should it not?—then I will count myself a failure.* Given his distrust of most sorts of success, that put Timothy Skaggs in a very hard place.

Kent, England

THE PRINT ROOM of Great Chislington Manor contained 133 woodcuts, etchings, and lithographs, nearly every one pasted directly to the walls. The only sounds were the hiss and pop of the coal in the fireplace and the scratch and inkwell clink of Sir Archibald's pen. He sat at his desk, carefully dipping and furiously writing, composing his account of the events of the day, as he did every day.

His son stood at the entrance, unseen, watching his father scribble away, the top of the white feather flicking. Would he never switch from goose quill to steel?

Ben rapped on the door. "Father?"

"Nearly ready," he said. "Sit. What are Darwin's islands called? In Spanish America?"

"The Galápagos," Ben said as he removed his coat and lowered himself into one of the stuffed chairs near the fire.

Some seconds later, Sir Archie finished writing, waved his hand over the page to fan the words dry, stood, and walked to the fire. "Friday, the tenth of March, 1848, is *done.*"

"He seems intelligent and interesting, Mr. Darwin. I was most pleased to meet and talk with him."

"Of course he is '*intelligent*' and '*interesting.*' He's Charles Darwin! He is also very industrious for a man of his type. As well as a father already of *five.*" Sir Archie was fussing with the fire as he spoke, jabbing and beating the red-hot coal with a poker to make sparks fly. He sat down across from his son, brass rod still in hand. "Did the professor convey any . . . anxiety about the family's financial situation?"

Ben never failed to startle at his father's perspicacity. "A little, yes, actually, he did."

In the firelight the corners of Sir Archie's mouth tweaked upward, suggesting a smile. "A flatulent man," he announced, "is an anxious man."

As Ben wondered whether The Diary of Archibald Knowles was filled with such aphorisms, the author turned to face him.

"What is the awfully important business that we've convened in the middle of the night to discuss?"

Ben sat forward and leaned his forearms against his knees. "Father, I have decided to take leave of here soon. Very soon."

"Of Kent? So shall I—on Monday I am off for Malvern to try Dr. Gulley's cure—cold springs, sweathouse, Indian hemp smoke . . . they say Her Royal Highness the queen swears by Dr. Gulley."

"No, I mean that I shall be quitting the firm, sir. And, in fact, quitting—"

Sir Archibald tossed his poker onto the marble hearth slab, where it slammed with a clang against the fender.

"*Quitting* the *firm*."

"Yes, sir."

"Benjamin, I understand how Ashby's death has upset your good sense, but the frogs' revolution is a war of blacksmiths and swinkers and paupers *against* the likes of Ashby—and every bit as much against you, my boy."

"I am not—"

"You are an industrialist, Ben. Despite your costly upbringing, as you shouted tonight at dinner, you *enjoy* the steam and the machine tools and our workingmen lined up on the floor."

"Indeed I did, but—"

"An 'everyday opera,' you once called the Manchester works. Why in God's name would you pretend sympathy for the loom-smashers? It is *those* clods and half-wits who want to return to the old days and repeal our modern ways. With more passion than any monarchist."

"You misunderstand me," Ben told his father. "It is not street battles against kings in which I am inspired to enlist. It is the *American* revolution into which I intend to throw myself."

Sir Archibald regarded his baffling son for a long moment. "How drunk are you? The American Rebellion finished fifty years ago! What sort of joke are you attempting?"

"Sixty-five years ago, and no joke at all, sir. I am sailing for New York." Ben was relieved to hear himself finally say it out loud. He felt gooseflesh rise on his arms and neck. "I am emigrating. To America." *Emigration:* he had never gone quite this far in his own mind.

Archibald Knowles guffawed, a horselaugh that after a few seconds devolved into a cackle. His eyes glistened in the firelight. *My wafting romantic boy,* he thought as he looked at his earnest child in shirtsleeves, *my beautiful contrary baby Benjamin.* Why are the cosseted children of this supremely fortunate generation not content with their golden lots?

"Ben," he said, shaking his head, "life does not resemble one of your storybook tales. The real America is not the same as your pretty pictures of free Yankee backwoodsmen and wild red Indians and big whopper locomotives steaming alongside four-hundred-mile canals." He turned and pointed up to John James Audubon's paintings of a bald eagle and a golden eagle that hung above the door to the gun room. "I have no doubt that my pictures of the place are far nobler than the place itself. There is no business that a gentleman of your sort has in that strange, scruffy roughcast of a country."

"The strange roughcast is what I want! *This* country I find all too well finished and furbished."

"Your love of America was a lad's hobby, Ben. You are well nigh twenty-seven now. Your salad days are nearly past. You are a grown man."

"Yes! Precisely! I have been a dawdler these last ten years, a truant, and now I haven't a minute to waste."

His father made a short, sharp, puffing sigh and stood, wincing as always. He began to pace the Chinese carpet between the fireplace and his desk. Whenever events threatened to slip beyond his control, he paced. He had paced for hours at a time during the weeks his wife was dying.

"If it is an adventure you're after, we could have Philip find you a situation with the Colonial Office . . ."

"Father . . ."

". . . or I might speak to the gentlemen at the East India Company. A year in the Punjab gunning for Sikhs should be plenty strange and rough for you."

"No. I am headed west."

"Sir Henry is running things in Madras now, and I believe if your brother and I asked him—"

"I am going to America, Father."

But what good father would not endeavor to outflank his rash child? Mr. Knowles was quiet for a moment as he formed an idea.

"All right. I see that you are determined. But allow me to propose a *plan*.

The firm is joining with Spencer and Company to extend their guano fertilizer business into the United States. We need a man to serve as our director general of the enterprise."

"You wish me to become a jobber of puffin shit? To sell heaps of bird dung to the Americans?"

Ben's father stopped walking, grabbed the back of his chair with both hands, lifted the weight of his gimpy left leg from the floor, and, feeling every one of his fifty-nine years, looked over at his son with excruciatingly mixed feelings of pain and pleasure. He had raised a son who scoffed at his stratagems and accomplishments, who looked with disdain or pity at both the swamps from which Archie Knowles ascended and the fine hill on which Sir Archibald Knowles now stood. Yet Knowles the elder felt that he had thereby won the game. He had succeeded in producing offspring of such sensibility and refinement that they did not merely *affect* indifference to trade and profit, but were filled with a real, visceral contempt for the ordinary work of the world. And Ben's tongue was no less glib and insolent—*a jobber of puffin shit!*—than any young earl's. Ben Knowles, mocker of aristocrats, was himself an aristocrat in everything but title.

But, of course, old Archie Knowles would never admit his delight or his misery that his son was such a different species of Englishman than he.

"Then apprise me, Benjamin, of the details of your magnificent American plan."

"I have no details," he said. "I wish only to become the architect of my own fortune . . ."

His father was an instant away from interjecting a disparagement—*How very grand!* or *The poet speaks!*—before Ben added:

". . . the same as you have done, sir."

More tears seeped into Archibald Knowles's eyes.

"*America*," he said, shaking his head, disguising his soup of emotions as mere disapproval. "Why must it be America for you?"

"America is the next stage."

"The 'next stage'? Stage of what?"

"Of social development. England is the zebra, and America is the horse that the zebra becomes. I want to ride the horse."

"The zebra and the horse? What rubbish! Is this *science,* according to your farting friend Darwin? America is the newer model, is that it? A carriage with a rubberized hood? A dress with an extra inch of padding on the hips?"

"Yes, a better mode. A more advanced model."

"Because in America every idiot can pretend he is nobody's inferior? Unless, of course, he has the rotten luck to be a nigger . . . I trust you do know that your beloved America has its own classes of men in society, from very high to horribly low. Oh, the hypocrites! Did you not read Dickens's accounts of the place?"

Archibald Knowles citing literature! "Do you refer to *American Notes*, Father, or *Martin Chuzzlewit*?"

His father ignored the quiz, since he had never read a word of Dickens. "The country teems with brutishness and poverty."

"The country teems with possibility. Here we grip the illusion of permanence. The Yanks delight in change. America is a place in flux, perpetually in flux, by design . . ."

" 'Flux,' yes, precisely, *flux*, as when a man with the dysentery shoots bloody shit from his arse."

". . . which means that in America, no dream is deemed impossible—"

"You sound like an overexcited vicar."

"—not even the impossible ones!"

"A boozy vicar inventing riddles."

Each was enjoying this duel, the universal and eternal struggle of father versus son, generation versus generation.

"And every American is an inventor," said Ben, now unstoppable, "if not of some electrical gimcrack or new tool to clean corn, then an inventor of new customs, new ways of speaking—or, I daresay, of himself."

"There it is! A demented improvisation in the forests and deserts, a million square miles of schemers and impostors who piously *believe* every one of their frauds."

"Yes, there it is—a nation of improvisers."

"Where everything was forged the day before yesterday and nothing lasts longer than a season."

"Yes."

"The half-baked nation," Sir Archibald said, "where speed trumps all."

"*Yes.*"

His father shook his head again, sat back down at his desk, and shut his eyes. Sir Archibald had grown fatigued by his own inexpressible confusions. Did he sincerely wish his son to capitulate, and abandon his dreams of America? He did not. But did he want the boy to leave England for years, or forever? He did not.

"Father?"

The old man opened his eyes. "Who will"—he waved a hand—"remove and clean your soiled boots? Who will heat the bathwater? Dennis and Rose will not be accompanying you."

Ben had to admit—to himself—that while his imaginary picture of life in America did not specifically exclude servants, his bold scheme had not yet extended to such details.

"I can order coal, and light a fire. And perhaps I'll even learn to undress myself."

"You mock . . ."

"I mock only the mocker," Ben replied.

"But how do you propose to *pay* for the necessities in America? Surely no fancy-free young American expects an income from his retrograde English father . . . Maybe you will make a shilling a day selling tobacco and biscuits in the street. Or—I know!—you should construct *railways*—yes, you and ten thousand Irishmen can cut pine trees and lay the tracks through the wilderness . . . and wipe your arse with leaves . . . and hunt grizzly bears with your bow and arrow."

"You are a comedian, Father."

"No, I am a practical man wondering how his second son will survive. What money will you use?"

Ben glanced away, and found himself staring at the portrait near the door of eight-year-old Philip, six-year-old Isabel, three-year-old Benjamin, and the infant Caroline in profile, smiling wide-eyed at their unseen mother. Ben's living memory of Caroline, who died only a year after Mr. Haydon painted the portrait, was now faint, and merged entirely with this picture of her.

"Are you quite finished gathering wool? Do you care to give an answer?"

"I have some savings. As well as Mother's bequest."

"Her Scottish *pin money*? Am I meant to laugh or cry?"

When Ada Knowles died, Isabel found deep in the drawer of her dressing table a yellowed envelope containing forty-four £5 Scottish banknotes issued thirty-odd years earlier, in the year of her marriage to Archie Knowles. Packaged with this secret cache was a recent note explaining the money's origins (a confidential bridal gift from her father intended as a hedge against matrimonial disaster) and her wish that upon her death it be shared equally by her two younger children, "preferably in the exercise of some noble, interesting & hopeless indulgence."

On the £28 a week Ben earned from Knowles, Merdle, Newcome & Shufflebotham, he lived well—indeed, lived more or less oblivious to money. But he had no other income, and without the job at the firm, he knew, he would need a fortune to generate an equivalent sum. His half of his mother's bequest had grown to £120, which would throw off an income of . . . two shillings a week—a fraction of what he paid his servants. But in America, he would not need four new suits of clothes and ten new shirts and two new pairs of boots each year, nor two servants, nor clubs, nor a whole house to live in. In America, he would wear a plain American costume and find some gainful occupation and live like other Americans, by his wits. He figured that his mother's money and his £82 in savings could last him a year.

"You are, I suppose," Ben told his father, "meant to admire my determination to survive without your assistance, and without any rich wife, by my own efforts."

"Yes, yes, so you say, the architect of your own fortune . . ." But instead of continuing to shout about Ben's improvident, quixotic ways, Sir Archie decided in that instant to surprise him. "Well, I should think your mother in heaven, bless her large liberal heart, will be pleased. 'Interesting and hopeless' were her words, were they not?"

Ben was shocked. In fact, he had been so certain of the response that he was now silently reciting his father's actual words to be sure that they contained no trap. And then, given the void he suddenly faced, he stumbled into an argument with himself.

"And 'noble' as well," Ben said. " 'Noble, interesting, and hopeless.' To tell the truth, my American ambitions are far more selfish than noble."

"Like all ambition. All sensible ambition."

"But perhaps Mother meant for us to use the money to build a . . . refuge for prostitutes in Shepherd's Bush or . . . or a parsonage in Belize."

Sir Archibald shook his head, then turned and started toward the door. "Come with me to the gun room, Benjamin," he said, limping heavily. "As long as you are bound for the frontier . . ."

"I am bound for *New York*, Father . . . Your wound seems especially vexing tonight."

"Admiral Nelson won at Trafalgar with one arm and one eye," he said quickly, as he always said when anyone expressed concern about his bad leg. "If you are headed for America, you had better be prepared to shoot, and you might as well take your ten-gauge. I believe it is still in the gun room closet."

Sir Archibald was confident, without turning around to see, that he had surprised Ben again. He was pleased that his younger son no longer seemed frightened of The Game.

Ben felt dizzy. His check rein had been unfastened, the whole bit jerked from his mouth, the harness suddenly pulled off and tossed away. He had control of his own destiny, and the fear and joy were indistinguishable. As he followed his father out of the print room, he turned and glanced once again, for a passing instant, at the portrait on the wall of little Benjamin. *How strangely hungry I appear,* Ben Knowles thought. And then he was gone.

8

———→>•◄←———

March 16, 1848

. . .

Paris

*P*ARIS WAS A chaos.

A month into the new republic, almost every last wisp of exuberance had disappeared, replaced by a dour nausea, like a drunkard's the day after a binge. The stock exchange had reopened, but share prices sank. Banks were collapsing. Businesses remained closed. No one had money to spend.

Three weeks to the day after the monarchy fell, thousands of national guardsmen had gathered in the streets to protest their own official disgrace as well as the socialist drift of the new government.

One of the angry men marching down the Boulevard Bonne-Nouvelle— "Good News Boulevard"—was Gabriel Drumont, a forty-seven-year-old former sergeant of the former Municipal Guard. He was, like half of Paris, without work. He had been a member of the guard for sixteen of its eighteen years of existence, the only job he ever held after the army, and now the service had been declared defunct by the radicals. Yet because he was from la Garde *Municipale*—the *Municipal* Guard, a mere gendarme in the view of the men of the Garde *Nationale* who'd organized the demonstration— Drumont had been instructed to march near the end of the parade. For sentimental reasons, he brought along a paper parcel containing the bloody private's cap and blouse in which his brother Michel had died.

Among those lining the sidewalk, watching the soldiers' parade, was Marie Brasseaux, a twenty-year-old daughter of a bookseller who had been a member of an underground political club before the February Revolution. She stood on the curb with a few of her young comrades, watching and heckling the *contre-révolutionnaires*. And as it happened, she was wearing the same maroon dress she had worn a month before, the evening the Drumont brothers had arrested her for making bombs.

Because some of the soldiers were chanting—"Nous sommes des hommes *fidèles!*" *We are* loyal *men! We are* loyal *men!*—the sidewalk hecklers raised a chant of their own. "Le peuple dit *non!*" Marie and her chums shouted. *The people say* no*! The people say* no*!*

Gabriel Drumont was on Marie's side of the boulevard. She spotted him just as she snarled a final ". . . *non*," and for a few seconds she was stunned into silence. His hair was now short and he wore a mustache, but *it was he,* no question, the sergeant of the Garde Municipale who had grabbed her a few blocks from this very spot, threatened to let his men have their way with her, promised to lock her in a cage in Sainte-Pélagie along with the other subversive vermin, and whose underling had bruised her neck and wrists.

She pointed at him and shouted, "C'est *vous*! *Brute! Criminel!*"

One of her friends grabbed Marie's arm, but she jerked from his grasp and strode into the boulevard to confront this brute, this criminal who had abused her, who had resisted the people's will at the crucial moment on the night of February 23.

Gabriel Drumont didn't remember Marie until she was close to him, walking alongside him, jabbing her finger toward his face like an angry lover or wife.

He did not stop walking, which fed her anger.

The heat of her rage and this public contretemps had in one stroke improved Drumont's mood.

"Où est l'arme de mon grand-père?" she demanded. "Je la veux tout de suite!"

Now Drumont looked her straight in the eye.

The audacity of these radicals—especially the bourgeois radical brats, like this girl. You want your pistol returned immediately—your grandpa's "antique" pistol and dagger with which you would have happily killed me?

He grinned at her, saying nothing.

The sergeant's smile made Marie Brasseaux want to snap his neck then and there. When she swatted his hand, his parcel, Michel's uniform, fell to the pavement, and he lunged down to retrieve it from the grime.

She had succeeded in making his smile go away. He met her glare. He knew what honor and decency required him to do. He forced his face to relax and stepped up on the curb.

"D'accord, mademoiselle," he said as her friends gathered around protectively, *you must forgive my surprise, I am very sorry, not yet accustomed to the new order. Your old P-P, the dagger and pistol, shall be returned to you tomorrow, if you would kindly provide the address.*

In the Latin Quarter, she told him. *Number 7 Rue Neuve-Sainte-Geneviève, above the Brasseaux bookshop, the door at the back.*

"Très bien," Drumont said. "Demain?"

Marie, now feeling very pleased with herself, amended her instruction. *If it's to be tomorrow,* she said, *have it sent in the* morning—*before I leave to join* our *great march in* defense *of the revolution . . .*

She was showing off for her friends. Tomorrow they and tens of thousands of other democrats would be in the streets, not on the sidewalk, endorsing the socialist drift of the new regime and protesting today's protest—a *counter*-counter-revolutionary demonstration.

Tomorrow morning? Why not? "Demain *matin,* oui, mademoiselle," he replied with a mask of courtesy as he turned back toward his march.

Marie Brasseaux had one final instruction for her former tormentor. *And under no circumstance,* she said, raising her voice as Drumont trotted away, *send your stupid little boy on the errand, do you understand, your soldier you shot in the street that night.* "Votre petit stupide garçon," she said.

He stopped and turned around.

It required all of his strength not to curse her—not to kill her on the spot. *No,* he assured her, *I shall personally return your antique to you.* He didn't have her dagger-pistol, of course, had never even touched the thing. The corporal had deposited it in a weapons closet that same night.

Drumont made a small bow, and before he left raised his hand toward them, palm open, and said, "Fraternité, mes citoyens!"

Two of Marie's friends, impressed by the sergeant's progress along the path of rehabilitation, replied in kind. "*Fraternité,* monsieur," they said.

the next morning—March 17, 1848

MARIE BRASSEAUX WAS among the hundred thousand Parisians preparing to march on the Hôtel de Ville in support of the radicals in the new government. But before she could join them, she needed to await a delivery.

When the Garde Municipale sergeant arrived at her apartment carrying a bundle, she let him inside. It was only as she tore away at the pasteboard that her surprise gave way to suspicion. There was only a stuffed black-and-white bird.

"Qu'est-ce que *c'est?*" she asked. "Un *pingouin?*"

Yes, the penguin of your English comrade, Drumont replied. *I thought you might wish to return it to him.*

The Englishman? Don't be a fool, he was not my "comrade," I have no idea who he is, or where.

Alas, Drumont thought. But it had been worth a try.

"Je veux mon poignard," she said.

The dagger! Yes, of course, miss. Here, he said, revealing a brass scabbard under his coat and pulling out a bayonet. Before she was able to say, *But that is not mine,* Drumont had grabbed a handful of ringlets, yanked her head back, and sliced twice, back and forth, deep across her neck. Then, as she gurgled, and crumpled to the floor, her hands grabbing at her open, pumping throat, he jammed the knife straight into her left breast, and her heart.

Drumont used the shredded pasteboard from the penguin to clean his hands. *A mere six weeks ago,* he thought, glancing down at the dead girl and pool of blood, *back when everything was different, I would have been within my rights to execute her, a treasonous would-be assassin of the king caught practically in the act.* He dropped the wads of paper on the floor, then wiped both hands, backs and palms, across the penguin's smooth feathers, leaving a set of red smears on its white belly. *And in any event, it's one fewer marcher for this afternoon.*

As he turned to leave, he was startled by someone in the back of the room and reached for his bayonet—but it was merely his own reflection in a looking glass. And there on her dressing table, sitting on a velvet pad beneath the mirror, he noticed something gleam and glitter . . . an old gold brooch covered in pearls and diamonds. Another antique from another grandparent, no doubt, but in any case no longer of any use to Marie Brasseaux. Whereas Drumont was now embarked on an expedition of uncertain length and cost.

By the time the revolutionists' demonstration finished that afternoon and Marie's friends discovered her body, he was already speeding north from Paris, 450 francs in his purse. As the train had approached Boulogne, he had released his pawn ticket for the piece of jewelry from the open coach window into the winds. And by the time the police of the fifth arrondissement had begun investigating the Brasseaux murder, Drumont was on the deck of a ship, watching steam blow from the end of its funnel into the darkening sky over the Channel.

Though he was a native of Corsica, Drumont loathed sailing. An irony, and there it was. One or two days at sea was all he could stand—from Aiacciu to Cannes as a young man, now from Boulogne to Guernsey. At least he had managed to sleep for some of this present hell.

He walked to the bow and pulled his collar up over his neck as he faced the wind. There was no turning back. And his way forward was clear, unambiguous. Decisions seemed to be making themselves, as if he were taking orders from a higher power. His dispatch of the girl had been an obligation, not really a choice but a matter of defending the defenseless Michel's honor and his own. And fulfilling those duties had required him to escape his subverted city and nation, which in turn pointed him in one direction—to England, where he would avenge his brother's death. He knew only a surname, Knowles, and the fact that this young coward Knowles was a revolutionist. But those were a beginning.

Precisely where should he go? As he fled Paris, he had assumed that he would sail directly for one of the English coastal towns, then proceed immediately to London. But did Knowles live in London? Drumont didn't know—indeed, he realized during his trip north, he knew almost nothing of England. He had killed the girl somewhat rashly; from now on he needed to plan with care.

On the train he had hatched a scheme. He would take time to learn what he needed to know. And so he was sailing for the island of Guernsey, where his cousin Baptiste worked in a shipyard. Drumont had not seen him since Baptiste left Paris in the thirties, but they were the same age, and they had been close as boys on Corsica; he would help; he was Corsican. And while Guernsey was English territory—stolen from France—the residents spoke an old French patois, Guernésiais, that Drumont hoped he could understand. He would reconnoiter on Guernsey for a few weeks, learn what he could about the English and their ways in a half-French place. There was no rush; let Knowles imagine himself safe, let him relax his guard.

From which harbor should he sail? That choice was a more patriotic one. He sailed from Boulogne, of course, because Boulogne was the port from which the Emperor Napoleon had prepared to launch *his* invasion of England a half century ago. And while Napoleon's army had been frustrated, perhaps Drumont might now succeed, as a lone guerrilla, and in his small way vindicate the emperor posthumously, as a good son fulfills a father's incomplete dream.

Might he truly *be* Bonaparte's bastard, as his dirty-minded friends used to tease back on Corsica when they were boys? Drumont was born in June of 1800, precisely nine months after Napoleon Bonaparte's final visit to the island, just before he became emperor. And Gabriel's mother, like so many of her Corsican generation, claimed she had known Napoleon when she was young, back when his surname was still Corsican, with four syllables, Buona-par-te. Like the emperor himself, Gabriele Tremonti had Frenchified his name when he immigrated to the mainland.

All his life, Gabriel's wish to believe his mama was not a slut had overridden his wish to believe he was Napoleon Bonaparte's secret elder son. But now, with his whole family dead, he found himself indulging the wishfulness concerning his patrimony.

In the distance he spotted a bonfire at St. Peter Port, on Guernsey. He had spotted Britain.

9

March 18, 1848
. . .
New York City

OR MORE THAN a year afterward, whenever Skaggs tried to parse out the events and emotions of 1848 for the memoir he intended to write—*Wonderstruck,* he would call the book—he debated with himself about when and where to fix the start of the present age of wonders.

There could be no doubt, he was certain, that the year constituted a true annus mirabilis. Surely the revolutions in Europe and the discoveries in California and then the cholera everywhere were the equals of the wonders of 1665 and '66, the original annus mirabilis, when London was wasted by the Plague *and* the Great Fire, and Isaac Newton explained gravity *and* invented the calculus. In 1848 God the gamester had certainly spun his wheel again. But for the purposes of the book Skaggs planned to write, when did it make sense to begin?

Was it the instant of magnificent dumb luck in January in California, when the no-account boob from New Jersey, an incompetent mill-builder standing half numb in the waters of the American River (which was at that time still a few days shy of actually being American), leaned down and plucked from the gravel a speck of gold no bigger than a piece of snot? The moment's absence of spectacle would displease Skaggs when he learned of it.

Or should he begin his chronicle in Europe a month later, when the first of a hundred kings and princes ran from their palaces like a frightened herd of overbred animals? The revolutions were *pure* spectacle, a whole continent on a spree.

Public events of large consequence did occur a month after that, on the third Saturday in March—democratic passions boiled over in Milan and Berlin, San Francisco's eight-week-old newspaper reported the discovery of the golden snot in the American River—but it was a date that would be marked in no chronicle save Skaggs's own as the commencement of the new age.

ON SATURDAY THE eighteenth, admittedly, Skaggs's judgment may have been colored by the bit of opium he'd stirred into his luncheon tea. He had finished his day's work for Bobo, a double portrait of the magician Signor Antonio Blitz and his favorite wooden dummy. He decided to use the rest of the afternoon to start writing an essay, inspired by Poe's talk, on the ways that rail travel and photography and the telegraph were warping the perception of time.

And he'd decided that a taste of opium, just five or six grains, would be a propitious way to prime his pan for the task.

And so it was. By the time he stepped out into West Broadway at five o'clock, he had filled two large double-elephant sheets and started on a third.

No! Not merely five o'clock, he noticed as he looked in at the clock-maker's, but precisely *seven past* five—*no,* seven minutes forty-three, -four, *forty-five seconds* past. He had been writing all afternoon about "the useful tyranny of clock time," and here it was, displayed two dozen different ways in a shopwindow. Today he had scribbled out his theory: because watches in every pocket and clocks in every factory and railroad station had stimulated in people an acute awareness of time passing, that new awareness had in turn stimulated an unhappiness with the status quo, and the new demands for still-speedier progress. "Shall we adapt and submit to the useful tyranny," Skaggs had asked in his final sentences today,

and all of us become automatons in wrappings of skin and blood, mere androids? Or will the ultimate ism *of our day, this driving* precision-ism *of schedules timed to the very minute, instead so fire our impa-*

tience that we revolt against the clock-mad bosses in the factories and countinghouses and railway offices? Lovers of liberty and poetic justice must hope for the latter.

Ten square feet of fresh words! Sentences that trickled and flowed over his mind's topography all in their own time and for their own sakes, not forced out on some publisher's account for ten-words-a-penny.

"Schveep for half a cent?"

Skaggs blinked. Occupied by his own overheated thoughts, he had hardly registered the presence of the city, let alone its people. He saw now that he was in the crowd huddling along Broadway, waiting for a landau and a city wagon to pass. In the landau were a pair of rich ladies dressed for a party, each smiling and holding a tiny candle out the windows of the carriage. Piled in the wagon were dozens of street carcasses—mostly dogs, some rats and cats, a couple of pigs, the whole heap covered in an inch of lime, which sifted out between the boards as the wagon rolled, leaving a fuzzy trail of white on the pavement.

"Schveep for you, sir, please?" A street arab of nine or ten was tugging at his coat with one hand and with the other held a broom as tall as she. A patina of filth made her chestnut hair black, and she had no right eye.

"*Ja,* bitte," he said, tapping his walking stick on the stone.

The girl smiled.

"Which I'm afraid," he continued, "is practically the entire extent of my German, which I acquired in Buffalo. Haben sie von Buffalo? Und *million* Deutsche im Buffalo!"

The girl giggled now at this *wirklich verrückt* American, this crazy New Yorker, and started furiously brushing away the dirty feathers and bits of dried manure from the patch of Broadway in front of him, making the odors and motes rise and swirl as she cleared a place for him to step. When she came for her wage he noticed that his writing pencil was still gripped tight in his hand, so he ceremoniously placed both it and a penny in the girl's open palm. She glanced up quizzically, registered his smile, winked her good eye, and plunged the pencil like a bodkin into one of her braids, shouting "*Danken* Sie!" as she dashed off down . . . *Worth Street,* Skaggs saw on the sign bolted to the lamppost. The single Negro among the city's troop of lamplighters stood on his ladder wiping soot from the street sign with a rag.

Skaggs had walked quite far, he realized now, in this pleasantly addled state. And that was part of the problem with his current life, he reckoned—his familiarity with almost every board and stone and step of Manhattan, his habitat by now so well known that even in an opium haze he was able to wander for a mile in a trance, chatting silently with himself.

As he crossed Worth, he watched the lamplighter gingerly poke his torch, like a wizard's wand, up inside the glass globe toward the jet of gas. Duff Lucking had suggested Skaggs make a portrait of this man to include in his eventual "Daguerreian of Fire" exhibition.

The bloom of light surged and enveloped Skaggs. A moment earlier it had been late afternoon, the sky still indigo; now, from within the glamorous bubble of white-hot golden glow, it seemed as if night had fallen over the rest of the city. Skaggs's favorite hours in New York had always been the gradual, liminal recession of day into night, the daily autumn, with each of its slow, soft, ambiguous gradations of deepening color and shadow. But twilight had been rendered obsolete by the New York Gas Light Company. Half the city's streetlamps were gas now.

Skaggs did not believe, as many people did, that gaslight harmed one's eyes. But expanding its territory in every direction, the new light allowed New York—forced it, really—to remain awake longer, to ignore the earth's rotations. The interminable glow had turned tens of thousands of New Yorkers into night-crawling scamps, instead of the select fraternity that stayed out late carousing when Skaggs had first arrived. Back then a city inspector had patrolled every gassed street every evening, and by midnight would pound his cane on the sidewalk and yell "*Lights-out.*" Now the lights burned practically all night long. And Skaggs did wonder if the city's gas-fired wakefulness had begun to overstimulate its inhabitants, make them merrier, louder, funnier, stranger, greedier, crazed. As he stepped now from the luminous Worth Street blossom back into the ordinary mid-block evening, the whole view down Broadway struck him as unusually bright, saturated with light.

To be modern, he thought, *is to be artificially aglow.*

Nor was the new luminosity only a matter of gaslight spreading into every parlor and respectable street. There were also the laughably large new panes of plate glass that amounted to architectural magician's tricks, erasing the boundary between indoors and out. And the unearthly rays of light beaming from burning lime that transformed any actor on a stage into a shining angelic or demonic figure; the magic-lantern shows of Jesus on the cross and Halley's comet scaring a tribe of Indians; the new, exceptionally *yellow* yellow paints and bright red printer's inks, all mixed up by chemists in laboratories; the telegraph wires that sparked and blushed against the night skies like grapevines beset by St. Elmo's fire.

Skaggs thought of his Latin master at school, forefinger extended at Skaggs, warning him yet again, *"Cave ignis fatuus!"* Beware the fictitious fire!

Modernity glows.

Then, however, he recalled the world's other great modern metropolis— murky, sullen, dun-colored London, which he had visited for the first time last winter en route to Bavaria. It was a city that seemed to darken a little more every day from the soot belched by smokestacks and chimneys.

All right then, an amended declaration: *Modern* America *glows.*

On the sidewalk in front of him, a telescope man had set up for business: five cents for a five-minute look, money Skaggs had often spent to gawk at the moon's craters and Saturn's rings and the nearest stars, such as Vega, in the constellation Lyra. Tonight there was already a queue of people hoping to see GOD'S OWN ILLUMINATIONS, as the man's wooden sign promised.

What a funny puff to peddle astronomy, Skaggs thought as he prepared to cross Thomas Street—when five drummers in army uniforms stepped directly in front of him. He had bumped the nearest man.

"Oops, pardon me," he said, and only then noticed behind the drummers a whole *band*—ten trumpets, ten trombones, another ten men carrying larger horns. They were all silent but for the soft rhythmic stomping of their boots as they marched in place. And then, all at once, they moved forward into Broadway and began playing "Yankee Doodle" so loudly that Skaggs was blown backward by the sound. He thumped his right elbow against a bystander's belly—and as he jerked away and prepared to apologize, accidentally brushed his left hand across the lightly upholstered buttocks of the man's young wife.

Modern America: artificially aglow, preternaturally loud—*and unreasonably crowded.* Then Skaggs remembered why. Tonight was the peace festival, to celebrate our crushing of Mexico. The bands and General Scott and some of his New York troops marching up Broadway from the Battery and, by order of the mayor, the *illuminations,* a patriotic obligation for all New Yorkers to stick candles in windowsills, twist open the valve on every gas lamp, wave torches, build bonfires—that is, to come as close as possible to burning down this flammable city without actually setting it afire.

In the short pause after the first verse of "Yankee Doodle," Skaggs heard another familiar tune insert itself. He turned and saw that behind him, marching out of Worth, another regimental band had appeared, playing one of the inescapable songs of the moment, "Strike for Your Rights, Avenge Your Wrongs." The musicians were arrayed in a single line from Broadway curb to Broadway curb. Leading them were a pair of ensigns, one carrying the regular twenty-nine-star American flag, the other a gray banner painted with a crude red star and crude red silhouette of a bear—a replica of the flag raised by the American rebels in Mexican California back in '46.

As the band reached the last bars of their first verse, pedestrians around Skaggs began shouting the words and clapping along in time.

"Felt Mexico's foul tyranny,
Upon the Rio Gran-dee!"

More voices joined in on the chorus:

"Sing to the Rio Gran-dee,
The rolling Rio Gran-dee,
Our foe shall bow the knee!"

Almost none of the enthusiastic citizens knew any of the lyrics except the chorus and the final lines of each verse. All the words people had memorized, and now gloried in shouting out, were the angry ones, the ones that smelled of bile and gunpowder and blood.

Skaggs watched a group of girls tossing bouquets at the survivors of New York's decimated Second Regiment. One of the men stopped to pick up a hyacinth and began to place it in the tip of his musket barrel when a large bomb detonated in the sky—followed shortly by a second, smaller explosion. The soldiers and the girls and everyone in the street stopped and smiled and looked south. The fireworks were going up from the Battery. Skaggs adored fireworks, and these days the displays were beyond brilliant—not the pale flashes and pops of his childhood, but reds and blues and greens burning in apocalyptic splendor. At one astounding bloom of purple, he cooed and chuckled along with the rest of the crowd.

Artificially glowing, artificially noisy, artificially jolly America . . . and in these protean times, it occurred to Skaggs as he stared at the fire in the sky, modern artifices turn from toy to tool to toy and back again: gas lamps had begun as theatrical geegaws, just as weapons of war had been turned by the pyrotechnicians into entertainments.

He hustled down Duane Street back toward West Broadway, away from the mob, against a column of people holding tiny star-spangled banners on foot-long sticks and all eager to join the bloody-minded festival of peace. Ten yards ahead of him one other escapee was making his way west. The fellow had both hands shoved into his coat pockets, and his glazed leather cap was pulled down low.

"Señor *Lucking*, please to be halting *now!*"

DUFF STOPPED SHORT. Who was calling his name? Should he run? Should he stand his ground and deny everything? But then there was no more time to decide: he felt the tip of a gun barrel poke between his shoulder blades. His left hand froze around the thick roll of cord in his pocket, the right around his pistol-shaped match safe.

"Ees tonight *la fiesta* of *victoria*, Meester Señor *Lucking?*"

The voice was a few feet away. The man had a long gun, not a pistol. Still, Duff thought, perhaps he should run. Wouldn't it be better to die in the street here and now, shot from behind by a cowardly foreigner? Rather than have the whole truth about his time in Mexico revealed to Polly and the world? No, even better: he would pull the tin toy gun from his pocket and turn toward the man, surprise him, force the stranger to fire point-blank, guaranteeing Duff his own hero's death . . .

No, no, *no:* why should some aggrieved Mexican want to assassinate Duff Lucking, of all people? The poor fellow is simply misinformed. Duff could tell him the truth. He had to tell him the truth.

Who are you? "¿Quién es usted, hombre?" Duff asked. He had not spoken a word of Spanish in six months.

The assailant did not answer.

"Por favor, señor," Duff asked, "¿de dónde es en Mexico? ¿Cómo se llama, hombre?" *Please, where are you from, what is your name?*

"*No*, señor!" came the reply.

Why did none of the flag-waving New Yorkers stop to intervene? Were they so jaded? The man had a gun!

Duff tried again to engage the man, lowering his voice to a whisper. "Este no es una *victoria* para *mí*—soy un *amigo* de su República. *Viva* la República . . ." And then he reduced his voice to a whisper. "¿Conoce la Legión de Extranjeros?"

Still no reply, but finally he felt the tip of the gun barrel lift away from his spine. His resort to plain dealing had worked. Duff opened his hands wide and removed them gingerly from his pockets, then, with a hopeful smile, twisted his head around slowly to look over his shoulder and find . . .

"*Skaggs!*"

"I know I failed to keep up my end of our conversation, but Latin is the only foreign language I have, apart from my pathetic bits of—"

"You *bugger*! You goddamned son of a *dog*!"

"Don't come any closer," Skaggs said, now pointing his walking stick at Duff's face, "or I swear I'll shoot. And at this range, it's unlikely I'll miss."

Duff swatted the cane out of his hand and into the street. "I nearly crapped my pants, you fool!" Passersby were looking at them now. "*Damn* you, Skaggs. I ought to thump you." He was panting. His face was bright red.

Skaggs felt bad about embarrassing the boy. "Forgive me, Duff. Honestly, I meant no disrespect. I'll buy you a brandy, or two. We'll celebrate the victory indoors. I mean to say, *your* victory."

"I don't want a drink. I don't need a drink."

"Please, man, do not tell me that you have taken the pledge and sworn off liquor. You have not joined some gruesome temperance fraternity, have you?"

Duff shook his head. "I want no blunting of my anger," he said with the even tone of a man who had spent time pouring and measuring his vitriol. "Not tonight." He raised his right hand, finger pointed like an orator. "Understand—it is no true victory these windbags and fools are celebrating." He continued walking. "When it began, you know, when *I* enlisted, we understood ourselves to be fighting for a Mexican *revolution*." He was angry. "Such a lie."

"Yes. Yes it was."

"Your friend Whitman, in the *Eagle*—"

"Yes, I remember."

" 'Mexico must be thoroughly chastised,' he said. 'America knows how to crush, as well as how to expand . . .' " Duff was frothing. "Now this 'peace' is nothing but the end of a successful . . . of a transaction."

"It's Polk's Mexican gratuity has you riled up, eh?" Skaggs said. "The six-bit tribute for the damage you and your fellows wreaked down there."

Under the terms of the peace treaty being celebrated, the United States had agreed to pay Mexico $15 million in reparations—seventy-five cents on behalf of each American man, woman, and child, the six-bit tribute. Just before the war started two years ago, President Polk had offered $20 million to buy California, Texas, and the rest of the 338 million acres of Mexico the U.S. wanted.

"It was nothing *but* a deal of business," said Duff. "Forty thousand dead men nothing more than . . . garnish. A means of reducing the price five million dollars. Twelve dollars per corpse."

Skaggs knew that, in fact, $5 million divided among the 40,000 war casualties amounted to $125 for every dead man, not $12. And almost *$400* apiece if one made the calculation using only the 13,000 American dead— that is, *U.S.* dead, since a majority of the force were not Americans at all, but Irish and German immigrants the army had purchased and scooped up like so many musket balls to fire across the Rio Grande. But Skaggs thought it best not to correct or clarify just now.

"In the end," Duff continued, "it was all a negotiation for some real estate, wasn't it? American bankers and Mexican bankers using men with cannon and rifles to bargain hard."

Yes, Skaggs further refrained from saying, *and why should* this *war be different from any other?*

"I do not blame you a bit," Skaggs said instead, hooking his right arm through Duff's left. "If it were me that my own country had misused in such a fashion—" His hand happened to press against the thick coil of cord in Duff's pocket. Skaggs patted and grabbed it through the cloth, as if to ask, *What is this?*

"Fuse," Duff said. "Forty-second-a-foot safety fuse."

"Ah. Gas fitter's matériel."

Duff shook his head.

"A*ha,*" Skaggs said, "for your *own* illuminations! So then I take it you are not altogether in the dumps about tonight's festivity?"

"I'm not blue now," Duff said.

He had swallowed two double doses of the little pills he took to fight off his depressions—Blue Mass, little gray-blue balls of mercury that tasted like licorice and roses. He had found himself crying in bed that morning even before he was entirely awake. Exactly one year ago he had made his choice in Mexico, after watching for forty-eight hours as they blasted Vera Cruz with their cannon.

And this afternoon in the Vauxhall Gardens he had hidden behind an oak tree and finally run away down the Fourth Avenue after he spotted a corporal from his company, a Pennsylvanian named Pishey Wetmore, roaming with a group that included Fatty Freeborn. Duff had not known Wetmore well, and was one of the few in Company A who had never teased him about his name, but ever since Duff's return from Mexico he had lived in dread of encountering men like him by chance.

With the Second Regiment volunteers back in the city and mustering out, his chance of encountering some inconvenient former associate was increasing by the hour.

"Are you hungry, then?" Skaggs asked. "I was headed to Budd's—I'll buy us a big fry of oysters."

From somewhere nearby they heard a bull's deep, long, sad bellow. For a couple of seconds the sound bounced from stone to brick to stone, and the echo provoked the answering cries of a half dozen more animals, then a chorus of moos beyond numbering.

The men exchanged a look. Duff's expression did not include surprise.

"The beeves' parade," he said. "The spring march."

Now Skaggs inhaled to catch the aroma, and nodded. It was a Saturday, and only three days until the vernal equinox. The weather had been unusually warm, and the river ice was fracturing and bobbing and disappearing all the way up to Albany. The season's first boats, steamers and sloops with cattle cribs lashed and bolted to their decks, had arrived at the city's piers loaded with fattened animals from upstate. As it happened, tonight was the night hundreds of head would be driven through Manhattan's streets in celebration of the thaw and the spring, a remnant of the time before railways, when all livestock walked or boated from the countryside to their deaths in New York City.

The animals appeared. Ten, twenty, fifty, and then more, a widening herd of chocolate-brown Durhams and reddish Devons coming into West Broadway a block below where Skaggs and Duff stood. They were a clattering rather than a thundering herd. On the tip of every horn was some seasonal decoration: a daub of green paint, a red ribbon, the spiraled peel from an orange. They were gay beasts.

"I suspect," Skaggs shouted, "that no one thought to inform the visiting herdsmen about tonight's Mexican War gala."

Duff smiled. It was a mischievous smile, entirely uncharacteristic. "Come on," he said as he darted left down Reade Street, ahead of the cattle. "You are going to see your first *stampede.*"

"My what?"

The cattlemen, wearing leather pants, walked quickly along on each side of the animal mob, snapping their sticks against their beeves' shoulders and barking "Yo, yo" and "Yah, yah."

Their intended route would take them north to Greenwich Village, and finally all the way west to Abattoir Place, the riverfront block of Twelfth Street. Before dawn these animals' blood would be pouring into the very river current that had floated them down to the city today.

By the time Skaggs caught up with his friend, Duff held a burning match in his left hand and one end of the stiff black safety fuse in his right.

"Duff? Is that wise, just now?"

"What, are you a copper now, Skaggs? Are you going to march me over to the Tombs?"

"With all these animals in such unfamiliar territory . . ."

The cattle were just about to turn north into Church Street, a long block away from the mobs of musicians and merrymakers and speakers' platforms that filled Broadway.

Duff touched his fire to the fuse and threw the whole coil onto the stones just behind the herd's lead animal, a large Durham bull that sniffed the air, made a full stop, turned its head to see the snake of sputtering fire a yard from its rump, snorted, and began running—not up Church but straight toward Broadway.

The nearest drover saw the sparks just as the bull did, and leapt into the street to stamp out the fuse, but the animals' panic was quicker than the man's. In an instant there was an impassable wall of bawling cattle cantering east. When the unlit end of the coiled fuse looped around a Devon's foreleg, turning that bull into a one-ton firework, the drovers' task became hopeless. All they could do was run after their animals toward the urban throngs on their illuminated boulevard.

Duff was walking calmly in the opposite direction.

"What have you *done*?" Skaggs asked.

"As long as America wants to own half of Mexico, well, they ought to know the customs of the place, oughtn't they?" Duff turned, stretched out his hand, and pointed toward the marauding herd. "A stampede."

The Broadway crowd parted and the cattle rushed through the sudden channel. One cow stepped into a drum and dragged it along with her, as if she'd been outfitted with an elephant's peg leg. Several animals kicked at dropped trumpets and flutes, which spun like whirligigs in the street. People screamed. People laughed. Horses reared. A beer cart was upset, sending bottles tumbling across Broadway like tenpins. A block farther down Broadway, the melee spread.

The lead bull, followed too closely by too many of his fellows, was pressed against one of the giant illuminated windows of Stewart's department store. The glass shattered, and suddenly the bull and two other animals were inside the display cabinet, thrashing and yelping, smashing the Viennese bentwood chairs and precious English china, blood from the cattle's gashes splattering onto French tulles. When the last animal to escape Stewart's leapt to the sidewalk and bounded all alone across the street into the Park with an American flag wrapped around her horns like a bandanna, the crowd nearby, only moments out of harm's way, cheered, as if it were a grand finale.

FROM TWO BLOCKS away, Duff and Skaggs heard the shouts of people and cattle recede, and the band music resume.

"You are a strange outlaw, Duff Lucking. Have you no desire to go and see the trouble your mischief provoked?"

"That would be vanity." He remembered something. "Tell me again your Latin phrase . . . ?"

"Vanitas vanitatum—"

"No, no, the one—'Beware the fictitious fire' . . . ?"

"Cave ignis fatuus."

"Yes, exactly."

Skaggs looked at Duff, awaiting some elaboration, a coherent *quod erat demonstrandum* about the clownish new American imperialists and revelrouts.

"You know," Duff said instead, "there are too many people hereabouts."

"What, do you mean tonight, in this neighborhood? Certainly, and too many cattle, and I'll wager that your stunt—"

"No, Skaggs, I mean in the city." Duff was thinking again about Pishey Wetmore, and the hundreds of other veterans whom only luck and prayer had so far kept from crossing his path in New York.

"Ah well, yes, now you're speaking of sociology."

"Sociology?" Duff thought he knew all the *ologies*.

"So many people crammed together in our nest, we're the same as bees in a tree or ants underground or bacteria teeming in a drop of spittle. We are, in cities, insects of a more monstrous kind, obeying rules we do not

even realize we are obeying as we crawl and slither through our days."
Skaggs was virtually reciting a piece he had written for *The Subterranean*.
"In these last fifty years New York has doubled and more than doubled
again three times. At that rate—why, the city of our grandchildren will contain *eight millions*."

Duff wanted to remember *bacteria* and write it down later. "So, then we
are agreed," he said.

"We are? Agreed on what, precisely?"

"Our manifest destinies," Duff said.

"What? Are you joking, Duff? Not a moment ago you were railing at
everything which that ridiculous phrase—"

"Not the nation's destiny. I can't pretend anymore to understand a nation's destiny. But mine, yours—those we can figure." His scar itched. "We
ought to leave, the both of us. To light out."

"For the West? I have been there, and found it overrated. My dream of
pilgrimage runs easterly—if it is morning in America," he said, stealing a
phrase from his former editor at the *Mirror*, "and high noon in England,
then in Italy it is evening with the human race. The mellow early evening, as
you know, is the part of the day of which I am fondest." Skaggs had mused
about becoming an expatriated daguerreian in Rome.

"I mean beyond Illinois," Duff said, "beyond the Mississippi and the
Missouri. Out to the Territories, I mean."

"Ah, my cowboy friend . . ."

"Where it's still pure. Blank."

Skaggs smiled lovingly, skeptically, and said nothing.

"It is ours for the taking."

"Well, here we are, the wild-blazing grog shop appears at last." They
had arrived at Budd's, and when Skaggs opened the cellar door they were
enveloped by a warm blast of saloon fumes—ale and brine and burning tobacco. "After you, sir."

But Duff was agitated, insistent on making his murky meaning clear.
"*All* of it is *all* of ours," he said, gesticulating with his hands. "Out there we
can make of it whatever we wish. It's you who talk of 'living life as a perpetual experiment.' "

Skaggs used the phrase generally to justify some minor personal mischief.

"Out there," Duff said, shouting now, "we can experiment! It's a frontier
of, of—of *infinity*."

" 'A frontier of infinity,' eh?" He pulled on Duff's hand. "My restless lad, you need a drink."

They had each finished three brandies and two dozen oysters by half past eleven when a squad of newsboys burst into Budd's, their arms full of papers, and started shouting.

"Revolution in Europe!"

"Extra Herald*!"*

"The king is gone!"

"Extra Sun*!"*

"Got the last news from Paris!"

Men actually left the food table—abandoned the platters of free sardines and black bread—to get the news. In a few minutes, fifty of the newsboys' papers were being devoured by the patrons of Budd's.

Here and there a man whooped as he read, or chuckled. An actor Skaggs knew was reading aloud from the *Herald*. At the bar a workingman stood on his stool, raised his glass of porter, and cried, "America welcomes the republic of France into the world of the free!"

A cheer rose up.

Duff stared into his glass. Skaggs tapped a finger on his head. "No happy huzzahs from my young democratic hero? One of the old empires has fallen. Despots running for their lives from the people."

"Huzzah," Duff said quietly, and took another swallow of brandy. "As an old one falls our new one rises up. What kind of fool celebrates the vanquishing of Mexicans at ten and the freedom of the French at midnight?"

"An American fool," Skaggs replied. He shrugged. "In any experiment, there are surprises. That's part of the point."

A MILE AWAY, at Heilperin's Studios in the Bowery, the news from France gave Polly Lucking an inspiration. She would not portray the Venus de Milo at tonight's second performance. Instead, she borrowed the Heilperin boy's red woolen cap, and into the muzzle of Mr. Heilperin's broken musket wedged a kitchen knife as a bayonet. For the French tricolor she tied red, white, and blue scarves to a broom handle. She had worn her oldest, plainest buff calico dress out tonight—perfect, as it happened, for the costume she was improvising.

In honor of the revolution, she had decided to play Marianne, the symbol of French liberty heroically leading her insurgents into battle. Before she took the stage, Mr. Heilperin announced the news from Europe and showed the gathered "artists" the front page of the night's extra *Sun*. And when Polly appeared in the famous pose—holding the gun in her left hand, the French flag hoisted in her other, the dress pulled down to expose her chest—the fourteen men put down their drawing papers and pencils and crayons and stood. "*Hurrah*," they shouted, "*hurrah* for the republic of France," and applauded for a full minute. Several of them cried.

10

March 25, 1848

. . .

New York City

$\mathscr{S}$IXTEEN YEARS EARLIER, when Timothy Skaggs was deciding to leave Dartmouth and enroll at Columbia's medical school instead, his father had warned him that New York City "has the air of the permanent carnival about it, as if half its population were on a spree."

New York really had taken on the air of a permanent carnival this spring, and now there was another happy mob, even larger than last Saturday's Mexican War gala. A slow-moving eighty-foot-wide herd of New Yorkers— a Festival of the Peoples celebrating the European insurgency that the newspapers were calling the Springtime of the Peoples.

"Must we really go all the way up to Madison Square?" Polly had asked Skaggs. "Why are they starting the rally so far north?"

"To frighten the rich," Skaggs had said.

At twelve o'clock they spotted Duff, a member of the Order of United Americans and an official marcher. There were some women in Broadway, but Polly remained on the sidewalk, arm in arm with Skaggs. The crowds passed Union Square (where dozens stooped down to drink from the new fountain) and through the neighborhoods of the well-to-do.

As the first marchers approached City Hall and the Park, various factions began trying out various three-syllable chants—"*Death to kings*" and "*Anti-rent*" and "*Liberty.*" Duff was a Liberty man.

"Your brother seems to have passed out of his funk," Skaggs said, remembering Duff's mood at this very spot a week earlier.

"Spring," Polly replied. "And I do believe that *this* allows him to feel like a kind of soldier again, as if he's doing righteous work, a member of a movement."

"Then he'll need to let his whiskers grow and buy some country clothes. Duff doesn't look the part of a rad."

She smiled. A large fraction of the crowd wore beards, and most of those with cravats had them hanging loose around their necks, flapping in the breeze like banners. Skaggs had not seen so many rough, broad-brimmed hats since he left Illinois. Were the New Yorkers impersonating the European democrats? Or were the European democrats impersonating Americans? Polly found herself moved, both by the passionate fraternal fever and by the events prompting it in cities thousands of miles away.

THAT AFTERNOON IN Broadway they had only rumors and hopeful hunches about the revolutions fevering through Europe like a contagion. They knew for certain only what had happened in France a month before. They had no idea that news of those events had been transmitted by telegraph to every capital in Europe. Spring arrived on the Continent unusually wet and warm and stormy, and with the extreme weather were coming imitations of Paris in dozens of different cities and towns—uprisings, revolts, and revolutions, undertakings variously heroic and madcap, sometimes both at once. Even on the rustic edges of the Continent, in places like Spain and Ireland and Romania, republicans and socialists and rioters of no particular creed were shouting and burning, shooting at the kings' men.

No one in New York yet knew that two weeks before, the Austrian monarchy had ended press censorship, granted a constitution, and forced its chancellor, Prince Metternich—*Metternich,* old Europe's presiding genius and tyrant—to resign and leave Vienna. They had no idea that those events in Vienna had in turn inspired crowds in Berlin to stage their own protests at the palace of the Prussian king, who had capitulated the previous Sunday; or that on Monday in Munich, Bavaria's King Ludwig had abdicated, just as radicals in Milan had launched an insurrection that by Wednesday was entirely victorious; or that on Wednesday in Venice a group of liberals had taken the arsenal and declared a republic; or that at this very hour in his Winter Palace in St. Petersburg, Czar Nicholas was writing a proclamation that Russia would resist forever this evil of revolution.

People all over Europe were sobbing and babbling, shuddering at what might happen next. Others, maybe fewer or maybe more, were laughing and singing over what had happened already. The people arise and kings quake, monarchies defeated and republics born, *voilà*.

IN NEW YORK CITY, at the edge of the New World at the dawn of the new age, there were no soldiers aiming muskets, no desperate rulers. On the platform in the Park near City Hall, geysers of oratory spouted from some of the city's most powerful politicians. A few spoke in German or Gaelic as well as English. In speech after speech, the proposition that provoked the loudest and most general acclaim was for a ten-hour working day, although three of the listeners applauded only politely, since Skaggs and Polly worked fewer than ten hours a day already, and Duff voluntarily worked many more.

Finally, as the bells of St. Paul's and Trinity chimed four, Skaggs decided he had eaten as many hot yams and cold sausages and listened to as many harangues as he could stomach.

"May we take our leave?" he asked Duff and Polly. "My old legs are sore."

"But they say the *Hutchinson* Family is to appear," Duff replied.

"As an ensemble, or each of the hundred of them, one at a time, performing one of the hits?"

"They say just the three brothers and Abby," Duff replied. A few years ago, before they were the most popular musical artists in America, thirteen Hutchinson siblings had sung and played together with their parents onstage. "And I do aim to see Abby."

"Well, I guess we must be approaching the finale now," Skaggs said. "The Fourteenth Ward's most celebrated debtor is taking the stage."

"Mad Mike" Walsh walked to the front of the scaffold slowly, so that applause would have time to break out and build before he reached the podium to speak. After Walsh had lost a libel case the previous year, his paper, *The Subterranean,* shut down—owing Timothy seven dollars for two book reviews. Skaggs was still peeved about the debt. But for the rest of this crowd of shoemakers and bookbinders and tailors and porters and students and even the odd clerk—and for Duff—Mad Mike was a beloved rabble-rouser, a Democrat who ranted in the state assembly the same way he ranted in the saloons of Mulberry Street and the Bowery.

"He looks old," said Polly, seeing him for the first time.

Skaggs knew that Walsh was only thirty-eight. "Perhaps hoeing the socialists' beans and tomatoes," he said, "aged the Irish scoundrel."

"The struggle that our victorious brothers across the sea have heroically *begun*," Walsh shouted, the accent of County Cork still thick, "is only just the beginning! It is time now for *this* country truly to become, as the song says, 'the land of the *free*'!"

Duff and the thousands were clapping again. Skaggs had to admit it: Walsh had a knack for stirring passions.

"Our European brothers and sisters are burnin' the thrones, refusin' to remain as serfs—and so must *you*! Your bosses and their elected apologists tell you that your labor is a-buildin' America. But it is a-buildin' only their *fortunes*! They tell you that you are creatin' a new city on a hill here. Well, *I* tell you *this*—that sometimes *creation* must be preceded by good, clean, righteous *destruction*."

The audience clapped and whooped. A claque of young men in the back of the crowd, members of Walsh's political club, the Spartan Association, chanted "*Walsh, Walsh, Walsh, Walsh*" until the applause subsided.

Duff put his lips close to Polly's ear. " 'Destruction and creation, the cycle of life,' " he told her, "just as Daddy said."

Walsh resumed. "Do *not* believe the dogtricks and sharkings and friendly falsehoods handed to you daily by the *demagogues*."

Skaggs smiled and shook his head. Was there a more titanic demagogue in New York than Mad Mike Walsh?

"The demagogues *tell* you that you are free men. But they *lie*! You are *slaves*! You are slaves, and none are better aware of that fact than the heathenish *dogs* who *call* you free men. No *workin'man* is free! Everything he buys, every step he turns, he is robbed by some worthless . . . wealthy . . . *drone*."

This time, Polly joined in the applause. Skaggs, however, was stunned, not by Walsh's sentiments but by how he had expressed them. "Worthless wealthy drone" was *Skaggs's*, a phrase he had coined last year to describe the elderly author Washington Irving—in one of his unpaid articles for Walsh's *Subterranean*.

"*Thief!*" Skaggs shouted, cupping his hands around his mouth. "*Thief!*" he shouted a second time. People nearby smiled encouragingly and nodded as they clapped harder. They thought he was affirming Walsh's attack on their capitalist oppressors.

"*Amazing,*" Skaggs said. "On top of everything else, the man is a barefaced plagiarist."

"Plagiarist?" Duff asked.

"He filched *my phrase!*"

When Walsh finished, but before the Hutchinsons took the stage, Duff carefully wrote down P-L-A-Y-J-R-I-S-T in his journal.

The applause and shouts for the Hutchinsons were even more rapturous than that for Walsh, like the glee of children when Christmas candies are handed out. And as the four siblings began to play and sing, the sounds of their violin and violoncello drew scores of passersby off the streets to watch and listen, people who didn't care much about upheaval in Europe or the prospects for democracy. Asa, John, Judson, and Abby Hutchinson were young *celebrities*.

Skaggs was so pleased that they did not perform "King Alcohol" he declined to point out that Mike Walsh, a defender of Negro slavery, remained onstage tapping his foot as Abby sang her solo on "The Slave's Appeal," one of the Hutchinsons' abolitionist tunes. And near the end of the rally, while they fiddled and sang the final verse of "There's a Good Time Coming"—

> "*In the good time coming*
> *Nations shall not quarrel then,*
> *To prove which is the stronger;*
> *Nor slaughter men for glory's sake—*
> *Wait a little longer.*"

. . . Skaggs held his tongue again. As he glanced over at the smiles of his young blond friends—Duff mouthing the lyrics, *Slaughter men for glory's sake—/Wait a little longer*—he did not see fit to remind them that Walsh's political power was enforced entirely by the brutal shoulder-hitters of his Spartan Association, young men such as Fatty Freeborn who *lived* for quarrels, slaughter, and glory. Hypocrisies be damned. The day was fine.

March 30, 1848
. . .
New York City

OU ARE GIVING me the sack on account of that god*damned* toady bootlick Mathew *Brady?*" Skaggs had said to Ninian Bobo twelve hours earlier. He regretted his public whining, but it was the publisher who had chosen to announce his decision at Shakespeare's at the end of a night of drinking.

"Brady and the *hundred others* who have set up shop a stone's throw from here," Bobo had replied. "What choice do we have, Timothy? These days I could hire my own camera operator and assistant, full-time, for fifteen a week." He had gone on for another half hour as if he were being pinched, not caressed, by the market's invisible hand, until Skaggs had abruptly stood and walked out.

He was now considering the implications more coolly. On the one hand, the end of his barter arrangement with Bobo would let Skaggs devote himself to his own pictures instead of Bobo's paper *carte de visite* portraits of the pseudofamous, and give him more time as well to contribute to *The John-Donkey,* maybe grind out another eighty-dollar novel or two, and finish the essay about time.

On the other hand, he had never laid out cash for the studio. Could he bear to take some ordinary scribbler's job to subsidize his photography? Just how much humbling was he willing to endure in order to pay the rent Bobo was demanding? Could he consent to work as one of Greeley's "news collectors," a *Tribune* harbor-crawler, a glorified errand boy? Even at the rather lucrative wage of three dollars per four-hour errand?

Yet the end of his photographic hackwork for Bobo was already paying Skaggs in the currency of time, affording him the freedom to laze at home. Which he was doing this gray morning, wearing his tattered blue and orange Turkish slippers, purple velvet smoking cap, and paisley dressing gown as he walked downstairs from his apartment on the third floor to fetch his morning papers. He tended to act the part of a raffish swell when he was hard up, and his little stretch of West Broadway from White to Walker, lately teeming with French picture-painters and wood-carvers, lent itself nicely to Skaggs's ruined-aristocrat illusion. He wondered if all the local cheese eaters and cigarette smokers would return home to their revolutionary republic now, or if instead more of their kind would join them here.

He wondered also, crouching in the drizzle to scoop up his papers, whether his eighty-one-year-old great-uncle Gaster would make good on his (drunken, late-at-night, onetime) promise to bequeath his favorite nephew his house in Greenwich Village. From two blocks west, Skaggs heard the chorus of sledges slamming iron for the Hudson River Railroad, under construction along Hudson Street. *When dear old Gaster does finally succumb and I take up residence in Barrow Street,* Skaggs thought, *I could make the trip downtown in ten minutes once they've finished laying the tracks from Christopher to Chambers . . .* He sighed.

Back up in his parlor-library-study-dining room, he made his way to his one comfortable chair and glanced at the *Tribune*—his eye moving directly, as if guided by God, to the great story of the day, of the week, of the month, a piece of news that excited him as much as any European revolution. His spirits lifted. To hell with Bobo and earning a living!

John Jacob Astor had pegged out, fallen dead, *finally,* at age eighty-four.

Skaggs had once written in the *Mirror* that hatred of Astor, more than any other thing, provided a common bond for New Yorkers of every class, every race, every language, every creed, every age. He was the richest man in the city, in the nation, perhaps among all billion humans in the whole world, kings and queens aside. The official reckoning was $3 million, but Astor's total wealth—the value of half the ground in Manhattan and Lord only knows how many millions of acres of the western wilderness—must be ten or twenty times that. Yet it was not simply the size of his fortune that fueled Skaggs's and others' loathing. Astor was hated because he was New York's first great landlord. Despising landlords had become an obligatory sentiment.

Astor was also despised because he was both rich and well known, and yet unlike other celebrated men of wealth (such as Barnum), he never made any concessions at all to popular sentiment, or displays of magnanimity. Astor was the ultimate democratic product, a foreign pauper (Johann Jakob Ashdor) who had declared himself an American and scrabbled a fortune from nothing. Yet he never stepped up to his obligations as America's first famous rich man. His public performance was always that of the peevish antidemocrat, crabbed and miserly and by every appearance contemptuous of the moaning mob of paupers and hustlers who dreamed of moving in and up like him.

He was resented by some because he remained so very foreign, and by all, whether they knew it or not, because he seemed immortal and unchanging. Every other thing in America was new. Some Americans (such as Skaggs) were unsettled by the *pace* of change, but their own hopefulness depended upon the *fact* of ceaseless, shocking change. Astor, however, had been rich and famous forever. Astor had arrived as a young man in America before it was the United States, and yet he was still enlarging his fortune, still buying up swaths of Manhattan, still building mansions, still, impossibly, alive.

But now dead.

Hooray! Skaggs smiled recalling the anti-Astor rants of his Buffalo friend Herman Swarr, and the dollar wager they'd made one night on whether either of them would outlive Old Skinflint.

Ordinarily Skaggs devoted an hour a day to reading the papers, but today he would spend two. Each morning delivery boys dropped three papers on the doorstep—the *Tribune,* opposed to all evils; the *Herald,* opposed to all celebrated individuals, but in favor of violence; and the *Sun,* which couldn't decide whether or not it supported slavery, or if it would sell advertisements for condoms and abortions, or if it was in the business of publishing fact or fiction. At least one evening a week, Skaggs stopped in at the gaslit reading room of the Society Library on Broadway to skim the other half dozen half-decent dailies. For *The Scorpion, The Flash, The Rake,* and the rest of the sporting papers he spent his own pennies in the street. How could he resist the catalogues in *The National Police Gazette* of the week's foulest seductions, rapes, and murders, entitled simply "Seductions," "Rapes," and "Murders"? He had stopped reading *The Whip*, however, after it published a list of alleged New York sodomites on the pretext of moral righteousness.

Not all of today's tasty bits of the papers concerned Astor. A page and a half of the *Herald*'s eight were devoted to journalism on the subject of journalism, a dispatch under the byline "*Mr. John Nugent, in the Custody of the Sergeant-at-Arms.*" Nugent was a Washington correspondent, and had been charged with contempt and arrested by the Senate over the weekend because he declined to reveal which government official had slipped him the secret copy of the Mexican War treaty the *Herald* had published. The paper announced it was increasing Nugent's salary by 100 percent for as long as he was confined at the Capitol. Skaggs was envious of this trick: double pay plus free room and board plus painless punishment plus the honor of martyrdom.

It was past noon. Even before the familiar knock on the door had finished—two slow, two fast—he was up and on his way to greet his visitor, letting the *Tribune*'s two big sheets separate and float to the floor.

He had not seen Polly Lucking since the Festival of the Peoples, nor entertained her privately for weeks. And he had never seen such an electrically blissful smile on her face.

"And to what do I owe this surprise—"

"*Skaggs,*" she said, "I believe my luck has turned at last!"

As he shut the door and took her shawl, she grabbed his head between her hands and kissed his forehead, astounding him.

"Good *God*! Evidently so has mine."

Polly was burbling. "I have just come from Mr. Burton's new theater in Chambers Street—"

"*Burton?*" Skaggs was suspicious.

"The comedian. And impresario."

"I know Burton."

"I sensed good tidings the moment I entered, and smelled the fresh sawdust and plaster. It's just down the block from Stewart's, you know."

"Naïve child! Seduced once again by the perfume of the brand-new. And, of course, by a Brit—a low, lecherous Brit, by the way, who preys on pretty girls like *you*."

When William Evans Burton was running his *Gentleman's Magazine*, he had turned down a comic story by Skaggs about life in Illinois. And some years before that, Burton had scandalously abandoned his wife and son in London for a sixteen-year-old girl.

"I am not naïve."

She poked his belly with her umbrella. He grabbed it by the silk and dropped it in the corner.

"A Brit," he added, "who is considerably portlier and older and gamier than even I."

"His first production at the new theater, in the summer, will be a dramatization of Mr. Dickens's latest!"

"Dombey and Son?"

"The first time on any stage! I read for the part of the *heroine,* who is called *Florence* Dombey. And do you know Mr. Dickens's birthday, Skaggs?"

"I do indeed, the seventh of February in 1812—the man is more than thirteen months my senior."

"February the seventh is also *my* birthday! And do you know my middle name?"

"Dickens?"

"Florence! Mary Ann *Florence* Lucking!"

Her eyes were bright, her nostrils flared. She was hot with hope. Polly was prone to this sort of mumbo jumbo—fortune-tellers' cards, meaningful bumps on the skull. Skaggs attributed her lurid credulity to the votive candles and communion crackers of a Catholic childhood. It saddened him a little.

"I am extremely pleased for you, Polly."

"According to your friend Miss Chapman, whom I also saw at Burton's, if he invites me to join his cast, the pay would be fifteen dollars a week." Caroline Chapman was the disrobed English actress who had been trapped in the closet with Skaggs at the burning theater when Duff rescued them. Until today, Polly had disliked her. "At that rate, and with my savings, I should be able to end my association with Mrs. Stanhope entirely."

They looked at each other for an extended, somewhat uneasy moment.

She had never so baldly expressed to him a wish to abandon the brothel. Indeed, she and Skaggs had never discussed any particulars of her professional occupations apart from acting.

She had always felt comfortable in his company. And for this last year, she had enjoyed their intimacies, despite the beard and his fondness for brandy. Indeed, it was in the fall of '46, when she started spending two or three evenings each week at Mrs. Stanhope's, that she'd decided she *required* a Skaggs—that is, one worthy, congenial man to whom she would give herself without charge.

He had enjoyed her company even when she was Duff Lucking's quiet and intelligent sister, before she'd ripened into this strong-minded woman. When Duff left for Mexico, perhaps never to return, Skaggs's scruples concerning Miss Lucking diminished—he had started calling her Polly almost as soon as her brother sailed. And once he discovered she had become an associate of Mrs. Stanhope's, his reticence toward her disappeared entirely.

They were playmates, not soul mates.

He had been worried that her new utopian, quasi-vegetarian, Greeleyite ardor might lead her to some extreme and inconvenient doctrine. Some weeks ago, in her maternal tut-tutting about the girl Priscilla, she had quoted lines from a new book, *The Origin of Life and Process of Reproduction,* which had left him dumbstruck. " 'A child cannot walk out,' " she'd read aloud, " 'but his eyes and ears are assailed with sights and sounds all bearing on this subject,' " *this subject* being sexual intercourse. What next? Would she be persuaded by the lunatic masochism of "spermatic economy," which prescribed a maximum of one ejaculation per month? Skaggs fretted that the fine ideas of "free love" that Polly was picking up might lead to *less* love for him. But for now, like every wise man who wants what Skaggs presently wanted, he was the picture of discretion.

"Congratulations, my dear," he said as he guided her to the sofa. "I have been offered a new part as well—in Mr. Greeley's troupe." As he poured himself a thimble of brandy, he held the bottle toward her and raised his eyebrows as a matter of courtesy only, since Polly never indulged during the day. He sat down close to her and told her about the proposal from the *Tribune,* how Greeley had very flatteringly recalled his article last year about the coffin ship disgorging its load of starving Irish into South Street; how he had not disabused Greeley of his mistaken notion that he, Skaggs, was fluent in European languages ("Is not *Latin* a language of Europe?"); and how the editor thought he was "ideally suited to seek out and report, with the correct mixture of sympathy and skepticism, travelers' stories of the spreading revolution."

Polly appreciated the hard exigencies of work for wages. But Skaggs's *Tribune* news distressed her a little. Only a few hours a week, as he said, and plenty of fresh air . . . but wasn't he too old and too qualified a man to become a sort of glorified errand boy?

"Would you row out each time into the harbor to meet the ships?" she asked, her voice all earnest and curious girl.

Row? Skaggs disguised his wounded feelings. "Greeley and the other news titans, my dear, have leased a little *steamer* to make the trip every day out to Sandy Hook."

She was surprised. "The newspapers have joined their forces? But aren't they meant to compete *against* one another?"

"Modern times," he said, shrugging. He changed the subject again, hoping that with enough detours in the conversation the true purpose of her drop-in, their violation of the seventh commandment together, would somehow naturally . . . present itself. The word *fornicate* had formed itself in his brain like a monk's chant.

"Astor has died!" he said abruptly.

"So I've heard. From Mr. Burton this morning."

"I think the specter of revolution smote the bastard. He saw history moving against him and chose to make a strategic retreat."

Skaggs lifted Polly's left hand and lightly brushed his lips against her knuckles.

She was not yet in the mood.

"Skaggs," she said, removing her hand from his, "what did you mean the other day, about Walsh, his 'socialist beans and tomatoes'?"

He was sensing that Polly and he would not be gamboling together beneath the linens anytime soon.

"A few years ago, Mad Mike lived for a stretch at Brook Farm."

"Which is . . . ?"

"*Was*—one of the utopian colonies, editors and writers living together at a plantation outside Boston growing their own food. Another folly . . . another failed fanatical Fourierist phalanx folly. The place went bust last year."

Polly was intrigued. She had read about the socialist colonies sprouting up across America, many of them "phalanxes" organized according to the principles of a Frenchman, Fourier, whom all progressive people seemed to admire.

Skaggs, naturally, had made a sport of deriding his ideas. In a review of Fourier's book *The Social Destiny of Man,* he had called the scheme "hilariously and elaborately self-satirical in the French fashion." Each community was to assign twelve work teams to raise one of twelve different varieties of Bergamot pear. Eventually, Fourier wrote, the people of the planet would be organized into precisely 2,985,984 phalanxes. Constantinople would be the capital of the new world government, presided over by an omniarch, 48 empresses, 576 sultans, and a Chancellery of the Court of Love. Peace would prevail, the climate everywhere would become temperate, disease would disappear, wild animals would become tame, the seas would turn to lemonade, people would grow tails containing eyes, dead bodies would evaporate into fragrances that would drift forever through space, and six new moons would appear in the heavens.

Nevertheless, the basic underlying idea—like-minded people of good will coming together to share their goods and labor, all for one and one for all—sounded right and sensible to Polly.

"But perhaps the time has become ripe only now," she said. "The revolutions in Europe did not occur *last* year, they are occurring *this* year. *Now.*"

He nodded, but he could not hide his doubt. Polly was growing angry.

"You speak," she said, "of 'living one's life as a perpetual experiment,' yet you invariably ridicule such experiments as these."

Again! Did the young Luckings, brother and sister together, rehearse their attacks on his hypocrisy? Should he simply let her rail, decline to thrust or parry in reply?

Polly continued. "The people engaged in projects like the Book Farm—"

"Brook Farm."

"—are surely driven by the finest intentions, even when their schemes are flawed."

"Ah," he said, unable to restrain himself, "the *finest* intentions! I suppose those pave the very *depths* of hell."

"You sneer. You mock Astor and the factory owners and upper-tens, but you also mock their enemies, like Walsh, and all those who would dig the rot from society to reform it. On which side do you stand, Skaggs?"

He smiled and took her hand again. She jerked it away.

"Which?"

"Why must I enlist on either side? I mistrust parties and pigeonholes. Am I a journalist or a photographer? Am I witty or ridiculous? Why must I choose one or the other?" He paused. "Are you a good woman, or a bad one? *Which?*"

At last she smiled a little, and relaxed against the arm of the sofa.

"Evidently neither," she said.

Again he kissed her hand. This time as he released it she let it rest on Skaggs's knee.

"You are acquainted with Mr. Burton?" she asked softly.

"Barely so. And years ago. I doubt he remembers me—and if he did, I am certain that our friendship, mine with you, would be unhelpful in your ambitions."

His answer was chillier than he wished.

"Which is to say, my dear Miss Lucking, that your talent alone shall win you the part in his production of *Dombey and Son*."

Polly blushed.

SKAGGS HAD NEVER used the lightning line. Therefore he had not known, until it was explained to him by the agent at the telegraph office in Exchange Place, that the minimum charge to send a message was seventy-seven cents, for which one purchased the right to send fifteen words. Therefore, the insanely concise message to Herman Swarr he had composed this morning—ASTOR DEAD! YOU LOSE—was wasteful, since he would be paying for eleven unused words. As a professional paid by the word, Skaggs was accustomed to padding prose on command. But it struck him as unjust that he had to do so now, when he was the one *paying*. And he had only a half-dollar in his pocket. So after getting the agent to agree that "seventy-seven" was a single word, and persuading the man to extend credit of twenty-seven cents, he completed his message at precisely the correct length.

> *ASTOR DEAD! IF YOU AREN'T,*
> *YOU OWE $1. PLUS SEVENTY-SEVEN CENTS?*
> *(WHAT HATH GOD WROUGHT!)*

He watched the agent tap away in Morse's code. When telegraph keys were common appliances, as the Wall Street promoters insisted they would someday become, installed in every house and shop from Maine to Texas, might this funny new telegraphic style become the ordinary way of writing and even of speech, every document and conversation pared and crushed and minimized? A minute later, the last of his fifteen words was turned into electric pulses and sent in one five-hundredths of a second over 397 miles of copper wire into Swarr's offices at the *Buffalo Republic*.

According to Skaggs's receipt, the message had been sent at precisely "3:16 P.M." Outside, the rain had diminished to a mist, so he walked up to his studio to find the money he owed the agent. He made himself a meal from the still life he had photographed the day before—a half cheese, an onion, an apple, brandy—and after taking the shortcut through Jews' Alley, he was back at the telegraph office by four. The agent took his two dimes and seven pennies and passed back a folded paper.

"Your reply, sir."

He thought the man was joking. But there was not even the slightest smile on his sallow face.

Skaggs looked at the dateline of the message he had been handed— "March 30 Buffalo *3:09* P.M."

He had discovered a ruse, some capitalist's secret grand sham! The telegraph wizards were charlatans, humbugs, thieves!

He still had his receipt, which he pulled from his coat pocket and held in front of the agent, side by side with the new paper.

"*Sent* at sixteen minutes past three," Skaggs said, "and *answered* by my friend at *nine* minutes past three? I think *not,* sir."

Skaggs tossed the paper to the counter. His tight, angry smile twitched in triumph.

But the agent did not blink. He took a deep breath and said, very evenly:

"Buffalo is one half hour earlier than we are here, sir."

"What? What?"

"When it is twelve o'clock in New York, it is half past eleven in Buffalo. And ten past eleven in the city of Detroit. And ten minutes before eleven in the city of Chicago. And et cetera."

Had Skaggs ever felt quite so undone?

"Your Mr. Swarr," the man continued, "received our message before three on his time, and sent his reply immediately."

Of course. Skaggs had never thought about the existence of such small time differences. As a schoolboy he had learned that when it was night in Europe it was daytime in America, but this had been a merely theoretical truth, a fact he'd taken on faith. Now he had the hard evidence in hand.

"Ah," Skaggs said, "I see. Yes. Thank you."

What *hath* God wrought? And what was the need of opium now? The world was strange enough. His unfinished essay on the nature of time, filled with half-baked intuitions, suddenly seemed sensible and pertinent. He must finish it.

Wishing to escape the gaze of the telegraph agent, Skaggs waited until he was outside to read the message from Buffalo.

WILL YOU TAKE $1 WORTH OF NEW NEWS?
NIAGARA FALLS FROZEN SOLID.
ALL-TIME MOST AWESOME SHOW.
THOUSANDS GATHERING. CAVALRY COMING.

He read the sheet again. He hadn't seen Herman Swarr in eight years, but he was a man of great natural rectitude who never fabricated stories or played pranks.

He read the message a third time, then looked up, considering his options. In the sky, a rainbow stretched from above the Greek temple front of the Merchants' Exchange toward the Battery. *An omen,* Polly would say. Swarr's incredible dispatch was certainly worth a dollar, quite possibly more. Skaggs hurried up Nassau Street to find a buyer while the news was still fresh.

———→•◦◄———

12

April 2, 1848

. . .

New York City

 HE SUGARHOUSE, ONE of a dozen in Duane Street near the East
 River, was called Collins's because an old sugarman named
 Collins managed it. But Duff Lucking thought of the place as
Prime's. Months ago he had read in the paper it was owned by a cabal of
London and Wall Street merchant bankers that included Prime, Ward &
King. This group's fleet shipped opium from Bombay to Shanghai, South
Pacific cane from the Sandwich Islands to Chile, guano from Chile to New
Orleans, cotton from New Orleans to Liverpool, and Caribbean cane from
Nevis to New York. At Collins's the cane from Nevis was boiled into sugar.
Sugar packed in barrels makes an excellent fuel, so when sugarhouses
burned they tended to go for a long time, and this place was big, rigged up
with gas-fired cookers.

By midnight there were a hundred and fifty firemen scrambling around
the block like ants. The light from the blaze made their lanterns moot. Men
from nearby had taken the front positions—hose companies from Elizabeth
and Chambers streets, and 21 Hose, from just down the block. This fire was
farther south and east than 15 Engine ordinarily came, but Duff knew early
that it was a big one, so his crew had been among the first to arrive.

Duff felt proud.

Destruction and creation are the essential cycles of life. This was a *big* blaze, still spreading. And not a soul had been hurt or killed—Duff personally made sure the building was cleared of people.

The Old Dutchman was already on the block. To most of the men who ran with machines below Houston, the rants of the old man with the long beard no longer registered as words, only as one more part of the discordant song of fires—running, ringing, grunting, shouting, swearing, pumping, splashing, chopping, sizzling, sputtering, crashing . . . and the Old Dutchman's sermonizing. No one knew who he was or where he had come from (his accent might just as well have been Norwegian or Hungarian as Dutch or German). But during the last year he had become a regular fixture at big fires.

As usual, he was pacing back and forth on the wet sidewalk across from the blaze, hands clutched behind his back, bellowing Scripture. At the beginning of a fire, he would recite mostly from the Old Testament—often a single verse, over and over again—and then later, once the blaze was defeated, he took most of his excerpts from the New Testament. Tonight, for now, he was the prophet Nahum.

" 'The chariots shall *rage* in the streets! They shall *jostle* one against another in the broad ways! They shall seem like torches, they shall run like the *lightnings!* ' "

Looking into a window on the first floor of the sugarhouse, Duff saw the broken gas pipe hanging cleanly away from the wall like a broken arm, and stared. As he watched a flaming splinter shoot past it from the ceiling like a falling star, he suspected what was about to happen, and immediately it did: the gas from the pipe ignited, the ball of flame blasting the glass out of the window toward him. Other men instinctively ducked, but Duff continued staring, and watched the free end of the pipe as it swayed to and fro, gushing fire like some war machine of the future.

Duff considered himself a warrior.

" 'The chariots shall rage in the *streets*! They shall jostle one *against* another in the broad ways!' "

Duff had been gone, fighting in Mexico, when the Old Dutchman made his first appearance. He still listened to the words, could not resist trying to make sense of their meaning.

The second wave of men and machines was racing onto the block now, companies from all the way north of Houston and west of the Sixth Avenue. 35 Hose and 38 Engine came careering down Chatham Street side by side, both pulling hard left to try to make the inside turn and arrive at the fire first. Making the corner, 35 bumped hard against 38, smashing the glass in one of its lanterns.

"Lousy goddamned bastards!"

Duff smiled. It was his old pal Henry Fargis, 38's assistant foreman, making the curse.

" 'They shall *seem* like *torches!*' " the Old Dutchman yelled.

Fifteen minutes later, Duff heard a thick, low hissing and looked up. Smoke and steam and red cinders were surging from one of the round windows in the top floor. He stepped back three paces, four, away from an assistant engineer named Kerr and the scrambling men from 35 Hose, then took yet another step back, behind 38's engine, next to a pair of men spraying a pipe against the fire.

"Lucking!" boomed a cheerful voice from just inside the sugarhouse. "You damned chickenhearted *bystander!* To work, man!"

Duff saw only an approaching silhouette, man and ax, illuminated by the orange flames and red timbers behind him, but recognized the voice of his friend Fargis. Fargis was inside the building, thirty feet away, walking out.

"I'm acting *foreman*," Duff shouted back, "overseeing my boys." Up above, the gush of smoke and steam pouring out the window was growing thicker and louder. "And if I were you, Henry—"

Duff did not see the wooden cornice above the round window buckle and drop away from the wall, bringing hundreds of bricks flying out with it.

"—I'd step lively!"

" 'They shall *run* like the *lightnings.*' "

"What's that?" Fargis asked, pausing, a smile on his face, as he stepped from the building, the very instant before a chunk of carved, painted black cypress collided with his head and shoulders, smashing him to the sidewalk. The shower of bricks, a ton of them, slammed down like cannon shot.

DIVERTED FROM HIS work by the sounds in the street, ready as usual to surrender to any interruption, Skaggs laid down his pencil and walked to the window. An unblemished white fire engine was barreling down West Broadway. The engine was bright in the moonlight, a big four-wheel carriage with a dozen running men pulling the rope on each side and a huge *40* painted in gold on its rear. The bell ringer was doing his job, but unnecessarily—not much traffic was in the street so late at night. As the engine rolled south, a sow and her four piglets feeding at the corner scrambled to their feet and ran away for dear life, and a pair of boys shot out from North Moore Street, running after Engine Company No. 40 and the terrified swine family.

Skaggs had nearly finished his lampoon about two children communicating by Morse's code with the ghost of John Jacob Astor. He ought to have been writing his philosophical essay on time, the piece that might in one stroke transform his reputation from scabrous jester to visionary sage.

But for now he needed to earn his bed and board as a jester. He knew *The Spirit of the Times* would want his ghost-of-Astor piece immediately— even more so as soon as the New York papers published the news of the actual spirit-talking children upstate. People around Rochester were all atwitter, Herman Swarr had written him today, over two little girls, sisters named Fox, who claimed to converse with a ghost in their house by means of knocks on walls and bedposts.

Meanwhile, a bit farther west, in Buffalo and the surrounding towns, the churches had been holding special services, according to the Sunday papers: the Christians of western New York considered this week's forty-hour-long cessation of Niagara Falls a sign of the Lord's displeasure at heathenish modern life, a portent of the imminent apocalypse.

Whereas here in the capital of heathendom, the men in charge of the newspapers had at first disbelieved the very fact of the Niagara marvel. Skaggs, flushed with excitement and breathless after his run uptown from the telegraph office, had barged into the *Tribune* with the news. They were convinced he was playing a prank. It was almost April 1. Greeley would not stop smiling, and the fact that Skaggs was waving an actual message sheet from the New York, Albany & Buffalo Telegraph Company only entertained him more. "Getting started on your All Fools' Day shenanigans early this year, eh, Brat?" At the *Herald*, Dickie Shepherd, sniffing a bit of Skaggs's lunchtime brandy, had loudly suggested that he was intoxicated. At the *Mirror*, where he had not set foot since the night three years ago he had let the sainted editor step into the river and drown, they'd considered his excited shouts—"I *swear* it, the Niagara has *stopped*, the Falls are no more!"— the hallucination of a sorry, guilt-racked madman.

And at the *Sun*, they had accused him of "trying to pull a Poe." The *Sun* had not lived down its publication of an extra by Edgar Allan Poe featuring the news that a famous aeronaut had completed the first transatlantic balloon trip. The story was pure fiction. And unfortunately, it had been published "four years ago practically to the *day*," a subeditor at the *Sun* noted as he shooed Skaggs away. "Nip your fifty dollars elsewhere, man." The next morning's papers were about to be put to press, and Skaggs, rebuffed four times, decided to give up. "You paid Poe *fifty dollars?*" he said to the *Sun* editor on his way out. "My God, you fools *did* get sucked!"

The next day, the *Herald* received the story itself by wire from Buffalo, and on Saturday—April 1—it published an excited two-column "exclusive." A queer sequence of weathers—high temperatures, gales, sudden freezing temperatures—had formed a solid ice dam at the end of Lake Erie where it emptied into the Niagara River. And the Falls had disappeared. A wonder of the world had for two days and a night become an even greater wonder, a supernatural place.

The waterwheels stopped, so mills and factories emptied. Thousands of townspeople and tourists made their way down into the suddenly naked rocky gorge to wander in awe, each of them wearing an expression—dumb, smiling, a bit worried about what might happen next—like a soul newly arrived in heaven. Fish lay flapping by the thousands in the riverbed, tons of catfish and bass available for the taking to anyone with a basket. People filled boxes and baskets with souvenirs that had been underwater—bayonets, musket barrels, tomahawks. And Swarr had been right about the cavalry: a squadron from Fort Niagara rode grandly down and back up the American half of the empty riverbed as a display of order in the face of the astounding. On Friday evening, after the temperature rose to 64 degrees, today's newspaper reported, "a great wall of water roared and gushed back into its customary place, like the Red Sea after Moses and his Hebrews had passed." Skaggs hoped that some fugitive slaves had used the opportunity to walk across to freedom in Canada.

Looking out his window, he watched Engine 40 turn east into Franklin Street and disappear. He checked his watch—twenty past three in the morning—and returned to his desk and the children's-séance-with-Astor's-phantom story, resisting the impulse to go downstairs for a refreshment at the French café on Lispenard Street. However, he wrote only one sentence before pausing again. He stared vaguely across the room toward his cold stove, thinking. Ever since his brain had been invaded by Poe's remarks on the creation and destiny of the universe—"*Within the original unity of all matter and energy in the universe lies the germ of their inevitable annihilation*"—the familiar contours of life seemed as warped and wavy as an opium moment. Had a cosmic whimple turned the world upside down? Every day's news was a fresh stanza in some deranged epic poem. Kings tipping over like china dolls, free America suddenly a conquering empire stretching coast to coast, Astor dead, Niagara Falls gone, the telegraph reversing time, little girls speaking in knock-knock code to spirits . . .

As he forced his gaze back toward the page, he spotted a shelled walnut on the floor a few feet away, leaned down, and grabbed it. Still just as tasty as this morning; the small, rude pleasures of living by oneself.

DAWN WAS A few minutes from breaking. Shortly the sun's rays would tint the cloud of smoke that hovered around the ruins of the sugarhouse.

The Old Dutchman paced the sidewalk, preaching at the final fifty tired, disconsolate firemen who remained. But he was no longer shouting.

" 'If we say that we have no sin,' " he said to them, " 'we deceive ourselves, and the truth is not in us.' "

Had he chosen his New Testament verses this morning in light of the terrible circumstance? Or were they the random church memories of a confused old wretch?

" 'Whose sins you shall forgive, they are forgiven them; and whose sins you shall retain, they are retained.' "

The sharp, chalky miasma of charcoal and dust and water, the familiar smells after a fire, were mingled with a strong caramel aroma, dreamy and luscious, the smell of twenty tons of burned sugar.

Duff laid his ax in the box on the back of 15's carriage, then crouched to pull the lead bags blocking each wheel.

" 'If we confess our sins, he is faithful and just to forgive us our sins, and to cleanse us from all unrighteousness.' "

The Old Dutchman was directly behind Duff now. The wagon that had come for Fargis and the other dead fireman, Kerr, was rolling away.

" 'If we say that we have not sinned, we make him a liar, and his word is not in us.' "

"Tad?" Duff called softly to his lantern carrier, a boy of thirteen who was staring at the undertaker's black wagon. "Come on now and gather your things, and your wits."

The boy wiped the tears from his cheeks with a coat sleeve. "No one had died since before the Old Dutchman started coming around, had they?"

"Lots of people have died since then," Duff replied. "Off now, Tad, go run and get Gray and Jim and the rest." Most of Engine 15's men had wandered off to a grocery for a drink of something strong. "It's time to push off."

"No, no," the boy said. He regarded Duff with a dreadful curiosity. "The *Great* Fire, in '45, Duff. And that was the last time."

"The last time *what*, Tad?"

"The last time a fireman died."

" 'I tell you,' " said the Dutchman, very quietly now, as if saying words he had never heard or spoken before, " 'there will be the same kind of joy before the angels of God over *one* repentant sinner.' "

13

April 7, 1848
. . .
New York City

WHEN DUFF, AT age five, had asked his father why Ma forced them to eat eels for supper every Friday, Zeno Lucking answered, "She believes it's *penitential* for you, son." For years afterward, Duff believed that if he ever dared to eat pork or lamb on a Friday, his mother would send him to the penitentiary, which he imagined was operated by angry, armed priests. When he finally summoned the courage one morning in the woods to ask his father if Ma would *really* send him down the river to Sing-Sing if he stopped eating fish on Fridays, Zeno Lucking laughed so hard and long he had to lean against a tree.

Eel had not touched Duff's tongue since they'd moved to the city, but he continued to eat no meat on Fridays. Lately it had been his main nod in the direction of piety, and given the price of oysters, it was very easy to keep the faith.

Skaggs had been saying that New York this spring seemed like a permanent carnival, but to Duff the city was like an unending Mass. The night of the Mexican War celebrations, when he had sniffed the burning sulfur and then tossed his fuse into the street, he'd been an altar boy swinging his smoky censer down the nave. On Tuesday he had walked in the funeral procession for Kerr and Henry Fargis. Duff had never seen such a crowd, so large and so peaceful, tens of thousands of silent people filling the blocks from the Bowery most of the way to the East River. For a pair of dead firemen! Duff did not understand this outpouring of grief, but on top of his sadness it made him feel proud and a little envious.

He also felt guilty, of course, about Fargis and Kerr. A sense of contrition burned in him. Duff had always scrupled to make sure, at any fire he attended, that no one was burned or killed. The puncture in the gas pipe at the sugarhouse had been an act of righteous vandalism against the *property* of the propertied class, part of a campaign of retribution against Wall Street (on behalf of his father) and in particular against the Primes (on behalf of his sister). But except for Nathaniel Prime himself, Duff had never taken pleasure in anyone's death, not even in Mexico. Indeed, wasn't his true wartime bravery his *refusal* to kill innocents? "Justice is a messy thing," the major had said to the brigade last summer in Churubusco at their final assembly, "and none of us but God himself can be certain of how and when it will be meted out." The truth of that was proved in the war: by what lottery luck had Duff survived? He was reassured by today's papers that Fargis and the others had not died for nothing: the collapse of the wall was being blamed on the moneymen who built and owned the sugarhouse. He'd also read that the injured man from 35 Hose had succumbed to his injuries as well. Another funeral.

And now he was at St. Patrick's Cathedral, waiting in a line of people that snaked out the front door down Mulberry to Prince Street, over to Mott and then back up toward Houston. He had arrived just before two, and he had already heard the bells strike four. His shadow on the high brick wall was now taller than he. Duff decided the long wait was a down payment on his penance.

When he was a boy in Dutchess County, there was no Catholic church within a half day's drive, so every two months a young French Canadian priest riding circuit out of Albany would celebrate Mass in the barn of another Catholic family eight miles from the Luckings, with a portable confession box trucked along for the occasion. The risk of fire was considered too great for burning incense, so until Duff attended a Mass in a real church for the first time at age ten, the odor of church was dried hay and corn husks and manure.

And although the sacrament of penance had been the aspect of religion he'd liked best as a young child, he had not confessed his sins since he was thirteen—not since he'd committed his first mortal sin. And he had lied to his mother, again and again until she died, about this neglect of the sacrament, a fraud that amounted to hundreds of additional sins he had never confessed.

But now he was contrite, truly and sincerely sorry, and with all the sincerity he could summon he was seeking God's forgiveness.

As for his neglect of the sacraments, for most of the year in Mexico he had been *forbidden* to attend Mass or confess to the ear of a priest. Practically every officer had considered any priest doubly suspicious—not just a Mexican but a soldier of Rome, apt to deliver Lord-only-knows-what secret messages in Latin to the homesick Catholic troops.

Beginning on that final terrible day during the siege of Vera Cruz, though, Duff had found a moment of privacy to cross himself and recite the Act of Contrition. *Pray for us sinners now and at the hour of our death,* he'd whispered as he'd watched the gunners load their cannons with "hot shot," big eighteen-pound balls glowing red. He'd learned that day that iron does not melt until it reaches 2,800 degrees. "Twenty-*seven* hundred is plenty hot to broil Mexicans," a sergeant had explained cheerfully. *I detest all my sins, because I dread the loss of heaven and the pains of hell.*

"Hot honey doughnuts!" cried a woman with a basket as she walked along the line of waiting Catholics. "*Hot* doughnuts a penny apiece!" Duff was hungry, but in the interest of propriety as he awaited his tribunal of penance, he abstained. A man had also been up and down the queue three times offering little paper portraits. "I have excellent souvenir pictures of Dagger John," the fellow said softly, "but only five more . . . The latest lithograph of the bishop, and they're almost gone."

"One for myself, sir," the old lady in front of Duff said, and handed the man her five cents.

Dagger John was John Hughes, the bishop of New York. And it was he for whom Duff and four hundred other Catholics were standing on the sidewalk along the fortress wall of St. Patrick's. For one day during Lent each year, on the first Friday of the month, Dagger John personally heard confessions and administered penance and gave absolution. For the last several Lents of her life, Charlotte Lucking had come home practically whistling with pride at having confessed to Bishop Hughes. Her children had always wondered what sins their mother had to confess.

Duff had never visited St. Patrick's before. As he walked inside, the noise of the street diminished to nothing. His glance, as always, first found the crucified Jesus. The statue was smaller than he had expected, and not as bloody as some. He dipped two fingers into the holy water and made the sign of the cross. As he touched his head he felt the scar on his cheek sting and pulse.

Should he call him "Bishop" or "Bishop Hughes" or "Your Excellency"? Duff had not come today because he idolized Dagger John. Rather, he knew that to make a clean breast of it, he could not depend on an ordinary priest to do the job. When he was fourteen, one of the altar boys, Sponge McCain, had stolen a handful of Holy Eucharist one Sunday and eaten them like cookies with two of his friends—his *Presbyterian* friend and *Jewish* friend. A girl from Transfiguration had happened upon this sacrilege in an alley off Hester Street, the three boys laughing, their mouths full of communion wafers—and informed Sponge then and there that she knew for a *fact* that desecrating the Holy Eucharist was grounds for automatic excommunication, and therefore he was no longer a Catholic and bound straight for hell. When he'd gone to confess the next day, he told Duff later, Father Varela had shocked him by saying that he lacked the power to absolve Sponge for such a grave sin—that he would need to seek the *bishop's* approval. So today Duff had decided to come straight to the bishop.

He was staring at the banks of candles, wondering what had ever become of Sponge, when the old lady opened the door of the box and let it slam shut, kissing her new picture of the bishop and making the sign of the cross before she passed by Duff on her way out. His turn had come.

"In nomine Patris . . ." he said as he once again touched his head, then his heart—"et Filii"—and then each shoulder—"et Spiritus Sancti"—before kissing the tips of his fingers.

"Bless me, Excellency, for I have sinned. It has been . . . eight years since my last confession."

Duff strained but failed to hear any reaction behind the screen—tongue clicking, lips parting, a sigh.

And then he began listing sins he had committed. The bishop uttered only an occasional "yes" in reply. A few minutes into the recitation, which jumped and bounced forward and back through the years, he came to the pressing reason he was here.

"I caused the big fire that burned in Duane Street, Excellency . . ." He decided against saying *Sunday;* it had been after midnight when he lit the gas. "Early last Monday morning." He heard the bishop rearrange himself, as if he had leaned closer to hear.

"*Caused* it, my son? What do you mean by that?"

Duff found his Irish accent hopeful, reassuring. He had never in his life confessed to a native-born American.

"I started that fire in the sugarhouse. I did it because the people who own the place ruined my father and took the most awful liberties with my sister when she was a child."

"Three good men died fighting the blaze there."

"I know that, sir, Excellency. I know that terribly well. I run with—with an engine, and one of the men who died was a friend of mine. No one was meant to die there. It was not . . . a murder."

Now Duff heard a heavy sigh.

"I am deeply sorry for this sin and all the sins of my whole life, Excellency."

"And is that the all of it? Every sin you have to confess?"

Duff took a deep breath. "There were some other fires. One at a distillery, in February, a swill-milk hell that killed my baby brother and sister. And when I was young, three others. Three other fires."

Bishop Hughes said nothing.

"Fires seemed to be a mania with me."

Still no reply from Dagger John.

"No one at all died in those other fires, Excellency," Duff said, "not one person. I took precautions always. And I helped extinguish them as well. At one I saved a man and a woman from death."

His confessor remained silent.

"I am grievously sorry for my sins, Excellency. I wish to be reunited with God the Father and Jesus. I do."

Finally the Irish voice returned. "You have sincere sorrow and contrition and purpose of amendment?"

"*Yes.* Oh yes." A couple of seconds passed. "I have . . . a question for you, Excellency."

"Ask it, then."

"I fought in the war, and I killed men there, in Mexico."

Many of the priests in the diocese were hearing such confessions now from the returning troops. Bishop Hughes had a reply at the ready.

"Of course, my son. I expect you have concerns about the sinfulness of your acts as a soldier, and whether the war was a just one."

Duff hesitated. "I *did* have those questions. I had, I had a . . . crisis. In Vera Cruz."

"Yes."

"In Vera Cruz, that is a city down there, a beautiful little city, which we bombed and bombed and burned."

"I know of it."

"Well, I prayed to God and he made me understand that I must no longer follow the orders of my *officers* to harm innocents." Unspoken but understood by Bishop Hughes, embedded within Duff's pronunciation of *officers,* were *heartless* and *Protestant*.

"I see."

"Innocent Catholics we were murdering, Excellency. What choice had I but to try to stop those murders?" *Like your heroic Irish brothers now rising treasonously against their savage English overlords*. "I had to stop if only in order to protect my own soul from damnation." His apologia was sincere.

"I see. I see."

"I took up arms against my fellow Americans, Excellency."

"The Lord does not recognize the flag or the bullet of one nation as better or worse than any other, my son. War is wrong. Even when we must wage it."

"*Yes,* Excellency, *yes,* that was—that was the way I thought of it, too." He struggled to open his throat and stop the tears.

"My young sinner . . . You are now *truly* sorry for all the sins you have committed?"

"I am," he sputtered, "*grievously* so. Yes."

"And you have confessed to each and every serious sin, everything which in your heart separates you now from our Lord Jesus Christ?"

He sniffled, and tried to catch his breath. And in that moment Duff thought of one of Zeno Lucking's sayings—not *destruction and creation,* but what he always said with a wink when he decided to camp out overnight in the woods with Duff so they could keep digging for buried gold in the morning, or to take a second piece of mulberry pie after dinner, or to instruct Polly to draw yet another patent forgery: *May as well be hanged for a sheep as a lamb.*

"No. There is another." He paused. "A mortal sin, when I was thirteen. I told you about the abuser, the vile old banker who ravished my sister when she was a girl? I avenged the crime, Excellency. I killed the man. And I am sorry to God for that sin, as I am for all the lives I have taken—in the war, I mean, in Mexico. And deaths I may have been responsible for. And for all of my other sins. I pray and promise I will never take another life again. I am a repentant sinner, and I wish with all my heart for God's forgiveness."

Would Bishop Hughes want details of that remarkable morning eight years ago in Nathaniel Prime's house down on Bowling Green? Duff had watched the house almost every day for weeks. He knew that at five each

Wednesday afternoon, a wagon arrived and a scullery girl left open a cellar door for ten minutes while the iceman lugged in his twenty big blue-white blocks. Duff knew that each trip took the man a little longer than the one before, as he tired out, so that the chance to slip inside unseen would be best after the eighteenth or nineteenth ice block. If anyone spotted him, he had planned to announce himself truthfully—"I am Duff Lucking, I have worked for the Primes at Hurlgate"—and say that he was there to let Mr. Prime know that his mother was ill and the family needed a small loan. But none of the staff spotted him as he ran and hid, ran and hid, from mudroom to pantry to nook and up the back stairs, as if he were playing a game. Would he do it? He was not absolutely sure until the moment he saw the old man sitting by a window in the library with the *Journal of Commerce* laid over his belly, snoring. All alone and asleep—Duff took this stroke of luck as destiny's pat on his back. By the time he was standing over him he had drawn the razor from his pocket, and by the time Prime's blood was soaking the newspaper Duff had placed the razor in the dying man's right hand and run back to the door, seeing if the way was clear to make his escape.

But Dagger John demanded none of that. Bishop Hughes instructed Duff that for the rest of his life he must say an entire rosary twice each day, the Act of Contrition twice each day as well, and a novena once a month. And he was to perform "works of mercy in the name of Jesus Christ to please your Lord God and Savior. Do you understand?"

"Yes, Excellency."

"And no more fire-setting, eh? You're *finished*."

"Yes, Excellency."

Duff waited for some additional penance. But he heard only an energetic clearing of Hughes's throat.

"O my God," Duff said, "I am heartily sorry for having offended thee. I detest *all* my sins because I dread the loss of heaven and the pains of hell. But most of all because they have offended thee, my God who art all good and deserving of all my love. I firmly resolve with the help of thy grace to confess my sins, to do penance, and to amend my life. Amen."

"*Ego te absolvo*," replied the bishop. "I absolve you from your sins in the name of the Father and of the Son and of the Holy Spirit."

DUFF HAD NEVER imagined that Mexico would be all cornbread and fiddle music, ruddy boys on holiday in the tropics. He had been only nineteen when he'd enlisted in the summer of '46, but not stupid, or, he thought, naïve. Hadn't he attended school for eight years? And was it possible to grow up a half orphan a mile from the Five Points burdened with a lot of sweet, creamy illusions about life being painless or pretty? But he'd figured that "the Mexican difficulties," as everyone called the war at the start, would be more or less familiar. As he had chirped to the bald, sweaty recruiting sergeant that morning two summers ago at Fort Columbus on Governors Island, "I've marched for four years with a target company—Bobo's Sharpshooters?"

"A *target* company, eh?" The target companies were clubs that had sprouted during the thirties. Each autumn the target companies put on their costumes, some playing the parts of soldiers and others of mountain men, and paraded into the parks to fire muskets. A smile broke across the recruiting sergeant's face, which Duff misapprehended as encouragement.

"Yes, sir, and for many years I've run with one of the finest, bravest machines in town—Engine Company Number 15?—so yes, in answer to your question, I think I do have a strong hunch about what it is I'm volunteering for. I have seen men fall in battle, battling the flames."

"Have you, now? A lot of them?"

Duff now heard the doubt in his voice. And, in fact, in all the time Duff had lived in New York City up to his enlistment in '46, only three firemen had died fighting fires. Yet on one night back in 1840, just after Duff had become a full member of Engine 15, he witnessed one of the deaths, amid the rubble of a collapsed wall.

Duff had looked straight into the army sergeant's eyes, unflinching. "A single death is plenty if you love the man," he'd said.

The army man's smile had lost its sarcastic skew. He'd asked if Duff was born in America, if his parents were living, and if he was married; yes, no, and no had been the right answers. After Duff said he had attended school until age sixteen, the sergeant asked how many inches were in twenty-six feet, and Duff had replied "Three hundred twelve. I'm a gas fitter, sir, and we cut lengths of pipe all day long." The sergeant had handed him a book of army regulations and instructed him to read any paragraph out loud.

Finally, he had asked if Duff also happened to be an experienced hand at digging holes in the ground. When Duff had replied that half his boyhood was spent shoveling ditches with his father through the woods of Dutchess County, part of a perpetual search for buried Spanish gold, the sergeant had laughed. And then announced that he was enlisting Duff Lucking as the seventy-eighth and final private in the Corps of Engineers' new Company A, the so-called Company of Sappers, Miners, and Pontoniers.

"You will be a *pioneer,* Mr. Lucking," the sergeant had said.

Duff had sensed he was meant to be grateful, and thanked the man, although at that moment he had had no good idea what a sapper, miner, or pontonier did. Nor did he know the original military meaning of *pioneers*—the troops who march ahead of the main army to ready the terrain for conquest by destroying enemy earthworks.

It was a few days after he'd signed up, when Skaggs had explained to Duff his understanding of sappers and miners ("I believe you will be burrowing and blowing up"), that he realized he did have experience in precisely the work Company A was being assembled to perform. Early one morning a year before his enlistment, as an awful blaze spread from a sperm oil warehouse, threatening to incinerate half the city, an older engineer had pulled Duff and another young fireman aside, handed over canisters of black powder and fuse, and pointed them toward the cellar door of a saltpeter warehouse. When the warehouse exploded, a fire engine was hurled across the street, two adjacent buildings crumbled, and the blast shattered windows a mile away. At the end of the day, the fire had burned hundreds of buildings to the ground. Nine people had died. But the engineer told Duff afterward, as he swore him and the other boy to secrecy, that it would have been twice as bad if not for the firebreak they blasted. He also said that Hart, the fireman from 22 Engine, had suffered only a sprained ankle. Hart had been standing on the roof of the building next to the saltpeter warehouse at the moment of the blast. He was blown through the air across the street to the roof of another building, as if carried by an angel.

The events of that day in 1845 had had several marked effects on Duff. They confirmed to him the virtue of taking great risks for the greater good, and of performing heroic, dangerous, violent deeds secretly. He began to believe in the possibility of just and happy endings, as in the books he had read as a boy. And Hart's survival was the first miracle he had ever encountered personally. For the year after the Great Fire, until he left for Mexico, he had attended Mass with renewed enthusiasm.

HE HAD CROSSED with his company into Mexico in October of 1846, and crossed back into the States, all by himself, in October of 1847. For Duff the war had lasted exactly one year. But whenever he revisited his memories of

Mexico, that middling term—*a year*—seemed all wrong. It was an accurate lie. When Duff thought about Mexico and tried to fit all of it into his retrospective gaze, it consisted of a pleasant three-month preface (training, sailing, marching, construction, demolition) *followed* by The War—which he remembered as either one careening, roaring, explosive nightmare, or else an interminable sentence in hell, either a confusing, sickening instant of blood and terror and anguish, or an eternity.

But it had lasted a year. In the beginning he had enjoyed the army. It was like the church and the firehouse both, as strict and serious as the former and as bluff and manly as the latter. He had reveled in his weeks of basic training in sapping and mining at the military academy up the Hudson. He had adored the nightly lights-out ritual of the bugler's tattoo. He had not gotten sick at all on the voyage south, and picked up Spanish easily. He'd respected and envied his officers their West Point educations. Lieutenant McClellan was no older than Duff. In Texas he had helped construct—in only four days, under Captain Lee—a magnificent, 300-yard-long rubber pontoon bridge across the Rio Grande, which remained the single proudest accomplishment not only of his time in Mexico, but of his whole life so far.

Not his happiest moment in Mexico, however. That had come the following month, when he and a small detachment of engineers had been dispatched to destroy an arsenal in Michoacán, west of Mexico City. The depot, in a forest of pine and fir on the side of an extinct volcano called Nevado de Toluca, had been empty when they reached it, and they'd decided to camp overnight. When Duff awakened before anyone else early the next morning, he'd decided to hike a mile higher to take in the sights—a pair of little lakes filled the dead volcano's crater, according to the map. And there they'd been, deep blue and cool and gorgeous in the very first light of dawn.

As soon as he'd begun his walk back down to camp, he'd realized he was uncertain of the way. At half past six the trail looked very different than it had in the darkness of five. He'd stopped to decide which fork of a path to take, and noticed the lower limbs on the evergreens around him were bowed, and covered from trunk to tip with what appeared to be some odd fungus. He'd stepped closer for a look and shook the end of a branch. Hundreds of butterflies had arisen—no, *thousands*—fluttering off their perch, startling him. *Fairies,* he'd thought for a moment. And then tens of thousands more, all of them orange and black monarchs, left a hundred other branches of that tree, awakened by the rustle of their airborne brothers and sisters. They'd formed a swarm, gathered their bearings, and all at once flown off together to find a new, uninhabited tree on which to spend the rest of the Mexican winter unmolested.

Duff had been ecstatic, and without thinking he'd run and stumbled after the butterflies. As he'd raced through the woods, keeping an eye on them as they fluttered through the shafts of morning light above and ahead of him, he'd seen that the whole forest was filled with millions upon millions of monarchs, covering not only trees but much of the ground as well. He'd felt as if he'd come upon a miracle, some reassertion by God and nature of their power and wonders, heedless of arsenals and enemies, miners and sappers, guns and war . . . and then he saw that he had returned directly to his camp.

Then, as he'd watched the butterflies rise together and hover near the treetops, beautiful as a dream, he'd decided their appearance was both a providential gift and a warning. For they could have led him anywhere—to the Mexicans, or over a cliff, or deep into the woods, like a lost boy in a fairy tale. He'd given thanks, and made the sign of the cross.

BUT AFTER THAT, Mexico had no longer seemed like a camping expedition and became a real field of war, with men he knew dying all the time. At first, Duff's responsibility for killing had been modest and shared, the violence he caused delayed and distant. He'd helped *arrange* destruction—by filling caissons with powder, sneaking them at night under a Mexican rampart or lookout tower, laying fuse. It was not until the Battle of Buena Vista that he'd shot men, and seen the men he'd killed after they died.

Making Buena Vista even worse was the grim, disillusioning winter that had led up to it. Most of their meat had been rancid. The coffee tasted of vinegar. Nearly everyone caught the dysentery they called "diarrhea blue." Duff pitied the ragtag volunteer militia troops, who dropped like dogs from injury and disease. But he grew also to despise them when they stole chickens and corn from Mexicans and then shot the poor people dead if they raised a fuss.

He had begun praying for guidance. *Wait on the Lord: be of good courage, and he shall strengthen thine heart: Wait, I say, on the Lord.*

Duff and the other army regulars had a better time of it than the volunteers. But the Catholics among them—a third of the regulars had been born in Ireland—were subjected to insults and gratuitous whacks from their officers, called "papist clowns" and "Romish dogs." The fact that Duff lacked an Irish name or accent meant that he escaped the catcalls and thrashings, to his everlasting shame.

Jesus, prince of all heavenly truths, you have commanded the virtue of honesty, it is the power against all deceptions. Direct your spirit of honesty upon me . . .

Duff had known deserters. Everyone had. By the end of the winter a tenth of the regulars had run away. Most just disappeared, and scuttled back across the Rio Grande to their lives in the States. But a small fraction— nearly all of them Catholic, most of them Irish—had stayed in Mexico and formed El Batallón de San Patricio. It was at Buena Vista that Duff had fought against the St. Patrick's Battalion for the first time. In one minute at the beginning of the battle he'd watched a volley from their twelve- pounders fly in with incredible accuracy and disintegrate the wagons of a company of Kentucky volunteers, as if God were firing the rounds. He had never seen such artillery skill.

Even while he'd tried to kill them for twenty-four hours, and vice versa, he'd admitted to himself that he regarded the St. Patrick's boys as . . . not heroes, but certainly not cowards, either. They weren't risking their lives and reputations for the Mexican money and land they'd been promised, but because they sincerely believed that the Mexicans, fellow Catholics and fel- low peasants, had more right on their side. He'd been happy, of course, when General Taylor had arrived to save the day at Buena Vista. But he'd also been happy when he'd heard that nearly all the San Patricios had gotten away.

PREPARATIONS FOR THE great landing at Vera Cruz began only weeks after Buena Vista. Duff had been dispatched with a platoon from Company A to go ashore and divert several streams by means of explosives and timbers. As they'd pulled their surfboat onto the beach, Duff had finally asked the most congenial sergeant the purpose of blocking streams—were they navigable? *Nah,* the fellow had said with a chuckle, *this is a siege, Lucking.* Their or- ders were to cut off water to Vera Cruz. *Water to the forts, you mean?* Duff had asked hopefully. The sergeant had looked at him, but for a long moment made no reply. Reality outran apprehension. The scheme was to deprive the whole local population of drinking water for the duration. Duff had ached to raise objections, to demur. But he'd said nothing as they spent days going about their business of making life impossible for the people of Vera Cruz.

And there shall be upon every high mountain, and upon every high hill, rivers and streams of waters in the day of the great slaughter, when the towers fall . . . Blessed are they which are persecuted for righteousness' sake: for theirs is the kingdom of heaven.

Duff's next task had been to build two field furnaces just outside the city to heat the Martin's shells, a new and improved version of incendiary hot shot. A Martin's shell was a hollow sphere that shattered when it struck a target, spewing the molten iron that filled its center.

So shall it be at the end of the world: the angels shall come forth, and sever the wicked from among the just, and shall cast them into the furnace of fire: there shall be wailing and gnashing of teeth.

On the second day of spring, the American bombardment began—from the hot-shot battery, from the giant siege guns Duff and the engineers had dragged ashore, and from the decks of navy battleships in the harbor. He'd stood only two hundred yards from the city wall. For four days he watched the fire and iron rain down, a hundred tons a day smashing and burning not just forts but the ordinary Mexicans' houses and stables and shops and dispensaries and even—he saw a flaming steeple and cross—their churches.

Near dawn on Sunday, before the fifth day of shelling began, he and some other men from Company A were sent on a reconnaissance foray. In a little yard behind a ruined, smoldering tavern they'd found five people curled and sprawled on the ground, broken and burned and bleeding, whimpering and groaning, barely alive. Duff had asked his sergeant if they could put the dying Mexicans out of their misery, but a lieutenant accused Duff of recklessness—of proposing to "waste good American ammunition on a few Mexican goners."

That was the moment Duff stopped obeying orders.

His squad continued its way around the edge of Vera Cruz, but he'd fallen back and returned to the tavern, where he'd performed his acts of mercy, then finished a quart of *mescal*.

As he stared up at the orange disk of the sun in the cloudless sky, drunk, miserable, tears streaming down his smooth cheeks, from somewhere he was sure he actually heard Saint Paul's words . . .

And I persecuted this way unto the death, binding and delivering into prisons both men and women . . . As I made my journey, and was come nigh unto Damascus about noon, suddenly there shone from heaven a great light round about me. And I fell unto the ground, and heard a voice saying unto me . . . "Why persecutest thou me?" And I answered, "Who art thou,

Lord?" And he said unto me, "I am Jesus of Nazareth, whom thou perse-
cutest" . . . And I said, "What shall I do, Lord?" And the Lord said unto
me, "Arise, and go . . . and there it shall be told thee of all things which are
appointed for thee to do."

The next day the Mexicans had surrendered Vera Cruz. But by then Duff
Lucking was long gone, walking west. A week later, he had found the San
Patricios.

"Soy un católico, soy un amigo de su República," he had said to the Mexican sentries. They'd searched him for knives and pistols, then said "Bienvenidos" and escorted him into the camp. He'd heard a familiar Latin chant
in the distance and smelled the incense before he saw his famous fellow deserters, two hundred white Catholics from America, all kneeling outside on
blankets in their white canvas trousers and Turkish blue coats with red collars and cuffs—their Mexican officers' uniforms. It was the end of Easter
Mass. Four Mexican priests wearing white robes were blessing the San Patricios, one by one, and sprinkling holy water on each of their guns as they
passed down the ranks.

14

April 10, 1848

. . .

London

B ARELY A MONTH had passed since Ben had left his family in Kent, but it seemed like an age. The last day at Great Chislington Manor had dawned in standard March fashion, cold and pitilessly gray. Breakfast was the kind of country feast that gave a bad name to English bounty: eggs, anchovies, prawns, kippers, fried lampreys, lobster meat floating in tureens of butter, then chocolate cake, treacle pies, candied bananas, cream and hazelnuts. Throughout the meal, his sister Isabel, eyes rimmed red, clutching a handkerchief, had been unable to speak for fear she would start crying again.

As the sweets were served, their father had invited Philip to make a wager on when Ben would return to England, chastened and broke, asking for his position back at the firm: would it be before the end of 1848, or after the New Year? Philip had only grinned, shook his head, and kept his *Economist,* refusing even to acknowledge that his brother was about to do something exceptional. Philip had seemed infuriatingly blithe that morning. Perhaps he was cheered by the prospect of Ben's departure and presumed failure abroad.

Ben had kissed Isabel goodbye, shaken hands with the men, and just climbed into the brougham next to Joseph when Tryphena suddenly ran out the open front door of the house. She wore a red wool dressing gown embroidered with a riot of peacocks and palms. Its top several buttons were unfastened, revealing her chemise, and the belt was slipping loose. Philip was so shocked he said nothing, as if he did not wish to believe it was happening. And Tryphena ignored her husband. She was smiling, with a look on her face of almost horrific excitement.

"Oh, *brother*-in-law," she said to Ben as she ran toward the carriage, "they tell me you are sailing for *America*! And I had just that instant awoken from the most wonderful *dream* in which we were children, you and I, living with other children in some red Indian's lodge built of logs, put up like wickets, on a lake in *America*! With a telegraph machine that played music!"

She was at his side, breathless. Isabel approached gingerly, to clothe and calm her. But Tryphena's dream was still pouring out, as if from a child.

"The prettiest yellow . . . *orbs*, like croquet balls but shiny and ever so bright, were scattered across the ground, around the trees, like big magical nuts! And fires blazed all around, but the flames were *soothing*! Oh, it was heaven!"

"Sounds like hell itself," Archibald Knowles grumbled.

She kissed Ben's hand. "Goodbye, dear Benjamin. Will you return before September, so that we may play croquet?" Croquet and the summer flowers were Tryphena's country passions.

"I rather doubt it, I am afraid, my dear. We shall play another summer."

"If my dream should come true, Benjamin, will you write and tell me?"

"I shall." And off he had driven.

PREPARING TO LEAVE England kept him as busy as he had ever been. He had to choose which of his books and prints and personal effects he would send to a warehouse, and which he would let the secondhand man cart away. Sir Archie owned the house in Bruton Street and offered to "rent it out for too much money to some foreigner for the year, while you are abroad," but Ben insisted that he sell it, and Sir Archie was happy to oblige, given property prices lately. Ben spent days finding suitable positions for Dennis and Rose, his steward and cook. He spent hours at his desk in King William Street writing to each of his clients about his imminent withdrawal from Knowles, Merdle, Newcome & Shufflebotham. Every few nights he attended a small farewell gathering in his honor, each of which left him a little melancholy—not because he was emigrating but because he realized, with each tired joke about America and each final drunken expression of bafflement over his leave-taking, how little he would miss most of his London friends. The one he would miss dearly was gone already, lost in Paris.

Ben had looked over the schedule of departures and found himself considering which vessel to book the way he had picked racehorses at Epsom—by his affinity for their names. He liked the idea of sailing to America on the *Flying Scud,* the *Santa Claus,* the *Climax,* the *Sweepstakes,* the *Rip van Winkle,* the *Skylark,* or the *Brooklyn.* The *Mischief,* however, was putting out from the London Docks and sailing sooner than the rest, at 1:00 P.M. on Monday the tenth of April. So *Mischief* it would be.

And now the morning had arrived. His luggage, nothing but two bags he could carry himself, was packed tight, sitting on each side of him in the hired Hansom cab. One bag bulged where his books and the pieces of his shotgun pressed against the leather. The mist turned intermittently to drizzle. As he rode through Trafalgar Square, past the new statue of Admiral Nelson standing atop its comically tall column, he found himself next to an omnibus pasted with Cunard advertising bills—THE UNITED STATES OF AMERICA! *Weekly sailings!*—with the letters spelling the country's name rendered as if they consisted of rough logs and twigs. Ben smiled—it was his sister-in-law's dream version of America.

The two letters he'd received in the post this morning were in his pocket, to be answered from aboard the *Mischief.* The first was from Roger, his brother-in-law, wishing Ben "an unmolested and uneventful journey" and confirming that, with Philip's help, he had been named to the government's new Lunacy Commission at "the remarkable salary of £1,500." *Good for Isabel,* Ben thought; *poor Isabel,* he thought as well. Roger Warfield had once filled an entire weekend in Kent with this lately acquired expertise—how he had discovered, for instance, during his "tour of one of the finest asylums," that "the madman's rages can often be calmed by quiet, straightforward conversation."

The second letter was from Paris. The Count de Tocqueville had responded to Ben's plea for information concerning the whereabouts of Ashby's remains; no word and no encouraging prospects, alas, for the provisional government remained terribly disorganized. But he said he was "pleased beyond measure" that Ben was headed for America, "a democracy in which I invest more hope than my own. You inquire about *my* view of the volcano that erupted here in February. You saw it—did you not have the feeling that my countrymen and I had staged a *play* about the French Revolution, rather than *continuing* it in actuality?" Indeed, he wrote Ben,

the new Government laid down the rule that we must all wear the dress *of members of the revolutionary Convention of 1792—the white waist-*

coat with turned-down collar as they are always worn by actors *playing Robespierre on the stage.*

And on this wet, dark Monday morning in London, as his driver headed east along the Thames toward the docks, Ben saw no one quaking or laughing. At several large intersections he saw groups of impassive soldiers and constables gathered around sawhorse barricades, requiring carriages and wagons to turn away, and pedestrians to pass through in single file. And he saw thousands of Englishmen diligently trying to join in the Springtime of the Peoples, making their way toward the bridges. The Chartists had called a rally for eleven at Kensington Common to *hip hip hooray* their charter one last time, and then finally deliver their millions of petition signatures to Parliament. These were England's revolutionists, Ben thought as he watched them waiting silently to cross Fleet Street and head toward Blackfriars Bridge. In England, the revolutionists carried affidavits and umbrellas.

The drizzle became a steady rain and then a deluge. Ben saw lightning over the Houses of Parliament. The costermongers outside Hungerford Market rushed to cover their carts with canvas. And there was the new iron and steel footbridge over the river, packed with hundreds of soggy radicals shuffling to the south bank for their demonstration. Tasteful people loved to hate the Hungerford Bridge; Ben found its giant swooping iron chains not only impressive but actually beautiful—as he did its architect's greatest work, the new tunnel beneath the Thames that had been under construction during Ben's entire youth.

He burned to be on his way to America. But a few minutes after arriving at the docks he'd discovered that the sailing of the *Mischief* was canceled due to the weather and, according to one of the ship's officers, "circumstances beyond the control of management of the line." A porter told him that "a quarter of the crew are off marching from Kensington Common up to Whitehall, even after the captain stood right there under that boom and called them mutineers who deserved to hang."

Ben put down his bags and looked up at his ship, considering his situation. He would not be leaving for America today. There were no cabs in sight. And even if he had found one, the crowds would make the drive even more tediously slow, if not actually impossible.

He left his two bags at a luggage shed, unable to bear the ignominy of returning home this afternoon. Perhaps he would take a room at Brown's Hotel until he could book a new passage. That would deprive Philip and his father of the pleasure of his setback. *Well, how perfectly apt,* one of them would be sure to say, unbearably, *that it was your Chartist mob, your own revolutionary chums, who prevented you from taking your clipper to America!* But one of their friends might well spot him at Brown's, his subterfuge thus producing an even worse comeuppance. He sighed. He would amble upstream, get a bite to eat, then head home to Bruton Street after all.

The last time he had walked along quays, in Paris, Ben had seen and heard and smelled revolution. These docksides were calm. Insurgency had not broken out. No shots had been fired, no omnibuses burned, no rocks thrown, not a single shopwindow cracked. The rain stopped.

Finally he leaned against a stone embankment, ignoring the schooners and sloops, watching each ferry pass right to left, packed to the gills with marchers now heading home to Greenwich or Barking.

A steam packet, the *Gravesend,* landed noisily thirty yards in front of him. He watched its first passengers, most of them carrying luggage, step onto the pier.

Then he saw a face he knew. The sharp, high cheekbones were familiar, and the long nose, the pouty lips, the black hair . . . but the mustache? Was it the newsagent from Berkeley Square—or his former bootmaker, the Italian? Or—Lord—could it be the old head clerk dismissed from Knowles, Merdle, Newcome & Shufflebotham after he was caught rogering one of the errand boys in the cellar? But that poor fellow had not worn a mustache.

Then Ben imagined the face shaved clean. He recalled the expression of ice-cold rage; the hand gripping the pistol, and the high-pitched yowl.

It was the sergeant from Paris.

No. The soldier had been younger and much taller, Ben was sure. This fellow was probably a cabdriver he had once hired, or a doorkeeper at the Athenaeum, or no one at all.

The instant the man happened to glance up and meet Ben's stare, even before his dark eyes squinted and widened and squinted again, both of them knew.

Ben steadied himself. This was *London!* No French maniac could simply throttle or shoot him in broad daylight in the middle of Wapping High Street. But the Frenchman was dead set. Ben watched him stride through the crowd of passengers on the gangway shoving men and even women out of his way as he made for the landing stage.

Ben bolted.

A minute later, he reached the gray stone tower that led down into the

Thames Tunnel, and he blasted through the doors without pausing, taking two slick steps at a time, nearly slipping—"*Careful*, sir," said one of the special constables—surprising the crowd shuffling through the exit turnstile as he rushed past them, barely stopping at the tollbooth, throwing his penny across the counter toward the agent, who opened his palm flat to catch it when it fell.

Ben rounded the bend and entered the narrower space of the tunnel proper, a barrel vault of a million bricks glazed white and illuminated by the flames of hundreds of coal-gas spigots, an otherworldly tube that seemed to extend infinitely, like a telegraph wire in which he and the others passing to and fro were electrical dots and dashes, each person a particle of energy, unconscious of his final destination or the message he carried.

From well behind him, back at the gate, he heard snatches of a loud argument, commands and threats in French and English echoing off the brick and stone. The tollbooth agent would not accept Drumont's Guernsey coins, but Drumont shouted in French that he had no time to wait for change from his British banknote. The three lounging special constables, happy at last for the chance to suppress some insurgency, surrounded this wild and— good God! *armed*—foreign troublemaker.

By the time one of the specials ended the exchange by pulling his baton against Drumont's neck from behind, Ben was almost halfway to the other side, running at full speed into the depthless white glow.

New York City

THIS, POLLY DECIDED the moment she stepped out of her building and took a breath, was the sort of sunny spring day that required celebration. So she bought carrots and cheese and a loaf of raisin bread as well as some butterscotch candies, packed her art things in a basket with the food, and waved down a big two-horse, two-seat landau. First down to West Broadway, where she awakened Skaggs and dragged him downstairs while the driver waited. His sleepy confusion and wild, uncombed hair and Turkish slippers made her laugh. And then they drove far to the east, toward a block of rotting, unpainted wooden houses.

Skaggs and the driver were having an argument about whether he would make the turn into the alley—too narrow and muddy, the man said, too many animals and children messing about in the road. But then Polly spotted Priscilla, a bucket in hand, walking down a boardwalk. She was moving in a careful zigzag, attempting to avoid the jets of green and brown muck each of her steps caused to spurt up from between the boards.

"Miss Christmas!" Polly said, more loudly than respectable women spoke in public. "We are here to kidnap you!"

Priscilla looked up, a slight panic in her eyes. The fear turned to mere bewilderment, and then—her embarrassment about the squalor of Daggle-Tail Alley overcome by the appearance of a large carriage containing Polly in a pretty dress and Mr. Skaggs—to joy.

"Polly Lucking!" Priscilla said. "How did you find me here? And . . . and *why?*"

Polly felt like crying, so she laughed and said, "Why? Because today is the start of your Easter holiday and because I have never seen a sweeter spring morning. We are off to have a picnic and draw pictures and enjoy the bliss of profligate leisure on a regular working day. Come along!"

Priscilla shook her head and held up the empty pail. "My dad needs beer. He'll be too angry when he wakes if I haven't brought his growler home full."

"He's passed out, is he, already at this hour?" Polly asked.

Priscilla nodded. Polly sighed. But Skaggs was unwilling to let this moment turn into some cautionary anecdote about the evils of drink.

"Well, fine then," he said cheerfully, hopping down onto the boardwalk, extending his hand toward Priscilla, "we'll have you back here with a *gallon* of ice-cold lager before the old sod realizes you've escaped. Trust me, Miss Christmas—I am an expert in the science of inebriation."

She smiled, took his hand, and stepped aboard. Her face powder did not entirely hide the purple and green on her bruised left jaw.

THEY WALKED ALONG the Battery and settled on a shady spot between two pear trees in full flower. After they ate, Polly helped Priscilla sketch a sloop, then left her on a bench at the water's edge to draw alone and joined Skaggs back on the grass. He spread out his coat as a blanket for her and lay back on one elbow to read his newspapers.

"Lovely, isn't she?" Polly said. "There in the breeze with her pencil and picture?"

Skaggs looked up and agreed, but then reflexively inserted his distressing glimpse of the future. "Beautiful—and obsolete, alas, in our age of the all-mechanized. The sketchbook is doomed. Damned Daguerre." His friend and physician Simon Solis had once diagnosed him, only half in jest, as a victim of "anticipatory nostalgia." Skaggs sipped from his pint bottle of German wine. "Speaking of which, I am sorry I haven't brought along my camera today. Such a sad and lovely photograph this scene would make."

"Your camera is only a different sort of pencil," she said. "New devices breed new types of artists."

"An 'artist'? Not I. No, the new devices permit the unskilled and untrained to *impersonate* artists."

They sat in silence while Skaggs read his *Tribune*.

"What news of the wars in Europe?" Polly asked.

Skaggs turned the page and placed his finger on the top of an article—A BRAVE INSURGENCY REPRESSED *by the Tribune's correspondent via Sandy Hook*—that he had written yesterday based on a brief conversation with a fifteen-year-old prince shipped from Poland to America for temporary safekeeping. "Only what my horrid little Polish friend told me on Friday, about a massacre of peasants by his uncle in the province of Posen." He pointed at another headline. "But elsewhere in Prussia there's some new Parliament convening. I am afraid, however, *that* is when I lose all interest in revolutions—the moment they form subcommittees and start debating the boundaries of Schleswig-Holstein."

Down at the water, Priscilla was now drawing a picture of a fisherman on the bank. Polly smiled. She had decided to end her own nascent career as an artist's model. The Heilperins had called her performance as *Liberty Leading the People at the Barricades* "genius," and proposed that she become the featured member of their troupe. But while the tableau vivant felt *almost* like acting a part in a play, she had seen too much pitiful carnal hunger in the eyes of the men drawing her. One of them—a huge fellow with flour in his hair and eyebrows—had simply stared at her, sniggering and licking his lips, not even pretending to draw. If she were going to earn a wage indulging men's animal appetites, she decided, she would rather do it without the elaborate charade that Heilperin's entailed. She would be an actress *or* a whore, but she would not split the difference to work as a phony artist's model.

And indeed, she was feeling hopeful about getting a part in one of the plays opening at the Broadway or—she fervently dreamed—in Burton's production of *Dombey and Son*.

As Skaggs finished with his paper, turned over on his back, and laid his head against the basket with his eyes closed, Polly had a question.

"Is there any further news about our own little revolution?"

Skaggs opened his eyes.

"In Albany," she added. "The women's bill." The Married Women's Property Act would for the first time allow married women to keep any property they owned or money they earned. "I saw it yesterday in the *Tribune.*"

Skaggs decided that it would be unwise for him to joke that it was unladylike of her to read the newspapers. "No mention today at all, I think." He reached for the bottle lying next to him. "But I am certain that you, Polly Lucking, shall be able to keep your fortune out of the clutches of the otherwise lucky fellow you finally marry." He lifted the bottle to his lips and swallowed his last dram of wine. "Yet another reason why *we* shan't ever be husband and wife."

Smiling now, she rose onto her knees, grabbed his hat off the grass, and pushed it down hard over his face.

"At Mrs. Stanhope's," she said, "I read your article about the two sisters in Rochester who speak with the ghost by knocking. She thought you had invented them. When I told her they were real girls, she became quite feverish with excitement. As if she had seen a sign from God. She says we *must* turn this to Priscilla's advantage. That a golden opportunity had arrived. That Priscilla will be the first Spirit Girl in any New York house, the first on earth. That gentlemen will *beg* to pay ten or *twenty* dollars for an evening with her."

Skaggs shook his head. "Margaret Stanhope is the Barnum of your world."

"Of her world. But in any event," Polly continued, watching two daddy longlegs stepping across Skaggs's newspaper, "I shan't allow her to turn Priscilla into . . . *that.*"

A strong gust blew the newspapers and spiders sprawling across the grass, and as he scrambled to his feet to catch the sheets, they heard Priscilla shouting cries of distress. Polly stood. Skaggs ran.

A very small black spaniel puppy was in the water, six feet out, paddling frantically, barely keeping its head above water and bobbing away from the shore. The owner, a rich girl of about nine, was sobbing, and the girl's elderly nana stared at the struggling dog and slowly shook her head. Priscilla had borrowed her fisherman's nine-foot leader and tied it to the handle of the beer pail, which she was shoving as gently as possible into the water as a lifeboat for the puppy.

Polly and Skaggs exchanged a look—sweet, hopeless. But the breezes sent the bucket floating toward the puppy quicker than he was drifting out to sea. And then he started sniffing eagerly in its direction. He was only a couple of feet away.

"*Swim,*" Polly shouted. "Climb inside!"

Skaggs was delighted. "He smells the ale."

"I think the lard," Priscilla said. At her father's insistence, she always rubbed the inside of his pail with lard, which reduced the foam and so gave Mr. Christmas an extra couple of cents' worth of beer.

Miraculously, the puppy reached the edge of the bucket and started to scrabble inside. But each time he tried, the rim of grease around the top edge kept him from getting a good purchase, and his paws slipped and scratched down the side, shoving the bucket farther away and leaving him paddling more desperately than ever. The dog was fatigued, and drifting out beyond the nine-foot limit of the bucket. The old lady was trying to make her weeping granddaughter turn away and leave. The rescue attempt was more awful than the predicament—*as always,* Skaggs thought.

Polly put a hand on Priscilla's shoulder. "Let the line go," she commanded.

"Let it *go?*"

"If the pail reaches him quickly, he might still manage to get inside. It is his only chance."

"*Her* chance," the dog's owner cried, "she's a girl, *Cindy,* I only just *got* her."

"But . . . but, Polly," Priscilla asked, "what kind of chance? Even if she should climb inside, she'll float away and probably drown." Tears lined her cheeks. "She looks like my Jonathan." Priscilla was referring to her stuffed dog, the only store-bought toy she had ever owned.

"But she might survive," Polly said. "One of those men in the dinghy there," she said, pointing at a boat fifty yards away, "might snatch her out of the water." Or, more likely, the wake of one of the ketches or ferries would flood the bucket and sink her. "At the very worst, we shall enable her to survive another minute, or another ten. Unless she swims to shore on her own, without the bucket she has no hope at all. Drop the line, Priscilla. Now."

She did. And less than a minute later, the puppy managed finally to heave herself into the bucket, headfirst. The little crowd of spectators applauded.

"That's ten cents you owe me, miss," the fisherman said to Priscilla the next moment. "That was a brand-new leader of the best silkworm gut."

Priscilla looked forlorn.

"*I* shall pay," Polly said. But the rich old lady interceded and gave the fisherman his dime.

So Polly handed her own coin to Priscilla. "For your father's new beer pail."

She took it, but her spirits did not lift. "I knew," Priscilla said softly to Polly. "Before the girl and her granny came by, in my mind I saw a picture of—I had the feeling of someone sailing away." Polly took her hand.

The old bucket, although yawing precariously, remained afloat, for the wind had subsided. The puppy, occasionally peeking over the side as she licked at the lard and residue of beer, appeared happy enough to be bobbing south and east into the harbor, in the direction of the Atlantic Ocean.

15

April 15, 1848

. . .

Liverpool

*P*RINCES DOCK, ON the north bank of the river Mersey, was built at the swirling, murky border between the waters of the sea and those of the river, at the point where the lively blue-gray of the salt water disappeared into the stinking flat silty chemical flow from Liverpool's bleach factories and lead mills. And lashed to the dock's longest pier, aglow in the smoky Liverpudlian light, lay the new *America*. The low roar from its guts vibrated the keel, dispatching from the waterline manic little waves that wind and water could never produce on their own. All sixteen furnaces were lit and stoked, and both engines were coming up to speed. It was after eleven. At noon the sidewheel would engage with the gears of the engines, sending Cunard's latest out on its maiden voyage, bound for New York.

One of the second-class passengers stood in Bath Street, hands in his trouser pockets, bags on the sidewalk, staring up and smiling like a half-wit at the gleaming, steaming, smoking ship.

It was now a hundred hours since Ben had made his escape from London. And he had begun to doubt himself again. Had it really been the French sergeant who'd chased him into the Thames Tunnel? In the cold light of Liverpool, it seemed incredible, impossible.

After sprinting through the tunnel, Ben had waited until nightfall, then crept back across London Bridge and taken a cab to Isabel and Roger

Warfield's house, figuring that his pursuer might somehow know his own address in Bruton Street. After a breathless explanation, he'd persuaded his sister and brother-in-law that he was being stalked by the soldier who'd murdered Ashby in Paris. He'd rejected their suggestion that they ask Philip to organize an official Foreign Office hunt for the rogue—indeed, he'd pleaded that they not tell his brother or father of this bizarre circumstance, since he was leaving for America anyway and it was therefore moot. Ben feared—he knew—that Philip and Sir Archibald would manage to use the Frenchman's pursuit to embarrass him.

But he had accepted Roger's offer to conscript men from the new detective branch of Scotland Yard to secure his departure from London. And so early the next morning, a pair of special officers had appeared with his bags fetched from the dock, and drove Ben away in a large closed coach with metal bars across its windows and LUNACY COMMISSION painted on the back. At Euston Station the constables had insisted on waiting with him inside his London and North Western Railway carriage—"*explicit* orders from Lunacy Commissioner Warfield, sir"—until the train began rolling in the direction of Liverpool.

During the stop in Birmingham, Ben had watched with interest as a group of lunatics in the next carriage were led by uniformed attendants out to the platform and then into a private asylum that seemed to be part of the railway station. "Isn't that *strange!*" he'd remarked to the passengers around him. "I am not certain if that is civilized or monstrous." The others had only nodded. Ben had been unaware of the awkwardness of the next several minutes, as his carriage mates waited for the attendants to return from the asylum and take this well-dressed and well-spoken but oddly talkative young stranger away as well.

When the train had started moving again, the man beside him breathed a sigh of relief and asked, "Is Liverpool your final destination, then?"

"*No*, sir," Ben had replied more emphatically and cheerfully than necessary. "I am sailing to America."

"Ah. And on which vessel?"

He chuckled. "I am afraid I do not know. I left London strangely, in a terrible hurry." In the view of the people sitting near him, Ben's sanity was once again in question.

In Liverpool, as soon as the ticket agent had informed him that Cunard had established direct steam service to New York, and that the line's newest ship, the RMS *America*, would make the first voyage that very weekend,

Ben had without another word handed over a £20 note for his passage. It seemed God had smiled.

Standing at quayside now, adoring his ship, grinning at its paddle wheel as big as some of the buildings behind him, he found himself thinking of God again—as the *America*'s mammoth steam whistle blew, it sounded like a low, flat chord from the biggest church organ on earth.

The dockside crowds about did not consist mainly of the regular collection of sailors and travelers and longshoremen and drunkards. He was surrounded by families of scrawny children in tattered dresses and trousers shuffling along behind mothers and fathers carrying dirty, ripped, overstuffed canvas bags and searching for a street sign or a relative's face or *any* plausible remedy for their confusion and fatigue. They were immigrants. Two ships had docked this morning at the other end of Princes Dock, pouring several hundred Irish newcomers into Liverpool.

Ben had read about the horrors since the famine began, eyewitness stories that seemed like accounts of medieval or Asian misery, not life today in the United Kingdom just across the Irish Sea. But he had never seen *the starving Irish* so clear and distinct.

A few yards away, one family was standing in the gutter, facing away from him. The parents were barely older than Ben. The father searched his pockets for something—a paper with a name or some instruction, or perhaps the £4 fare for a berth in steerage to America. The mother appeared dazed. One child, maybe seven, was almost bald and had pus oozing from red sores on the scalp. Another, younger boy was shirtless; Ben stared at his bony arms, the skin tight against his ribs, the tiny belly protruding over his gunnycloth pants. A soggy scrap of gray animal hide hung from a younger sister's mouth and flopped against her chin like a newt's tail as she chewed.

The *America*'s whistle bellowed again. It was time for him to go aboard. But just then the fourth and oldest of the Irish children, a fierce-looking black-haired girl in a muslin smock belted to resemble a real dress, turned to look at the ship's stacks and saw the gentleman staring at her family. Ben touched his hat. The girl approached him.

"Is it Mr. Cavanaugh, then?" she asked in a gravelly voice. "Or Mr. Shanley? We're the Kellys, off the *Free Trader*. There's jobs for me mum and dad here in Liverpool, and a passage for myself to the States? *Oona* Kelly."

"No, miss, I'm sorry, I am afraid I am neither Cavanaugh nor Shanley."

She nodded without emotion. Disappointment was her expectation.

Ben smiled. "But while I am also a stranger to this city, I have come to know its streets rather well during the last few days, so perhaps I could help you and your family find . . . whatever place it is . . . ?"

"*No,*" Oona Kelly said. She had been warned back home in Balbriggan about the "runners" and "mancatchers" in Liverpool who appeared as friendly as the serpent in the garden in order to cheat Irish newcomers.

Ben was startled. He knew the Irish could be tetchy, but this was only a girl, maybe thirteen, and he was offering to help. He maintained his smile and reached into his coat. He would give her a few shillings.

"*No,* sir," she said more firmly, and returned to her family, certain that this sharper was attempting to ensnare her family in some slick English fraud.

Defeated in his attempt at charity, he showed his ticket and climbed aboard. Up on the bridge a mate pulled and held the chain once more, and the whistle blasted a third time. Now Ben could feel the sound in his gut. By the time the last suppers were served, with every oil lamp in the cabins and corridors and saloons lit against the darkness, the ship was making its broad starboard turn toward Cape Clear. Nothing but a rocky crumb of Ireland stood between the virginal *America* and America itself.

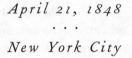
April 21, 1848
* * *
New York City

HIS MUST BE her week's punishment.

Priscilla had learned long ago to expect at least one or two punishments every week, and to accept each without complaint. Argument and tears never reduced the severity, anyhow, and sometimes aggravated it. So she always endeavored to remain quiet.

Last week upon her return home from the picnic on the Battery she had made no plea for mercy, not even a whimper, when her father struck her for disappearing all afternoon, and then slapped her twice more for attempting to pass off the new beer pail as his dear old one.

Then a few days later came the necessary unpleasantness in Dr. Solis's examination room, and the attendant pain.

And now Fatty Freeborn was pounding away at her, soiling her just an hour after her Friday bath at 101 Mercer. Half standing and half crouching, both wrists pinned against grimy bricks and her face pressed into the damp, stinking, suffocating shirtfront between his heaving breasts, she was taking this week's punishment.

"Good Friday, eh?" he had said to her a minute ago as he pulled her by her arm into Amity Alley and put his jackknife to her throat. It was indeed Good Friday. "You think a slut like you, missy, can just do it as she pleases without paying a regular price for the sinning? I'm the one that has to show you the straight truth, make you sacrifice, show what happens when fierce little *cunts* think they're too fine to open up for good b'hoys."

Fatty Freeborn's anger, more than his lust, was red hot today. Last night after work, he had paid for a whore in Mulberry, down in the Five Points. *"What?"* his pal Charlie had exclaimed when Fatty bragged this morning about gaffing a sweetie in Bottle Alley. "You *fucked* Bottle Alley Sally?" The girl, it turned out, was a young man who not only dressed as a convincing woman but had fitted himself with a simulated vagina—a pair of raw pork chops held in place by a raccoon-pelt girdle. The truth of the whore's gender had somehow escaped Fatty in the dark and in his boozy, ruttish condition. Charlie began howling with laughter, and could not wait to tell every man in the firehouse, if not every b'hoy in the ward.

Fatty Freeborn made Priscilla's flesh creep. She supposed he *wished* to make her flesh creep, so now she willed her face smooth and calm—dead— so that it betrayed no wrinkle of disgust.

"You want me to squeeze them nice little dugs of yours, don't you, *slut?*" he said as he pawed and pinched at her nipples with the fat fingers of one hand. She made no noise that he might construe as pain or pleasure. *Look at the good side of things,* Polly Lucking had told her, *whenever there happens to be any good side at all.* The only good side Priscilla could figure just now was her recollection of the four yankums she had given Fatty Freeborn— they had never lasted as long as a minute, so his awful grunting minute here and now must be almost through.

17

April 22, 1848
. . .
New York City

B<small>Y HALF PAST</small> three, when Duff and the other men of 15 Engine arrived in Wooster Street, accompanied by their daguerreian chronicler, Timothy Skaggs, the whole corner was aflame. Nine companies, among them three double-decker machines, were already fighting the blaze. Fire had consumed four buildings as it rampaged down Spring Street. It had also burned toward Prince Street through six buildings, and now threatened a seventh. The eighth, next door, was the house of Engine 11.

After 11's foreman asked Duff to pump Engine 15's stream onto the building just south of the firehouse and "wet it down good," there was some mumbled wisecracking among the boys of 15. The building they were drenching was Mrs. Clara Swan's parlor house, a brothel for gentlemen that also, in neighborly fashion, occasionally invited in small groups of the butchers and plumbers who volunteered at Engine 11. Six young women in evening clothes, two of them crying, stood together on the opposite side of Wooster Street, watching the fire do its work and the firemen do theirs. The prettiest wore a shiny red silk dress and caressed a tabby cat at her bosom. Skaggs set up his tripod to take a picture of the girl in the red dress as she stared past the camera at the fire, engrossed—and then, once he aimed his lens at her, only pretending to be engrossed. In this good sun, her rouged and powdered whore's face would make an excellent picture.

Among the hustling firemen there was the usual quick, excited, confused small talk about which companies were on the scene and which were expected.

And the Old Dutchman was already on the block, preaching as he walked.

" 'I will not *punish* your daughters when they commit *whoredom*,' " he said, " 'nor your *spouses* when they commit *adultery*—for you *yourselves* are separated with *whores*, and sacrifice with *harlots*.' " Duff had heard this reading from the Old Dutchman before. He asked the foreman of Engine 11 to take the coot aside and persuade him to replace the verse with another for the remainder of the afternoon.

This was Duff's favorite sort of fire—neither puny nor a monster, but complicated. It was a dozen fires burning together, an orchestra of flame, each fed by a different fuel—taffeta here, hemp there, molasses here, straw there, spruce and curly maple in the violin maker's here, solvents at the jeweler's workshop there—and the buildings all had different arrangements of doors and windows and interior walls. Each fire burned at its own rate of speed, and each had its own sound and light and smell. He liked this blaze.

I did not light it. Now that Duff had sworn a sacred oath, he found himself pleased to know that God knew he had not started this one. But he found himself worrying that after the papers described it, Bishop Hughes might think he *was* responsible.

"Try the *old* hydrant, Jim," he said to a man searching for more water to pump. "In Prince, round the corner!"

Now he chastised himself for his presumption and hubris: Dagger John Hughes had more important matters on his mind than what a penitent had told him two weeks ago in the darkness of St. Patrick's.

An old Negro suddenly staggered out of one of the burning warehouses and fell to the cobblestones. His ankle appeared to be broken, he was coughing blood, and where his smoldering shirt was half burned away Duff could see patches of charred, bubbled flesh. He asked one of 15's new boys to fetch a doctor from the infirmary in Grand Street.

The kid hesitated and gave Duff a funny look. "For the nigger?"

"Listen," Duff said, "I'm no bleeding heart for Zip Coon, but this one is burned bad, look at him . . ." Ever since he'd discovered that the sugarhouse that burned in Duane Street was a local station on the slaves' Underground Railroad to Canada, Duff had been saying even more extra rosaries in penance. He might have ordered this whippersnapper to get help for a colored man in the past, but now it was one of Duff's necessary works of mercy in the name of Jesus Christ. "*Go*, I mean it, *now*."

The right side of Mrs. Swan's roof had started to billow smoke.

"Crispin! Tommy!" Duff shouted to two men aiming their gooseneck nozzle at the third floor. "Throw it all the way up top, go on, get that wood soppy before she takes fire!"

Bishop Hughes might pay no attention to this blaze, but Duff knew that the local *Protestant* divines would find it irresistible, that in his Easter sermon this very Sunday some preacher would note with angry glee that in this *Holy Week* a well-known *brothel* had burned with *hell's own fire*, proving that this city's own *whores* and *whoremongers* were *not* exempt from the judgment and earthly *punishments* of the Lord. And Duff wondered if that might be true.

" 'For the *wrath* of God,' " the Old Dutchman said as he returned up Wooster, pitching his voice louder now to be heard over the roar and crack of the fire, " 'is revealed from heaven against all ungodliness and unrighteousness of men, who hold the truth in unrighteousness . . .' "

Duff steeled himself. He would not turn and see the ancient face and look into those startling, rheumy blue eyes. He refused.

" 'Being filled with all *unrighteousness. Fornication. Wickedness.*' " The old man took a loping step forward as he pronounced each word.

Skaggs, surprised to find that he remembered the words of Romans after so many years, began reciting in a whisper along with the old man as he lugged the camera across the street. " '*Covetousness. Maliciousness. Envy. Murder. Debate. Deceit. Malignity. Whisperers. Backbiters. Haters of* God . . .' "

The Dutchman passed by the boys of 15 Engine and continued around the block again, his catalogue of torments finally becoming inaudible to Duff, who was examining an inch-long split in the seam of one of his hoses.

" '. . . *spiteful* . . . *proud* . . . *boasters* . . . *inventors of* evil *things*.' "

" 'Inventors of evil things,' " Skaggs repeated in the direction of the old man's back. "I wonder if he is referring to my camera," he said to Duff, now beside him.

"He doesn't mean anything at all," Duff replied. "He's insane."

"Look *there*," one of the tearful young women from Mrs. Swan's shouted as she pointed at a window on the parlor floor. "It's Mr. Polk! He's trapped! He's done for!"

Mr. Polk was Mrs. Swan's other tabby. The cat stood, hind feet on a windowsill in the parlor, scratching furiously at the panes.

Skaggs returned to his ground glass as he prepared to take another picture. How odd that for the second time in as many weeks, circumstances had made him a witness of emergencies involving imperiled pets and their distraught female owners.

"Please," the girl in the red silk dress pleaded with the firemen, "I beg you—save President Polk from the flames!"

If Duff dispatched any of his men to save a cat from a brothel—a cat named after the president—he and the rescuer would become the butt of jokes for weeks, perhaps years. However, he could not ignore the desperate animal or the crying girl. He was a good distance from the flames, but he felt the scar on his cheek burning.

"*Please*, boys?" the girl asked again, looking from fireman to fireman.

Duff turned and saw Tad, his lantern boy. The lad longed to join the fray and fight a fire. And he would recover from any dishonor before he was a grown man.

"Tad," he said, "take an ax and smash the window and chunk that cat out of there. OK?"

Tad did not move. He looked as if he might cry.

"*Go!*"

Even as they unspooled their hose and checked the pipe and put on their double-thick leather gloves, the other men were watching and listening to this encounter between Engine 15's new assistant foreman and the apprentice.

"Duff," the boy whined quietly, "*please*, I, I, you, it's nothing but a *cat*, if it were—"

Duff's posture of command, so sure a moment before, was being resisted. He wanted to beat the boy. Then he wanted to make the sign of the cross. *Forgive me, Father.* "Tad, "he snarled loudly, enunciating each word carefully, "go get that goddamned pussy out of there before it burns!"

Only one of his men guffawed, but another six or seven covered their mouths or suddenly coughed or ran toward the fire to avoid laughing right in Duff Lucking's face.

President Polk was saved, but before the blaze was finally quenched his home was damaged badly. Eleven buildings were gutted in all. Skaggs had exposed five plates—three portraits of Mrs. Swan's girls, a picture of a pile of charred, unfinished violins in the gutter, and another of Tad the lantern boy's dirty, bloody open palms, cut by the glass shards of the window he'd broken to rescue the cat.

"You know, Duff," Skaggs said as more and more of the men slowed their pace, lit up cigars, took off their helmets, and dug out the brandy and whiskey, "I cannot run like you boys. In the future, if I'm going to continue to immortalize the men—"

"Shut up, Skaggs."

"—I shall need to *drive* directly to the sites of these grand catastrophes of yours. A suggestion: *horses*."

This was a sore point among the firefighting fraternity. Only a few companies kept horses to pull their machines—stabling them was expensive, and they were spooked by fire. And Duff grasped the sad, inexorable logic as well: the more that horses pulled engines, the fewer firemen you'd need, and half the firehouses in New York would become obsolete. And once the engines were horse-drawn, the superiority of heavy steam-powered water-pumpers would be inarguable . . . and before long fighting fires would be just another two-dollar-a-day job of work. He knew Skaggs was right about horses. In all other things Duff was an enthusiast for progress. But he knew that this way of life—packs of New York men running out of their private clubhouses and risking their skins for the wild, noble sport of it—was done for. It counted as one more reason to strike out for the West sooner rather than later.

But . . . why had Skaggs put it the way he did? "What in the devil's name do you mean," he snapped, "these catastrophes of *mine?*" As Skaggs only stared at him, startled, Duff realized his mistake. "I'm sorry, I, I was, I have been thinking that horses make good sense as well."

This wasn't entirely a fib. Out west, men *lived* in the saddle.

A small gang from Hose 25 came stomping around the corner from Spring, ostensibly to inspect the damage on Wooster, actually to tease and roister a little bit.

Among them was Fatty Freeborn.

"*Ohhh,*" Fatty shouted from the end of the block, "you lousy little *rats* don't have no *dock* here—do you, boys?" Fatty's men smiled at his lame joke. Number 15 had been called the "dock rats" for years, a nickname from when they sucked water for their hoses straight from the river.

Duff made no reply, not even a grimace. He turned back to his friend. "Say, Skaggs," he asked, "do you know the word 'materialism'? I read it someplace, and my *Webster's* says it's a philosophy, about how there is no soul at all separate from our body and brain—but this magazine article was all about ladies shopping for goblets and paintings. It puzzled me."

" 'Materialism'?" Skaggs gave him a quizzical look. Duff did not appear feverish. "Well, yes, it is a philosophy . . . an extremely sensible ancient Greek philosophy which many respectable people, my father included, consider to be identical with atheism. The idiot writing in your magazine, however, apparently trumped up some stupid new meaning . . ." He stopped. Duff was staring and nodding like an overeager schoolboy. "Are you feeling well, Duff? Do you need to sit down?"

Duff shook his head in a casual, ordinary way. No glance over Skaggs's shoulder or flicker of his eyes indicated that someone was approaching them from behind.

"Hey, Mr. Money Changer," Fatty Freeborn said to Duff, "I've got another bag of pennies saved, and I'm good to let bygones be bygones." He removed his cigar from his mouth to take a swig of whiskey from a tin canteen.

Skaggs turned to look, so Duff could no longer ignore the swine. He did not extend his hand.

"That is," Fatty continued, "as long as you stop jewing me on the trades. From here on out, I'll take your dollar for ninety-*eight* of my pennies."

Duff simply turned back to Skaggs.

"Well, *this*," Skaggs said to Duff with a smile, "exactly this single-minded concern with copper and gold, is, I believe, what your magazine writer meant by 'materialism.' "

"*Saaay what?*" Fatty chuckled. "You're a regular walking, talking encyclopedia, ain't you?" He offered his little canteen. "Care for a taste of the spirits, Professor?"

Skaggs took a polite sip.

"And congratulations, Lucking," Fatty said, "on saving Mrs. Swan's flash-house from burning out completely. You and your boys'll be in line for your *gratuities* from those ladies, huh?" He grinned, then pinched each of his jowls with thumb and forefinger and rapidly pushed and pulled the flesh of both cheeks at once, rhythmically, to produce a squishy noise meant to resemble the sound of fucking. His b'hoys snickered. When he finished, he cackled and punched at Duff's shoulder in a jovial fashion—but Duff grabbed Fatty's wrist hard before he could withdraw it.

"You aim to go at it right here in the street, do you, Lucking? Have our knock-down and drag-out?"

"Hey," Skaggs said, "no, no—no need for a fracas." He had been caught in the middle of street brawls between fire companies before, and during a melee last year had a whole box of exposed plates smashed and ruined. He put his hand on Duff's other shoulder. It was five more seconds before Duff released Fatty's wrist.

"Do not bother that girl again," he said to Freeborn. "Priscilla Christmas. Stay clear of her." His scar stung.

"Why, I never heard her right name before. Thank you, Mr. Lucking. That is, if you and me is talking about the same chicken. From right over here in Mercer Street, the skinny schoolmaid cunt?"

"*Damn* you, Freeborn, keep your rotten ugly ideas in your own mucky head! Miss Christmas is a *friend* of my *sister's*!"

Fatty grinned again. "Uh-*huh*. Yeah. *Riiiiight*." He turned to go.

Skaggs squeezed Duff's shoulder harder, trying to hold him in place.

"Oh," Fatty said, swiveling his head as he remembered something. "Me and one of my bubs, Toby here, happened to see your sister *perform* last month."

Toby giggled. Duff turned away and walked toward his machine and his men.

"On*stage*, you know?" Fatty said a little louder.

Duff was blind with rage. He kept walking.

"At Heilperin's," Fatty shouted, "the art studio in the Bowery! We thought she was prime, Lucking. *Prime!*"

Skaggs shut his eyes, took a deep breath, and shook his head.

Duff Lucking did nothing, did not turn or stop or talk back. But he felt that he was about to explode, as if ten pounds of black powder were packed into his skull in place of brains, and the hot scar on his cheek was a curlicue two-inch fuse. He imagined the wreckage his bomb head would produce as an aerial charge five or six feet above the ground. (The shattered window glass alone! In Mexico there had been next to no glass to shatter.) He imagined the thousands of people for a mile around who would stop what they were doing for a moment and frown and wonder what on earth *that* had been.

POLLY LUCKING WOULD have felt the blast, might have even seen bits of flying debris erupting into the sky. As it was, she had smelled the fire burning. She sat 250 yards away, in the privy behind 101 Mercer, craning her neck to peek out through the vent at the backs of the two buildings in Greene Street that abutted Mrs. Stanhope's. She watched a man lugging ten-gallon canisters into the backyard of the bakery.

The other building, No. 94, was the rich widow Gibbs's old house. The draperies on its tall rear windows were open. Polly had never been able to see inside the house so well. Through the middle window she could see a painting of an old man with long, curly white hair. The portrait, of President John Adams, had been commissioned by Mrs. Gibbs's late husband and painted from life. Polly amused herself admiring the old fellow's likeness to Prosper Skyring. Skyring was currently dressing upstairs in Three South, having just completed his hour of bliss with Polly.

She had pledged that she would finish her association with 101 Mercer and with harlotry in general, but her affection for Mr. Skyring was real, and until she definitely had one of the theatrical parts, she wanted his monthly ten dollars. He was the only man with whom she had faddled for money in weeks and weeks. She conceived that she was now passing through a moderate temperance phase before swearing off commercial lewdness altogether.

As she closed the privy door behind her, she glanced again at the back of the house in Greene Street and saw five Negroes in profile, men and women, country-looking people, standing in the middle of the parlor, as if they were students in a class. How curious. She stopped to watch. But then Mrs. Gibbs appeared at the window and hurriedly reached up to close the draperies. The show was over.

In the kitchen, one of the new girls stood at the sink. Mrs. Stanhope stood over her, holding a water bottle fitted with a tin valve, spraying mist over the girl, who wore a simple, straight, loose gown of nearly translucent white tulle and muslin. The dress was an old one of Mrs. Stanhope's, fashionably "classical" when she'd been young. The dampening enhanced its tendency to cling to the curves of the wearer's body.

As Polly passed through on her way back upstairs, Mrs. Stanhope made her familiar, loud *tsk* sound—Polly had used the outdoor privy, which she preferred in the warmer months. Polly rolled her eyes and Mrs. Stanhope said, "Does little Laura not look positively *dewy* and *sweet?*"

"As delicious as an Easter trifle and pretty as an angel," Polly said.

"An angel! Yes! Exactly!" Mrs. Stanhope patted Laura's back to send her upstairs. "We *must* have a certain conversation before you go, Polly."

They sat in the pantry that had been fitted out as a tiny office. Mrs. Stanhope spoke at length about her multiplying competitors and rising expenses. In addition to the cost of the Croton pipe, there were nickel-a-gallon jugs of water from Poland Spring in Maine that she continued to stock for fashion's sake. And she recounted in great detail the conversation she had had with her landlord, who was proposing to raise her annual rent by 30 percent beginning the first of May. It was customary for houses of bad fame to pay a certain premium. But Mrs. Stanhope had argued that her house was now so well known among the finest gentlemen of New York, and that "101 Mercer" was now such a trusted and desirable name, like Delmonico or Tiffany, that her occupancy had actually *increased* the value of the landlord's real estate. And so did she not deserve some financial consideration for the "upper-ten cachet" she had attached to his building? "You conduct a *brothel*, Mrs. Stanhope," the landlord had said, and she had practically turned on her heel and left the brute, but then she'd remembered Mr. Skaggs's clever notion, and told the landlord that she was an "entertainment broker," no different, really, than Mr. Barnum with his performers.

"In the end," she said to Polly, "I agreed to a rent of five hundred sixty dollars, which necessitates that we generate an additional thirty dollars per week of earnings. I am paying the new doctor more than I paid Madame Restell—and did he not, by the way, cure *Priscilla's* problem at my expense?" A week earlier, Polly had taken Priscilla to Skaggs's friend Dr. Solis for an abortion. "And now that *you* have made such a sudden and extreme reduction in *your* participation in the affairs of the house, Polly, in the interest of teamwork we must take advantage of opportunities as they present themselves. Mustn't we?"

Polly said nothing.

"Priscilla told me only days ago that she *prefers* her hours here to all her hours at home in her slum with her beast of a father."

Priscilla had said much the same thing to Polly. But Polly made no reply as Mrs. Stanhope twattled on.

"And I spoke to a quite impressive young fellow from Palmer's about the spiritualist aspect of the enterprise. He had read about the excitement in Rochester over those sisters and their rappings. He was *very* enthusiastic."

"Palmer's?" Polly asked. "The coal company? Of what relevance is a coal seller's opinion?"

"Palmer's now conduct an 'advertising agency' from their offices as well. They purchase advertisements on behalf of tradespeople. In any newspaper one wishes, or in *all* of the newspapers." Mrs. Stanhope wore a supremely pleased expression. She had discovered a new sector of respectable society in which her business was regarded simply as . . . a business.

Polly could contain herself no longer. "And you intend to pay this 'advertising agency' to place *advertisements* about Priscilla and her powers in the *newspapers*? 'Come one, come all, to experience in person the astounding Magnetic Whore!' "

"*Shhhh.*"

" 'Ten dollars for twenty minutes!' "

Mrs. Stanhope was both crestfallen and disgusted. "Polly, *nooooo.*"

" 'Communicate with your grandfather as you tidder a girl as young as your own granddaughter! Every familiarity available, in the here and now *and* the hereafter!' "

"*Shush* now with your joking, Polly. Nothing vulgar or blatant. Only discreet notices in the papers. The man from Palmer's mentioned *The Flash* and *The Scorpion*, but he said that even the *Sun* and the *Herald* were possibilities. And *we* would pay not a penny for Palmer's services," she added gleefully. "The *newspapers* pay their fee!"

Polly stood. "No, Margaret. I said from the first that Priscilla's arrangement would be limited, involving only Mr. Prime. And now I have decided it is also temporary." She would wait until later to ask Mrs. Stanhope for any of Prime's money that Priscilla was owed, and for Priscilla's velveteen dress from the locker upstairs.

Mrs. Stanhope stood as well. "But, Polly, we are *friends*, are we not? How shall I possibly manage?"

"We must all manage ourselves, Margaret," Polly said, and left the little office without another word. As she put on her gloves and bonnet, she heard from upstairs the canaries' nervous tweets and a familiar plummy southern voice instructing Laura to "be very sure to convey to Miss Bennet Mr. Skyring's dearest, fondest farewell."

"I beg your pardon, sir, Miss . . . *who*?" Polly heard Laura reply to Skyring. The new girl had not been informed of Polly's various aliases. She had never heard of "Elizabeth Bennet," "Catherine Morland," "Emma Woodhouse," "Betsy Bowditch," or "Presence Goodnight." And never would.

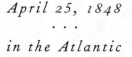

18

April 25, 1848

. . .

in the Atlantic

EN STOOD ON the foredeck looking out at the long, fractured reflection of the moon in the water off the starboard side. The ceaseless steam-powered breeze rustled his hair and the bottom of his coat. The streak of moonlight moved along in the water at exactly ten knots. Up here, one could almost ignore the pitchy odor of coal smoke and the muffled clash and thunder of the engines.

He was alone. It was not yet eleven o'clock, so both bars were open, and most of the hundred saloon passengers were working conscientiously to finish their daily quotas of wine—twenty-one glasses apiece, a ship's officer had told him, including six of champagne. Ben was failing to consume even half his fair share, although the alternative to a perpetual bibulous haze was drinking the fetid water stored in giant iron tanks below deck.

He was happy to be alone. He had finished reading the new Melville novel, *Omoo,* and had repelled two English shipmates when he had informed them that the tale was "more or less a comedy whose hero engages in mutiny." He'd repelled several others one afternoon when he read *Manifest der Kommunistischen Partei* sitting in the sun on the foredeck. Ben's desire for company had been sated after spending his first few nights aboard in the main saloon listening to the same string quartets performed in the same order, listening to the same grumps complain about the constant rumbling and the cheap papier-mâché paintings, playing whist and backgammon with the same several strangers.

And only now, forty-eight hours after their endless and exceptionally boozy Easter dinner, did he feel fully resurrected. Rough weather had struck during the meal. The ship pitched even more violently than during the storm a week earlier, since it had in the meantime burned through a million pounds of coal that had served as ballast.

"Whales-a! *Whales*-a there, *sweeming,* off the *port!*" The voice came from the other side of the bow, ten yards away.

Ben had seen shoals of porpoises swimming alongside and then racing away twice as fast as the fast ship could move. But *whales,* alive, swimming in the open sea? He hurried over to the port side to take a look.

The man who'd called out was a slight Italian of about forty. Some nights earlier they had stood near each other on deck in the darkness, squinting to see the lamps of the Black Ball Line's *United States* as it steamed east on its way to Liverpool. When the *America* had fired twelve Roman candle balls to signal the other ship, the faces of the gawking Cunard passengers were illuminated in the blue light, which made them nervously, gigglingly sociable. Now it was just the two of them, and the Italian was pointing with his left hand and holding a monocle to his right eye with the other.

Ben spotted the three distant forms, like rocky hills on the dark horizon. Whales!

"They appear to be, what, at least five hundred yards away," he said.

"Not black enough for *right* whales, eh?" the Italian replied. "Belugas, maybe, because they white, eh?"

As far as Ben knew, all whales were gray. "They seem to be moving very slowly," he said. "And remaining above the surface for a considerable period of time."

"Is now understand why we can so very easy to *kill* them with the *gaff,* huh?" He made a harpoon-throwing motion with his left arm. The *America* was heading toward the whale pod. "We *pursue* them now, huh? Ha!"

The stranger introduced himself as Mr. Memmo, and the two men stood watching and chatting for another five minutes before Ben realized that the whales were not a few hundred yards off but some miles away, that they were not right whales or belugas or bowheads, and that the vertical outcroppings were not dorsal fins. They were three icebergs, huddled together and slowly, grandly rotating in the vortex of Atlantic currents. They looked in the moonlight like the skyline of a fairyland. Both men stared together

silently for a long time. Around eleven, when the windows of the main saloon were opened to clear it of tobacco smoke, Ben heard the musicians
playing Mozart, the string quartet called *Dissonance*. If opera were like
this—no singing, no libretto, nothing but exquisite playing and magnificent
natural scenery—then he might become a devotee.

The ship came no closer than a half mile, but near enough that Ben and
Memmo could see that each piece of ice was a hundred feet high. Before
they passed completely, a score of fellow passengers had gathered at the bow
for their first and last peep at icebergs.

But soon the Italian was aiming his monocle in a different direction. A
twinkling point of light was straight ahead. They had made landfall. "We
arrive New York in the morning after tomorrow, eh? What a *spanker* we are,
eh?" Across the Atlantic in less than thirteen days would indeed count as a
spanking fast run. Memmo pointed with both hands toward the light, as if he
were introducing Ben to an old friend. "Mr. Knowles? America!"

"Yes, yes indeed." But Ben knew that he remained within the British Empire. He had not yet escaped. "Canada, actually."

"This, sir, I know, of course. New-found-land. The discovery of
Caboto." He bowed his head slightly, as if accepting congratulations. "The
discoverer 'Mr. John Cabot,' before he made himself English, he was Signor
Giovanni Caboto, the citizen of Venice. Like myself, before."

Memmo tucked his monocle into his breast pocket and held out his hand,
which Ben took. The Italian's handshake was more violent than any he had
ever felt, as if he were about to wrestle.

"And I take it that you, sir," Ben asked, "no longer reside in Venice?"

"*No!*" he said, his tone of bemused surprise verging on offense. "I live in
New York City for seven years. American! I make myself American. And
you, Mr. Knowles?"

19

April 27, 1848
. . .
New York City

GIVEN THAT HE had to board the newspapers' steamboat this morning at the inhuman hour of *six,* Skaggs had stayed up all night. He had finished drinking at midnight—"To temperance," he said to himself as he'd clinked his glass against the empty brandy bottle—and switched to an herbal tea of his own concoction, nutmeg and pennyroyal fortified with the tiniest pinch of opium.

Just as the sun rose, he strolled down to the foot of Cortlandt Street. The air really was cleaner at this early hour, as people said. And as much as he enjoyed the ordinary fleshy commotion and clangor of midday and evening, he had to admit the superior beauty of these quiet, nearly empty streets, the unpeopled city gently frosted in immaculate pinks and yellows. At six in the morning, an hour he had rarely experienced since leaving New Hampshire (and until this morning never sober), the stinking, skimble-skamble metropolis was actually sublime. If he could force himself awake and out into the early-morning streets regularly, imagine the photographs he might chance to take.

"I presume this is the SS *Monopoly,*" Skaggs said as he stopped at the little gangway of the *Newsboy.* He was already acquainted with his boat mates from the various papers, including upright young Dickie Shepherd of the *Herald.* Shepherd carried with him a neat list of every passenger ship scheduled to sail to New York from every European and Pacific port since the first of the year, with their respective dates of departure.

As the *Newsboy* steamed slowly and noisily into the river channel, Skaggs watched a sloop loaded with chickens glide across its bow and wondered how many years remained until steam mooted sails and wind entirely. Closer to New Jersey, he saw gulls circle above two oystermen kneeling on the bottom of their boat and raking the invisible bottom mud with their long tongs. In the water, bobbing in the *Newsboy*'s wake, he spotted a rusty tin cup atop a large snarl of string and wondered what had become of the little spaniel Polly and Priscilla had failed to save.

The fellow from the *Express* had stepped to Skaggs's side and caught him staring at the twine. "You know, when Professor Morse and the rest finally lay their submarine cables," he said, "goodbye to old-fashioned harbor journalism, eh, Skaggs?"

"That is true, sir." Skaggs filled his lungs with the cool air. "And do you know what else? Good riddance."

An hour later, as they approached Sandy Hook, they saw four ships anchored behind the long, skinny finger of land, and a fifth out in the open sea. Dickie Shepherd studied the nearby vessels, referred to his list as it fluttered in the wind, then announced that the packet was the *Oscar* from Rotterdam; the famous *Sea Witch*, recognizable by her Chinese dragon figurehead, now about to set off once more around the Horn to Hong Kong; the clipper *Samuel Russell*, arrived from China in twelve weeks—a week longer, Dickie noted, than the record time set last month by the *Sea Witch;* and the steamer, Cunard's new *America*, out of Liverpool only the Saturday before last.

Dickie Shepherd decided he would go aboard the arriving China clipper, while all the others but Skaggs picked the ship that had come from the Continent. The consensus was that the Liverpool steamer would prove useless—filled with two hundred John Bulls who had nothing useful to say about wars in Asia or revolutions in Europe and six hundred tween-decks Irish who had nothing useful to say about anything.

So Skaggs was hoisted onto the Royal Mail Steamship *America* all by himself. He was on the hunt for Europeans, particularly Prussians and Italians, whose regimes had been the latest to fall. Interviews with Britons or returning Americans would likely be a waste of time; therefore, as he scanned the tables in the dining saloon, he immediately eliminated from consideration the passengers speaking English, eating crimped cod, drinking water, or chewing tobacco. An Indian chap wearing a white dress and brimless black cap and gold medal looked interesting, but unpromising for the *Tribune*'s purposes. There was one likely prospect—a middle-aged fellow with a bright blue jacket and a mustache, using a monocle to examine his toast and slice of cold peppered tongue. French? Prussian? Milanese? Certainly foreign, certainly not a Yankee or English.

"Bonjour, monsieur," Skaggs said quickly as he pulled out his pencil and notebook and sat down across from the man, who was plainly not comprehending, "ich schreibe für die New York *Tribüne*—eine Zeitung, un journal, un periódico? Scusi prego—sprechen, parler, comunicare?"

"Hallo," Memmo said, extending his hand, "John Memmo of New York City. Mr. Greeley's paper I read her every day! I subscribe!"

"I see, *fine*, I'm Timothy Skaggs." He would resign that afternoon. He was too old for such foolishness. But since he was aboard and mortified already, he might as well earn his three dollars. "As a member of the *Tribune* clan, sir, perhaps you will help—I could deputize you for the morning."

" 'Deputize'? This word 'deputize' I do not know."

"To assist me, by making introductions to any gentlemen or ladies aboard who might wish to share their personal accounts of the uprisings in Europe."

"I have now the very man for you!" Memmo said to Skaggs, jumping to his feet and scampering toward the door. Ben was just entering the saloon for breakfast. "Mr. *Knowles!*" he shouted in Ben's ear as he grabbed and shook his forearm. "This good newspaperman depends on a conversation with you to collect his necessary intelligence. *Please,* come to join us now for breakfast!"

Skaggs glanced left and right as he stood, noting which nearby diners were most visibly appalled by Mr. Memmo's outburst. The crimped-cod eaters—that is, the English. The young man Memmo had called over, on the other hand, *looked* English but was responding casually, even jauntily. He reminded Skaggs of his brother when Jonah was young, before he had married and become a lawyer and stiffened up.

WHEN BEN FINALLY directed his attention to the face of the man next to Memmo, he was startled, and for the briefest moment stepped forward to greet him as a long-lost pal. He was five or ten years older and two stone heavier, he wore eyeglasses and scruffy tweeds, but otherwise this bearded man was Lloyd Ashby's doppelgänger.

"Mr. Knowles of London, I would like you to know Mr. Skaggs, of New York City. And vice versa, please."

"Please forgive me in advance for waylaying you this morning. I am a paid curioso. How do you do, Mr. Knowles?"

The hard twang of a real American! Uttering a real American *how do you do*! Yet from that improbable face. "Good morning, sir," Ben finally managed to say.

"Have we been introduced before?" asked Skaggs. "I was a week in London a year ago, and perhaps—"

"No, sir, I do not believe we have been, I—forgive my groggy state." Ben motioned both men to sit and took the seat next to Skaggs.

"What information of any use at all to you, sir," Ben asked Skaggs, "might I possibly have?"

Memmo explained to Skaggs that Ben had been in Paris "upon a business trip, as *l'entrepreneur*" during February's revolution, saw the fighting break out "with both his own two eyes," that his "dear and oldest friend" was shot dead, and that he had been stalked around Paris and then even to London by "a dog-mad French sorehead." And then Ben retold the tale himself, in detail, which Skaggs scribbled down between sips of coffee, since he knew— well-to-do Englishman, acquaintance of revolutionists (make it "an intimate of"), eyewitness to history, tragic young death of an artist, et cetera—it would suit Greeley and the *Tribune* perfectly.

Ben made Skaggs laugh with his descriptions of the stuffed penguin and the girl with the bomb. Skaggs made Ben smile when he asked if his father's firm "was Knowles, Miter, Newcastle & Shafflebottom," and made him chuckle when he explained that he had read about the firm in the newspaper when "they became hooked up with Prime, Ward & King of this city in the Chinese opium and Peruvian bird-dung businesses."

A half hour later, Skaggs was nearly finished.

"May I know your given names, Mr. Knowles, for my little article?"

Ben took a breath. "I am Benjamin Motley Mactier Knowles."

Skaggs wrote, then suddenly looked up. "Motley . . . Are you therefore, perhaps, kin of the wife of America's second favorite Frenchman?"

"I beg your pardon?"

"No need to beg my pardon, sir," Skaggs replied. "I was asking if one of your Motley relatives—so to speak—is married to the Count de Tocqueville."

Ben was heart-struck with surprise. How could this random, smiling American stranger know of his relatives? His mind groped for an explanation. Was Skaggs a deceiver of some kind, a thief who had ransacked his cabin and found the letter from Tocqueville? But *why*? Or perhaps he was a hireling of his father's, engaged from London by Sir Archibald to spy on Ben in America? Or, worse, an ally of the French sergeant's . . . who bore some grudge against Tocqueville . . . ? *No*. Ridiculous.

"I apologize, sir," Skaggs said, "if I have unsettled you with my question. It was intrusive of me to inquire. It was, I am afraid, as you shall discover, quite American of me."

Ben took a breath. "My cousin Mary Motley is indeed married to the Count de Tocqueville. But how did you *possibly* know that?"

"I am blessed and cursed with a knack for recalling stray and trivial facts. Some years ago I wrote a review of the books of your cousin-in-law (the very great books, may I say) and in the course of my research discovered that the count had—and let me apologize for *this* in advance—discomforted his family by marrying an English commoner called Miss Motley. The rest of it, connecting you to her, was my lucky guess."

"Congratulations, sir. And may I ask you—which Frenchman ranks *first* in the affections of your countrymen?"

"The savior of our revolution, of course, General Lafayette—or, if you please, the Marquis de La Fayette." Skaggs returned to his notes. "And finally, sir, may I ask your business in this country?"

"No business at all, apart from . . . adventuring, I suppose."

"I shall describe you as, quote, 'a refugee former London merchant banker and cosmopolite of independent means.' "

Ben snorted and returned Skaggs's smile, pleased as could be by this American's jolly familiarity. He enjoyed the idea that he was a refugee.

"Well, I must write *something*—'traveler'? Or 'immigrant'?"

Ben thought for a moment. "Perhaps both. Probational immigrant. Permanent traveler, possibly. You may say I am embarked on an *expedition*, but one with no particular goal as yet."

"How very mysterious and gnomical you are, sir." Skaggs closed his notebook. "Particularly, if I may be impertinent, for a person of your race."

Ben laughed out loud. The man joked like Ashby as well.

And if Skaggs was not already fond of Ben, that laugh confirmed the bond.

"*Ha!*" Memmo interjected.

They chatted a little more, and Skaggs mentioned that Astor's recent death was "giving our local celebrations of this Springtime of the Peoples their own special mirth and sense of progress."

"Astor," Memmo noted, "he was the *immigrant*, like Mr. Knowles and yours truly."

"Are you joking with us?" Ben asked Skaggs. "Are Americans truly taking a close interest in the European uprisings?"

"Why do you suppose I'm sitting here on behalf of the *New York Tribune*, begging to serve as your amanuensis, sir? Why is the *Herald* paying for steamship shipments of *La Presse* from Paris? We are *avidly* curious here—cracked with pleasure over the disgrace of foreign kings and princes. It proves the point of America, does it not, of our own grandfathers' rebellion against George III? It feeds our great conceit concerning our own special greatness."

Memmo was nodding. "America is *best*, you will surely come to agree, Mr. Knowles."

I do agree, Ben thought, *and I have not yet set foot there.*

"Come to think of it," Skaggs said, "there would be a tidy income for you on this account, in this country, if you could bear it. Not that you require . . . money."

"An income?" Ben and Memmo asked at once.

"Yes indeed, by means of the lecture racket. You can speak to audiences here about the revolutions there . . . eyewitness to the dramatic and violent events themselves . . . expert on the forthcoming, well, *Americanization* of free republican Europe, and so forth."

Memmo was excited by such an idea. "And he is paid how many dollars to make his speech?"

From outside came the sound of very loud, watery gurgling and convulsive mechanical bleats.

"Good God, man, I know people, not remotely celebrated or accomplished people—former drunkards, newspaper hacks who exchanged a few words with General Scott on his way to Vera Cruz . . . Transcendentalists . . . mesmerists . . . in one instance, actually, a combination of all four of those—these sharpers are paid fifty dollars for a lecture, the lucky fools."

"*Eleven* pounds nine shillings!" Memmo calculated for Ben's benefit. "For a *speech* only? *Incredible!* America!"

"And there are some at the top rank," Skaggs continued, "who earn one hundred and two hundred dollars a night."

"I appreciate your good thoughts on my behalf, sir," Ben said to Skaggs, "but I am no expert. As I say, I was present in France for only two days, and for a good part of that time I was asleep."

"Ah, but you had the good luck to *be* in Paris, and to be there during the *crucial* days! You participated in the very beginning of the revolution and witnessed its triumph! You may be imperfectly learned in the politics, but—"

"Entirely ignorant."

"—but you have a *ripping good tale* to tell, sir. Americans demand nothing more than that. And nothing less."

"Two hundred dollars," Memmo said, nearly giggling, "to *speak!*"

The *America*'s steam whistle finished clearing the water from its pipes and finally blew a long, honking blast. The pilot had come aboard, and was ready to steer its two thousand tons into the harbor, through the bay, up the river, and into its pier. Before the whistle ended, Memmo had started vocalizing the note loudly.

Skaggs applauded. "Excellent—Duet in C-flat for Alien and Steam Engine," he said. "And you should know that I am a former professional reviewer."

"*B*-flat!" Memmo corrected. And then: "I am no alien, by your way. A citizen, naturalized since before last year. I am your *fellow* American."

Skaggs stood and handed Ben a strip of paper from his notebook. On it he had scribbled his full name—*Timothy Bailey Skaggs*—and his addresses at home and the studio. "My card, if you please. When I am not engaged in one or another vice or folly, you may find me in those places."

"You are most kind, Mr. Skaggs. I am fortunate to have met you this morning."

"The good fortune and lucky timing are all mine. May I ask where you will reside in New York?"

"Until I get my bearings, I shall be at the Astor House."

"I shall forgive you that, since the owner is now dead."

"Are you not landing in New York along with us?" Ben asked.

"I regret to inform you that *you* shall be putting into port elsewhere."

"Quarantine, is it?" Ben asked.

"New Jersey," Memmo said.

"The medical inspectors will undoubtedly permit a non-Hibernian gentleman such as you to escape the detour to Staten Island"—the immigrants' quarantine hospital—"but Cunard has built his docks across the river, in Jersey City. My employer's foul little boat is scheduled to snatch me off this vessel at half past eight."

From some distance away, the *Newsboy*'s nasal steam whistle sounded twice.

"Speak of the devil," Skaggs said. "Mr. Benjamin Motley Mactier Knowles, welcome to the United States of America."

Part

TWO

20

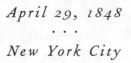

April 29, 1848

· · ·

New York City

*E*VEN IF HE had not had his rash cupid's moment on his first night in the United States—imagining that he had fallen in love with a stranger across a public dining room—Ben Knowles would have spent his first hundred American hours in a permanently roused state, wandering and looking and listening. He walked up and down and back and forth through New York, miles and miles.

All day every day, most of the city was as noisy and bright as the West End on a Saturday night. As nearly as Ben could tell, no quiet quarter existed south of Fourteenth Street. Practically every shop stayed open for business past six, and even some respectable-looking places did business at *midnight*. The taverns and bowling saloons seemed never to close.

American buildings were as bright and wide-eyed as the people, every façade filled with as many windows as it could contain. What's more, glaziers walked the streets everywhere, crying, in German accents, "*Glaꝫ* put in, *glaꝫ* put in, *glaꝫ* put in."

A few days had fully confirmed the London caricatures of tobacco-loving Americans chewing and spitting, chewing and spitting, in every place and circumstance, heedless. He bought a cake, bit off a tiny piece to chew, and spat it out after a few horrid seconds.

The riot of advertising was not, as it turned out, a peculiarity of the wharves. The city was painted and plastered with words and words and more words in a hundred different fonts. The bombast was ubiquitous. Broadsides as big as the biggest newspaper sheets covered walls and fences, and on some busy streets the sandwich-board men outnumbered the ordinary pedestrians. As an experiment, walking up Broadway his first time, he had accepted every handbill and trade card thrust at him. At the end of twenty minutes, the stack of paper and pasteboard was thick as a book.

Although in unfamiliar cities he had a knack for losing his way, he found himself unable to become lost in New York. He had known, of course, that the city was on an island and growing straight up, like a trained shrub in a hothouse box. And he knew that it organized itself nowadays according to a strict grid. But during his first full day on land, as he roamed north, he was astounded to discover that after a couple of miles, apart from Broadway and the Bowery and Madison Avenue, New York abandoned street names altogether, in favor of numbers—not merely the Fourth Avenue, the Fifth Avenue and the Sixth Avenue, but First Street, Second Street, Third Street, Fourth Street, Fifth Street . . . and evidently on and on, up into the suburbs, the exurbs, namelessly toward infinity. It was like a *Punch* lampoon, the American worship of the efficient and practical extended to the point of absurdity. But after a little while his reflexive English sniffiness passed—Eleventh Street, Twelfth Street, Thirteenth Street—and he began to relish the plain audacity of the system. It was the famous American confidence and directness. If civilization was sprawling forward in a particular direction, *presume* that it would never stop, *let* the empty land ahead of settlement be plotted and stamped by the simple rules. Abandon the arbitrary and sentimental residue of history—of Church streets and Market streets and the rest; history be damned. Numbered streets would permit the blank slate of this new city and new land to remain fundamentally blank as a blackboard, even as the lines—Twenty-third, Twenty-fourth, Twenty-fifth—were filled by the quick provisional scrawls of people and buildings and lives.

As he came to what appeared to be the northern edge of the city—Thirty-first, Thirty-second, Thirty-third—he saw a great stone building looming ahead. Was it the national bank? It had no windows. A cathedral? There was no spire. Some old fortress against the Indians? The Dutch had shoved the last of them away into the northern woods two hundred years earlier. At Thirty-seventh Street he realized that it was, of all ridiculous things, a brand-new Egyptian temple. And when he reached Fortieth Street he saw it was something more bizarre still: the Croton Distributing Reservoir, a rectangular water tank bigger and deeper than any he had ever seen or imagined, a lake constructed aboveground with granite walls as high and thick as a row of houses and a perimeter hundreds of yards long. It was filled with 20 million gallons, a man told him, pumped underground into the city from *fifty miles away.*

He climbed the steps and found a promenade at the top, and joined the people, scores of them, strolling along the granite walks and surveying the city. Along the western precipice he stopped to gaze at the North River, as the Hudson was called where it flowed past Manhattan. At this latitude it was not quite so jammed with boats and ships. When he finally turned to leave he found himself looking at the back of an organ-grinder, and into the face of a tiny monkey on the grinder's shoulder. The monkey was still. Ben grinned at it and it slowly shook its head, looking away from Ben only when its master turned the crank of the grinder and began playing "Yankee Doodle." How Sir Archie would revel in reviling this moment: a monkey dancing to a clinking machine rendition of the great patriotic American tune.

A HALF HOUR later he was in an office at the address in Fourteenth Street he had been given by one of the clerks at the hotel that morning. When he announced his business, the real estate broker, a Mr. Magoffin, smiled and lunged toward him as if they were brothers, then grabbed and shook his hand as if it were a stubborn pump handle.

"OK then!" Mr. Magoffin said.

"I beg your pardon?" Ben had never heard or read "OK."

Instead of explaining himself, Mr. Magoffin ("Call me *Jim*") began rapidly reciting the particulars of a dozen apartments available to let— "quaint but clean," "absolutely apple-pie order with gas *and* water piped," "in the stretch of the Fourth Avenue where many young professional men reside," "in MacDougal Street, adjacent to the black-and-tan zone, but inexpensive." Within fifteen minutes, Ben had signed a lease, and the exceedingly jovial stranger had taken several of Ben's American banknotes as advance payment on the rent for his $180-per-year rooms in Sullivan Street.

When Mr. Magoffin—"*No*, Ben, I implore you, it's *Jim*"—suddenly turned away and opened a book, then glanced repeatedly back and forth between the money and the pages he turned, Ben asked what he was doing.

He lifted the book up to show its binding. "Need to see if your bills are in Bicknell," he said cheerfully. The title was *Bicknell's Counterfeit Detector and Bank Note List.*

Ben had heard his father tell and retell the story of how he had made his first true fortune in 1837 "owing to the childlike and very nearly insane financial recklessness of your heroes the Americans." So Ben more or less understood the basic quirk of the U.S. monetary system—that paper money was printed and issued not by a central government bank, but in thousands of different colors and sizes by hundreds of different private banks in every state of the union. Faced with the real thing now, he was agog. He thought Magoffin might be one of the confidence men Memmo had warned him about.

"Do you mean, sir," Ben asked, "that you must determine the authenticity of each and every piece of money you receive against that . . . entire . . . listing?"

Magoffin had found a description of Ben's ten-dollar note that satisfied him, and he shut the book. He smiled and shrugged and winked all at once. "Eternal vigilance is the price of freedom! Our wildcat USA, don't you know!" He paused for a moment, then for the first time turned a little solemn. "May I ask you, Ben, for your frank impression so far of our great nation and city?"

"They have exceeded my most extravagant expectations." He thought of Tocqueville's unhappy feeling that the French had staged a *play* about radicals' overthrow of a king, rather than conducting an actual revolution. But for Ben in America the comparable sensation was in no way dispiriting. "It seems almost," he said to Magoffin, "as if you and all your countrymen are staging a wonderful pageant for my benefit *about* America."

Magoffin did not know quite what he meant, but he laughed enthusiastically, slapped Ben on the back, and instructed him to appear no later than noon with all his belongings ready to occupy 171 Sullivan.

"But it's well past noon already," Ben said.

Magoffin hooted. "Noon on *Moving* Day—Monday. Day after tomorrow. Monday's the *first*, don't you know!"

"Ah."

"So it's just blind luck, is it, then, that you've come to me *now, today*? In the nick of time? You are one lucky Englishman, sir," he said, suddenly rubbing Ben hard on his shoulder with his fingers as if he were scrubbing a stain. "Give *me* some of that luck of yours!"

By city law, Magoffin explained, no lease could last longer than twelve months, and every lease expired on the same date each year. And Moving Day was more correctly Moving *Morning*, since the law required that every tenant vacate his rented apartment or house by 9:00 A.M. on May 1, and take up residence in his new quarters by noon the same day.

Once again, Ben wondered if he was listening to the fictions of a confidence man or prankster.

London

GABRIEL DRUMONT HAD endured worse conditions as a soldier. But his weeks sleeping on Baptiste's kitchen floor on Guernsey now seemed like a vacation compared with his weeks living among the enemy in their grim, graceless capital. He had spent two days in their jail after the two English municipal guardsmen—the awful irony of it!—had grabbed him at the river tunnel and allowed the fugitive Knowles to escape justice once again.

Their threats to deport him had ended when their superior officer had seen that he was no vagabond but a man of some means—he was welcome to spend his three hundred francs in Great Britain.

The shack he rented behind the cottage of a Huguenot silk weaver in Pleasant Place was cold and shabby but hardly worse than barracks life. A bed was a bed, a pisspot a pisspot. And while these London French seemed half British—their talk a mess of French and English words, without the excuse of the Guernésiais—they did eat real sauce and loaves of real bread. And if they drank beer and gin, that was a result of persecution: the British government taxed wine from the motherland so onerously that the Frenchmen here could not afford to buy it. At least as long as he remained in the French streets of Spitalfields, he could understand and make himself understood.

And Knowles was here in London. He had seen him. He was close.

But Drumont despised the city nevertheless. He wanted to damage someone. He wasn't a murderer. Yet he needed to execute those responsible for sweet Michel's death. Tears filled his eyes, still, when he thought of Michel, which meant he cried more than once a day.

He shared the truth about his mission with no one. He told these French Protestants only that his dear younger brother had been shot dead in a street in the ninth on the first night of the revolution. He was spending the spring in London, he said, because he was too distraught to remain in Paris just now. Let these strangers believe that Michel had been an insurgent. Let them believe that Gabriel Drumont was a weakling on holiday from his anguish.

He had no training as an investigator, but he had once engaged in conversation with Eugène-François Vidocq himself at Monsieur Vidocq's private detective agency on the Galerie Vivienne, No. 13, the famous Bureau des Renseignements. Vidocq was a hero. Indeed, one of the few books Drumont had ever finished was the old man's *Mémoires*, a mammoth chronicle of his criminal youth and redemption as the original and ultimate police detective. From the night Michel was killed, he had asked himself more than once: *What would Inspector Vidocq do* now?

Drumont had arrived knowing only two useful facts about the criminal Knowles—his surname and his democratic sympathies. The fact that the Jacobinical little bastard had been there among the crowd on the riverbank the day he arrived in London—a crowd, he learned later, that had consisted of English socialists returning from their demonstration—confirmed for Drumont that Knowles was indeed a revolutionist, that he had been a confederate of the bomb-thrower Marie Brasseaux that night in Paris, a foreign agitator.

This afternoon Drumont had found a gun shop called Rivière where a man spoke French. He spent fifty-five francs on a small American revolver—.31 caliber, less than a kilo, what the clerk called a "Baby Dragoon."

Seeing Knowles that first day had been so lucky, so tantalizing, so exasperating. In the last three weeks, he had visited dozens of socialist outposts all over London, lecture rooms and clubhouses and publication offices and taverns, posing day after day as "a man of the Paris streets" in search of his "missing February comrade Mr. Knowles." And he had found nothing, no new clues.

Some days he wandered the streets aimlessly, looking at each passing face, thinking he might see Knowles. This was not what Inspector Vidocq would do. The trail was cold.

Despite living meagerly, he was running through his money. One afternoon in Spitalfields, as he'd paused in front of the place in Fashion Street where they gave away free food to the Jewish poor, an attendant had mistaken him for a Jew. He'd wanted to throttle her, but he'd only smiled; he thought he might need their free soup and bread and figs before he was through.

Most evenings he passed an hour or two in a French newsroom reading the imported papers to keep abreast of the insanity in Paris, and to search for any story about the killing of a certain Mademoiselle Brasseaux in the Latin

Quarter. He also read every article about other Frenchmen driven out of France, like the one tonight in *Le Figaro* that mentioned an industrialist and inventor called Thimonnier who escaped across the Channel with a new sewing machine and was now doing business in London with an English bank in King William Street. Drumont wondered if one of these rich French refugees in London might find a way to give a fellow exile some respectable job temporarily.

How was he to live? Even after he had avenged his brother, he could not return home, where the regime of radicals and fools would call him a murderer. But as a man of France who spoke the English of an infant, what work could he get in England? A job as a common laborer? Impossible. He had not invested years in the army and the Garde Municipale, honing his skills as a paladin and warrior, in order to slip back down into the common muck now. He had spent a quarter century feeling superior to his Corsican boyhood pals who earned their livings cutting stone and sawing wood or stealing. He had taken Marie Brasseaux's brooch, yes, but he was not a thief. He was an officer of the higher law, bound to mete out justice on behalf of Michel and of France.

21

May 1, 1848
. . .
New York City

O N MONDAY THE first Ben arose before the sun and decided to use his extra hours to shop for groceries and supplies to furnish his new home. Sure enough, as his cab took him west toward the river, he saw families in every block already making ready to leave their old houses and tenements, boys and men lifting chairs and mattresses into the backs of wagons, women and girls lugging clothes and carpets and open crates packed with lamps and pots and books.

The Washington Market covered all the riverfront blocks north of his ferry landing. It was like Covent Garden but much bigger and more comprehensive, overflowing with stalls and the stalls overflowing with every sort of meat and fish and green and grain for sale, as well as cakes and butter, coffees and teas and spices. He figured there must be fifty oystermongers alone, and a hundred butchers.

In his twenty-six years, Ben had bought only the odd apple or handful of flowers in Drury Lane, or cherries and cake from a cart in the Markt in Bonn; he had never shopped for groceries, not once filled a basket with meats and vegetables to make a proper meal. He bought a canvas bag and started wandering, asking for some of everything that looked good, without any menu in mind—a two-foot-long loaf of bread, Spanish oranges, a Bahamian pineapple, a bunch of Cuban bananas, peaches from South Carolina, two Quebec cheeses, half a small German ham, a pound of peas, three pounds of huge bright red American apples, and two whips of Italian sausage. His bag was already heavy, and he had not yet bought a pan or a pot or a knife or spoon, so he resisted the impulse to get a watermelon, which he had never seen before. He stared for a full minute at a pile of green lobsters from Maine—hideous monsters, still living, all engaged in a constant futile clawing dance.

Outside, he found his cab waiting in Fulton Street, still parked next to a public hydrant gushing water into the gutter. Ben wondered how many hundreds of gallons were being wasted. When he had asked the driver if the stopcock was broken, the man had shrugged and said, "It never runs out."

The driver jerked the reins, said "Yo, *get*" to his nag, and rolled up Washington Street. "You're an Englishman, are you, sir?"

"I am."

"Fresh in?"

"I beg your . . . *What?*"

"You just arrived here?"

"Yes."

"Tired of old England, eh?"

"Yes. Exactly true. I had grown very tired of it indeed."

The driver nodded.

"You don't have to be telling me how great you consider America," the fellow said.

"I beg your pardon?"

"No need to beg anything here. But I know a lot of our natives squeeze every foreign visitor to say how much better and freer and finer and richer this country is than other countries."

"So I have been told. Are you, sir, one of those dissidents who do *not* consider this nation the finest on earth?"

The driver turned back again to look at Ben, to see if he was joshing or losing his mind.

"I only think it's sad and girlish if *I* need for *you* to tell me so. I know it already. If America weren't better 'an all the other places, what does every foreigner want to turn himself *into* an American for?"

"Your argument has merit, sir," Ben said.

"But we don't have to *brag* about it all the time, do we?"

Before long they turned east from the river and found themselves entering the heart of Moving Day. The system Mr. Magoffin had explained on Saturday sounded insane. "It is like a celebration with damned little gaiety," he had said, "a holiday on which New Yorkers labor *more* feverishly, not less."

Presently the carriage was stopped on a block of Provost Street. A big coach, a carriage, and two cabs—and their six horses—were all jammed in tight behind them. Directly ahead was a wagon sitting crosswise in the street, blocking traffic. It contained a mountain of furniture covered by a canvas cloth lashed down with ropes. Men were being offered a half-dollar apiece to unload the wagon and pull it onto the sidewalk so that its broken front axle might be replaced. The wife of the owner of the pile wailed at her husband, with tears trickling down her cheeks, as he shouted in turn at the driver who had allowed his axle to snap. A small boy picked up moist nuggets of horse dung from the street and carried them carefully, like eggs, one at a time in each hand, to the house his family was leaving, and placed them in a neat line along the doorsill.

A celebration with precious little gaiety indeed—like ten thousand tiny simultaneous riots all over the city. When Ben's carriage finally passed through the jammed block and turned up West Broadway, he got a glimpse of the whole helter-skelter panorama as it stretched north, like a painting by one of the Brueghels. A hundred overladen coaches and carriages and wagons and vans and carts raced in every direction, blocking intersections, while a thousand people carried burlap bags and boxes, some of them trotting or running. Even the horses and dogs jerked and brayed as if they had been infected with the Moving Day anxiety.

As Timothy Skaggs walked down West Broadway toward the *Tribune*, he did not spot his English acquaintance in one of the carriages passing in the opposite direction. He carried with him his latest article about the revolutions, in which he'd mingled the accounts of several arriving travelers with whom he had spoken during the last few days—a woman visiting from Munich, a Canadian couple returning from Naples, and the Englishman, Knowles. Until he'd stepped out the door of his building, he had forgotten all about Moving Day.

He decided to walk east on the quieter streets down to Nassau. He stared fondly at the ancient New York Hospital, the untended trees and stone pesthouses beautiful now in their abandonment. He paid no attention to the brand-new factory and warehouse going up across the street, nor to the bustle of carpenters and plasterers wandering in and out of its cast-iron front.

. . .

UPSTAIRS, ON THE empty top floor, stood Duff Lucking. He had been there three hours already, cutting and crimping gas pipes and installing jets. He was taking a break, eating a cinnamon bun and sipping apple juice from his canteen, staring out one of the windows down at crowded Broadway.

Duff was envious of all the people moving, particularly the families. He lived in a boardinghouse, and over the winter had considered finding a proper apartment to rent. The low cost and regular meals and proximity to the firehouse were the reasons he gave for his decision to stay put, but he knew, looking down at the hundreds of people rushing to their new homes, that the choice to remain temporarily was really an admission that he had decided to leave New York for good.

More and more veterans of the war would be drifting into the city. There were too many fires, and too many temptations of every kind. Life had become too complicated. He knew he had no choice but to take off. He was saddened, however, by the idea of forsaking the pleasures of civilized life, by which he meant Timothy Skaggs, and at the prospect of abandoning his sister, whom he loved more than—

A monarch! The first of the season, fluttering and hovering inches from his face, just beyond the windowpane, a sentinel come to warn him or lead him to safety. *¡Bienvenidos, mariposa!* Duff was pleased he remembered the word for butterfly. *¡Hola, amigo!* Until that cool morning in Mexico, wandering through the pine grove, he had never thought about butterflies.

As soon as he'd returned home last fall, he'd begged Skaggs to take him to the Society Library. And what he discovered was a kind of mystery and grace and miracle of faith as wondrous as anything in the Bible. Each spring, the monarchs left their winter roost in Mexico, at the Nevado de Toluca, and flew across the Rio Grande and the Territories to meadows and woods in Michigan and the Carolinas and New York that they had never seen or smelled . . . and then, at the end of the summer, their descendants flew the same thousands of miles in reverse, returning south—incredibly, inexplicably—to the very Mexican mountains from which their grandparents had flown the previous spring. Of the 165,000 species of butterflies and moths, Duff had read, only *Danaus plexippus,* the monarch, undertook a journey of such ambition. The question that perplexed him still was whether God had created them on the fifth or sixth day of Creation—that is, did they appear first as butterflies flying across the face of the firmament of the heavens, or as caterpillars creeping on the earth?

And now the lone, jaunty Manhattan monarch left him—*¡Adiós, mariposa! Buena suerte!*—not diving lower or climbing higher but flying straight off in Duff's sight line. His gaze followed it into the westerly blue sky until it disappeared. For an infinitesimal fraction of the next moment, as his eyes swept back across acres of city to the pine-and-plaster-scented room where he stood, his sister—that is, his sister's Broadway omnibus— was in his purview.

POLLY WAS EN ROUTE to the Greenwich Theatre to inform the manager that he would need to replace her as Queen Gertrude for the last week of the run, when she had to begin rehearsals for *Dombey*. She looked out the window of the bus and spotted a young woman whose name she could not recall, a page-folder at Harper Brothers who had worked every night at 101 Mercer for ten days last fall—as an "experiment," she had told Mrs. Stanhope, and a means to buy Christmas gifts for her family in Connecticut. She was on the sidewalk walking slowly south, carrying two enormous carpet-cloth bags, one of the Moving Day multitude. Polly had renewed her lease for her two bright rooms on Third Street near Washington Square. But she thought now. *I am moving, leaving behind 101 Mercer and my own eighteen-month experiment in whoredom, moving securely into the profession*—she glanced down yet again at her name on the folded *Hamlet* playbill—*the profession for which I am suited and even (dare I say it?) destined.* She wondered whether the Connecticut girl was relocating to better or worse rooms—whether she was returning to the higher-paying work at 101 Mercer or had been sacked from her publishing job and needed a cheaper place . . .

The theater was now only a block ahead. She reached and pulled the leather signal strap. As her fingers searched inside the silk of her coin purse for the fare, the bus driver reined his team.

London

PERHAPS IF HE had been more forthcoming with the local Huguenots about his true business in London, if he had not worried so much about keeping his quest a secret, he would have been guided straightaway to the directory. He would have saved himself fruitless weeks of walking and riding and searching. But no matter. The secrecy was important. It was what Inspector Vidocq would do. And the weeks of failure had improved Drumont, made him a more careful watcher and listener, and taught him humility and patience and some rudimentary ability in the gawky, tight-jawed language of the English.

In any case, success was now his. The other evening at the newsroom in Old Bethnal Green Road, he happened to see the proprietor consulting a big tattered book as he addressed correspondence. It was the London Post Office Directory, Drumont learned, and he had spent the next two hours copying out a list of the names and addresses of forty-four Knowleses living in the city.

Drumont posed as a Parisian cabinetmaker come to London to collect a bill his workshop was owed. He even forged an invoice for 1,100 francs made out to "Mr. Knowles, London," which he would show at every doorstep. During his first four days, he spoke to a Mr. Humphrey Knowles, a Mr. Garrick Knowles, a Mr. Fernando Knowles, and fourteen other Mr. Knowleses or their wives or children or landlords or servants.

And on Friday, the morning of the fifth day of his census, he knocked on the red door of a small house in Bruton Street, No. 24, according to the directory the residence of a Mr. Benjamin Knowles. The carpenter who answered the door said that young Mr. Knowles no longer lived there, and his fancy old man no longer owned the house besides. But he dug out for Drumont a card with Sir Archibald Knowles's office address printed on it—17 King William Street. And as he walked off, Drumont *remembered*, in a glorious burst of Vidocqian deduction: the French sewing machine manufacturer he had read about in *Le Figaro*, Thimonnier, was associated with a London financial firm *in King William Street* . . . A Frenchman exiled by the February Revolution to King William Street; a young Englishman named Knowles in Paris during the revolution; a rich old Englishman named Knowles in King William Street—these connections did not strike Gabriel Drumont as accidental.

Sir Archibald would return from shooting the following week, Drumont learned from his talkative confidential secretary at the office in King William Street, when an audience might be arranged, but young *Mr.* Knowles had indeed visited Paris during the February disturbances, and had the most awful adventures there . . .

And so as Drumont talked haltingly with the secretary, aided after a while by a Monsieur Cecil Shufflebotham who spoke French badly, he altered his masquerade, posing no longer as a tradesman collecting a debt but as an officer of the Sûreté investigating the senseless murder of a young woman in Paris who was reported to have been . . . *quite friendly* with the young Monsieur Knowles before she was killed. The two Englishmen told Drumont they were certain that Mr. Benjamin Knowles would wish to assist the police inquiry in any way he could, but that he would need to do so by transatlantic post, since he had sailed for New York a month ago . . . perhaps, Shufflebotham suggested, Drumont might wish to write to Knowles *fils* in care of their associated New York firm of Prime, Ward & King?

The secretary wrote down the particulars and, as Drumont prepared to leave, Shufflebotham asked if the authorities in France had made any headway in finding "le cadavre absent de Monsieur Lloyd Ashby." Drumont had no idea who or what on earth he was asking about. A corpse? What would Inspector Vidocq do *now?* Drumont thought it best to shrug and refer, vaguely but sympathetically, to "les affaires confidentielles de la police." Which seemed to satisfy the English idiot completely.

22

May 7, 1848
. . .
New York City

*N*OT SINCE HIS university days had Ben been deprived of entirely private hygiene. And he did not, to be honest, enjoy this aspect of his new democratic life. Although a girl came around each morning to empty the chamber pot and bring water for the sink, all three sets of tenants (eleven people in all, including four children and a servant) shared one necessary in the rear garden, which the adults called "the backhouse" and the children "the gong." The landlord, a professor of chemistry at New York University who lived nearby, promised Ben that he planned "as soon as feasible to equip each household with a patent dry-earth commode—a handsome oaken chair, really—so that everyone's excrementitious affairs may be managed more comfortably and privately indoors."

In addition, all the other places where Ben had lived by himself—at Cambridge, in Bonn, in Manchester, in London—had been furnished for him before he took up residence. He had enjoyed his New York furniture-buying expedition, however, and found himself quite satisfied with his secondhand chairs and bed and somewhat stark living quarters. He'd never realized before how many dozens of inessential objects had cluttered his house and every fine house in London. Here in his plain whitewashed flat above Sullivan Street there were no end tables, no tea tables or card tables, no butler's tray table, bill-paying table, or secretaire. A tattered trunk with broken hinges left by the previous tenant served as his nightstand. The building was equipped with gas, so he didn't require lamps, or tables for them. His new home looked to him not empty or impoverished but spartan and serene. Given that he spent most of his waking hours immersed in the foreign excess and clutter of the streets and shops and markets and theaters, he found himself relieved to return every evening to his private oasis of austerity, like a cool swim at the end of a hot summer's afternoon.

Not that he didn't still adore the foreign excess. He devoured a dozen large round sweet American oysters each day—an entirely different breed from the puny, brackish English variety. He had discovered during his first evening walks that a district of concert saloons and bordellos lay just south and east of his neighborhood. And now he understood what the real estate broker had meant by a "black-and-tan zone"—every nearby block of Sullivan Street and the next street over was filled with colored people. Ben had never seen so many Negroes in one place.

He walked and walked for hours every day across the city. On the afternoon of his second Sunday, he set out to post a letter to his sister, pick up any mail that might have arrived for him at the Astor House, and amble in the neighborhoods east of Broadway. When he crossed Lafayette and came into Delancey Street for the first time, he might as well have been back in Bonn on the Pisternenstrasse. He had known nothing of New York's Kleindeutschland, and this "Little Germany" was not little at all. Streets with German shop signs and conversation continued for blocks to the east, and for even more blocks, he found, after he turned down into the Bowery. And notwithstanding the Christian Sabbath, the streets were alive with people and commerce, and smelled of bread and burnt sugar, coffee and beer, tobacco and shoe leather and varnish. Every second shop was a baker or cabinetmaker. Indeed, it seemed that everything brown and fragrant and pleasantly bittersweet in the city was sold by Germans.

Ben stopped in Chrystie Street to watch some men on ladders removing the cross from the top of a church, and inquired of another bystander, a young man wearing a derby and a jacket of bright red and yellow checks, what they were doing.

"Changing that old church they bought from the Methodists into their sinny-gogue," the young man said with a wink as he puffed on his cigar. "They're makin' it into their own"—he pronounced this slowly—"Temple Emanu-El."

They? Their? Was this fellow not a Jew himself? Ben had seen sidelocks like his in London, in Houndsditch Street and at the Rag Fair, on Jewish tailors and peddlers. And a *church* turned into a *synagogue*? On a *Sunday*? Ben suspected he was being teased.

But in fact, the fellow was telling the truth—and he was not a Jew at all, but simply wore his hair in the fashion of the b'hoys, with long, thick curls flopping around his ears.

"Strange days, eh?" the b'hoy said, shaking his head. "Who needs to go abroad? America turnin' into a foreign country here before our very eyes." Then, recalling that Britons were foreigners too, he added, "Not meaning to give offense to you yourself."

As Ben watched, the cross descended on a rope, swinging and twisting as it went; he noticed that one of the men on the ground reaching up to catch it wore a skullcap.

Around the Bowery's intersection with Canal Street, the distinctly German character became just one racial strand among many. *Now,* Ben thought, he had arrived in the heart of mongrel America. Paddy Worden's Worden House was across from White's Ethiopian Opera House (NIGGA MELODIES! the billboard over the doors announced), which was adjacent to Toby Hoffman's saloon, where he stopped to eat a plate of deviled eggs and, for the first time in his life, pickled cucumbers.

One whole block, on both sides of the street, consisted of nothing but a pair of beer gardens, both already filled with men and women at this hour, lounging, laughing, drinking, and listening to a musical hodgepodge. He tried to pick out the different tunes as he passed—a polka, a Negro song, an imitation of a Negro song, a Haydn divertimento, and some Teutonic dirge, all played simultaneously by five different bands on trumpets, castanets, violins, harmonicas, oboes, tubas, accordions, and drums. Scattered around the gardens he saw two jugglers, a team of three acrobats, and a plate-spinner, and for a few minutes watched a Punch-and-Judy show featuring a marionette which, at the finale, appeared to snip its own strings and walk off the stage under its own power.

He ate some shreds of grilled beef from a cart, then turned right to make his way toward the Astor House, passing into a zone of increasingly gamy saloons. A boy in front of Big Jerry Tappen's offered Ben a card advertising that night's boxing matches. And then he was in a neighborhood of back slums. It was revolting, but no more wretched or dense with humanity than Whitechapel. The houses tended to be smaller than in London's poor quarters, almost all one or two stories, and of a hastier, more recent construction.

Cracks and holes in windows were stuffed with rags and wadded newspaper pages.

There were nearly as many Negroes in these streets as in his own neighborhood. And he heard Irish voices all around.

He saw a girl and a boy sitting cross-legged on a stoop with a pile of potatoes between them, peeling off the skins with their fingernails.

He saw two boys at the side of a hovel, standing on their tiptoes and staring inside. (He could not see what they saw—a stranger, still wearing his waistcoat and trousers, shogging himself against the boys' aunt, lying half naked on a pallet of gunnysacks and straw.)

Half a block farther on, a barefoot, bareheaded woman standing in the doorway of a grocery caught Ben's glance. She poked her tongue out of her bruised, unsmiling mouth and slowly licked the full circumference of her lips, paused, then licked again.

On one block he counted fourteen saloons and grog shops and liquor groceries. He turned left down a little side street, and a few paces later passed into an enveloping stench—no mere smelly breeze but an oppressive atmosphere of putrefaction, human excrement as well as that of horses and hogs, old beer, fresh vomit, decomposing rats, plus the steamy fumes of fat renderers. In the shadows on his right, a little flood of wastewater suddenly coursed down the gutter . . . and as it flowed into an area of sunlight and pooled, Ben saw that it was blood, gallons of it. His stomach fluttered, but he regained his composure and turned back to the main road, called Orange.

At least half the businesses in Orange Street sold old things (watches, guns, umbrellas, hand mirrors, chairs, jackets, hats, dishes, and more, on and on), and every shop bore an Irish name (Hart, Buckley, O'Breck, McBride, Costello) until he was south of Cross Street, after which every shop had a Jewish name (Seixas, Noah, Gratz, Myers, Judah). As he came to a weedy green, he stopped to read a sign nailed to the door of a shed called Paradise Grocery that advertised BEER OR CROTON I PENNY A GLASS, PRINTED SCENES & OTHER SOUVENIRS OF THE FIVE POINTS FROM 5 CENTS. Of course—he had stumbled into the Five Points, New York's most celebrated stretch of geography, an international synonym for urban poverty.

"It ain't the *actual* Croton water, mister," a boy on the sidewalk half whispered to him. His accent was Irish. "If you were considerin' spendin' the penny."

"I beg your—excuse me?"

"There ain't a stopcock between here and the Bowery south of Walker

Street—none of the pipes come over into the *Points* at all, of course." He gave Ben a moment to absorb the information. "Clean and polish for three cents, sir? Make it two. Best blacking in the Sixth Ward."

The boy made a show of taking his cleanest rag from his box and began wiping Ben's boots as if his hands were cams on an engine. Directly across the street, Ben saw a pair of identical signs that said DICKENS'S PLACE, each painted with a green arrow that pointed down to a bright pink door below grade.

Again, the bootblack caught Ben's glance and anticipated his question. "Yes, sir, that *is* Pete Williams's famous drinking and dancing place, the very one Mr. Dickens writes about in his book."

The book was *American Notes,* which Ben had read as soon as it was published a few years earlier. Its scene in the cellar saloon in the Five Points was the most memorable—whites and Negroes packed together watching the impossibly talented young black man Juba dancing like an imp. He had intended to visit.

"But in Mr. Dickens's *Notes,*" Ben said to the bootblack, "it was called Almack's, was it not?"

"An *English* gentleman, I hear now!" He spit on the toe of each boot and continued wiping. "So it was, sir, and our Mr. Williams across the way is a colored man with a genius for business, which is why he's changed the name of his place to Dickens's."

"Is that so?"

"Sure! To inveigle visitors like yourself to pay their shillings to stop and watch the reels and heel-and-toe tappers. Back when I was young," said the boy, no older than fourteen, "Almack's was for the locals only. Now they get mostly foo-foos, sir, Bostonians and foreigners and upper-tens down for the night from the Fifth Avenue and that like."

Ben lost all interest in paying a visit to the former Almack's. He was reminded of his family's holiday stop one summer in Cornwall at "King Arthur's Castle." When an actor dressed in a Merlin costume and speaking in pseudo-Chaucerian rhymes had accosted them, his brother shoved the man away—"Leave us alone, you ridiculous fraud"—and it had been the one time in his life Ben remembered being grateful for Philip's easy cruelty.

Now the Irish boy was about to inveigle Ben. "I can take you there, sir, as a special guest of Pete Williams—or just down Cross Street for a personal tour of the Old Brewery." Ben knew of the Old Brewery, renowned as the world's worst tenement, a hundred jerry-built flats housing a thousand of the unluckiest New Yorkers. "I can show you the green slime, the piss-drip ceilings, the murder rooms . . . I can show you everything. Andy Kelly is my name."

"Thank you, no."

Ben's boots were clean.

"Are you here in New York for some time, sir?"

"Yes, I believe I am. I've let a flat."

"Ah! You'll need a girl to clean and wash for you, then, eh? Perhaps shop for your food and so on as well?"

As Ben considered the suggestion, the boy half turned his head and shouted—"*Oona!*"—then resumed his patter. "My cousin is just now over from Balbriggan, a country girl, all by herself, and she's honest and healthy and hardworking and never takes a sip of liquor. *Oona!* Come!"

From out of a narrow side yard strode a fierce-looking girl with dark circles under her eyes and tousled black hair, wiping her wet hands on a dirty apron.

"Oona, you have soap on your chin," her cousin said, and she wiped the white foam away with the back of her hand.

Oona Kelly was shocked by the sight of the Englishman from the dock in Liverpool. She wondered for a panicky moment if he had followed her to America. But then she saw in his eyes that he had no idea they'd met before.

"This good gentleman," her cousin Andy said, "requires a maid of all work." He looked Ben over, calculating quickly. "Just yourself, is it? Two rooms? Maybe . . . two hours every second or third day. Eh, sir?"

"I haven't much money to pay . . ."

"Ah, we all of us run short now and again, right? As expatriated compatriots of the United Kingdom of Great Britain and Ireland, we can offer you a good discount, sir. Instead of the usual . . . fifty cents for six hours a week of faultless labor, instead, only for you, sir, only *forty*." Ben's face registered a jot of uncertainty. "That's one and ten, more or less—eight shillings a month, give or take. Not even five pound for the whole year."

"A *year?*" Oona said to her cousin. "Don't get ahead of yourself and frighten the gentleman, Andy."

Hearing the throaty Irish voice, Ben suddenly remembered her. She was smiling now, as she had refused to do in Liverpool. Ben smiled back, and nodded.

And so he walked out of the infamously filthy, depraved Five Points wearing absolutely clean boots and employing a witty housemaid. After

passing by another huge new Egyptian temple (the Tombs, as they called the
city jail), Ben found himself stepping directly into the familiar genteel quarter of the Park and City Hall and the Astor House and the Broadway stores.
This instant transition from stinking Five Points to silken High Street made
him a little dizzy. He stopped and turned around, thinking he had lost track
of time and absentmindedly walked farther than he imagined . . . but *no*, behind him still in view were the ramshackle wooden buildings. Just ahead was
a parade of merchants and bankers in fourteen-guinea suits and shiny beaver
hats and their wives and sisters riding in fine two-horse carriages. He looked
back again at the slums. It was like a trick, as if he were living inside a story,
whisked capriciously and instantly from one realm to its opposite.

Up ahead, just past the Park, he saw the flags of ten nations flying atop
the American Museum, and he realized he had in fact walked from one entertainment district to another and now to another still, from the Bowery to
Five Points to Park Row, each one a museum of curiosities with its own
character and themes. New York was a pleasure garden of many parts.

As he gave his quarter dollar to the man at Barnum's door, the fellow said
in a rushed monotone drone, "Good afternoon sir welcome to the American
Museum our next performance of 'Ignominy A Shocking Tragedy of the
Five Points District with Music' begins in the lecture room in ten minutes
thank you."

Although Ben had been hungrily attending the theater since arriving in
New York, and while Barnum's scenery was remarkable—a reproduction of
the gutted interior of the Old Brewery constructed on three levels—the
play itself was beyond dreadful. (*"I may be a mere immigrant pauper girl,
but not so destitute of virtue that I shall let the grog peddlers and fleshmon-
gers soil and sell me!"*) Ben left the hall at the end of the first act, but roamed
through all four stories of the museum until it closed.

In fact, he spent the better part of the next two days at Barnum's. Such an
array of amusing nonsense! He saw the jewel-encrusted yellow suit Tom
Thumb had worn for his audience with Queen Victoria two years before,
and a waxworks figure ("superior to those by Madame Tussaud in London")
of the queen herself. He saw a six-foot-tall magnet. He saw the late President Jackson's actual shoes and a pair of smiling microcephalic Mexican
boys called "Maximo and Bartolo, the Aztec Children." He spent half an
hour watching a score of live animals called "the Happy Family," all locked
in a great cage together—monkeys, rabbits, mice, an eagle, a South American armadillo, and an African giraffe. The two boys next to Ben visited the

Happy Family frequently, he heard them say, in order to see the eagle swoop down and grab a mouse. He saw a sniffling, red-eyed child and his mother put fifty cents and a dead cat on a metal counter in front of a museum employee with a badge that read STUFFING ATTENDANT. ("She'll be ready to go home in three hours, ma'am," the man told her, "after lunchtime.")

He looked for a long time at a mummified Chippewa Indian standing inside the largest glass cabinet he had ever seen. Most of his fellow onlookers agreed that the Indian, except for the glass eyes, was real, but Ben had his doubts. Next to the mummy, also standing, was an Indian horse club, which looked authentic to Ben—it was like a cricket bat wound with red leather string, the leather forming a thong that held a spherical stone the size of a cricket ball tight against the tip of the blade end. He returned to the lecture hall for a show that featured "Sioux Indians"—alive but unquestionably fake—performing tomahawk combat and paddling a birchbark and cedar-strip canoe back and forth in a long, narrow tank of water onstage. Swinging from "vines" (ropes dyed chartreuse) above and among the Indians was a howling ochre-skinned Wild Man of the Prairies, an acrobatic actor known as Signor Hervio Naño, who had tiny legs and wore a fur and leather costume. Ben had understood that the prairies mostly lacked trees, and thus vines.

On his second visit to the museum, he returned to the lecture hall to watch a brief interview with "Kaspar Hauser," the celebrated Prussian "wild boy" who was supposed to have been murdered fifteen years earlier. Now a wild *man*, this Kaspar was in fact Signor Naño, minus the orange paint but clad in the identical fur and leather and wearing a hat.

On his third afternoon at Barnum's, Ben happened to see the beau (or husband) of the tall, blond, beguiling girl from the Astor House dining room. He spied on him as the fellow examined a diorama of a New York blaze that had, according to the label, burned 241 buildings in 1845. And then a bit later in the basement shooting gallery, he was firing a percussion-cap pistol when Ben arrived. Ben paid fifteen cents to try his hand at what the attendant had described as "an exclusive prototype of Mr. Sharps's amazing new breech-loading rifle" that used paper cartridges and enabled "a trained shooter to fire ten balls in a minute." The scar-faced young stranger glanced over, fired once more from his little pistol, and quickly left the gallery.

FATTY FREEBORN NEVER considered himself lucky. He had always had to fight and grabble and scrooge for any measly advantage. The night that two strokes of luck presented themselves inside of a minute in Greene Street, he was quick to exploit the first but slower to recognize the other.

It was his turn to work the ovens alone all night at the Enggas Bakery. Around midnight, waiting for the last of the morning bread to bake, he had fashioned a game for himself, hurling a knife at every rat he saw running through the kitchen, then drinking a swig of rye each time he retrieved the knife. (In fact, the parade of rats consisted of only two, running back and forth along different paths, every time escaping Fatty's throws.) By three in the morning his bottle was finished; when he awoke at half past four, lying on a mattress of six dozen warm white loaves, he couldn't even remember having taken the bread out of the ovens. He shoveled the squashed and dirty-crusted breads into a bin, locked up the bakery, and stumbled out to head home.

Ten yards ahead in Greene Street was a woman in a dress with big flounces around the neck and hem, walking with her back to him. Her bonnet was askew. Given the hour, Fatty figured she was a whore. When she stopped to take off the bonnet and retie it, he thought her hair looked very short. And then he realized who it was—Bottle Alley Sally, the punk nance rigged up with the fake cunt. By the time Sally heard Fatty lumbering up from behind, it was futile to run, especially in his ladies' heels.

The whiskey bottle didn't break when it slammed against the side of the boy's head, and didn't break as Fatty whaled it against his lower back after he fell, moaning, to the sidewalk. Fatty was deciding whether to lift up the dress and rip open the drawers to see if his pal Charlie had been telling the truth about the raw pork when two other young men, Negroes, sprang from behind the swill tub where they had been hiding across the street, next door to the bakery.

Fatty, surprised and confused, started to run, then turned and threw the bottle in the Negroes' direction. It shattered against the swill tub, but by then the two men were already scrambling into the cellar of No. 94. A hand holding a lantern closed the door quickly behind them. The light in the cellar was extinguished. *Burglars at the rich widow lady's house,* Fatty thought. He had no desire to get mixed up in such a mess, so he turned away from the nance, who was spitting blood between sobs, and went on his way.

23

May 9, 1848

. . .

New York City

EN HAD ALREADY seen more plays in two weeks than he had attended during the last six months in England, including one he had meant to see in London, *This House to Be Sold: (The Property of the Late William Shakespeare) Inquire Within*, featuring Shakespeare and his most famous characters singing and dancing together. Theaters became his fixed destinations at the end of each long day of wandering. He enjoyed the crowds—and such crowds: *four thousand people* the night before last at the Broadway. He had always paid for a box in London, but here he was happy being jostled by hoi polloi in the shilling seats. He liked the warm, oily *"peeeeeanuts"* sold by the strolling vendors; he had never tasted one before. And he also found that his new life, so thoroughly uncluttered (not to say empty and feckless) and filled with solitude (not to say loneliness), predisposed him to *believe* much more easily in the stories and characters depicted onstage.

Theater in America seemed devoted to blurring the distinctions between the players and the ticket holders. At the first play he attended, *How to Settle Accounts with Your Laundress*, he was shocked when members of the audience started whistling and yelling and stamping their feet *during* the performance, and when they tossed nuts and a lit firecracker onto the stage, and when they shouted not only praise and ridicule at the actors and actresses but advice to the *characters*.

The playwrights and performers did their parts as well. During *A Glance at New York,* a stew of comedy and drama about raucous young working-men that Ben had seen last week, the hero started to leave the stage to join a fictitious brawl when the actor playing his friend stopped him, pointed out at the audience, and said, "Mose . . . remember *them?*" Whereupon Mose turned and delivered an aside: "Look here, ladies and gentlemen, don't be down on me because I'm going to leave you . . . I'll scare up this crowd again tomorrow night, and then you can take *another* glance at New York!" And that was the end of the play. At the Drury Lane in London, the managers had started charging £20 to watchmakers and tailors to paint advertisements on the scenery flats, but Ben had never seen any play conclude with a winking advertisement for *itself.*

He had been eager to sample all of the indigenous extravaganzas. In London, two or three minstrel shows appeared during an entire season. Here he discovered that he could, if he had wished, attend a different one every night for weeks. He saw Cool White and the Congo Melodists. He saw an *Othello* in which the star, Thomas Dartmouth "Daddy" Rice, embraced a white-powdered white man in a wig and a dress playing Desdemona and used a raccoon skin for a handkerchief. Ben was delighted by Rice's new ending for the play—instead of committing suicide, this Othello impregnates Desdemona and they live happily ever after, their baby's face painted half white and half black.

But as he watched a matinee performance by Christy's Original Band of Virginia Minstrels, he found himself bored listening to still more banjo-playing, bone-rattling, and tambourine-shaking, watching another break-down dancer waving his limbs like a marionette, listening to yet another strenuously satirical "Negro lecture" (this afternoon on "The Joys of Communism") and another too-antic rendition of "O, Susanna" . . .

I jumped aboard the telegraph
And trabbled down de ribber,
De lectrick fluid magnified,
And kill'd five hundred Nigga.

He was even bored by his own continuing attempts to decipher the lyrics. (Did the Negro singer somehow murder five hundred fellow Negroes? Or did they drown in the Mississippi? Or did the electricity in the telegraph wire kill them? And were the journey and the deaths literal or metaphorical?) *Bored in America!* Not two weeks ago he would have considered such a thing impossible.

As he stepped out of Mechanics' Hall at the second interval in Christy's Minstrels' show, he encountered the bearded journalist he had met aboard the *America,* now struggling to enter with a large wooden box and a complicated folding tripod. Ben was very pleased to see him. Perhaps in this country where he knew nobody, a sympathetic acquaintance did count as a full-fledged friend.

"Sir! Well, hallo!"

As Ben held the door open, Skaggs passed through and continued speaking.

"I received your kind note proposing we meet, and let me apologize for the lack of reply—my secretary has not attended to the social correspondence for days . . . weeks . . . probably years by now."

"Christy's show is nearly over, I'm afraid," Ben said.

"Oh, I've not come for the ridiculousness onstage—I'm here to practice my own foolish art."

"You—you—as well as a newspaper reporter you are a *minstrel performer?*"

Skaggs chuckled. He explained to Ben that he worked as a reporter only occasionally these days, and that photography was now his true profession. He had wheedled an appointment to take pictures of Mr. Christy and his troupe, in the little alley-yard behind the theater.

"May I help carry your things? I hadn't any idea so much equipment was required," Ben said.

"I am sure you have far more pressing business this afternoon, but I should be delighted to have you join me."

In the dressing room, Skaggs introduced Ben to Christy as his "well-known colleague Mr. Knowles of Mayfair," and announced his intention to make not one but two portraits of the minstrels—one right away, in which Christy and the other players would remain blacked up—and another after they washed off the blacking, for which they would pose identically, in costume, as white men. "Mr. Knowles tells me that in London," he explained, concocting a lie, "the Ethiopian Serenaders have just sat for a famous portrait in Oxford Street entirely au naturel."

And so for one afternoon in May in a hidden well of sunlight between Grand and Broome streets, Ben Knowles served as a daguerreian's assistant. Afterward he agreed to accompany Skaggs down to his studio.

"Thirty-*two*," Skaggs suddenly said, shaking his head, as they climbed into a cab.

"What's that?"

"*Christy*. He told me he is only thirty-two years old."

"I miss your point, sir. I am younger than that myself."

"But you, my boy, are not earning a hundred dollars a day for two hours of clowning. You are not famous and beloved by the world—not, like Daddy Rice, preparing to retire at age forty with a fortune of forty-five thousand dollars. Even Christy says they are now about to change the name of Mechanics' Hall to Christy's American Opera House." He sighed. "Ours is an unjust world."

They passed a sign on the front of the theater promising, in letters two feet high, GENUINE NEGRO FUN!

"I have wondered why," Ben asked, "there are not more *Negroes* singing the tunes and dancing the jigs in the shows in this *nation* of Negroes."

" 'This nation of Negroes'! I might have to borrow that phrase."

"Honestly," Ben said, "it has surprised me that I have seen not one colored performer in the theaters here. Even in London, they nearly always include at least one true American Negro, such as Juba, or Thomas Dilward . . ."

"Mr. Lane"—Juba's actual name—"is a virtuoso, better at dancing than *any* drunken white kickshoe in blackface. He simply cannot be denied. And Dilward has the added virtue of his dwarfism. Only if a colored man is *superior* to his white counterparts, by virtue of sheer talent or freakishness, is he permitted to join this new minstrels' guild.

"As you surely know, Knowles, we Americans loathe and fear the Negro—"

"Do you, sir?"

"Not I, but Americans in the main. They despise him—but they also *envy* him his supposed innocence and gaiety. Slavery may be a crime against God and the American idea—indeed, it certainly *is*—but does the slave fret about paying his rent or paying for her children's school or the pew at church or which fine shawl to buy? The slave is in fact free, free of every bourgeois worry. And so we pay Christy a thousand dollars a week to enact the fantasy that he is a Negro. His is the double freedom, the impossible freedom, which Americans want for themselves—the freedom of a Negro to sing and shout and dance and laugh and fornicate, but the freedom of a rich man like Christy to upbraid his bankers and live in a mansion and wear laundered clothes every day and eat roast beef every night. We democrats want to live as aristocrats."

"You have considered this question before, I take it."

Skaggs smiled. "I have, sir." He liked Knowles. "A piece I wrote in a magazine last year provoked a mammoth rumpus. I proposed that a special tax be imposed on the minstrel shows to subsidize the costs of operating the Colored Sailors' Home, the Colored Orphan Asylum, and a House of Refuge for Colored Juvenile Delinquents. And I suggested that this craze among whites for impersonating Negroes is part of a secret abolitionist plot to blur the differences between the races."

Ben gave him a doubtful look.

"The second notion was satirical," Skaggs explained, "although neither the local abolitionists *nor* the Negro-haters appreciated my comic intentions. And, indeed, I have come to think I may have been more correct than I realized. *Left,* sir," he said to the driver, pointing across Broadway.

"So you are no devotee? Of minstrelsy?"

"I confess I am not, no." He looked at Ben. "As a young mechanic I know puts it," he said, quoting Duff, " 'nigger-singing in the theaters is too mean and disrespectful to the *real* niggers.' "

In London, minstrel shows had seemed to Ben charming, prankish, good-natured celebrations of black Americans and America itself.

"Perhaps you are not aware, sir," Skaggs continued, "that Delaware, a ten-hour coach ride from where we sit, is a proud slave state. Right here across the river in New Jersey they abolished slavery only months ago. In liberal Connecticut they permit it still, as they do in New Hampshire, the province from which I escaped as a boy." Even today, whenever his father launched one of his diatribes against New York City's immorality, Skaggs would reply by asking his father how the last remaining slave in New Hampshire was faring these days.

"And therefore shenanigans such as Mr. Christy's," Ben said, "offend you. I understand."

" 'Offend' me? A word I seldom use. Indeed, have never used, as best I recall. But even given my rickety moral compass, these lampoons of black men performed in a nation where black men are still bought and sold . . . fail to amuse me much."

"Do you know slave-owning men?"

Skaggs shook his head. "I drank with one once at Niagara Falls, where a colony of plantationists summers. A Mr. Martin, from Alabama—*Athens,*

Alabama, I shall never forget, because Mr. Martin took pains to remind me that the glories of *ancient* Athens depended upon slavery."

Even now, Skaggs explained, slaves who fled north to New York were often apprehended and returned like stray livestock to their owners in the South.

Ben felt guilty and foolish. His father's and Philip's critiques of the United States had only redoubled Ben's adoration. He was pleased to have an American friend to enlighten him about America's flaws and impurities . . . which, he realized, he had hardly considered before. He recalled what Ashby had often said in defense of himself or others after some wanton behavior: *To be pure is to be uncomplicated, and to be uncomplicated is to be a cretin or a trout or some inanimate thing.* Ben's love for America had been like a boy's infatuation with an actress or a princess from afar.

"Thank you, Mr. Skaggs."

"My good God! Timothy Skaggs providing ethical guidance. This must remain our secret."

24

May 10, 1848

. . .

New York City

EN HAD ALREADY seen one New York *Hamlet*—a production starring the young son of the English émigré actor Junius Brutus Booth—but he had read for years about the odd American theatrical fashion for "infant wonders," and so now he prepared to watch his second *Hamlet* in as many weeks. And was already regretting the choice. The woman next to him reeked so strongly of otto of rose that he considered changing seats. And as soon as the curtain lifted—with comic speed, as always in America—he found the show embarrassing for everyone concerned. The oldest boy on the stage was eleven. The lines were recited as Shakespeare wrote them, and the actors performed earnestly, but most of the audience chuckled and hooted as if the play were a comedy, laughing at the boys' terror when the ghost of Hamlet's father appeared. Local custom did not oblige audience members to remain in their seats for a full act, and Ben was tempted to walk out. He hesitated too long after the first scene ended, however, and settled himself for the second to begin.

How odd, he thought, that only Claudius and Gertrude and the ghost of Hamlet's father were played by adults, and he wondered about the rationale, speculating that the implicit carnal liaisons would offend American sensibilities if those parts were performed by children—

The woman! From the Astor House two weeks ago! She is Queen Gertrude!

Was it truly? With her heavy makeup and gray-powdered hair, in the glare of limelight, he wasn't certain . . . but then she took her place down-stage and turned to face the audience. It was she, the tall, electrifying girl from the Astor House, the young woman he had mused about every busy day and lonely night since. An actress! It made sense. He reached into his pocket for his playbill with such haste that he elbowed the sweet-stinking woman on his left.

Mary Ann Lucking.

The audience looked at Claudius and Laertes and Polonius as each delivered his lines, but Ben stared at her. He had never looked so long or hard at an unspeaking player onstage. He felt like a Peeping Tom. He could not glance away.

"Good Hamlet," she said to the pouting eight-year-old playing her son the prince, "cast thy nighted color off,/ And let thine eye look like a *friend* on Denmark."

Ben was growing more entranced by the second. Her voice was deep and musical, but her style of acting was the most extremely American he had seen so far—understated, unaffected, almost as natural as genuine conversation. She was like a woman speaking, not an actress playing. Albeit a woman speaking in iambic pentameter and wearing a tiara of paste emeralds and rubies.

When Claudius whisked her offstage in the middle of the scene, Ben was bereft. Ordinarily he tended not to sympathize with Hamlet (in the prince's adolescent indecision and funks he saw too much of his own least attractive side), but now he felt real anger against the usurping king for taking Gertrude out of sight.

For the remainder of the show, when she was absent he paid no attention, and when she returned he gazed only at her. When Polly delivered her final lines ("The drink, the drink! I am poisoned") and slumped to the floor, dead, Ben's eyes actually watered. In the play's last minutes he saw only her body twisted and sprawled on the planks of the stage, and heard only his own mind's cries of longing for her. To Ben, all the rest—the final, squeaking, tragic speeches by Hamlet, Laertes, and the other little boys, the trumpet-and-drum funeral march, the applause of the crowd—was silence.

London

THE FEELING THAT energized Drumont was a mixture of emotions—righteous rage that the murderer had escaped again, a flattered sense of his own power, the simple old pleasure of inspiring fear in other men. He found the very familiarity reassuring, given the odyssey he now faced. But it pleased him too to wield a fearsomeness that was all his own, not on loan from the army or Municipal Guard. And he felt his mission more passionately than ever.

It astounded him that his hunt had actually caused Knowles, a rich man, to flee his family and country. *As I was forced to leave my own,* Drumont thought. *But he is a coward, running to* escape *his moral responsibilities. Whereas I am running to* fulfill *mine. And only a guilty man runs. I must track him as if he were a panicking boar in the swelter of a Corsican August. And I shall finish this round-the-world hunt, this great* battue, *as I finished the day-long* battues *of my youth—exhausted but victorious, covered in blood and glory.*

A more prudent man in Drumont's circumstance might have considered his dwindling capital, now less than two hundred francs, and thought first of securing his own safety and future. A different man, cast out of France by tragedy and history, would have sailed off to fashion a new life in some cheap, warm, and faraway place that was French but not too French—a former colony in the Caribbean like Haiti or Grenada, perhaps.

But Drumont would not retire from this fight. The moment he had discovered he could buy a one-way fare to New York for only a hundred francs, sailing from Plymouth in a few weeks, his course was certain. For his honor, for Michel and for France, he must be man enough to overcome his hatred and fear of the sea. There would be no turning back.

And would it not be better to be exiled in America than in enemy England? Montreal and New Orleans, as he understood it, were essentially French. The whole continent was filled with foreigners. Hadn't Inspector Vidocq once planned to immigrate to America with a stake of stolen francs? And Drumont's other idol was the ultimate American, a man he imagined to be something like himself—John Charles Frémont, the famous explorer and soldier, bastard son of a penniless Frenchman, a natural leader of men, pushed out of military service by political opponents, a gambler driven to journey west, a man who made and obeyed his own rules.

New York City

BEN CALCULATED THAT his money would last him only until winter. And he had no plan yet for earning more, apart from Mr. Skaggs's suggestion that he deliver lectures about the February Revolution. So he began to husband his coins and notes, denying himself luxuries like wine and books. Yet he paid to see *Hamlet* again the following night, and a third and fourth time the week following. And then a fifth.

Happily, his parents and governesses and vicars and schoolmasters had all neglected to hector him as a boy about the debilitating consequences of the sinful and abominable practice of onanism. And so for the last two weeks, now that he had ogled Mary Ann Lucking directly for hours on the stage (*luminous, supine, eyes shut, lids barely fluttering, lips parted*) and knew her name and the sound of her voice, his flat in Sullivan Street had become a regular den of self-pollution, night after solitary night.

But that pleasure had come now to seem like a pitiful, snively ritual. Thus he found himself this evening with a condom in his pocket listening to a pianist play as he chatted with a young woman called Debby in the parlor of a house operated by a Mrs. Shannon downtown near Columbia College. He had last visited a bordello at Christmas, with Ashby in Soho. Debby was a plumpish brunette with a nasal voice and too many ringlets bouncing around her face. She had an exceedingly familiar manner.

He finished the cocktail Mrs. Shannon had brought him—gin with lemon and cherries and a great deal of sugar, what Debby called a "Seminole Sunshine"—and had a second.

"Can I ask a question?" she said.

"Of course you may."

"As a foreigner, how much superior do our American ways here strike you, as a foreigner? Is this country *so* much better than England and France and the rest? I've never been to anywhere else, except Long Island. And Morristown."

"Well, Debby, I myself have visited only Jersey City and Brooklyn and New York to Fortieth Street. And I have been delighted thus far by almost everything I have seen and everyone I have met in this small strip of America." In fact, his single disappointing day was the one in Brooklyn, only a penny each way across the East River, but no wonder—no gas streetlamps, too many churches, too little strangeness, too much of a provincial air, like one of the forgettable cities in the north of England, Bristol or Sheffield. "Delighted by every bit, including and perhaps especially the very lovely present company."

She smiled. "Aw, you're buttering me now, huh?"

" 'Buttering' you?"

"Uh-*huh*." She poked his necktie with her forefinger. "You tell me you're some kind of gallivanting guy"—this is what she had called him earlier after Ben said he'd sailed to America without prospects and only a general hankering for adventure—"but you're also my own sweet English King Albert!" She touched his necktie again. "*Ain't* you?"

"*Prince* Albert is German, actually. I read philosophy with him in Bonn." Why did he say such a thing?

"Skylarkers with education and *manners* too. Those are the guys I favor."

"You do?"

She nodded slowly, very deliberately, and put her own glass of Seminole Sunshine on the mantelpiece. "You set?"

"I beg your pardon?"

She leaned close and said softly, "Are you OK to go upstairs now?" She lowered her voice more, to a squeaky whisper. "Shall we have our nice fuck, then?"

Ben was fairly staggered. His face reddened. But he closed his mouth, offered his arm, and let Debby lead him to her netherworld. Embracing her nakedness against him in the darkness, he tried to make himself believe that she was not Debby, a foulmouthed whore who smelled of patchouli, but Miss Mary Ann Lucking, the luminescent actress. Or *Mrs.* Lucking, he feared.

LESS THAN AN hour later, Ben was walking home, thinking about a possible new use of Knowles & Company's Malay rubber. Ashby's old pig-bladder oil paint tubes had been replaced by pliable tin . . . and if gutta-percha could be molded thinly enough to insulate even telegraph wires, why, he wondered, could condoms not be manufactured from gutta-percha or India rubber? And would Sir Archie be disgusted or amused or intrigued by such a business proposal?

He had gone only a few blocks when he spotted three young men posting advertisements for a circus.

The foreman wore a peacoat and glazed leather cap, and held the sheaf of dry posters. He glanced up and down West Broadway, watching for policemen. The two other, younger boys did the work, one holding a bucket and brush and the other using a two-by-four scantling to smooth down the pasted bills.

As Ben approached, Duff heard his footfalls clicking on the stones and turned to look. Each man recognized the other with a start.

The shaggy aristo rifleman who eyed me in Barnum's basement.

The man who dined with Mary Ann Lucking at the Astor House.

Both looked away quickly.

He must be some kind of investigating detective, Duff thought. *Dispatched by whom? The Primes? The army? Some secret association of bankers and distillers?* He felt lucky to have the two boys at his side. He glanced up the street. *The stranger is not stopping, or slowing. He's conducting a surveillance is what he's doing, pretending to happen by . . . At half past midnight!* Duff decided he must begin carrying his pistol.

Ben had never felt such instant unreasoning anger toward a stranger. *That £2-a-week American yob, a dirty billsticker, is her lover . . . the bastard, with his monster mark.*

But by the time he arrived in Sullivan Street, his jealous rage was spent, and he had begun chastising himself as a dirty un-American whoremonger who performed no useful work and longed pointlessly, like a boy, for a woman he would never meet.

CHARLIE STRAUSBAUGH, the smartest man in Hose Company 25, was shaking his head. "It wasn't no colored *burglars* you saw the other night in Greene Street, Fatty. Sure as anything those were *slaves,* run away from somewheres. That house next to your bakery must be one of their hiding places. Like they say about Downing's, the oyster house. One of the cellars where they lodge during the run to Canada."

"But the Downings are *niggers,*" said Toby Warfield, "and I don't think no *nigger* owns such a nice house there in Greene Street."

This remark triggered one of the regular 25 Hose amusements—teasing Toby.

"The old lady that owns that house is whiter than *you,* Warfield," Fatty said.

"Toby, ya dolt," Charlie added, "most of the abolitioners are white. You think Horace Greeley's a colored man, do you?"

Everyone snorted and chuckled.

"The sugarhouse down there in Duane," added Bill Boyce more seriously, "the last one that burned, Collins's, that's owned by Wall Street, the *Herald* said, and that's part of their 'Underground Railway' too, it had been."

It was after midnight, and five of the Hose 25 boys were passing the flask, having a nightcap at their firehouse on Anthony Street.

"Goddamned rich bedpressers," Fatty said after he took his next swallow of whiskey. "When you spend it to help niggers like that, it means you got too much."

"Well," said Charlie after a while, "I reckon we might've got a way here to make *us* a few dollars. *More* than a *few.*"

"Sell the tip to a blackbirder, you mean?" Dick Owen asked.

"No, I mean doing a bit of blackbirding ourselves, and keeping the bounty for ourselves."

Charlie's plan was for all five of them to bunk at the firehouse for a week or two, as long as it took, and post one of the young lads each night as a watcher near Mrs. Gibbs's house on Greene Street. When any suspicious Negroes appeared on that block, the lantern boy would sprint the five minutes down to Anthony Street and they would all come running, with weapons and chains. And in the morning turn in the runaway slaves for their cash.

"Turn 'em in to who?"

"For how much money?"

"Boys, boys—I only just hatched the scheme! I reckon I still have a little time to parse the details."

"But wait," Bill said, "if we did that, wouldn't it make us . . . snitches?"

There was an uncomfortable silence.

"They break the law of the land by escaping," Charlie replied. "Wherever they come here from, they're *criminals.*"

Everyone nodded. And Fatty went straight to the real point. "Besides," he said, "killing a rat ain't murder, and snitching on niggers ain't really snitching."

25

May 18, 1848

. . .

New York City

HE WAS FLORENCE DOMBEY. That is, she was wearing one of
the new Florence Dombey costumes she had bought at Stewart's. It was dark blue twill with a high silk collar, plainer and a
little more chaste than she would ordinarily wear, particularly to a dinner
and dance party on Gramercy Park. But it was new. And tonight she wished
in her appearance to err on the side of respectability. She had applied color
to her lips and cheeks, but only a little. Her favorite bonnet, the red velvet
that flared out to expose her cheeks and ears, sat on the table just in front of
her. She looked into the mirror as she pinned little pink and cream flowers
into her hair.

Duff had come to Third Street to escort her, and sat behind her, studying
the passages he had marked in one of his etiquette books. He looked up at his
sister.

"The flowers are pretty," he said.

"Thank you, brother."

"And expensive."

"They're narcissus. And less than a dime."

"Not daffodils? They look like the daffodils Ma grew in the Clove."

"Narcissus and daffodil are the same flower. And jonquil."

He considered making a note in his journal. "May I read another part of
my book out loud, Polly? Just one more passage."

She sighed and smiled as she glanced at him in the mirror.

"*Cramming* to be convivial," she said, "seems a cross-purpose."

"This is about intercourse with the *help*. You are to speak to them as little as possible. Did you know that? Will there be *many* servants at this shindig, do you think?"

Polly was finishing with her last flower. "Skaggs said it is to be a large party, one of the largest of the season." Polly blushed; she had never before used "the season" in reference to any subjects but the weather and the availability of fruits and oysters. "So I imagine there will be servants galore."

" 'A good servant is never awkward,' " Duff read. " 'His boots never creak; he never breathes hard, has a cold, is obliged to cough, treads on a lady's dress, or breaks a dish' . . ."

"It sounds as if the perfect servant," she said, "is a dead servant."

Duff still had his finger on the passage, and resumed reading. " 'Dish after dish comes round, as if by magic; and nothing remains but to eat and be happy . . .' "

ON THE SIGN behind Ben were the words "Colored Persons Allowed," but not one of his fellow bus passengers was a Negro. One sunny afternoon earlier in the month, riding up Broadway, he had been appalled to see his driver flick a whip at the hand of a black man about to step aboard, causing several passengers up front to laugh. Ever since, he had, whenever possible, hailed buses bearing "Colored Persons Allowed" signs. Tonight's was one of the larger, brighter coaches, with a glassed-in clerestory roof and benches running the length of each side. The man sitting next to him smelled of onions and spices and wore loose canvas pants and a soft yellow flannel shirt that looked like the costume of a prison inmate. A book of children's stories lay open on his lap, and he silently formed the words with his mouth as he read.

Ben checked his watch. Half seven, the very time he was to meet Skaggs. And then he looked again at the address Skaggs had scribbled—No. 57 Gramercy Park North. Such remarkable American hospitality: who in London invited a complete stranger (let alone a foreign stranger) to attend a friend's private soiree? Ashby would have, but no one else.

The fragrant passenger suddenly touched a forefinger to the page he was reading and turned to face Ben, as if they had been conversing. "Tell me, sir . . ."

Ben ought to have been accustomed to it, but every time a stranger touched his arm or spoke to him out of the blue, he was still taken aback.

"You read English, yes?" the fellow asked. Astounding. His accent seemed Polish or Hungarian, eastern.

"I can," Ben replied as softly as he could without actually whispering. "Yes."

"You please say these words for me, please? To pronounce correct in English?"

"You—you wish me to read a sentence from your book aloud?"

"Yes." The man tapped a spot on the page with his finger. "This."

" 'During the next fortnight,' " Ben read in a whisper, " 'little Jemima walked one hundred miles along rocky trails and through muddy gulches.' " The man watched Ben's mouth as closely as if he were examining some rare wiggling insect.

"One *houn-dred*," the fellow said carefully, and then, with greater difficulty: "*Moody gulches. Moody gulches.* I do not know this 'gulch.' What is this, 'gulch'?"

"I'm afraid, sir, that I don't know either."

The bus was nearing Gramercy Park. Ben pulled the strap and stood, smoothing the back of his tailcoat. The man regarded him with a wounded, skeptical look.

"It must be an Americanism," Ben offered. "I am sorry."

"You joke. OK."

"I beg your pardon?"

But the man snapped his book shut and turned pointedly, proudly away.

Ben stood and reached up through the hole in the roof to pay the driver—another Americanism.

As he walked down Twentieth Street, the noise of Broadway faded. Ahead he saw the green edge and iron railing of a large garden, and a moment later, as he entered the square, he stopped. If the other afternoon he'd had the uncanny experience of stumbling from a back slum directly into High Street, just now he had passed directly from New York City to London, from the teeming commercial clank of Union Square into hushed, pretty, respectable Bedford Square. Gramercy Park, it turned out, was a reproduction of the city he had fled.

Across the garden he saw a fine old Georgian house twice as wide as its neighbors, every window ablaze with light. Even at a hundred yards he could hear a low, happy roar from the open windows. It must be No. 57, the home of Skaggs's friend Herbert Backhouse Rumpf. As Ben got nearer he realized that notwithstanding its Georgian style, no such mansion could have been built here a century or even fifty years ago—its eighteenth-century English grandeur was freshly fabricated, like that of every other house on the unfinished square.

Inside smelled of butcher's wax and paint and perfume. Every inch was bright and perfect. The ballroom occupied the whole third story, and it was filled with two hundred chattering, laughing, expensively dressed people in their twenties and thirties. A few of the men wore tight pantaloons, and even old-fashioned breeches. Overhead hung six big crystal chandeliers, all burning gas, and on the floor precisely beneath each one was a Chinese porcelain pot: six spittoons. The music was a polka, performed by a five-man band—a pianist and cellist on the floor and, wedged into a cove in the wall just above them, a trumpeter, flutist, and banjo player. Ben watched a man light the cigarette of a chic young woman, then smelled the sulfur and smoke as she resumed fanning herself. From a distance, except for the spittoons and the banjo, he might have been in Mayfair or Belgravia.

"A Gin Sling for my well-dressed English friend, or a Brandy Smash? Take your pick, sir!"

It was Skaggs, holding a glass in each hand.

"Good evening, Mr. Skaggs." Ben took the gin.

"We can also arrange for an ordinary, sugarless *man's* drink if you find cocktails fulsome."

"Your Mr. Rumpf is very grand."

Skaggs glanced around. "More profligate and jovial than very grand, in fact. The wife is now the grand one." He had introduced Sally Blair to Backy Rumpf ten years ago, when she was a concert saloon singer and Backy a would-be young publisher. The two men became friendly after Skaggs had arranged to keep Rumpf's name out of the *Sun* in connection with a certain trivial case of sexual and financial impropriety. And Rumpf had agreed to invest in his scurrilous, satirical new illustrated magazine, called *Bedoozled*—the very week in 1840 Skaggs was suddenly compelled to flee New York for the West. And so the smoking, drinking, whore-loving capitalist heir had invested his ten thousand dollars instead in Horace Greeley's new anti-tobacco, pro-temperance, puritanical, socialist *Tribune*.

Skaggs and Ben touched glasses.

"Cheers," Ben said.

"Az isten lova bassza meg," Skaggs replied.

"What?"

"Az isten lova bassza meg," he repeated. "The Magyar tongue."

"You speak *Hungarian,* Mr. Skaggs?"

"Certainly not. But I was briefly in Transylvania last year, and on my first night in Brașov I toasted a drunken stranger in a tavern. Well, the fellow became very angry and shouted, '*Az isten lova bassza meg!*' In Transylvania, I discovered, clinking glasses is not done."

"What on earth took you to Transylvania?"

"Some business in Munich."

"But Munich is days away."

"It is a long story . . . I had been led to understand that the *Gazeta de Transilvania* wished to pay an experienced American newspaperman a hundred dollars to tutor them for a month in sound American newspaper practices. As it turned out, I was misinformed."

"You are a man of many adventures."

"Entirely profitless adventures. Although I did discover the meaning of 'Az isten lova bassza meg,' which is the most remarkable curse I have ever heard in my life."

"Yes?"

"I oughtn't," Skaggs said, but proceeded with barely a pause. "God's horse," he whispered. "shall *fuck* you. *God's horse* shall fuck you. A very strange people."

Ben smiled and shook his head. He was blushing.

The little orchestra was playing a new piece by Johann Strauss, Jr.

As Skaggs gulped his sweet brandy, he caught sight behind Ben of someone he knew. "I am afraid," he called out, "that this thirsty gentleman has filched your drink."

"My goodness, a cocktail thief?" she replied. "Here on Gramercy Park?"

Ben did not recognize the low, gay voice until he turned and saw the lips from which it was purring. The shock caused his decorous 30-degree swivel to extend itself into a wild 90-degree swing to face her.

"*Mary Ann Lucking!*" he sputtered. With both hands he offered his glass to her.

"Thank you, no," Polly said, smiling.

She lifted her little goblet of clove liqueur to show Ben. He looked faintly familiar, and she had a moment of panic that he might be a patron of Mrs. Stanhope's. But she reminded herself that no visitor to 101 Mercer Street had ever heard her true name. Perhaps they had known each other as children in Dutchess County?

Ben, speechless, took a long sip of the gin she had refused.

Skaggs was pleased to see his new English friend flustered—indeed, Skaggs was always pleased to see almost any placid, respectable surface disturbed by passion or wonder.

"I am redundant, I see," he said, "since you have already been introduced."

"No, *no,*" Ben replied, as if a misunderstanding were about to snatch away bliss, "I—I attended Miss Lucking's performance at the Greenwich Theatre, in *Hamlet.* I know her only as a fine actress. Extraordinarily fine."

Now Polly was shocked. Strangers had seldom recognized her from the stage, and none, ever, had praised her acting so enthusiastically. And he was English, which gave his praise a certain imprimatur.

"Well!" Skaggs exclaimed as he looked at the delight and hunger in his friends' faces. "As I have said, good fortune is all in the timing, eh? Did my heart *love* till now? *Mademoiselle,*" he said to Polly, "permit me to introduce you to Mr. Benjamin M. M. Knowles, formerly of Mayfair, London."

Both bowed more deeply than they had since childhood.

Ben was caught off guard again when Skaggs announced the latest arrival by speaking loudly past him over his left shoulder.

"A brand-new song for you, Duff—and you too, Knowles," Skaggs said, raising his brandy toward the musicians, "The 'Revolutionsmarsch.' Composed in the streets of Vienna as they ran off Prince Metternich. Imported to free America through the good offices of our host."

Ben did not want to look away from Polly.

"*Mr.* Lucking," Skaggs said, grabbing Ben's attention as if with a slap, "let me present Mr. Knowles."

As they reached to shake each other's hand and exchange the minimum necessary greeting—"Sir," "Sir"—both simmered with contempt.

Duff's scar turned a bright scarlet. He now knew for certain that their earlier encounters—shooting at Barnum's gallery, walking on West Broadway after midnight—hadn't been accidents. *And now the dirty sneak,* he thought, *has insinuated himself into Skaggs's affections so as to observe me at close range.*

Mary Ann and Duff Lucking: Ben now knew for certain that this gangling, grim-faced blond whelp was indeed her husband, her deeply undeserving husband, and that his own love was doomed.

"Who is your employer?" Duff asked Ben sharply.

"*Duff Lucking,*" Polly said to her brother. She was mortified. "Are you drunk?"

Skaggs was amused by Duff's surliness. "Mr. Knowles was formerly a banker in London, Duff, if that is what's troubling you—but I believe he has now repented of both capitalism and l'ancien régime."

"A moneyman, eh? *English*, are you?" Duff asked, his suspicions changing form from the specifically sinister (*detective, spy, skulking assassin*) to the more categorically objectionable (*banker, British*). In Mexico among his Irish mates, his native American suspicion of the mother country had been honed to the beginnings of hatred. "You've come here from *England*?"

Ben glared. "I have," he replied.

"And how may we be sure of that?" Duff asked. "Your accent aside."

Skaggs was as bewildered as Polly by the men's instant mutual antipathy.

"Because, my churlish young fellow," said Skaggs, laying a palm gently on Duff's shoulder, "it was *I* who *discovered* Mr. Knowles last month at sea, aboard his steamer from Liverpool."

Duff started to relax. It seemed wildly unlikely that the army or even rich, ruthless Knickerbockers like the Primes would import a detective all the way from England on his account.

"And I am afraid that *you*, Mr. Lucking," Skaggs continued, grabbing a glass of whiskey off a passing waiter's silver tray and handing it to Duff, "require this urgently. And let me explain to you why Mr. Knowles here should be your *hero* . . ."

As ever, Polly had an urge both to comfort and wallop her brother. And to explain him to this long-haired, sweet-eyed, strangely eager pal of Timothy Skaggs's whom Duff had offended for no good reason.

She pushed her face to within a few inches of Ben's. His fragrance was . . . effeminate, she thought at first, and then realized why—no sour tobacco-juice funk, the characteristic aroma of the American male. He could smell the clove on her breath.

"I am terribly sorry for the rudeness you've suffered, Mr. Knowles," she said. "Permit me—"

"Oh no, no harm done, Mrs. Lucking, I only—"

"*Please* permit me to apologize on my brother's behalf, Mr. Knowles. He has been under a terrible strain."

Ben's mood improved so quickly and completely, as if by magic, that he was not yet consciously aware that she had called Duff her *brother*. The little orchestra was now playing the fourth movement of Beethoven's Ninth Symphony—*Ode to Joy*.

"He took our mother's death in '46 very hard," Polly continued, speaking softly, "and then he shipped off straightaway to the war. In Mexico? He has suffered greatly . . . as you can see. And he was always a terribly passionate boy."

Deliriously, just short of delusionally, Ben heard her last whispered words—*passionate boy*—as a lover's fond, teasing coo. As she spoke, his eyes darted to her mouth, to the pink daffodil over her ear, to her flicking tortoiseshell fan, then to her lips again, and her green eyes.

Skaggs delighted in what he called "moments of ordinary alchemy," when people and sensibilities were flung together and transformed into some new glowing thing, like gold and silver into electrum. But tonight he had been the alchemist, and his dangerous experimental alloys—Duff with Ben, Ben with Polly, Duff and Polly with *bon ton* society—already looked strange and marvelous.

As soon as Duff learned that Skaggs's English friend knew about engines, had abandoned his titled family, and risked death in a battle with the French tyrant's army across Europe, Ben was remade in his eyes as a noble knight-errant.

Ben had never met a fireman, or any young man who had fought in a real war. He was full of interested, respectful questions about both.

When Ben mentioned that he had been absolutely entranced by the sight, in his fourteenth year, of the old Houses of Parliament on fire, Duff practically fell in love.

"As it happens, the new buildings are actually much superior, I think," Ben said.

"Destruction and creation are the cycle of life," replied Duff.

Indeed, having simultaneously learned each other's true identities, Duff and Ben both experienced deep, almost identical surges of relief and shame which in turn reinforced in each man a sudden strong sympathy and bond that neither altogether understood. Each wanted to protect the other.

As THE NIGHT crackled along, Ben grew more spellbound by Duff's sister. So often in London or Kent he had admired the hair and smile and figure of some pretty new girl in the park or across a room until the moment she spoke and revealed herself as a ninny or a spoiled brat . . . whereupon her comeliness would ebb and disappear before his eyes. But not here, not her, as the drinks and conversation gave way to—good Lord—*dancing*. Each time Ben and Polly danced together (two quicksteps, a quadrille, an ordinary polka, and a slow, divine schottische), he wanted to pull her close and breathe her scent and tell her more, to utter every excessive, worshipful, and foul thought coursing through his brain.

And watching Skaggs quickstep with her, and chatter and roister around the party, alienating or charming everyone with whom he came in contact, Ben thought of Ashby's similar knack for inspiring instant fondness and contempt, and realized that his new friend and his late friend had blended in his mind. *All for one, one for all!* Ashby had shouted in Paris an hour before he died, and now in New York, as they all rose and left the dinner tables, Ben felt a little embarrassed by his own infatuated whimsy that he was d'Artagnan joining these intimates, this band of three musketeers, as their fourth.

Polly was delighted to see her brother suddenly so loose and easy and curious, the way he had been before the war had twisted and darkened him—he even danced with her twice. And Skaggs always pleased her best not alone in his rooms but playing the twinkling mischief-maker out in society.

She found this Mr. Knowles a little fascinating—his accent and recent adventures and promiscuous praise for her acting, of course, but also the fact that he was a man devoted to turning over a new leaf when the old leaf (family, work, income) sounded so fine. And his looks—the height, the shaggy hair, the long nose, the reticent smile, the alert brown eyes—she found appealing. He was if anything too solicitous, offering to fetch another éclair or clove liqueur and paying her compliments (the shine of her boots, her knowledge of Voltaire) that exceeded even her appetite for flattery. She was sometimes unsettled by gentlemen at 101 Mercer who worked themselves into rhapsodic frenzies . . . but then she remembered that Mr. Knowles was no customer, that she had deserted whoredom. It had been a very long time since she had flirted at such length with a stranger without any prospect of payment.

For a few minutes Ben found himself surveying the party alone, smiling.

"And what mysterious thought amuses you so, Mr. Knowles?" Polly asked, returning to his side. "Some peculiar local buffoonery?"

"No mystery at all, I assure you," he replied. "I am the only buffoon in this place making myself smile. I find everything—*everything* is perfectly . . . perfect."

She looked at him a little askance. Earlier he had not seemed arch or jocular at all, nor did he seem drunk now. "Are you toying with me, Mr. Knowles? Or perhaps your fondness for Voltaire drives you to impersonate not Candide but Dr. Pangloss."

"*Dear* Miss Lucking, my love of—in *this* best of all possible worlds, Mr.

Rumpf's castle is the most magnificent of all castles . . . and my lady the best of all possible ladies."

She blushed, he grinned like a fool, and she smiled at his grin, which made it grow more ridiculously wide, which finally caused her to giggle and shake her head.

Duff and Skaggs happened to arrive at the same moment from opposite ends of the room. Now all four looked from one to the other, exchanging smiles and, for a long moment, saying nothing.

It was queer.

"*All for one and one for all,*" Skaggs finally said, waving his hand in the air as if he held a saber.

ALL AROUND THEM the servants were treating the tablecloths like tarpaulins, wrapping into bundles all the dishes, cutlery, and scraps of food where they sat.

"Mr. Knowles," Skaggs said, "if I may impose upon you—several self-important gentlemen are begging to arrange an audience with you before we leave. They *crave your insights* into the European revolutions."

Duff had taken out his watch and turned to his sister. "Shall I drive you home, Polly? It's nearly twelve. I have—I have some work to finish before dawn."

No! She knew Duff was conscientious about his postering jobs, which were only done late at night. And she had picked up her copy of Burton's *Dombey* manuscript this afternoon; the cast was gathering on Saturday morning, the day after tomorrow, to read the play aloud together for the first time. She ought to spend all of Friday studying her part. She ought to get some sleep. *Yes.* "Yes," she said, "we must go."

She took Skaggs's hand in both of hers. "You are a good and generous friend." They exchanged a complicated look.

"Mon plaisir, mademoiselle." He bowed and kissed her hand, and then her cheek.

"This was a great fandango," Duff said, shaking Skaggs's hand. "Thanks!"

" 'Fandango'?" Skaggs repeated. "I need to start a word journal of my own."

"You will give Mr. and Mrs. Rumpf our heartfelt thanks?" Polly said, like the respectable girl her mother had trained her to be.

"Mmm, well," Skaggs replied, "perhaps another time. Backy is nearly unconscious, and Sally is angry with me for what I told her ridiculous snobby friends about their ridiculous snobby scheme to rename 'their' stretch of the Bowery '*the Third Avenue.*' "

Polly turned to Ben. "I very much enjoyed making your acquaintance, Mr. Knowles." And she sincerely had. "Thank you for disguising so well my ignorance of the polka."

A thick cable of her hair had come loose and dangled over her left temple. As she smiled, the corner of her mouth stretched up toward that loose lock. To Ben she radiated the kind of glamour one reads about in stories and poems, the bewitching glow he had been certain did not actually exist. *God, how I love you, my dearest darling Polly Lucking, and ache to have you in my arms now and forever, to follow and lead you, to adore and caress you, to see and taste every sweet exquisite corner of your body and soul.*

He took her hand. "I consider myself extremely fortunate, Miss Lucking, to have met you. And your good brother. I hope we may see each other again before very long."

DUFF HAD NOT lied to his sister—he did have a job, seventy-two posters to stick up around Greenwich Village. But he also had another task to accomplish before morning, well to the east.

No one lived there, and the shackly little shed wasn't worth a hundred dollars anyway. He would confess to a priest what he was about to do. Although he wasn't certain it would even count as a sin, given the sinful acts Fatty and his b'hoys undoubtedly committed there, at the place on the vacant lot in Avenue D they called their "jamboree penthouse."

But Duff did not delude himself. He knew that this would not be the kind of destruction that cleared the path for some act of creation. He was enabling no cycle of life. He was simply executing some righteous punishment, doing a small bit of the Lord's work. He prayed that the Lord would agree and, despite his promise to Bishop Hughes, forgive him this one last little fire.

FOR THE EIGHTH straight night, Fatty Freeborn, Charlie Strausbaugh, Toby Warfield, Bill Boyce, and Dick Owen had gone to sleep on pallets at the firehouse. For the last seven nights, their scouts had spotted no groups of Negroes anywhere near the intersection of Greene and Spring streets, apart from tubmen and carters and some parlor-house musicians leaving work late. Charlie had talked to one of the brokers who worked with Aetna and

New-York Life, and learned that the insurance companies paid $250 for any returned slave on whom they held a policy. But among Fatty and the other fellows, enthusiasm for the blackbirding scheme was on the wane.

"*Hey, wake up,* Fatty, wake *up!*"

It was one of the lantern boys, breathing hard and pounding on the wall.

"It's your penthouse, Fatty, over on Avenue D," he said, still breathless, "burning like a bonfire, it is! I could see it from my window in Sheriff Street."

BEN AND SKAGGS had left the Rumpfs' and walked east on Fourteenth Street, past the last of the upper-class shops and tradesmen, past stables and chandlers and lime kilns, past a workingman's tavern blaring with the sound of guitars and tambourines and fists pounding on tables in time to the music. But now they heard only their own steps. The gaslight had ended two blocks before, and the East River was two blocks ahead. The buildings grew larger, the chimneys taller, the brick walls higher. The chance that they were actually about to meet up with some of Skaggs's acquaintances for a "special midnight soiree," as he had promised, seemed to Ben increasingly remote.

"Sir," he asked with a smile, "I hesitate to ask, but given the neighborhood, are you certain that we are—"

"Shhhhh! In this bleak wilderness, I am the pathfinder. You must trust that I know where—" He stopped and turned to Ben with a serious expression. "Do you trust that I know where I am going?"

"Why, yes, I do. Of course."

"You do? You *do?* Well!" He resumed walking, now at a ridiculously fast clip, and swung right. "Such a reckless innocent skylarking fool you are, Mr. Knowles." Ben practically leapt to keep up. "I am very fond of that in a man, particularly in one who has something to lose."

They raced along for another block, then another. It seemed as if Skaggs might be about to break into a run. The odd spirit of intimacy and urgency decided Ben to find out, here and now, the meaning of Skaggs's quick kiss with Mary Ann Lucking at the party.

"Sir, may I make a personal inquiry?" he asked.

"If my choice is either that or some technical, professional, or political inquiry, by all means, yes."

"Mr. Skaggs, are you—do you court Miss Lucking?"

"A *very* personal inquiry."

"I apologize, but I must know the nature of your affections for her, and of hers for you. You see, I find myself—"

Skaggs abruptly stopped at a tall iron gate near a small sign—BROWN & BELL—and turned to Ben. "Polly and I are on familiar terms," he said briskly. "We are good and intimate friends, as I am with Duff as well."

"I see, but do I therefore understand you correctly to suggest that I might make—"

Skaggs turned away and said "*Rumpelstiltskin*" into the darkness.

A tall, burly man in a leather cap stepped from the shadows behind the gate. "No, sir."

"I meant *von München.*"

"That is a no-go, sir," said the guard. "That was for the last one."

"Ah *yes,* right, damn," Skaggs said. "What is it? The tip of my tongue . . . *Cosmopolitan?* No. Suburban . . . it's *suburbanism*! No? Hell . . . Wait! Yes! Metropolis? *Metropolis!*"

"Afraid that ain't quite it either, sir."

"Ain't *quite* it?" Skaggs pleaded. "But surely close enough."

"Megalopolis?" Ben guessed, having finally understood that a certain polysyllabic password was being sought.

The man threw the bolt and pulled open the heavy gate. "Good evening to you, gentlemen," he said.

Skaggs led them across a gravel-covered yard, and then through ten-foot-high stacks of milled lumber. Ben could smell the cedar. They crossed railway tracks and turned down a long, barrel-vaulted passageway. Finally, Skaggs heaved open a tall, heavy sliding door.

They stepped into an empty hall a hundred yards square, every surface painted white. The space shone with the glow of the full moon through the skylights. Hundreds of boards cut to different lengths leaned against the walls all the way around the perimeter. On the floor just to their right was the word ORIENTAL, eight feet long and a foot high, written in green chalk. The rest of the floor was covered with huge geometric drawings in half a dozen different-colored chalks.

"Forgive my detour," Skaggs said. His voice sounded tiny. The sound wanted to echo, but instead disappeared as if into the void. "My cathedral."

Was Skaggs crazy? "What *is* this place?" Ben asked.

"Where clippers are dreamt and born. Yankee clippers, China clippers, coffee clippers, tea clippers, extreme clippers, all clippers, faster, faster, faster still."

Ben stared at him quizzically, making no reply.

"We are in a *shipyard*," Skaggs said.

"They—they *draw* the ships on the floor?"

"Think of a ship's hull as a giant potato."

"A giant potato?"

"A *half* of a potato, I should say, two hundred feet long, cut lengthwise— the shape of a ship." He held out one cupped hand. "This imaginary new ship's hull is sliced, like the potato half, into a stack of horizontal slices." With his other hand he performed a potato-slicing pantomime. "Do you understand? Each of these great ovoids chalked on the floor is one of those slices of hull, drawn at actual size. They call this a mold loft. It is the pattern book for Brown & Bell's next new clipper . . ." He pointed to Ben's feet. "The *Oriental*."

They stepped through another doorway into a smaller attached building. In the center was an open tank sixty by forty, and four feet deep. The moonlit surface of the water was perfectly still. Here, Skaggs explained, the engineers performed tests of scale-model clippers.

"Extraordinary," Ben said. "Otherworldly. Sublime." A cloud passed over the moon, and the glowing space at once went dark. "Thank you for bringing me here, sir. This *is* a special midnight soiree."

"What? *This?* You misjudge me, you poor dreamy man. I am the crassest sort of literalist." He turned for the door and beckoned.

He led Ben to another side of the shipyard, and into a building that smelled new, where Skaggs repeated "*megalopolis*" to a second guard. They were in a warehouse, each of the first three floors filled with shelves and tables crammed with matériel—ropes, sailcloth, hooks, screws, pipe. But as they ascended the stairs, Ben could hear music and laughter.

At the top story, Skaggs stopped to catch his breath, stepped aside to wave Ben through the open doorway, and announced: "A genuine New York blowout."

The space, illuminated by candles, was a storeroom empty of all fixtures and devoid of decoration. Waiters were passing and pouring glasses of water and champagne. Ben had never attended or even imagined a party in such a place. Nor had he ever seen a more colorful mishmash of people gathered together. Half the crowd looked rich, and half of those were the sort of rich men who wore gold waistcoats and striped blue neckties and large emerald shirt studs. A few were accompanied by wives or fiancées. There were some ship's officers in full-dress uniform, including a captain. But there were also publishing clerks and watchmakers and painters, tavernkeepers and actors, even truckers and stonecutters. At each end of the loft were two clarinetists, one pair playing Chopin études, the other popular tunes.

"Who are our hosts?" Ben asked.

"Ah, the great riddle—one does not know. For a time, I spread the fiction that Astor was the secret patron of these affairs—that his agents in attendance chronicled these goings-on as a means of blackmailing the old man's business associates. They are held every second month, more or less, each one at some highly improbable location, never announced but rather . . . feverishly *rumored* among certain circles."

On the nearer side of the room sat four men hunched over a table, one of them a Negro wearing a fine suit. On the tabletop were two oil lamps and a chessboard with 160 squares and two complete sets of pieces.

On the far side of the room, thirty yards away, were three sofas, arranged to face the windows. Several people sat on each sofa, women as well as men, all staring at the moon and darkness and twinkling lights outside. None of them were speaking. A woman sat in one of the men's laps, her arm around his neck and their heads leaning together as if they were at home alone. Arrayed on a table behind the sofas were several brown quart bottles, a cake on a silver plate, and two large hookahs. Five people stood close to this table, most with their eyes closed, all breathing deeply—from the hookahs or from folded handkerchiefs covering their noses. Another dozen people, grinning and yammering, awaited their turns.

Skaggs saw his friend staring at the arrangement. "The instant awe and bliss of chemistry," he said by way of explanation. "Medicines for the super-strained American soul."

A man in a waiter's suit sprinkled dried rose leaves and candied sugar into the big bowl of one of the hookahs and then crumbled in a small piece of the cake.

Ben tried to sound nonchalant. "It's opium they're taking."

"From the hubble-bubbles, yes, or"—he sniffed—"possibly hashish. *Something* balmy and Indian."

"And the others?"

"Do I understand that your fashionable Kit-Kat Club circle in London is innocent of opium and chloroform frolics?"

"Perhaps only I am innocent," Ben said. Once again, Ben felt as though he had been whisked out of America and returned home to some secret Soho haunt of peers' decadent sons. "None of these . . . prosperous fellows works for a living, then? All of them are men of independent means?"

"Like *that* jack-pudding there?" Skaggs pointed to a well-dressed man sitting in a chair, jerking his head in time to "Turkey in the Straw" and attempting to spin his hat like a top on the floor. "He made his million as a dry-goods jobber. Nearly all of these nabobs are self-made men. Important ones, one or two of them."

Ben was surprised. "Merchants, you mean? And industrialists?"

"Investors, mostly. *Speculators.* Capitalists of the purest kind—financial magicians, really. Businessmen who sell nothing, operate no factories, and employ no laborers or artisans. Who have somehow divined the mysterious Wall Street spells to create fortunes, by means of private conversations and the signing of papers. Would that I had the brain and stomach for it."

"And all here dissipating on a Thursday at two-thirty in the morning in a shipyard warehouse . . ."

"Why do you suppose the opening bell at the Exchange doesn't ring till half past ten?"

"This is not the usual conception of America."

"New York is not 'America,' sir, not precisely, not yet."

From near the drug table came an explosion of laughter: a man on his hands and knees with his mouth open and his tongue hanging out rubbed his head and shoulder against a woman's red silk skirts as if he were a dog. The woman smiled and shook her head in both real and mock disapproval. Skaggs recognized her—she was one of the disorderlies-and-profligates he had photographed in Wooster Street a month ago, during the fire that drove them from their parlor house. That afternoon, wearing the same dress, she had been merely a chance subject. Tonight the bodice was removed, and she looked as tempting as the hookah.

Ben noticed him eyeing her. He was encouraged by the implication, emboldened.

"Mr. Skaggs, I—"

" 'What prodigious queer feelings will leap into the breast,/And make us feel funny in more parts than one,/If a fine girl is only transparently dressed,/And shows what would take a seraph to shun.' "

Ben chuckled. "You are a poet."

"Alas, no. I swiped that from a deceased pal."

Ben didn't quite register the queer coincidence (on his last night alive,

Ashby had also quoted a comic poem by a departed friend) because he was so anxious about posing his question to Skaggs. "Sir, if I may impose upon your sympathetic nature, I must ask you—"

"To initiate you into the pharmaceutical feast of wonders by yonder window? By all means, man, come along . . ."

"No . . . no, thank you, another time."

Skaggs kept walking, and Ben left him to the smoke and vapors and the woman in the red dress. Instead, he followed another party guest up the open timber stairs to the roof of the building, where a group of men stood near the edge chatting, smoking cigars, contemplating the city. Occasionally one of them glanced at an orange flicker to the south, a burning shed down Avenue D near Sheriff Street whose immolation, from this distance, looked pretty.

Ben fell into conversation for a while with a thin, fit older fellow with gray-white hair down to his shoulders, a dancing master called Prosper Skyring, who soon sidled off to greet a man who wore a cape and a patch over one eye.

Then he introduced himself to a man who seemed to be studying the dry docks and ironworks that stretched beneath them for a mile downriver. Carrow was a merchant officer, first mate on a clipper. Ben enjoyed looking down with him as he explained the silhouetted forest of iron trestles and cranes and half-finished hulls and masts and thirty-ton steam engines.

"That's William Webb's yard there," Carrow said, adding, with a sailing man's distaste, that the steamer at Webb's dock was the SS *California,* a new mail steamship built for runs to Oregon. "She puts out tomorrow . . . they'll float her just up here to get fitted out with engines." He sighed. "Between here and Grand Street they must be laying down a dozen ships, but hardly a one being made for the wind. Nothing but these *steamers,*" he added in a tone other people used for saying *harlots* or *niggers* or *Irish.*

"What are your routes?" Ben asked.

"Bombay and Canton."

"Tea, spices?"

"Opium," Carrow replied.

As Ben considered whether to mention that his sister-in-law was the opium-shipping heiress Tryphena Matheson, Skaggs appeared at his side, moaning.

"*Alooone,* Knowles! For yet another dawn I shall be all alone! That splendid-looking girl, if you can imagine, after flirting outrageously with me for the longest time, demanded that I pay her a sum of *money* in return for her private company! 'But I am not that sort of gentleman!' I told her. 'And I am broke besides!' But the stony-hearted goddess was unrelenting. So here I am, come to micturate into the gloom." He looked up. "My *God*, the stars are fantastic tonight, are they not? And I am pixilated tonight, am I not?"

The officer bowed. "I am Bailey Carrow, sir."

Skaggs was about to comment on the man's name, but a falling star caught his eye. Its long trail glittered for a second or two. "*Lord*, what star-shoot," he said.

"Mr. Carrow and I were discussing the business of opium," Ben told him.

"The *business* of opium, eh? As ever, the conversation returns to the late John Jacob Astor."

"May he rest in peace," said Carrow.

"May he burn and rot in hell," Skaggs replied.

Mr. Carrow excused himself.

"I take it," Ben said to Skaggs, "that Astor was in the opium trade."

"For years I would not touch the stuff for that reason alone. By the *ton* the hypocritical scrooge sold it, contraband to the Chinamen, to the English, to any weakling with a dime."

"My relations are in the same business."

"So you *are* very well off, eh? I've speculated on that subject since we met, and thought yes and thought no, to and fro, is he rich or is he . . . *po*'. My God! I *am* a poet."

"My father is rich. My brother is rich. But not I, the second son."

"And a black sheep as well. Well done."

"I have no income at all. I cannot even afford to buy wine, or books."

"I shall secure a Stranger pass for you at the Society Library, which considers me a member in good standing. You may read and read and pay not a penny. And the drinks they provide on credit."

"Thank you. I should be very grateful. Thank you very much."

Skaggs did not respond. He was pointing at individual stars, and very slowly turning around with his face pointed up. Ben worried that Skaggs might step off the roof, and linked arms with him to keep him safe.

"Are we walking?" Skaggs asked, a little surprised.

"Sir, I must tell you that I find myself bewitched by your friend Miss Lucking, perhaps even obsessed, but if you are in any way—"

"Polly Lucking is not my truly beloved, my betrothed, or my certified kicky-wicky. You are free to pursue her as you wish, sir. As her comrade, I welcome it. And now I must piddle."

Skaggs pulled away and strode off. "*Kicky-wicky,*" he had said; Ben had heard the phrase only once before—in Ashby's line of Shakespeare, in Paris, just before they took their turn down the Rue du Helder. Strange.

On the opposite side of the roof, Skaggs pissed off the edge of the building, his stream angled high, attempting in vain to reach the East River. Ben joined him. A moment later, a few yards away, the caped man with the eye patch stepped to the edge as well. Standing very close beside him, a young servant reached with one hand into the man's trousers and removed his penis for him, then held it out as the master relieved himself. When the man finished, the boy shook the member dry, replaced it, and, using both hands, buttoned up the man's trousers.

Ben glanced at Skaggs, who nodded discreetly. After the stranger left, Skaggs explained that these soirees were "famous for the good champagne and excellent pizzle-holders. I believe certain people attend only to partake of the pizzle-holding. Shall I call the boy back to attend to you?"

"You jest, sir."

In fact, the caped man was from a prominent family, a lieutenant with New York's Second Regiment who had lost his eye and both arms in Mexico. The young man assisting him was employed by his family.

"Not at all," Skaggs replied, giving no hint that he was joking. "Do you mean to tell me that none of the London clubs staff their water closets with . . . intimate hautboys? These days they are practically de rigueur in all the fashionable New York places."

Skaggs sat down on the precipice, his legs hanging over the side, and idly kicked his heels against the bricks. Again, Ben joined him, and accepted a cigar.

Before long they were alone on the roof. Skaggs pointed toward the rim of gray and periwinkle on the eastern horizon beyond Brooklyn. "Dawn," he said. "Damn. The universe becomes invisible for another day. Farewell, Alpha Centauri. Farewell, Neptune."

"Neptune is visible? With the naked eye?" The newest planet had been observed for the first time only two years before.

"Alas, no. One needs a telescope. A quite expensive telescope."

"You are an astronomer as well?"

Skaggs fixed him with a guileless and hopeful look.

"If only that were true. I have wondered if astronomy is perhaps the true and proper . . . my destiny."

The sudden sincerity surprised Ben.

Skaggs continued. "Do you know the writer Poe?"

Ben shook his head.

"He delivered a lecture this winter, about the stars and galaxies and the beginnings of existence, and I—I was tantalized and moved by his remarks. Which I understood only intermittently. But . . . he spoke of time and space as 'precisely analogous' to one another. He suggested that time and space constitute a single entity—as I imagine it, like water and steam, or clouds and rain, different forms of the same substance."

"Science, at that exalted philosophical level, baffles me, I am afraid."

"Yes, of course—as it does all of us. It's more akin to religion than to chemistry or electromagnetism. (Of which I am also ignorant, by the way.) But *this* is my first fuzzy glimpse of a sort of religion that I have ever found . . . not only beautiful but wholly plausible. My idea is to fit my camera to a telescope and make lunar and stellar daguerreotypes."

"Is that possible?"

Skaggs shrugged. "I believe so. Although it has never been done."

Their faces were faintly bathed in pink light. Only a few stars and Venus remained in the sky.

Skaggs stood, groaning with the exertion, and offered his arm. "Shall we walk? Before the shipbuilders arrive and thwack us?" He suggested they go to Buttercake Dick's for some doughnuts or peach pie and cream.

As they waited for a cab, Skaggs plucked one of Polly's pink daffodil petals from the collar of Ben's coat and displayed it to him between thumb and forefinger. " 'The summer's flower is to the summer sweet,' " he said, and let it flutter to the ground.

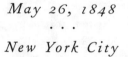

26

May 26, 1848

. . .

New York City

UST BEYOND A group of willows that waved and shook in the breezes, a short allée of elms led to a short pier. The setting sun gave the dark red sandstone walls of the theater at the end of the pier a golden glaze, a shimmer magnified by the reflection from the water.

As he stepped off the tip of Manhattan he heard the new bronze bells of Trinity Church chiming half five. Walking the planks now toward the little stone island, what Mary Ann Lucking had called a "concert saloon," Ben recalled playing pirate as a boy with the cook's sons in Kent, brandishing real swords borrowed from his father's library mantel, climbing the mizzenmasts and yardarms of the oak trees that lined the river embankment.

"Yes sir?" said an older man behind a counter in a yellow gatehouse. The man did not remove the cigar from his lips as he spoke. "What can we do you for?"

"I would like to buy two tickets, please."

The man stared at Ben for a long moment. "Balcony tables dollar and a quarter. Pit's fifty cents. I expect you'll be wanting *up.*"

"You 'expect' I will be wanting . . . ? I don't understand."

The man reached across the counter and pressed a pair of tickets into Ben's palm. "One dollar and twenty-five cents for a table upstairs."

"I have a question for you, sir, if I may," Ben said as he handed over the coins.

"Free country."

"Why was the theater built in this manner?" Ben asked, nodding toward the wall to which the ticket shed was attached. "As if it's a military fortress, in miniature? Even the door—iron, isn't it? And there at the top, running all round beneath the upper tier," he said, pointing past the big letters spelling CASTLE GARDEN, "appears to be a parapet. It's a very authentic-looking simulation. But why was the *military* theme chosen?" This seemed to be a New York fashion—the Negro doormen portraying hussars outside a store, now a concert hall built to resemble a garrison.

"This *theme*?" As before, the man paused a few seconds, puffed, then spoke. "This is the *Battery*, mister. This *is* a fort—the Southwest *Battery*. Built for our second war against your King George. The last time, in eighteen and twelve."

"Ah," Ben said. "Yes, of course. I see."

"Your navy never did attack New York."

"No."

The ticket clerk puffed again. "The fort did its job fine, I guess."

Passing through the door, Ben saw that the walls were eight feet thick. Every ten paces around the circumference were holes for cannon. The ceiling, decorated with yellow stars and crescent moons against a mauve field, and the balcony level, reached by cast-iron stairways, were recent additions. Castle Garden was plainly a real fort, now given over to entertainment.

Such a shameless freak, America.

In the lavatory, Ben was surprised to find that he was alone at the urinal, although a young man stood nearby at the washbasin. He exchanged a glance with the fellow and smiled—the American way—and then proceeded with his business. The man stepped closer, put one hand on Ben's shoulder, and softly said, "Yes?"

Ben assumed he was a pissing attendant, one of America's pizzle-holding hautboys Skaggs had told him about.

"No, I'm nearly finished, actually, but thank you very much. Perhaps another time."

Only when the bewildered fellow turned and scuttled quickly from the room did Ben understand that he had been the victim of a joke by Skaggs. Stupidly, he had never imagined the United States having sodomites. The practice seemed somehow antique, arcane, un-American.

Back at the main entrance, waiting, he watched a procession of cabs discharge passengers. As a loud, swaggering group of young men entered the fort close to where Ben stood, he felt a sudden spot of wetness on his skin, like a large raindrop. He lifted his hand to look—a teaspoon of brown jelly, one of the rowdies' tobacco spittle, clung to his knuckle.

And then *she* approached, smiling, only a few paces away.

He whipped his hand toward the ground. The brown phlegm, now a strand, clung to his finger, and he finally wiped it on the sandstone behind him. He removed his hat with his left hand, a little awkwardly, and bowed.

"Mr. Knowles," she said. "Are you . . . well?"

"Miss Lucking! No, I am sorry, it seems, I—an *insect,* or something, on my hand, but I—I am very pleased to see you again."

She put her arm through his.

Both found themselves more nervous than they had expected to be.

"Beautiful summer evening," she said, regretting her triteness.

"Yes, it is indeed! Almost." *Idiot.* "Almost summer, I mean." He grabbed at a new thought randomly. "On my walk down Broadway just now, I stepped over a lovely illuminated sidewalk. Have you seen it? It was made of glass coins set within an iron grid."

"Yes, there are quite a few now." He had *walked?* They were miles south of Sullivan Street. Maybe he was not rich. "But they are not decorations for our benefit—the glass allows daylight to shine underground. In order that cigar makers and tailors can be put to work in cellars."

"Ah." He was head over heels for her strong-minded manner. And her eyes, and neck, and the curve of her hips.

"But I do agree, they are very pretty," she added.

As Ben led her to the stairs, Polly was relieved; they would not be sitting in the pit on a crowded bench. And as they ascended the top step, they were both struck by the impossible beauty of the moment—by the view of the harbor (empty market boats racing home, a steamer thundering into its Hudson pier, a brig gliding toward the East River) and the gust that rustled Polly's yards of bombazine and blew her beribboned hair away from her face.

Her blithe spirit nearly dissolved a moment later when she spotted a young man she recognized from 101 Mercer. Mr. Mattson? Mr. Mathews? Mr. Mattingly?

"Good evening, Miss Morland," he said, touching his hat brim. She made no reply, and a moment later said to Ben that the man obviously mistook her for someone else.

At their table, Ben looked up from a list of available drinks and asked, "Tell me, have you tasted this . . . Mathews?"

She gasped. "Excuse me?"

Ben read from the little advertisement in the menu: " 'Mathews and Company's lively and healthful carbonated water, bottled in Manhattan exclusively from fresh Croton.' Have you tried it? Is it like seltzer water?"

She exhaled. "Yes, yes I have drunk it. Some evenings they make punch with it at, at my boardinghouse. My former boardinghouse."

"A boardinghouse serving punch to its tenants! Is America really such a gay place as that?"

"The city of New York is gay."

"You remind me of Mr. Skaggs."

"A man too gay for his own good."

"Are you a volunteer in the great war against the liquor fiend?"

She did not smile in return. "Liquor destroyed my father as surely as his gun, but no, I have enlisted in no crusade. In our late war against the Mexicans," she said, "my brother was nearly killed. That was enough war for me."

The waiter returned for their orders.

"A mint julep. And for the lady . . ."

"Water, please."

"I'm famishing for a beefsteak," he said. "Two?" She nodded. "And some strawberry ice cream."

So he was apparently not *poor*. Rather than look at him during the silence, she examined the brass capitals of the green iron columns that formed a sort of loggia—and then glanced back to see that he was staring at her.

"Cast iron is remarkable these days," she said, filling the moment. "I was admiring the . . . fronds on the tops. I should like to draw them."

"A lover of music, an artist, *and* an architectural savant. The Germans would call you *kultiviert und Kulturschaffenden*—a cultured culture-maker."

Was he teasing her again? "I am acquainted with an architect," she said. "I am especially fond of one new building on Broadway . . . just north of the Park? Stewart's, the big store they call the Marble Palace?" Polly turned her face toward the harbor, feeling the breeze, deciding whether to plunge forward all the way. Yes. "It is built of a dolomite marble quarried north of the city. And modeled after a certain palazzo in Florence, in Italy. They say it is done upon the London style."

"You truly are a student of architecture."

"No, no," she said. All of that information she had learned from one of Stewart's architects, a Mr. Snook, whom she had met in the parlor at 101 Mercer. "I attended school . . . my mother was determined that I become a teacher. She was appalled by my passion for acting."

"A badge of infamy! A blot on your escutcheon!" Ben grinned.

She met Ben's eyes straight on, but carefully to avoid the hint of any look that might be considered wanton. Flirtation in the regular world was a much more elliptical affair than it was at 101 Mercer. Each required its particular style of playacting.

"Lacking an income, one must sometimes risk infamy in order to earn a decent wage," she said, surprised by her waspishness. But why not? This was no professional engagement. She was free, free to speak sincerely.

"As you know, I am avid for the theater," he said, worried that his joke had insulted her. "I have tickets to the Astor Place next week, a new play, by a Russian." Now he was being forward—proposing another evening to-gether when their first had barely begun.

"I should like to see it, but the Astor is a black house."

"Mixing with Negroes is offensive to you?"

"No, *no*, a 'black house,' " she said, smiling as she pointed at Ben's black sleeve. "An audience consisting only of *men*."

His foolishness, he hoped, could pass as the charming idiocy of a for-eigner. At least it amused her. "Have you any roles in the offing, Miss Luck-ing?"

"Do you know *Dombey and Son*?"

"*Yes*, of course—Dickens. You . . . you are to play Florence Dombey? I read the chapters every month these last two years, and feel as though I know Florence well. But," he added, "I did miss the final installments. What happens in the end?"

"Mr. Dombey ends broken and alone, but Walter did not drown, after all."

"Walter?"

"Florence's lover. The two are reunited." After a sizzling pause, Polly asked, "And you, Mr. Knowles—you are not an enterpriser come to this country on business?"

An "enterpriser"? Another word he did not know. "I suppose I shall have to be one, for I have no alternative means of survival."

Aha: he wasn't rich. "My father was an enterpriser," she said.

"So Mr. Skaggs told me—in which line of business?"

"All lines," she said. "Any line. An inventor. An investor. A treasure hunter. Oil was the fever dream that finally finished him."

"He was a whaler?"

"He poured every last dollar he had, and some that he did not have, into a scheme to transport oil east from the Hudson River whalers to Hartford by canal and rail."

"A visionary."

Polly paused a long moment before answering.

"He had not counted on the appearance of kerosene. Nor the credit panic, in the spring of 1837. After that, he was done for."

Polly didn't know that the panic of '37 had nearly ruined the Primes as well. The firm had been saved by the timely arrival of British gold in Wall Street that fall, a loan that Archie Knowles had helped arrange and the delivery of which Polly, as a girl, had chanced to witness during her first visit to New York City.

"I am so sorry," Ben said to Polly about her father's misfortune. The same American banking crisis, he well knew, had enabled his own father to transform himself from the very prosperous manufacturer Archie Knowles into the extremely rich Sir Archibald Knowles.

The waiter placed Ben's julep in front of him, in a glass the shape of a globe that held more than a pint. The mint sprig floating on top had five leaves and was big as his palm. Polly could smell it across the table.

"The julep custom," she explained, "is to toast, sip, and pass the glass along to one's partner."

He lifted the drink with both hands. "To your impending success, Miss Lucking, as Florence Dombey. A toast to my evening's partner." As he gulped, a bit dribbled down his chin and onto his collar. She reached for the glass.

"You do indulge in ardent spirits."

"I suggested only that I know from experience how liquors debauch the weak and unwary. I hope I am neither." She lifted the drink. "To my new friend, and his grand enterprise, whatever it may be."

She sipped and exchanged a long glance with him that was friendly, impish, not quite demure.

Was it a wanton look? Neither knew for sure.

She was pleased to be with a suitor who seemed to have the heart of a boy (a different sort of boy than Timothy Skaggs) and treated her like a lady. She was pleased to be sipping a julep in the harbor breezes at twilight. And she was pleased by the preparatory disharmony of the orchestra, the sound of the instruments tuning. *Perhaps,* she thought, *I really am a student of culture.*

The musicians stopped bowing and blowing, and the audience hushed. Down below, the conductor, an elderly Bohemian by way of Kentucky named Anthony Philip Heinrich, had stepped up to his podium. He announced that the orchestra would play, for the first time in America, the overture to the great Herr Wagner's new opera *Tannhäuser,* and then, for the first time in any hall, one of Mr. Heinrich's own works, which he called the *Barbecue Divertimento.*

Ben laughed, shocking the people sitting nearby, who assumed he was drunk. "I apologize," he whispered to Polly, "but did he actually say '*Barbecue* Divertimento'?"

She nodded, and both smiled smiles of unabashed and unpracticed pleasure.

27

May 31, 1848
· · ·
New York City

*S*KAGGS HAD INVITED Ben to the theater as a gesture of apology for his pizzle-holder joke, and the embarrassment it had caused him at the Castle Garden urinal. They walked up the Bowery outside the theater where they had seen *New York As It Is,* a new play about Mose, the carousing, plainspoken New York fire b'hoy—the sequel to *A Glance at New York,* following the premiere of the original by only two months.

"You were unimpressed, I take it," Skaggs said. "Except when the chicken bones struck me"—someone had dropped dinner scraps from the third tier onto the parquet—"I believe you did not even chuckle."

"And where were your great howls of delight, sir?"

"Ah, but for *you,* Knowles, life is now all spring, sparkling prospects, and new vistas, your young man's fancy lightly turning to thoughts of love— *you* ought to giggle at the slightest tickle. *My* gloom, on the other hand, has good cause." He stopped at the door of one of the dozen noisy saloons and cellars they had passed in a few minutes' walk. "No filthier than the others. And German, so they have chairs."

They spent the next two hours drinking gin and slurping oysters. Ben was happy to learn that his friend's dark, spleeny mood had no connection to his own courtship of Polly Lucking.

At the beginning of the week, Skaggs explained, he had delivered a eulogy at the Greenwich Village funeral of his dear bachelor uncle Gaster Skaggs, in which he had marveled that Gaster had been among the last of that New York generation "who remembered a field of golden wheat growing at Broadway and Fulton Street." After the service at St. Luke-in-the-Fields he had strolled through what he imagined would soon be his neighborhood—noting the new houses at the bend in Grove Street and the cluster of cottages under construction in a cul-de-sac off West Tenth.

But the next day he'd learned from his uncle's lawyer that Gaster Skaggs's house at 36 Barrow had been bequeathed to something called the Greenwich Village Asylum and School of the Arts for Unfortunate Boys. The legacy to Timothy consisted of two hundred dollars, the old man's parrot, and a first edition of William Blake's poems. A minute after he'd left the lawyer's office, having disclaimed the bird, he had been assaulted in the street—struck with an umbrella, hard, three times, on his neck, elbow, and buttocks—by a rich brewer-turned-novelist whose first book Skaggs had reviewed harshly. When he'd arrived home that afternoon, a bill collector was waiting in the hallway, dunning him for sixty-eight dollars the man insisted Skaggs owed the Brevoort House Hotel for a room and a week of meals last summer—a week of which Skaggs had no memory at all.

"My poor dear fellow," said Ben after Skaggs asked the bartender to replenish his ice and leave the bottle of gin in front of them. "You *have* had a wretched time of it."

"A wretched time? Oh, but it goes on, sir, it goes on. Today, my so-called career as a penny-a-liner winked out completely."

In the morning mail he had learned that *The John-Donkey,* the satirical magazine that had been paying him a few dollars a month, was going out of business.

Then at midday his essay about time had been turned down by two editors, its third and fourth rejections. The fellow at *The Knickerbocker* was baffled by what Skaggs called the piece's "original and disturbing new scientific epiphany"—that the maximum speed of printing presses had precisely doubled during each half decade since the beginning of the century, and that this acceleration might proceed without end. The editor of *The Living Age* not only turned down the essay but had lectured him. " 'As an *old pal,*' the little pickthank had the brass to tell me straight to my face, 'let me explain—Timothy Skaggs is a *humorous* writer, a fine *jester,* from whom such sentiments and ideas as these are like being served a glass of beet juice when one is expecting a refreshing beer.' "

And then later in the afternoon, when Skaggs had dragged himself over to the *Tribune* to ask Greeley if he might read the piece as a favor, he'd learned that his services as a three-dollar-a-trip harbor journalist would no longer be required.

"And do you know the very worst of *that?*" he asked Ben as he poured more gin into both their glasses. "The *profound* melancholy? That they are not sacking *me*. 'I am certainly not displeased with your articles, my dear Brat,' Horace said with that horrible smile of his, 'you are simply an unfortunate victim of progress.' " He gulped his gin. "A *victim*," he repeated bitterly, "of *progress*! Of his shitty *cartel*, I am the victim." Greeley and the *Sun* and the owners of four other New York dailies had organized what Skaggs called "this monstrous 'Associated Press,' " which would soon employ its own harbor reporters whose work would be shared by all the member papers.

Skaggs spotted a burly man with a battered-looking face coming into the saloon. "Why, look here—another good fellow of the old school they want to make a victim of progress." He lifted his glass and shouted, "To *Young America*!"

Heads turned, and more than a smattering of hurrahs and applause broke out. Skaggs had shouted a nickname of Tom Hyer, the champion prizefighter and neighborhood fixture. Hyer smiled and nodded, acknowledging the acclamation.

"After the Christian busybodies finally do away with his occupation," Skaggs said to Ben, "at least Tom can still earn an income from selling liquor." Tom Hyer's, his saloon, was just up the Bowery. "Until they manage to outlaw drink, of course. Why, sir, must we let the new and soulless *always* replace the natural and sinful?"

"Mr. Skaggs," Ben said, "you are a conservative in bohemian's clothing. A radical beset by nostalgia."

Skaggs sighed. "You know, that was a true *disease*—nostalgia. The diagnosis and coinage of a medical man, a Swiss, once upon a time."

"But, Skaggs, you are a *daguerreian*. The epitome of the new. And the 'unnatural.' "

"Yes, and I am nostalgic already for the early days, five or six years since, when people were shocked and *unnerved* by photographs. When my mother saw a daguerreotype for the first time, a portrait of my brother's infant daughter, she called it 'obscene.' " He cracked a smile at the memory.

"I am afraid," Ben said, "that I pine for the renaissance of no bygone age at all. Not merry old England. Not ancient Greece or Rome. I have no real faith in the superiority of yesteryear."

"Callow youth." Skaggs emptied his glass. "Although nor do I, to be honest." He chewed his ice dregs and stared at his hand. "Yet even if I don't wish actually to *return* to the past, I am vexed as the very recent past disappears before my blinkard's eyes. The pull-down-and-build-over-again spirit saddens me. One day I counted the demolitions of *thirty-three* buildings on Broadway. I do not gainsay real progress," he concluded. "But I mourn all the victims of progress."

By the time Duff arrived, Skaggs had downed a pint of gin and was juggling hard-boiled eggs from the basket on the bar. As he juggled, he recited the Lord's Prayer to welcome Duff, and then asked if "your great entertainer Jesus" could perform tricks such as this.

"Don't, Skaggs," Duff said. Skaggs's blaspheming always distressed him.

"Your priests should take up juggling, right at the altar, at the end of Mass, amuse the Irish . . ."

Duff ignored him, turning to Ben to ask if they had enjoyed his firemen friends' new play.

But Skaggs continued the patter as his gaze flickered from the flying eggs to Duff to the eggs—and then to the door, through which another famous local character had just tottered. It was the Irish prizefighter and neighborhood saloonkeeper known as Yankee Sullivan.

"Speak of the devil," said Skaggs, still juggling. ". . . The Irishman in Ireland, you know, starves himself trading his chickens' eggs for tobacco . . .

"Then happily smokes his pipe in his hovel . . . his hovel, already thick with peat smoke . . . so Irish . . .

"Then instead of building a chimney, he builds a special chair . . . low to the ground, to keep his lounging head beneath the peat haze . . . *so Irish*— adjust to the squalor instead of fixing the problem . . ."

"*Enough*, Skaggs," Duff said.

Ben stood. "Shall we go and find a real meal somewhere?" he proposed. "As my treat."

Skaggs continued juggling—four eggs at once now. "My own Irish grandpa said they cultivate their misery . . . gives them a *reason* to drink . . . Do you know *half* the arrests in the city now are Irishmen . . . ? And half those for drunkenness . . . needless to say . . ."

"Yes," Duff said to Ben, "let's go."

"Was it the strong drink, Duff, *damn*"—an egg had dropped to the floor—"the liquor that caused such a number of your Irish brothers to desert the fight in Mexico . . . ?"

Duff snatched one of the airborne eggs out of the air and crushed it in his hand. "*Stop*," he said.

And Skaggs did, but not because his friend was angry. On the other side of the room, Tom Hyer and Yankee Sullivan were suddenly all over each other, punching and kicking, knocking over benches and glasses. Everyone in the place gathered around to cheer them on. Sullivan was bigger, but Hyer, with the advantage of sobriety, quickly got the upper hand. Within a few minutes, it was no longer much of a fight. Hyer had Sullivan bent over, one arm locked around his neck while with the other he punched his face like a sledgeman hammering, a blow a second. Finally he finished, shoved Sullivan away, wiped his own wet hand on his pants, and coolly pulled a pistol from his coat pocket and began to prime it.

"No, Tom," Skaggs said, "that's a *foul*, no guns permitted by the London Prize Ring rules." Hyer smiled, but before he replied, a policeman pushed his way to the front of the crowd.

"Put up the pistol." He showed his copper star.

"Any minute they're going to bring his gang in here," Hyer explained, "and I'm not going to let them murder me without a fight."

But the cop persuaded Hyer to flee with him instead. And not three minutes later, a shouting, snarling pack of Sullivan's men did indeed stomp into the saloon looking for Hyer—and found instead only their own insensible hero sprawled on a table.

Before Skaggs left for dinner, he turned to one of the angry Sullivan partisans, who was loudly demanding that the bartender pour a restorative drink for poor Yankee. "You know, sir," Skaggs said with a smile to the Irish fellow, "it was the whiskey that *did in* your man. *Abstaining* from the national elixir might be his best course just now."

The man's single punch to Skaggs's face sent him to the floor, knocked out.

28

June 2, 1848

. . .

New York City

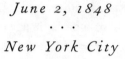

A S SOON AS Ben learned that Polly would be leaving soon for Philadelphia with Burton and the other *Dombey* players, his wooing acquired an even greater urgency. He would have taken her out every afternoon and every night to plays and dinners and for walks and conversations in the Park. And she would have gone, too, had she not been required to learn and rehearse her part in *Dombey*. And sometimes she declined a particular invitation from Ben for what seemed to him capricious, inscrutable reasons—that is, for fear of encountering at certain pleasure gardens or theaters men she had known at 101 Mercer.

"I confess, Mr. Knowles," she had said to him the third time they were together, "that I feel with you the way I do when I have begun to draw a picture I like."

Both felt reborn this spring, and now hurtled toward summer together, like a pair of birds in flight. Every day seemed sunny, every tree in bloom, the very air effervescent. Neither had ever engaged in a courtship so goggled and feverish.

The fact that he had kissed her only twice during the week after their Castle Garden outing, and had so far sought nothing more, filled her with gratitude and desire. The fact that after knowing him so briefly she had permitted him to kiss her twice, on the lips, filled him with gratitude and desire.

Their affinities of mind and spirit were strong as well, and served for both to roil their passions. At the theater, they agreed about which scenes were funny, which were moving, which were mawkish. The day after Polly told Ben she had read and loved the adventure story *Typee*, he brought her his copy of *Omoo*, by the same author—and as she eagerly opened the book to read, each of them was literally hot with passion for the other. One afternoon she mentioned that she was Catholic, a fact he found faintly exciting. Sitting on a bench in the Park that evening, Ben asked Polly if she remained a believer. She shrugged, then shook her head no, and quoted a sentence she had memorized by a Protestant minister in Tennessee—" 'Eternal doom or damnation is a hideous fable of a barbaric age; a dream of the fanatic, and a curse to all who receive it.' " For Ben this was another provocation to ravish her.

For the first time in the two weeks since they had met, they planned to spend a whole day together. They would rehearse scenes from *Dombey and Son*, see an exhibition of paintings at the Academy of Design, and then have an early picnic dinner. In his whole adult life, the only women with whom Ben had been alone in an apartment were his sister, his mother, various housemaids, and perhaps a dozen prostitutes. Her brother aside, Polly had never been with any man alone in her rooms, not even Skaggs. And so Ben pulled the bells in the vestibule of her building when (only four blocks from Ben—more kismet), both he and she felt an excited flutter, and took deep breaths to steady themselves.

"A good morning to you, Mr. Knowles."

"A splendid morning, Miss Lucking." The weather was clear and cool, but that was not all he meant.

Her building was a respectable tenement house, and her sitting room was furnished sparely but fashionably—to Ben's eye, like that that of a young don at Cambridge. Two Oriental rugs covered the floor. The tables and chest of drawers were creamy, golden maple and pine, not dark, lugubrious mahogany or walnut. Several of her drawings and watercolors were tacked to the walls, and he stepped close to look at each, one at a time, which pleased and rattled her.

"Very lovely," he said about a view from a hilltop of a town on a river. "Such precise detail, yet drawn with such a quick hand. Is this the village where you grew up?"

"No, it's Astoria, one of the towns across the East River . . . We lived nearby for a short time, before we moved into the city."

"Astoria? Another of Mr. Astor's property holdings . . ." *What a tedious clod: why had he turned the discussion from flattery and art to real estate and dead millionaires?*

"Actually, no," she said. "Just as we arrived, the town fathers renamed it in *honor* of Astor—with the hope that the great man might build them a lecture hall." She glanced at her drawing. "He declined."

Ben smiled. Wit in women had always charmed him; wit in young women, of which he had known rather little, aroused him. He moved on to the next picture, which depicted six small panes on the exterior of a greenhouse—an orchid was visible inside, through the glass, and in the foreground was the reflection of a girl's face.

He read the title aloud—" 'Self-portrait, Conservatory at Hurlgate.' *Remarkable.* And you were a mere, what . . . fifteen at the time? Fourteen?"

"Somewhat younger," she answered. "It was a rich man's greenhouse on Long Island. I adored the odors and even the feel of the dirt." *What a silly slut: why had she allowed the conversation to drift from craft and beauty to her deflowering and her plow-girl's sensibility?*

She led him to the upholstered wingback, and pulled a wooden chair alongside so that she could consult the playscript as necessary.

They rehearsed for more than two hours, Ben playing old men and young women, sea captains and countinghouse drones and governesses.

For a scene near the end of the play, on a moonlit ship's deck, the stage directions instructed that the actress playing Florence "sit with her head laid down on his breast, arms around his neck."

"Oh, Walter, dearest love," Polly said, her cheek against Ben's chest, "I am so happy!"

" 'He holds her to his heart,' the instructions say." He clasped her.

"As I hear the sea," Polly read, "and sit watching it, it brings so many days into my mind. It makes me think so much—"

"Of your brother, my love. I know it does."

The scene was finished. But for a long extra moment, neither moved. Finally Polly rose—but stopped short when she found one of her braids had snagged on his shirt button. Only after some seconds of fiddling, fingers on fingers, reddening face an inch from heaving chest, was she able to sit up.

After she retreated into her bedroom to prepare for their outing, Ben leafed through a small sketchbook on the table. The portraits and scenes were recent—the clock tower atop City Hall in winter, canaries in a cage, Timothy Skaggs grinning, a young girl with her chin in her hands, Duff Lucking asleep . . . He flipped to the end. On the last page were two columns of names, six female names on the left and a score of men's names—Mr. Snook, Mr. Skyring, et cetera—on the right. From each woman's name lines radiated, connecting it to two or three of the men's names.

"All ready," she chirped when she reappeared, hair back in place and bonnet tied—and then realized what Ben was examining.

"Forgive me for *snooping*," he said, using a word he had learned from her, "but I could not resist the pleasure of seeing more of your work." She nodded.

"Is this a list of your friends—Miss Bennet and Miss Bowditch . . . Miss Morland? And, perhaps," he speculated with a smile, "the matrimonial matches you hope to see them make?"

"No, no. Those names, the women are only *characters*. Elizabeth Bennet is from Jane Austen's *Pride and Prejudice*, Catherine Morland from *Northanger Abbey*. Do you know Miss Austen's books? I am very fond of them." She knew she was prating like a fool. "And the other names are merely—are inventions, my inventions, characters I imagined writing about one day, perhaps."

"A writer as well as an artist and actress! Your powers are promethean, Miss Lucking."

She was breathless, and blushing bright red. "A silly game is all. Idle fancies."

"I have the impression that none of your fancies is idle."

THEY STOOD IN a picture gallery at the National Academy, arm in arm, admiring an enormous picture of a forested Catskill mountain gorge at sunrise.

"More heaven than earth," he said. "Rather a fiction, I suspect."

"I suppose," she replied, "but captivating to my eye."

"Beauty trumps truth?"

She made no reply for a long time, looking hard at the picture. "Perhaps truth and beauty defer each to the other, taking turns, like good friends, or partners."

"And when both shine at the same time and place, the result is art."

She smiled, and squeezed his hand with hers, silk on kid. Beneath his trousers, flesh rose.

"You know, it is as if the painter . . ." he said, leaning in close to look at the name and birth date on the frame, ". . . as if young Mr. Church here shares a muse with Mr.—the German . . ."

"Wagner, our bit of German opera at Castle Garden."

"Yes, *Tannhäuser,* Wagner, exactly," Ben said. Now his member was swollen. His face flushed as well.

A few minutes later, when he told her he had never visited a panorama, she was amazed, and he in turn suggested that they find one right now.

They entered the sanctum sanctorum of the Minerva Room through a narrow, dim tunnel into a darkened room the size of a large parlor. The viewing platform on which they stood was cantilevered six feet above the floor, and a young mother and daughter joined them just before the show began.

From an invisible alcove, a pianist played one of Beethoven's sonatas. Above them, skylights inched open by means of pulleys and gears to simulate dawn, gradually illuminating the panorama. Beneath them was revealed the entire city of New York, from the Battery to Fiftieth Street, every pavement reproduced in gray plaster, the parks made of moss, every house and church and bank and pier carved and painted at impeccable pixie scale. A huge painting that circled round the miniature city depicted Brooklyn and all the suburban towns. Ben felt drugged.

Polly found each of the places that shone brightest on her mental map— the schoolhouse she'd attended for five years in Elizabeth Street; Chrystie between Hester and Canal, where the family had lived; her building in Third Street. Gas lanterns high on the wall lit an overhead canopy covered with a hundred paintings of well-known New York sites. Polly recalled Skaggs asking her to paint a mural of the moon and stars on the ceiling of his bedroom; Ben thought of his visit to the Sistine Chapel, where Lydia Winslow had whined about the pain in her neck from looking upward. The girl beside them on the platform whispered elaborate descriptions of everything she saw to her mother, who Ben and Polly realized was blind.

The lights dimmed, the skylights rumbled shut, the music finished, and the girl led her mother away. Polly paused for a last look at her tiny, enormous city—and finally let herself find Mercer Street just above Spring, Mrs. Stanhope's—before taking Ben's arm to leave.

Two paces into the dark tunnel, he paused and faced her and, raising his fingertips to each of her cheeks, kissed her on the lips. She smelled of lavender. He tasted of plums.

As he started to break away, she reached up with one hand to touch the back of his head with something more than a caress and less than a push, keeping his mouth pressed against hers for an extra moment, and then another. Soon he was encircling her with both arms as he had never done any respectable woman, fondling her shoulders and hair and neck, pressing her whole body, from bosom to hips, against himself. He shivered, she breathed sharply, he made a quick sound combining a hum and a moan, she dropped her bonnet, they kissed again, and didn't stop kissing. A minute passed in a blink.

When they finally separated and took a step toward the light at the end of the tunnel, they found themselves facing two boys on their way in for the next show, standing still and staring, one sucking a lollipop and the other a cigar.

As Ben and Polly walked out into Broadway, grateful for the air, chatting about what they had seen, she said she would like sometime to try drawing a picture of New York from a certain middle distance—far enough to see a whole swath of the city in a single glimpse, but close enough to make out barrels on a wharf or a particular window of a house. "Something like the scene," she said, "at the Minerva Room."

And so not an hour later they were sitting in a dinghy, rented for fifty cents from an old man who may or may not have been its owner, putting into the river. The picnic gear, his coat, and her sketchbook and box of pencils lay on the seat next to her in the bow. A folded wool blanket served as her cushion.

The oarlocks wiggled and creaked noisily as Ben rowed. Polly faced Ben, looking alternately from his eyes squinting against the six o'clock sun, to his straining arms and shirtsleeves streaked with perspiration, to the receding city, the stone and brick all luminescent and coppery. Her legs extended straight out before her, and she lifted her feet an inch every few seconds, the rhythm timed to keep the hems of her skirts out of the little bilgewater waves that washed across the bottom as the boat pitched and yawed. When they were a hundred yards out, he paused and looked at her.

"This should do perfectly," she said.

He stowed the oars, dropped anchor, pulled his hat low on his head, and leaned back, elbows propped on the gunwale. The traffic in the river was thin at this hour. The air was still. As she drew, he stared at her face for a few minutes (such fierce concentration), then shut his eyes, then stared again, daydreamed, back and forth.

An hour passed before either of them spoke. The sun was just splashing into the horizon. Polly put her pencils away.

"May I look?" he asked, sitting upright.

She had not, after all, sketched the western edge of the city in detail—no candlelit windows, no cargo stacked on wharves, only the outlines and shadows of big buildings, the spire of Trinity Church, the busy smudge of the Washington Market. A meticulously rendered human figure dominated the foreground of the picture, a man in shirtsleeves lounging in the stern of a rowboat with his hat nearly covering his eyes. She had drawn a portrait of Ben. He felt a gratitude and longing not simply greater than he had known before, but altogether different in kind.

Will you be my wife?

"The hat, I know, appears rather comical," she said. "And your hands look like sheep's hooves. I simply cannot draw hands properly."

"It is extraordinary." He looked up. "You, Miss Lucking, are extraordinary."

Must I tell what sort of woman I have been, who I truly am?

"You, sir, are buttering me terribly."

The wake of a schooner slapped against the boat. Ben rowed them closer to shore and dropped anchor again. Polly moved to the stern, carrying the blanket so they could sit together and watch the western sky. It was a deep, blazing orange.

"Even the sunsets in this country," he said, "seem grander and wilder."

"The colors are still more spectacular in the West, so they say. According to Timothy, the main redeeming feature of life on the prairie was the setting sun."

"When I was small, we had a nanny," said Ben, thinking of the woman hauled off to Newgate when he was ten for stealing two of the Knowleses' silver serving spoons, "who taught us that a spectacular sunset meant that God or the Holy Ghost had a nasty fever, and that we should pray for them to survive."

"How frightening for a child!"

"No, it was quite gratifying, actually, because it flattered us that our prayers were effectual—since the 'fevers' always passed, and the Lord always recovered completely."

They talked on and on, meandering from topic to topic and recollection to recollection as the boat bobbed on the leash of its anchor rope. During the hours they talked, eating the bread and cherries from the picnic basket, the rising tide lifted them two feet, twilight became night, and one by one the city's million flames were lit.

She shivered. He offered his coat, and irresistibly his decorous tugs and smoothings of fabric around her shoulders gave way to strokes, pets, squeezes . . . and at the same moment they seized each other. The boat tipped and rocked, then righted itself, and then both blanket and lovers were spread on the bottom of the boat in a wet, twisted dishabille.

Ben had never before put his fingers and palms on breasts and buttocks and legs and belly through layers of silk and linen and cotton; every prostitute had undressed before he'd touched them; and with Lydia Winslow and the three other girls he had courted, his hands had never moved beyond the tops of their backs, shoulders, and arms.

Polly and Ben breathlessly plucked and pulled at buttons and straps and strings. Their elbows and shod feet rattled the oars and knocked against the hull, each resonant thump sending the curious underwater loiterers—fluke, whiting, shad, bass—darting away.

Bliss was it in that night to be alive, and to be young was very heaven!

Ben knew she was an actress, a modern girl, a freethinker, even a radical, and so he had suspected that her chastity was not intact. Now he felt certain. And that knowledge, in this delirious moment, did not disturb him. After a while he sat up and took a deep breath.

"I love you, Polly Lucking." Filthy water dribbled from one of his cuffs.

"Oh, and *I*, I think—you are very flattering to say so." She was back in her seat at the bow, rebuttoned and relaced and now reshaping her bonnet in her lap, which had been crushed in the excitement. She was flustered. She had abandoned the whore's life, yet she had never before indulged in a copulation as whorish as this—in a swampy boat bottom, bedraggled and grunting and banging away in the open air. Although now, at least, he knew half the truth: *Polly Lucking was a fornicatress.* "And if I may add, you are rash to say such a thing. You needn't say it."

"I love you better than I have ever loved anyone. I think better than I ever shall love anyone."

"And I am exceptionally fond of you. I have never enjoyed a man's company more." She reached down for his hand and rubbed his knuckles with her thumb. "I suppose that I am only . . ."

"Abashed? *Do not be.*" He kissed her hand.

"Confused. Slightly deranged." She looked around. "We are in the middle of the river in the middle of the night. In a boat." She splashed the toe of her boot. "A leaky boat." Now she sounded to herself like a spoiled girl, which wasn't what she'd meant at all.

He hoisted himself back into his seat. "I am sorry."

"No, no . . ."

"I have taken advantage of the situation, and of your honey-sweet temperament. And in my great impatience turned what ought to have been splendid and fine into . . . this . . . higgledy-piggledy embarrassment. But understand, Polly: if you can return my love, I shall never leave you."

She had never said to anyone outside her family that she loved them. She thought of the passage that she had underlined in Fanny Wright's book, about sexual ardor being "the strongest and at the same time, if refined by mental cultivation, the noblest of the human passions."

"What does it gain us," Polly asked Ben, "to call our strong feelings 'love'?"

"What?"

"The great fondness and stirrings—the *erotic* feelings that I harbor for you, surely anyone would call these love. But love, love is—what *is* love? Between a man and a woman? What is it beyond a lucky affinity for a person's character and beliefs, together with a . . . with the sensual hunger."

"Yes, I suppose you are right." He had never expected to have this conversation with a woman he loved. Of course, he had never expected to find himself in precisely this circumstance. Astonishment built upon astonishment.

"And I believe 'love' exists," she continued, "as a means to lash those two feelings together—as a respectable word for the unspeakable half of the mixture, for our lustful feelings. So may *we* not call *our* intellectual affinity a great friendship, and our sensual affinity a passionate attraction?" She exhaled deeply. These thoughts had been boiling in her mind and heart for a long time. She was relieved to have spoken her piece.

It took Ben a little time to collect his thoughts. " 'Love' is prettier," he finally said. "And simpler."

"It is ornery of me, I know, to refuse the ordinary word . . ."

Ben shook his head. This was the moment which, forever after, he would remember as his moment of true and total capitulation. "We may use whatever language you wish." He lifted the oars and started hoisting the anchor.

"Truth trumps beauty," she said.

As they docked and he looped the line around a post, she pointed behind him. Just above the tip of Trinity's spire was the merest sliver of a new moon.

"Goodness," he said as he tied the knot.

"Shall we watch it rise?"

And so they sat together again in the back of the boat. She snuggled into his embrace and closed her eyes.

Ten minutes later, she was asleep against his shoulder. Had he been more contented, ever in his life? He had not. He felt as if he had been cured finally of a chronic headache or nervous tic. His craving for change and surprise and speed was gone. He was calm.

And then he was agitated. From the river came voices and the sound of oars and banging hulls as people boarded a small boat from some larger vessel, and a moment later from the land end of the pier he heard wheels rolling onto the boards, followed by two pairs of heavy footsteps. He saw the light from a swinging lantern.

He thought it must be men of one of New York's famous night-roving pirate gangs—the Buckoos or Gorillas or Baxter Street Dudes—come to thieve cargo ships at anchor. But now, given the opportunity, what evil might they perpetrate on Polly? He glanced around the rowboat. He grabbed one of the anchor's sharp flukes and hefted it; twenty-five pounds; it might pass as a weapon. But while he was willing to do anything to protect her honor and her life, could he fend off cold-blooded cutthroats with an awkward piece of iron?

The sounds of wheels and boots grew louder. One of the murderers was whistling a tune—"O, Susanna," rendered as clear and sweet as a nightingale's song, here and now as black-hearted a sound as Satan himself could conceive.

Ben decided their only chance was to remain perfectly quiet, shrink to nothingness, disappear. He slid down with Polly until they were nearly flat, athwart the bow. She wriggled into his arms and whispered a dreamer's breathy nonsense phrase.

The two men and their cart were now still. Their lantern light flickered down through the cracks in the dock. Ben lay face down, but he had the dreadful sense that the men were standing directly over them, staring at the rowboat's defenseless, motionless occupants.

And he was right. They were here to do a job—two jobs, actually, one they had done ten thousand times, the other improvised tonight on the spot.

Neither man spoke. Ben wondered if they were aiming guns. Should he cover Polly with his body to take the shots himself? Should he spring up and challenge them? His mind was still racing, undecided, when in the next instant their big wheelbarrow tipped up and over. Gallons of stinking mud came splashing down over the side of the dock and into the rowboat and water around it.

By the time Polly awakened and Ben stood unsteadily to look, the two men had trotted halfway back down the pier. And as he realized what had happened, he began chuckling, which alarmed Polly more. Then, as sludge trickled and dropped in chunks off his head and onto his shoulders, he started to laugh. Finally smiling herself, grudgingly, disgustedly, she wiped a thick splatter from her cheek with the edge of her palm. The two men had not been thieves at all, but night scavengers, two of the Negroes employed by the city as "necessary tubmen." It wasn't mud they'd dumped into the river from their night cart, but muck—400-odd pounds shoveled during the last couple of hours from the privy vaults of thirty households. Ben and Polly were drenched in a slurry of piss and shit.

They cleaned off the worst of it with handfuls of river water and their picnic blanket, then headed toward Skaggs's apartment, which was only a few blocks away—Timothy would be at home nursing his concussion and black eye from the other night in the Bowery, he would have soap and towels, and he would find their predicament deeply amusing.

And so the downpour of sewage had had its intended effect: the two interlopers, the white lovers, had been driven away by what appeared to be a foul but unremarkable accident—every night, tons of excrement were dumped from riverbanks and piers by scores of tubmen. A minute or two after Ben and Polly had walked out of sight, a one-horse wagon rolled down Hubert Street to the river, and another dinghy nudged the tip of the pier. It was the boat that had alarmed Ben a few minutes earlier. The boatman was a Negro who lived close by, a cousin of one of the tubmen. His passengers were five more Negroes—three men, a woman, and a little girl—whom he had met tonight across the river in New Jersey, aboard the fruit sloop that had carried them up the coast from Washington, D.C. The five were slaves. They had crept out of a fine new brick house in Georgetown a week ago, and hoped and prayed that a week from now they would be free in Canada.

"Go on," the boatman whispered, and the five climbed up into New York City holding their ragged satchels, then hurried along the pier, stepping lightly. "Don't need to *tiptoe*," he said after them.

He lit a torch and waved it slowly above his head as a signal to his white confederate at the other end of the pier, the Quaker wagon driver who would take these five to their next stop, the cellar of a house on a certain block of Greene Street.

"IT'S A WHOLE *wagon* of sambos coming up the street real slow, with a white man driving," the lantern boy had said as he'd burst in the door of the firehouse this time. "Real scraggly, too, they look like." Fatty and the other four had been awake, playing cards, so within a minute all five were armed, squeezed into the borrowed phaeton and racing north as fast as the horses could run.

They leapt out at Spring and ran toward No. 94 Greene. Three of the Washington Negroes, two of the men and the woman, were already near the cellar door. A white man shoved them inside, slammed the door behind him, and announced to Fatty and his gang that they were "acting in clear violation of due process, as well as all of the relevant city and state laws," and threatened to send for a police officer.

He was ignored. The third colored man had been collecting his belongings from the wagon and minding a little girl. Charlie Strausbaugh held a pistol on him.

"*Go*, Peggy, right now," the black man commanded, "run to that house. Your daddy *always* loves you."

Toby pulled a sack over the man's head, and Fatty pinned his arms behind his back. The girl started to cry, but did as she was told. And a minute later, the carriage was racing south back toward Anthony Street, some of its white passengers laughing and hooting as the others tied the hands of a Negro named Elmer Armstrong, late of Washington, D.C., his one week of freedom over.

→ ⊱•⊰ ←

29

June 13, 1848
. . .
New York City

EN OPENED THE windows facing Sullivan Street to let in the breeze. He returned to his writing table. For the moment, however, he was reading instead of writing. "In our one meeting in '37," his father's letter explained, "the young Mr. Prime seemed very tolerable for an American, although he is a man of your brother-in-law's type—like Roger, a little rabbity, frightened of The Game."

Rabbity Roger Warfield, Ben thought, *is only frightened of* you, *Father.* "Frightened of The Game" was Archie Knowles's peculiar, dismissive judgment of any man who had no obvious flaws, such as dishonesty or laziness or being Catholic, but who lacked *verve.* The purpose of the letter, his first to Ben in America, was to announce that he had written an introduction on Ben's behalf to Samuel Prime, a partner in the Wall Street firm with which Sir Archibald had conducted business for years. "Your mother would have wished me to provide this help to you, and therefore, whether you believe it to be meddlesome or not, I have done so."

The crusty, hearty, insinuating manner was somewhat easier for Ben to appreciate on paper and at a remove of three thousand miles, but as he read he could hear the old man's voice like he was spouting off right there in the apartment. The last thing Ben wished to do was to meet this Mr. Prime. He had come to America *fleeing* wellborn bankers.

Ben looked up from the letter to glance around his sitting room. The wall he faced was now a virtual reproduction of a wall of his library in Bruton Street, covered with the dozen framed aquatints and lithographs that Dennis, his former steward, had taken it upon himself to ship to America, as a final fond obeisance. There was the Pawnee warrior who had black silhouettes of bull's heads painted on his chest . . . the side-wheeler *Fanny* steaming down the Ohio River . . . the Indian boy with the silver ring in his nose and red and green stripes running down one side of his face . . . a pair of snorting, head-butting bison at sunset, a herd of peaceable bison at sunrise . . . and the Dakota chief who could have passed for Lydia Winslow's mother.

"Like sending coals to Newcastle, I am afraid," Dennis had written in his note, yet Ben was nowhere near such scenes as these. Except for the exhibits at Barnum's Museum, he had witnessed no war dances or tomahawks or eagle feathers, and remained a thousand miles from bison, log cabins, Conestoga wagons, and armed roughs in leather, half a continent away from frothing wilderness cataracts and infinite treeless prairies.

When he'd arrived, the city had seemed as unlike London as Paris or Bonn, and ten times more exciting. But now, not two months later, as he learned the dialect (*I guess that guy out on the sidewalk by the bakery is the storekeeper* meant *I believe that fellow in the footpath near the bakehouse is the shopkeeper*) and became more or less accustomed to the odd local practices (mail deliveries on Sunday and the ceaseless back-patting, tobacco-spitting, approval-seeking, and liquor-drinking), the differences between London and New York had come to seem equivalent to those between London and Glasgow or Dublin. There were more newspapers and Jews than in London, about as many theaters and Irish, fewer coffeehouses and Frenchmen. The workingpeople were, as billed, oblivious to their inferior station, but the New York rich seemed hardly different from the London rich.

When he had decided to leave England, he'd been inspired by a vision to change the course of his life entirely. And yet his life in this strange new city and country was beginning to feel familiar and ordinary. He was settling down, fitting in.

"You seem less and less a fish out of water," Polly Lucking had told him the night before.

Yes: there was the shocking and bedazzling Polly, who made all the difference. She was wilderness cataract and infinite prairie incarnate. Perhaps Polly herself was his staggering American adventure. He had Polly. Or believed he had her, anyway, every time she smiled or called him "dearest" or squeezed his hand.

"Isabel," his father's letter said,

> *was abed with chills for a week and some. She misses you. The doctor persists in trying to feed me laudanum for the frog wound (which pains me terrible even with winter over). Ah!—I am reminded of two matters additional. While I was traveling a Frenchman arrived at Prince William Street to enquire of you about the murder of a woman in Paris, one of your "revolution" friends. Shufflebotham told him you had left this country and that he had no fixed address for you apart from the Primes in New-York. Secondly, your brother's relatives have hatched a plan of business for America, which Philip believes you might helpfully assist. He will write you under separate cover with details & etc. Your father, SIR Archibald Knowles.*

Marie the stinkpot girl had been killed. It did not surprise Ben. The soldiers must have executed her in the streets that night, hunted her down after she waddled away in her fetters. He shook his head at the suggestion— *ridiculous*—that Philip and the Mathesons wished to enlist him as some kind of local agent.

He dipped his pen and returned to composing the lecture, his first, for which he had been promised twenty dollars.

Those extraordinary events which I witnessed? . . . No . . . *which I experienced personally in February in the streets of Paris, ignited my lifelong . . . fascination?* No . . . *my lifelong passion for America . . .* He paused. He dipped. . . . *for America, both as a place and as an* idea, *a promise, the promise of limitlessness.* The promise of limitlessness? Excessive sibilance. He scratched out two words and dipped again . . . *the promise of unbounded liberty in all things, and the robust embrace in polly . . .* He smiled; he scratched; he dipped . . . *the robust embrace in politics as well as ordinary social intercourse of new, untried modes . . .*

June 22, 1848

THE LECTURE HALL was called the Temple of Reason. On the first day of his first American summer, 316 people came to hear "a FIRSTHAND ACCOUNT by a native-English-speaking EYEWITNESS to the late REVOLUTION in the streets of PARIS which inaugurated the present GREAT & STIRRING EVENTS RIPPING ACROSS EUROPE AND THE WORLD!" The audience was a New York microcosm: cabdrivers and brickmakers and lawyers and newspapermen, intelligent Unitarian ladies, a few homesick Frenchmen, one old Negro, jumpy students from New York University and the Free Academy, frowning German leather-crimpers and corset makers who whispered translations to one another as Ben spoke. Sitting together on a bench near the front were a gas fitter (and poster-sticker and former soldier), an actress (and former strumpet), and a photographer (and hack novelist and former newspaper writer).

Ben spent most of his ninety minutes at the podium recounting everything he had seen and felt during his February night and day in Paris (omitting the fact that the "makeshift African weapon" he'd used against the king's military force had been a stuffed penguin). But he also delivered opinions. He said, apropos the killings and burnings that attended the current revolutions, that "even Nature herself uses lightning and flood and fire to effect rebirth," Duff nodded at that. When Ben said that the chance of an insurgency overthrowing Queen Victoria was equal to the chance of a coup d'état murdering President Polk and canceling the Bill of Rights, Skaggs chuckled softly and someone in the back of the auditorium cheered loudly and applauded.

As he reached his peroration, Ben said he was certain that the revolutions in Europe were irreversible, secure against the plots of counter-revolutionists. "Time and history move in one direction," he said. "My friend killed that night in Paris was a painter, and he said to me more than one time, 'When the paint is squeezed from the tube, you cannot put it back inside again—you must *paint* with it.' In Paris and Vienna and Berlin and Milan and Budapest, the paints have been squeezed from the tubes.

"But the effect on *me* of the remarkable events I witnessed was to arouse my love for wild, hopeful, virgin America . . ."

Polly, Skaggs, and Duff all smiled.

"My dream of America as an untamed physical wonder . . . as a great experiment"—Skaggs arched his eyebrows approvingly and exchanged a glance with Duff—"a haven of unbounded liberty, and an eagerness in every man and woman to embrace new and untested modes of living. And so, ladies and gentlemen, I humbly offer myself to you here now as a new volunteer in your continuing American revolution."

Ben was pleased with his performance. He had endeavored to be thoughtful and sincere but also cheerful, rousing, full of gusto, American. However, the applause was polite and perfunctory. The handbills and posters had not advertised the fact that Benjamin Knowles was English. For quite a few of his listeners—particularly the workingmen, like the two Irish hod carriers who had gone to the lobby to demand their money back as soon as Ben opened his mouth—Ben's nationality made everything he said dubious. And quite a few had come to the lecture wishing to be told that the United States itself was ripe for armed uprisings.

Several people stood to ask questions. The first, from a boy wearing eyeglasses, was the most cogent: "I am confused, sir, about whether or not you and the late Mr. Ashby actually intended to bear arms on behalf of the republicans in Paris or if you were, rather, content only to . . . *observe* the insurrection. And if the latter, why so?"

"The truth, I suppose, is that I am not French, and therefore I had no proper business plunging into their political fights to the death. For his part, Mr. Ashby was under the impression that the uprising would not succeed. And perhaps as well, I am not at heart a revolutionist of the gunning kind."

The answer caused people to murmur, and several to grumble.

The man who had applauded the prospect of President Polk's assassination asked Ben about the story appearing in one of the local papers concerning a secret brigade—composed of Parisian revolutionists, Jews from Berlin, and Irish traitors from Mexico—which was now assembling in Florida to lead a revolt among the Negro slaves. Skaggs snorted. Duff clenched his jaw.

"I haven't a clue about any of that," Ben replied, "but four months ago, none of us would have believed the upheavals now occurring across Europe. What seemed fantastic yesterday becomes commonplace tomorrow."

A German man asked how Ben had come to be "familiar with the sentiments of the British proletariat. Are you one of that class?"

"My father was the son of a wheelwright, sir, and while I certainly cannot claim to be a member of the laboring classes, I spent a recent year in a weaving mill."

"Doing *what*, then?" shouted one of the Irishmen who had unwillingly stayed for the lecture, "ballaraggin' the loom-tenders and countin' your gold?"

A few people laughed, but a handsome woman stood, frowning, and pointed at the Irishman. "*Shhhhh!*" she said.

"Ah, *shush* yourself, ya huffy little bluestocking," the Irishman replied, "it's a free country."

"Sir!" said a fellow sitting behind the Irishman, "in *our* country one is free to debate, not to hurl insults at ladies!"

"*Our* country, eh?" said a second Irishman. "To hell with ya."

Skaggs shot to his feet. "Mr. *Knowles,*" he boomed, trying to reimpose order and defend his friend without appearing to do either, "I understand that you are a close relative of the great lover of democracy and America, Monsieur de Tocqueville . . ."

Ben nodded.

". . . as well as a political associate and very close personal friend of Mr. Frederick Engels, the communist leader."

Ben nodded, and the audience's murmuring had changed from querulous to curious and respectful.

"My question, then," Skaggs said, "is whether it would be possible for you to arrange for Tocqueville and Engels and also, perhaps, men such as the great Italian . . . Mr. Giuseppe . . . uhh—"

"*Garibaldi,*" shouted someone in the audience.

". . . yes, and other celebrated friends of democracy and justice from around the world, to convene here in New York for a great symposium, an international parley, if you will, perhaps in the fall."

The audience was excited by the prospect of such a grand revolutionary symposium.

"Well, sir," Ben replied with a straight face, "that is a remarkable idea, an incredible plan, and I should welcome it."

Skaggs applauded, then Polly and Duff, and nearly the whole audience enthusiastically joined in. The lecture promoter strode up onto the stage and stood shaking Ben's hand longer than anyone had shaken it ever before.

A RECEPTION FOR forty people had been organized in a parlor off the front lobby of the auditorium. All but Polly and a teacher from the Brooklyn Female Academy were men, only two chewed tobacco, none was Irish or German. Skaggs informed Ben that a dozen were "*Tribune* editors and writers and other Harvard bores from Greeley's claque."

Duff and Polly stood among half of the *Tribune* men, Skaggs and Ben with the other half.

"Do you believe, Mr. Knowles," someone asked, "that Vienna can reassert imperial control in the East?" Before Ben could answer, Skaggs replied, "As my Hungarian friends say about such matters, 'Az isten lova bassza meg.' "

The *Tribune* men, most of them accustomed to Skaggs's mischief, tried to ignore him. The young city editor asked Ben his business in New York, "apart from enlightening the likes of us."

"My business here . . . my business seems to be," he said, "endeavoring to discover precisely what my business here ought to be."

"You see, Mr. Knowles," Skaggs interjected, "is a devotee of the Indian prophet Buddha—and thus his destiny is a never-ending search for his true destiny."

"And does what you saw in Paris," someone else asked Ben, "incline you to foresee the same sap rising in America if—"

Skaggs interrupted. "I do believe Mr. Knowles has said all he wishes to say tonight on the subject of France. But *I* certainly find the hundreds of new newspapers a worthy result," he said, referring to the post-revolutionary effervescence of journalism in Paris, "and if an insurrection in New York could be assured of the same result, I'd wave a red flag in Washington Square tonight. But I cannot imagine any politicians, not American or French or even Prussian, managing to employ a million laborers sensibly." In Paris, a hundred thousand workers were being paid by the government under the new system of National Workshops. The *Tribune* men were enthralled by the scheme. They had no idea that the great experiment was already over—that days earlier, the French Assembly had voted to abolish the workshops.

"But, Skaggs," said Bayard Taylor, a friend of his and one of the younger *Tribune* men, "surely you are not on the side of the bankers and industrialists in this fight? Why *not* let the poor men who toil take control of their own arrangements?"

"Because, Bayard, if I, like our comrades in the new French republic, am *guaranteed* one and a half francs a day to dig trenches and sew flags, or, alternatively, one franc to loaf patriotically, I should certainly choose loafing."

The others shook their heads.

Across the room, Polly and Duff were listening to the other *Tribune* men question a Mr. Noyes about Oneida, the community he had founded upstate, and its new offshoot at a house in Brooklyn Heights. The men were arguing the differences among the various utopian schemes, discussing a half dozen of them—Perfectionism versus Fourierism versus a more general Associationism, socialism versus Noyes's "Bible communism." Through this fog of jargon, Polly was intrigued by the glimmers of life at Oneida.

When one of the *Tribune* men, Mr. Brisbane, asked Noyes whether "your fourscore members of Oneida truly practice *free love,*" both Luckings snapped to attention—Duff because he had never heard the phrase, Polly because she had discussed it recently with her new friend Mary Gove.

"If by your slippery term 'free love' you mean the invidious caricatures that appear in certain newspapers, then by all that's holy, sir, *no,*" Noyes replied. "But if you mean a righteous opposition to tyranny over the form of any individual's affections, man or woman, why then, yes indeed."

He shot Polly a quick, magisterial smile, which she returned. Duff glared at him.

"Though a man loves apples," Noyes added, "may he not relish a peach too?"

Free love as Polly understood it meant freedom from the dreariest oppressions of marriage. And these new colonies, whatever their particular philosophies, sounded splendid to her, like her country girlhood but reorganized as an idyll: bed, books, companionship, civilized conversation, fresh food, clean air, free water, green fields. She listened closely as the *Tribune* fellow, Brisbane, like a kindly schoolteacher, described for her such places that he had visited.

Noyes and most of the other guests drifted out. Those remaining formed one circle, and the conversation returned to Paris, not the new utopia but the swoony old one—a breakfast of eggs and absinthe overlooking the Seine at the Café Cuisinier, the twenty thousand dollars paid to George Sand for her latest novel, the summer fragrance of the carnation beds and apple orchard in the Jardin du Luxembourg . . .

NONE OF THEM imagined as they chatted that Paris was at that moment a frenzy of gunfire and explosions and death. Thousands of unemployed ditchdiggers and weavers and carpenters, and some of their wives and children (as well as men like Ashby's friend Théodore), had gathered in two hundred different blocks of the city and once again heaped together wreckage and garbage to block the streets. At the summits of their great piles they affixed flags that bore hand-painted slogans—*Du travail ou la mort!* . . . Work or Death! . . . *Du pain ou la mort!* . . . Bread or Death! But this time, unlike in February, the great mass of Frenchmen were more frightened than sympathetic, and this time the regime—the new, liberal rulers of the republic, including the Count de Tocqueville—were resolute. This time, it was not a lark on either side, but war, determined and horrible.

As soon as the barricades had been raised, the Assembly declared a state of siege and the battle began—and still raged now, through the Paris night and into morning. Against the Paris revolutionists, the army *and* National Guard *and* Mobile Guard—more than one hundred thousand uniformed men in all—unleashed not only cavalry charges and musket fire but artillery assaults. In the course of five minutes' bombardment, a flurry of 20-pounders striking near the Pont Saint-Michel turned the Café Cuisinier to a ruin. Thousands more national guards were racing toward Paris at superhuman speed, on the railways. By the next twilight, when forty-nine prisoners (including Théodore Surville) would be shot by a squad of guardsmen in the Luxembourg Gardens, the battle would be all but finished. And by Monday morning, the corpses would number in the thousands and the prisoners in the tens of thousands. In only three days in February the republicans' revolution had been won, and in only three days in June the socialists' revolution would be defeated.

ANOTHER THREE WEEKS would pass before eyewitness accounts of the counter-revolution reached New York City—the same date that news of the original, February upheaval would finally make its way to San Francisco, thereby inspiring the editor of *The Californian* to publish an extra under the headline THE WHOLE WORLD AT WAR. In fact, it wasn't properly an extra edition; by then *The Californian* hadn't published at all for a month, because almost every man in San Francisco had quit work and headed for the hills to hunt gold. And *that* news—gold by the ton, gold sand and gold pebbles and hefty gold rocks, glittering in the water and dirt and all free for the grabbing by anyone with the luck or pluck to get himself to the California hills *right now*—would not reach New York until the late summer.

—»•≪—

30

June 26, 1848

. . .

New York City

*S*KAGGS HAD INSISTED on the dinner at Shakespeare's to celebrate Ben's twenty-seventh birthday—his treat. Polly and Ben sat together on the bench across from him.

"Just look at you nubiles," Skaggs said. "Like a happy married couple." He put up his fingers to form a frame in front of his face. "Portrait of young love."

"Please," Ben pleaded, "she will flee if you suggest she resembles a wife."

"Ah yes, well," Skaggs said to Ben as if Polly were not present, "now that she has fallen under the influence of these *Tribune* Crazyites and Mrs. Mary Gove, she will be an ultra by the fall, a regular come-outer, cutting and stitching all her French dresses into pants."

Polly sipped her gin and rolled her eyes.

From the bag at his side Skaggs lifted a stack of little books he had tied together with a red ribbon. "A happy birthday to you, Ben."

Ben untied the bow and briefly examined the paper covers—all seven were by T. Bailey. "Thank you very much, Skaggs—I take it this Mr. Bailey is a great favorite?"

"Mr. Skaggs," Polly said, "*is* this Mr. Bailey."

"A pen name," confessed the author.

"You are a novelist as well! What a remarkable secret to have kept."

"Alas, a quite unremarkable one," Skaggs replied, "a mere scribbler of lurid tales that require a week to write, two bits to buy, and a day to read. You now own my *oeuvres complètes*."

The titles were *Passions Down South, Satan's Romp on the Hartford and New Haven Railroad, The Moonrakers of Capitol Hill, A Private History of a Certain Shocking Donnybrook, The Fancymonger and the Maniac, Too Much of a Good Thing,* and *Ruined by a Nunnery.*

"Pulp pamphlets," Skaggs said as Ben looked at each one, "smutty trifles, a mangy literature of the epithumetical."

Ben chuckled and looked up. "Of the what?"

"Epithumetical? Embracing the animal passions. From the Greek." Skaggs pushed his face across the table toward Polly and whispered loudly, "Shocking what a Cambridge man doesn't know these days, eh?"

"Timothy," she explained to Ben, "has made and memorized an index of every word in the dictionary with a definition that includes the word 'lust.' I'm surprised you're unfamiliar with the recitation."

"Well," Skaggs said, "since your chaste baby brother has not yet arrived . . ." He stood, teetered, and cleared his throat. "*Bawdy,*" he said. "Brothel. Carnality. Concupiscence, corruption, cupidity, debauchery, enslave—"

"Wait," Polly interrupted, "what of 'desire'?"

"Damn! Yes." Skaggs sat. "I defer to my understudy, Miss Mary Ann Lucking."

Ordinarily she would have smiled and shaken her head in more or less ladylike fashion. But with the blush of gin in her cheeks mingling with the blushes of embarrassment and glee, she accepted his challenge. She remained seated but began reciting, counting off each on her fingers: "Debauchery, desire, enslave, entice—"

"*Go,* hussy, *go,*" Skaggs said.

". . . flagrancy, inflame, lasciviousness, lechery, lewd, lewdster, libertine, libidinous, loose, pander, pimp . . . uhh, provocative."

"And?" Skaggs said, making small, quick revolutions with one hand. "*And?*"

"You may finish, sir," Polly said. She realized that even after two gins she could not bring herself to say the next word.

"*Rut,*" Skaggs shouted, "sensual, tempt, unbridled, and—most significantly in our land of the free—*voluntary.*"

Ben felt slight jealousy and great affection for Skaggs, slight fear of and great desire for Polly. He had befriended a libertine. Was he also in love with a trollop?

Ah, *words,* mere prim and hoary English *words.* He thought that in these last giddy minutes he had stumbled across some final threshold into America, that he was in any case freed from the nervous fetters of his former life, relieved of the morbid fear that his father or mother or schoolmaster or vicar was hovering nearby, disappointed and disgusted, hissing reproofs. Shockingly, Ben found himself not shocked at all by Skaggs's and Polly's ribaldry.

"Bravo," he said, applauding, "and brava as well."

Which is not to say he had really cast off a lifetime of propriety. He was still capable of shock, as he discovered only a few hours later, naked with Polly in his bed in Sullivan Street.

31

July 3, 1848

. . .

in the Atlantic

A s Drumont's vessel slipped from the pier at Plymouth a week earlier, he had watched a Channel steamboat dock a hundred yards away. The boat had carried the first Paris papers with news of the weekend's combat. By the time translations of the news of the counter-revolution had spread up and down the quay, his ship, the *Ivanhoe,* was outside the breakwater, nosing into the Atlantic. And so Gabriel Drumont left Europe and England unaware that General Cavaignac, his old commander in Algeria, had pacified and exterminated a whole brigade of insurrectionist scum in Paris, and now ruled France under martial law. If he had known these happy facts, perhaps he would have sailed east instead of west, returned home. If, perhaps; if, perhaps.

On the second day out, the weather had turned squally, and so it had remained. The *Ivanhoe* left Plymouth with 22 passengers in cabin and second class and 373, including Drumont, crammed into three steerage holds. The count in steerage was now down to 362, a death rate—not quite two corpses a day hurled overboard—that the crew considered unremarkable. There was no priest aboard, but the sobbing and wakes and amateur funeral Masses were almost continuous, the song of steerage.

The smell of steerage was, at best, the ordinary miasma produced by the sweat and belches and farts of several hundred unwashed people subsisting on bread and a porridge of barley and smashed peas and the occasional boiled maggot, and, at worst, the smells of mingled excrements and vomits. (A string of horses and a flock of sheep were also aboard.) Any draft of fresh air was a very occasional gift, since stormy weather required that the hatches remain shut for safety's sake.

Drumont was glad to be among the Irish. They were Catholics, at least, dirty and sick but people with *heart*, unlike the frigid English. Drumont gambled with them, winning with a game of dice drinking rights to the favored water barrel—the better cask had carried wine on the previous crossing, rather than turpentine. He also got drunk with them once, and barely restrained himself from flashing his wad of pounds sterling to prove he did not *need* to travel in such miserable conditions.

Except when he was seasick, he kept to his berth. The bed was narrow, but it was the top in a stack of three (another dice game won), and it was better than perpetually stooping to stand or walk in the five-foot hold. At least he had a mattress. Which he had taken without asking from his Huguenot landlord in Pleasant Place. He also had two big books, Vidocq's *Mémoires* and a new one, a guide to America lent him by the Huguenot's wife. It was called *La Démocratie en Amérique,* by a count, Tocqueville. (Leave it to the aristocrats to explain democracy.)

As the *Ivanhoe* pitched in a bad wind, Drumont was particularly heartened by one of the Comte de Tocqueville's sentences, and read it a second time, his lips forming the words to be sure he understood. America is "a nation of conquerors . . . which shuts itself up in the solitudes of America with an axe and a newspaper . . . a restless, calculating, adventurous race which sets coldly about the deeds that can only be explained by the fire of passion." *Les conquerors, les solitudes, une hache, froidement calculan, le feu de la passion*—a country perfect for Gabriel Drumont.

The old man in the next berth down blew his nose again, his snot flying onto the sleeping man below him.

New York City

As ILLINOIS GLIDED past and Mrs. Banvard played "Jim Crack Corn" on the piano, Skaggs felt a little envious (the celebrated Mr. Banvard looked thirty, maybe younger) and a little foolish: *why,* when he had stood on the bank of the real thing four years before, had he not traveled that last half mile, *across* the Mississippi, to smell the air and step on the earth of the West?

Ben had read last year about Banvard's Grand Moving Panorama, its depiction of the whole length of the great river, and when he'd noticed one of Duff's posters advertising "FINAL DAYS in this City before its departure for a theatrical tour in BRITAIN & EUROPE," he'd suggested they all go to commemorate Polly's final days in this city before her departure for her theatrical tour in Philadelphia. As he watched the painted panorama of limestone bluffs and cottonwood forests unfurl and disappear, listening to the lively music and narration, he wondered why he had waited months to experience this marvel.

Polly was also charmed by the pictures of dreamy, spacious western arcadia, but she tried to ignore Mrs. Banvard's music and Mr. Banvard's jokes and anecdotes to concentrate on his painterly technique. Her study was made difficult, however, by the constant passage of the canvas from right to left across the stage. Around the Iowa-Missouri border she concluded that the movement of the picture served two functions—to simulate the experience of traveling downriver, of course, but also to disguise the artist's mediocre skills with brush and paint.

Duff took notes. But he wrote down not just the unfamiliar phrases, as usual, like "stogies" for work shoes and "broad horns" for the flat-bottomed riverboats, but also shorthand highlights of what Banvard said about the enormous boils and swells in the river, about the telegraph line that was strung nearly all the way from Dubuque down to New Orleans. He stopped scribbling to stare when the scene of a burning Memphis wharf glided by.

None knew it, but this Manhattan hour of watching a two-and-a-half-mile-long picture of the heart of the American continent—"THE LARGEST PAINTING IN THE WORLD!"—was the last they would all be together for a long while.

On the sidewalk outside Duff bid Polly goodbye, kissed her cheek, and promised again that he would look after Priscilla Christmas and "defend her against all trouble." Skaggs lifted her hand to his lips and kissed it. "Travel safely, act as if you are not acting, and we await your triumphant return next month. And beware Mr. Burton's greasy inveiglements." She was to leave with the *Dombey* company the next day, the Fourth of July, for Philadelphia.

"And thank you, brother-in-law," Duff said to Ben, "for treating us to the excellent show."

"*Ah,* Duff," said Skaggs, "how fortunate that neither of you is an Arab or an African, for in those regions, to address a man who is not one's brother-in-law as 'brother-in-law' is a sordid insult. It would mean, in this instance, that you had enjoyed extreme intimacies with Mr. Knowles's sister."

As BEN ESCORTED Polly home, they passed a pack of boys all whistling some tune in unison and one of them drumming on the doors they passed. He saw a worried look cross her face. She sighed. He worried that Duff's "brother-in-law" remark had distressed her.

"What's the matter?" he asked, using the American argot.

She shook her head. "Nothing, I hope."

"Is it the conference with Mr. Burton that upsets you?" At the end of the *Dombey* rehearsal that morning, Burton had asked her to meet with him "to discuss privately some aspects of the production" that evening. "If you wish," Ben said, "I should be pleased to accompany you . . ."

She gripped his arm more tightly. "My fears are for Priscilla." Polly had told Ben that the father's rages when he drank were growing worse, and his condition when he failed to drink more dire and pathetic. But Polly's greatest worry now, she said as she prepared to leave for Philadelphia, concerned a ruffian, an acquaintance of Duff's, who lurked about, insulting Priscilla in the streets and presuming familiarities, *imposing* familiarities . . .

Ben did his best to calm her, offered to look in on Priscilla himself. By the time they'd reached Third Street, their conversation had turned to Polly's latest drawings. She innocently invited him in for a viewing and a glass of tea, and he innocently accepted.

He picked through the sheaf of new cityscapes and portraits and complimented each, but when he reached a charcoal self-portrait of Polly at a mirror, smiling, looking more impish than angelic, he brought the picture close and inspected it carefully, longingly, almost reverently. She told him to take it with him, as a gift.

He grasped her right hand in his, then her left, and a few minutes later, after she had run to the other room to apply a preventative syringe and returned, they were embracing and shimmying together on her bed. A week ago, during their night together after his birthday dinner, she had taken his member into her mouth, sodomized him, which until that moment he had never imagined any woman but a whore would do. And now, during their hour of play on this afternoon of their last day together, Polly once again behaved shockingly, both by initiating a second act of intercourse and then by *straddling* him as no whore had ever done, the open front flaps of her drawers fluttering as she huffed and twisted and heaved.

Afterward, they lay together silently on the damp sheets, both facing the window, which despite the curtains brightened and darkened as clouds passed over the afternoon sun. He held her lightly at the waist. He was naked. The small chair in the room had almost disappeared, draped and piled higgledy-piggledy with her dress and petticoats, his coat and trousers and shirt. His undershirt and her shift formed a white linen puddle on the floor. A single fly buzzed in and out of one of his boots. They silently counted church bells striking one, two, three, four, five.

"I must go soon," she said.

"I know that you must." He hugged her, and felt her buttocks and the silk of her drawers against his thighs.

"Will you marry me?"

She looked down at his hands beneath her breasts and said nothing.

"Will you marry me, Polly Lucking?"

"I am yours already."

He was irritated. "Will you *marry* me?"

She turned over to face him. "I love you, Ben, I will say that. I love you." She had never said it before. His hopes blossomed. "But what bliss more would a priest's words and a stamped paper give us?" Their faces were inches apart. "I am yours. But let us not, not"—she stammered, then re-membered something she had heard in a lecture—"not put the police badge on a great passion."

His irritation now contained a tinge of alarm as well. "You oppose mar-riage as if it were a vice. And yet, yet, *here*, you . . ." He could not bring himself to say it outright. He did not wish to say it outright, but she under-stood his meaning.

"I make love wholeheartedly? Would you prefer a meek, immobile girl? Or a statue? I am not that." She had startled herself by her boldness.

He did not want to make her angrier. He did not want to accuse her of immorality; he did not want to believe that he considered her immoral.

He raised himself on one elbow and assumed an earnest tone he imag-ined to be loving. "This is a difficult matter to discuss." He paused. "Polly, do you—are you familiar with an illness called . . . nymphomania?"

She did not know the word. But she thought she suddenly understood Ben's quixotic, almost desperate wish to marry, and for that matter his sudden, inexplicable abandonment of his family and career in England. She looked at him now with the deepest sympathy. *He suffers from a fatal illness, some exotic, incurable disease*—nymphomania. *He wanted to see America and now to marry before he dies.*

She reached up to put her hands on his cheeks. *So young and sweet and romantic.* Her eyes watered. She shook her head.

"No? Perhaps," he attempted, "you know the condition called 'furor uterinus'?"

Polly shook her head again, now struggling not to cry. He seemed so stoical to her, so heroically serene about his sickness, whatever it was . . . Of course she would marry him now.

"These are true illnesses," he continued, "medical conditions, not matters of . . . of *sin.*"

"Oh no, my darling, certainly not." His malady, nymphomania, was apparently some consequence of alcoholism, or drug addiction, or venereal disease . . .

"And there are physicians of my acquaintance, specialists, among the most advanced men in London, who have devised treatments to cure the condition . . ."

"Yes, *yes.*"

"And if you wish, I might write them to inquire about your case."

"Oh, Ben, I . . ." For a moment she did not register what Ben had said. "*My* case?"

It took a long minute for each to sort out the mutual misunderstandings. Finally Ben forced himself to define her supposed illness precisely as "uncontrollable sexual desire, morbid lusts."

Her anger was fierce, righteous, and resolute. She stepped from her bed and started to dress, pulling on her chemise, kicking at his boots, grabbing a petticoat. He tried making excuses for himself, but she said nothing.

He finally said, "It isn't as if I'd called you a, a, a *whore.*"

She stopped dressing for a moment and looked at him coldly. "You ludicrous prude. What a tiresome and common combination—fornicator *and* prude. A hypocrite like every other piddling '*gentleman.*'"

"Perhaps I—"

"I don't care."

He tried to summon anger. *You foulmouthed freethinking Yankee slut.* She was leaving for Philadelphia in the morning. *Dearest love of my life.*

"Polly, if in my ignorance and innocence of the world, and of your modern American sensibility, I've presumed—"

"*Shut up.* And go."

"Shut your smart mouth, you lyin', thievin', *stinkin'* little dandiprat," Peregrine Christmas said as he wiped his nose with his sleeve, "and set down, *there,* on the floor in front of me where I can see you right."

Priscilla had just come from school to the dank brown room she shared with her father, and mentioned to him helpfully that the mucus beslubbering his upper lip was about to fall into his beer. Perry Christmas was sitting in his chair, as usual, with the beer pail between his legs on the seat, the tin cup floating on top. But the chair was turned away from the open window to face the door. He was red-faced and seething, as usual, but this afternoon there was some elation whipped into his anger as well. In his right hand he gripped his wooden cudgel, nasty with bits of dried meat and fur and feather, which he employed to bang mice and pigeons. In his left, she finally saw, he held the little muslin bag that she kept hidden in the straw of her mattress.

She started to sit down on the floor where she stood.

"*Closer,* Prissy, so I can *see* your lyin' eyes."

He shook the bag in her face, jangling the coins. "Forty-seven U.S. silvers buried in your bed. *Forty-seven* shiny dollars." He had never earned more than twenty dollars in a month, and barely forty-seven dollars altogether during the last six.

"Savings, Papa. I was going to tell you about it when I had fifty." This was true, after a fashion. Fifty dollars had been her goal, and when she reached it she had planned to write him a letter explaining herself.

He wheezed, but did not otherwise reply.

"Savings for a new start in some better, clean, green town on Long Island, like Middle Village—or Gravesend, 'by the same sea that touches home,' like you always say." Perry Christmas referred to West Sussex, in England, as "home," although his family had emigrated when he was seven. His self-pity was inflamed by the ignominy of living as an Englishman among so many Irish in the Five Points.

He only stared at Priscilla, saying nothing.

"Savings to move out of here once and for all," she said. This was true as well, but only narrowly, since Priscilla's plan of escape from Daggle-Tail Alley and the Points had never included her father.

"I don't judge you wrong for pinchin' it, whoever you nimmed it off, Prissy—but keepin' a fortune like this here secret from your poor *dad* is *very* naughty. It's ungrateful and unfair and god*damned* un-Christian of you."

His accusation stirred her spunk, and before she could think better of telling the truth, she blurted out, "I swear I did *not steal* that money."

Her father knew his daughter well enough to see that her indignation was sincere. And after only two growlers and a half of beer (it was just past six o'clock), he was not yet too boozy to make the inevitable inference. If she had not stolen the money, there was only one way a girl could have *earned* forty-seven dollars. And this epiphany—the surprise more than the fact of it—made him angrier still.

"You *punk*. You *whore*."

She quickly considered various alibis—selling flowers in the streets, odd jobs performed for Mr. Skaggs and Miss Lucking—but found none of them convincing.

"You sneaky little damned crack-for-sale! Like *mother*, like *daughter*, eh?" In fact, Mrs. Christmas had never prostituted herself, but she had abandoned her family in 1844 and left for Michigan with a handsome German widower she had met in a line for free firewood. "You know, I could've let 'em keep you in the public home, but *no*, I worked and sweated all alone for goin' on five years to give you a real home here." He shook her bag of dollars again. "So this is the *reimbursement*, eh? This is *mine*. Thank you, Prissy. And you're welcome."

"I'll give you half, Papa."

He smiled.

Just then, a mourning dove landed on the windowsill. They both turned to look and the dove started to coo, filling the room with Priscilla's favorite song in the world.

In the corner of her eye, she noticed her father's cudgel flutter. She had seen him hurl it at pigeons on the sill a hundred times, once or twice breaking a wing or leg, another time knocking out the pane that was now stuffed with oilcloth.

"No, *please*, don't bang him," she said, and began to make for the window and shoo the dove to safety.

He had not intended to throw his club at the bird. But faced with Priscilla's lies and now this impertinence, he flailed it at her, backhand, as she started climbing to her feet, and missed.

"I *hate* you, Papa."

She knew what would happen now. For one thing, he was consistent—indeed, Peregrine Christmas believed that his consistency, no matter how rough, made him a good father. Also, when the dove had landed on the sill, the hairs on Priscilla's neck had stood up: she knew—in that way she knew certain things—that her father would strike her.

He was apoplectic, and literally roared as he sprang from his chair, spilling his pail.

If the floor had been dry, Priscilla might have made it to the door a step ahead of him. But the puddle of beer slowed her just long enough that his first standing swing struck her squarely across the shoulders, and when she stumbled to one knee he hit her on the back a second time, which knocked her head onto the side of the stove. As she collapsed to the floor, he paddled her one last time on her bum for good measure.

He was out of breath, which he hated to be. He was not a cruel father, in his view, since he seldom hit her very *hard*. He pulled the filthy little pillow from his chair and laid the bag of silver and the cudgel down in its place. Priscilla's eyes were shut. She was not moving. He looked down at her. He sincerely hoped she was not dead. She was his only daughter, and he loved her. Besides, as long as she was already selling herself to men—he'd always suspected she was an early-ripener—she could keep at it now and then and start paying her way in the household.

He squatted down next to her, turned her over, and shook her shoulder, then patted her cheek. She did not awaken. He held the back of his hand near her mouth and nose. He believed she was breathing. And she didn't seem to be bleeding. He slipped the cushion under her head, then pulled the hem of her dress down to cover her calves, for modesty's sake.

He took his hat from the nail and the money from the chair. Before he left, he glanced back and saw that the string of her bonnet was stretched very tight around her neck. He walked back, bent down, and untied it. *Not such a bad dad,* he thought, feeling happy and even gay for the first time in years, and stepped out, eager to spend some of his booty.

The mourning dove returned to the sill, cooing as the dusk turned from gold to fuchsia to dark blue. Priscilla did not stir.

FIRECRACKERS AND CANNON and rockets were lit at sunset, beginning the twenty-four-hour-long racket of July Fourth celebrations. Polly barely noticed, for despite her best efforts, her mind was filled with images of Ben Knowles and stray lines of *Dombey* dialogue. She was packing her luggage for the next day's trip and silently repeating to herself Mrs. Pipchin's line to Miss Nipper from the play—"*Does that bold-faced slut intend to take her warning, or does she not?*"—when the knock came at her door. Priscilla was pale and (despite the summer heat) shivering. She began sobbing as soon as Polly took her into her arms.

Polly listened and sympathized and soothed, and checked carefully that Priscilla wasn't too badly injured. But she was calm and clear and resolute.

Polly had a plan.

She would enlist Duff and some of his boys from Engine 15 to find Mr. Christmas and retrieve Priscilla's money. And tomorrow Priscilla would join Polly on her journey. They would leave New York together and find some better, happier place and way to live, away from the mean, filthy, hypocritical city.

It was four in the morning before Duff and his two pals finally did find Perry Christmas, passed out in the weeds and muck behind the backhouse of a dive in Mulberry Street. He was, of course, dead drunk, and he had been robbed of his treasure bag hours before. His hair and clothes were soaked in the robbers' urine.

Priscilla started crying again when she heard this news from Duff, who badly wanted to be her rescuer, her savior, her avenging knight—and had no idea what to do. Polly took her aside and bucked her up. She had enough money for the both of them, she promised, and they would go together to Mercer Street to make Mrs. Stanhope hand over the four dollars she still owed Priscilla—and, yes, of course, she said when the girl asked, while they were there they would also pick up her velveteen dress and *Phantasmion*.

At dawn on the Fourth every church bell in the city started to ring, and artillery began blasting from the Battery up to Madison Square. As the rest of the city descended into the merry holiday hell, Polly and Priscilla remained unsmiling and diligent, walking and riding like soldiers on their various missions—back to the tenement in Daggle-Tail Alley to gather her few belongings (two dresses, underclothes, a bonnet, a hairbrush, schoolbooks, and her stuffed toy dog), to Mrs. Stanhope's, to a dry-goods store for supplies (including a packet of blank drawing sheets), back to the ticket broker to book Priscilla's passage, back to Polly's rooms. They felt themselves to be the only serious people in the streets, ignoring the drums and trumpets and drunken *Hurrah*s and pop of Chinese crackers, nearly oblivious to the sulfurous haze and drifts of paper debris covering the pavements.

Their boat was scheduled to depart at three, and they were standing at the foot of Barclay Street with their luggage by two, ready to board.

"Nice hot corn, smoking hot, smoking hot, just from the pot!" The season's first hot-corn girls wandered up and down the piers and through the waterfront crowds with their baskets, hawking snacks at a penny a cob.

" 'We hold these truths to be self-evident,' " an old man declared to a small crowd in Washington Street, " 'that all men are created equal, that they are endowed by their Creator with certain unalienable rights, that among these are life, liberty, and the pursuit of happiness.' " He was one of ten thousand American men reciting the Declaration of Independence aloud at that moment, standing before crowds from Boston to Chicago to New Orleans.

At the next pier upriver from Polly and Priscilla, a cattle boat was docking, and the animals were skittish, pawing at the deck and lowing. They were frightened by the July Fourth ruckus, but unaware of the slaughterhouse knives that would actually kill them before sunset. *We're right to be scared*, Polly thought, *but in our ignorance we are scared of the wrong things.*

Priscilla was excited about their trip. Wedged into her new canvas sack was Jonathan, whose ragged brown beaver-fur head she discreetly petted. Nothing in her manner suggested that she (and her father) had been robbed and beaten nearly to death during the last twenty-four hours. "I have never traveled on a steamer before," she said, "nor on any boat overnight."

Polly smiled. She herself had been on a steamboat only once, one-way, down the Hudson when she and her mother and brother and the twins had moved from the country, half her life ago.

She would write Duff soon. And she would write to Ben as well. Her throat tightened, and tears threatened to come. But she took a deep breath. She hefted her purse to feel the weight inside, the pair of paper tubes each packed with a pound of gold eagles, her savings from the last year and a half and her wage from Burton. She reminded herself that she was grateful to be steaming out of New York on a bright blue and gold summer's day, to be starting with a new dream in her head.

And with a new sister she was duty-bound to save. The black and purple from her father's blows covered Priscilla's back from her neck to her bottom. Priscilla reassured Polly that the injuries were not as bad as they looked. She removed her bonnet carefully to show the goose-egg bump on her head. It was enormous.

"Wow," Polly said, and very gently touched it.

"*Ow,*" Priscilla said, then smiled at her accidental rhyme.

A rocket exploded overhead. "*Pow,*" Polly said.

The cattle responded to the aerial bomb with a chorus of frightened moos, and Priscilla's eyes brightened. "*Cow,*" she said.

They clasped hands and smiled at their nonsense.

One of the hot-corn girls, younger than Priscilla, came toward them. *"Hot corn! Hot corn! Here's your lily-white . . ."*

The Declaration-reader had been handed a bullhorn, which gave him the voice of God. " 'When a long train of *abuses* and *usurpations* . . . evinces a design to reduce them under absolute *despotism,* it is their right, it is their *duty,* to *throw off* such government.' "

". . . corn! All you that's got money, poor me that's got none . . ."

" 'Nor have we been wanting in attentions to our *British* brethren. We have warned them, from time to time, of attempts by their legislature to extend an unwarrantable *jurisdiction* over us.' "

Polly thought again of Ben Knowles.

Priscilla looked up at the steam funnel on their boat, and a few seconds later the whistle blew.

". . . buy my lily-white corn, and let me go home."

" 'With a firm reliance on the protection of Divine Providence, we mutually pledge to each other our *lives,* our *fortunes,* and our sacred *honor.*' "

Polly picked up her bags and nodded to Priscilla to do the same. "We're off," she said, and they were.

32

July 15, 1848

· · ·

New York City

*H*IS FOREIGN ACCENT and poor English did not seem to provoke New Yorkers, he'd discovered, the way it did Londoners. Americans were no more humane than the British, he decided, but too pleased with themselves and too busy to waste precious seconds sneering at a Frenchman.

And besides, here he was merely one among numberless foreigners, an outsider in a city of outsiders. It seemed as if every second American was not an American at all. In his hunt for Knowles, he'd found that the New York radicals' clubhouses and taverns and newspapers were mainly German. There was even a small *quartier* where the French clustered, and he had rented a cellar room in that district.

Tonight at Ricard's, the French café in Lispenard, it was so hot he had taken off his coat and drunk as much water as an American. And he had drunk more wine than usual as well, due to the good news from Paris, what they were calling "the Bloody Days of June." The strongest and sanest men in the new regime had turned on their dangerous bedfellows, the smug social tinkerers and bandits disguised as reformers. The forces of order had defeated the sowers of chaos. Marie Brasseaux brats had been shot dead in the streets, and many more would be transported—ha!—to Algeria, and soon the reckless shits running their "free" newspapers would be required to show respect once again.

Drumont had drunk an entire carafe to celebrate, but also to numb his new pangs of confusion and regret. Now that the worst of the madness had been slapped down in Paris, he wondered if he had acted too rashly by killing the girl and exiling himself. He realized now that *nothing* endured anymore, not kings and their loyal armies, but not the revolution either; an irony. Perhaps France would return to normal. Perhaps he could have stayed. Perhaps he should have waited.

But Michel's honor could not wait. Gabriel Drumont had had no choice but to follow the killer.

Tonight he had said nothing to the Lyonnaise bitch at the next table at Ricard's as she had first shouted and cried to another woman about the Days of June—*la tragédie et l'horreur, l'horreur et la tragédie,* bah. But a minute ago, when she had called the troops in Paris "dumb savages" and "murderers" and "demons," then it had become a matter of duty. Drumont had turned and told her that she ought to take her ranting outside, where it would only annoy the pigs and dogs, and that she was unworthy of calling herself French. She had slapped him, began sobbing, and rushed out the open door with her friend.

Now Drumont noticed a man walking directly toward him from the other side of the café. If he wanted trouble, Drumont was ready to give him some; the Baby Dragoon was in his pocket, if it came to that. But the fellow, maybe a decade Drumont's junior, did not look angry. He had the face and strong body of a workingman but the clothes of a gentleman. America was confusing.

"Vous êtes *corse,* oui?" the man said, extending a hand. "Je m'appelle Alexandre Roux."

Drumont said yes, he was Corsican, by way of Paris, and shook the man's hand.

Drumont's forthrightness and firmness with the woman, he explained, had impressed him—very American. Would Monsieur Drumont allow Roux to order two cognacs and join him?

Roux had a close friend in the French army, and a cousin in the Garde Municipale, it turned out. He himself had emigrated twelve years ago, and now conducted an excellent business over in Broadway—making modern cast-iron chairs and sofas but also, he said with a wry smile, gilded rosewood pieces in the style of Louis Quinze, good fake-aristocratic furniture for the good fake aristocrats of New York. He asked Drumont how he planned to earn his living here.

"Un détective privé," Drumont replied. *A private detective.*

"Ah, l'Inspecteur Vidocq d'Amérique!" *The Inspector Vidocq of America!* "Mais parlez-vous . . . do you have English, Monsieur Drumont?"

"Un peu. Very little. I learn."

"And I shall help you, if you wish. Je vous aiderai."

Over their second brandy Roux offered Drumont work as his night manager—to join the truckers on large evening deliveries, when necessary, and to guard the workshop until dawn, when the first woodworkers arrived. And Drumont accepted, of course.

His previous lie—that he was a cabinetmaker from Paris in London to collect a debt—would now become a fact, more or less; another irony. And the job was ideal: he would be entirely free to hunt for Knowles during the day.

BEN MISSED POLLY terribly, ached for her, despised himself for what he had said to her, for every scared, embarrassed, vicarish bit of pseudoscientific bunkum he had spouted.

His trip to Connecticut to deliver another lecture on the European revolutions had helped take his mind off her temporarily, although he'd found himself insensible to the flirtations of the young women who flocked around him before and after his talk. A mere sixty-four Hartfordians had bought tickets, but at least none of them were angry Germans, mistrustful Irish, or madmen.

Back in the city for the last week, he had hoped every day for some word from Polly. Most days he loitered in Sullivan Street until midafternoon in order to meet the postman when he arrived with the second delivery. But no letter from Philadelphia arrived. And he had repaired nearly every evening with Skaggs to a customary haunt, Budd's or Shakespeare's or the Belle of the Union.

On this sweltering Saturday night they were drinking at Joe Orr's Saloon in Greenwich Street, whose clientele was a mixture of workingmen and men of Skaggs's type. Duff was supposed to join them, but never did; they assumed he'd been called to a fire. The front doors were propped open wide to catch any river breezes. Most of the patrons had taken their coats off, and Skaggs was wearing his collar open, with no necktie at all. A few men wore only cotton undershirts.

Ben ordered a three-cent whiskey instead of a five-cent gin to conserve his limited funds. "Perhaps," he said, "I shall be forced to become a guano broker for my father after all." His career as a lecturer was probably over—Ben's inspiring tale of the February Revolution, according to the agent who booked his engagements, had been "rendered moot by the counter-revolution."

"Ah," Skaggs said, "so the audiences will now demand eyewitness accounts of the more recent slaughters. The latest, the newest, faster, faster . . ."

"No—the lecture fellow said the problem is with the *nature* of the events in Europe. 'It's just too darned hard now for us to know who are the villains and who are the heroes,' " Ben said, clenching his jaw and pronouncing his *r*'s and vowels in the hard American fashion, "and 'Over here we are not so interested in unhappy endings.' "

Skaggs smiled. "Your imitation of the accent has become excellent. As has your understanding of our addiction to sunny simplicity."

For the next hour or so Skaggs explained American presidential politics to Ben—why President Polk was not running for reelection ("no western deserts remaining for him to invade or buy"), and why he, Skaggs, planned to vote for Zachary Taylor, the Whig, rather than Cass, the Democrat, or Van Buren, the former president and presumed candidate of the new little antislavery party.

"Because," Skaggs said, "number one, Cass favors the infection of the West with slavery, and number two, because he is a New Hampshirite of the most embarrassing kind. And he is ancient—as is Van Ruin, of course. 'Van, Van, *is* a used-up man,' " he said, quoting the Whig slogan. "The former president is a virtual *dwarf* as well, and a cadger of the usual political type. Now the evil geniuses behind General Taylor are no better, of course, peddling him like a bottle of Brandreth's Pills. In the *Tribune,* Horace is already retailing the humbug every day that Taylor was a yeoman, Old Rough-and-Ready, Mr. Buckwheat Bumpkin."

"He is, in fact, a man of means?"

"Owning a hundred Negroes makes one a man of considerable means. Though that suggests, at least, that the prospect of twenty-five thousand a year isn't his only reason for running. Taylor seems to me more or less sensible, and more or less honest. For better or worse he risked his life on our behalf killing Indians and Mexicans. And on the slavery question, at their convention in Philadelphia his fellow southerners loathed him but the Greeleyites disapproved as well, which together predisposes me toward him." Skaggs slurped the last of his second whiskey. "I call myself a member of the Anti-Boredom Party, and yet now I have bored you completely. You are quiet tonight."

Ben had stopped listening after the word "Philadelphia." "Today," he said, "is the fifteenth—"

Skaggs raised his empty glass. "Beware the ides of July."

"—nearly a fortnight she has been in Philadelphia, and not a single letter."

"Sir! The lady is making her debut in a role which, at long last, might give her real standing as an actress. Your days and nights, on the other hand, are spent dissipating with me. You, Mr. Knowles, might take the initiative yourself and write to your true love."

"I have—three posted to her at the theater."

"Ah. Hmm. Have you really?"

"As well as a message by the telegraph this week." Ben knew he had drunk too much the moment he started to recite the message he had sent her. " 'Am entirely sensible that I behaved like a monster July third.' "

Skaggs was counting with his fingers. "*Eleven* words? Did you know they charge in units of ten, which until I—"

" 'Beg forgiveness. Will make amends. Longing to see you.' And still no reply."

"Well. Hmm." Just then, behind Ben, Skaggs was surprised to see a certain man he knew coming through Orr's open doors. "*Franklin Evans!*" he shouted. "The prodigal son returns *already?* Presto!"

Ben turned to look. A pair of well-dressed young men had stepped inside, one slight and epicene, the other a tall fellow with a beard who traded nods and smiles with several patrons as he lumbered in. He had a loose tie, a big lopsided grin, and huge brows arching over bright blue eyes. Despite his graying hair, he was about Ben's age.

"Hallo, friend," Skaggs said to the big, smiling fellow. They hugged and pounded each other's backs.

Ben stood and began to introduce himself. "I am Benjamin Knowles, Mr. Evans, it is very—"

The man slugged Skaggs playfully as he stopped Ben. "No, no, my name is *Whitman*, sir, Walter Whitman—your disreputable companion harries me by that ridiculous moniker whenever he can."

"Not whenever, sir," Skaggs said, "only in groggeries, only in groggeries." He explained that Franklin Evans was the fictional, reformed-drunkard hero of an anti-liquor novel Whitman had written for money. "To his credit, however, Walt is the only man in New York sacked by more newspapers than I myself. And Mr. Knowles here, Walt, was in the streets of Paris in February."

Whitman's face brightened and he took Ben's right hand in both of his. "Terrible what's befallen Paris now, terrible, ten thousand dead, they say— and *splendid* what they have been attempting, eh?" He gripped Ben's hand hard and shook it. "How *splendid* to see the grip of the people on the throats of kings, eh?"

Whitman introduced his friend, an actor named Henman Platt whom Skaggs knew slightly. He had called him a "spastic little clodhopper" in one of his pseudonymous reviews for the *Evening Mirror.*

"I take it, then, that slave-land did not suit my favorite abolitionist after all," Skaggs said to Whitman. "I had figured you to continue west to become a free-soil pioneer, a mountain man, an honorary Indian."

After Whitman's celebrated falling-out over the slavery issue with the owner of the *Eagle* last winter, he had decamped to New Orleans to work for a newspaper there.

"The city was a fine, gay place. Opera four nights a week! *You* would thrive there, Skaggs. But the proprietor of the paper—an awful skinflint and dissembler, as it turned out. And, I must tell you, it *was* a horror, truly, to see with my own eyes men and women sold like animals. A salutary horror. We shall be starting a new paper in Brooklyn for which I should be pleased to have you write, if you are still writing, and not *only* making pictures."

"Alas, I continue to wordsmith, and would be honored to earn a few pennies from you, sir . . . as long as I am not required to pledge myself to your used-up Van."

"Slander!" Whitman replied with a smile, and turned to Ben. "Are you a member of our sorry guild as well, Mr. Knowles?"

"Not a newspaperman, no, sir," Ben said. "A recent immigrant, unemployed and quite possibly unemployable."

"A London man of affairs," Skaggs said, "and perhaps the most rapturous lover of this country I have ever met. Present company excluded."

"*Hurrah,*" Whitman said, tapping Ben's shoulder as if he were a friend, "and may your love be requited."

And may my love be requited, Ben thought to himself. *I love you, Ben,* she had said at last, in her bed, the very moment before he'd dashed it all. He had returned to that memory, her lips saying those words—*I love you, Ben*—a hundred times in the last twelve days. *I will say that. I love you.*

As Whitman and his friend began to move toward the bar, Henman Platt paused and turned. "Oh, Mr. Skaggs—I was distressed to hear of your friend Miss Lucking's hard luck with Burton. Do send her my kind regards."

"*What?*" Ben practically lunged at the man. "What's that you said?"

Platt put both hands up reflexively, as if he feared an assault.

"Mr. Knowles," Skaggs explained, "is Polly Lucking's"—*fiancé?*—"beau."

"I—I—I," Platt said, "only wish to express my sympathies, sir, for a fellow thespian . . . so badly cogged and so . . . ill treated by, by mean gossip and backbiting."

"This is all news to us, Mr. Platt," Skaggs said. "Please explain."

According to Platt, the impresario and star of *Dombey* had been persuaded by another member of his troupe that Polly was insufficiently . . . innocent to play Dickens's virginal Florence Dombey—and that some terrible embarrassment might accrue to the new Burton's Theatre and certain of its investors if Polly Lucking appeared in the leading female role in its debut production. Burton had dismissed her from the company the very night before the players were to leave for their debut out of town.

"Although I am led to understand," Platt added, "that he had the good graces to pay her a full month's wages when he sacked her. Fifty dollars."

Ben's feelings churned and spilled in every direction, from jealousy to pity to rage to fear, bewilderment, and self-accusation. But he realized that his missives to Philadelphia had not gone unanswered, but had never been received. *I love you, Ben. I will say that. I love you.*

NOT A MILE to the east, crouching on a greasy stone floor and working by the light of the full moon, his trousers smudged with flour, Duff Lucking was also filled with a toxic and desperate admixture of emotion on Polly's behalf. But Duff's sorrow and shame were anticipatory. At moments such as this, a part of his mind always became, as he imagined it, a kind of holy parrot, screeching, *Forgive me, Father . . . Forgive me, Father . . . Forgive me, Father . . . Forgive me, Father,* even as other thoughts drifted through his mind as usual.

And tonight those thoughts were all the odious ones that had driven Duff to break and enter the Enggas Bakery in Greene Street and take vengeance, his promises three months ago to Bishop Hughes and God notwithstanding.

He thought of all the squalid rumholes and gambling pits through which he had tracked down Priscilla's father on the nightmarish eve of Independence Day. He thought of the snatches of whispered conversation he'd overheard late that night between his sister and Priscilla about "101 Mercer" and their plan to "visit the house one last time" to collect Priscilla's things "from Mrs. Stanhope." And he thought of his mortifying exchange one evening last week at the firehouse, after he'd heard one of the boys sniggering about his cousin's "night and *morning* of happiness at 101 Mercer."

Now Duff knew the nature of 101 Mercer's business. Now he understood why his sister could afford to buy so many good dresses and books and chalks and pads of paper. Now he understood that the ugly things Fatty Freeborn had said at the blaze that afternoon in Wooster Street were true, understood that the "bit of regular, indoor work" Polly had arranged for Priscilla Christmas had not involved laundering or sewing. And after he understood all of that, he resisted the urge to break his promise and strike once again, but finally he realized what he had to do before he left New York City for good. From his reconnaissance he had discovered that the old lady at 94 Greene had closed her house and moved to Long Island for the summer, and that on Saturday nights the Enggas Bakery at 96 Greene baked its last buns and loaves by ten o'clock.

And so there he was, past midnight on Saturday, with his leather satchel of U.S. Army sapper's tools he had meant to put away for good; cutting fuse with his folding bowie knife and placing three charges inside and out; and arranging open canisters of coal oil like a line of pickets against the fence of its back neighbor, the house at 101 Mercer. He laid out plenty of fuse, a fifteen-foot length for the first charge, to give himself a full ten minutes to run around the block and warn the women of 101 Mercer that the bakery adjacent to them was ablaze, that they must evacuate their house. Although he thought it might serve their visitors right—the men, the whoremongers— to be incinerated.

"The Lord rained upon Sodom and upon Gomorrah brimstone and fire," he said out loud.

The flour in the air made Duff sneeze. He was packing his things, maybe a minute from striking a lucifer and touching the fuse, when he heard a pound and a slam and a heavy footfall from the front of the building.

"*Hey!*" came a shout. "*Carl?* That you? Still baking so late!" The voice was getting closer. "Who you gabbing with in there? I come back for my rye whiskey I left."

Duff grabbed his bag and his coil of fuse from the floor and tiptoed in four long, fast strides to the darkest corner of the room.

"Carl?"

The voice sounded familiar.

"You hidin' back there in the dark, tossin' off in the lard like the dirty boy I knows you are? Show yourself, hoss, and we can take a nightcap together."

It was Fatty Freeborn—this must be the bakery where he worked. Duff got a whiff of his cigar and then saw the profile in the doorway not ten feet in front of him, that crapulent face and sideways mountain of flesh. He held a liquor bottle.

"Carl?"

Some grains of flour tickled Duff's nose and he strained to stifle another sneeze. But Fatty heard the choked strain of throat and sinus in the dark and turned sharply to his right.

"Hallo, Freeborn," Duff said as he stepped toward him, into the moonlight.

"*Hey!*" Fatty shouted, and jumped back, but then relaxed when he saw who it was.

"Why, what—you creepy goddamned sneak! I oughta smash you, Lucking! What are *you* lurking in here for?"

"Working."

"What? Horseshit! There ain't no gas hooked into this place yet. You've gone from shylock to thief now, is that it? Down to filching bread, are you?"

Duff could see that Fatty was beginning to enjoy himself.

"You know, this don't surprise me altogether, Lucking, on account of what I heard about you the other day from a army bunkie o' yours I met."

Duff started to rummage through the satchel.

"Pennsylvania boy working here in the city now as a boilermaker, living at my boardinghouse. Pishey Wetmore? From your Company A. Pishey told me about how you disappeared in Vera Cruz, and at first they thought you turned chicken and run away . . ."

Duff acted as if he were not dismayed in the slightest. He had just found the tool he needed in the bottom of his bag.

". . . but how then he heard they found you joined up with those Irish traitors down there, the St. Patricks, killing your own American brothers on the orders of the Mexicans."

Duff set the satchel and the coil of fuse on the floor.

"So not only is Duff Lucking the cat-lick brother of a whore—a whore, by the by, who I can fuck four different times at ten dollars a crack, now that I got some extra cash in the pocket." He patted his coat, in which he had his blackbirding fee. "Not only is Duff Lucking a traitor and a whore's brother, but a regular little bread burglar on top of all that." Fatty shook his head, stuck out the forefinger wrapped around the neck of his whiskey bottle, and stroked it with his other. "Shame on you, ya sinful little bastard, shame! Shame, sh—"

At the first "shame" Duff had opened his knife, and at the second he had propelled himself forward, and before the fourth "shame" left Fatty's mouth, the blade had pierced a lung and nicked the heart. As Fatty stumbled backward, he hit a cask of whale oil and knocked open its bunghole, then slipped in the resulting slick and fell. Now sitting on the floor, he saw Duff's hand flying toward him a second time and tried to duck from the thrust, but instead merely presented his neck as the target instead of his chest.

Duff stood up and looked down at Fatty in the moonlight. He was supine, pints of blood and whale oil puddling together around him on the floor. This wasn't like in Mexico, where none of the men he'd killed had deserved to die. *I have slain a monster,* he said to himself. He needed to light the fuses and go. *Destruction and creation are the cycle of life.*

Fatty grunted and squeaked and shook, tried to groan. His eyes were open wide, and filled with terror. Blood streamed down his chest. His shirttail had pulled out of his pants, exposing his hairless pink belly. He looked like an animal in distress, which made Duff feel sorry for him. Duff had butchered dozens of sheep as a boy in the Clove Valley, and had learned to cut the throats fast and deep, with a single stroke, two at most.

This knife was barely half as long as the one they had used on the lambs at Easter. But it would be barbaric to let Freeborn gasp and quake and suffer any longer, so Duff crouched down and did what he had to do. Unfortunately for both men, the blade was too dull to make a good slaughter knife.

July 16, 1848

"WE WAITED FOR you last night at Orr's until one, or later. God, was it hot." Skaggs was making small talk. "But later, coming east on Canal, I saw a great blaze up in Greene Street, and decided that must be what kept you from joining us. You look tired, Duff." Skaggs was filling time, trying to await Ben Knowles's arrival so that he and Ben might together deliver the unpleasant and mysterious news about Polly they had learned from Whitman's actor friend. They were standing in Prince Street, outside St. Patrick's Cathedral. Skaggs knew that since the spring Duff had been attending morning Mass there every Sunday.

Of course, Duff already had learned the most unpleasant news about his sister. And he was surprised by this odd encounter with Skaggs, which made him suspect that Skaggs suspected him.

"We were over there in Greene until dawn," Duff said, "Fifteen Engine was, along with seven or eight others. It was a big bakery burned, gallons of oil they stored were lit, and *kaplow.* Some houses next door and behind in Mercer caught afire as well."

"Arson, do they believe?"

He shrugged and shook his head. For someone who hated to lie, Duff Lucking found himself lying rather a great deal.

"True they pulled a body out?" Skaggs asked. "That's what some old loon this morning was saying. *'Baked* to a crisp in a *bakery.'* "

Duff nodded. "Burnt beyond recognition." He paused. "But not any other deaths or even an injury."

"Good. That's good."

"Skaggs, I have a letter to post downtown." He touched his pocket. He was indeed carrying an urgent letter, which he needed to deliver to an office in Fulton Street. "I must go."

"Of course," Skaggs said, but he was looking up at the trees behind them in St. Patrick's cemetery. "You know, those elms there have grown a good twenty feet since I came to the city. Which demonstrates how elderly I've become."

"Why have you met me here, Skaggs? What do you want?"

"Knowles and I decided to surprise you for your birthday—"

"My birthday was in May."

"—*belatedly,* and treat you to a good Sunday meal. A young man cannot survive on communion wafers and priest's wine alone."

Skaggs now spotted Ben coming down Mott Street and hailed him. He looked grave and forceful. Before even a greeting could be uttered, Ben addressed them both.

"I have received a letter from Polly. She is not in Philadelphia, Duff. I know where she's gone. And I am leaving in pursuit as soon as possible."

When they sat down to lunch, Ben recounted the salient points of her letter. A young protégée of the actress Caroline Chapman's, a girl of seventeen, was now playing the part of Florence Dombey. Polly had been sacked from the *Dombey* company because Miss Chapman had persuaded her good friend Burton of Polly's "notoriety."

There was an awkward moment before Ben continued.

Burton had told Polly he was especially anxious to avoid any embarrassment for one of his investors, who Miss Chapman had informed him was an old friend of Polly's—Samuel Prime.

"Prime!?!" Skaggs and Duff said in unison.

"You know Mr. Prime?" Ben replied, sincerely surprised. "He is an acquaintance of my father's as well."

Skaggs shook his head. Duff clenched his fists, yearning at that instant to dispatch Mr. Prime the younger as he had done Mr. Prime the elder—and might have acted on the impulse had he known of Samuel Prime's thirteen liaisons with Priscilla Christmas in the bedroom at 101 Mercer.

"She wrote," Ben said, "that her last several years in New York have amounted to 'an overextended stay in life's greenroom.' "

"Greenroom," Skaggs explained, was theater jargon for the parlor where actors await their turns to take the stage. And he explained to Duff why Caroline Chapman's name sounded familiar—she had been the half-clothed actress Duff rescued along with Skaggs from the closet at the Lyceum Theatre during the fire in 1844.

The long and the short of it, Ben continued, was that Polly had decided to abandon acting and the theater and the city. She was traveling with Priscilla Christmas, whom she now considered her ward. The letter was posted on the seventh from the city of Buffalo (which elicited a groan from Skaggs), and Polly's plan was to join one of the socialist communities in the West so that she and Priscilla could make a new start in a healthy place among people of good will.

Skaggs groaned again. "Good God, she's gone and done it, headed off to become some species of Shaker communist ascetic, eating vegetables and singing hymns and talking with the dead. Does she say for *which* of the western utopias she's bound? There are scores of such places sprouted now, like mushrooms in the dim wastelands."

"She says she has a list of some dozen prospects," Ben said, "from Ohio out to the Indian country, a list she acquired from your friend Brisbane at the *Tribune.*"

Skaggs shook his head and sighed.

"And there is nothing more?" Duff asked.

"No." In fact, yes: there was also the joyful and shocking penultimate paragraph, the one Ben had reread a dozen times: *You are the only man I ever loved. But during our final encounter I came to understand that you could never return that love once you were apprised of the true facts of my previous life & occupations. By which I mean this, plainly put: for seventeen months, from October 1846 until April last, I rented myself to men.* Before writing "rented myself," Polly had with a single fine line crossed out the phrase "sold my affections."

"And you, Ivanhoe," Skaggs said, "intend to find her and fetch her home?"

"I do intend to find her. If she is at the ends of the earth, I shall find her. And to stay with her forever if she'll allow me."

Duff stared in admiration: *the ends of the earth.* He had never heard anyone but a priest use that phrase. He felt a wave of love for Ben, and suddenly saw his chance. "I'll come along with you," he said, practically shouting, he was so excited. *"West."*

Ben smiled, and clasped Duff's hand, thumb hooked to thumb.

"Wait, wait, *wait* . . ." It had fallen to Skaggs, of all people, to challenge their quest on practical grounds. "How shall you possibly find her? She has been two weeks on the road already. They might be anywhere between Ohio and the desert."

"We shall obtain from Mr. Brisbane a copy of his little guide," Ben said, "and follow it like a map from east to west. The only question is our fastest route. Speed is paramount."

Skaggs saw that his friend would not be deterred. "Well, a steamboat to Albany, railways to Buffalo, then a steamer across Lake Erie. It sickens me even to describe the route. But you could be in Cleveland before the end of the week."

He paused. "I cannot believe that I am describing a speedy arrival in Cleveland as a *desirable* thing."

Part

THREE

33

❖❖❖

July 17, 1848

. . .

New York City

*L*AST EVENING, DRUMONT'S first day at his new job, Monsieur Roux had sent him downtown in a wagon with three other men to deliver a set of very grand étagères to an office of lawyers. When they'd finished, as they turned on Wall Street toward Broadway, he'd happened to glance at the number 42 and the name painted below it: PRIME, WARD & KING. And then he'd remembered—*this* was the firm that the grinning noddy at the Knowles office in London had mentioned. And at dawn, he had rushed to his room in White Street and found the scrap of paper— *yes*—then came straight back to 42 Wall to wait for the offices to open. Vidocq would be proud.

"Is that so?" Samuel Prime now said to Drumont. He was pleased by the visit, since he had been expecting a letter from Benjamin Knowles and had heard nothing at all. "And the two of you became acquainted in Paris, during the insurrections?"

"Yes." So far, Drumont had not even had to lie to this polite American banker.

"And you *both* decided to immigrate to republican America, inspired by that terrible confusion."

"*Oui,* yes, exactly true."

"Well, sir, you are in luck, I believe—since according to a missive from Sir Archibald, his father, young Mr. Knowles has been in the city for months. And I certainly do expect to meet him before long, now that he must be settled. His father wishes him to oversee some new business interests. And when I finally encounter him, Mr. Drumont, I shall tell him that you are here as well, and give him your address."

"No, *please*—I want to make a surprise?" Drumont forced his mouth into a big, stupid American grin. It worked.

"I see, of course. The *joie de vivre*, eh? In that case I shall post a note to you with his local address whenever I learn it."

Magnifique. He was closing in. And Drumont was interested to learn that even as Knowles was trying to spread the germs of revolution to yet another country not his own, he was still employed in his daddy's business— interested and *pleased*, in fact, since it meant the spoiled hypocrite deserved his punishment all the more.

Chicago

THE FIRST PART of Polly and Priscilla's journey—the evening cruise up the Hudson past a dozen different fireworks displays, the trains to Buffalo, the week on the steamer across Lakes Erie and Huron and Michigan—had felt like an extravagant summer romp.

They were now in Chicago, having been disgorged from the *Queen of the West* onto a dock a few blocks from their hotel. The city—all the brand-new buildings and plank sidewalks and paved streets, the noise and bustle of thirty thousand busy-looking men and women—had made both of them a little homesick.

They'd dawdled a couple of days, but only a couple, for the city also made Polly eager to get on their way to a green prairie Eden. Although they did not need the eleven dollars, Polly sold her bracelet and two necklaces and all but three of her fine dresses to a woman in a shop. And she started making inquiries about the communities on Mr. Brisbane's list. Mary Gove had given her the names of sympathetic Chicagoans—a reporter for the new *Chicago Tribune*, a phrenomagnetic experimenter, a homeopathic physician. All three encouraged Polly and Priscilla to investigate a certain farm in the hilly country between Terre Haute and Indianapolis, two days' drive south. Polly liked the sound of the place. It was called Lovely.

For their last evening in Chicago, Polly decided they should have one more taste of the soft, sugary city life. Instead of once again sharing sausage and apples in their hotel room with one knife and no forks, they had dressed and descended to the dining room of the Sherman House. They sat at one of the tables looking out on the twilight hurry of Randolph Street. They devoured fried lamb chunks and sweet corn drenched in butter, and ignored the glances of some young grain dealers two tables away.

"How *awful*," said Priscilla. "Do you know if any of the girls at number 101 were hurt?"

Polly had read an article in the *Tribune* about a large, suspicious fire in New York that burned three buildings in Greene Street and two more in Mercer. Given that the blaze had started in a bakery, and as far as she knew the only bakery in Greene was the big one that backed onto 101 Mercer, she deduced that Mrs. Stanhope's had been one of the houses destroyed.

" 'No serious injuries,' the paper had it—but one death, a man, inside the bakery."

"I guess that counts as a blessing. I wonder if your brother battled the blaze?"

Polly shrugged. *Poor dear Duff,* she thought. The next morning, before their departure, she would wire a message telling her whereabouts.

"Do you think often of Duff and Mr. Knowles and Mr. Skaggs?" Priscilla asked.

In fact, Polly had managed to go since noon without thinking of Ben Knowles, her longest abstention since leaving New York. Whenever she did think of him, she tried to flush away the sorrow and desire by reminding herself of every awful second of that humiliating final scene in her room.

Polly nodded.

"I have had gooseflesh on my neck for days," Priscilla said.

"Have you indeed?" Polly tended to ascribe Priscilla's psychic perceptions to the stormy mental weather of adolescence, a lonely and imaginative girl's fancies. On the other hand, if it was possible to send a letter a thousand miles through a copper thread in a second; perhaps . . .

"Yes. A very strong feeing that"—she smiled—"that you and I are both quite *longed* for in New York."

Polly's eyes flickered with skepticism as she took another bite of dinner.

"Honestly, I have the feeling quite strong," Priscilla insisted.

"Strongly."

"Strongly. Do you not think that Duff and Mr. Knowles miss us? And Mr. Skaggs as well?"

Polly finished chewing her lamb. "Friends come and go, and each of us has his or her own life to carry on, his or her own destiny to fulfill," she said. She softened. "I am certain that my brother misses us, Priscilla, yes."

"What do you suppose they are all of them doing right now? Duff and Mr. Knowles and Mr. Skaggs?"

"Your clairvoyant telegraph can't tell us that, eh?" She reached over and playfully tugged on one of Priscilla's corkscrew curls. "If you finish your salad, we'll ask for a strawberry pudding."

New York City

PRISCILLA'S SENSATION OF fervent male desire in New York was perfectly accurate, of course. But the strongest longing for Priscilla herself came from an unexpected party. Not Duff, though he thought of her often. Not her father, who assumed Prissy had gone off to board as well as fuck in her uptown meat house, wherever it was, and to give some slick pimp, whoever he was, the cut of her wages rightfully due her long-suffering dad.

No, the man in New York who fretted most about her, and craved her with the ardor (in his own fervid reckoning) of Romeo for Juliet or Heathcliff for Catherine, was Samuel Prime, Priscilla's own Sammy Boy.

After Prime had learned, on that Friday afternoon in May when he'd appeared for his regular appointment, that his girl was pregnant and had quit the hireling life, his first reaction had been shock and grief and anger, almost as if he'd lost one of his own children. She had *abandoned him*, he could not help feeling. He'd insisted that Mrs. Stanhope tell him the girl's true, full name, and the answer—Priscilla Christmas—had pleased him even more than her alias, "Minerva Spooner." He'd thought of going to Polly Lucking and asking her to intercede . . . but the prospect of that encounter—*Miss Lucking, you must persuade your protégée Miss Christmas to return to the brothel and submit once again to my animal passions*—was too mortifying and ridiculous to consider. After a few days, his second, sensible assessment of the situation prevailed: that Priscilla Christmas was too fine and pure a creature for harlotry, and had redeemed herself before her young life was ruined entirely, may she go with God.

But unquenched lusts finally overwhelmed Episcopalian virtue. In the last weeks and months he had indulged in assignations with other women and girls in other parlor houses—beautiful young women, pretty girls, the finest houses—but each served only to sharpen his hunger for Priscilla,

Priscilla, Priscilla. He was embarrassed by his feelings, but he could no longer resist or deny them. He knew it was mad, the love—the *love!*—of a respectable married man for a girl—a *whore!*—in her teens. But did the poets not say that all love is a kind of madness? And was not Romeo's Juliet only thirteen when she gave herself over to her one true love? Samuel Prime reveled in the first lovesick misery of his forty-six years.

When he had seen the article about Saturday night's blaze ("a well-known disorderly house in Mercer Street," the *Courier and Enquirer* reported, was among the buildings that had burned to the ground, as well as a bakery and "the fine old home of the late Colonel Gibbs and Mrs. Gibbs next door"), it was as if he had been delivered a terrible vision. Prime knew Laura Gibbs from Trinity Church, and at her behest made a donation each year to the American and Foreign Anti-Slavery Society; he hoped the dear lady had escaped the fire unharmed. But his instant terror and preoccupation as he dropped the newspaper next to his poached eggs concerned Priscilla Christmas: in his mind's eye he saw her dying hideously in the flames—she and their unborn child together.

So for the last two days, Samuel Prime, ordinarily the picture of Knicker-bocker calm and reasonableness, was like a man possessed. And when he finally found Mrs. Stanhope at the Arena, a sporting man's saloon, he pulled her aside and sputtered, *"Tell me she did not perish in the blaze! Tell me that Miss Christmas is alive!"*

"But of course she did not die," Mrs. Stanhope replied in her usual chatty and gracious fashion. "All of my ladies are just fine—and as you were informed in the spring, Miss Christmas is no longer associated with the house . . . Indeed, since her final and I trust quite satisfactory appointment with you, sir, she returned to the house only once, two weeks ago, to gather her personal things, for a journey west, I don't know where, in the company of Miss Lucking, I believe to one of those states with all the *i*'s and *o*'s in its name. Perhaps her father has the address . . ."

Prime could barely keep from sobbing (in relief and gratitude that Priscilla was safe, of course, but also that she had been sullied by no other man since their last encounter). He was so unhinged, in fact, that he asked directly about the other aspect of his lurid vision—"I must inquire, madam, if the young lady was *enceinte*"—and then spoke even more bluntly when Mrs. Stanhope failed to understand his question.

"Is Priscilla definitely *with child?*" he nearly spat.

"Is, what, is . . . ?" Mrs. Stanhope stuttered. She felt a panic, wondering about the most advisable answer. She had mentioned to him in May that Priscilla *had been* pregnant, using the past tense. But Prime was now in a deranged state, and Mrs. Stanhope wished to stay in the good graces of such a customer, given her plan to reopen her establishment at a new location. "Miss Christmas was indeed pregnant, yes, indeed, so I am reliably given to understand, sir."

Given Prime's reaction to this news—he appeared suddenly satisfied, calmed—she decided against mentioning the abortion that had ended the pregnancy. Whereupon Mr. Prime thanked her sincerely, gave her a five-dollar banknote "to atone for my presumption and your inconvenience," and strode out the door.

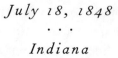

34

July 18, 1848

. . .

Indiana

ETWEEN NOISY, SOOTY, frantic Gotham and noisy, sooty, frantic little Chicago, they had traveled across a thousand miles of pristine waterways and bucolic countryside entirely by steam—that is, racing west inside screeching, jangling machines and stinking gales of cinders and smoke.

For their first hours in the stagecoach rolling through the meadows, marshes, and hills of Indiana, Polly and Priscilla felt not relaxed but anxious—the absence of tumult shocked their systems. Not that travel by stage is ever serene, with wheels bouncing in and out of ruts and thudding against stones, the four horses trotting and shitting a few yards away, the whole rig constantly shaking and swaying.

But when they stopped to change teams at a way station and the two women wandered off from the other nine passengers, out of the oak grove and down the road to stretch their legs, they felt as if they had suddenly been engulfed by nature. The sky and land were no longer parceled into little fragments of green and blue by the frames of the coach windows, and the clatter of town and travel was replaced by the oceanic whoosh of tall grass blowing in the breeze, the trills and whistles of sparrows and bobolinks and finches, crickets' chirps, grasshoppers' complicated clickings, and the soft buzz of cicadas. Three hawks circled high, high overhead. It had been a decade since Polly had set foot in such a rural precinct or ridden so long.

Priscilla had never been outside the city, nor ever sat on flowered damask inside a big, bright red-and-yellow Concord coach.

After another hour of riding during which they saw no sign of man, Polly marveled, "One wouldn't know that it is 1848 at all. It might as well be 1748 or 1448." She took Priscilla's hand. "I do believe," she said in a whisper, "that our luck has turned." With her other hand she knocked twice against the basswood wall.

Later in the afternoon, as they passed through the town of Raccoon, the driver blowing his horn as much to entertain as to alert the citizens, Priscilla spotted a magnificent Indian war bonnet of white and blue feathers hanging in the window of a dry-goods store. She pointed at it excitedly, exclaiming that they must finally be entering "Indiana *Indian* country." The local man sitting across from them informed them that, in fact, "the very last of our natives, the Miami, were sent west to Kansas year before last, at Thanksgiving."

When the driver announced they were approaching the intersection with the National Road, Polly thought of her father. When she was twelve, she had made an elaborate picture of a certain stretch of the road, drawn entirely from her imagination ("At Milestone 86 in Scenery Hill, Pennsylvania, the Site of a Prospective Lucking's Establishment"), to illustrate his business scheme for building a chain of a dozen dry-goods stores along the whole length of the National Road, from Maryland to Illinois.

When their coach reached the road, Polly was surprised to see that it was gravel, not paved with brick or macadam. The coach was turning east for Indianapolis, and as the women disembarked, the driver informed them that "your Reverend Danforth's farm is that way there." He pointed down the narrowing dirt lane on which they had been traveling. "A walk of twenty minutes, maybe thirty. I never been down there myself."

"And we shall see Lovely from the road?" she asked the driver, who had retaken his seat.

The man gave her a funny look. He didn't understand.

"Lovely fronts the road directly?" she repeated.

"It's pretty enough through there, I guess, sure. Flowers are up. Good afternoon, ma'am." He flicked the reins, shouted *"Heeyah,"* and was gone.

The driver had never heard of Lovely because that had been the name of the community only briefly. In fact, the place had been rechristened several times since its founding five years before by the Reverend James Q. Danforth and his sixty followers. Originally they'd called it Boza Kokapo, based on the reformist scheme devised by the late Stedman Whitwell, an English socialist who had been a member of the community of New Harmony, Indiana. Whitwell believed that the names of American cities and towns were dull and arbitrary. His code converted the degrees and minutes of latitude and longitude for any location to letters of the alphabet, generating a unique new name, according to a rational system, for each place on earth. New York City thus became Otke Notive, and London was Lafa Vovutu. Danforth and company calculated that the center of their four hundred acres in south-central Indiana was latitude 39 degrees, 32 minutes north, and longitude 86 degrees, 58 minutes west—which translated to Boza Kokapo. The local people had figured it was an Indian name, like Wabash or Kankakee. After a year the name had been changed to Equilibria, then Aspire, then Danforthia, and then Lovely.

After walking for half an hour, Polly and Priscilla saw two men and a woman at the edge of a field of sweet corn carrying baskets, picking ears. They were all dressed in shades of red and pink. Polly called out, "We are in search of *Lovely*."

The men put down their corn and wiped their hands on the bibs of their crimson overalls. Both smiled and waved. The woman looked pleased to see the female strangers as well, but her attitude seemed closer to relief than enthusiasm.

"This *was* Lovely," the older of the two men told them. The other, a blue-eyed, sweet-faced boy of eighteen or so, never stopped shifting his glance back and forth between Priscilla and Polly as if they were two different, irresistible flavors of ice cream. "But since the spring we have been Glee. I am Harlan, and these are two of my consociates, Billy and Presence. Welcome to Glee, friends."

"Welcome, friends," said Billy and Presence.

"I am Mary Ann Lucking," Polly said, shaking hands with each of them, "and this is Priscilla Christmas. We have come from New York to join your community, if you'll have us."

The woman nodded. The two men grinned. "*Welcome,*" they said in unison.

"Presence," said Harlan, "will take you to Persephone Spring to cleanse yourselves of filth—"

"To wash," Presence amended.

"—and then to the Hive, to confer with James."

on the Hudson River

DUFF AND BEN both relished railway travel, and had planned their trip for maximum speed. But the Hudson River Railroad's present terminus was only fifty miles upriver from the city, and the rail lines west started another hundred miles north in Albany. Thus they boarded a steamer at dawn. The *Isaac Newton,* named after the president of the People's Steam Navigation Company, was enormous—broader of beam and much longer than Cunard's *America.* The roar of boilers and engine and the paddle wheel's splash made conversation on the deck difficult, but both men were keen on sightseeing, so they stood together on the upper deck in the shade of the stern, taking turns staring at the eastern and western banks.

Duff was in a bonny mood, and not only because he was making his escape. The *Herald* believed the letter he had written two mornings earlier, and published it on the front page today. It was a confession to arson and suicide. "So my conscience is all clear with the good firemen that my actions might have troubled," it said, "I need to tell the following, which is the d— straight truth: I am the one who burnt the Granville distillery last winter and the sugarhouse in Duane in the spring and some other arsons too. And tonight I am going to set a blaze at Enggas Bakery in Greene St., because Enggas is a d— cheap & lofty cuss . . . and I plan to die there in the flames." The letter was dated July 15 and signed "Francis Freeborn, member, United States Hose Company No. 25." The *Herald* reported that since the confessed arsonist, known to his friends as Fatty, could barely write, Enggas's insurance company was looking for the scrivener who must have produced Freeborn's letter for him.

"Does it surprise you," Skaggs had asked Duff at their farewell dinner the previous night, "about Freeborn? He did not strike me as the type. That jumbo was a thug, surely, but a maniac?"

"I always figured him for nutty," Duff had replied.

"I must say," Skaggs had said, "to me he appeared no more crackbrained than half the young chuckleheads in this city."

Ben was thinking of their adieu as well. Near the end of dinner, Skaggs had grasped his hand and Duff's. "Now: *swear* to me," he had said, "that if on your journey west you *should* come across the ladies—in whichever God-besotted encampment in whichever godforsaken backcountry they're hiding—that after you accomplish the rescue you will return here? I am too old to make new friends to replace you."

Ben had hedged. "It is not our intention to abandon New York for good."

"Oh, 'not our *intention*,' " Skaggs had said. "I understand." His eyes had moistened. He had nodded. "You, Mr. Knowles, are as slick as snot on a doorknob."

BEN HAD ASKED Duff to identify several sites, and once again tapped his shoulder, pointing to a large marble building on the right bank. "A university?"

"No, Sing-Sing."

"Which is?"

"A prison."

After that, they traveled mainly in silence. Ben faced west. The view of bluffs and mountains and dense woods, all glazed gold by the morning sun, made him realize that the painting he and Polly had seen in the gallery last spring—the picture of a wooded Catskill ravine at sunrise—was not really exaggerated or sentimental.

A remarkable new sight came into view on the left—a stream falling a hundred feet down into the river. Ben touched Duff's arm again, directing him to behold Buttermilk Falls. Duff acknowledged them with a nod, but then pointed right. There a locomotive and train had appeared, gaining quickly on the *Isaac Newton*. A few minutes later, as the river narrowed and the boat slowed and steered toward the landing at Garrison's, Ben pointed again, back across the river.

Atop the high, broad plateau on the western bank, dozens of tents were pitched in neat lines. A company of two hundred men—each dressed in short gray coat, white linen pants, black leather cap—marched north to south. They reminded Ben of the toy soldiers he played with as a child, the Second Royal North British, lithographed wood-and-paper men on springs, perpetually charging toward Napoleon. Some distance upriver of the drilling cadets, a line of cannon, aimed away from the river, were firing one at a time.

"West Point," Duff said loudly, over the steamer's din.

Ben did not know the name.

"The *Academy*."

Still Ben did not understand.

"The United States *Military Academy,*" Duff hollered just as the captain cut the engine, "for the *army's* goddamned *officers.*" The nearby passengers all turned to look at the red-faced young man who had bellowed a curse against the U.S. officer corps.

Duff's mortification mixed with sudden fear. He had forgotten they would pass West Point. He knew that one of his officers in Mexico, Lieutenant McClellan, had returned to the academy to teach other young Protestants how to use picks and shovels and powder to blow up poor Catholics. What would Duff do if McClellan happened to board the boat? Or some other West Point officer who recognized him and knew what had happened after Vera Cruz?

"Excuse me," Duff said, "I need to check on my luggages," and disappeared below deck. Ben thought he had been driven away by embarrassment over his shout, but Duff did retrieve his bags, and from the bottom of the larger one dredged his folding bowie knife and put it in his coat pocket. He also pulled out his shiny black six-shot revolver. He could not very well carry the Colt's in his pocket—men in the East did not go about armed, and the thing was enormous. But he wanted it loaded and handy in case worse came to worst. He placed it at the top of his valise, which he proceeded to carry with him until they landed in Albany, finished dinner, and locked the door of their room for the night.

SKAGGS INSTRUCTED HIS cab to stop at every hotel along State Street. It took only half an hour to find the right place.

As he put down his bags and knocked on the door to the room, he could not suppress a smile.

The door opened two inches.

"Timothy?"

The door swung open wide.

"Indeed, it is I, young traveler," Skaggs replied, stepping into the room, "your Daniel Boone, come to guide you greenhorns west. Rise and shine, boys." Duff Lucking, dressed only in underclothes, held a huge pistol at his side. Ben Knowles was in bed.

"You—you are *joining* us?" asked Ben.

"Unless our friend here shoots me dead."

At first Skaggs joked about why he had impulsively decided to come along—the city heat, the mosquitoes, the end of oyster season, the fact that no one but the two of them would buy him drinks. But over breakfast he became more earnest. Ninian Bobo was demanding that he work as the editor of his new spiritualist magazine in order to pay off the back rent he owed on the Ann Street studio. And he realized that he needed "a restorative period in the country air to feed the creative fires." Indeed, he had decided that a stint of temperance would be good for his brain, and that New York's 4,528 licensed saloons and "equal number of friendly druggies" made such a trial regimen impossible in the city. "For all the glorious hubbub, my life in New York has grown . . . stagnant. I feel immured in the erstwhile city of my dreams. I require novelty and surprise. Therefore"—he spread his arms wide, palms out—"I come unto you." He checked his watch. "And if I'm guessing correctly, we have a westbound Albany & Schenectady Railroad train to catch in an hour. Good fortune is all in the timing, eh?"

35

July 21, 1848

. . .

Albany and points west

*T*HEIR DEPARTURE WEST would be delayed, they'd learned at the depot, by a crash. Somewhere beyond Utica, the smoking, battered wrecks of two locomotives and their seven derailed passenger coaches were being cleared from the tracks and roadbed. Neither engine had been running at full steam, so only two people had died. (An elderly passenger on one train had collapsed in terror, and the stoker of the other had been pinned and roasted beneath two hundred pounds of hot coals that poured from his furnace.) As with most railway collisions, the cause was not mechanical failure but human confusion concerning schedules—a regular problem given the endless disagreements and contradictions among all the various local times and railroad times.

"*What?*" said Duff, incredulous, after he listened to Ben commiserating with the ticket agent about the competing systems of time. This was news to him. "It can't be."

"Look at the timepieces here," Ben said, pointing at the three big clocks mounted around the depot, each owned by a different railroad and each showing a different time. The main ten-foot-tall iron clock of the Albany & Schenectady line reported the current time as eleven minutes past eight, which agreed with Duff's watch—but according to the brass clock of the Auburn & Syracuse Railroad, it was 8:20, and on the clock owned by the Attica & Buffalo the time was already 8:31. Each line kept its own time, according to the hour at its headquarters. "I believe you now follow *144* different times in this country."

Duff struggled to come to grips with this new disillusionment. How could the very incarnation of the new America, of progress itself—the railroads—be conducted in such a reckless and stupid way? "It is the capitalists' greedy doing, isn't it? They think they own *time,* too."

"A reasonable point, well put," Skaggs replied.

"In England," said Ben, trying to calm Duff, "the discord was solved only this past winter, when the railways agreed to abide by a single observatory time. I am sure the practical-minded citizens of America will correct the problem soon."

Skaggs shrugged. "Practical-minded to *selfish* ends, since we are pigheaded as well—liberty means having one's own way, doesn't it? Charleston will not agree to Boston's ideas concerning slaves, nor will Detroit agree to New York's idea of the correct time."

"And among *certain* Americans, I suppose," Ben teased, "the nostalgia for the old days, before railways and the telegraph, is another impediment to progress in this regard."

"Mind your own business, foreigner," Skaggs replied.

They finally left around noon. Before they reached Buffalo the next day, they would change trains six times and pay fares to seven different lines that ran on schedules geared to four different timekeeping schemes.

Ben was alert, as ever, to the national peculiarities. As in England, most of the trains included five or six passenger carriages—"cars" in the local vernacular. However, the American cars were distinguished not by first, second, and third class, but according only to sex (several gentlemen's cars, two ladies' cars) and race (a car, painted black, reserved for Negroes). What's more, the passengers could roam from car to car, and each one was enormous, big enough for coal stoves and seats running along both sides of a passageway.

As their train stopped west of Schenectady so that a dying sheep could be pulled off the track, Ben opened a window. The car filled with the sweet, spicy aroma of the pink blossoms that stretched out to the south as far as they could see. He inhaled deeply. "A *peppermint* farm!" he said.

Sometime later they passed a gang of men who had just finished levering and hoisting a two-story house from its foundations near the track onto a gigantic wagon. "Hearth and home shoved aside for the sake of this machine," Skaggs said. As the house began to move forward, pulled by more oxen than it seemed possible to harness together, its chimneys crumbled and fell to the ground.

AFTER THEIR SECOND change of trains the track doubled and they approached and then passed an eastbound freight. For an astounding minute, the passengers cringed and stared. The combined speed of the two trains was seventy-five miles per hour. Duff counted 120 cars. Half of them were piled with huge trees, stripped of limbs and bark, hurtling past only a few feet from their faces.

"That train," marveled Ben, sounding like a boy, "must be a *mile long.*"

"And somewhere in the north country," said Skaggs, looking up from the book he was reading, "a thousand birds and deer and bear are wondering why there is suddenly a hole in their forest."

"What rancid fiction has put you in such a crotchety mood, sir?" Ben asked.

Skaggs smiled and pushed his eyeglasses up from the tip of his nose. "Fiction, is it? No, an exposé of the *greatest* fiction." He held up the binding to show Ben—the book was *The Life of Jesus, Critically Examined.*

"Ah, Professor Strauss. In English now. *Das Leben Jesu* was the first German volume I attempted to read." During Ben's student year in Bonn, the heretical book and its author caused a sensation from Geneva to Berlin. "It was my German-language catechism."

Skaggs cackled.

"What?" Duff asked, confused by Skaggs's laugh, then turned to Ben hopefully. "Are you . . . are you religious, Ben?"

Skaggs laughed again.

"No, Duff, I am not—I mean that I used the book to learn German." He saw that Duff remained mystified. "The author purports to show—"

"Definitively *proves*," Skaggs said.

"—that Matthew, Mark, Luke, and John never witnessed the events they describe . . ."

Duff's eyes were wide.

". . . and that the Gospel of John in particular is more . . . fable than fact. And that the miracles in the Scriptures are in the nature of metaphor, or myth, or—"

"Fiction," Skaggs said, snapping the book shut with both hands. "Turning the water to wine, healing the leper, healing the blind men, *all* of his healings, five thousand people dining on five loaves and two fish, walking

across the Sea of Galilee, raising Lazarus from the dead—*all* of his wonders, according to Herr Doktor Strauss, fabricated by the Gospel writers.
Mere tales. Hoaxes. Fabulous lies."

No one said a word for a long time. Duff had tears in his eyes. His faith
was not shaken a bit, but he worried about Skaggs at moments like this.

"Excuse me," Skaggs said, exhaling deeply. "I apologize for the ill humor.
You have now witnessed the unhappy result of "—he checked his watch—
"forty-four hours without a drink of anything stronger than lemon pop."

Duff reached over and softly patted his shoulder.

The conductor entered the car. "*Utica* depot is the next stop, *Utica* the
next stop, the next stop is *Utica*."

"Lunatica," Skaggs muttered.

"What?" Ben asked.

"That may be the problem with my mood, as I come to think of it—this
region." He sniffed at the air. "Some strange poison or animalcule in the atmosphere, pressed into my blood and brain by our unholy speed . . ."

"What are you saying now, Skaggs?" Duff asked.

"My rant. Can it be chance alone that we are now traveling into the heart
of our national bedlam, the land where every second peasant believes that a
rainbow bridge from heaven touches earth?"

"The heart of what?" asked Ben.

"Have I not told you, Knowles, about the dementias that prevail in these
parts? I laid out the facts last year in a magazine, together with a handsome
map—the Lunatic Belt, three hundred miles long and one hundred miles
wide, the greatest concentration of every species of righteous fanatic, som-
nambulist, spiritualist, mind reader, necromancer, soothsayer, miraclemon-
ger, and fortune-hunting fortune-teller the world has ever known.

" 'The Poughkeepsie Seer,' Andrew Jackson Davis, a shoemaker's apprentice who gives trance performances in which he sees the future and di-
agnoses diseases while speaking pidgin Greek and Hebrew and Sanskrit . . .

"The Shaker insanity took root at a farm near Albany . . .

"William Miller, the farmer who persuaded thousands of desperate idiots that Jesus would return in 1843, or 1844 at the very latest . . .

"The well-intentioned fool Gerrit Smith of Utica has agreed to give
away two hundred square miles of his land in the Adirondacks to any three
thousand Negroes who want them . . . but has managed to recruit only a
dozen who will agree to move north and live according to the hard rules of
his goodyship.

"Soon we shall pass the Reverend Noyes's colony of Christian fornicators at Oneida . . . which is not far from the very place where attorney Finney saw Jesus's light and became the Reverend Finney." A lawyer named Charles Finney reported seeing a divine flash in his law office, and had become the most popular evangelical preacher in America.

"And the bleak precinct toward Rochester gave us the greatest of all, the counterfeiter Joseph Smith . . ."

"Of the Mormons?" Duff asked.

"*The* Mormon, the martyred prophet, the boy who spoke with Christ and Moses as well as Saints Peter, James, and John—in person, right here in Wayne County. And a few miles west is where our newest young charlatans, the Fox girls, chat with ghosts by tapping on their bedsteads."

The couple sitting across the aisle had moved to the back of the car with their daughter, and a man on the bench behind Ben and Skaggs had begun shaking his head more and more violently for the last several minutes.

"But if the miracles of the telegraph and the daguerreotype are now possible," Duff said finally, "then why is it nuts to imagine communication with spirits?"

"You and your poor, dear, trusting sister . . ." Skaggs said. "By the way, the meddlesome Mr. Brisbane, who supplied Polly her itinerary? Another native of the Lunatic Belt." He lowered his voice to a whisper. "I tell you, we are traveling through an accursed land."

"Ben," Duff asked, "do you disbelieve in all miracles as well?"

"No, lad, *no,* you misunderstand me," said Skaggs, sincerely vexed. "It is delusion and hypocrisy and fakery I loathe, not the *true* marvels, not an ice plug that halts the falls at Niagara, not plain wonder at the stars and planets."

"I believe in daguerreotypes, and in the telegraph and electrical engines," Ben finally said. "And in the stars and planets. And in your dear, trusting sister."

The rest of the afternoon passed quietly. They changed trains, napped, and nibbled on meat pies. Skaggs finished his book and stared out the window, wishing he could someday witness a miracle. Duff made entries—*immure, necromancer*—in his journal. They were heading directly into the setting sun when the conductor passed through the car repeating "*Syracuse . . . Syracuse,*" and Ben looked up with a curious smile: in the past day conductors had also announced cities called Athens, Troy, Rome.

Skaggs caught his glance and nodded. "And Attica tonight. A ridiculously modern country fitted out with ridiculously ancient names," he said.

"One means of reassuring ourselves that we are a great civilization. Perhaps we shall have the chance in the days ahead to visit the imperial city of Cairo, in Illinois, which the locals call *Kay*-row."

Ben was napping when they stopped after dark to take on wood and water and let off passengers in Auburn. He awoke to the sound of long, eerie howls coming from the deep forest to their right.

"Damned *wolves*," grumbled a disembarking passenger. It was the man who had shaken his head at Skaggs's tirade against the region's visionaries.

"Damned wolf-slaughtering *farmers*," said Skaggs loudly enough to make the man scowl.

"Wolves?" Ben asked. The animals had been extinct in Britain for a century.

"And thanks to *this* great machine," said Skaggs, "they are now marooned forever up there, on the north side of the tracks—along with the thousand arsonists and murderers forced to make silverware for the remainders of their miserable lives."

"I do not understand, sir," Ben said.

Duff understood. Skaggs was referring to the prison. More than once since the sugarhouse fire he had imagined himself sitting alone in a cell or standing on the gallows at Auburn. Now he was in Auburn, and gooseflesh rose on his arms. His scar stung. He stood.

"I need a coffee and a bun," he said, and shot out of the car toward the food peddler on the platform.

"It was your own French cousin, Knowles," Skaggs continued, "whose book on our prisons made the place famous, for its system of work and silence. It is why they can now sell *tickets* to tourists for a quarter apiece. It is our perfect Puritan factory—no choice but to work, and no complaining about the conditions or hours."

"But about the *animals*," Ben asked, "why do you call them marooned?"

"From the Hudson all the way to Lake Erie the wolves now remain strictly north of the railroad line—the creatures take the tracks for a colossal new trap, which they dare not cross."

They continued to listen to the wolves' howls until the locomotive fired up and drowned them out.

AN HOUR LATER in Seneca Falls, a small mob of very respectable-looking women boarded. There were so many that the ladies' cars filled, and the last several were forced to sit on benches in one of the smoky, spittle-strewn men's cars—across the aisle from Duff and Ben and Skaggs. Only one looked as old as forty, and all were in high spirits as they talked gaily about "the convention." One mentioned "a *brilliant* speech," and another called the speaker "surely the finest person of color on earth."

Around Geneva—between Waterloo and Vienna, Ben noticed, wondering why the nomenclature had shifted abruptly from Mediterranean antiquity to Napoleonic Europe—Skaggs could no longer contain his curiosity. He introduced himself to the eldest woman and admitted with a smile that he was "ignorant of the great and historic gathering" they had attended.

"You may trifle with us, sir," answered a girl of eighteen called Hannah, who earlier had wondered aloud where in Rochester she might purchase Turkish trousers to wear, "but we *are indeed* coming from a great and historic gathering."

"I do not trifle, and do not doubt you. But which party are you?"

The older woman, a Mrs. Experience King, explained that the convention had not been for any political party. It had been a gathering of hundreds of women and men, organized only during the last week, to discuss the conditions and rights of the female in America and to pass a Declaration of Sentiments.

The girl Hannah could not contain her excitement. "The preamble said we are oppressed and fraudulently deprived of our most sacred rights," she said, "and listed *eighteen* injuries and usurpations on the part of man toward woman. All the resolutions were passed *unanimously*."

Mrs. King and the other women were slightly chagrined by their youngest member. But all three men were charmed—and reminded, naturally, of Polly Lucking.

"May I know," Skaggs asked, "one of the eighteen crimes of which my sex stands accused?"

Hannah was happy to recite. "That man has endeavored, in every way, to destroy woman's confidence in her own powers and to lessen her self-respect."

Ben was agog. "May I ask if your declaration stands in opposition to marriage?"

Two of the women blushed.

"*No*, sir, certainly *not*," said Mrs. King. "The objections are only to the laws that turn a married woman into her husband's chattel, deprived of rights."

"Like a *slave*," added Hannah.

"I believe we overheard you make mention of the remarkable Frederick Douglass," Skaggs said.

"You gentlemen are familiar with our Mr. Douglass?" Mrs. King asked. Douglass, the former slave, had recently started publishing an abolitionist paper, *The North Star,* in Rochester.

"Why, yes, of course," Ben answered.

"And I," Skaggs said, stroking his beard, "consider him a great friend. Of many years' standing."

The women smiled and murmured with interest.

"In fact," he continued, "I consider him a blood *cousin* of mine."

One of the women tittered, but the rest looked dismayed.

"Mr. Skaggs here," Ben offered, "is a jester."

"And *white,*" Duff added helpfully.

"But, ladies—and gentlemen—I am entirely in earnest." One beautiful afternoon in September of '38, he explained, he happened to encounter a Negro friend, a fellow journalist, Mr. Ruggles, near his home in New York City. Ruggles was walking with a nervous young man, another Negro, called Mr. Stanley. Skaggs, momentarily flush and also eager to dine with two black men at a certain grand new hotel, treated them to a lavish luncheon—the finest food, Mr. Stanley said, he had ever eaten in his life. Afterward, on the street, once his guests were satisfied that Skaggs was not in league with any lurking blackbirders, they revealed to him that Mr. Stanley was a slave, on the run and new to the city, and that his name was actually Bailey.

Telling the story now, Skaggs paused, smiling broadly. Certainly the women but even Duff and Ben were wondering if he was right in the head.

"I mentioned to Mr. Bailey that Bailey happened to be the name of my mother's family in Baltimore. Whereupon he told me that *he* had been raised in Maryland, and that his father had been white. 'Cousin,' I cried, and hugged him right there in Broadway in front of the Astor House. When I learned a moment later that we were both born in towns called Hillsborough, our serendipitous encounter came to seem"—here he turned his gaze for an instant on Duff—"fairly *miraculous.*"

"But, Skaggs," said Ben carefully, "what on earth is the connection between your Mr. Bailey and Frederick Douglass?"

"Shortly after our meeting, Freddy Bailey changed his name—to Freddy Johnson." He paused for several perplexing seconds. "And then one time more, of course. To Frederick Douglass."

The women had fallen in love with Skaggs, who asked them, "And what did he tell your convention in Seneca Falls?"

"It was Mr. Douglass," offered Hannah, "who persuaded all the waddlers to approve resolution number *nine*."

"Hannah Victor!" Mrs. King said sharply. Some of the other women appeared anxious, as they dreaded this first broaching with outsiders of their most audacious act. "May I inquire of your gentlemen's business in Rochester?" Mrs. King asked, hoping to change the subject.

"You may, but the answer is none at all," Skaggs replied, "for we are going on to Buffalo tonight—but may I ask you, madam, the details of your resolution number nine?" He still had the rude curiosity of a journalist, if not the job.

Young Hannah Victor leapt in again. "That it is our *duty*, the duty of the women of America, to demand for ourselves the sacred right to *vote*. Mrs. Stanton *insisted* on it."

No one said a word for a long moment. Looks were exchanged. Throats were cleared. Duff blinked nervously. Female suffrage was a notion beyond radical, nearly inconceivable.

"I am *with* you," Skaggs told the women. "And indeed, I hereby volunteer to sacrifice my own franchise so that it may be transferred to any one of you. But who is this remarkable Mrs. Stanton?"

"Mrs. Elizabeth Cady Stanton," said Hannah Victor. "She was the organizer, and wrote the Declaration."

"A lady of Seneca Falls, from a great family of abolitionists," said Experience King. "You may know of her cousin—Mr. Gerrit Smith?"

Duff and Ben looked at Skaggs, afraid he was about to lodge some terrible insult against the man he had described earlier in the day as a fool.

"A great family indeed," said Skaggs.

After the women disembarked and the three men boarded a new train, Skaggs announced that his antipathy to anti-liquor zealots and haughty New York City bluestockings had led him to misjudge "the *normal* American Amazons, such as those good women."

"They were sweet on you, Skaggs," Duff teased.

"I am simply their latest Aunt Nancy man," he replied as he arranged himself for sleep. "And now that I am a temperance man as well, perhaps I shall be allowed citizenship in their utopia, this new petticoatdom." He shut his eyes and began to sing, in the manner of a lullaby: " 'There's a good time coming, boys, / A good time coming . . .' "

Ben smiled. He knew the song, a favorite lately among liberals, Quakers, Unitarians, pacifists, and the irredeemably hopeful of every stripe. It was written, Lloyd Ashby had informed him, by the author of the book *Extraordinary Popular Delusions and the Madness of Crowds.*

" '. . . Let us aid it all we can,/Every woman and every man—' "

"Hey! Quiet!" said a man sitting nearby.

But Skaggs's baritone grew louder. " 'There's a good time coming, boys . . . /The pen shall supersede the sword!/And right, not might—' "

"Shhhh!"

" '—And right, not might, shall be the lord . . . /In the good time coming!' Snooze well, comrades."

36

late July 1848

. . .

Glee, Indiana

AT THE START, life at Glee was like a dream. The sun shone all day every day the first week after they arrived, even on the one afternoon it had briefly rained. That day, a rainbow arched over the entire farm for an hour as two members of the Amusement Team, a soprano and a flutist, strolled the grounds playing Mozart songs ("To Isolation" and "The Song of Separation") whose English lyrics all the consociates seemed to know. Polly had not seen both ends of a rainbow or eaten apples straight from the tree since she was a girl.

Glee's orchard and vegetable and hemp gardens were planted among three big earthen mounds in the rough shapes of birds, and enclosed by a high earthen wall, with an opening at one corner. The mounds and wall were "a cemetery built thousands of years ago by ancient aboriginals," James Danforth told Polly and Priscilla that first afternoon, which made Glee "a hallowed place centuries before Jesus Christ was on earth. This land was inhabited," he said with a blissful smile, "at the time of Odysseus and Achilles and Homer."

The smells of the settlement (sweet honeysuckle and minty wild anis around the main house and the many nearby huts, the walnut sawdust hanging in the air of the mill, the rich cellar smell of the loamy earth itself) were fresh and alive. The residents were courteous and seemed kindly, the food good and abundant. Every meal was taken by all the residents together at three long tables arranged in a triangle and, whenever the weather allowed, outside on the grass behind the Hive, as they called the large main house. At the Saturday night feast where Polly and Priscilla were initiated as PCs, or probationary consociates, each of the other forty-seven current residents, one by one, sprinkled handfuls of wildflower petals—red royal catchfly, orange butterfly milkweed, pink lilacs—onto the heads and shoulders of the two new recruits.

Every evening after supper, Polly and Priscilla took drawing tablets and colored chalks up the cleared hill behind the gardens and sketched until sunset. The second night, Billy asked if he could join them. When it became too dark to draw, they watched the lightning bugs. Billy started to sing in a beautiful tenor voice—Polly and Priscilla knew only scattered verses from "Woodman, Spare That Tree!" ("Touch not a single bough! . . . /There, woodman, let it stand/Thy axe shall harm it not!"), but all three of them sang all the verses to "Buffalo Gals." And by the time they sang "Can't you come out tonight,/And dance by the light of the moon?" for the fourth and last time, the moon had just risen over the far hill.

The first week, even ordinary, tedious tasks—tilling the wheat field, weeding the garden, milking the cows—had a dreamy, enchanted aspect. For Polly, almost every sight and smell and sound became a revisitation to a particular place or moment in the Clove Valley of her childhood. And to Priscilla, each pastoral moment and agricultural task was thrillingly alien.

They were put to work the first morning, and Polly was happy for the chores. They kept her thoughts from straying too often to Ben Knowles and the rest of her former life. Labor was assigned without regard for one's sex—men cooked and laundered as well as plowed and sawed, women swung axes and drove wagons and spread manure. Young Billy, who had grown up the oldest of eight siblings, took turns with Priscilla caring for the community's several toddlers, and Polly was assigned to the Fencing Team (boiling wire in vats of linseed oil to rustproof it, lugging five-foot fence posts from the sawmill to the pasture) and the Dairy Team.

At first, even the queerest customs seemed agreeable. Surnames were never used. Greetings—between men, between women, between men and women—frequently involved pecks on the cheek. The service on Sunday was unfamiliar to Catholic Polly and unchurched Priscilla, but both of them enjoyed the references to Norse and Hindu divinities intermingled with allusions to God and Jesus. They learned most of the jargon—consociate, conclave, aspirationalism, PC—within the first few days. The Glee diet, with the exceptions of milk and cheese and butter, was vegetarian—or "Pythagorean," as James called it. Any consociate could request permission from the group to drink coffee or tea or eat fish, but permission was granted for only a month at a time, and fish eaters were responsible for catching their own bass from the river Xanthos—Danforth's name for what the locals called Skunk Creek. For Polly, grown accustomed these last years to clean rags in the privy, the corn husks and pieces of moss stocked in Glee's outhouses were (she told herself) charmingly rustic.

As probationers, Priscilla and Polly were assigned to sleep in one of the tiny sleeping huts that were big enough only for one bed and a sink. Everyone at Glee was abed by nine, not because the time was prescribed but because candles and lamps burning lard or tallow or whale oil—light that required the slaughter of animals—were prohibited. And bayberry wax candles were too expensive. After nightfall, Glee was completely dark.

None of the women wore bonnets. All the members of both sexes picked their costumes each morning from common closets and chests. And although Polly had never considered red a flattering color, she did not mind the female uniform—simple gingham dresses in various shades of scarlet and peach and pink, flannel undergarments all dyed the same colors. Priscilla was balky about the uniforms, having been required to wear one during her months in New York's Home for the Friendless. But Polly reminded her that Duff had sometimes worn a sombrero and serape when he was in Mexico, and that when Skaggs traveled last year in Transylvania, he'd grown a mustache—"When in Romania," he had said, "*always* do as the Romanians do." Glee was like a tiny foreign country where the inhabitants spoke English.

And the occasional bit of some dead language. James Danforth was a proud college graduate, and liberally salted his conversation with phrases from ancient Greek (he called it "Attic") and Latin. Although no Christian grace was spoken before meals, James always gave a kind of benediction before the first mouthful. "My dear *fratres et sorores* of Glee," he said at the first luncheon Polly and Priscilla attended, "before we gratefully share the gift of our earth's bounty, and delight in her warm and toothsome flesh"— by which he meant a hash of corn and tomato and summer squash—"may I remind us all that tonight is our evening cleanse in Persephone Spring. And the sun sets at half past seven." In his remarks at meals James always contrived to include some piece of celestial news—the remaining fraction of the waning moon, the precise length of the day just ending or the night about to come. The information came from his *Old Farmer's Almanack*, but the ritual announcements served to reinforce his casually godlike air. When rabbits invaded the gardens, or a pair of geese landed on the pond, James referred to them as "the beasts of the field" and "the birds of the air."

He was in his middle thirties, and he combed his very long, dark hair straight back from his temples and forehead. He was tall and moved gracefully. His demeanor was brotherly and fatherly in equal parts, grand and sometimes stern but also genial and with even a hint of mischief. As a young man he had been ordained in the Unitarian Church. He referred sometimes to "the difficulties in Burlington"—many of the consociates had been members of his congregation in Vermont. Polly believed, hopefully, that Glee's combination of discipline and eccentricity should suit her, since her mother had been a strict Catholic and her father a freethinker. But James Danforth was unlike any priest she had ever known.

He encouraged Polly and Priscilla, "our latest lovely PCs," to sit near him at meals so that they "might begin to commune deeply sometime sooner rather than later." Today at lunch they had discussed the hanging, just completed, of the new upper millstone in Sampo. (James had recently renamed the mill after a cosmic mill in Finnish myth.) Polly had said that the stone— a circle of granite five feet in diameter and ten inches thick—looked to her "like the wheel from the giant gig driven by some ancient race." James had practically shivered with delight, and placed his hand on her forearm. "Like a *chariot*, you mean, of the *giants* hurled into the pits of hell by *Zeus*! Yes, Polly! I had the very thought myself when I first glimpsed the millstones." She was happy to be praised by the leader of Glee, of course, but his slavering reaction reminded her of those she'd provoked in certain men at Mrs. Stanhope's when she would make some passably intelligent remark about politics or literature or art. Or like Ben Knowles on their first evening at Castle Garden, when she'd pretended to know about architecture.

Yesterday James had joined her for the evening milking, since one duty he always assumed for himself was ensuring that novice Dairy Team members knew how to milk properly. Polly had not touched an udder in years. James had put his fingers over hers as she milked, and after a minute declared himself pleased with her touch and the sure rhythm of her squirts into the pail. "Your fingers are excellent," he had told her. Making small talk as their hands tugged together on the Holstein's full, warm nipples, Polly had mentioned that she was doubly pleased that certain vegetables had not appeared on Glee's menu so far. She hated turnips and parsnips, she'd said, and had been taught as a child that for the sweetest milk, one never fed their scraps to cows.

"At Glee," James had explained, "you shall never see any *turnip* or *parsnip* or *radish*." The name of each vegetable he'd pronounced with a mild disgust, or . . . disappointment, as if he were listing the names of sinners. "Or *beet*. We eat no *root* vegetable here. Do you know why?"

"Because you dislike their taste, or texture?"

"Because we pity them. Because they are poor creatures who come to maturity *underground*, secret and dirty and ashamed. At Glee, we favor the *aspiring* vegetables that extend themselves *upward*, straight and true toward the mother sun."

Except for Timothy Skaggs, who after a few drinks might launch into an elegy for the gallant whale that sacrificed its life for the sake of a reading lamp and a corset stay, she had never heard anyone speak about such an ordinary matter in such poetic fashion. And she understood why at Glee she had eaten so much corn and asparagus, and not a single potato or carrot.

POLLY WAS IN the dairy barn with her fellow members of the Dairy Team, Presence and an older man named Granby, feeding the day's kitchen waste to Glee's six cows. Granby stood under the hayloft ten feet from the two women, stuffing wheat stalks into "the dog power," as they called the new device. One of Glee's two Great Pyrenees was harnessed inside the ten-foot-tall drum, the huge white dog's trot on the treadmill spinning a crankshaft that in turn operated a rotary blade that cut the straw.

Presence said that she looked forward this fall to hooking up their churn to the dog power for the first time.

"When does your buttermaking season begin?" Polly asked. She remembered her mother always making the first batch at Thanksgiving.

"Early this year, James says, in September, because now we can buy ice in Greencastle and needn't wait for the weather."

"And perhaps add more saltpeter to the recipe," Polly said, thinking that an extra ration of preservative would keep the butter from spoiling.

"*No,*" said Granby sharply. "No saltpeter."

Presence smiled slightly and shook her head. "At Glee we are opposed to such . . . medicines. As you might expect."

Polly thought she understood—the community's approach to health was homeopathic. "If we are starting to make butter as soon as that," she said, "should we not start soon to give the animals Indian meal and salt to eat?"

Every fall, Polly remembered, the Luckings would feed their cow rations of skim milk and salted ground corn to improve the taste of her butter.

Presence nodded. "For the cornmeal, I have already asked at Sampo for a hundredweight. But for salt, we no longer . . . some at Glee do not favor salt in our butter."

Granby glowered at her. "The vote was lopsided, Presence."

"Once you are a consociate," Presence said to Polly, avoiding Granby's look, "*you* may propose at the Conclave that we return to making salted butter."

The Conclave was the regular meeting of all the members of Glee, at which certain questions of governance were voted upon—whether orange fabric could be used for clothing (no), whether coal oil or petroleum might be adopted as lamp fuels (tabled), whether butter was to be made with salt (no). About more fundamental issues there was never debate.

"Do you feed the cows skim milk in butter season?"

"They refuse to allow it."

"The Conclave?"

"No," she said, nodding toward the cows, "*they.*"

"But if you withhold their water, they drink the milk. As I recall."

"Yes, but here at Glee, no animal is forced to do that which he doesn't wish to do. We use no oxen to pull the plow, for it requires a stick or a whip to make them move."

"And likewise," Granby said, "the two stallions that pull our wagon are *stallions.*"

Polly did not take his meaning.

"There are no geldings," he explained with a proud and slightly angry air, "at Glee."

Polly wondered how it was determined that the horses and dogs *wished* to walk in harness when they worked, but decided against asking just then.

37

July 22, 1848
· · ·
Buffalo, New York

"M Y *LORD*," SKAGGS said as their train pulled into Buffalo's new brick depot, "it has become a, a—what was your big word, Knowles?"

"Megalopolis."

The city had tripled in size in the few years since Skaggs's brief residence. They drove directly from the station to the harbor, where they discovered that the next steamer taking passengers to Ohio would not leave until the following morning. Ben wanted to board a smaller vessel sailing immediately, but Skaggs warned that "those lake schooners capsize every *week*." Besides, he argued, the extra day would give them a chance to stock up on provisions. He also had in mind an excursion.

"Excellent," he said as he took fifteen dollars from Ben. All three men had brought with them every cent they had—Skaggs because he didn't have much, Ben because he didn't know whether he would be gone a month or a year, Duff because he thought he was gone for good and didn't trust banks anyway. "You two boys wash and eat and rest, and I shall serve as quartermaster. I know the requirements of a journey west."

"And do you plan to make portraits of the shopkeepers?" Ben asked.

Skaggs held his camera case and tripod.

"Who knows what fresh wonders one might come upon?"

. . .

HE DID NOT return to their hotel room until after six, hatless and accompanied by a porter and a dozen boxes and packages of various sizes.

Duff smelled hops. "You fell off the water cart, didn't you?"

Skaggs gave him a dirty look. "I signed no *oath*, Reverend Lucking. When in Buffalo, one does as the Buffalonians do. And two beers with my old friend Swarr at the *Republic* does not make me a failure by my lights." He would leave unmentioned his quick trip by rail to Niagara Falls, and the glass of champagne he had there.

"What is all of this?" Ben asked, a little peevishly, about the mountain of goods.

"I spent half my day bargaining with half the shopkeepers along Michigan Avenue, and this is the thanks I receive from my slugabed partners?"

All of them tore open the parcels. Three pairs of goggles "for dust storms." A small brass telescope covered with black leather in a leather-covered wooden case. ("I returned the binocular opera glasses," Skaggs said. "Mother-of-pearl fittings are not rugged enough for trail life.") Something called Levinge's apparatus ("for keeping off vermin") and, "since I am to serve as the physician on this expedition," quinine, camphor, calomel, bandages, sticking plasters, and, in case Duff had a blue spell, a bottle of Blue Mass.

"I have no need for those any longer," Duff said. "I am jim-dandy now."

There was also paregoric ("for diarrhea"), laudanum ("for headache"), and morphine ("in case of injury"). Ben was surprised that Skaggs considered it necessary to pack three different opium derivatives.

And although Skaggs had brought his photographic equipment from New York—the portable camera and tripod, the plates and their sensitizing case, the fuming box and alcohol lamp for developing—he needed chemicals if he was to make pictures on the road. So from the Buffalo chemist he'd also bought mercury, nitrate of silver, iodine crystals, and a dark red liquid with a skull-and-crossbones label. Ben sniffed it and gagged.

"Careful," Skaggs warned. "That *will* kill you."

"Quickstuff," Duff said.

"Makes the plates more sensitive," Skaggs explained. " 'Quicker.' "

And he had bought maps—a large new atlas of all the U.S. states and territories ("Including Texas, California, and the Formerly Mexican Lands") printed on tough banknote paper and packaged in a red leather tube with gold-tooled lettering.

He'd also bought an atlas of the Indian country beyond the Missouri River "Based on John C. Frémont's Famous & Unexcelled Maps."

"We are not traveling so far west as that, Skaggs," Ben said.

"No, but since his court-martial last year—'conduct to the prejudice of order and discipline'!—I've had a soft spot in my conscience for Colonel Frémont. And we happen to be precisely the same age, besides. Also, the German at the shop let me have it for a quarter."

Skaggs unfolded and unrolled the maps and laid them out on the floor, beginning to plot a route. Because Albert Brisbane had sworn to them that Polly's list of prospective communities included none east of the Alleghenies, the search seemed daunting but manageable: fifteen places in five states—Ohio, Indiana, Illinois, Wisconsin, and Iowa.

LIFE IS ALL in the timing.

If Polly had arrived in Chicago a few weeks earlier, before the telegraph line reached the city, she would not have been able to wire her message to Duff, telling him that she and Priscilla were BOUND FOR DANFORTH'S COMMUNITY KNOWN AS LOVELY PUTNAM COUNTY INDIANA.

And if the men had delayed their departure from Manhattan by a day— by even a few hours—they would have received and read the telegram that now sat in a drawer at Duff's boardinghouse.

Life is indeed all in the timing, and timing is mostly a matter of luck.

—→·➤·◄·—

38

July 29, 1848

. . .

New York City

*P*ATIENCE! HE WAS a warrior, a man of action, but in this battle, he knew, patience and guile were the required arts of war. From reading Inspector Vidocq, Gabriel Drumont knew well that the scientific sleuthhound must expect to endure frustration. Sweet victory—the second of the English running dogs snared at last, Michel's murder avenged, France honored—would in the end erase all memories of discomfort along the way.

But he was dispirited nevertheless. This was his tenth day staring at one spot, waiting for one man to step into his sights. It had rained for four of those days, and it had been nauseatingly hot for all but two. And he was sleepy. Every morning except Sunday, he had arrived at the corner and stood at his post until half past six in the evening, attempting to appear nonchalant, eating cake and apples kept in what he had come to consider his food pocket (as opposed to his Baby Dragoon pocket), drinking water from a canteen, stepping a few paces back into the alley when he needed to piss, keeping a constant eye on the front door of the building at 42 Wall, which housed the offices of Prime, Ward & King.

From the beginning, Drumont feared that he had been spotted. The very morning following his conversation with Prime, his first morning of surveillance, he had watched the banker leave the building in a plainly agitated state twenty minutes after he had arrived, practically sprinting down the block to his carriage. And for the rest of that day he had not reappeared at all, or the next. But then on the third morning, Prime had come driving up just before nine as usual, and he'd stepped out of the barouche looking normal—dim and contented. Why had he been so perturbed two days earlier? Had he regained some piece of business that had threatened to go bad? Had his wife or a child sickened and then suddenly recovered? Or perhaps Prime *had* spotted him, and was now *acting* ordinary to give Knowles a chance to escape.

But surely not. Surely, sooner or later, Knowles would appear. He would do as his father had asked and pay a call. He would in any event need money, since all things in America except whiskey and meat were so dear. *I do expect to see Mr. Knowles soon,* Prime had said, *and I shall be pleased to give him your message.* But whenever Knowles finally did show himself, Drumont intended to deliver his message personally.

Alas, another wearying and fruitless day of vigilance was now ending, with no sign at all of his quarry. As always, Prime's driver flicked his reins when the first big bell of Trinity chimed the hour, the carriage rolled to a stop at the door on the sixth chime, and Samuel Prime stepped from the building to the pavement on the chime of the inexistent seventh.

Drumont sighed and began his walk to his job at Monsieur Roux's, watching Prime's barouche as it quickly became one of the evening herd of carriages racing up Broadway toward the Park and beyond. He always kept an eye out for Knowles as he walked, and he was now taking a second, hard look at a man crossing Canal Street toward him . . . late twenties, tall, slender build, light brown hair—but the wrong eyes, sleepy and green, not quick and brown like Knowles's. As Vidocq taught, the detective policeman must concentrate on seeing *the face,* not *le maquillage du coiffeur,* the mustache or curls that happened to decorate a face on a given day. Drumont was so busy mentally shaving another passing New Yorker, however, that he very nearly missed the dirty, crinkled advertisement on the wall directly behind and above the stranger's head.

In fact, he did not understand what he had glimpsed until he was three or four paces beyond it—whereupon he stopped, swiveled, and rushed back to the spot. He put his palms against the wall and looked up to make out what words he could.

A FIRSTHAND ACCOUNT by a native-English-speaking EYEWITNESS to the late REVOLUTION in the streets of PARIS which inaugurated the

present GREAT & STIRRING EVENTS RIPPING ACROSS EUROPE AND
THE WORLD!

  A VERY INTERESTING lecture on the DEMOCRATIC STRUGGLE,
VALIANT COMBAT, TRAGIC DEATH, AND INSTANT END OF
TYRRANY! Presented by Mr. Benjamin Knowles, a well-known Uni-
versity graduate.

"Alléluia," he said out loud. "Mon Dieu—merci, merci, mon *cher* Dieu!"

The two-faced parasite is indeed here, and not only is he still playing at
revolution, Drumont thought, *he is now puffing himself as some hero of the*
February streets! He is peddling his grotesque little Paris adventure—the
murder of Michel—as if it were something entertaining and lofty, "stirring"
and "very interesting."

The poster, for an event weeks earlier, had survived because Duff Lucking had pasted it so securely, and high on the bricks. But by standing on tiptoe (damn the Americans' stares) and stretching his arm, Drumont could
just grab the loose corner and rip away the bottom strip of essential information—the Temple of Reason, Broome Street—and stuff it into his gun
pocket.

39

July 30, 1848
. . .
Glee, Indiana

AFTER MORE THAN a week sharing their buggy little sleeping hut, Polly and Priscilla were happy when the first phase of their probation ended and they were moved inside the Hive. And Polly had been relieved to discover that every resident was assigned a private cubicle—including each member of the married couples—rather than the open barracks she'd heard that other communities maintained.

It was hard to know for certain who the married couples at Glee were, though, since everyone was always called by his or her first name. For instance, Polly hadn't known that Harlan, the older man she'd met picking sweet corn the afternoon they arrived, was married to Philippa, one of the pregnant women, until Abigail had caused a small ruckus one morning during work assignments by accidentally referring to Harlan and Philippa as "the Tarboxes."

On the same Sunday they were to sleep in the Hive for the first time, they were allowed to attend the weekly Conclave. Polly had warned Priscilla she might be bored, so she brought along paper, pencils, and a needle and thread to repair her old stuffed dog, one of whose tin eyes she sewed tight and whose seams she mended as the meeting proceeded. Billy sat on the floor beside her.

For nearly the whole first hour, James held forth excitedly on some new articles he had been reading—"in the German," he noted, which made Polly think of Ben—by Prussian and Swiss archaeologists and anthropologists. Their findings proved, he said, that all of the familiar ancient goddesses of antiquity, including Aphrodite, his favorite, derived from a forgotten but supreme "mother goddess" worshiped by even older civilizations, and that those earliest societies were "true, full, communist democracies." He smiled. "As well as gynecocracies."

Eleanor, a widowed former schoolteacher, raised her hand.

"A *gynecocracy*, Ellie," James said, continuing to smile, pausing meaningfully, "a society ruled by *women*."

Most of the female consociates reacted the way James had intended, as if they had been told something marvelous.

When James opened the floor for new business, Billy asked if regular Christian prayer might be introduced into the liturgy of Glee. From the exasperated reactions, Polly could see that Billy must have made similar suggestions in the past.

"You, my young sir, have been a consociate for a mere six months—"

"Seven and a half."

"—and I would suggest that as a new member of this community, Billy, still sloughing off your various Mormon . . . misconceptions, you give yourself more time to appreciate the full breadth and depth of our celebration of the divine at Glee. The Holy Bible—which *some* of us, sir, have studied since you were at your mother's breast—is but one of our sacred texts."

Billy stared at the floor.

Some votes were taken—whether the puce-and-red-striped stockings one of the consociates' mothers had sent as a gift were acceptable (no); whether children of eleven would be allowed to go without shirts during the group baths in the creek (yes—including "our naiads," as James called the girls); whether the limping, bloody fox found trapped in the silo should be killed to end its misery (tabled until next Sunday's meeting); whether a carrot someone had managed to grow in a jar of water could be eaten, since it had never touched dirt (no); whether the community declared itself in support of slave insurrections across the river in Kentucky (yes, "if performed without loss of life"); and whether Glee would take in fugitive slaves seeking refuge (yes, temporarily, but *not*—the male members were unanimous on this question—as consociates).

Then came the weekly Session of Mutual Criticism. Hackadiah, a man on the Housekeeping Team who spoke with a nasal New England accent, said that that very morning, when he'd swept out the sleeping hut "the new PCs had occupied," he'd discovered "three dead night-flies, two dead hawthorn-flies and another two mayflies, a dead gadfly, and the corpses of *many* honey-gnats." Hackadiah sighed and shook his bald head. "Each one was broken and smashed."

Polly was astounded. "I did not know," she said, "that your sympathy for animals—"

James raised a forefinger. "*Our* sympathy, Polly."

"We were not aware that, that *bugs* were to be spared as well."

"Whenever possible," said Harlan. Everyone nodded, and the insect massacre was noted in a large journal.

"And the guhr's dow," said a small man next to Hackadiah called Savage. Savage, missing a half inch of his tongue, could be difficult to understand.

"The *girl's doll*," a woman, named Charity, translated, pointing at Priscilla and her stuffed dog. A few other consociates nodded.

Now Priscilla was stunned. "I have no doll," she said. "Jonathan is not a doll."

"What earthly objection," Polly asked, "can there be to a child's toy?"

James sighed. "Priscilla is by no means a *child*, I should say first—but the Conclave has rather thoroughly debated and decided this question in many meetings long past. I happen to differ with the majority on this issue, but we are a democracy."

In the winter, back when Glee was still called Lovely, it had declared itself firmly opposed to "the doll spirit" by a 27-to-22 vote. "Whereas playing with dolls is acting and speaking a lie," the final resolution had declared, "and whereas playing with dolls tends to make us frivolous babies in thought and talk," dolls were banned. And the seven dolls owned by the children at that time were immediately collected and ceremoniously burned in the Hive's largest fireplace.

As the history of the doll issue was explained, Priscilla looked to Polly for consolation and tucked Jonathan deeper into her lap. Her breath quickened.

"It is a *dog* she has," Billy said firmly, "not a doll. I was present at that Conclave, it was my first, and at the burning, and none of them that burned was an animal. They were all little girls, those dolls. That vote concerned only *dolls*." He looked over at Priscilla. She was silent, but tears streamed down her red cheeks. "And she is a probationer, besides."

Billy's points of order carried the day, for the moment. It was decided that once Priscilla became a full consociate, the group would reconsider the issue of whether Jonathan—and stuffed animals in general—were contraband.

But the Housekeeping Team was not finished. Charity had her own criticism to lodge against Polly. This morning on the table in the sleeping hut "among the murdered flies," she and Hackadiah had seen "a proscribed female apparatus"—a rubberized belt-and-cloth contraption Polly wore during her menstrual periods.

A clock began to strike and James shot to his feet. "Ah, *six o'clock*," he announced with gusto, "and so we adjourn."

AND FOUR HOURS later, after the same clock dinged its bell ten times, and outside the million summer insects produced their synchronized sawing, Polly heard the quick, light, sharp taps on the door of her little chamber. She had wondered about the protocol of the Hive regarding open bedroom doors in the summer heat.

"Yes?" she said softly. Her bed, like all the beds at Glee, was constructed of big oaken timbers, and made not the slightest creak as she sat up.

The door opened, and a cooling breeze shot through the room before it closed. In the darkness she could not make out the figure who stood at the threshold a very few yards from her face.

"It is I, my dear," he whispered, "*James*. I have come for a love interview—to commune with you, if the prospect is pleasant."

He had already stepped in close enough that she could smell the soap and sun on the flannel of his nightshirt. *Commune?* Polly knew the word, but not as a euphemism for *copulate*.

"Do feel entirely free to decline," James said. "At Glee, no one is obliged or disobliged in these matters of affection and personal magnetism. Although I do confess that in sleeping with you, I expect something sublime."

She was not shocked. Yet nor did she feel especially eager to take him. She had enjoyed her month of sharing a bed with no man. This taste of abstinence had been refreshing, like a forgotten piece of music or a dessert she had not consciously craved but was pleased to experience again. The day before, as she had looked out from the hilltop at Glee's quilt of cultivated and fallow fields—wheat, oats, hay, weeds, wheat, oats, hay, weeds, wheat— she'd fancied that a piece of herself was now lying fallow, like the land, to replenish and rejuvenate.

On the other hand, it had been a month, as long as she had gone these last two years. And while she had been happy to disprove Ben Knowles's awful suggestion that she indulged her animal passions uncontrollably, and that she suffered from some kind of mental illness— *"nymphomania"*—nor did she wish to feel tyrannized in her own mind by Ben's disapproval.

Besides, James was handsome, and she was not immune to flattery—he had *chosen her.* (She did not know that during his previous two thousand nights at Glee, he had chosen, at least once apiece, all but four of Glee's women.)

"Have you a preventative?" she asked as he sat down beside her.

"We do not employ artificial means of that sort. If we do not *eat* the tasty flesh of the beasts, should we not also refrain from *disemboweling* them for our . . . convenience?"

Condoms, he meant, were cut from the intestines of livestock; since angling was permitted, grudgingly, at Glee, Polly wondered about the possibility of fish-skin condoms.

"*Our* way," he continued, sensing her reluctance as he lifted the sheet and climbed into bed, "is a matter of will. If you don't want butter, you pull the dasher out in time."

She took his meaning. (She also recalled Granby's angry reaction in the barn, at the time inexplicable, when she had suggested loading the real butter with saltpeter.) And soon she understood why James was touching and stroking her face and neck and breasts and hips with only the fingers of his left hand, and why in his right fist the whole time he held a small, neatly folded napkin—in which he would catch the buttermilk splatter from his dasher.

New York City

DRUMONT HAD BEEN very excited and very proud. He had imagined that victory was nigh. The morning after he'd seen the poster for the lecture he went straightaway to the hall in Broome Street, posing as one of Knowles's red republican friends, and easily wheedled his address from the manager.

He had proceeded directly to 171 Sullivan Street, where he found no concierge, and climbed to the second floor, knocked, then wedged open the door latch with the tip of his knife, and rushed inside . . . where he found himself all alone . . . and so altered his plan of attack from surprise to stealth, preparing to await Knowles's return . . .

But within a few minutes, as Drumont inspected the rooms, it became plain that the apartment was uninhabited. There was furniture and china and cutlery, there were dozens of pictures and engravings on the wall—such a *bourgeois*, this revolutionary on the run—but hardly any clothing and no candles, nor a scrap of food. Knowles had already fled. But to where on earth *now?*

What would Inspector Vidocq do? Drumont closely examined the return addresses and postage stamps on three unopened letters that had been left in a neat stack on the table, two from England, one from Chicago. On the trunk next to the bed he found a newspaper dated July 18—he had missed Knowles by less than two weeks, which exasperated and encouraged him in equal measure. He pressed a palm on the mattress: *feathers,* of course. Again he felt simultaneous anger (he had never slept on a featherbed) and hope (such a pampered man could not escape Drumont).

And now he saw the next play in the game, the only move open to him. He would revisit Monsieur Prime, and use the one soft aristocrat as the means of finding his way to the other. He had no other choice—which was the way he preferred life to unfold.

late July and early August 1848
. . .
Ohio

SKAGGS COMPLAINED ABOUT the heat and weak coffee, the niggardly soaps and stubby candles and dirty bed linens. But, in fact, much more than Ben he was able to enjoy their zigzag journey through "the fresh-baked America," as he called the states west of Pennsylvania. He would be pleased to see Polly again, and to rescue her from whichever species of utopia had bewitched her, but the hunt was for him secondary, a way to get the game going. He had come along to travel with his friends, to see the country again, to disorder his life a little.

And while Duff was eager to see Polly and Priscilla, and happy to be charged with a mission, mainly he felt relief to be where nobody was likely to know him.

All three men were traveling because they were restless, but two were wandering. Only one was driven by love, and that made Ben their commander. It was he who kept them on the move.

They galloped through Ohio. After two long days on stages from Cleveland down to the Tuscarawas Valley, they reached a well-established German socialist community called Zoar—and the moment they learned that Polly and Priscilla had not been seen, they said thank you and goodbye. It was the same the next day at the Social Reform Community, then at Every Class of Every Nation, and at the Columbus Phalanx.

At the Brothers and Sisters' Establishment, the eleven residents (down from twenty-nine two years earlier) were bitterly disappointed to learn that the men were not prospective recruits, and that the chance to enlist a pair of young female searchers had evidently passed them by. When the leader invited them to remain for a day to participate in a symposium on how they might persuade the state of Ohio to abolish capital punishment, as Michigan had done, the men begged off. After they boarded their next stage and went a few miles, Duff asked incredulously, "Is that right, they don't hang you in Michigan no matter what?"

Skaggs nodded. "Not for murder—only for *treason*."

Duff was silent for the remainder of the ride.

At the colony called Experiment, the founder invited them to stay on to talk about the European revolutions and Frederick Douglass and life in New York; Ben declined. "I'm afraid we must press on tonight to the Brotherhood Colony, and then to Mr. Warren's Utopia." After a brief bit of excitement at Brotherhood—where the community's new conscripts Mary Ann and Priss turned out to be sisters in their forties from Harrisburg—they stayed the night in a barn. Ben insisted that they leave for Utopia at dawn and, if Polly was not there, proceed to Evansville on the afternoon steamer.

UTOPIA'S FOUNDER, A printer and musician named Josiah Warren, had made his fortune as the inventor and manufacturer of a lamp that burned lard. In the years since, he had devoted himself to promoting his scheme for a new economic system, by publishing a newspaper called *The Peaceful Revolutionist,* and by setting up businesses and settlements in which profit was outlawed. The idea had sounded preposterous to Skaggs and Ben.

The town was parceled out with streets and alleys into eighty quarter-acre lots which sold for a fixed price of fifteen dollars apiece. A dozen good houses were already built; a dozen more were under construction. A brick kiln and a mill were running full blast. Utopia was tidy and prosperous-looking—"extremely spruce," Duff said.

When they entered the dry-goods emporium, the so-called Time Store, the bewhiskered shopkeeper greeted them. Beneath his apron he was well dressed, and looked to be fifty. Like the other Utopians they'd asked, he told them no, he hadn't seen Polly and Priscilla. He then turned to a large clock behind him—it read sixteen minutes past two—and moved a red-painted third hand forward to overlap the minute hand at the sixteen-minute mark. Duff and Skaggs and Ben exchanged glances.

Skaggs asked for soap and candles and the man apologized, explaining that his shipment was due later in the day—and then moved the red clock hand forward half a minute. "No change for disappointment," he said cheerfully.

Skaggs also wanted a soft country slouch hat to replace his hard, tall city model, which had blown off his head and into the river at Niagara. And Duff was looking to buy a good traveling cup.

"How much?" Duff asked about a particular pewter model.

"I could give you an estimate now, sir, but here in Utopia, we tot up the final price of the purchase only when we are finished."

Skaggs whispered to Ben, "A company of *riddlers.*"

Exactly fourteen minutes after they'd stepped into the store, they were finished—Duff had his cup, neatly wrapped, and Skaggs had pulled the new hat onto his head. The shopkeeper checked the clock, reckoned the sums in his head, and announced: "Thirty-four cents—twelve for the cup, and twenty-two for the hat."

The prices seemed impossible, half what they would be in New York, or less.

The shopkeeper was smiling broadly now, plainly accustomed to new customers' astonishment. He raised his palms and shrugged. "This is Utopia, gentlemen. No profit, and thus the lowest possible prices."

"*Viva* Utopia!" said Duff, surprising himself as much as Ben and Skaggs by the lapse into Spanish.

"And exactly how do you manage," Skaggs asked, "to operate without any profit?"

The cup and the hat were made by a tinsmith and a hatter living nearby, he explained, and had required about one hour and one and one-half hours of the makers' labor, respectively, plus the cost of pewter and felt. His own labor—the quarter hour he'd just spent attending to the sale, plus a half cent for the costs of lard for the lamps, freight charges, and the like—were added in as well. But no profit.

"The profit not taken, the two bits you saved shopping here, will be saved in turn on buying bricks across the way, or flour at our mill, or in paying the neighborhood physician. And if you boys lived around here, and we could therefore rely upon employing *your* labor at some later date, you would pay only for the costs of pewter and felt and lard oil with cash money, and we would transact the rest of the trade using *these.*"

From his till he pulled a banknote—rather, what resembled a crisp two-dollar banknote but was in fact a two-hour "labor note" printed by Josiah Warren for use along this hundred-mile stretch of the Ohio River Valley.

The fellow anticipated questions before they were asked. He said that dickering meant that prices in Utopia fluctuated, as in any economy, but eggs generally cost about twenty minutes a dozen, milk forty minutes per gallon, twenty pounds of corn one hour, a pair of shoes between three and nine hours.

"So much time spent calculating quarter hours and percentages," Skaggs said, "would unparadise me."

They all smiled.

"Not to mention . . . well, surely you enforce vegetarianism or Perfectionism or some other angelic regime for which a sinner like me is unsuited."

The Utopian chuckled, shaking his head and waving his hands. "No *ism* of any kind against any man or woman's wishes, I assure you. I have fought *those* bloody battles myself." A few years ago downriver in Evansville, he explained, he had built a blazingly fast new press for his newspaper, but "a rough pack of the local pressmen," worried the new machine threatened their livelihoods, had forced him to dismantle it.

"Well, sir," said Skaggs, preparing to leave, "as a fellow former newspaperman, I wish you great luck here." He held out his hand. "I am Timothy Skaggs. My friends are Mr. Knowles and Mr. Lucking."

"It has been my pleasure, gentlemen. I am Josiah Warren."

The founder was filling in for the regular shopkeeper, who was at home that day assisting in the delivery of his first child.

Before they left, Ben rummaged quickly through one of his bags and pulled out a green pamphlet to leave with Warren as a gift. Warren gave it a quick professional printer's assessment—rubbing the cover stock, examining the binding—before looking at the title. It was Engels and Marx's *Manifest der Kommunistischen Partei*.

"I'm afraid your kindness would be wasted on me, Mr. Knowles," he said, returning the booklet, "for alas, I know hardly any German at all."

Shortly they were steaming down the Ohio aboard the stern-wheeler *Financier*. The plan was to continue on to Evansville, but as they approached Cincinnati around dusk and saw the gaslights twinkling, Ben agreed to stop for the night. And once ensconced—eating pork chops, sleeping in clean, soft beds—they all found it harder to depart with the haste they had made during the previous two weeks. They were urban men, and while Cincinnati was known as Porkopolis, it was a true city, the largest west of Philadelphia.

Finally, after a glass of wine, even Ben was nearly decided to stay for a half day—"to refit and recomfort ourselves," Skaggs said, "to recuperate and reblossom from this"—he almost said *this wild-goose chase*—"from the rigors of our expedition. Frankly, Knowles, I need a break from our interviews with these smiling, doomed, moonstruck cenobites."

Duff checked his watch, took out his pencil stub, and scribbled s-e-n-o-b-i-t-e, 8:28 PM. For some reason he could not explain, he had started to note the precise time as he recorded each new word in his vocabulary journal.

"For all their occasional charms and considerable sincerity," Skaggs continued, "these people sadden me. So many of them seem so gloomy beneath their cheerful, hopeful masks. And we must pause here for a day if only that I might recover from those pitiful harpists." At the New Communia colony, the only music permitted was that played constantly on the farm's lyres. They'd heard "Auld Lang Syne" four times in as many hours.

"And Mr. Warren's arithmetic society," Skaggs said, shaking his head. "Oh my Lord."

"But you are good with numbers, Skaggs," said Duff.

"Yes, and I am adept at pissing as well," Skaggs replied, "but I don't wish to make *that* the foundation of my life, either."

Ben had been impressed by Warren—a sensible reformer, a man of vision but not fanatic. In Warren he imagined he saw an older version of himself, and all afternoon and evening he had daydreamed about some future Utopia of his own . . . reunited with Polly . . . building their own community together . . . perhaps in the beloved valley of her childhood . . .

"Mr. Warren is no humbug, Skaggs," he said.

"No indeed."

"And no zealot."

"I agree," Skaggs said. "He is a fine American specimen. Religious enough that he seeks to improve man's lot, and reasonable enough to appreciate that actual men only wish to be improved so far. Still, I am afraid that . . . in my case . . ."

"They permit strong drink in Utopia," Duff said. "I asked him."

"And of all the places we have visited," Ben added, "they seem to be laying practical foundations to grow and endure . . ."

"Gentlemen! I deny none of what you say! In a hundred years, the Ohio River Valley may well be a great democratic, socialist paradise from Pittsburgh to Cairo, with its capital in Utopia and a fine bronze statue of Josiah Warren calculating profitless sums. But for me, the problem of *joining* such a place would be the necessity of devoting so much of one's thoughts to— to one's own goodness, to the act of *feeling virtuous.* It would drive me crazy. In fact, I'm afraid it would only incite me to commit even greater antisocial outrages."

For a long time, Ben and Duff made no reply.

"I guess what you mean," Duff finally said, "is that it would be like praying all the time."

"Yes! Like perpetually praying and sermonizing and for all I know confessing one's meager sins. Precisely! *Every* day a Sabbath day, but with sweat and toil never ceasing—the worst of all possible worlds."

41

August 4, 1848

. . .

New York City

*D*RUMONT WAS BEGINNING to enjoy America, and not only because his English had progressed from the fluency of an infant to that of a toddler. Compared with England or France, America—New York, at least—was highly advantageous terrain. There were scarcely any police, and no uniformed guardsmen or soldiers at all. A country where passersby in the street looked you straight in the eye and smiled; where any muddy teamster *truly* considered himself the equal of a gentleman; where strangers engaged in intimate conversation—"What is that fish you're eating?" and "Never seen hair so short as you've got, like a beaver's backside!" and "Ah, *French*, it's all the news from over there, eh?" Such a madly fluid and eager place, he realized, was a perfect place for conducting espionage and guerrilla warfare. *Vive la démocratie.*

In Paris, would such a man as Drumont, without any letter of introduction, be permitted simply to wander into the Banque Rothschild and up to the private offices of Monsieur Rothschild? And then be recognized courteously by Baron James himself, and engaged in conversation? *Absolument pas.*

"*Certainement,*" Samuel Prime assured him in his office at Prime, Ward & King, "I recall you and our meeting quite clearly. You are an associate of Mr. Roux's furniture firm, and you are seeking to reunite with your English friend Benjamin Knowles, Sir Archibald's son. And you are Monsieur . . . Gabriel . . . Dumont."

"*Drumont*, yes, thank you very much, monsieur. I do not see Monsieur Knowles, I am sorry. Do you see him?"

"In fact, I have not, but after receiving another rather urgent letter from his family this week, I made inquiries, and according to his landlord in Greenwich Village, Mr. Knowles has departed the city for points west."

"Points West? He is there? I must go to it. Where is this place, Points West?"

"Ha! No, monsieur, 'points west' is no *place*—what I mean to say is that young Knowles has traveled west, to some locale in the western states, although precisely where, his landlord had no idea at all, I am afraid."

Drumont's heart sank.

"But the fellow did inform my man," Prime continued, trying to cheer up his French visitor, "that Mr. Knowles had paid his rent in advance through December, from which one may deduce that he expects to return. Do you—vous comprendre? Your ami il a payé à décembre."

This news did not cheer Drumont. "En décembre? He go from here until *décembre?*"

Prime shrugged and nodded wistfully. "C'est la vie, eh? The landlord said that Knowles has embarked on a lovelorn search for a certain young lady." He thought of his own dear smiling fugitive girl and sighed, feeling the sweet anguish of passion and longing, his obsession with finding Priscilla Christmas, his beautiful child, his lost love. "C'est la vie. C'est *l'amour.*"

Drumont, groping for some further clue, recalled one of the letters he had studied on the table in Knowles's room. "Is his lady, do you understand, if she is . . . Miss Christmas?"

"*What?* What did you say, sir? *Who?*"

"Miss Priscilla Christmas. I know she is a friend of . . . of Benjamin. Do he go to her?" Drumont, seeing he had touched a nerve, wanted to husband his precious bits of intelligence. He thought quickly. Perhaps he could use his information as leverage. "I know where Miss Christmas is."

Prime quickly shut the door to his office. "You *know?*"

"Yes, I know."

Prime grabbed both of Drumont's upper arms. "Oh! My good God, sir, you are a bearer of such good news! Such divine news!" Prime's cheeks reddened and his eyes widened. *"Gabriel!"* He laughed in a way that struck Drumont as slightly mad. "My *angel Gabriel*! You have no idea the lengths I've gone to find her! I am paying a detective in the West twenty-five dollars a week to hunt—and now *you* arrive out of the blue with the very information I require!"

Samuel Prime's run of luck was beginning to seem to him fully providential. First he had managed to find Mrs. Stanhope, and learn that Priscilla had left for Ohio or Indiana or Illinois or Iowa. The next day, while delivering his sympathies to Mrs. Gibbs about the bakery fire that had destroyed her home in Greene Street, she had told him she didn't believe the official story about the fire—she was certain that her house had been the arsonist's *intended* object, because of her work there assisting fugitive slaves. In order to apprehend these enemies of liberty, whoever they were, Mrs. Gibbs had engaged the services of a brilliant policeman in Chicago, a young Scot she knew through his work for the Underground Railroad. And so now, Prime was employing the same man, the finest detective in the Old Northwest, to oversee the search for Priscilla Christmas.

"Monsieur Drumont, *Gabriel*—where is my dear little dodger?"

"I may not say."

"What? Perhaps you do not understand—I wish to have her address."

The Sherman House, Randolph Street, Chicago, Illinois. "I may not say. I may *find* her for you." He would flash one tidbit of information, a piece of bait. "She is in your province of Eel-een-*wah*."

"In Illinois! Yes! You *do* know where Priscilla is living, don't you? You must tell me! Tell me where Priscilla is, and I shall pay whatever you wish."

"No, *no*, Monsieur Prime, not *money*, it is a question of . . . of my . . . *intégrité*, understand? My *respect professionnel*." He pulled his hand from his pocket and opened the palm to show his Baby Dragoon. "Understand, I too am a . . . detective. *Un détective privé*."

Prime complained that time was of the essence, but the Frenchman was unbudging, and Prime desperate. Drumont recited the relevant points of his résumé, only slightly embellished—his years in the Garde Municipale, half of those as senior sergeant of the ninth arrondissement, his work with the famous detective genius Eugène-François Vidocq. At length they managed to make themselves understood and came to terms. Prime would cover his travel expenses to the West, but Drumont would receive a fee only upon his successful return to New York accompanying the young lady. They shook hands enthusiastically, each believing he had gotten by far the best of the bargain.

Cincinnati

"You Englishmen are funny," Skaggs said the moment they walked out of the big soap and candle shop into the morning glare of Main Street. "You are an unemployed, unshaven young—what?—rambler, and he is a prosperous, hardworking, middle-aged man of affairs—and yet here in the heart of America, in his very own place of business, you intimidated him with your *accent*."

"Intimidated? Hardly, sir." But even as he denied it, and although it had not occurred to him, he knew Skaggs was right.

"Well, Ben," Duff said, "he is the boss of the whole place, but as soon as he heard you talk, he did trot out like, like a butler from the back to help . . ."

"I believe that Mr. Procter," Ben replied, "was surprised simply to encounter a countryman and fellow immigrant." And overwhelmed that the son of the great Sir Archibald Knowles had deigned to enter the Procter & Gamble Soap and Candle Company. "And pleased to satisfy my curiosity about his trade."

"You did ask a lot of questions," Duff said.

After six months' holiday from all thought of factories, Ben had, for a few minutes, found himself fascinated by the particulars of American manufacturing—by the thought of Cincinnati's slaughterhouses "doing" (as Procter had put it) one hog every second of every working day, a million hogs per year, and by Procter and his Irish brother-in-law being "the fortunate beneficiaries of an inexhaustible river of pure, creamy tallow," the rendered hog fat from which they made their candles and soap.

" '*Please*, kind sir, why *yes*, of *course*, governor," Skaggs teased, mimicking Procter in a ridiculous English accent.

"We were in the damned shop," Ben said, "for *your* 'real soap and good candles.' "

A young man wearing an enormous grin suddenly blocked their way.

"I'll be blowed if you three guys ain't just *passin' through* our dear Porkopolis for a day, maybe a week afore you move on? Yeah? Am I right? And maybe not afeared to head on out to the real Wild West, could be?"

He pronounced his New York Boweryese ("blowed," "guys") with a southern accent, and what Ben took to be antique Chaucerian words ("afore," "afeared"). And except for his slouch hat, he was fitted up in gaudy Bowery b'hoy fashion: a short coat with giant purple and gray checks, shiny silver waistcoat, greasy sidelocks that hung down beneath the brim of his hat and waggled as he talked. In one hand he held a cigar and a stack of pressed-paper handbills. He thrust the stack toward them, and like a card shark fanned out three of the bills. Printed by the American Society for the Encouragement of the Settling and Civilizing of Our Savage Western Territories, they were entitled AMERICANS *AND* FOREIGNERS: KEEP GOING WEST!

"You know, in all of forty-five," he said, "only a *hunderd* Americans jumped off, and now the Society believes it's that many every *month* like. The Society wants gentlemen such as yourselves to *keep going*, like it says, and let it rip out there. Before all the best opportunities is grabbed."

" 'Let it *rip*'?" Ben asked, prompting a hard glance from the man, who was no older than Duff.

"*Our* western territories?" Skaggs added.

"If you boys is maybe headed to set up shop in Iowa or Minnesota, let's say, then the Society wants to assist you to go on *further* west, past the Missouri, and settle in the lands out there free for the taking."

Duff was nodding as the fellow spoke.

"Free for the filching, do you mean, from the Indians?" Skaggs asked. "Tell me, is your society sanctioned by the Indian Office in Washington?"

"Sanctioned? I don't know for sure, sir, but they—"

"Because it makes *great* sense. As you know, the Department of War also operates the Indian Office, and your society enlists desperate romantics such as us to be . . . volunteer auxiliaries, an *avant-garde* to help conquer the unconquered Indian lands between Iowa and California . . . to create our rude little back settlements that the Army of the West will then be required to defend, by shooting Indians who are angry about all the new white squatters."

"Well . . . *sure*," said the promoter, thinking he had a live one hooked. "If y'all want to have a good fight with some red Indians, *sure*, hoss!"

Duff could no longer contain his curiosity about the fellow. "When did you live in New York?"

The young man was flattered by the question. "Naw, I'm from Owensboro, just across the river to Daviess County, but . . . did you truly think I was? From back east?"

"Well, I—I only wondered . . ."

"Your colorful manners of speech and dress," Skaggs told the boy, "are indigenous to the natives of a hundred acres of the Sixth Ward of New York City, six hundred fifty miles from where we now stand."

"Well, I got real friendly with some New York boys in camp at Cerro Gordo, down in Mexico."

There is no escaping the past, Duff thought as all the blood in his body seemed to rush toward the ragged oval on his right cheek.

"Duff," Skaggs said, "you fought at Cerro Gordo as well, did you not?"

"Yeah." It had been his first battle after he'd made his awful decision at Vera Cruz, nineteen days after he'd taken off his blue U.S. Army coat for the last time and walked away from the American massacre of his Catholic brothers and sisters.

"Well, *hey*!" said the local boy, extending his hand to shake Duff's. "Private Sponge Carpenter! Kentucky volunteers!"

Duff had managed to avoid an encounter like this for the better part of a year in New York City. *Lord, why here . . .*

"I'm Duff."

Carpenter shook his hand a long time, and chattered away all the while. "I was under Captain Gilmore? Cavalry? He was the one replaced our Captain Clay, y'know, after he and half our boys was taken by the greasers at Encarnación."

"Is that Cassius Marcellus Clay?" Skaggs asked the boy, "the emancipationist?"

"The famous nigger-lover Cash Clay, yes, sir, the very one. A *great* man, honest to God."

Captain Clay . . . Then Duff remembered. The recollection dredged up with it an awful sense memory that made him feel like vomiting—the airlessness of the Mexican high summer, the stifling cage in which he awaited death . . . Was this another coincidence? Or were these encounters messages from God, arranged to remind Duff Lucking of his divine omniscience? Or maybe there was no difference between coincidence and fate, as Father Varela used to say, and "coincidence and Providence share more than their last six letters."

"And you, Duff," Carpenter asked, "who was you with down there?"

"I was a regular, Engineers," he mumbled. "Company A."

"Yeah? Under Lieutenant Smith?"

"No." He paused for too many seconds. "No, McClellan," he said finally.

"*Whoa!* You are one lucky dawg, with the raking you boys took on that road at Cerro Gordo."

Duff nodded. In fact, he had been fighting from *south* of the National Highway, doing the raking, pulling the lanyard on an eight-pounder in one of the batteries firing *against* Lieutenant McClellan and his men.

"But we *took* Fat Hill in the end, didn't we, hoss? And not even six dozens of us made a die of it in the whole two days, huh?"

Duff nodded again. But a thousand Mexicans had died at Cerro Gordo— and Duff had been among the defeated, forced to run and run all alone to a hiding place in a little arroyo.

Carpenter mentioned the names of New Yorkers he had known down there, none of which, thankfully, Duff recognized. But Carpenter admitted he also knew how fashionable b'hoys dressed and acted in the city because he had seen *A Glance at New York* three times here in Cincinnati. It had played to a sold-out house at the National Theatre, he said, before the troupe steamed on to St. Louis and then up to Chicago.

"Thus helping to settle and civilize our savage middle-western territories," said Skaggs. "You realize, sir, that in my lifetime, *southwestern Ohio* was savage western territory." This was only a slight exaggeration.

The boy winked. "C'mon, you ain't *near* sixty." He pointed up to a banner directly overhead. "This city is ancient by now."

Walking up Main Street this morning, the three visitors had noticed the long red and white flags strung from the tops of the gas-lamp posts along Main Street. QUEEN CITY OF THE WEST, the banners declared, and ATHENS OF THE WEST and IN CELEBRATION OF OUR FIRST SIXTY YEARS! The city was advertising itself to its own citizens, cheering itself on.

"Ancient at sixty," Skaggs said. "Perhaps you, Mr. Knowles, should undertake to organize an anniversary celebration for London. 'The Queen City of Europe . . . the Athens of the British Empire . . . in celebration of our first two thousand years . . .'"

The Cincinnatian now turned to Ben suspiciously. "An English, are you, buddy? Well, I guess that figures, why you just stare and don't say nothing. We know what you English think of us hereabouts. From your *books.*" During the rest of Ben's hours in Cincinnati, he would encounter two more huffy Cincinnatians, still aggrieved, years later, by Charles Dickens's and Fanny Trollope's infamously snobby depictions of their city.

"Sir, I am already very fond of Cincinnati—of America," Ben said, "and I sincerely apologize if you have been offended—"

But the b'hoy plugged his cigar in his mouth, nodded goodbye only to his fellow veteran, and stalked off.

DUFF'S BODY WAS moving along Main Street in Cincinnati in the summer of 1848, but his mind and spirit had gone elsewhere. He had stumbled into a memory well, fallen back a year to the previous summer. And there he was trapped, jerked backward and forward and backward and forward, time's orderly sequence gone.

In early September, crammed with nine other captured Americans into a prison cell in Mexico City—the very cell, one of the Yankee guards remarked, in which the Mexicans had earlier held "an American *hero,* Captain Clay of Kentucky."

Then back to August, and the convent outside Churubusco, where the two hundred surviving San Patricios—by then the Legion of Foreigners, la Legión de Extranjeros—had gone to make their last stand, aiming cannon at the short white monkey jackets of the American officers (at Lieutenant McClellan himself), firing grapeshot from eighty yards, seventy yards, sixty yards . . . as the Yankees advanced through the mud, close enough to see white faces before they turned to red splatters.

Forgive us, Father.

Forward again to September, convicted at the court-martial, condemned to hang, ready to die—*Forgive them, Father*—but then he and a score of his fellows pardoned by General Scott . . . pardoned, ignominy of ignominies, shame heaped upon shame, only because he had been drunk when he'd run off at Vera Cruz, and the U.S. Articles of War named inebriation as a defense against the charge of desertion.

Standing for hours shackled in the sun outside Mexico City, watching thirty others choke and jerk on the gallows (including a boy who had already lost both legs to cannon fire); getting his fifty lashes; and finally, the red *D,* for Deserter, so hot it singed his eyelash as it came close, then pressed against his right cheek, and the smell of burning flesh as he rocked his face *into* the scalding iron, in order to muddle the scar and make the *D* an unreadable oval; and finally his own sobbing surprise at his terrible gratitude—not thanks for his life being spared, but for the redeeming pain of the whip and the hot iron.

Then back to August again, the unending shrieks and sweat and blood of battle, on the parapet of the convent at Churubusco alongside his pal O'Donnell, both of them furiously pulling down the white shirts some of the Mexicans had raised up on sticks, desperate to avoid the dishonor—that is, the unbearable *mortification*—of capture by their fellow Americans. And the worst and final memory, minutes after they'd pulled down the flags of surrender: sitting in the dirt with half of O'Donnell's skull and brain on his lap, suddenly surrounded by four bayonets from the Ninth Infantry of General Pierce's First Brigade.

Forgive me, Father.

SKAGGS AND DUFF took a cab past Little Africa, around the slaughterhouse district, and then through northeastern outskirts to the top of Mount Adams. Skaggs had promised Duff "a panoramic view of the whole valley," but in fact he was fulfilling his ulterior motive for stopping at Cincinnati. In his amazing Society Library lecture last winter, Edgar Poe had mentioned the city's remarkable telescope—a giant new refractor, the second biggest in the Americas and the third biggest on earth. Skaggs wanted to see firsthand how professional stargazing was conducted and inquire whether his wild fancy—to make telescopic photographs of the moon and stars and planets—was possible.

The observatory's director, Ormsby Mitchel, was a man about Skaggs's age but precisely his converse professionally—"a poor astronomer," he said, "attempting in middle age to become an amateur editor." He showed Skaggs a copy of his magazine, *The Sidereal Messenger.* Skaggs pulled out a dollar to buy a subscription on the spot.

Duff, who had not uttered a word since Main Street, was peeking past the vestibule into the darkened depths of the observatory. The telescope, pointed high, looked to him like one of General Scott's artillery pieces in Mexico—its 60-degree angle, Duff imagined, set to blast 64-pound iron balls the size of human heads five miles into the houses and markets of Vera Cruz.

"And *you,* son?" Professor Mitchel had turned to Duff, surprising him. "Are you one of us as well? An astronomer?"

"No, I only—only a mechanic, sir."

"The lad is too humble," Skaggs said. "In addition to fighting fires and saving lives and assisting me in my photographic endeavors, Mr. Lucking pursues *two* occupations, in the gas-illumination field as well as in advertising."

Duff blushed.

"What is more," Skaggs added, having noticed some military bric-a-brac on the wall near Mitchel's desk, "young Mr. Lucking is a brave veteran of the late war."

"Is that right?" Mitchel asked. "New York volunteers?"

Duff shook his head. "Regulars. Engineers. A private."

"Is that so? In Mexico? Under Robert E. Lee, by chance?"

Duff continued to redden. *Christ Almighty, not again.* "In the same regiment as Captain Lee, yes, sir."

"Lieutenant Colonel Lee now, eh?" Mitchel replied, smiling broadly and making a quick two-fingered salute. "In recognition of his adventures at Cerro Gordo and Chapultepec—*your* adventures, I should say."

"Right." Duff had known nothing of Lee's promotions. His scar itched. "Yes."

"Isn't it a small world indeed! Marble Man and I were at West Point together, class of '29. Only the other day I received a letter from him in Washington. In my reply I shall say that I had the honor of meeting one of his good young engineers."

Is there no escape, no refuge at all from the past? Duff could conceive of nothing to say. It was as if he had forgotten English.

Finally, Skaggs broke the silence. "Bashful young fellow, as I warned you, Professor . . ."

Duff was breathing rapidly and staring at his feet, still saying nothing.

"Are you all right?" Skaggs asked. "Do you have any of your medicine?"

Duff nodded, embarrassment now added to his panic. He had a packet of Blue Mass in his pocket.

Mitchel put a hand on his back. "Would you like a seat?"

"No, no thank you, sir," Duff said, "I need some air is all, I need to walk, I'll walk back down to town, Skaggs, I'll meet up with you boys on the dock there by Irwin and Foster's at six, *bye.*" And he shot out the door.

"A bit of a nervous condition since the war," explained Skaggs as Mitchel led him into the rotunda.

The telescope was as big as a sewer pipe or a pier piling, but it also looked fine and meticulous, like a bibelot in Tiffany, all shiny brass and chocolate mahogany. It made Skaggs smile. The telescope's very configuration— affixed firmly to the earth atop a mammoth granite plinth ten feet tall, but pointing at a gallant angle upward, always upward—struck him as . . . *noble.* When he stepped close and saw the engraving on the brass plate encircling the eyepiece—*Merz und Mahler, München*—he smiled again, thinking of his camera, and the Merz lens he had bought for it last year in Munich.

Mitchel checked his watch. "The moon is up. Do you wish to have a look?"

"Oh yes, sir. Very much indeed."

Together they heaved the rope that slid open the dome above them on a set of enormous iron ball bearings. As they pulled, light from the sky burst into the darkened space and then swelled to fill the great room. It was like an artificial, ultrafast sunrise, from gloom to daybreak to the glare of forenoon in ten seconds.

Mitchel turned cranks and dials to adjust the angle and aim of the telescope, looking up through the little finder scope as he worked. He installed an eyepiece and turned a knob to focus it just so. Skaggs removed his glasses, stepped up, and bent over.

He gasped. He had seen the moon through the little nickel-a-peek instruments at night on the streets of Manhattan. But the waxing gibbous moon he saw now looked incomparably close and sharp. This daytime moon was not just startlingly beautiful, its craters tinted sky blue, but appeared both more profoundly *real* than ever before, yet also more like some impeccable trompe l'oeil painting of the moon. Never under the influence of opium had Skaggs seen anything so wondrous. He was greedy for more. Two minutes passed before he took his eye from the instrument.

"Silent, upon a peak in . . . Cincinnati," Mitchel finally said, adapting the end of Keats's famous sonnet.

Skaggs had been required to memorize "On First Looking into Chapman's Homer" in school, and now recited the relevant line: " 'Then felt I like some watcher of the skies/When a new planet swims into his ken.' " He looked up through the open slice of dome at the sky and the moon. "Until this moment, I have always considered Keats ridiculous, and 'Chapman's Homer' a perfect *lampoon* of a romantic poem."

"I assure you that when even a tiny new piece of a planet does, in fact, swim into one's ken," Mitchel replied, "one *reels*. Now, sir, have you the time for a refreshment?"

They talked through an entire pitcher of iced tea and a plate of bacon and sliced tomatoes. Mitchel talked about the night he had discovered a mountain range near the Martian south pole. Skaggs posed question after question. In order to capture a picture of the heavens on a plate, Mitchel told him, he would have to arrange to use a fine, large telescope. (This one had cost—Mitchel's voice caught—nine thousand dollars.) And it would have to be outside New York City: given the city's smoke and lights, the more rural the better. To make the necessarily long exposures, the telescope mount would have to be equipped with a clock drive that continuously moved the scope to track the subject—the moon or particular star or planet—across the sky. But *yes*, Mitchel said, he thought it was possible. "Perhaps destiny has brought you here," the astronomer said, to which his visitor made no reply.

DUFF RAN THE whole way down to the city, where he gulped a beer, devoured a sausage, and stumbled into a large amusement hall. A lecture by a New Englander named Dr. Colton was under way. He had finished demonstrating a telegraph and several spinning, flashing, tinkling electromagnetic marvels, and was now describing the "new medical wonder" of nitrous oxide. At a table at the side of the stage, his assistants were preparing canisters of gas fitted with rubber tubes, and Duff was among forty or fifty men, women, and children who stood in line to inhale what the doctor called "chemistry's invisible, invigorating, and harmless ambrosia."

It tasted sweet—*Tastes like heaven itself,* Duff thought—and quickly made him feel very much happier. Indeed, he remained at the nitrous oxide table after all but two of the other members of the audience had returned to their seats to watch the next demonstration. Duff paid another ten cents for a few more minutes of bliss, and then another, and now his last dime just as Colton unveiled an enormous painting onstage, as high and more than half as wide as the proscenium. It was a picture of a luxurious cavern filled with ancient people painted large as life. Duff wanted to stroke the garments and kick the rocks and kiss the neck of the kneeling, bare-breasted woman . . . until the effects of the gas started to wear off, and he noticed that most of the people in the painting were distraught or frenzied, and he finally made sense of what Colton was saying . . . that "presiding over this painted court"— the shadowy hooded figure "at the center of the uneasy assembly"—was *Death*.

Then Duff got the idea that Colton was speaking about *this* very assembly, the people in this amusement hall. Duff thought he had been lured into this Court of Death, where he would be sentenced and punished. He started to pray. *Christ with me, Christ before me* . . . Perspiration dampened his whole face and neck. *Christ behind me, Christ in me, Christ beneath me,*

Christ above me . . . His scar stung. *Christ on my right, Christ on my left, Christ where I lie, Christ where I sit* . . . He had the strong urge to stand and turn and peer into the audience to see if a shadowy hooded figure was sitting there among the people. But he could not bring himself to look, and stared at his lap and continued to pray—*Christ where I arise, Christ in the heart of everyone who thinks of me, Christ in the mouth of everyone who speaks to me*—until out of the corner of his eye he saw the hand of the man on his left rise up quickly to strike him in the face, and he grabbed the man's right wrist, thrust the arm back against the villain's chest, and held it there fast . . . until he realized the sound filling his ears was not some apocalyptic storm but the crowd around him clapping. The show was over. The poor man next to him had simply wanted to applaud.

"Forgive me, sir," Duff said as the frightened fellow scrambled out of his seat and away. "I—I *misunderstood.*"

It was after five. He needed to stop at the hotel for his bags and make it to the dock by six, but the crowd ahead of him was shuffling slowly through the galleries toward the single exit. With shaky fingers he tore open the little envelope of Blue Mass and swallowed all six pills and prayed that he might soon be free, and saved. *Christ in every eye that sees me, Christ in every ear that hears me, Salvation is of the Lord, Salvation is of the Christ* . . .

BEN WAS TAKING in the sights of Little Africa, the colored neighborhood, still savoring the excellent luncheon he'd had in a charming, shady restaurant garden. Never before had he gnawed meat directly off the ribs of any animal, never had he tasted catsup or any other sauce so spicy *and* sweet. As he passed a Negro daguerreian's gallery and the fine showroom of a Negro cabinetmaker and looked at the Negro men and women and children of various classes passing by him—and stared back at the children who stared— he wondered whether it was every hour or every day or every week that they thought themselves lucky to be *here*, where they could work and shop and sleep as they wished, and not *there*, across the river, barely a mile south, where their cousins were being bought and sold for some hundreds of dollars apiece.

As he finally walked back across Cincinnati's Broadway—into Little Bavaria, as Skaggs had called the downtown, for all the German talk and German signs—he noticed a couple, a young man and woman arm in arm, five paces ahead of him. She was taller than her escort. Ben watched the man chuckle at something she said; watched her gesturing broadly with her left hand as she spoke; watched the coil of blond hair touch her neck as she walked; and then saw she was wearing *that dress,* the yellow silk she'd worn when he'd first seen her, in the dining room at the Astor House.

"*Polly!* Polly *Lucking!*"

Rushing forward, stopping only a foot away from her, he saw that the young blonde in a yellow dress was . . . wearing eyeglasses and speaking German.

"Oh, I beg your pardon, very sorry. Um . . . entschuldigen Sie bitte."

At six, as the starting bell rang and the side-wheeler *Liberty* blew its whistle, playing one of the notes in the calliope song of boats announcing their arrivals and departures, the reconvened travelers stood on deck, looking back on the city that had agitated each of them in his own way.

Ben felt drained by his foolish encounter with the German couple. Even when he was not consciously thinking of Polly, she lurked in his thoughts, exquisite and unavailable and taunting. Now he tapped his foot in time to the song being played on a pair of fiddles and a flute down on the public landing. There was no singing, yet in his head he sang the familiar lyrics—*I had a dream the other night, when everything was still, / I thought I saw Susanna dear, a-coming down the hill*—and in his mind's eye he saw Polly Lucking walking down a hill. What hill, where? The musicians finished—*I come from Alabama, with my banjo on my knee*—and paused for only three beats before launching into their next, a quickstep march.

Through the wide-open office windows of the steamboat agents Irwin & Foster, the young clerk tallying the day's sums could make out only intermittent bars of the music from the levee. But in his head he filled in every missing note, for he had written both songs himself.

Duff knew the music of the march but not the title. If he had—"Santa Anna's Retreat from Buena Vista"—he might have lost his grip on sanity then and there. He was watching a scruffy preacher pace in front of his riverfront mission, next door to Irwin & Foster, hectoring and inviting passersby—particularly *Duff,* in Duff's fevered imagination—to come inside and find Jesus. From the boat he could hear only some of the words (". . . *cowardly,* the faithless . . . for *murderers* . . . and all *liars* . . . lake that *burns* with *fire* . . . the *second* death . . ."), but those were enough.

As Skaggs surveyed the northern sky, he hummed along happily with "Santa Anna's Retreat from Buena Vista." He had heard it played by the Broadway marching bands the night of the New York war celebrations (and cattle stampede), and at the time had despised it on principle—even more so after learning that it was composed by the suddenly ubiquitous Stephen Foster, age *twenty-one*. But just now, here on the Ohio River at twilight, as sober as his own father, Skaggs liked the music despite himself. He decided to think of it simply as *Buena Vista*—"good view." And just then in the darkening blue expanse over the city, one star caught his eye and he remembered its name.

"Say, Duff? One night last winter you told me that *vega*"—*vee*-ga, he pronounced it—"meant . . . what was it, in Spanish?"

" 'Fertile valley,' " Duff replied in a monotone. "*Vay*-ga."

"Right, yes, fertile valley," and Skaggs just stared into the sky, smiling, and said nothing more.

"What?" Ben finally asked.

Skaggs pointed up at the star—"Vega"—and then spread his arms wide to indicate the Ohio and its green banks. "Vega presiding over our great American *vee*-ga, or *vay*-ga. A splendid *buena vista*, don't you two grumps agree?"

42

August 5, 1848

. . .

San Francisco

OR THE MOMENT, but just for the moment, no one in the States—*no one*—had any idea of what had happened in California these last months. No one knew of the discovery in the millrace on the Coloma River, and no one knew of the resulting money fever that had infected the whole region. The news of gold—gold for the plucking, trails practically paved with gold—was still moving east over the plains and across Panama and around Cape Horn only as fast as a horse or the wind. Some of the tales were exaggerated—alas, no special blue grease applied to the soles of one's boots for a day resulted in several dollars' worth of accumulated dust and flakes. But the essential, unbelievable news was true: the hills and creeks and rivers a hundred miles east of San Francisco Bay were riddled with gold, countless thousands of tons of gold, any single tiny ounce of which was equal to a very good week's wage. The giddiest, most fantastical part of America's dream—that practically unspeakable yearning for *instant* fortune, *easy* prosperity, and not merely liberty but no regulation at all—had finally, suddenly come true here at the far end of America. What's more, the weather was mild and the natives docile.

On the bright afternoon of the first Saturday in August, a gang of sailors off the clipper *Curious* from Chile and the Sandwich Islands, their legs still shaky from the sea, set foot on a dock at the place from which they had first sailed. The day they'd left, a mere four months before, the *Curious* had been the only three-masted vessel in the harbor. Now a grinning boy fishing from the pier told them why eight big ships lay at anchor in the bay, apparently abandoned, and why everyone—"honest to golly, *everyone*"—had left town since May and gone into the countryside with shovels and baskets and pans. The seamen thought the boy was playing a prank, but ten paces later an old Mexican woman swore that everything he'd said was true.

When their ship had cleared San Francisco Bay at the end of March, the town was a bustling port town with several hundred inhabitants. Now it was all but deserted. They had never seen such a thing. It was breathtaking, simultaneously frightening and funny. *Lord . . . shit . . . hell . . .* the sailors mumbled as they walked the dirt streets looking in windows and knocking on the doors of empty stores and unoccupied offices. *Skedaddled . . . Christ . . . ain't never . . .* The blacksmith's and groceries and stables were closed. The saloons were closed, as were the City Hotel and the Portsmouth Hotel and Ellis's boardinghouse, where they had stayed. *It's like the Indians came and kidnapped all the men . . . It's like a plague struck, wiped 'em out . . .*

In Kearny Street, they found the second mate of the *Curious* staring at a hastily painted "To Let" advertisement. The notice was for two houses— one over in Market Street, a mere $25 for the year, and the other a "farmhouse in the gold region near Sutter's," for *$375 per month.* The ship's mate, a Cornishman named Hardison, earned $375 in an entire year.

The evacuation was even more widespread than they could imagine. The whole of Upper California had become a vacuum, nearly all human energy suddenly and irresistibly concentrated into a few miles of the American River Valley, as if God or Satan had flipped an electromagnetic switch. From down in Monterey up to Bodega Bay and over to Sonoma, abattoirs and mills and farmhouses sat empty and silent, and livestock wandered loose through untended fields. Half the solders in northern California had walked away from their garrisons without leave and gone to the mines. During the last three palmy months, hundreds of sober and steady yeomen had abandoned their plows and hammers and routines and walked in a single direction, as if hypnotized.

In Washington Street in San Francisco, no sooner had several more awestruck similes been hazarded by the men of the *Curious* (*Like if Jesus Christ his damn self showed up and walked on the American River . . . Like everybody went and got killed in the war*) than they encountered a sailor some of them recognized—rather, a *former* sailor, not five days back from

China and already provisioned for his own mining trip up to the Sierras. He told them the *newest* news, which had arrived in just the past few days by U.S. mail from the south. The war with the Mexicans was officially finished, a treaty signed. All of them there were now standing in good *American* dirt.

"Wait—by *mail?*" said the boatswain of the *Curious,* as if by challenging this puny and mundane surprise he might rein in the gargantuan one. "What mail is that, fella?"

"Mm-hmm," said the man, "since spring, army's had a pair of riders running pouches between here and San Diego, back and forth every two weeks." He snickered. "But that one last week, that's the last of 'em, they say. 'Suspended.' " He nodded, but the new arrivals appeared not to understand. "The *gold,*" he said, as if that word should explain everything.

And in California in the topsy-turvy summer of '48, it did.

on the Ohio River

WHEN BEN AWOKE, he could just see his watch face by the dawn's early light—five past five. When he walked out to the bow, he was surprised to find Duff sitting on the deck, his knees pulled up to his chest, staring straight ahead. He had torn his KEEP GOING WEST! handbill into tiny bits and collected them into a neat pile between his feet.

"Another early riser," Ben said.

"I couldn't sleep," Duff said just loudly enough to be heard over the engines. "I didn't sleep." With a quick motion he scooped up the bits of paper and shoved them overboard. The breeze scattered them as they fluttered toward the water. "Some hours ago, we passed a steamer with its boiler blowed, some killed, it was still bellowing smoke, and an undertaker had already got there with his wagon, three in the morning selling coffins for five dollars. Just past Louisville, I saw a big mess of dead fish. Too many to count, maybe a hundred, maybe more. Big ones. Carp, I think.

" 'Cast the net over the right side of the boat and you will find something.' So they cast it, and were not able to pull it in because of the number of fish . . . So Simon Peter went over and dragged the net ashore full of one hundred fifty-three large fish.

"Some little critter, a muskrat or a mink, maybe, was holding on to a great big fish with both front paws, like it was his life raft. I hope he didn't get scooped up in the paddle wheel, but I couldn't see for sure what became of him. My cousin Flan nearly choked to death on a carp bone the same summer he drowned . . ."

Ben sat down next to him and listened as Duff went on like this, intermingling his chronicle of the night with Bible stories and memories of childhood. Once Ben realized he was not expected to make any reply, he observed the river traffic and the beginning of the day on both banks.

They passed a rowboat filled with five pale, nearly blue-skinned boys and girls dressed in tatters, the two oldest holding fishing poles over each side. Such a blue country, Ben thought: the faces of these poor children, Duff's pills, the tint of book pages and swill milk, the exceptionally bright blue skies. Presently they overtook a hundred-foot-long flatboat loaded with eight-foot-wide rolls of (bluish) paper . . . and then passed two others coming toward them, one heaped with hams and bales of buffalo robes and tobacco leaves, the other crowded with caged chickens. One of the boatmen from the chicken boat was floating in the river on its port side just upriver from the birds themselves, naked, gripping an iron bracket with one hand, soaping his furry face and shoulders with the other as he was dragged along. His long, thin, sudsy wake in the center of the river was making the notional border between Indiana and Kentucky fleetingly real.

"The flatboats look like arks, don't they?" Duff said.

"I have never seen an ark, but I suppose they do."

Their steamboat was closing in fast on another side-wheeler just as the river twisted sharply to the left and narrowed, forcing their captain to slow down until they were barely moving at all. For ten minutes Ben watched a pair of swineherds busily working on the shore. Using four of the countless stumps as posts and a hundred yards of rope as fencing, they had made a temporary pen for the little herd of hogs they had been driving to town. Another man arrived with a wagon, on which he had a press. One of the hogs had died, and they had butchered it there in the dirt by the river where it fell. The fifty pounds of fatty remains, still raw, had been shoveled into the machine. The two bigger men were pulling hard on the lever at the top of the press, turning dead hog into instant lard. If you stuck a wick in the center of that enormous cube, Ben wondered, how long would such a whopping American candle burn?

"And *this* little pig did not *quite* make it to market, did he?" It was Skaggs. "Good day, gents! A salutary peep for *you*, Mr. Knowles, eh, at our beautiful and sublime land?"

One of the swineherds was tossing bloody bones into the river.

"Hallo, Skaggs," Duff volunteered. He sighed. "Hallo."

"On this fine western morning, you're not still blue, are you, Mr. Lucking?"

"*This* isn't the West," Duff said, springing to his feet. "The West is the Rocky Mountains, and Oregon. In the West, there's next to no people." As he stood, the right pocket of his coat swung pendulously and clanked against the railing. It was his Colt's revolver.

Before long they were docking at Evansville. A steamboat in the next berth was loaded so heavily that the water was only inches from the lower deck. The top deck was filled with twenty identical new wagons, built narrow and long like the flatboats, but with both stern and bow canted inward. They were painted blue, with rear wheels much larger than the front. Over the bed of each one were a dozen tall bentwood hoops forming a kind of swooping archway. Ben would need to write Tryphena Knowles and tell her that one of the moments from her dream that final morning in Kent had come true: croquet wickets as big as garden sheds floating down a great American waterway.

"Conestoga wagons," Duff said. "*Those* are going to the *West*."

43

August 11, 1848
. . .
Chicago

THE CHICAGO POLICEMAN's thick Glaswegian accent was making it rough for his visitor to understand him, and the young deputy sheriff was in turn struggling to make sense of the Frenchman's English. In the new America, filling with foreigners, it was a typical encounter: two adults both slightly shouting at each other, smiling intently, eyebrows arched, as if conversing with a child or an idiot. Each time Gabriel Drumont and Allan Pinkerton managed to achieve a moment of mutual clarity, they were pleased. So far, it was understood by both that Mr. Samuel Prime had wired Pinkerton concerning his new arrangement with "a former Parisian gendarme and apprentice of the famous E. F. Vidocq" and that in addition to Miss Priscilla Christmas, Drumont was searching for his friend, a Mr. Knowles, who might be accompanying her.

"I have read Vidocq's *Memoirs,*" Pinkerton said, "and admire it very much."

"Yes. Also me."

"He is . . . a hero."

"Un *héros,* yes, also for me."

"You are employed by his Office of Information?"

"What?"

"Vidocq's detective agency? You? His bureau of *rand-send-ya-ma?*"

"Ah, le Bureau des Renseignements. *Moi?*" It was one thing to lie when necessary to ordinary people, people who mostly wished to be told lies and anyway had no knack for distinguishing truth from falsehood, but he worried that this intelligent American *flic* might have a sixth sense for detecting fibs. So Drumont would tell a careful version of the truth. "I now do not work with Monsieur Vidocq. He do not now . . . *s'est retiré*, he do not work with his bureau now. I do not see him in more from one year, not after his wife die. I am a *détective privé*, for myself all the time, like him, private detective."

"Ah well, I envy you that, Mr. Drumont. Now, Prime said that your friend Knowles is a fellow rather like me."

"A policeman? *No* . . ."

"No, no, I mean an immigrant from Great Britain—"

"Ah, un *immigré* . . ."

"—a fellow my age, and given that you two met in the streets of Paris, during the revolution . . ."

"Yes. We meet at the revolution."

"Therefore I deduce that Mr. Knowles is a bit of a red republican, a democrat, a radical—"

"Yes!"

"—probably a good Chartist, as I myself was before I left the sceptred isle."

Drumont's weeks searching the taverns and coffeehouses and lecture rooms of radical London had educated him in the vocabulary of British radicalism. "*You?* Chartist? Now? In America?"

"Mm, no, not exactly, but there is important work to be done even in America—three millions of us are *slaves*, you know."

"*Les Nègres*, the Negroes in . . . *le Sud*—'Go to *Alabama* with a banjo on my knee.' "

"Yes, from the South, and thousands escaping *here*, to our free states. Most of my work outside the official purview falls into that category—pro bono, for the Underground Railroad, as we call it. By the way, *hurrah* for the reform spirit in *your* country, sir—I was gladdened to hear the new regime in Paris has liberated every slave in all of your colonies."

"Yes." In fact, Drumont had been disappointed by the news. He had daydreamed about living a slave master's life in the Caribbean.

"Perhaps it might require a small second rebellion here in the States to free our slaves, eh? Well, sir, I welcome your assistance in this investigation on behalf of Mr. Prime. My time for private cases is limited—we have all of twelve men in the sheriff's department—only *twelve*, if you can imagine, to police this half-wild city of thirty thousand."

"Only twelve police." Drumont did not understand most of the words, but he happily took the meaning—the farther west, the fewer police, the easier his task would be.

"I propose," Pinkerton continued, "that we agree to split Prime's fee. To divide the money in half, same for you, same for me? You fifty, me fifty? Do we have a deal?"

Drumont was tempted to say: *Non, gardez l'argent, monsieur,* keep the cash for yourself, I want only Knowles. But that would make the man suspicious. And besides, after Drumont had apprehended his enemy he could use his half of the detective fee to pay his way to Guadeloupe or St. Martin or Martinique, some warm and fragrant island teeming with barely unshackled French-speaking slaves.

Pinkerton held out his right hand. "Are we in accord, sir?"

Drumont shook. "*Oui, en accord,* yes. Good. Tell me, please, is Priscilla, Miss Christmas, living now at the Sherman House, Randolph Street?"

Pinkerton lifted his eyebrows and smiled, surprised and impressed. "Why, you *are* a detective, sir, aren't you? Priscilla Christmas and her friend Miss Lucking are long gone from the hotel and the city. Precisely where they have gone is the question . . . although at no time in Chicago, at least, did they rendezvous with your Mr. Knowles. But come, Mr. Drumont," he said, placing a hand on his new collaborator's arm, "let me share the file with you, so that you may know what I know . . . and advance you some cash for your expenses."

Indiana

THE ROAD OUT of Evansville was rutted, but the coach would reach New Harmony by midday. If they failed to discover Polly and Priscilla there, they would catch a Wabash River steamboat, the *Telegraph*, leaving New Harmony that afternoon for Terre Haute. As they bumped along, Skaggs struggled to read the day's *Evansville Courier & Press*. Before they went five miles he came across an article that would have riveted his attention even if they had not been looking for Polly Lucking.

It was an editorial attack on "a certain notorious settlement" in the central part of the state. The community was said to be inhabited by "a most nauseous sect of socialists and, worse, *united fornicators,* who live according to a theory of promiscuous intercourse of the sexes so loathsome in its details, so horrifying to all the sensibilities of even the grossest of respectable people, that we shall not sully the columns of this paper with their narration." Among the communist fornicators, "who clothe themselves exclusively in satanic *red,*" the *Courier & Press* noted with relish, were "girls of only thirteen or fourteen, and an *actress,* formerly of New York City. This 'dramatic artist,' who calls herself 'Miss Lucky,' was the first of the sect to speak frankly and openly concerning the true and disgusting nature of their heathen way of life, which until now local residents had only suspected." The editors were pleased, they wrote, that the county's prosecutor was convening a grand jury with an eye toward "ridding his otherwise decent, Christian province of these blasphemous freethinkers and brazen adulterers." The colony, "called by Lovely and many furtive aliases in the past, has been known lately as Glee."

Skaggs closed his newspaper. Lovely was number eleven on their list, just after New Harmony. He was pleased at the prospect of being spared hundreds of miles more of jangling coach travel to Illinois and Wisconsin and all the way through Iowa. But he also felt some melancholy at the prospect of their adventure ending, and returning to life as it was in New York. Should he share the news, or keep quiet and let them discover it tomorrow for themselves?

He folded the paper in half, then quarters, and looked out the window of the coach. Ahead of them he saw a swamp rabbit race across the road toward a mangrove-choked pond, and seconds later a wild dog running after it. The dog stopped short at the water and started barking angrily, sending two geese into flight. Forgetting his rabbit, the dog turned and ran in the direction of the honking, ascending birds. A wild-goose chase. Skaggs sighed loudly.

"What is it," Ben asked, "that agitates you?"

Skaggs turned to face him. "I believe, sir, that we are close. Our great quest in the West is nearly finished," he said, handing the newspaper to Ben.

INDEED, THEY WERE very close, and before day's end would be absurdly closer.

A few hours after dark on the edge of Terre Haute, a stagecoach heading west along the National Road was stopped at the bridge over the Wabash River, waiting as the drawspan was winched open to let a steamer pass through.

The boat had just discharged passengers, including three from New York—two Americans and an Englishman—and now chugged north.

The coach, carrying Polly and Priscilla and the young Billy Whipple and five other travelers, would be at the drawbridge awhile.

Billy stepped outside to wait on the bank. Priscilla stayed in the coach. Sitting at the window next to her, Polly swatted idly at gnats and watched the ripples of moonlight on the black river. She felt content, as unburdened and hopeful as she had been when they'd steamed out of New York. She was happy to be wearing her own good clothing and not any shade of red or pink or peach. She felt liberated. This morning James had called her "damnably, tragically fickle and conceited," but hadn't he also said, again and again over the last month, that Glee was "a noble experiment on the human soul"? And during their second (and final) night in bed together, come to think of it, when she'd declined to be gagged with an apple and buggered, he had rather grandly said to her, " 'Experiment,' my dear, is a verb as well as a noun." So it was. And noun or verb, it meant a search for some unknown truth by trial and error. Starting today, Polly was going to continue to experiment—to conduct her own experiment.

Glee had been a trial and an error. At their first Session of Mutual Criticism as consociates, Priscilla was chided for "showing both coquetry and selfishness" in her attentions toward Billy. At their second Session of Mutual Criticism, a few days after Polly happened to mention that she had acted on the stage in New York, she was warned by Charity and Hackadiah that plays amounted to "the glorification of insincerity" and that actors were "paid professional liars." And it had been resolved by a majority vote that Polly and Priscilla would no longer be permitted to indulge in their "solitary and unproductive pursuits" of drawing pictures, particularly since "our real trees and grasses and water and sky are superior to any representations of them."

James, however, had suggested that Polly's "artistic impulses" be "harnessed productively for the good of the community." Since she was both "trained in techniques of public performance" and had been "at large in the world" more recently than the rest of them, he suggested that she be appointed "an ambassadress of Glee." Her mission was to travel among the neighbors to gather signatures on a petition affirming to the county authorities that Glee's members were "persons of good moral and spiritual character and lovers of good order who mind their own business."

Within the week, the most shocking details of Polly's far too candid descriptions of life on the notorious farm had reached the county courthouse in Greencastle. Angry sermons were delivered. Writs were delivered. Glee panicked. Some of the consociates accused Polly of being a "spy" and a "provoker." The members of Glee had voted that the two women should recompense them by contributing all of their savings to the general treasury, the money to be earmarked for hiring a lawyer to defend the community and for buying one of John Deere's new self-scouring steel plows to replace their miserable old iron job. Before James had voted aye, he'd pointed at Polly and quoted Scripture: " 'They that plow iniquity and sow trouble reap the same.' "

The next morning, in the grass not far from the breakfast tables, Priscilla had discovered the blackened remains of Jonathan, her stuffed toy dog.

And the day after that they had left Glee for good, with all their own money in hand.

The steamboat's stern passed beneath the big oil lamp bolted to the bridge's trestle. It was the *Telegraph,* and the name set Priscilla thinking. "Polly? Will you send another wire to Duff? Billy says the wire has reached St. Louis now. To let them know—let him know where we are?"

Polly had not received a reply from Duff. "I shall post a letter to New York. I needn't give another dollar fifty to the telegraph company."

For herself, Priscilla had this morning written to her father in New York informing him of her wedding plans. Peregrine Christmas had beaten her and stolen her earnings, but she was, after all, his only living child. He deserved to know that she was to be married.

Nor was this Priscilla's first letter posted east—last month, at the Sherman House in Chicago, Priscilla had written to Mr. Knowles encouraging him to tell Polly of his loyalty and love, if he still loved her. The note to Ben remained her secret.

"Polly?" she asked.

"Yes, dear?"

"Have you received any letter at all from . . . from Mr. Knowles, either?"

Polly shook her head. "No," she said softly.

When she had wired Duff, she knew that he would give Ben her address in Indiana, and she had hoped he might write. She had thought he would at least send her some clarifying gentlemanly epilogue to their affair. Several mornings at Glee, after awaking from dreams of him, she had dared even to imagine that he might write an apology. But did she deserve any apology? Perhaps, she worried, her animal desires did indeed amount to hysteria, a disorder of the mind. In any event, she realized now that her hope for a gallant farewell message was simply another of her romantic notions. Tears formed in her eyes.

"I am quite sure," she added, affecting a blithe tone, "that I am far from Mr. Knowles's thoughts."

"Perhaps," Priscilla ventured, "he is . . . bereft, and returned to England." She paused. "I had one of my daydreams . . . he was traveling on a steamer."

Before Polly could answer, the *Telegraph*'s whistle moaned one last farewell to Terre Haute. The drawspan was closing, and Billy climbed back inside the coach. He was still dressed in a uniform from Glee, but after dark, at least, his maroon coat could pass for black or brown, and his burgundy trousers for blue.

Polly was glad that Priscilla, at least, had come away from Glee with Billy. They'd communed rapturously, Priscilla had told her, practically every night she slept in the Hive. Polly approved of the boy. He smiled easily and sang well. He was kind to children. He also knew a trade, saddlemaking, and had mustered the conviction and resolve at age seventeen to deny his family's Mormonism and leave them. Priscilla and Billy had pledged to each other that if their affections thrived in the ordinary air outside Glee, and survived the rigors of the journey that lay ahead, they would marry on the twenty-sixth of August, the day after Priscilla's fourteenth birthday. Polly had extracted a further pledge from him disavowing "the law of the priesthood" and "celestial marriage" and any other Mormon euphemism for taking multiple wives.

"Westward ho," she said quietly, with a smile, as they rolled noisily onto the planks of the bridge.

Billy had crossed Illinois twice before. "We should make Teutopolis by morning," he said. "Hitch up a fresh team. And get a *good* breakfast," adding almost salaciously, "with *bacon*."

"But can we also buy you a new suit of clothes there?" Polly asked with a smile, making Billy blush.

She had come to think of her search for a new way of life as akin to drawing pictures—the blank sheet was always every bit as daunting as it was inviting, and she crumpled and threw away many more sketches than she kept. As for finding some congenial piece of the West to inhabit, she was still curious to try.

The fifteenth and westernmost place on Brisbane's list was a settlement on the far side of the Missouri River called Humblebee. It had been established by socialist farmers from New Jersey on frontier land. If they were lucky, Polly, Priscilla, and Billy would reach St. Louis on the thirteenth, the day after next, just in time to catch the steamer *Omega,* and a week later would step into Indian country.

DUFF HAD HIS gun wedged into his belt. It was a clumsy arrangement. The thing weighed almost five pounds, and the tip of the barrel reached halfway to his knee. But he had decided that western Indiana was far enough west that he could wear his revolver without dismaying the inhabitants. He was wrong. All the way from Terre Haute people had eyed the Colt's suspiciously, and when the coach changed horses in the village of Brazil, the fellow who operated the stage barn asked him directly why on earth he wore a pistol in such a fashion.

"He was wounded in the war," Skaggs answered, which shut up the man.

IT WAS DUSK when Ben knocked on the front door of the big house. Duff had his coat pulled back to expose the gun.

A woman in a pink dress opened the door and her glance went immediately to the enormous black barrel hanging on Duff's hip.

"Good evening, madam," Ben said, "I am Benjamin Knowles, and we are seeking—"

The door slammed shut. From inside they could hear frantic cries and squeals and running.

"You see?" Skaggs said to Duff. "You've only frightened her. Pack that blunderbuss *away.*"

Ben knocked again.

"Have you come from Greencastle?" asked a well-bred male voice from behind the door. "Is it the sheriff, and if so, do you have a proper warrant?"

"No, no, sir, we are travelers," Ben shouted. "From New York. We wish you no harm."

When the door opened again a fierce-looking codger had a shotgun pointed at their shins, and behind him stood a tall, younger man with dramatically long, dark hair combed straight back.

Skaggs gasped. Duff's hand tightened around the walnut butt of his pistol.

"Good evening, sirs," Ben said cheerfully. "We are searching for our friend Miss Lucking, whom we—"

"*Slicky Jim Danforth!*" shouted Skaggs. "My God! *You* are the nobodaddy of this place? You old rapscallion! The last time I saw you, you were drenched in rum and munching the tits of a Portuguese whore in Market Square! In . . . my Lord, when now? . . . the summer of '*32*! What *became* of you that night, Slicky Jim? We looked in every grog shop and whorehouse in Portsmouth. We worried you'd gone for a swim in the sea with your senhorita and drowned!"

During their freshman year together at Dartmouth, James Danforth and Timothy Skaggs had run in the same social circle. At the end of the school year, several of the boys spent a dissolute seaport weekend together in Portsmouth, New Hampshire. It was the last time Skaggs had seen him.

Granby, the codger with the gun, was now eyeing James.

"Hallo, Timothy," Danforth finally said. "What a great surprise to see you here. And you, good sir," he said to Ben more warmly, "are after Miss Lucking? I am afraid that you are an instant late."

"God*dammn*it," Ben shouted, stamping his foot on the porch.

Inside the Hive, they were presented with water and plates of cold corn and raw asparagus, and offered beds for the night in two sleeping huts. Presence, Charity, and Hackadiah joined them as they ate. Seeing that every article of clothing worn by every inmate was dyed some shade of red, Duff nudged Skaggs, who furtively nodded. Ben asked if they might light a lamp or a candle, but Danforth explained their prohibition on animal-fat illumination—including, he was sorry to say, the new Cincinnati candles Skaggs had in his bag. Duff asked if beeswax candles, expense aside, would be considered acceptably humane, which provoked an excited discussion among Presence and Charity.

As the visitors listened to the brief debate, each of them silently considered the more or less identical vulgar question: Could these ordinary, thoughtful, Quakerish women *really* be the sluts and slammerkins the newspaper had described? In Skaggs, the idea produced an erection; in Duff, embarrassment and pity. And for Ben, the thought was only a momentary stepping-stone, alas, to the inevitable contemplation of Polly in their orgiastic company.

When Danforth explained that Polly and Priscilla had resigned their places at Glee only twenty-four hours earlier, "by mutual agreement," because "they did not see eye to eye with our principles," Ben was cheered.

The women had left this morning, Danforth added, bound for St. Louis and then, they said, up the Missouri River toward the big Mormon settlements.

"*No,*" Skaggs said, "Mormons? Oh my good God. Our Polly has been persuaded by *that* lunacy?" He had lived in Illinois during the Mormon purges and murders in the early forties.

"She's *with* one," Granby snarled. "On their way to some place called Honeypot, or Birds and Bees . . ."

Ben turned on the old man still holding the shotgun. "What," he asked sharply, "do you mean to say, sir?"

"The girl, Priscilla," Danforth explained, "is apparently"—he paused, as if he had sniffed something foul—"*betrothed* to a young man who was raised a Mormon. Mr. Whipple. Their intended destination is a community not far from the Mormons called Humblebee, on the far side of the Missouri."

"The last one on her list," Ben said. "The very last."

"Polly has gone off," Duff said, his voice full of awe, "to settle outside the States. On the *frontier.*"

Skaggs turned to Ben. "It must be another, oh, five hundred miles, at least," he said.

"More than six hundred," said Duff excitedly.

"In the morning, when we may see," Skaggs said as the darkness deepened, "we can consult Colonel Frémont's atlas of the Indian country, and find our destination." His ridiculous purchase of the maps in Buffalo was suddenly vindicated.

"And we shall set out at dawn," Ben announced.

Danforth chose his next words carefully, and the consociates watched him closely as he did. "May I ask, Mr. Knowles, your precise . . . relation to Miss Lucking? Are you her . . . inamorato?"

Ben took a breath before he replied. "I devoutly hope that I may deserve to be once more."

"Ah yes," Danforth said, smiling and raking his hair back from his forehead with one hand, "our strong-minded Miss Lucking is no easy target for Cupid's arrows . . ." And then, realizing his tone was a jot too knowing, quickly amended, ". . . if I may presume, sir."

THE NEXT DAY in Terre Haute they learned that Missouri River steamboats running as far north as Hemme's Landing, Missouri—this side of the river from where Humblebee must sit, according to Skaggs's map—were still infrequent. Most of the packets went only as far as Westport, the big jumping-off spot for emigrants to Oregon. The *Omega,* the steamboat agent told them, bound for Fort Leavenworth, St. Joseph, and beyond, would leave St. Louis the following evening—and the next steamer going so far north wasn't scheduled for another two weeks. "*Damn* it to goddamn *hell,*" Ben said, to which the startled agent replied, "Guess you ain't Mormons after all, huh?"

And so, Skaggs's protests notwithstanding—"I would prefer instant death from an exploding boiler to enduring the slow, bone-shaking torture of another two weeks in a coach rattling down some prairie ditch"—Ben plotted an entirely overland route, due west by stagecoach through Illinois to Springfield and the Mississippi River, then straight across the state of Missouri and finally—two weeks hence, give or take a day or two—a ferry across the Missouri River.

"You know, Knowles," Skaggs told Ben as they walked into a nearby sa-loon for a lunch of hard-boiled eggs and cheese, "I retract what I said in Cincinnati. I believe you have been thoroughly denationalized."

"Meaning?"

"You are no longer English. You shave no more than once a week. Last night you shouted 'Goddammit' to Slicky Jim, a man—a *minister*—whom you'd just met. Now you have cursed again, in public."

"You do speak real familiar to strangers now, Ben," Duff said.

"Yes," Skaggs said, "that toadeater just now, our stagecoach agent, you greeted with a great *smile* as if he were a dear old friend. Before we reach the frontier I expect you to be stuffing your mouth with tobacco chaws and guz-zling bourbon and shouting 'Whoopee!' Benjamin Motley Mactier Knowles, son of Sir Archibald Knowles, has become American."

Ben remembered that he had already tasted bourbon—on his first night in New York, as he'd stared across the dining room of the Astor House at a beautiful, talkative, smiling, strong-willed young blond woman in a blind-ingly yellow silk dress.

"You flatter me, Skaggs."

"What's that?" the bartender asked Ben, who was reaching into a bowl of pickled cucumbers set out on the bar. "What'd you say?"

"I'd like a good bourbon whiskey, please."

44

A T HIGH NOON on a breezy, hot, cloudless August day, the Missouri River current nudged the flat-bottomed ferryboat five hundred feet south and west along a rope stretched between the two banks, out of Iowa and the United States and over to Indian country. Two canvas-covered wagons, two families, a handcart, eight oxen, and a mule shared the deck with another group of travelers—two young women from New York and a young man from Indiana—who were just off the *Omega,* their St. Louis steamer. As they approached the far side of the river, they watched two human figures who stood near the landing, two half-naked men, two *Indians.*

"Uh-huh," the ferry tender said, sounding bored. "They'll want a biscuit, or a coin, or what-have-you."

The men's black hair hung to their shoulders, and both wore only breechcloths. Neither was young. The older one had placed a large piece of bark on the dried mud in front of them, and held a large stick cut with notches in one hand and in his other a smaller stick. As soon as all the white people were off the boat, he started to hum a tune and rub the small stick across the notches to make a rhythmic rasp. His companion began to dance. The dancer looked to Polly as if he were pantomiming a run and playing a game of patty-cake. Unlike the gyrating Indians she had seen on the stage at Barnum's, these were unarmed and serene and sad.

She placed a penny on the bark, and then she and the others started up a trail toward the town, which appeared much bigger than St. Joseph, in Missouri, the largest place they had seen since leaving St. Louis. It stretched a mile along the river behind a picket fence that ran even longer.

They came first to a large corral, empty of animals.

Not far away, a gristmill's waterwheel spun freely in its creek, disengaged from the gears and stones inside.

Next to the mill was a log fortress thirty feet on each side, a building more than twice as large as any log cabin they had seen along any of the rivers. Its only windows were cut into the thick earthen roof.

Nearby were stores and workshops, and dozens of houses—no, *hundreds* of houses. Some were built of sod bricks, but most were made of logs, with roofs of straw and willow branches and turf. Each had a surname painted or carved on its door.

The three visitors walked slowly down a wide dirt main street, crossing two, three, four streets, and stopped; ten streets remained before them. It was a small city. Every building was new. And there was not a soul in sight. The only noises were whip-poor-wills and turkeys, and the flapping of waxed-cloth squares tacked in the window openings of the log houses.

ONLY TWO YEARS earlier, this had been an empty bluff where birds and deer were occasionally shot, a mere hundred out of the million acres hunted by the local Indians.

And then suddenly—*weirdly* to the Oto and the Omaha, who had become accustomed to the trickle of laughing, angry, frightened, childlike wanderers and their wagons passing through on their way, the whites believed, to some western ocean—one particular horde of white people and their cattle had crossed the river and stopped, here, on this good scrap of the Indians' land, and stayed. They'd called themselves "Saints." They declared the riverbank their "Winter Quarters," which sounded reassuringly temporary to the natives, although the whites had remained for *two* winters before moving west. For two summers, two falls, two winters, and two springs, the Saints had jammed themselves into their queer square city, and outnumbered all of the Oto and Omaha by two to one.

But then, only a few months ago, the last of them disappeared into the sunset as suddenly as they had arrived, loading up and driving their thousand wagons toward the bleak country occupied by the Arapaho and—may the whites' god protect them—the *Dakota,* and over the mountains to the great desert. *Why?* They had simply *abandoned* all their buildings (and burial grounds), into which they had so recently invested so much furious sweat and pride. If they'd really known beforehand that they were going to leave two years after they arrived, why had they constructed permanent houses and stores? Not to mention their inexplicable wooden fence that stretched for two miles along the river. Was it all a monument to themselves or their god, or some utterly bewildering folly? And why had such busy, *busy* people failed to harvest and store enough wild grapes and plums and berries and roots and leaves in the summer and fall so that during the winter their flesh would not become scrawny and sick and black and dead? The Saints had promised the Indians that after they left they would never return, and said that any Omaha or Oto was free to take up residence in the square houses, to live in the city as if it were their own. And the offer apparently had been intended neither as a trap nor as a joke.

From the start, the Saints had explained their ways by saying they were "a peculiar people"—"a white *tribe,*" in the phrase of the interpreter. But to the Oto and Omaha, the Mormons were simply insane. Their "tribe," they'd told the Indians, without smiles or embarrassment, had been created *sixteen years before.* (The Indians were sure there had been some mistake in the translation.) No wonder the other whites in the east had driven them west across the big rivers, to be rid of them for good.

Since last spring the Oto had been debating whether their descendants would believe, a century hence, long after all the log houses had rotted into the earth, the story of the ten thousand white Saints appearing from the east, building a city, and then almost immediately—*for no good reason at all*—disappearing into the west forever. Would the children of their children's children consider it an exaggeration or hallucination or some ancient fable? But since such an event had actually happened here on this very spot before their own eyes, some of them said, well then, all the old tales of talking bears and shape-shifting women must be true as well.

"IT IS *exactly* as Absalom described," Billy said again and again as they walked up and down the empty streets and among the abandoned buildings.

He had stayed in touch with the eldest of his brothers, thirteen-year-old

Absalom. Billy had come here to see the Winter Quarters, where his family had lived since he left them. In particular he wanted to unearth the little treasure his brother had left for him. In Absalom's last letter, he'd written that he had buried nine china marbles, each decorated differently, each representing one of his parents and his siblings, "right next to the BIG cottonwood near B. Smith shop." He'd also written that he prayed every day that Billy would join them in the promised land, at the Great Salt Lake, and that when he finally did, he could "stop at the Winter Quarters at the Camp of Israel to dig up my marbles and hold the whole family in your pocket until you reach Zion and hold us in the flesh."

After Billy's apostasy in 1846, he had been part of the exodus out of Nauvoo—when the Whipples and the twelve thousand other Saints had gone west, he had headed east to Chicago and later to Glee. Although he knew from Absalom's and his cousin Truman's letters that the Winter Quarters were to be evacuated this summer, he was nonetheless astonished to find this new, perfect, instant, vacant Mormon town in the middle of nowhere.

It was the strangest scene the two women had ever seen. Polly was reminded of a big Italian book of etchings her father had shown her when she was eleven in a library in Washington, with its fabulous pictures of the ruins of Roman antiquity. Unlike those abandoned Roman buildings, though, these were still tidy, slightly overgrown but none of them crumbling or collapsing—not really ruins at all, not yet, and they were the very opposite of ancient.

They had passed two blacksmith's shops, but neither was close to any cottonwood trees. Billy stopped and turned to Priscilla. "Dearest, may I ask . . . if it isn't too much trouble for you, if you might . . . *think* about where Absalom's little buried treasure could be." She had told him, of course, about her occasional psychic sensations.

Priscilla smiled at the request and his bashfulness. "I am not a dowser, Billy." She wiggled her fingers. "I have no divining rod. But yes, I shall try for you." She took a deep breath and tilted her head back. Her face was expressionless. She closed her eyes, then opened them, staring straight up into the blue. Her curls waved in the breeze. Billy watched hopefully. For most of a minute she stared into the sky.

Polly was about to suggest they continue searching on foot, with their eyes, when suddenly Priscilla shivered and stroked her neck from one ear to her shoulder. She lowered her gaze and then shivered again as gooseflesh arose on her arms as well. Her breathing became rapid, as if she'd run from somewhere.

"I think your *brother—your* brother," she said excitedly, nodding toward Polly, "and Mr. Knowles and, and another man are—I don't know exactly how to put this into words. But . . . they are *aiming* at us, and they have lately occupied some place that we occupied as well."

"Some *place?*" Polly was baffled. "In New York, some theater or store . . . ?"

"No, not a city at all. It's green and quiet. Could they . . . might they be back at Glee?"

Polly snorted.

"Perhaps not . . . Perhaps I have it mingled with the other picture that came to me." Now Priscilla looked at Billy. "Your brother's buried things are here. A ways back that way," she said, pointing west, to the higher ground away from the river, "maybe up there."

On a bluff, they found the cemetery. And near an elm tree, not a cottonwood, in a section of newer graves, they found those of Eliza Whipple, age four, and Absalom Whipple, age thirteen.

Billy sat down next to his brother's patch, looking over toward his sister's. "I had a letter from him in the spring, and *none* had passed at New Year's," he said, sounding as if he had been tricked. But he did not cry.

Later, walking back through the empty town toward the ferry, Billy spotted his father's name, G. WHIPPLE, painted in white on the front door of a house—his family's house. And three cabins down the street, Priscilla saw the house of a certain B. SMITH. Behind it they found a shed that had been used as a pottery shop, and just behind that was a cottonwood tree that looked a hundred feet tall. The nine marbles were there, wrapped in a piece of waxed cloth Absalom had signed with his full name.

THIS HAD NOT been the only unhappy surprise of the last twenty-four hours. The day before, they had disembarked at Hemme's Landing, across the river from Humblebee, which they'd expected to be their new home. The Humblebeevians had arrived in 1846, and already planted a pear orchard and built houses and a small brewery. In addition to bartering beer and guns to the local Indians, they had been traveling among their neighbors to proselytize—to persuade the Oto and Missouria and Pawnee to reorganize themselves into cooperative "phalanxes," without private ownership of land or "the means of production." The Indians had been mystified, and had tried to explain that they were already organized in such a fashion.

Unfortunately for them, Humblebee had been colonizing Indian country, in violation of the U.S. Indian Intercourse Act. Furthermore, the colony was on the Nemaha Half-Breed Reservation, which the government and the Indians had agreed to carve out as a home for all the inconvenient products of . . . Indian intercourse throughout the Missouri Valley.

The grizzled little fellow in charge at Hemme's Landing had informed Polly as soon as she'd stepped off the *Omega* that Humblebee was no more. A cadre of army dragoons from Fort Leavenworth had ridden up in June and evicted the Humblebeevians, escorting them across the river back into the States, where they belonged. Their houses and brewery had already been dismantled and scavenged by whites. "But we should be pleased to have you stay here in Missouri, ma'am," the man had said cheerfully, glancing at Priscilla and Billy, "unless you all are Mormon. And if you are, you better get back on the boat and don't get off until you reach Hart's Bluff."

"Where is Hart's Bluff?" Polly had asked.

"Up in Iowa, ma'am, what the Indians used to call Council Bluff. Lately people've called it Miller's Hollow." He'd spat his dripping chaw on the dock. "It's where all the Mormons have gathered up like a bunch of hungry rats in a corncrib."

"Actually, sir," Billy had said, "*now* they have renamed that town Kane."

"So I heard," the geezer had replied quickly with a self-satisfied sneer, pleased that the boy had fallen into his little trap, "named by those banished murdering Mormon heathens after the banished murderer *Cain!*"

And with that they had reboarded the steamer and proceeded upriver to the Mormons' temporary frontier metropolis.

THEY CROSSED BACK from the empty Winter Quarters to the bustling Iowa side and found the cabin of Billy's relative. Truman Codwise was at home, and delighted to see his cousin, prodigal or not—and said that God must have guided them here for a reunion, because in only a few days he was leaving for the Great Salt Lake—Zion. When he learned they had come because Billy wanted to be married in Truman's presence, if he could bear to witness a gentile wedding, Truman chuckled and then cried, which made Billy start to bawl as well. Both young men continued to sniffle as they prepared a dinner of catfish and watercress and mulberries.

Lately there were two gentiles living in town, Truman said, a new storekeeper downtown and a miller out east on Mosquito Creek, and he had heard that one of them was a Christian minister of some kind who would probably marry the two of them for a dollar . . . *unless,* he said, they did want an eternal marriage, in the temple, in which case he could quickly arrange for Priscilla's baptism and conversion . . . Billy declined, and Polly said they would remain only a short time after the wedding, and then make their way back east to find a place from among the several communities on Polly's list that they had skipped along the way in Iowa and Wisconsin.

"You are welcome to stay here in Kanesville, ma'am," Truman said as she put a second piece of fish on her plate, "as long a while as you wish."

Kane had been rechristened Kanesville. It occurred to Polly that these makers of new communities, from James Danforth at Glee to the Mormons' leader Brigham Young, were as fickle as little girls about naming and renaming their creations.

Suddenly someone knocked on Truman's door. Given the small size of the cabin, they could feel the heavy raps.

"Whatever it is you have frying in there, Codwise," called a young male voice, "could not smell finer." The man had an English accent.

Polly and Priscilla exchanged a glance and a thought: *Ben Knowles.*

"*Lawrence,*" Truman and Billy both shouted as they rushed to the door. All three hugged and whooped and laughed and cried some more.

Billy Whipple, Lawrence Grafton, and Truman Codwise had been friends in Nauvoo. The Mexican War began in earnest just as the Saints came west, and the army had offered to let the squatters remain on the Indians' land at their Winter Quarters for the duration—but only if five hundred of their young men would enlist to form a Mormon Battalion and fight in Mexico for a year. Thus the newlywed Grafton joined up, gave his forty-two-dollar army clothing allowance to his pregnant wife, and marched west in the summer of '46. He had turned eighteen as a private in southern California, he said between bites of catfish, while they were occupying the Mexican town of Los Angeles, and had turned nineteen as a laborer in the northern California hills, camped last fall and winter with four dozen other mustered-out members of the battalion on the American River, a day's ride from Fort Sutter. "The Indians in that part are very tame," he said. "We worked right with them, digging and sawing and hammering for our dollar a day."

What Lawrence was most excited to describe for Truman and Billy, however, was his journey of the last two months. As soon as the spring melt had allowed, he'd started riding back from California to Iowa to rejoin his wife and baby daughter. He had reached the Great Salt Lake in June—on the very day, he said, a great flock of white gulls flew into the valley and started eating the crickets that had plagued the Saints' six thousand acres of new wheat and corn, and driving the rest of the insects into the lake. And every morning, Lawrence said, the white birds returned to battle the crickets. "I tell you, if that was not a true holy miracle I witnessed, boys, a happy message from the Lord to the Saints, then I *am* a fool or a maniac!"

And the biblical pageantry had continued as he rode east and passed company after company of westbound brothers and sisters who had left the Winter Quarters for their New Jerusalem. At Fort Bridger, he had seen the seven other surviving Whipples. "Your sister," Lawrence said about Jemima, who was exactly Priscilla's age, "has become a woman since you saw her last."

Lawrence had returned only this morning, but had already signed up as a bullwhacker to help lead the last westbound company of the year, leaving Wednesday next, meaning that he and his family should celebrate Thanksgiving at Salt Lake.

Truman was grinning. "Brother Lawrence, I hesitated to say so before, but *I* am riding with the company leaving Wednesday as well—we are going to Zion *together*."

There was another round of hugs and whoops and laughter and tears.

As Lawrence prepared to return to his cabin for the night, Polly asked him about California. After describing its diverse terrain and gentle (but changeable) climate, he mentioned, as an afterthought, shaking his head, that during his final weeks there, "an unholy rumpus developed."

"A rumpus of what sort?" she asked him.

"Oh," he said dismissively, as if he were talking about children's shenanigans, "some boys building a mill found itty bits of gold in the river, some gold gravel, and then they scrabbled up some more in another place not far away, and in no time everyone was boiling with greed, nearly all the brethren as well as the gentiles. By the time I rode out, there was some new stranger or two appearing every day, men from San Francisco and Monterey, hot to find their fortunes.

"You remember little Azariah Smith?" he asked Billy and Truman. "He was right there building the sawmill when they found the first teeny bit. He held it up next to one of his army five-dollar pieces and said, 'Uh-*huhnhh—gold*.' " The three laughed, because back in Nauvoo, Azariah Smith had always answered questions "uh-*huhnhh*" and "uh-*unhhh*" instead of "yes" and "no." They proceeded to reminisce about other mutual pals and enemies from their youths on the Mississippi, but after a while Polly could no longer contain her curiosity.

"Excuse me, Mr. Grafton—"

"Lawrence, ma'am."

"—Lawrence, I am curious about the gold you mentioned earlier. When you say they simply found it in the water, you do not mean that they . . . actually plucked it out with their fingers, like pennies from a fountain?"

"I surely do, ma'am, yes."

"But it will run out soon, surely. The area will be picked clean."

"I don't know. Just before I left, some of our boys from the battalion found a whole fresh sandbar full of it. There was more to dig and wash than there were men to do it."

"And who *owns* this land?"

"Out there in the Coloma? Nobody, I guess. Quite a few Indians live close by. But now since America won the war, the States owns it all, everyone figures. All of us own it. Nobody and everybody."

"And those who went searching," Polly asked, "found how much gold in a day of looking?"

"Oh, anybody might pick up, oh, fifteen dollars in a day. The end of my time there I helped a couple of the boys use what they call a rocker to sift gold out, and we took a pound of dust. Nearly three hundred dollars. In those five days I got as much as I earned for my year in the army." From his pocket he pulled a leather purse, and into his palm he carefully spilled out a small mound of golden flakes and gravel.

Everyone stepped close to Lawrence's open hand to stare. Priscilla grinned. The men shook their heads and whistled, sincerely impressed that Lawrence had resisted temptation, choosing his wife and baby and a new life in Zion over the prospect of more easy wealth.

And Polly was hatching an idea. "Lawrence," she asked, "may I keep you just a few minutes more? I am very curious about California."

Illinois

WHEN THEIR STAGECOACH arrived in Springfield in the afternoon, Skaggs had once again pleaded that they stop and rest overnight to gather their strength for the final rush to the border, and to allow him to look up some friends from his years working at the *State Register*. Ben was persuaded only when Skaggs suggested they could make up any lost time by taking a railroad train most of the way to the Mississippi River—the most westerly train line in the States—the next morning.

"If you are so fond of this town, Skaggs, why did you leave it?"

"Why? Are you serious, Knowles? There are only a couple of thousand people living here. And half of those," he said, pointing across the street at the grand new limestone state capitol, "are politicians, politicians' wives, favor-seekers, bribe-payers, and lawyers. I left because I was offered a position back in New York at double my salary—and because around the same time I was informed that a certain overzealous and stiff-backed Hoboken prosecutor had died. Which freed me to end my exile and return at last to the vicinity of New Jersey."

Skaggs left Ben and Duff at their hotel, crossed the street to Tinsley's dry-goods store, and walked up to its third floor, where several attorneys kept offices. Before he gave himself over to the pleasures of Springfield society—to pals at the *Register*, and to a loose young Swedish seamstress whose company he'd kept—he needed to square an account. He needed to seek forgiveness.

"Good afternoon, sir."

"My Lord, is that Timothy Skaggs? The scoundrel has returned! Alive and well! And in a beard."

"Yes, Mr. Herndon, my hair has waxed, while I see that yours"—he pointed at the balding pate of his twenty-nine-year-old friend—"has waned."

They shook hands warmly. Seven years ago, Billy Herndon had studied his law books every morning in the same tavern where Skaggs had written his articles for the *Register*, and the two young men had become friendly. Standing at Herndon's desk now, Skaggs explained the odd circumstance of his visit.

"Billy," he said as earnestly as he knew how, "I have come here to see the congressman this afternoon, if he'll see me, so that I might make my apologies for the things I wrote and said about him."

Herndon was dumbfounded.

"The congressman" was Herndon's law partner. When Skaggs had moved to Springfield, the congressman had been a Whig state legislator on the make, and Skaggs had attacked him relentlessly in the Democratic *Register.* He had taken up his paper's standard critique—that the Whigs were squandering public money on railroad lines. But in the case of Herndon's man, Skaggs's ridicule had gone well beyond fiscal disagreements. He'd accused him in print of "practicing the cynical and nauseating politics of the gutter" for trying to besmirch President Van Buren's support of Negro suffrage with the fact that his vice president kept a black mistress. He'd written that Herndon's partner was "a remorseless bully" after the fellow caused another young politician to cry and run off a public stage by impersonating his peculiar manner of speech in front of a hooting, laughing audience. Skaggs had also suggested that the fellow's teetotaling caused his well-known mental depressions, and called his notoriously difficult wife "Scary Mary, Quite Contrary."

"Your *apologies!*" Herndon said finally. "Have you got religion, Timothy?"

"No, I have just—I have been exceptionally impressed by everything I have read of him this last year, Billy. No one in Washington was more sensible about the war." Amid the patriotic jubilee last winter over the U.S. victory in Mexico, Herndon's law partner, as a first-term member of the House, had dared to call President Polk's prophylactic invasion unnecessary and unconstitutional and "half insane." "On the slavery question as well," Skaggs added, "I am strongly on the free-soil side. And by the way, I am a temperance man—"

"*No!*"

"—more or less, yes, lately. And in the morning I shall be a westbound passenger on his own beloved railroad line."

"Your news is all as gratifying as it is surprising, Skaggs. I am sure he should be very surprised and pleased to hear it too."

"And where is he? At luncheon?"

"He is in Washington still, I am afraid."

"Drat! But I read that he was not seeking reelection . . . I meant to congratulate him for that as well—retiring from the House and from office-seeking altogether, leaving the District of Corruption for good."

"Oh, he *is,* he has. He's rejoining me here shortly—Lincoln & Herndon endures."

"Hurrah, then. Please do convey to Mr. Lincoln, Billy, the sincere regret of a man no longer so youthful or benighted or dog-hearted as I once was."

434 · Kurt Andersen

They shook hands again. "You know, Timothy, your appearance in town today will shock people—we had heard that you'd left the States to seek your fortune, and . . . had *died*."

"Really? Wishfulness! You seem to have mistaken me for George and Jake Donner."

"*Skaggs*. That is a travesty in appalling taste, even for you. My nephew Noah was a teamster with those poor people." Two Springfield families had formed a wagon train to California in 1846 and become snowbound in the high Sierras for months. A little more than half of the eighty-three lived, half of those by roasting and eating the flesh of a dozen of their dead companions.

"Yes, I know—and young Noah was one of the lucky survivors, I was interested to read, now a famous man, no doubt, living a happy life in California. Please send him my congratulations as well."

August 22, 1848

As THEY CROSSED west into Hancock County on the Sangamon & Morgan Railroad, Skaggs was recounting for Ben and Duff the excitement of his one and only visit to these parts four years before.

In June of 1844, dissidents in the Mormon town of Nauvoo had published the first issue of a newspaper in which they'd called their prophet and founder Joseph Smith a tyrannical organizer of "whoredoms and abominations." In response, Smith had declared martial law and ordered his thugs to sledgehammer the dissidents' press and burn their papers.

The moment word of this battle reached Springfield, Skaggs had hired a surrey and raced across the state to report on it for the *Register*.

Meanwhile, the Hancock County authorities had arrested Smith on charges of treason and jailed him in Carthage, the county seat.

And Skaggs happened to arrive in Carthage just an hour before a mob of armed citizens had stormed the jail to deal with the tyrant freak themselves.

"I saw Smith jump from the second story of the courthouse, as if he thought he was going to fly away on angel's wings. On the ground, he pleaded for his life, but the gentlefolk of Carthage shoved him up against the wall and shot him, point-blank. I had never seen a man murdered." The *Register* ran Skaggs's eyewitness scoop—and after he published an even more purple dispatch on the lynching in the New York *Evening Mirror*, he'd been offered the job that returned him to Manhattan.

"So Mr. Smith's end," Ben concluded, "was a new beginning for Timothy Skaggs."

Duff nodded. "Destruction and creation," he said softly.

IN THE CITY of Quincy, Ben and Duff went to inquire about their ferry across the Mississippi to Hannibal, and the stagecoach schedule west from there. Skaggs, minding the luggage on the docks, encountered a bachelor gentleman he had known during his time in Springfield. Kenner Loring, it turned out, was now an investor in the reconstituted local railroad—the railroad on which Herndon's partner Abraham Lincoln and his partisans had so enthusiastically spent the public's money. Loring and his associates had just bought the bankrupt million-dollar line from the state for twenty-one thousand dollars.

Skaggs congratulated him. "*Capital*, you sharper, absolutely capital. And I see your fortune has made you exceedingly well fed." Loring had gained fifty pounds since Skaggs had seen him last.

" 'The righteous shall still bring forth fruit in old age; they shall be fat and flourishing,' " Loring replied.

Both men laughed, and Skaggs pointed at the three large trunks on the dock. Loring explained he was visiting a lady in New Orleans whom he had met last spring.

"On my annual vacation through the South, with some fellows from Chicago, bucks of the blunt—your type of rover, Skaggs. We book a private steamer from St. Louis, and stop at the best places along the river, Memphis, Vicksburg—and *New Orleans*, of course. Is there any American city more devoted to *pleasure*?" He grinned, winked, then leaned close to Skaggs and whispered, "We also have our little slaving spree. Very naughty, very jolly."

"What is that, sir—a *'slaving spree'*?" Skaggs was sincerely mystified.

"*Shhhhh,* " he said, lowering his voice even more. "This city is a hotbed of ultras," by which he meant abolitionists. "We visit the dealers in St. Louis—the respectable ones—and then proceed down the Mississippi with . . . our enlarged crew." He was still smiling.

"Do you mean to tell me you and your friends go south on an expedition to buy slaves? For sport?"

"Skaggs, I don't expect sanctimony from *you*. You know, in New Orleans, I discovered, there are thousands of *Negro* slaveholders. In any event, I assure you that our little troop treats them well, very well, even affection-ately, I daresay. Not one has ever attempted to escape—for the coloreds it really amounts to a month of vacation as well. For us, you see, it is only a hobby, not any true deal of business. As one of the fellows says—he's a col-lector of art—'I can buy a marble *statue* of a man in Rome or a *man* in St. Louis, costs a thousand dollars either way.' And we do not keep them, for goodness' sake."

Skaggs only stared.

"Indeed," Loring continued, sounding proud, "we have established a means by which they can win their freedom. A contest. On our way back up-river at the end of the journey, we dock in St. Louis and hold a banquet, a gala to mark our last night all together in slave country. And after dinner our ten or dozen darkies put on the most *amazing* show—singing, juggling, act-ing, joking, hilarious dancing, acrobatic leaps. And at the end of the evening, we vote as a jury on who has performed best. And the prize for that lucky man is manumission. He is put into a skiff and sent off to Illinois, free and clear."

"And the others?"

"Sold back to the dealers. At a discount from the purchase prices, natu-rally . . . although the firms do pay the insurance for the time we have pos-session, a dollar and a half per month for each sambo . . ."

By the time Ben and Duff returned from their errand, the bellowed name-calling back and forth—*fanatical bastard, vile poltroon, un-Christian pig, barn burner, drunkard, New Yorker, sinner, criminal, fool*—had sub-sided. Loring was red-faced with embarrassment and anger but also from the smart slap Skaggs had given his cheek the instant he'd uttered *sambo*. At the height of the donnybrook, Skaggs had knocked his hat off, and as Lor-ing had run in vain to catch it before it flew into the river, he'd tripped over one of his steamer trunks. And none of the amused spectators had inter-ceded when Skaggs picked up Loring from the dock by his necktie, like a noose, twisting it tight around his throat.

As Duff and Ben approached Skaggs, the crowd expected an all-out tus-sle and scuffle, with eyes gouged and ears bitten. One of the quarrelers might even demand satisfaction. But no duel took place. The fellow in blue eyeglasses straightened his waistcoat and, without a further word, turned and walked off with his seconds.

On the way across to Hannibal, Duff leaned over to sniff at Skaggs's face. "No, I have *not* been drinking, Father Lucking—but just now even that disgusting rum treacle," he said, nodding toward a man with a tray selling cups of cherry bounce, "tempts me sorely. No, gentlemen, what you witnessed back there was once again the frazzled result of Timothy Skaggs *denied* the calming effects of strong drink. Teetotaling makes me dangerous."

45

August 26, 1848

· · ·

Iowa

*B*EN HAD BEEN more steadfast than ever as they'd traveled without pause for three days across the state of Missouri, confident that he was on the verge of finding Polly at last. He had thought of the pleasure she'd taken in his prints of the western plains, his Bodmers and Catlins, and then realized he was following those artists' very routes west along the Missouri River. Perhaps they had painted the hills and valleys of Humblebee. Humblebee! Cheerfully anticipating their imminent reunion, he had even grown fond of the name.

But now it was a bad joke. Humblebee had ceased to exist. Their final destination was defunct, a mirage at the end of the road.

Skaggs had said he was beginning to imagine they were the victims of a three-card monte game rigged by God, where their chosen card—Polly Lucking, the queen of hearts—repeatedly disappeared at the last moment. And while they would continue the search, Ben's hope and determination were flagging badly. For the first time, he felt the expedition was foolish and doomed.

They were on yet another stagecoach, rolling north on yet another rutted rural track toward a frontier camp of pious fanatics, this time entirely on the say-so of a snaky stranger. "You boys are the second eastern crew this week come to see that damned place," the small man at Hemme's Landing had told them. The others, he said, had been a pair of young women, "one real young," and a young man—"Mormons traveling *incognito,* if you ask me; I believe *both* gals was married to the fellow, the way they do it, you know." His descriptions of the women sounded like Polly and Priscilla. And back at Glee, Danforth had said that the man accompanying them was a young Mormon . . .

So off Ben and Skaggs and Duff had set for Iowa. What if Polly had converted to Mormonism? What if she *had* married? And what if she was not there at all? Where would they look next?

When Skaggs spotted a big beaver's dam in a stream alongside the road, and thus had a new excuse to attack the late John Jacob Astor—"his compulsion to murder beavers, *that's* what's driven America west, *there's* our manifest destiny, a thousand a day killed every day for fifty years by his damned American Fur Company"—Ben asked him to "try to be quiet awhile, please."

As they finally rolled into Kanesville, his new pessimism fed on itself. It was a big place, and its thousand new log cabins looked identical. Night was falling. It was a fresh opportunity for disappointment. She could be anywhere. Or elsewhere.

But nearly every one of the town's inhabitants was a Mormon, and most of them had lived together for years in Nauvoo, and in Missouri before that. Strangers were notable. Thus the second man Ben asked about the whereabouts of a young Mr. Whipple sent them directly to the cabin of Truman Codwise.

There was no answer at the door. One of the neighbors thought that Codwise, Whipple, and their visitors—"the two women"—had gone off that day for a wedding ceremony, but another had heard that the visitors had left for good.

The cosmic confidence trick continued: she had been there an instant ago, now she was gone. And so, exhausted from their travel, the three sat down on the ground behind the cabin to wait. Hours passed. None of them spoke. Their hopelessness grew. Before long, it was dark, the insects' summer lullaby was playing, and then all three were asleep, using their bags as pillows.

Chicago

"Sir, I have twenty-one dollars from what you give me," Gabriel Drumont announced as soon as he entered the sheriff's office at the courthouse. When Allan Pinkerton sent a deputy to his boardinghouse to wake and fetch

him, Drumont had assumed that Pinkerton thought he had absconded with
the thirty dollars in expense money.

"A week and a half in Chicago on nine dollars? *Scrupulous,* monsieur,
thank you. And altogether reassuring given the assignment which we—
which *you*—must now undertake. You must immediately go west, to Iowa.
Miss Christmas was bound for a town at the far end of the state called"—he
brought the paper in his hand close to a lamp—"*Kanesville.* She intends to
marry there before the end of the month."

Pinkerton had that evening received an urgent message by telegraph from
Samuel Prime in New York. One of Prime's men in New York had learned
from Miss Christmas's father of her marriage plans. Prime, of course, was determined to prevent the wedding, and had authorized Pinkerton to offer the
girl a cash sum to cancel her plans and return to New York, where he would
see to it that she and their newborn child were well cared for. Prime was willing to reward the fiancé, one William Whipple, for his cooperation—and also
suggested, conversely, that if necessary Pinkerton and Drumont should provide Whipple with the details of Priscilla's whoring past.

"We has time to reach the . . . Iowa? To Kanesville? Before the marriage?"

"*Scant* time."

"Is Benjamin Knowles travel also with her?"

"My single report on him is from Terre Haute, a stage office, more than
a week ago, accompanied by two men."

Pinkerton handed Drumont a pasteboard portfolio. In it were a Frink &
Walker stagecoach ticket, maps of Illinois and Iowa, and an envelope containing $350—*2,000 francs,* a year's pay—in banknotes.

"That should cover your traveling expenses and any necessary . . .
bonus payments to Miss Christmas and her young man. I am informed that
the final stretch through Iowa is a very rough track indeed. Therefore, when
the going gets slow you ought to buy a horse and take leave of the coach.
You ride, of course?"

"I have ride." But not since he'd left Algeria sixteen years ago, and never
very well.

Kanesville, Iowa

THEY HAD RETURNED to Kanesville well after midnight. The new bride
and groom and Truman Codwise were asleep. Polly awoke, and was making

her way in the moonless dark to the privy when she noticed the bodies in the dirt of the backyard.

For an instant she wondered if the bodies were dead, since Truman had talked more than once about assassination plots against the Mormons. But even in the darkness the position of the nearest body was familiar—knees pulled up almost to his belly, each hand wedged tight into the opposite armpit, the funny, knotty way her brother had always slept.

In his first startled moment of wakefulness, sensing a face and body hovering above him, Duff plunged his hand into his pocket for his revolver.

"Duff . . . ?"

"Sister!"

"How on *earth* . . . " she said as he scrambled to his feet and embraced her.

The two others awoke. Skaggs remained supine, but raised himself on his elbows as if he were lolling in his bed at home.

Ben, farthest away from Polly, slowly stood but did not move toward her. He needed to give her a moment to adjust to this remarkable new fact.

Polly saw him over Duff's shoulder. She stepped back from her brother.

"What brought you here?" Ben said. He had planned to say *I love you unconditionally* when he first saw her.

"Our friend Billy Whipple . . . it is complicated."

Both spoke softly, just above a whisper.

"We have waited since the afternoon," Ben said. He had intended his second sentence to be, *I cannot bear to lose you again.* "I dreaded that I had lost you again."

"We needed to drive some distance, and returned after a dinner—after dark. It was a wedding."

Ben's stomach turned.

"Priscilla has married," she added. "A good young man."

Ben walked to her. Seconds passed as they stared at each other in the darkness.

"You have come a very great distance," he said, "in search of your arcadia."

"And not found it yet, alas, but *you,* I, you must have, I . . . I thought I had seen you for the last time."

"I felt sure that I would find you, Polly."

"Priscilla had one of her . . . sensations that you were coming. I thought it was only, nothing, a dream." She took a deep breath. "I am still so amazingly startled to see you standing here before me in the flesh."

"But not displeased?"

She smiled and wiped the tears from her cheeks with the back of her hand as she shook her head no. "Not displeased. Not displeased at all."

Then they collided into each other's arms, both trembling, both squeezing tight, as if for dear life.

Duff was so happy for them both that he had difficulty swallowing. Skaggs, still on the ground, was looking up at the stars contentedly, smiling, drawing the lines of the constellation Lyra in the air with his forefinger.

"I love you," Ben whispered in Polly's ear.

"Oh, dearest, and I *you*," she replied. "And I you."

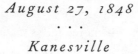

46

August 27, 1848

. . .

Kanesville

T<small>HE NEXT DAY</small> was Sunday, so for most of the morning the five gentiles and Billy Whipple had Truman's cabin to themselves for their reunion. The mood was mellow and lazy.

Ben and Duff were restored to primordial states of happiness, gazing at Polly's tanned face whenever she spoke, chuckling as Skaggs hunted in vain for "even a *smidgen*" of coffee or tea. One of Joseph Smith's divine revelations had proscribed not only tobacco, wine, and liquor for his Saints, but all "hot drinks." So they sipped water and elderberry juice as they chatted. Billy Whipple remained silent while Skaggs told his stories of Mormon Illinois— how he had bought a coffee *and* a pint of whiskey at Smith's own grocery in Nauvoo, and about the "reassuring number of drunkards" he'd been surprised to find rambling that city's streets.

Priscilla told them that Truman Codwise and Lawrence Grafton had invited Billy and her to join the train of fifty-eight wagons leaving Kanesville on Wednesday, bound for the Salt Lake Valley. After Skaggs asked the boy to reveal to "the present company, confidentially," the secret Mormon handshakes and passwords necessary for admittance to heaven, "in case we die before your erstwhile coreligionists have converted us," Billy excused himself for a walk along the river, and Priscilla joined him. Whereupon Polly gave Skaggs a familiar look—chastising but not unamused—that warmed him as much as any steaming pot of tea.

She turned to her brother. "Mr. Grafton is a veteran of the war—of the regular army. And there are many more, he says, *dozens*, living here in this place."

Duff's smile had frozen, as if his own face were now an instantly outdated daguerreotype image of itself. He was trapped. His scar stung.

"They all served together in Mexico," she continued, "in their own Mormon Battalion."

"*Ha!*" Skaggs barked. "Perhaps *the* most cynical of Polk's numberless cynical transactions. But these Mormon"—he paused, looking around as if someone might overhear—"mercenaries made a cute bargain. I understand they fulfilled their devil's deal as combatants by avoiding combat entirely."

Polly was nodding. "Mr. Grafton told me they went from here to California and left service a year ago without taking or firing a shot."

"They . . . they never marched all the way south?" Duff asked, exhaling a great gust as if he had been holding his breath. The hot lead ball spinning directly toward his head suddenly veered off.

"No, he never crossed the Rio Grande, he said, and never knew anything of the true war down there."

Duff listened to the shot plink away harmlessly. *The Lord is my strength and my shield; in him my heart trusts.* "I should look forward to meeting Mr. Grafton." In fact, he felt a confusion of emotions, admiration of the fact that these Mormon troops had neither seen death nor caused it in Mexico, but also both envy and contempt for such innocence of battle—as well as plain relief, of course. *So I am helped, and my heart exults, and with my song I give thanks to him.*

"He is quite certain," Polly said, "that God protected them."

"I wonder precisely how the Lord chooses," Skaggs asked, "as he looks down upon our wars, which men should survive and which must be eviscerated. Does he employ a bureau of angels to consider the merits of each case, or does he make certain decisions by wholesale—'five hundred Mormons, *saved.*' Oh, the medieval, deluded, poor white trash of this nation . . ."

"Mr. Grafton," she said, "is an intelligent and well-spoken man, and he is English also."

"Is that so?" Ben asked. "And why did he remain in California for an extra year?"

Polly collected her thoughts. "A whole company of them stayed. And in the spring, they found gold. Pounds of gold, on the eastern slope of the Sierra Nevada. In their 'foothills,' he says."

"Ah yes, of course," Skaggs cried, "of *course* these flamed followers of Joseph Smith say they've discovered *gold*! Just as young Smith happened to find God's own golden tablets lying in the dirt near his New York cottage. The grand delusion continues."

"No, Skaggs, this gold is quite real. I saw a handful of it, which you can look at for yourself. And Billy says that Lawrence Grafton is the straightest, most honest man he has ever known. He swears the gold is plentiful, for the taking, in country that no one owns."

She seemed as excited as she had been about winning the role of Florence Dombey. She was on fire. A large Carolina parakeet, bright green with a yellow head and orange mask, flittered through an open window and quickly out, and then back inside with a partner, landing on the sill.

"But the digging of shafts and grinding out of the ore," Ben said, "is all a laborious and unpleasant business." He had once been dispatched to Cornwall to inspect the arsenic and copper mines in which Knowles, Merdle, Newcome & Shufflebotham had an interest. "It requires considerable capital and machinery."

"But not this *gold*," she said, "not in California. Mr. Grafton says it is simply lying in the sand and the streams, in the mud and rocks, sprinkled practically everywhere. Available for any ordinary person to collect, working for himself. Beyond a shovel and a sieve, Mr. Grafton says, no great engines are necessary. No *capital* is required."

She glanced at her brother, knowing that he would be intrigued by the prospect of an enterprise independent of bankers.

"A finders-keepers game, eh?" Skaggs asked.

"How extraordinary," Ben said. As a boy, his favorite biography had been *The Life of Sir Walter Raleigh*, especially the passages about sailing up the Orinoco River in search of the golden city. "El Dorado."

Duff did not know the phrase, but he knew Spanish. " 'The . . . the golden one'?"

"Yes," Polly replied evenly to all three of them at once. "Democratic fortunes, available to any and all willing to work. Mr. Grafton says there is more gold in two or three small valleys than all of the several hundred men there could manage to pick up and carry away in a year or more." She looked around at the faces of her friend, her brother, and her beloved. "We could take as much as we wanted for ourselves. And we could establish our own good and just community on those empty common lands."

"We could if we were in California," said Ben. "But is California not as far from here as New York is in the opposite direction?"

"Yes," she answered, "exactly right, it is no farther than New York. If we intend to make so long a journey, why travel backward? Why retrace our steps?"

For a long while, the only sounds were the crickets outside and the nervous peeps of the parakeets. With their coloring, it seemed to Polly, the birds might have been emissaries from California, awaiting a decision.

She exchanged another look with her brother. They were both thinking of their father, and his serial thralls to financial fevers and schemes during their childhood. When Polly and Zeno Lucking went to Washington, he had been so impressed by the Chesapeake and Ohio Canal that he had impulsively invested his remaining hundred dollars—the savings he had not already invested in the last Hudson River whaling fleet, and in the proposed Hartford & Poughkeepsie Railroad that would have passed near the Luckings' house. But apart from his peculiar passion for buried treasure, the problem with their father's tragic hopefulness, Duff and Polly believed, had been his unfortunate *timing*. He had invested in whaling and canals a decade too late, and in the railway a decade too early. The time for this California gold seemed precisely right; perhaps it was the destiny of Zeno Lucking's surviving children to redeem his miscalculations and fulfill his dreams.

"I am in favor of 'What is now proved was once imagined' and all that, and I do not enjoy playing the fogy," Skaggs said, "but, Polly, my dear: you have searched for perfection all summer long. Up to now, in vain. So have *we* searched for *you*—and here, mirabile dictu, found you healthy and reasonably sane. You now suggest that we gamble our remaining capital to travel to *California*, and create there some sort of . . . communist settlement, our own wilderness utopia that does not survive by growing wheat or making butter or selling pewter cups and slouch hats, but . . . by gathering gold?"

She nodded. It did sound foolish, she knew. She wanted to yell at him.

"The four of us, *goldfinders*," Skaggs said, using a slang term for men who empty privy pots. "Deep in shit again, all right."

Now she wanted to punch him.

"You know, of course," he continued, "there are no steamers or railroad trains or stage lines across"—Skaggs waved a hand toward the river and beyond—"*that*. It would be a trek of fifteen hundred miles across desert and mountains. Civilization—and I use the word advisedly—ends right here."

"But exactly, Skaggs," she said. "Why should we not proceed to a wholly *new* place? A place far beyond what *is*, beyond the Mormons and the anti-Mormons, beyond the priests, beyond the upper-ten snobs and the revolutionist shouters, beyond the Whigs and the Democrats, beyond *this* world, a place of plenty where we might fashion our own world."

"A fresh, blank sheet of paper," Ben said finally.

She nodded. She wanted to leap into his lap and kiss him.

" 'One should live one's life as a perpetual experiment,' " Duff said.

"Ah, my own petard," Skaggs said, "and I am hoisted."

"As for our route," Polly continued, "proceeding west from here happens to be out of the question. By the time we reached the California mountains, they would be impassable with snow. By an overland route, we could not arrive in California for nearly a year. And by then, the gold and land might be all taken up."

"But, Polly," Ben said, "is that not a consideration in any event? Others will learn of the gold, and flock there. The competition will become fierce."

"Mr. Grafton believes he may be the only eyewitness from the gold country to cross back to the States so far."

Duff's hand was in his pocket, fingering his gold Saint Barbara's medal. Saint Barbara was the patron saint of firemen and gunners—and all kinds of miners. "So," he said, "we are blessed with a jump on pretty much everyone."

Skaggs's skepticism was now starting to give way to curiosity, and speculation about how people in New York would react to the news. He began thinking out loud. "The smart ones will doubt the first stories. They'll say it's a puff, or a hoax. Once it's been proved, though, they *will* get the mania. But to mount expeditions . . . it will take them a half year to round the Horn; even aboard a steamer or the fastest clipper, four months . . ." He stopped short. "But how do you propose that we reach California any faster from here, Polly?"

"According to these two gentlemen," she said, holding up two of Truman Codwise's books, *The Latter-Day Saints' Emigrants' Guide* and *The Emigrants' Guide to Oregon and California*, "it is possible to travel by ship, in the main."

"But, my dear, to return to New York and sail around South America, would, as I said—"

"*No*—by means of a southerly *shortcut*. The steamer *Omega*, which brought us here, will pass again very soon on its return downriver. Then from St. Louis it is five days more to New Orleans, and then a week across the Gulf of Mexico to the town of Chagres in New Grenada. The isthmus crossing, by canoe and mule, requires only a few days. And at the port of Panama City, on the Pacific side, one awaits the arrival of a northbound ship—the books say even the occasional clipper or steamer stops regularly. To San Francisco it is three more weeks. If our luck holds, we should be in the gold region by November at the latest."

Skaggs had opened one of the books, and read the author's name. "Lansford Hastings . . . Young Mr. Hastings was the expert guide who personally told Jake Donner about *his* shortcut over the Sierra Nevadas." He slapped the book shut. "But why should I mend my reckless ways at this late stage? I am ready to be an American prince of Serendip. I am willing to become rich with you, Polly."

"But you," Duff said, "are 'indifferent to wealth.' So you always claimed."

"Until now," Skaggs replied, "I have lacked any good purpose for spending a large sum. Polly has her project to undertake—and I, sir, have formed my own scheme for squandering some of our hypothetical fortune. I wish to build a great observatory in El Dorado. Beyond the smoke and light of any city, where I shall take the first pictures of the moon and the planets and the stars through a telescope.

"And I must say I find the . . . *poetry* of crossing the isthmus for gold irresistible—the very route the kahn-*kwist*-a-doors employed. *Ho* for California!"

Polly wanted to hug him.

"Cone-*keest*-a-doors," Duff corrected.

"And you, my brother," Polly said, "shall be essential as an interpreter—if you agree to join the company."

Duff was nodding before she finished her sentence.

No sign or word of affirmation was required of Ben. He already held her hand in his. He had crossed the whole United States and rummaged through a dozen desolate crannies in his quest for her, heedless of the discomfort, the expense, the odds against success. Of course he would go with Polly to California, or the Congo, or the North Pole.

A THOROUGH PLAN was formed over the rest of the day and the next. They decided they had enough money to get to California. After Skaggs and Duff counted out less than a hundred dollars apiece, the men were slightly stunned when Polly announced her savings ($364), and in order to avoid even a slightly awkward pause Ben immediately announced his remaining capital ($296), and Skaggs almost as quickly informed them of the total sum—$837. The *Omega*, they learned, was scheduled to arrive Tuesday on its way to St. Louis.

Billy and Priscilla had decided they would join Truman Codwise and the Graftons in their wagon train west, leaving the following day. Billy had no intention of returning to the church, but he did ache to see his family again; he and Priscilla would winter in the Salt Lake Valley, earning wages helping the Mormons build their new city, and in the spring continue on to California and the gold fields.

SKAGGS HUNCHED OVER his camera, looking down into his ground glass, the cloth covering his head. He ordinarily declined to make pictures of large groups, but sentiment demanded it that morning. A farewell portrait of Ben, Polly, Duff, Priscilla, Billy, and himself was required. For the picture, he had given Duff permission to return the big Colt's pistol to his belt. And since they would be standing in front of Truman's log cabin, he decided to use *"all* of our frontier props." He had Ben assemble and hold his shotgun, and he brought out the Indian club for which he had traded his spyglass the day before across the river. (Skaggs had asked the Oto if his "squaw" had used it to kill puppies for their stews, as he had read in a book about the prairie natives, but the man had failed to understand, and only laughed when Skaggs barked like a dog, tapped his own head with the club, and pantomimed dying.)

"Now, sir, to reiterate," he said to Lawrence Grafton, "when I say so, remove the cap from the lens and hold it back *here,* careful not to nudge the camera a bit—and then the instant I finish my count to five—which will only be *noises,* since I cannot open my mouth—replace the cap swiftly and firmly. Are you ready?"

Skaggs trotted from behind the camera over to his spot by Ben and held the Indian club with both hands, its stone head next to his, imitating the New York Knickerbocker baseball player he had once photographed holding a bat. "Everyone?" he asked. They each struck a pose and took a breath. Ben plunged his hands into his coat pockets. Duff turned his face to the right so the camera would not record his scar. Polly lowered her chin. Billy looked down at the top of his new wife's head, and Priscilla, uncontrollably, briefly shivered in the late-summer sun.

"*Now,*" Skaggs ordered, and started his count: "Mmm . . . mmm . . ."

From a mile away, they heard the blast of a steamboat's whistle, like a giant blowing with pursed lips into his giant's bottle.

". . . mmm . . . mmm . . . *mmm.* Excellent, Mr. Grafton. Everyone may relax."

Their steamboat was arriving an hour earlier than expected. The anxiety of the pose had been replaced by the anxiety of a suddenly hasty departure.

Polly dashed into the cabin to finish packing up. Priscilla waited an extra instant, squinting up at the sky with a perplexed look, then steeled herself and followed Polly inside. Duff put his revolver in his pocket and started dismantling the tripod. Even in this empty frontier, life's natural meter was being upset and transformed by machines and schedules.

"We lack the time for the picture to be developed, do we not?" Ben asked. "We must gather our things and make for the landing."

"We have time," Skaggs said, "we have time. Duff? Into the shed. Light the spirit lamp and heat the mercury. I will break down the camera and bring the plate . . ."

Within half an hour, chemical baths had been poured and used and re-bottled, hands shaken, tears wiped away, affection professed, good luck and godspeed wished. The four travelers stood together at a railing on the *Omega's* middle deck; Polly waved goodbye to Priscilla, who forced a smile but looked sad and resigned; Ben examined and reexamined the tiny smiling face of his true love on the daguerreotype portrait, to which the salty chemical tang still clung; Duff watched three monarch butterflies flying together in a tight circle just over the bow, a tiny kinetic figurehead of orange and black about to lead him back toward Mexico; and Skaggs had just spotted a sign on the pier for Astor's American Fur Company. "No escape," he muttered.

A FEW HOURS later they were steaming down the Missouri through the twilight, and while Skaggs retired to the saloon to drink coffee and smoke a cigar, the others lounged in chairs on the starboard side of the upper deck. They looked between and over the cottonwoods lining the western bank, across miles of empty prairie, at what they took to be the last vivid minutes of a remarkable sunset.

Ben considered how the limpid void of the landscape earlier in the afternoon—*exactly* like the pictures by Bodmer and Catlin—had become a lurid J.M.W. Turner sky of blazing orange on gray-black, with low clouds that seemed to ooze along the horizon. But it would be pretentious to say it, so he kept quiet and stared.

It reminded Duff of the night before he'd fought the Battle of Buena Vista, looking out at the line of bivouac bonfires along the desert horizon. And he also thought of what Truman had mentioned the other day about the new name of their Iowa county, Pottawattamie, after the Indian tribe they had displaced—Pottawattamie, he had said, meant "makers of fire." But Duff decided to keep his thoughts to himself, for fear of sounding like an absolute bug for flames and war. And if it was some kind of message to him from the Lord, he should keep that private too.

"I do wonder why it is," Polly said, "that not only the colors of the sunset here are so much more vivid, but the glow *lingers* for such a long, long while there at the horizon."

"Let such magnificence dawdle," said Ben, still a little giddy three days after their reunion. "Let beauty be dilatory."

"No, ma'am, and sir, if I can inter-trude, that ain't a sunset nohow," said a large man wearing a big bushy beard and leather shirt sitting near them. He was a bison hunter who had spent the last several years living up north at Fort Pierre, and was trembling with excitement at the prospect of talking to a well-dressed white woman. "The *sunset* is all done now, sometime since. That there's your fire on *earth,* maybe ten miles out. That's your whole *prairie* burning. That's what it starts at doing this time every year, when the buffalo grass gets dry and drier. If there weren't this good east wind blowing back of us, we'd be smelling her stink awful good now."

They were acknowledging this new information with murmurs and nods when Skaggs came up the stairs and joined them. The stranger, embarrassed that he had just said "smelling her stink awful good" to a woman, used Skaggs's arrival as cover to stand up and slink away.

"*Ignis fatuus,* " Skaggs declared as he took the hunter's empty chair, his brain now stoked with a quart of strong coffee. "The great American night-fire, Duff! 'Tiger, Tiger, burning bright/In the forests of the night,/What immortal hand or eye/Could frame thy fearful symmetry?' Oh, would that we could take a photograph of *that.* And capture those true reds and or-anges!"

"I suppose that some of the grasslands need to burn," Polly said, "in the natural order of things."

"What is the proverb, Duff, your epigram," Ben asked, " 'Annihilation is creation' . . . ?"

"Destruction and creation are the cycle of life. But it isn't mine. It was our daddy's."

Ben thought of his own father's red and lively face as he said goodbye on the steps of Great Chislington Manor, and then recalled again Tryphena's dream that she had rushed outdoors to recite: Ben a child in a fantastic America, playing with other children among Indians and fires . . . and the shiny yellow orbs scattered on the ground.

He would have to write Tryphena from New Orleans and recount everything he had seen, and tell her that he was on his way to California to collect pieces of gold from the ground.

September 4, 1848

· · ·

Iowa

*D*RUMONT HAD SPENT several of his army years in Algeria, freeing white Christian slaves, pacifying Berbers, exterminating pirates, and making it a *département* safe for French settlers. He hadn't enjoyed Algeria.

Iowa was like Algeria. Or anyway, after nine days traveling five hundred miles in a primitive coach, the thinly inhabited western half of Iowa reminded him of the dreary Algerian interior—dusty, windy, and hot, towns of a few souls called cities, houses built out of earth and straw, trenches that didn't deserve the name "road," unsmiling suspicious faces, no wine to be had. He had even seen a goat roasting over coals. And the Indians—he had spotted seven, some of them dressed like people, in shirts and trousers and skirts—might as well have been Arabs.

No surprise that this used to be France, he thought, *and no wonder Emperor Napoleon sold it to the Americans.* But at least Iowa was more green than brown. Gabriel Drumont had no idea how bleak and utterly Algerian the landscape ahead would become.

He could not find anyone who would sell him a horse to ride the last rugged seventy miles to his destination. The first yokel he'd asked had understood him to be looking urgently to pay for "the cheap whores, the good cheap *whores,* to ride her hard and come fast," and had circulated this misapprehension to everyone in his village and its environs. Which was just as well. Drumont and horses had never really trusted each other.

And would it be so bad if he failed to reach rich Prime's little *fille de joie*, Miss Christmas, until after she'd married? She was only a job, a means to a wage. It was the English demon for whom he had spent three weeks vomiting into the Atlantic and traveled five thousand miles. And he was closing in at long last. He needed to keep his eye on the prey.

At the last stage stop, the new team had been harnessed and the driver was ready to *heeyah* by the time Drumont stepped back up into the coach and sat down next to the talkative man who had ridden with him across Iowa. When the man asked if he was constipated, since he had taken "pretty near a quarter hour in that outhouse," the Frenchman answered that, no, his "pistol chamber was empty," which made the man cackle, since he thought that was a funny foreign way of saying one had successfully shat. But Drumont was only telling the plain truth: before he arrived in Kanesville, he wanted to reload his London pistol with the fresh powder and caps he had bought at Fort Des Moines.

When he first saw Fort Des Moines spelled out, the name had intrigued and amused him: *Fort of the Monks?* It reminded him of the tales his priest on Corsica used to tell about the Crusades. And the old American chatterer in the coach had said that the town of Kanesville was inhabited almost entirely by thousands of Latter-Day Saints, members of a bigamist religious sect embarked on some kind of pilgrimage to their promised land in the American desert. Out in these parts, Drumont thought, Americans were *daft* with piety, like the Crusaders—or like the damned Mohammedans, in Algeria.

It was late in the day as he began to walk the dirt streets of Kanesville. He had the pistol cocked in his right pocket, his hand on the butt and his forefinger on the trigger guard. Who knew where or when Knowles might appear? It did not take long for the news to circulate that a Frenchman was looking for William Whipple to give him money he was owed. And so less than an hour after he arrived, Drumont was told by someone that Billy Whipple had indeed married Prime's beloved little *cocotte*—"Yup, Christmas," the young man told him, "that *was* the girl's name." And much worse, Drumont learned, "Whipple and the new wife and all the rest of them have left here for good."

"They *go?*"

"Uh-huh. They surely did, may the Lord protect them."

"They go when?"

"Wednesday last."

Drumont took a moment to translate and count the days. *Mercredi* . . . *merde*. It was now Monday. Five days ahead of him. He should have stolen a horse in Iowa. Vidocq would have done so. "To *where* they go?"

"Why," said the young man with a smile, "to Zion, of course."

"Zion, this is your desert holy place, far to here?"

"Yes, sir, real far. Ten weeks' travel with the best luck, fourteen or more without it."

"She travel, Miss Christmas, with . . . uh, um . . ." Drumont patted his belly. "*Un polichinelle dans le tiroir* . . . the duck in her oven?"

"She is not with child. Not that you could see, anywise, not a bit. *Skinny* little girl. Pretty, but skinny and pale."

So Prime's great abiding vision was so much misinformation; the fugitive *pute* was not carrying the fool's sperm-blossom. "And the man with them, from *England*? The English friend travel with Miss Christmas and Whipple also?"

"The Englishman?" This fellow had never spoken to Ben Knowles during the three days the gentiles had stayed at his cousin's. Lawrence Grafton came from England, however. "Sure he's with them, and his wife, they're all driving together. Last train of wagons this year."

"Putain de *merde*!"

"Are you cussing at me, mister?"

Drumont was tempted to answer this cow-eyed American by shooting him in the face. But he wouldn't squander his rage on this cretin; it must be used against the vile and devious Benjamin Knowles.

"No, only I have anger to lose my English friend. Not to you."

Drumont's obligations had not been canceled. For all Prime and Pinkerton knew, Priscilla Christmas was still pregnant and unmarried. And for all Drumont knew, she and her husband might be persuaded, either with the carrot or the stick, to end their week-old marriage. Besides, she fucked for money; why wouldn't she *stop* fucking for money? His unending need to find Knowles could still be served by his unfinished assignment to find Priscilla Christmas. "It is possible I go for them in a coach from here? To follow?"

The Mormon smiled again. "No, sir, you cannot. No coaches to there. This here is the end of the line. The States is *over*. To go on west, you need your own horse or your own wheels. That's why it's the *frontier*, don't you know. Rough country. Indian country."

The sun had just set, the hour now *entre chien et loup,* between dog and wolf, a phrase that fit Drumont's own hungry, half-wild mood. He still had $229 in the envelope Pinkerton had given him, enough to reach wherever he needed to go, and to return. Knowles must think himself very clever, finding new ways to discomfort his pursuer at each stage of the chase. Drumont would be forced to ride a horse not for a day or two through the bunghole of America, but to gallop for a week or more through the very shit itself, his own ass a target for the arrows of savages. Well, he was a man of the city, a Parisian, but he was still a Corsican too—he could buy a goddamned horse and a saddle and a camp outfit, the tent and bedroll and knapsack and tin pans, the packets of food and a rifle and more powder and balls.

He was a soldier. He was tough. And this was his purpose.

The next morning, with the help of the postmaster, he wrote the briefest letter to Pinkerton in Chicago—a message from the battlefield—telling him the truth, or most of it, anyway no lies: *Miss Christmas she go west now, far west, & I go after her for you as far as necessary, sir.*

As he trotted from the ferry landing on a track that followed the big river south along its western bank, he was encouraged by the matted grasses. When he reached the village called Bellevue (another encouragement) and passed a new mission church for Christianizing the natives (*precisely* like Algeria), he turned right onto the broad trail west and slowed the horse to a walk to watch the rivers mingle, the shallow blue waters of the Platte disappearing into the deep brown Missouri. *The great John Charles Frémont himself probably stood at this very spot,* Drumont enjoyed thinking, *as he embarked on his explorations of America.* Drumont decided he needed to feel the recoil and smell the sulfur and rejoice in his own tenacious manhood, so he pulled his pistol from its holster in the saddle, cocked it, and fired into the air.

Whereupon the goddamned $115 Mormon mare whinnied and jumped and proceeded to gallop, very nearly dropping Drumont in the grass, and refusing to be reined in until she had run half a mile into the western wilderness.

48

early September 1848

. . .

on the Mississippi River

*B*EN WAS CONTENT to abdicate managerial duties to his dear-loved for the duration of the trip to California. Yet as hard as she pushed to waste no time and move on, all four were freed of the anxieties that had beset them for the last months. Ben no longer fretted about Polly, and Polly no longer fretted about Priscilla or her brother or Ben. Duff was happier traveling down rivers *past* civilization than moseying through towns and cities where unknown enemies might lurk. (On the docks in St. Louis, he'd exchanged a fleeting glance with an army lieutenant in uniform; Duff remembered him as the officer who had handed him a lemon on the beach at Vera Cruz after they'd landed the siege guns.) Skaggs endured the worst of the jimjams after his month of teetotaling, but the coffee improved as they got nearer to the jungles where it was grown.

Skaggs and Polly had been to Washington, D.C., so they had seen slaves. Still, all four travelers were prepared to be appalled by the sight of gangs of them at hard labor deep in slave country, and their expectations were promptly fulfilled. They stared with pity and disgust at the sight of Negroes working on the levees and in the fields of Arkansas and Tennessee. And they could see dozens every mile as they steamed farther south, for the frenzy of the cotton and sugarcane harvests had just gotten under way. They wondered if they might chance to witness some special horror when they passed plantations and docked in cities like Natchez—a whipping, a beating, naked bodies manacled in carts, the choked sobs of husbands and wives sold apart on a slave block—but they did not. Observed from the deck of their shiny new side-wheeler at a fast and steady twelve knots, after a few days the fact of slavery mostly reverted to the abstraction it had been back in New York and London. By the time the boat reached Baton Rouge, they had become not indifferent but accustomed to the sights.

Polly was relieved that they had to remain less than a week in New Orleans awaiting a schooner bound for New Grenada, and Skaggs was ecstasied that the shipping schedules required them to spend nearly a week in this loose, booming, Babylonish city.

He found that watching drunkards in his sober state amused him now almost as much as being drunk had before, and that coffee seemed to enhance his animal charms and fortitude. He sent a letter to his brother Jonah in New Hampshire informing him of his new life—his temperance, his immigration to California, and his passion for astronomy. "I should be unspeakably grateful to you, Jonah, if you agreed to indulge me." He had requested a loan against his eventual inheritance, asking that his brother order from New York a five-inch refracting telescope (preferably one made by Lerebours et Secrétan, Paris), lens (Merz und Mahler, Munich), and mount (Molyneux & Cope, London) and have them shipped to San Francisco.

All four made good use of the metropolitan opportunities. In New Orleans, Ben and Polly shared a bed again. After he discovered that the city was wired to New York, he sent a message to his father's Wall Street associate asking Mr. Prime to inform Sir Archibald, if he would be so kind, of his California plans. Anticipating wilderness living, Polly paid a seamstress to refashion two of her three dresses into overalls by cutting the skirts in half and then sewing them up as loose trouser legs. Duff shopped for the equipage Lawrence Grafton had said they would need at the mines in California—tents, stove, pick, shovels, pans, perforated sheet metal, hammer, jigsaw, work gloves, scales, tweezers. He also bought a leather holster for the Colt's called a Slim Jim, made to clip over his belt, and buckskin shirts for himself and the other men.

On their last day in the city, a hot Sunday, they heard music through the open windows of their hotel and crossed the street to a weekly market, the stalls and carts set up in the corner of a field. All the sellers and nearly all the patrons were Negroes, several hundreds of them, both slaves and free people of color. There for the better part of an hour Polly and Ben and Duff and Skaggs drank lemonade and ate bananas and warm little *bâtard* loaves and listened to a quartet—a fiddler, two banjo players, and a drummer—as they performed one or two familiar tunes in double time, and many others, simultaneously jovial and melancholy, of a type they had never heard. The cries of a vendor carrying a freezer on his head—"Ice crreeeam, ice crreeeam"—formed a chorus to every song.

Polly and Skaggs had resisted the obligatory visit to the river end of Esplanade Avenue, on the opposite side of the Vieux Carré, to gawk at the buying and selling of human beings, and Duff said he had already visited on his own. But Ben was, on this last afternoon, insistent. After fifteen minutes of confused wandering, Polly asked a pair of young nuns on Rampart Street for directions, and one of the sisters informed them that the market was closed, of course, on Sundays—and the other added in a fastidious whisper that the *Spanish* used to permit the slave trade on Sundays. As the nuns walked on, Duff crossed himself.

Each was as happy as he or she had been in years. As summer became autumn—a fact of which they were unaware as they crossed the 30th parallel and prepared to cross the 20th and then the 10th into the latitudes of perpetual August—none was burdened with any doubt about what they were doing, where they were going, or why.

September 1848

. . .

the Platte River Valley,
Indian territory

RISCILLA CHRISTMAS'S MOOD was blithe as well. No distraught soldier had arrived in Kanesville before they left, despite her premonition; perhaps she had misconstrued her own agitation at leaving Polly, or perhaps Duff was the soldier. Billy wondered if she had foreseen an Indian. Small packs of them—Pawnee, Lawrence Grafton said—regularly rode within sight of the wagon train, and last week an Oglala warrior had seemed very distraught indeed when his proposed trade—five buffalo robes for one of the Mormons' brass trumpets—was refused. Perhaps Billy was right. In any event, she had had no more of her daydream shivers during their month on the trail, no gooseflesh divinations or skyward hunches at all.

The Mormons were brittle and guarded people, to be sure, but no stranger than the people of Glee. Their drumming and trumpeting each daybreak struck her more as a frolic than the herald of a military maneuver. The day they left Fort Childs they passed a camped train that included wagons covered in blue and red and bright yellow canvas as well as the customary dirty white. The sight had delighted her, as if she had been surprised by a pack of clowns.

But her favorite sight of the whole month was the balloon. Priscilla had been the first to see it. She had turned round as her gaze followed a small flock of passenger pigeons flying east—she hoped to see one of the enormous flocks of millions of the birds, miles long, that Grafton had said looked "like a great arrow fired by the Lord." When she spotted the shiny purple onion floating above the northeastern horizon, shimmering in the morning sun, she thought for the briefest moment that it was one of her hallucinatory messages, taking a startlingly crisp, clear new form. But it was a real balloon, as big as a bus, and after she called to Billy, he shouted down the line to the rest of the company, and soon scores of Mormons were waving and yelling at the sky behind them. The men in the basket, a pair of rich St. Louis excitement-seekers and their pilot, were many miles distant, unaware of the shouts as their balloon drifted north on the wind into the empty blue.

Priscilla had grown to adore the emptiness. It had never occurred to her before that *horizon* and *horizontal* were, as she thought of it now, parent and child. These plains, here in their baked, brown heart west of Fort Childs, were the very opposite of New York City. The country was pure and clean and simple, devoid of people and buildings and money and fashion and rotten smells. Back in the Five Points, danger and misery were always present, and like everyone else, she had steeled herself to ignore the ghastliness; here in the vacancy of the Great American Desert—a phrase she pronounced gaily—the peculiar dangers (falling from a wagon, getting kicked by a horse or murdered by an Indian's arrow) seemed slight and even manageable in comparison with those of the Sixth Ward. Even the puddles were different—instead of the city's foul bowls of watery blood-and-shit soup, the puddles here were alkali pools that smelled like strong soap. The buffalo gnats that tormented almost everyone else did not bite Priscilla.

Perhaps the frontier was the place she belonged. Perhaps it was the heavenly blue-and-golden emptiness of this country that had finally relieved her of her unnerving shivers and visions. She had never prayed in her life, and agreed with her father that the idea of "asking God for any favor is a *damned* sure path to disappointment." But at the ends of some days this last month, after walking for fifteen miles between two seas of tall brown grass, looking ahead into the sky, hearing only the grass rustling and the burbling music of the train—wagons' squeaks and shakes, oxen's shuffling stomps and thousand tinkling bells—she would realize that her mind had been empty of thoughts for an hour or more, and wondered if those blank, languid, wide-awake spells amounted to prayer.

On this cool late September afternoon, she was in a particularly good humor. Three days ago the featureless western horizon had suddenly sprouted a feature, straight ahead. And although they had not altered their route a bit, she found herself pleased that they were now traveling not on faith but toward a landmark they could actually see—"a thing yonder to draw a bead on," as Billy had said. She had watched it grow taller every day, like the giant's beanstalk in the story, only petrified, or like one of the turrets of the castle in *Phantasmion*. During the last three noonings, while the Mormons and their beasts had rested and eaten, she had drawn pictures of the rock.

Now the tip of its afternoon shadow was touching the front of the train. As they grew close enough to see a herd of bison near the base, the tower's true height became more apparent—over the last few minutes, the petrified giant beanstalk had grown. Priscilla smiled. She now reckoned it must be twice as tall as Trinity Church, which was the tallest building she had ever seen. Why, Priscilla wondered, was such a heart-robbing wonder called Chimney Rock? It was so much weirder and grander than any chimney. Why not Spire Rock?

"Yo, *Whipples!*" shouted one of their fellow travelers from three wagons back.

Priscilla and Billy, walking side by side, turned to look behind them. The two rear sentries, both holding rifles, were riding toward them, flanking a stranger who rode alone. He was an older man, maybe fifty, with sharp, high cheekbones and a long nose. His horse was panting, and covered in sweat.

Drumont had let his hair and beard grow, thinking—like Inspector Vidocq—that a tactical change of appearance would improve his chances of catching Benjamin Knowles unawares. But he had not counted on the guards. The sentries had taken his guns. He was unarmed.

As Priscilla's eyes met Drumont's, he touched the brim of his hat and smiled like an old friend.

He saw that she was not pregnant. She was pretty, he thought, in a wan, raw way, but worth Prime's huge expenditure of lust and money? *Chacun à son goût.* To each his own.

She felt no apprehension at all. The man looked tired and confused, but hopeful, even convivial. She felt sorry for him.

The train, of course, kept moving as they had their interview. Priscilla climbed up to sit on the lazy board of Truman's wagon as Billy and the stranger walked alongside, Drumont leading his horse. The moment he learned that Ben Knowles was not there among them, and was instead a thousand miles away, en route to California by sea to dig gold, the Frenchman's eyes widened and then shut, his neck and shoulders slackened but his jaw tightened, as if he were at once relaxed and agitated. Priscilla had never seen muscles express such disappointment. And then he was silent for a while, as if deep in thought.

"Your baby, he is inside the wagon?"

"We have no child, sir," Billy said. "We have only just finished our honeymonth."

Now he looked even more lost.

"But, sir," Billy asked, "surely you have not come all this distance simply to reunite with Ben Knowles, did you, sir?"

Drumont was so certain he had finally reached his goal that he had neglected even to imagine what he might say under this circumstance, how he ought to dissemble. He was no Inspector Vidocq.

"No," he finally said. "I did not. No . . ."

He was thinking and calculating as quickly as he could manage. If he were able to bribe the couple with Prime's cash and take the girl back to Pinkerton in Chicago, and then to Prime in Manhattan, he would earn his fee, enough money to start a life in the Caribbean . . . or to sail from New York to California, where Knowles was now fixed in place at last. But it would take him another two months to make his way back out of this godforsaken Algeria to New York . . . and then, shit, six months on a ship nearly to Antarctica.

No. He had already crossed the Atlantic. He was already halfway across this empty continent. Only a thousand miles remained between him and Knowles's final destination. Drumont would keep Prime's remaining cash for himself. And he would continue west with these natural fools, and make his way directly to California, right now, by land, on the back of this excitable goddamned mare. It was not ideal or pretty. It was a soldier's decision in the heat of battle.

". . . come to America for going to California also, like Benjamin. For the gold"—he pulled a ten-dollar coin from his pocket—"c'est de l'or? Yes? Now I get gold."

"Traveling by yourself?" Priscilla asked. "From all that I understand, that is not wise."

"They say the Indians never attack a train proper," Billy explained, "only the stragglers, or individuals on the trail alone. And besides, you can't reach California this year for sure."

"Not in this year? Why? It is not so far."

"It isn't the distance," Billy said, "it's the weather. Winter's coming. You passed no other wagons on your ride out here, did you?"

No, he had not. Theirs was the last Mormon train west in 1848, and no prudent emigrants for Oregon or California had jumped off across the Missouri since June. The first snows would fall in a month in the Rocky Mountains, and the Sierra Nevadas would be snowed in by the end of November. Priscilla and Billy were going to spend the winter in the Great Salt Lake Valley, they told Drumont, but in the spring they planned to leave for California to rejoin the others—yes, including Ben Knowles—in their golden camp. If the Mormon elders agreed to it, perhaps Mr. Drumont could join the wagon train and then winter in Deseret. They would surely pay a fair wage to a strong, experienced man to assist in building their utopia . . .

L'utopie. Why was this new insanity infecting every sort of person everywhere? The radical swine in Paris wanted to remake France into their own disorderly *utopie*—along with rich, reckless British *boulevardiers* like Knowles and his laughing friend. New York City was filled with shouting German *utopistes*. Pinkerton (who wasted his time assisting runaway slaves) had told him the woman, Miss Lucking, had left Knowles to search the back settlements for her little *utopie*. And now these Protestant fanatics. *As the whole world goes mad*, Drumont thought, *I am a member of a dying breed, one of the last completely sane men on earth.*

"Thank you very much," he said as he shook Billy Whipple's hand and smiled up at Priscilla. By accompanying them he would be adhering strictly to his assignment from Pinkerton and Prime, would he not? "I should be very much happy to join with you to the Salt Lake."

—+>•◦<+—

50

September 22, 1848

• • •

the Isthmus of Panama, New Grenada

THEY SPENT THEIR first days on the isthmus marveling and ex-claiming and smiling again and again. The trip across the Gulf of Mexico had had its exotic moments—the sailors harpooning dol-phins and catching albatrosses with baited hooks hung from kites—but this dense, humid, impossibly verdant land made Ben feel as if they had been de-posited in a giant greenhouse.

"I have never really been in nature before," he said. "The whole country is a hotbed."

He had read about the jungles of Hindustan and Africa, and listened to his brother Philip's accounts of shooting elephants and commanding natives in the bush of Ceylon. But this forest was more profuse and teeming with blossoms and creatures than he had ever imagined. Squeezed into their canoe, he was reminded of a recurring dream from childhood in which he was crouched in some warm, watery, dark, secret undercroft, immersed in a flux of throbbing sound and colors.

The music of nature was both louder and more complex here than in the peopled and cultivated north. The tropical symphony contained a few famil-iar sounds (woodpeckers' rat-a-tats, quail doves' coos), but many more they had never heard—parrots' chirps, the frantic choruses of howler monkeys' yips, and, one time, the throaty, explosive growl of a jaguar, close enough that it caused Skaggs to cry out and Duff to touch his pistol.

Each of the two native paddlers wore three articles of clothing: a straw hat, a yard of cotton cloth fastened around his hips, and sandals made of black leather and rope. Polly sat in the prow of the long canoe so that she would not be required to stare at their wet, dark, naked backs in the moonlight as they stroked.

She breathed deeply. The perfume—rose and orchid and lime and orange—was extreme, so wildly sweet and rich that whiffs of perspiration and rot were refreshing. Even at night, the light of the moon shone bright enough that the reds and yellows of flowers at the river's edge were visible. "This country is almost *too* vivid," she said. "It seems"—she struggled to recall the French word Ben had used to describe the old French paintings in one of the New York galleries—"rococo?"

"Rococo!" Skaggs said. "Excellent word for it. Another would be outré." As soon as he had glanced at a map in New Orleans, he had seen that the Panamanian isthmus itself, the lithe and brazen curvature of the geography, resembled a recumbent woman in her heedless instant of ecstasy. He had kept that thought to himself. But all night long, from the moment after sunset their long, tubular dugout canoe—their *bongo*—had glided upriver into the narrowing mouth of the Rio Chagres and then into the dense, fragrant, blackish thatch of vines and tendrils, past pendulous yellow bananas pointing down at gaping pink orchids, Skaggs had been unable to see anything but a sexual fantasia. And that had been last night, before daybreak, when they had watched an owl monkey furiously masturbating on the riverbank just beside them.

"To me," Duff said blissfully, "it is all an Eden."

"The Garden of Eden and Gomorrah merged into a single estate," Skaggs said. "Maybe it is no accident that *green* and *obscene* is a rhyme. Perhaps God himself was the first pornographer."

After another hour of paddling toward the brightening horizon, they pulled ashore and made camp in the shade for the day. One did not want to be under the sun on the river during the five hours either side of noon. They slept on beds of ferns, and when they awoke they ate a good stew of hardtack, smoked pork, guavas, and mangoes.

After the meal, Skaggs read. Polly lay on her back and used every one of her pencils (red, yellow, and blue as well as black) to draw a double portrait of a three-foot-long macaw perched just above her and of a toucan on a higher branch. She laughed when she first saw the toucan, its enormous mask of a beak, aqua blue with smudges of orange and crimson and a delicate little frieze of zebra stripes. And flying above the river and the canopy of treetops were dozens of enormous vultures, a slow black cyclone that made the sunshine flicker.

The three white men stripped down to their drawers to swim while one of the Indians stood guard, watching for alligators and crocodiles. When the men came out of the river, Polly noticed that her brother maneuvered to keep his back turned away from the rest of them, but she nevertheless got a glimpse of a crosshatch of red scars as big as fingers. She presumed, correctly, that it was another war wound he did not wish to discuss. Skaggs, shameless about his naked paunch and his drenched, drizzling hair and beard, squinted his right eye shut and muttered curses as he carefully pulled off two leeches that hung from his right earlobe like a big onyx pendant.

"Ahoy, Skaggs! I have never seen a better buccaneer," Ben called out.

Skaggs handed the leeches to the closest Indian. "Vicious little hermaphrodites," he said.

Just then, on the opposite bank, an enormous animal splashed and scrambled noisily out of the river on four legs. Duff thought it was a boar, and Ben said it appeared to be a small hippo of some kind.

"No, no," Skaggs said as he dressed, "*Tapirus terrestrisa*—a tapir."

"I wonder if these boys ever *ride* the tapirs," Duff asked, pointing his chin at the closest Indian, who was currently using a twig over the fire to turn Skaggs's leeches into a snack.

Ben remembered the provocative notion Professor Darwin had practically whispered to him after dinner in Kent, that the tapir might be a kind of ancestor of the horse, and the rhinoceros a more ancient ancestor of the tapir—that nearly all creatures may be, in effect, redrafted and improved editions of earlier species. And then he was reminded of his specimen-gathering task—the professor had asked him to collect and send back to England certain California barnacles.

The tapirs across the river had lain down together on the bank, and Polly took out a sheet of paper to draw the adorable scene. When the animals started copulating, she blushed and shook her head. Skaggs whistled. Duff looked away. For Ben, both the rutting and Polly's embarrassment excited his passions.

The next moment a large raindrop splashed onto her drawing paper, and another. The daily downpour had begun. Everyone scurried close to the trunk of the nearest tree, their giant umbrella. Some of the vultures landed in the boughs overhead, and the tapirs unfastened and trotted into the forest. Polly was relieved that the rain—rather than her own modesty—had caused her to stop drawing, and Ben was pleased that the same act of God caused him to be pressed up close against her. Their fire hissed and steamed.

"La estación de lluvias," said the leech-eating boatman. "Es bueno." Duff translated. " 'The rainy season. It is good.' "

Chicago

CHICAGO SEEMED TO grow louder each month, each week, each night. Allan Pinkerton lay awake in his bed. As always, he was trying to make productive use of his insomnia by sorting and culling the characters and facts from his current investigations, and trying to fit the pieces together. He had come to understand in his four years as a detective that the most confounding cases were nothing like making barrels and buckets, his previous occupation, not a matter of binding together neat, grooved wooden staves within a neat iron hoop. Rather, he had come to think of the most challenging investigations as akin to imagining a new constellation in the sky—putting lines between unrelated stars until a picture appeared. And sometimes, apparently *distinct* cases intersected and overlapped, which only made sense, given that outlaws and troublemakers naturally associated with other outlaws and troublemakers. Tonight, as he stared into a dark corner and listened to his wife breathe, *three* different constellations threatened to merge.

At the behest of his abolitionist associate in New York, Mrs. Gibbs, he had undertaken a private investigation of the fire that burned her block in July. Despite the newspaper stories about the suicidal Bowery b'hoy Francis Freeborn setting the fire at the bakery next door, Mrs. Gibbs smelled a very different rat. She surmised that the arson was actually aimed at *her* by some secret conspiracy of southern slaveholders—that it had been a disguised attack on her house, which was one of the city's Underground Railway stops.

Sure enough, a week ago Pinkerton had learned from a man he knew at the Aetna Insurance Company that Francis Freeborn had indeed led a gang of blackbirders to Mrs. Gibbs's house, where they'd grabbed a slave on the run from Washington, one Elmer Armstrong, and turned him over to Aetna for the $225 reward. Evidently Mrs. Gibbs's suspicions were more than the sinister delusion of an old lady . . .

And now today, through a piece of work for a client in Chicago—a real estate title company engaged by the fire insurance firm that held the policy on the Greene Street bakery—Pinkerton had learned another piece of relevant news. Freeborn had spoken of a grudge against a brothel adjacent to the bakery that had also burned, and the late arsonist's confession was apparently written and delivered for him by a fellow New York fireman with whom he had transacted business in the past. On the morning after the fire that killed Freeborn, a newsboy had spotted his acquaintance dropping the letter at the *Herald*'s front door, and recognized him as "the daguerreian Skaggs's helper," a young man by the name of Duff Lucking.

And *Lucking* was the surname of the woman who had accompanied Priscilla Christmas to Chicago—Mary Ann Lucking, the actress for whom Sir Whoever's second son, Mr. Knowles, had gone searching.

Very curious indeed.

Might these three constellations really constitute some improbable, complex panorama of liaisons and misbehaviors and deceptions? (And why were the insurance companies always so much more nearly omniscient than any police department? Perhaps because they were working for real money.) It made him eager for Drumont's return from Iowa, so that he could question him and Miss Christmas about the young Mr. Lucking. Pinkerton's Frenchman had left Chicago a month ago; he should return any day with the girl.

The client, Mr. Prime, was desperate for hopeful intelligence.

That night, Pinkerton never slept.

September 24, 1848
. . .
the Isthmus of Panama

"THIS DAUNTLESS ANIMAL is my friend," said Skaggs, stroking his mule's withers and leaning forward to speak into its ear. "I hereby promise, my darling, that I shall never ride a high-strung *horse* ever again." He sat up. "A jackass for a father, a mare for a mother, but at least as strong as either and a disposition so far superior to both."

Their progress up the track through the forest of the Darién had been calm and steady. Among the travelers, only the son of a titled British millionaire had been on the back of a mule before—as a child Ben had once ridden for an hour around Hampstead Heath. At the little town of La Venta de Cruces (whose name Duff reluctantly translated as "the sale of crucifixes"), they had left the river and paid a muleteer to take them and their baggage the

last twenty miles across the isthmus to the town of Panama. They had imagined peaks like those they had seen in pictures of the Rockies. But these were
large hills, mere Catskills.

The road, only a few feet wide, consisted of half-ruined cobblestones,
and was covered in deep mud for several rods at a stretch. Osvaldo, the
muleteer, explained to Duff that it had been laid three centuries earlier by
the Spaniards and their local Indian slaves—his very people—as a causeway
for the transshipment to Europe of gold they had taken from the South
American Indians. But before long the English pirates had also used the
road, Osvaldo said, to ambush the Spaniards and steal their stolen gold.

They occasionally encountered other travelers on the road. When they
passed a group of Negroes coming in the opposite direction on foot, Osvaldo said they were headed home for Belize. Ben remembered his last conversation with his father—and his own glib reference to building "a refuge
to save prostitutes in Shepherd's Bush or a parsonage in Belize." *And here I
am with a saved prostitute, near Belize.*

Skaggs was still thinking about mules. "Hybrids. *Hybrids.* I have seen the
future, friends. Why are flower beds in New York and Boston now entirely
bloom, no foliage, gaudy patches of solid color? The science of hybrids,
which lets us improve upon God's repressed palette. The Creoles of New
Orleans, *hybrids,* and to my eye more vigorous and attractive than the pure
French *or* the pure Africans. Our stalwart and happy guide here is no doubt
a great improvement over his hard and dour Spanish grandfather and pi-
geonhearted Indian grandmother. Or consider *mechanical* species—the
steam engine is mated to the omnibus, and what is the result? A triumphant
new species, the railway. Or a newspaper—cross a newspaper with a litho-
graphic print, mate the progeny in turn with an advertising handbill—and
voilà, the magazine, a new species."

I am the indolent and coddled English jackass, Ben thought, *and she the
wild, energetic American mare. Our children shall be of a vigorous new
species, an improvement over us both.* "And the American nation too," Ben
said, "is a hybrid of English and Dutch and Irish and German . . ."

"And also even the colored and Indians, in a way," Duff added.
"Maybe."

"We are a mongrel howling," Skaggs shouted, "the eyes of all people
upon our new American species! *Hybrids.* That's the ticket, friends, for better or worse. Mark my words."

"But the mule," Polly said, "is not a species at all, is it? Because mules cannot procreate?" She was right. "So do you claim, Skaggs, that progress consists in a movement toward the sterile?"

"*La primera gran vista del mar,*" the muleteer said, "*ya estamos allí.*" He reined his animal.

Skaggs nodded, as if he understood Spanish. "I believe Mr. Osvaldo makes the excellent point that since the mules' animal passions are undiminished, their infertility is rather a boon to them." Skaggs had composed a similar argument on behalf of sodomites that not even the most scurrilous New York publications would publish. "The mules' very barrenness makes their lusts for life all the stronger."

"No," Duff said, "what he said was that the vista, the good view, is . . . Well. Here we are."

Duff's translation was suddenly superfluous. Their drove had halted. They were atop a treeless ridge with a clear view for miles across the remainder of the Isthmus of Darién. Far below and still hours ahead was the Pacific Ocean, so much bluer than the Atlantic blue they knew. They all stared, saying not a word.

Ben was the first to speak. "The peak in Darién."

"Yes," Skaggs replied with a smile. " 'Much have I travell'd in the realms of gold, and many goodly states and kingdoms seen . . .' "

Ben joined his recitation of Keats's poem. ". . . 'Round many western islands have I been / Which bards in fealty to Apollo hold./ Oft of one wide expanse had I been told . . .' "

Osvaldo thought the two men were saying a prayer. When he made the sign of the cross, Duff crossed himself as well.

" '. . . Then felt I like some watcher of the skies/When a new planet swims into his ken;/Or like stout Cortez' "—one of the pack mules whinnied loudly—" 'stout Cortez when with eagle eyes/He star'd at the Pacific—and all his men/Look'd at each other with a wild surmise—/ *Silent,* upon a peak in Darien.' "

While they continued down the mountain toward the sea, Osvaldo held a brief discussion with his translator. "It was not Cortés who came here first from Europe," Duff finally said. "It was a different Spaniard."

"We know," Ben and Skaggs answered in unison.

"The poet made an error," Ben explained. "It was Balboa who discovered the Pacific."

"It was in Vera Cruz and Mexico City," Skaggs said, "where *Cortés* and *his* war dogs tore apart the kindly natives . . ."

Duff swiveled around in a frenzy, but saw that his friend had not meant to make any insinuations about Duff's own war service. No, he decided, the gibe was a private message to him from the Lord. Not an hour earlier, Osvaldo had mentioned to Duff an old town hereabouts called El Nombre de Diós—the name of God.

". . . And you know," Skaggs chattered on, "God *punished* the young poet for his mistake. After Keats finished the sonnet he dropped dead, hardly older than you, Duff . . . And for that matter, come to think of it, after Balboa left this peak in Darién, his compatriots convicted him of *treason* and chopped off his head . . . There's your sic transit gloria mundi for you."

Upon arriving in the little city of Panama, they found that no one could say with any certainty when the next northbound passenger ship might arrive. Weeks? A month? Polly's spirits sank, and therefore so did her lover's and her brother's.

But only four days later, as Duff stepped out of Panama City's dark, cool cathedral into the glare of the noonday sun, a boy from the American Hotel rushed up and said that "una *bergantín* para el norte está llegando *ahora*"— a northbound ship was coming into port. The British vessel, sailing from the islands off Peru with a hold full of guano bound for the west coast of America, had docked at Panama briefly to make repairs.

Yes, the severe Welsh captain told them when he came ashore, he did plan to make port at San Francisco, but no, he certainly could not take on four people (including a woman!) for the trip—he hadn't proper accommodations, and besides, the rules from No. 15 Bishopsgate absolutely forbade running passengers, no exceptions.

Skaggs replied that they didn't wish to board his "floating dungyard anyway," and that the ship's destination, John Jacob Astor's Fort Astoria in Oregon, was an ill omen. (Besides, he was in no hurry to leave a cheap city that provided excellent grilled mullet fish called *bobo*, ten-cent pitchers of orange juice, very strong coffee, and half-naked girls taking surf baths in plain sight.) But Ben made another try with the captain.

"Fifteen Bishopsgate Street?" he repeated. "I believe I am acquainted with your employer, Mr. Antony Spencer . . ."

And not five minutes later, as soon as Ben mentioned who he was, and that his father's firm was lately in partnership with Spencer & Company, Captain Owen invited Sir Archibald Knowles's son and his three American friends to come aboard his humble guano barque, as soon as the foremast was fixed, and coast with him up the sunny Pacific shore to California. The ship had plenty of wine and, thanks to a terrapin-gathering stop on Indefatigable Island in the Galápagos, thirty-seven succulent tortoises remaining in the hold.

"And do you know, by the way, sir," the captain asked Ben, "that it was Sir Archibald himself who rechristened my ship this past spring? She was launched the *John Wesley,* but before we cleared Plymouth she became the *Caroline.*"

"Indeed?" Skaggs asked cheerfully, turning to Ben. "After your late King George's homely German slut of a wife, Queen Caroline?"

Caroline had been the name of the fourth and last Knowles child, Ben's baby sister who'd died when he was small. "No," he answered, "I believe Queen Caroline is not the ship's namesake."

51

—→•◄—

October 1848

. . .

in the Great American Desert
and Rocky Mountains

NLIKE THE ALGERIANS, the Indians had a religion that permitted them to booze openly. But like the Algerians, these brown American savages apparently lacked any scruple about intimacies among men. At Fort Laramie, Drumont had watched each of several Indians drink mouthfuls of whiskey in turn and then spit the liquor in a fine stream into the open mouth of a friend.

Lawrence Grafton said the natives seemed to him childish and imprudent and tragic. Take their overdependence on hunting bison. "The Indians are the Irish of the New World," he said, "doomed by their single-minded bisonmania the way the Irish have been undone by their dependence on the potato—and don't both races love liquor and storytelling too much?"

"At least the Irish bury their dead," Truman Codwise countered. All the Saints had been disgusted when the train passed an Indian corpse lying hacked and bloody at the bottom of a large, lonely poplar—a Dakota Sioux, Grafton surmised, defiled by a band of Crow after a natural death and funeral. However, it was not the desecration but rather the Sioux custom of ceremonially arranging their dead in the boughs of trees, out in the open air, which had struck the company as the most unfathomably savage of the savages' habits.

The plains were so devoid of incident that the occasional detritus of death and defeat was not entirely unwelcome. Any remnant of humanity was pretext for conversation. They discussed whether a grave, marked by a sawed length of wagon board with only the letters of a surname, BYARS, burned on with a hot iron tip, contained a man or a woman, an adult or a child. Where they crossed the Sweetwater, they saw a dozen pieces of large, fine furniture dumped like trash by wagoneers who had judged that pulling their tons of oak and mahogany treasure across another river and over the Rockies was, finally, an unaffordable vanity. A large looking glass lay flat, silver side up, in shallow water near the bank, a glowing, dazzling rectangle of reflected ripples and sun and sky. On a sandbar were velvet-upholstered chairs, and two Chinese porcelain pots shattered into pieces. Drumont was reminded of the barricades in Paris last February.

Billy Whipple returned from gathering firewood one evening carrying an enormous dark brown bone five feet long with two-foot-wide fanlike knobs at each end. It was unlike anything any of them had ever seen, and prompted a conversation among the whole camp the rest of the night. Priscilla thought it looked like a bone from the paw of a dragon, and wondered if it might be a giant relative of the little lizards that sneaked across her bedroll at night.

She sometimes felt as foreign as the Frenchman in this company. But she was content to stare in silence at each splendid new sight. The morning she'd first seen snowcapped mountain peaks on the horizon, she'd grinned. The air had been scented with lavender. "This is perfect," she'd said to Billy. She remained happily free of all murky hunches and inexplicable forecasts. She stared up at the sky only to examine a cloud or an eagle or the stars. She got goose bumps the same as everyone else—at night, from the cold.

As they came down the last Rocky Mountain through the canyon of the Wasatch Front into the valley, a light, slow snow was frosting the pine boughs and red sandstone ridges. Back in New York City, winter had always been a special tribulation. But here, even the season of dying was gorgeous.

"We arrive now?" Drumont asked, waving toward a distant fort, miles of straw-covered fields, and, on the far western horizon, the shore of a vast lake. "This is your place?"

52

October 20, 1848
. . .
Chicago

HE LAST LETTER Pinkerton had received from the loquacious Mr. Prime was six pages long. All of the man's roundabout language, however, had amounted to a single command: *I no longer care about the girl, but*—"as for my outstanding charitable proposal"—*I very much want you to retrieve my offspring.*

By contrast, Drumont's latest communiqué from Iowa—"Miss Christmas she go west now, far west, & I go after her"—carried brevity to an extreme. Somewhere in the two million trackless miles of the western half of North America, a Frenchman in his employ, supposedly a detective, was chasing after a fourteen-year-old New York City whore, supposedly pregnant.

But in fact, Pinkerton thought he knew exactly where in the "far west" everyone—Priscilla Christmas, the baronet's son and his beloved, now Drumont—was bound. Since news of the gold had appeared in the *Tribune,* it seemed as if half the men his age in Chicago were scheming to go west, right away by steamship to Central America or overland in the spring. He felt the pull himself. What robust young man would be numb to it? He had fled Britain and traveled thousands of miles west to find fortune and freedom in America. If not for his own babies, and if not for his own schemes to give up public policing in favor of private investigations, Allan Pinkerton himself would be en route to San Francisco.

It was merely a hunch about all of them going to California, but it was a sensible one. And today he had developed another suspicion. He was being paid to track only Priscilla Christmas and her hypothetical infant, and he didn't care about most of her companions—not the Englishman nor the actress nor the daguerreian, all of whom had disappeared from New York around the same time. But he had his own worries about Miss Lucking's untoward brother, Duff, and his intentions in California.

Duff Lucking had been an accomplice of the late arsonist Francis Freeborn. It seemed likely to Pinkerton, therefore, that Duff Lucking had also been part of Freeborn's June blackbirding crew at Mrs. Gibbs's house. And when Pinkerton had looked into Lucking's past, he'd discovered that the boy had been one of the San Patricios in Mexico—that is, a righteous scoundrel with a violent history.

Yesterday the *Tribune* had printed an article about the appearance among the gold miners in California of Negroes, fugitives as well as freedmen. They were starting to gather in their own camps—Negro Bar, Negro Slide, African Bar, Nigger Tent, Nigger Hill. And so now Pinkerton had an awful boding that Duff Lucking was on his way to California not only in search of gold but also of runaway slaves to capture or kill. It was just another hunch, a hypothesis, but it was certainly worth forty cents' postage to test out.

"Dear Mr. Drumont," Pinkerton wrote in care of the post office at San Francisco, "I trust this letter finds you well after your long journey west. I write concerning some slight alterations of your previous assignment. Mr. P— of New York no longer demands the return of Miss Christmas herself, but his interest in rescuing and returning any offspring remains strong . . ."

in the Pacific off California

THEY HAD VISITED the pilothouse of the *Caroline* often during the trip from Panama. The inescapable ammoniac fumes were almost tolerable there. The price, though, had been listening to Captain Owen's disquisitions on guano. ("Each bird, you see, drops an ounce of dung each month . . . earning your father's enterprise eleven pounds sterling per hundred birds per year . . . plucky Peruvian tykes pick it up off the ground like garden candy at an Easter party . . .") But now, at last, a new subject presented itself.

"Port the helm," Captain Owen ordered the man at the wheel, then turned to Benjamin Knowles and his party and pointed over the starboard bow toward the rocky shore. "Frémont's Golden Gate."

Polly smiled at Ben. "Here we are," she said.

Pushed by a good breeze from the west and a tidal current flooding through the rocky gap, the *Caroline* fairly flew into San Francisco Bay. John Charles Frémont had named the strait the Golden Gate only a few years earlier, before he was an international celebrity, and before any white man knew that the hills and streams nearby were fraught with gold.

It was late afternoon, and the light on the hills enclosing the bay was tawny and resplendent—that is, golden. They saw red deer wandering the hillsides, and tents pitched above the town. The ship sailed in and out of a cloud hovering just over the water.

Frémont had renamed the cliffs, and last year other Americans had renamed the town San Francisco, as the Americans named and renamed almost every place when they arrived.

"The Mexicans called it Yerba Buena," Captain Owen said.

Duff translated. " 'Good grass.' " He was eyeing the adobe buildings on the shore to the right. The captain said it was the *presidio*, which the U.S. Army had occupied since the start of the war. "It means fort in Spanish," Captain Owen said, although Duff knew the precise translation was 'military prison.' This presidio was nearly empty, though. Most of its soldiers had deserted, and headed for the hills.

To Duff and the others, San Francisco appeared sweet and soft, downright luscious, especially after living for weeks (as Skaggs had said more or less daily) "cooped up in a hundred-foot cask atop a million pounds of bird shit." They watched cloud shadows race ahead of them over the bay and across the town and the hills behind, like an armada in a wonderland where their earthbound barque was bringing up the rear.

"Such perfection," Ben said.

"Yes indeed," Skaggs agreed, "assuming I shall be able to dine tonight on a meat other than tortoise. But in any event, if it should turn out *not* to be the perfection of which we have dreamed, please spare me that truth for as long as possible."

Captain Owen remarked on the sixteen ships at anchor, twice as many as he had ever seen there before. He was even more surprised to spot the clipper *Curious*, which he had seen leaving Valparaíso, in Chile, three months earlier, bound for San Francisco and then Canton. Why was she still here? It did not occur to him or to anyone else aboard the *Caroline*, as they furled their own sails, that most of the vessels had been abandoned at their moorings by the men who had sailed them through the Golden Gate last week or last summer, that the crews and even most of their officers had scrambled off into the enchanted woods and ravines like overexcited boys, running away from regular employment and duty and order to camp out and play at being back country loafers, to run wild, live free, and get very rich very quickly.

Polly had finally worked out her reply to Skaggs and Ben. "As for finding perfection," she said, "I believe the task is to use our good sense and good fortune to *make* our part of the earth more perfect. Is that not, after all, the idea behind our—the foundation of, of the whole . . ." As she searched for the words, she fluttered both hands toward land.

Ben finished her sentence: "Of America."

"Yes."

Part

FOUR

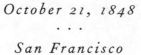

53

October 21, 1848

. . .

San Francisco

*I*N THE DARKNESS of the liquor and gambling saloon in the City Hotel, a homesick diner noticed Ben's accent (as well as Polly, the only woman in the place) and joined their table. Jory Hardison, a vicar's son from Cornwall, had been second mate on the clipper *Curious*. Along with half his crew, he had jumped ship almost as soon as they'd docked at the beginning of August. He had spent his last two months at the diggings, and had now returned to San Francisco for the first time to buy winter provisions and sleep on sheets and eat restaurant meals for a few days. He answered all of the neophytes' questions clearly and straightforwardly. His absolute lack of hyperbole made the account all the more amazing. His sourness and doubts only kindled their excitement.

The area around Sutter's Mill, he said, was "completely dug out over the summer, done and finished." And the gold region was both more distant (a week's ride) and much larger than they had understood before. It was no longer a "small zone around the mill," as Lawrence Grafton had said, but a fifty-mile-wide swath of central California "half the way up to Oregon and south all the way to Santa Barbara by now, I don't doubt."

"Why, that's twice as large as the Home Counties," said Ben, referring to the south of England, encouraged by the expanse Hardison had intended to seem daunting.

The Spanish names pleased Duff. Sacramento meant "sacrament."

"Santa Barbara?" he asked Hardison hopefully. Saint Barbara was his patron saint.

"Spanish town," Hardison said. "With a fort full of American soldiers," he added.

The essential choice for miners, he explained, was between the hard labor of "freezing your shins digging and sifting river gravel ten hours a day for the gold dandruff, as I do," or else hunting in the mountains "on the risky gamble that you'll come across the lode." By common reckoning, he said, there were fifty new miners a day arriving "to find your fortune before you do," and the rainy season was about to hit, which would make the work much more difficult. "And it's getting almost as deadly as London around here," he added. Two weeks earlier, the region had had its first murder—a miner living inside Sutter's Mill itself, stabbed to death by "an Irishman too drunk and too stupid to find gold."

Hardison explained that during his first weeks at his first placer claim, working alone and with only a pan, he had taken no more than an ounce and a half of color a day and sometimes less than an ounce. Ever since he and three other men of the *Curlous* had formed a company and constructed a good, large cradle, however, they had been rocking out an average of a pound every day—no less than eleven or twelve ounces, and occasionally two pounds. *Placer,* he explained, was the Mexican word for a patch of ground that had gold buried in it.

"But *placer,*" Duff said, pronouncing it as a rhyme with "*affair,*" "in Spanish means 'please,' 'to be pleased.' "

"That does not surprise me," Hardison said, nodding ruefully. "Another troublesome feature of this place." He lowered his voice. "One cannot even trust these Mexicans to tell the truth about their own *language.*"

Ben realized that none of his party knew the fundamental fact concerning their prospective enterprise. "How much, sir, is an ounce of gold worth here, in dollars?"

"Ah well, there you are. Not as much as it was even in August. It was nineteen dollars when we started at it, but here today at Mellus & Howard"—a San Francisco dry-goods emporium so new that the mortar between the bricks was still wet—"they're giving no more than *sixteen* an ounce. There's too many of us now taking out too much of the stuff. Flooding the market, as they say. Twice as many men back at the mines now as when we started."

Skaggs was calculating and recalculating quantity times price . . . "*What?*"

he finally cried. "*Two thousand dollars'* worth of gold every *week?*" Anyone but an Astor would have been pleased to earn two thousand dollars in a whole year.

"That is shared four ways, sir," Hardison said.

"With a capital outlay," Ben said in the excited tone his father would assume when presented with some unusually attractive deal of business, "of practically nothing. And an expenditure on labor of zero."

Hardison was shaking his head. "Our rocker is large, and would cost thirty ounces to buy—you will find that everything, even ordinary timber and nails, comes terribly dear out here. Even I now own a *four-ounce donkey.* Up from three when I bought him."

For an instant they imagined an itty little rodent-sized pack animal, until they realized all prices here were denominated in ounces of gold.

"Up in the stores around the mill now they get three for a shovel, and nearly that for boots or a shirt. And yes, it is true, as you say, that our little company pays wages to no one," Hardison continued, "but many do employ Indians, and unless you're a sheriff"—he had already described the jailer from San Jose who'd arrived in the gold fields with ten shackled Indian convicts to mine his placer—"half an ounce of wages to each digger a day is no pigwidgeon, now, is it?"

"But, sir," Ben said, "do I understand you to say that, as an *average,* you and each of your partners has been digging up and keeping at least fifty dollars apiece, every day—"

"Not on Sundays."

"And occasionally," Polly asked, "one hundred twenty-five dollars to each one of you for a day's work?"

"Yes, sometimes, but in two months we've had no *very* large nuggets at all. Not like some. Why, Saturday last at Tuttletown, a little girl, the daughter of a Californian, picked a dirty *seven-pounder* out of her creek. No such luck has come our way."

Hardison excused himself, he said, since he was no gambler and "dreaming in a real bed" was one of the main purposes of his visit to the city. In the morning, he would start the return trip early to Timbucktoo, his camp on the Yuba River.

"Do you remember," Polly asked her brother after Hardison had gone, "the stories we read to William and Grace in bed that first winter in the city? The Brothers Grimm and the Andersen?"

It was an odd question to pose at midnight in a liquor saloon. Nearby a pair of Chilean sailors were placing dollar bets on which of the two could drink more, and they were now up to five dollars and five brandies apiece—*cinco piscos*. Next to them two men were gambling on a dice game called chuck-a-luck, and beyond them a table of five was playing poker. The players bet not with coins or bills but with pinches of gold dust that each plucked almost daintily out of his leather purse or glass jar—their "*pokes,*" Hardison had called them.

The four New Yorkers had each had a drink themselves to celebrate their safe arrival in El Dorado, and Skaggs was treating himself to a smoke as well.

"Of course I remember reading the storybooks," Duff replied. The first winter in New York was the twins' last on earth, and Polly and Duff were only moments out of childhood themselves. "I loved them," he said, not sure if he meant the tales or the babies or both. "Why do you ask?"

"Because everything I have heard and seen since we arrived here," she said, "*all* of it"—a thousand ordinary men each plucking a banker's income from the dirt, tailors and farmers and seamen making gambling wagers like pashas with gold powder, a child finding a golden ball in a creek, three-ounce donkeys, Timbucktoo, a river called Yuba, chuck-a-luck, a ship's cabin pulled onto a lot down the street and turned into a store, the witchy Mexican woman greasing and combing her hair in the Portsmouth Square plaza, the breezes scented with piñon and bay and sweet shrub, the sunlight that made shadows inky black and colors exceptionally bright, *all of it*—"is perfectly fantastic. Every scene here could be from a fairy tale." She looked around at all three men. "A hundred dollars a day sifting golden dandruff!"

" 'The Midas Touch,' " Duff offered.

"Or 'The Children of Hameln,' " said Ben, thinking of the deserted streets outside, "the story in which the children are lured away into the mountains forever."

"That was a real historical incident, you know," Skaggs said. "The children of Hameln actually did leave en masse one summer day. The story came to *seem* imaginary only when the Grimms put it in their book of fictions."

Unlike the boys and girls of Hameln, San Franciscans were already starting to return. Because there were now so many miners desperate to spend money on pans and blankets and beefsteak and whiskey, the invisible hand—and wasn't *that* a fairy-story term of art?—had pulled the departed shop owners and saloonkeepers back behind their counters and cash drawers. The weekly *Californian* was about to resume publishing. And the City Hotel was not only open again but full—Ben and Polly took the last room, in the cellar, and Duff and Skaggs were paying a dollar apiece to sleep on their bedrolls in the ten-pin bowling alley across the plaza.

Polly had not been thinking of King Midas or the Pied Piper. Rather, it was a certain Hans Christian Andersen story that had occurred to her as she watched and smelled Duff light and relight Skaggs's cigar with a sulfur match. "Do you remember 'The Tinder-Box,' brother, from the Andersen book?"

Duff wondered if Polly had learned mind reading from Priscilla Christmas. He had not thought of "The Tinder-Box" for years—not until one day last fall, when he was making his way home on foot from Mexico into Texas, carrying his knapsack, and passed an enormous hollow oak tree in which a dead campfire was smoldering. The hero of "The Tinder-Box" is a young soldier making his way home from the wars on foot with only his knapsack. He encounters a witch who sends him into a magical hollow tree, where he fills his pockets and knapsack with gold and retrieves the witch's missing tinderbox. Back outside in the world, he cuts off the witch's head and discovers that her tinderbox allows him to summon magical dogs to do his bidding. They fetch him endless gold and chase off the king so that the soldier can marry the princess and become king himself.

"I never understood that story very well," Duff finally said. He had considered the soldier's murder of the witch and resulting windfall unjust. "It lacks any moral. Stories are to have morals—like with the Pied Piper, taking revenge against the town for his unpaid debt."

"Your tale has a German moral," Ben said. "Seize what you wish by force of arms, without remorse."

"Perhaps one day, in some future century," Skaggs said, taking a long pull on his cigar, "all of this—the gold, the easy fortunes—will be considered a *fairy tale* of El Dorado, nothing but make-believe."

"And the four of us," said Polly, "characters in the story?"

Skaggs smiled. "Minor characters."

54

late October 1848

· · ·

the Sacramento River Valley
and the gold region

*J*OHANN SUTTER HAD been the first white man to settle in the
Sacramento River Valley that formed the heart of Upper California. It was in Sutter's millrace that his employee had found the
first flake of gold nine months earlier. And it was on Sutter's
schooner that Ben, after he happened to meet the old man at the City Hotel
and charm him by speaking German and displaying "the fine tender manners of *ein Edelmann,*" a gentleman, cadged a ride up the Sacramento River
to his fort for himself and his three companions.

The first afternoon on the river, Duff was kneeling on one side, mum-
bling his rosary and staring down at the water as it began to boil and glisten.
He stood, thinking he was witnessing a miracle. But then he realized that it
was fish churning the surface, hundreds of red and silver sea beasts swimming upriver. Polly and the others were on the deck not far away, chatting
and reading.

"*Fish,*" Duff shouted. "A mob of furious fish!"

They all rushed over to look. Their two fellow passengers, a Scottish
miller and a storekeeper who had just arrived by sea from Oregon, joined
them at the railing.

"I believe," Skaggs said, "the correct term is 'school,' not 'mob.' "

Ben had fished for spawning salmon with his father and grandfather, and
explained what they were now watching—the years at sea, the return to

fresh water, swimming for miles against the current in order to reach the stream where they were born and to produce offspring.

"How fatiguing," Skaggs said.

Ben recalled his father telling him that once the salmon hit fresh water, their throats shut tight, so that they are unable to feed. To make them take the bait on a hook, Archibald Knowles had said, "one must annoy them" so that they bite instinctively. "They cannot eat," Ben said, "but they are powerless not to try."

"How awful," Polly said as she looked out over the jostling, speeding mass of salmon.

"How very like us all," said Skaggs.

"And after they spawn," said the miller from Scotland, "these Pacific salmon die, every one of them. Not like ours back home. These are all in such a hurry to swim to their doom."

"How sad," Polly said.

"Or heroic," replied Skaggs, "in a Sisyphean way." He glanced at Duff to see if he would jot down *Sisyphean*, but Duff now wrote mainly biblical verses in his vocabulary journal. He simply stared at the water.

"I find it monstrously pointless," Polly insisted, shaking her head.

"Must it be one or the other," Ben asked, "*either* heroic or pointless?"

Later in the trip, Captain Sutter, as he preferred to be called, told Ben that the stupid salmon reminded him of the raving idiots rushing into his valleys and hills to find gold. *Ach,* this *Sinneslust,* he said to Ben, was a curse as much as a blessing for him. He had tried to deal fair and square with "our diggers," as everyone called the local Indians, by signing a lease (at two cents per acre per year) for the mining rights around his now-famous sawmill—but Colonel Mason, the damned American military governor, was insisting the Maidu Nisenan had no title to the land. Since the spring, Sutter told Ben, both as brag and complaint, he had let space in the fort to a hotel and two dozen new stores, but now he was going broke faster than ever. He could manage to keep only two mechanics in his employ, and only by paying them a week's wage every day to fix wagons and shoe horses. Even his Maidu laborers were quitting to go pick out the shiny bits that had been sitting there untouched for the hundred centuries they had inhabited the land. Half the able-bodied Indians were out digging for gold! Squaws as well as men! The world these last months had become like a terrible dream, he told Ben, *ein Tollhaus der Möglichkeiten,* a madhouse of possibilities . . . which is why his eldest son, whom he had not seen since the boy was seven, had just arrived to help sort out the affairs of New Switzerland, as Sutter called his eighty square miles. The boy, he said, was already sketching a true town— *Sacramento City* would sprout *here,* at the wharf, this *embarcadero,* he told Ben as the schooner docked. Sutter invited the young Englishman and his friends to attend a feast for the boy's twenty-second birthday.

But Ben had already endured days of Sutter's grandiose, self-pitying, half-German gab. Polly called him "King Lear without the charm," and Skaggs was threatening to take Duff's revolver and "kill the boozy old Switzer myself." For his part, Duff was unnerved by the sight of several young army officers camped out on the bank of the Sacramento near Sutter's compound.

"We are in a terrible hurry to get to the mines," Ben told Sutter as they reached the landing.

"*Ach,* like all the rest," Sutter said.

THEY SPENT THE last Sunday of October in a wagon, Polly up front with the Mexican driver, her three companions sitting in the back between barrels of flour, riding across a brown plain at dawn and then up into the splendidly autumnal Sierra foothills.

As they approached the town of Coloma, the driver nodded toward a structure on the south bank of the American River. "El Molino," he told Duff. It was Sutter's sawmill, where the first gold had been discovered. They all stared in silence as the wagon passed and then turned south.

"I feel as though we are entering the Holy Land," Skaggs said, "and seeing the manger in Bethlehem." Duff made the sign of the cross.

The road became narrower and rougher. Duff asked the driver about the large burned-over patches of ground. "La quemadura, de los indios," he said, "cada año. Fertiliza la tierra—la destrucción causa la creación, ¿ésa es la vida, entiende?"

"*Sí,* claro," Duff answered, nodding emphatically in agreement. The man had told him that the local Indians burned the dried grass and flowers and shrubs every year to encourage new growth in the spring. He had said that destruction causes creation.

They arrived finally at Old Dry Diggings—"diggins," as it was pronounced locally, and called "old" even though the first gold had been discovered there only a hundred days earlier. Like all of the gold hunters' communities, it was not called a town or a village but a camp.

Now they saw why. Like the Mormons' towns on the Missouri River, Old

Dry Diggings was conceived as temporary, a frontier limbo in which to sleep and eat only until all the gold was snatched up, and then abandoned. But unlike the Mormons' sturdy log cabins and orderly streets on the prairie, this place made no bones about being ephemeral. Everything was jury-rigged.

There were two basic sizes of lodging, a smaller type for one or two men, the larger housing six or seven. And there were two basic modes of construction as well. The more regular were canvas tents, roped and staked approximately square, perhaps seventy-five in all—some army-issue, some the kind that hunters and anglers used in the States. The other sort—hut? bush-harbor? hermitage? hovel?—was more various and numerous. There were a score of lean-tos constructed from tree limbs, one having a gabled roof of blood-spattered oxen hides. For another, a Conestoga wagon cover was stretched out and nailed to the trunks of three trees to form a ceiling, then a second piece of canvas was nailed a few inches above it and covered with piñon boughs to make a roof. A tepee consisted of wagon axles and barge poles set on end and wrapped with rugs, buffalo robes, and an American flag. And a ladder led down to a cave home that had been dug out of the earth.

The Diggings appeared to be as populous as San Francisco and as densely packed as Manhattan, yet the dwellings were placed across the hillsides and ravines according to no discernible geometry, as if the only rule of planning had been to exhibit no plan whatsoever. It was squalid, but an energetic, festive, wholly intentional squalor.

When their wagon came to the center of the camp, they saw in one panoramic view a majority of Old Dry Diggings' population. It was the Sabbath, and hundreds of men in their twenties and thirties milled about on the grass and dirt and rocks, strolling, sitting, drinking, smoking, spitting, chatting, whittling, writing, reading, wrestling, gambling at faro, pitching horseshoes. A bonfire burned. One large group was bowling on a packed-earth alley using eight-pound cannon shot rolled at pins whittled from split pinewood. An accordionist and a trumpeter played. Everyone was tanned, and in a few cases permanently brown—Mexican, Chilean, Polynesian, Negro. Nearly everyone wore a beard and soft slouch hat or no hat at all. And not one—none of the beachcombers and quondam millwrights and truckmen nor even any of the former merchants and schoolteachers and lawyers—wore a necktie or buttoned collar. Dozens were in their undershirts, and many were barefoot.

The new arrivals stared. And the residents of Old Dry Diggings, as soon as they noticed Polly, were returning the stares.

Ben's fondest boyhood fantasies had merged and come to life. He was Sir Ivanhoe arriving with Lady Rowena and Friar Tuck at Robin Hood's secret camp, but this Sherwood Forest was on the American frontier and filled with rollicking Davy Crocketts and Natty Bumppos.

"I have never imagined that such a place existed," he said. "It is so utterly ad hoc. So . . . so . . ."

"Improvised," said Polly.

"Our protean, plastic nation in a nutshell," Skaggs said as he climbed over the cargo in the wagon, "this ad hoc, improvised, shining squatters' city of trash upon a hill." He finally heaved himself out of the back of the wagon to earth.

The driver had stopped his team near the camp's one quasi-building, a grocery consisting of two adjacent tents with a shed built to join them. It was operated by an apparently well-liked man called Dutch John, who was also known as "the Jew."

A crowd formed around the wagon. When Polly stood and they saw that her skirt was in fact a pair of billowy green trousers, their murmuring rose audibly. As she prepared to step down from the driver's box, she looked out over her audience, smiled, nodded—and gave one quick, modest wave acknowledging them. "*Hurrah,* miss!" a young man shouted, and then the whole assembly applauded.

THE REST OF the afternoon was spent in a ravine a quarter mile away, at a gold-hunting tutorial conducted by several good-natured and very eager volunteers. Among the squad of teachers were two "old-timers"—a pair from Sonoma who had started panning a stretch of Weber Creek on the Fourth of July, one of them explained, "back before this horde of Johnny-come-latelies showed."

The ground at the bottom of the ravine was upturned as far as they could see, not like furrows plowed in a field, but as if a thousand tiny graves had been dug. They watched one of the miners sink a new placer hole, which appeared no more complicated than preparing to plant a rosebush or set a fence post. They watched another man demonstrate panning, which amounted to staring into a pie pan and swirling an inch or two of water and sand and gravel in order to separate any bits of color from the gray slurry, and looked to Polly and Duff like their childhood game of making mud-pebble soup.

And they watched three of the men demonstrate a rocker, which was like a large wooden thresher mounted on a cradle, with kernels of gold instead of grain meant to shake out through the holes drilled in the bottom.

"How remarkable," Ben said, by which he meant *How utterly unremarkable*. On a page of Duff's journal, Polly carefully sketched the apparatus as the men talked.

Lawrence Grafton had told the truth. Gold mining in California was hardly "mining" at all. It was more like gardening or washing. There was no racket of blasting and furnaces, no arcane skills or great and costly machines. The reason was simple. The iron that capitalists extracted from the Luckings' Clove Valley and the copper Ben's father's company took out of the Cornish moors sold for less than $50 a ton. Gold, on the other hand, was worth $400,000 a ton. A man using his own two hands could dig out only a bit of gold, but those bits could make him rich.

Ben asked how far it was to Weber Creek.

"You're standing in it, pard," a man called Schoolcraft said.

"The smaller streams dried up two months back," explained his friend Hipwood, "although with winter coming, that's the rainy time, so we'll have water again, more'n we can stand."

Since all of these men had arrived in California during the previous two years and none had ever searched for gold before last spring, they were all equally expert.

"The thing is," said another, "it'll be harder and easier in winter. Harder 'cause of being drenched in the rain all the time, but easier too 'cause you got the rivers and creeks running again."

The youngest of the miners, a boy named Anson, slapped his own cheek. "The god*damned* mosquitoes go away in winter, though," he said in a New York accent. "Excuse me, ma'am."

"You do need water to get the gold," said Barney, one of the men from Sonoma and the de facto leader of the group.

A little later, he happened to spot something in the dark muddy rind on one of the rocker's iron cleats. "Looks as if somebody," he said to his friends, "got sloppy at the end of yesterday." He licked his forefinger and touched it to the mud, then reached over to touch and gently rub his dirty finger against one of Polly's—leaving a tiny shimmering yellow grain on her fingertip.

"A flake of *gold*," she practically sang.

Ben and Duff and Skaggs leaned in to have a closer look. The dusky five o'clock light made the metal appear particularly bright.

"Naw, not a real *flake*," said Barney. "A fleck, more like."

As they started the hike back to the center of camp, the men explained the nomenclature that had been adopted over the summer. After dust (or "flour") came specks, then larger flecks, *then* flakes. There were small pickers—"You can pick a picker up with your finger and thumb"—nice pickers, and big pickers. All sizable nuggets were also known as plinkers.

Skaggs suggested that for clarity's sake, they might contrive distinct names for each of the two larger classes of pickers, such as "smidgens" and "boogers."

"Why, I don't expect the magistrate out here would approve of names like those, Skaggs," Duff said.

"Ain't no magistrate or sheriff or *alcalde* or any other such a person out here," said Barney's partner, George.

"There's just . . . us," said young Anson.

"Really? You have no formal governance," Ben asked, "no oversight by the county—"

"No county yet."

"—or by the state of California—"

"No state, neither."

"We call a meeting every fortnight or so," George explained, "like the big camps all do, and change any rules we need to change about sharing water, or choosing a new claims recorder when the old one starts whining and whining about the chore of it"—one of the other men slugged his shoulder—"or whatever such matters as that."

Near a long ditch that the newcomers thought was another zone of placer diggings but which turned out to be one of the camp's latrines, Skaggs spotted a flag hanging from an oak limb. It had a picture of a bear, just like the one he had seen waving in the Mexican War victory parade on Broadway. Barney and George said the flag was the very one they had raised at Sonoma during Captain Frémont's all-American anti-Mexican revolution that had briefly established the California Republic during the summer of 1846.

"Officially," Barney said, "it's the army in charge of things here, officially."

The cheerful backwoods anarchy had made Duff drop his guard completely, so this news came with an extra jolt. "The *army?*" he barked.

"Uh-huh. We've seen some of the officers, the big colonel—"

"Mason," George said.

"—and his West Point boy with the Indian name—"

"Sherman, William Tecumseh Sherman," George said.

"—who came through here in July on their inspection tour."

Duff filled with dread.

"But I believe they've all gone back to Monterey," a Mr. Queen said, "although Sherman and another one of 'em are backing a new store at the mill."

"As long as they aren't any of them *mining,*" said Hipwood, "or out here trying to *officer* us."

The army is not out here. Duff relaxed as quickly as he had become agitated. *Thank you, Lord, you are my strength and my shield; in you my heart trusts. So I am helped, and my heart exults, and with my song I give thanks to you . . .*

"Mr. Hipwood," Barney explained, "and young Anson, and Schoolcraft and Queen," he said, pointing at four of his fellows in turn, "are all just mustered out of Colonel Stevenson's regiment, the New York Seventh—volunteer soldiers in the late war. They count as seventy of us in all at Dry Diggins these days."

Duff winced. When he'd sailed out of New York Harbor for Mexico two Septembers ago, he had passed the regiment's ships at anchor—the *Loo Choo* and the *Susan Drew*—readying to leave for California.

Perhaps Hipwood and Anson and Schoolcraft and Queen had seen him then. And now they were here, all around. *There was no escape.* His pistol was in the luggage back at Dutch John's store.

"My brother served in the regular army in Mexico," Polly said, thinking that Duff's nervous look was a result of embarrassment, "but he returned to his real life last winter."

Let it be done, Duff thought, *take me, scourge me, crucify me.* "Lucking, Private Horatio Duff," he said, "Company A, Corps of Engineers. Buena Vista, Cerro Gordo, Vera Cruz . . ." He took a breath. "And Mexico City."

"Well, sir, what do you know," said Barney with a trace of a smirk as he grabbed Duff's right hand and wrist—not to thrash or arrest him, but to offer thanks and, by the way, to tease his four friends. "At long last, I have the privilege of meeting an *authentic* hero who risked his life in the *true* war against Mexicans bearing arms."

During the five months Colonel Stevenson's regiment of volunteers had been at sea, the war in Upper California had been fought and won without their slightest participation.

"Oh, *gas,* you old dope," Anson said to Barney. "The Seventh Regiment served *proudly.*"

Although the New York soldiers had arrived too late in California to fight the war, they had been among the first Americans in gold country. In the spring, one of Stevenson's men had literally stumbled across a twenty-four-pound piece of gold on the bank of the Mokelumne River. So they were doubly lucky.

The thousand men of New York's other regiment of volunteers, however, had sailed directly to Vera Cruz aboard the brig *Empire* and the barque *Jubilee,* and most of them had died in Mexico.

Life was all in the timing.

Duff felt wobbly from his second wave of fear and relief in as many minutes. Like Grafton and his Mormon Battalion, he realized, these men here had been in California for the duration, and so knew nothing of the war in Mexico proper, and probably nothing of the San Patricios and the courts-martial and hangings and brandings and whippings in Mexico City. *I hank you, Lord.*

"The Seventh Regiment of *New York* Volunteers?" asked Skaggs. "Yes? Why, all four of us are Gothamites as well!"

Hipwood said that Anson and he were from Brooklyn Heights and Charlton Street, respectively, and that another two dozen of the regiment here in camp were from New York City. "Maybe you boys are even acquainted with some of them."

"You never know," said Skaggs.

You never, never know, Duff thought.

As they approached Dutch John's, Anson walked double time to catch up with Polly.

"Miss Lucking," he said, "I have a proposal to make that I hope is not too impertinent. If you wished to take in washing for money, I would pay a dollar per article, and, also, ma'am? If you wanted to bake a gooseberry pie, I would pick the berries and be more than glad to pay ten dollars for it."

"Anson here struck a bonanza on Tuesday," Barney explained. "He's dug out eighty ounces."

"Hey, eighty-*six,*" said Anson, now grinning.

The boy had unearthed thirteen hundred dollars during the last five days, as much as his father, a master house-joiner in Brooklyn, had earned in the last two years.

DUFF INSISTED THEY pitch their tent a quarter mile beyond the main encampment, ostensibly to secure Polly's privacy from the wanton glances of five hundred lonely, goatish men. But his companions also thought they understood Duff's strong disinclination to mingle with so many former soldiers—that he'd had his fill of military camp life in Mexico, and did not approve, as he said sincerely, of deserting one's army post on account of mere greed.

They remained at Old Dry Diggings only two nights and a day, long enough for Ben and Skaggs to gather intelligence about other camps and the latest discoveries of gold so that they could determine the best place to establish their own community. They studied a map of the region and discussed their options and plans all day Monday, feasting on extremely expensive sardines and crackers. They wanted to be near proven deposits and close by a stream, of course, but they worried that too rich a lode would draw in too many other miners who did not share their social and cultural ideals. "We can keep the news of any bonanza we find to ourselves," Skaggs said, but Polly argued that secrecy and lying "would be contrary to the principles we mean to embody." They wanted to create a settlement apart, with its own spirit and protocols, but not so isolated that the pleasures of California society would be inaccessible. They wanted a site that was picturesque and salubrious, with a good hilltop for building Skaggs's astronomical observatory.

They decided against going up the American River's North Fork to settle near North Fork Dry Diggings after they discovered why the camp was also called Soldiers' Springs—another group from the New York regiment predominated there. Then they decided against heading down to Volcano when they learned that it was also called Soldiers' Gulch by the men from the New York regiment digging there. Duff proposed going much farther south to the rich district suddenly thick with Mexican miners. But Skaggs said that he didn't wish to learn Spanish, and Polly and Ben argued that journeying to the southern mines—to Angels Camp or Savage Diggings—would require too many wasteful weeks of hard travel. Finally, Skaggs took a pencil, pretended to shut his eyes, and jabbed at the map. He made a mark on the Middle Fork of the American River near a place called Ford's Bar, about twenty miles due north of Old Dry Diggings. Skaggs and Ben walked immediately to Dutch John's, where they learned the first placer there had been dug last spring by a certain Mr. Ford, who had taken out thirty ounces every day for three weeks before moving on.

"A half ounce in every pan," Ben said, repeating what he had just been told. "The fellow called it 'fine paydirt.' "

Duff wanted to study the various possibilities some more before making a decision.

Skaggs, growing exasperated, said that prices at Dutch John's were so high that he figured their own stock of equipment and supplies bought in New Orleans for forty dollars was worth a thousand dollars or more. "We can sell everything tomorrow and return home," he said. "Your knife, Duff, would get another twenty, and your Colt's a hundred more for sure. A fellow up at the store just now offered me thirty for my eyeglasses."

They were sitting on the ground outside between their two tents. The afternoon shadows were long.

"Is this choice not indeed somewhat . . . arbitrary?" asked Polly.

"Yes," said Ben. "Like most choices."

Duff found this philosophical tangent disconcerting. The wind ruffled the trees and deposited a swirl of golden yellow aspen leaves on the map. "OK," he said, relenting. "We must buy a mule. Or a donkey. And a cart."

"A most excellent plan," said Skaggs.

55

October 30, 1848

. . .

*on the Middle Fork
of the American River, California*

N O ONE HAD said a word for half an hour. They could finally see a true mountain peak in the distance. A falcon swooped and shrieked overhead.

"We have come so far," Ben said.

None of them, including Ben himself, was certain whether he meant the seven-mile walk from Ford's Bar east or the three thousand miles from London and four thousand more from New York City down rivers and through jungles and over two more oceans—or something more metaphorical.

Skaggs, huffing and puffing, looked at the nearly treeless hillock beside them and imagined his observatory atop it. "Quite far enough, I vote."

And so they had picked their spot, a five-acre glade tucked between a wide, calm stretch of the American River and a low double hill, bordered on the east by a rocky promontory and a deep, fast stream flowing downhill into the river. Late in the afternoon, while Ben and Duff finished pitching the tents and Skaggs gathered firewood, Polly took off her clothes for a plunge in the frigid stream, her first bath in more than a month.

Ben heard her brief scream in the distance. "Are you all *right?*" he shouted.

"*Yes,*" she replied. Clean cold water, a barrelful a second, free and unending. "*Absolutely fine.*"

They had discussed the nature of their prospective utopia dozens of times during the journey, and were agreed on basic principles. But not until their first night on the riverbank of the Middle Fork, after a meal of ham and dry biscuits, sitting on a fallen incense cedar tree in the darkness, did they formally debate and approve the rules that would govern the community. Polly unrolled one of her last big imperial sheets of drawing paper, a paper (they imagined) the size of the Magna Carta or the Constitution, and by the light of the campfire transcribed their eight bylaws.

> 1. *All labor required by the community shall be determined by a majority vote.*

Although this first vote and those for the other seven bylaws were unanimous, they unanimously voted against *requiring* unanimous votes, since as the community grew, they knew, unanimity would be impossible.

> 2. *All necessary labor is deemed to be of equal value.*

Each of the four was eager to dig and wash gold, but it was assumed that Skaggs would do more of the cooking, since the others had virtually no experience at the stove. Skaggs had also hunted deer and turkey in New Hampshire every summer and fall of his youth, so he would be their huntsman, and thus exempt from scullery and laundering duties. Polly could use a needle; Ben had overseen an industrial enterprise (although none without steam engines and a hundred workers to do the hard labor); Duff knew carpentry; and so on.

> 3. *Each member, male or female, shall work at some necessary labor nine hours a day for twenty-four days in each month unless prevented by illness, injury, weather, or other acts of God. And each member shall determine the best means of conducting his or her work.*

In addition to Sabbath days, Skaggs spoke forcefully of the need for an additional number of monthly "free days," to be chosen at the discretion of each member, "for making pictures, writing nonsense, observing the heavens, and restorative time-wasting and meditation, as necessary." He had pressed for five such holidays every month; they compromised on three. The final clause of Bylaw 3 was the result of a small argument concerning the proper cleaning of their dishes after dinner—whether they would boil water for washing twice a day (Duff and Polly) or rely on the local custom of wiping plates and pans clean with a handful of turf (Ben and Skaggs).

4. *All members shall share equally in the expenses and profits of the community.*

They'd talked about devising some scheme of fixed rates of exchange for labor and money and gold, but decided that because unearthing any given nugget could as easily require five seconds' or five days' work, and since the prevailing price of gold was anyway beyond their control, any such mechanism was impractical.

5. *All placer claims filed by members of the community are the property of the community as a whole, not of any individual member.*

Miners at every big camp had established a local code governing the size of gold claims—in the vicinity of Ford's Bar, each was to be 30 by 30 feet or its equivalent. Thus the four of them were entitled to work 3,600 square feet of ground at a time, and each new recruit to the community would enlarge the community's claim by another 900 square feet.

6. *Members shall endeavor to be openhearted, open-minded, kind, and loyal.*

Each of the founders was allowed to insert one cardinal virtue. These were Polly's, Skaggs's, Ben's, and Duff's, respectively.

7. *Moderation in all things is encouraged, but any formal regulation of private behavior is beyond the purview of the community.*

The other three had persuaded Skaggs that his proposed amendment specifically prohibiting "any future ban on cursing, ardent spirits, tobacco, or the Oriental substances" was unnecessary.

8. *All sympathetic persons (including females and any Mexican, Indian, Jew, Kanacker [i.e., Sandwich Islander or similar Polynesian], Chilean, Negro, Irish, Mormon, Transylvanian, Turk,*

Transcendentalist, or refugee of New Hampshire) may apply to join the community, and shall be admitted by a majority vote of the present members.

Skaggs had insisted upon appending the last four categories of welcome races, and despite Polly's complaint that he was mocking her progressive ideals, they approved the final bylaw.

Finally, each of them suggested names for the community. Polly wanted to call it Arden, her brother proposed La Dorada, and Skaggs argued long and hard on behalf of Flabbergast or Manifest Destiny. But Ben's sentimental notion prevailed. He would not be there, he said, and in all likelihood none of them would be, if not for the death of his friend Lloyd Ashby. And so in a grand hand at the top of the page, Polly wrote *The Charter of the Community of Ashbyville, California,* and they all retired for the night.

56

—➤•◄—

THEIR JOURNEY WAS OVER, but all four were filled with the spirit of industry. Surrounded by nothing but heedless, timeless nature—by infinite sky and virgin forest and ancient rock—they were impatient to get on with their enterprise. The unceasing sound and sight of the rushing river was itself a kind of taskmaster. The woodpeckers' perpetual tapping was a metronome. The shortening days and falling leaves made them a little anxious.

They needed to make money. After buying a cart, two donkeys (male and female), and lumber to build their rocker, they had only $93 left. Skaggs shot birds, Ben caught salmon, and Polly and Duff gathered berries and greens, but everything else—flour, bread, beef, onions, salt, sugar, coffee, apples— was $2 to $4 dollars a pound at the store in Ford's Bar. A candle cost more than a good lamp in New York, and whale oil went for $20 the quart. One could put a girl in New York or London on staff to light and snuff wicks all day long for the price of five friction matches in California. The Ashbyville treasury would be empty by the middle of November unless they found some color.

Their first cloudy morning in the cold river, Skaggs yelped with each step as he waded in, which made Duff laugh, and Ben called the water "frig-orific," which made Polly laugh. Skaggs had boasted that his and Duff's two years of making and developing daguerreotype plates, carefully stirring and

tipping the shallow chemical baths, would make them panning prodigies. He
was wrong. They all did the work clumsily. At first they stood in water too
shallow, only up to their ankles, so that they had to bend over too far to reach
the current. They swirled their pans in the water too rapidly, so that they
were losing half of any gold hidden among the sand, and then they swirled
too slowly. Each managed to wash only a few dozen handfuls of gravel the
whole day. The group's little mound of dust and specks and flakes weighed
half an ounce.

But on their second morning, a brilliantly clear day, Ben was facing Duff
and saw him suddenly stop swirling, stand up, press his wet pan flat against
his chest, and with his right hand in a fist make the sign of the cross. Then
he slowly opened his fist and brought the palm closer and closer to his face.
Ben watched reflected sunshine flutter across Duff's cheeks and nose and
awestruck eyes.

"Is it a nugget, Duff?" Ben shouted to be heard over the river.

He nodded.

"Well, then," Skaggs said, "the custom is to shout, '*Eureka*, I have *found*
it!' "

"Hoo-*oww!*" Polly whooped, a kind of rude, manly cry none of the men
had ever heard her (or any other woman) make. It so startled Duff he
dropped his plinker. Without pausing, he plunged his head and hands and
whole upper torso into the water, and after an anxious couple of seconds
shot upright, his right hand in a fist again and raised above his sopping head.

Back on the bank, they each examined their first plinker, grinning as they
rubbed and scraped at its sandy black-and-brown crust with their fingers. It
was the size and rough shape of half a walnut and weighed just over an
ounce.

"A much dirtier thing than I imagined," Ben said, "but even more beautiful."

"She is indeed," said Skaggs.

Together with the specks and flecks they managed to collect, their second
day's total was two ounces and a half. Their skills improved quickly, and
once the rocker was built, they were rocking out a half pound almost every
day, nearly a thousand dollars each week. It was dull, enervating work, but
it was not difficult. They required no special luck, of course, because a stu-
pendous stroke of luck had befallen the whole region, like strange weather.

November 1848

. . .

Ashbyville

*T*HE SMALLEST OF the three tents—where they stored barrels of
flour and oil and lime, and where at the end of each day they set
the trays of soggy gold-flecked sand on the ground to dry—
served as Skaggs's laboratory. It was dim enough to protect the exposed daguerreotype plates from sunlight, but bright enough for him to do the work
of fuming and washing and fixing his pictures. Back in New York, Skaggs
had not been fond of fixing, a purely mechanical process of gilding the surface of each finished plate with a foul-smelling solution of gold chloride.
But in El Dorado, a few paces from a free supply of the main raw material,
he took special pleasure in preparing his own batches of solution—a pinch
of Ashbyville's gold dust dissolved in a bubbling vial of the acid the ancient
alchemists called *aqua regia,* royal water. Skaggs fancied himself a modern
California alchemist, turning gold into supernaturally realistic pictures of
the gold district.

One afternoon a few weeks after they made camp, he took a picture of
Polly and Duff and Ben peeking out over a four-foot-high log wall of one of
their half-finished cabins. Back in the tent, he suspended the plate in his fuming box, carefully poured the mercury into the box's iron tray, and struck a
match to light the naphtha lamp to heat the mercury to 200 degrees and release the developing fumes. But when he tossed aside the match, still hot and
smoking, it fell to the ground inches from a squirrel cowering in a corner.

The animal panicked and ran, leaping and scrambling across the developing table as it escaped the tent. Skaggs, surprised, swiveled and lurched, narrowly missing the lamp flame but knocking his tray of mercury off the pine plank—splashing several ounces of quicksilver onto a tray of wet placer sand.

"*Damn.*"

But when he squatted to examine the spill, he noticed that where the mercury had dribbled onto the wettest areas of the sand, it had collected tiny bits of gold. With his pliers he dug a little mercury canal through the wet sand and saw that it worked like a liquid magnet, picking up still more gold—and, from the look of it, gold alone, leaving the other mineral grit behind. The quicksilver naturally amalgamated with the gold.

He looked up and stared at nothing for a few long seconds. If he heated the amalgam, he realized, and thereby vaporized the mercury, only pure gold would remain. And then he smiled. *Eureka,* he thought. A whole flask of mercury, seventy-six pounds, cost $30. In his bottle right there he had more than a pound of the stuff—and there was more among his medicines, and in every percussion cap for any gun. The New York newspaper hacks had ridiculed his daguerreian enthusiasm as a dilettante's fad, had called him "the photo fool" and "Mr. Mercury." Mr. Mercury *indeed:* he had literally stumbled upon a way of making every scoop of placer sand a little richer, perhaps much richer, by retrieving grains of gold that would otherwise wash away, lost. *Eureka.*

"Comrades," he said as he trotted into the roofless cabin where Ben and Duff were ramming a log into place while Polly plastered a chink with lime paste, "I have made a momentous discovery."

They looked at him curiously. He was apparently not joking.

"A nugget?" asked Ben.

"No, a new process by which we shall take more gold. *Amalgamation!*"

Now they were sure he was joking, or delirious from his chemical fumes. "Amalgamationist" was the catchword used to disparage liberals on the Negro question—it referred to someone who approved of sexual congress between people of different races.

"*Quicksilver,* " he said quickly, "using quicksilver, we can sift out more gold from every pan and shovel."

OF THE TWO dozen newcomers who had made claims within a mile or two of Ashbyville, two inquired about becoming Ashbyvillians. The first was an extremely friendly Philadelphian, a passionate abolitionist, who stayed a week before they caught him hiding gold in his pockets. The second was a fellow from Oregon, by way of Kelsey's Diggings, who was driven off by Duff at gunpoint within hours of arriving, after he'd asked when he might take his turn in the tent with Polly.

Others with whom they discussed membership failed to appreciate the special attractions of Ashbyville, since most miners had formed ad hoc companies that shared the work and earnings, but had none of what one man called Ashbyville's "hoity-toity rules." And until they received a patent on Skaggs's amalgamation process, Duff was adamant that it remain secret. The others were willing to share the mercury technique, and Skaggs was dying to tell the world of his discovery. But Polly understood her brother's strong feeling, which derived from the failure of their father's endless schemes to profit from patented inventions.

A third potential Ashbyville recruit had preceded them to the neighborhood by some months. Duff discovered him camped with his son a half mile upriver, using rough woven straw baskets to wash placer gold. He was an Indian called Jack. Jack was short for "jacksnipe," he told them, the English word for the bird that formed part of his name in his native language. His clan lived five days' walk to the south—in the valley of the Stanislaus River, he said, which had become overrun with outsiders looking for gold.

Skaggs asked Jack why the Indians had not taken up the gold for themselves, before the influx of whites. Jack shrugged and smiled and said that his people "did not know before."

"About the gold?" Skaggs asked, surprised.

"About whites' *love* of the gold."

Polly invited Jack to return with his son on Thursday the twenty-third, to join them for a special annual dinner. He accepted, though he had never heard of Thanksgiving.

SKAGGS MANAGED TO shoot a turkey, so the essential tradition was observed, and Jack and his son, Badger, brought a crisp, savory acorn-meal bread. Everyone, even the boy, had brandy.

Jack explained over dinner that the whites called the Indians "diggers" not as an idiomatic twist on "niggers," as Ben had presumed, but on account of their dietary dependence on acorns, which they dug from the dirt. "Also, some Indian," Badger added, "call him own person 'digger' too." Their name for themselves, the Maidu, was simply the phrase for "people," just as their name for the Sierra Nevadas was Hedem Yamani, or "these mountains," which Skaggs called "a very handy recourse to tautology."

After the meal, the white people performed a little play from a book of parlor theatricals Polly had bought in New Orleans. It was a comedy called *Irresistibly Impudent*. Jack and Badger were highly entertained and completely confused. At one point Polly, according to the script, pretended to forget her character's lines, whereupon Skaggs, playing the character called "the Prompter," took the stage to pretend to chastise her. At the end of the play Ben, playing "Dick," turned to Jack and Badger and delivered the final lines directly to them—"You knew it would end that way, didn't you? Farce always does. The parent relents, the lovers are made happy, and as a matter of course, down comes the curtain."

The guests thought it was their turn. Jack stood and recited the prayer of grace he had been taught as a boy at a mission school: "Damos las gracias por todas, el Diós todopoderoso, que vive y reina por siempre . . ."

And Duff joined him, in English, for the end. ". . . And may the souls of the faithful departed, through the mercy of God, rest in peace. Amen." Duff made the sign of the cross, and suddenly remembered that Sunday would be the eighth anniversary of the death of old man Prime, in honor of which he would say a special third Act of Contrition.

In the end Jack politely declined to join Ashbyville, but he was very eager to learn to build and use a Long Tom, as the biggest cradle rockers were called, so he proposed that he and Badger become temporary members of the camp until the next full moon—a little more than two weeks—and remain friendly allies thereafter.

—➤•◄—

58

December 1848 to February 1849
. . .
Ashbyville

AND SO AS 1848 ended, the socialist community of Ashbyville consisted of two tents, two new cabins, and an ingenious means of drawing more gold from the earth using mercury. It had signed a treaty of peaceful coexistence with Indians. After expenses, it had already amassed a profit of $5,786. But its population remained at four.

As December turned to January, the sky drizzled as often as not. Just after New Year's it snowed. By and large, however, the worst of winter in California was no harder than late fall in New York, with a warm, sunny day once a week. They bought heavy woolen jerseys—for seven ounces apiece, a rough knitted tunic for $120! But they got used to the prices. Eggs $1 each. Butter $16 the pound. It was California.

Little by little, though, all four grew restless. After six months in one another's constant company, they were familiar with all of the others' recitations and songs and stories. The parlor theatricals and charades that had diverted them easily in November had grown stale by February. The new amusements—as when Skaggs pronounced their names the way Jack and Badger did, "Pen" and "Pully" and "Duh-vuh"—palled. Each of them had read all of the books they had brought (except Skaggs's blasphemous *Life of Jesus,* which Duff refused to open), as well as several new ones Skaggs and Ben had acquired at the big camps. There was one four-page newspaper only once a week. They had named everything in Ashbyville that deserved to be named. The rocky promontory was Mount Aetna. The stream, now gushing with winter rain, was Generosity Creek. The main trails leading west and north and east were called Chrystie, Broadway, and Piccadilly.

The single men withdrew into their own pursuits. Duff grew quiet and very, very calm. He put in his hours at the placers and helped Skaggs build the observatory, a simple twelve-by-twelve cabin constructed directly atop the promontory's naked granite, but left the camp for hours each day before dusk to walk alone in the woods and pick blackberries and coffeeberries, and to say his rosaries and novenas and contritions out loud, and thank God for delivering him to the safety of this wilderness. The others were appalled by the recent murders in the south: the Irishman who had stabbed the miner at Sutter's Mill in the fall had formed a gang that robbed and—with axes and swords—slaughtered a rancher, his pregnant wife, and eight others at a ranch down at Mission San Miguel. But while the news did prompt Duff to dig a hole in which to hide their treasure, he was struck more by the swiftness of justice than the horror of the crimes. Only days after they read about the murders, they learned that two of the outlaws had already been tracked down and shot by a posse as they ran into the Pacific surf, and the other three were executed by an army firing squad just after Christmas in the center of Santa Barbara.

Skaggs spent most of his time reading about astronomy. He occasionally made a daguerreotype picture—of each of them gripping pans, of their little redwood chest half filled with gold, of piles of dead salmon ("ideal portrait subjects"), of Jack and Badger pointing toward the nearest Sierra peak, of a doe that happened to step in front of the camera where he had set it up to take a picture of the observatory under construction. But he was more eager to contrive a means for photographing stars through his telescope, whenever his telescope finally arrived. And he busied himself with correspondence—ordering new books, writing colorful accounts of life in California to his friend Taylor at the *Tribune,* replying to a generous letter from his brother Jonah, sending specifications to the Mexican maker of his observatory's dome.

He and Ben were the official Ashbyville quartermasters, but it was Skaggs who usually made the one- and two-day trips to and from the stores, where he would smoke and drink and gamble a bit.

Polly and Ben had each other's company, which ought to have been sufficient.

Every couple of weeks, on a provisioning trip, or from a miner passing by on his way to new diggings, they got the news of some fresh discovery of gold. The stories were amazing but true, most of them. The woman living up on the Yuba River who one day, while tidying her hut, swept away just enough dirt from the earthen floor to expose two pounds of embedded nuggets! And the Mexican near the Sonoranian Camp who in a mere eight days of pecking and scratching dug out fifty-two *pounds*—a pound for every two hours spent mining, $16,000 in a week and a day! And the man along the Tuolumne whose rifle shot at a black bear sent the dying animal flying over the lip of a canyon and onto a ledge some yards below—a ledge of silvery white quartz, the hunter discovered when he climbed down to retrieve the carcass, that was laced with long, thick veins of gold, like some bejeweled czarist bauble expanded to the size of a house. And still another impossibly lucky hunter—Mr. Raspberry, down at Angels Camp, who fired his musket's jammed ramrod into the dirt of a hillside, in which he then found three pounds of gold hidden in a tangle of tree roots . . . and ten more pounds the next day . . . and twenty-five more on the third day. "In the Grimms' tale," Duff said, "the boy cut down the tree and found his goose with gold feathers sitting in the roots."

At Ashbyville, however, there were no such grand accidents or fairystory bonanzas. The largest nugget they had found was three ounces, and Duff's plinker from the second day of panning was the next largest. Their success was merely steady.

There were so few women in the gold country, perhaps two dozen, and so many thousands of men, Polly found it unpleasant to visit the camps. Even at little Ford's Bar, each of her visits inspired a ruckus. And so she seldom left Ashbyville. As the winter passed she found herself drawing fewer pictures. Back in New York, drawing had served as a private respite from moneymaking and society and worry and the clamor of the city. In California, however, there was hardly any clamor or society to escape, and no real cause for worry. Skaggs bought her jars of red and blue and yellow tempera, but she found she lacked easy facility with paint.

The shock of losing Ashby had led Ben to admit his dissatisfaction with life in London, and propelled him to America. The torture of losing Polly had sent him racing across the continent. In California, however, there was no shock or misery to fire and form his next ambition. The greatest trauma they suffered that first winter was the death of a donkey, the one they called John Donkey.

In California, the fabulous was real and the most abnormal and remarkable things quickly came to seem normal and unremarkable—the endless free gold, the crazy prices, the haphazard camps packed with hundreds of wild boys and men, Ashbyville's own fortuitous mercury dribbles and cache of buried treasure, the observatory, the friendly natives named after animals, the absence of poverty, the peaceable anarchy.

And so perhaps it was inevitable that Polly and Ben's particular good fortune—that is, their love and their reunion—also came to seem ordinary, as wonders do.

Paris had been an adventure for Ben, as had his narrow escape from the French soldier who'd followed him to London. Once Polly left Mrs. Stanhope's, she had started to see the brothel in retrospect as an adventure, as she did the rescue of Priscilla. To both Ben and Polly their meeting and lovemaking and separation had been adventures. Her search for a utopia and his for her were adventures. Reuniting at a log cabin amid a religious exodus, steaming down the Mississippi through slave country, crossing from one sea to another in a hollow log and on the backs of mules, sailing atop a mountain of excrement through the Golden Gate . . .

Now, in 1849, the adventures were occurring elsewhere, to others. Their very experience of time's passage, Skaggs said at the campfire one night, had been altered, accelerated by the wondrous speed of recent events. Kings dethroned overnight, the nation ribboned with rails and telegraph wire by the day, California conquered and turned into a gold mine, their own settled lives in New York and London abandoned in a flash . . . According to Skaggs's theory, they now *expected* outlandish surprise and speed and high adventure—even needed them, as people acquire a taste for spiced food or drugs. "Perhaps the quiet meandering and murk of ordinary life," Skaggs said, "is now too ordinary for the likes of us. We've been spoiled."

59

February 9, 1849

. . .

Ashbyville

AND THERE WERE Polly and Ben, dirty and sweaty on another gray Friday, two days after her twenty-fourth birthday, working the rocker alone in silence. Skaggs had left early for his fortnightly ride to North Fork Dry Diggings. Duff was off on one of his rambles. He had panned for an hour at dawn and pulled up two one-ounce plinkers—or *chispas,* as he now called nuggets, Spanish for "sparks"—so according to the third bylaw, as amended in the new year, he was exempt from mining duties until tomorrow.

Ben carried the day's ninety-eighth shovel to the Long Tom and tossed the earth onto the perforated iron sheet at its mouth. A small stone ricocheted off the iron and struck Polly's cheek.

"Ouch." She had often suggested that he gently *spill* rather than *throw* the gravel onto the sieve.

"I'm sorry." He had often suggested that she stand back with the pails of water until they were ready to rock and wash.

She poured their gallons over the pounds of earth while he rocked the cradle, washing the worthless dirt and sand down the tilted length of the rocker's trough toward its tail.

Sometimes as they rocked the cradle Ben could not help thinking about babies. If they had a girl, perhaps they would call her Caroline.

And sometimes as Polly looked at the cradle—a pinewood box seven feet long, two feet wide, and a foot deep—she could not help thinking of her mother and father and especially her baby brother and sister. The morning she saw William and Grace washed and neatly dressed and squeezed side by side into a single three-dollar coffin—that was the moment Polly had decided she would not remain poor for the rest of her life.

Ben dripped quicksilver onto the riffles before he and Polly rocked the Long Tom, both of them staring at the nine iron bars nailed across the floor of the trough, watching for color to catch against the metal as the muddy slickens slid past. There were many specks spangling the drifts of dark sand on this washing, then some flakes, and finally two good pickers as well. The product of their labor of twenty minutes was worth a decent week's wage in the States. Neither of them said a word.

Polly squatted and used a slat to scrape the bits of gold and wet, gold-studded sand through the holes and into the tray on the ground beneath the tail of the cradle.

Ben walked back to the placer and resumed digging. *We have turned ourselves into proletarians,* he thought. *Very rich workfolk, one of the great American oxymorons.* He recalled a passage from Engels's pamphlet about how work has "lost all individual character" and "all charm" thanks to engines and the division of labor. But where was the craftsmanship or charm of this work? They had twelve more washings to finish.

"You have not yet told me what you truly think of my idea," he said at the end of the day, as they carried another of the heavy wooden trays covered with sludge into the tent. "The flume." A week earlier he had conceived the construction of a permanent, fixed, sixty-foot Long Tom—a Supremely Long Thomas, as Skaggs called it. It would run parallel with Generosity Creek down the slope at the eastern end of the camp, with its tail at the river. They would build a sluice gate at its head and dig a new channel to divert the creek through the long trough, like a millrace beneath a waterwheel, so that the running water's own current would wash the gold from the sand and gravel, automatically and constantly.

They had not yet mined that stretch of Ashbyville in earnest, but it looked rich—Duff had dug out his morning's two acorn-sized *chispas* from the riverbank there. Ben calculated that they would clean out five or maybe ten times as much gold each day, even with the labor required to carry the loads of earth twenty paces uphill. (And for that extra labor he had a second phase of construction in mind, involving wheeled wooden barrows drawn by ropes and pulleys.)

"It is very clever indeed," Polly said. "I am extremely impressed by your designs. I am."

A light rain had started to fall.

"However . . . ?" Ben said.

She was quiet for a moment. "To pluck Generosity Creek out of its bed, forcibly and unnaturally, for our own ends, strikes me as somehow . . . oh, I am afraid it is too ridiculous to say."

"What is it? Please."

"It seems a little . . . mean, a *blow* against the land. A kind of defiling. It reminds me of the greedy kings in stories—like Midas, and the one in Rumpelstiltskin, who get their comeuppance when they go too far. Careful of the skink, Ben." A tiny lizard with a bright blue tail raced between his feet. "It sounds awfully silly, I know."

Ben said nothing but smiled, just as he'd smiled when Lydia Winslow had asked him if he thought it would be impossible to marry at St. Paul's Cathedral, or, if it had to be St. George's Church, whether Sir Archie might arrange to clear Hanover Square of traffic on the morning of the wedding. Polly's scruples about the stream sounded very silly indeed to Ben— whimsical and mystical and girlish. Her flights of fancy were part of what had made him fall in love with her. But he was bored with simply digging and rocking and pouring buckets of water all day long. He was proud of his plan. It had for the first time ignited his passion for the mining enterprise it- self. And was not *any* extraction of gold from the earth a matter of plucking and defiling?

"Besides," she continued as they walked slowly, careful not to tip the tray they carried together, "as you have said, to efficiently operate such a mining *manufactory*"—she pronounced the last word with a touch of distaste— "we should need many more members in the community."

THIS WAS A somewhat sore subject. Californians' general lack of interest in joining Ashbyville had surprised them. At first they'd ascribed it entirely to the gold fever and competitive temper of the time and place—every miner imagined that *he* would be the one to pull out the next little $10,000 gold baseball, or find the great lode, and had no wish to share his imminent for- tune unnecessarily.

Back in November, Polly had suggested that they advertise for members in the newspaper, and then in December that they reconstitute Ashbyville as "a kind of *scattered* community of the like-minded," an archipelago of sympathetic miners from the Feather River all the way down to the Tuolumne who would share costs and profits equally.

But as Ben and Skaggs made the circuit of the booming camps in the vicinity, they came to understand the true reason for Ashbyville's failure to grow. Their little utopia was redundant.

Back in the States, even the most liberal towns and cities were rife with social arbiters and moral aldermen and church ladies who all but forced the come-outers and freethinkers among them to become exiles, to form their own phalanxes and colonies—the Oneidas and Brook Farms and Glees—in rural isolation. But in California there were no Mr. Pecksniffs or Mrs. Grundys, no churches or right-thinking committees, no censoriousness or opprobrium, let alone tyranny or oppression. There were Christian ministers among the miners, but none of them preached. Everyone talked and dressed and behaved as they pleased. What revolution in thought or manners was required?

And the new economy, the economy of gold, had revolutionized the system of labor and capital as radically as the socialists had proposed. It was the rare man who worked for a wage paid by an employer. Rather, each miner's very work was unearthing money. For an outlay of fifty dollars, any able-bodied person was as likely as any other to earn a living or get rich. Almost the whole country between the Pacific and the Sierra Nevada was a commons, where on any unclaimed patch of earth anyone had a right to dig and wash and keep the metal he found.

And because rich new veins and placers were discovered every day in California, there was no scarcity of wealth to fuel the otherwise universal and age-old resentment of the poor for the rich. No one in California felt he was *permanently* poor. Greed and envy prevailed, just as it did in the settled world, but so did a spirit of rough cooperation.

In the gold district in early 1849, a community of reformers was superfluous. The Ashbyvillians' neighborliness and fairness toward Jack and Badger and the other Indians mining on the Middle Fork amounted to the main virtue that distinguished them from most of the other thousands of white newcomers in California. "In *this* free and rich country," Skaggs had said just after New Year's, "I fear that nearly all of our noble intentions are at the present moment moot." Finally even Polly had agreed.

. . .

Ben had estimated that the Supremely Long Thomas would need at least eight men (or seven plus Polly) to operate it properly. "If the flume washes as well as I believe it should," Ben said to her now, "its output of gold ought to be great enough to attract others to our side."

"That might be. But then I fear we would draw in members the way a business draws in investors, only for the sake of a better profit. We would cease to be a community of the like-minded."

She was right, he knew. But he also thought they could hire Indians to help them conduct the larger operation he envisioned.

They lay down the gold tray in the drying tent and wiped their hands on their damp, filthy work clothing.

" 'Output' is a queer word," she said. "I have never heard it."

And until then Ben had never uttered it. His father had sometimes used the term.

"Hallo! *Hallo!*" It was Skaggs, back from a shopping expedition.

"The quartermaster and his Jenny Lind are returned to quarters with bounties galore!"

Jenny Lind was their surviving donkey. She was laden with bags and parcels, and Skaggs's pockets were stuffed with rolled newspapers. He had bought the first several editions of the *Alta California,* the San Francisco newspaper that only a month earlier had been called *The California Star & Californian.* They were all hungry for periodicals, since none of the magazines to which Skaggs subscribed had begun arriving.

The two men lugged a ninety-pound sack of potatoes into one of the tents, and Polly carried a little wooden firkin of butter imported from the States, a bag of corn flour, and several yards of jerked beef.

Even after hours riding in the open air, Skaggs still stank of Mexican cigarettes and brandy, *cigaritos* and *aguardiente.* His hair and coat were soaked from the drizzle.

"The mingled aroma of liquor and smoke," Ben said, "all of creation damp and gray, and we two hairy unshaven louts grunting to pull a bushel and a half of potatoes out of the rain. We might as well be in Ireland."

Skaggs considered making some reply about his entirely abstemious Irish grandfather, or the Luckings' Catholicism, or Ashbyville's un-Irish absence of children. But he could see that his friends' day in Ashbyville had been less blithesome than his in North Fork Dry Diggings, and said nothing until they had finished unloading Jenny Lind.

"Ah, *foolish* me!" he suddenly cried, digging into his coat pockets among the newspapers. "We have *mail*, via San Francisco!" He pulled out five envelopes. "Two from New York for me"—a book, and correspondence concerning his observatory's clock drive—"and three from London for you."

Ben took his mail. Two carried the seal of the British Foreign Office; they were from his brother. He slipped them unopened into his pocket. The third was from his father's firm. This he opened, but it contained nothing from Sir Archie himself, only two forwarded pieces of correspondence—a pair of drawings from Professor Darwin, and a letter from his friend Engels that had been sent from Geneva in care of Knowles, Merdle, Newcome & Shufflebotham.

For a moment Polly had dared to hope she might have a letter from Priscilla Christmas—before she remembered that the mountains to the east and west of Salt Lake Valley meant that nothing and no one could escape or enter until spring.

"There is talk of a great new bonanza at Old Dry Diggings," Skaggs told them. "This latest story sounded absolutely fabulous to me, but they swear it is true." A fellow from Georgia or Mississippi had arrived at the camp with his slave, but they had been allowed to stay. (It was only large-scale slavery that worried the miners, since any true industrial operation would have an unfair advantage in digging out too much gold too quickly.) The Negro had dreamed repeatedly of a certain miner's hut in the camp. When his master dreamt the identical dream, he bought the hut for cash and the two started to mine right there in the floor. Since New Year's they had taken out almost a hundred pounds. "And with a roof over their heads while they work," Skaggs added.

"I wonder," Polly said, "how large a share the master has given to his man."

The tale from Old Dry Diggings did not improve the mood at Ashbyville that evening.

NOR DID THE two letters Ben received from his brother. Each contained news of a death. Last summer their father developed rheumatic fever and severe dropsy in his lungs and heart. Despite the attentions of the best physicians, Archie Knowles had died. Philip had written two pages describing the funeral. "I know that Father would have been exceptionally pleased by the new archbishop's kind remarks, and by the list of mourners, who included Lord Palmerston, of course, as well as HRH Prince Albert." He had signed himself *Sir Philip Knowles*. And to be certain Ben understood that he, Philip, had inherited the baronetcy, he had added *Bart*. after his signature.

60

※・➤・●・◄・※

the winter of 1848 and 1849
. . .
Salt Lake City

*T*HIS NEW JERUSALEM was cloudier, windier, and much colder
and snowier than New York. The mercury had not marked as
high as freezing in weeks, and the drifts were three feet high. But
Priscilla did not mind the weather so much. In fact, she found nothing very
objectionable about life among the Saints in their latest instant city on the
frontier, certainly not the burnt taste of the parched-barley coffee Billy
complained about. She had lived through far worse.

When Billy and she had appeared that evening in early November at the
door of the log cabin, his parents had been overcome. The return of their eldest son, apostate or not, was a miracle. The five younger brothers and sisters started jumping and laughing and wailing at once. And then they
embraced Priscilla.

Billy Whipple hadn't intended that wintering in Salt Lake City and repairing relations with his parents would draw him back to the church. But as
the weeks passed, Priscilla could see his resistance dwindling. And why not?
He was with his family again, and Salt Lake City was a place of order and
fairness. Polly had inculcated Priscilla with her hope for virtuous social experiments, and Salt Lake City seemed a plausible version. The winter was
hard, but all five thousand Saints there were predisposed to share and share
alike. When the Whipple family needed extra firewood, it was donated to
them, and since they had stored a surplus of potatoes from their garden,

they gave away a bushel to the hungry. Unlike James Danforth and his favorites at Glee, Brigham Young and his bishops and apostles seemed sensible to Priscilla. And the Mormons had the steely temperament to survive the rigors of living in a utopia.

To Priscilla, who had been to church only for funerals, the religion seemed no stranger or more onerous than any other. Their germinal miracles had occurred recently and in America, rather than two thousand years earlier in some foreign desert, but she failed to apprehend any essential difference between the magics. And perhaps it was the freshness of the Mormon revelations and martyrdom that accounted for the fever of the Saints' faith. They believed in prophecies and visions and speaking in tongues—but who was Priscilla Christmas, given her years of inexplicable premonitions, to gainsay any of that? Furthermore, she entirely approved of the absence of priests. (On a breadline in the Five Points when she was little, a Catholic priest had made her cry when he'd told her she would get only a single loaf because she was not baptized. And an Episcopalian divine, one of her regular customers for yankums in the Bowery Theatre alley, had insisted each time on ejaculating onto her hair beneath her bonnet, for which he'd paid her five cents extra.)

"I think I am beginning to know that I am a Saint after all," Billy confessed to her one day in January. When she replied that she knew that already, he blanched, after a pause asking very softly if her premonitions had returned. She smiled and told him no, she had simply watched him blossom among his family and old pals, despite the bare-bones conditions.

She offered, if he wished, to join the church and remarry him in a Mormon sealing ceremony. He started to cry, and reaffirmed that she would be his one and only wife for eternity, which made her very happy—although she did not disapprove of the Mormons' custom of plural marriage. To the contrary, she found its lack of hypocrisy astounding and noble. Every man of means in New York, as far as she knew, bought women to serve his carnal needs for one night at a time, in secret and without further obligation; Brigham Young, on the other hand, kept more women than Priscilla could count, all of them wives, none whores, and he was proudly building each of them a cabin in the center of town.

"Perhaps we should stay a while longer with your parents and your friends," Priscilla said when he had finished crying. "We needn't leave as soon as spring comes."

"Do you not miss *your* friends?" her husband had asked her. "They will wonder what has become of their girl."

"Poor Mr. Drumont can take the news ahead of us. He can tell Polly and Ben that I am well and happy here." She thought for a moment. "And if they have become rich now, they can hire their own coach and four to drive them *here* for a visit whenever they wish."

"But what of gold for you and me? Time is wasting. There is no buried treasure in this valley. Only fields to plant."

Priscilla shrugged. "Both are rugged, and in either place," she said, "we would be digging in the dirt to earn our livings."

GABRIEL DRUMONT SHARED a cabin on the edge of Salt Lake City with five other bachelors, away from the women. Four of his five bunkies were young Mormon veterans of the American war against Mexico, and the other was a childless widower. It was a barracks, which suited him. In fact, he had to admit he found the military air of the whole place admirable.

His days were spent sawing and hammering, which suited him as well. His English was improving. The city provided his food and bed and firewood and four dollars a week, although he had liked it better at the beginning when his salary was paid in California gold dust, rather than their new handwritten scrip. Would these priests' one- and three-dollar notes be worth a *sou* in California or anywhere outside their own snowy Algeria, this bleak Protestant valley? No matter. He had no choice, as he'd had no choice when they'd asked him at Chimney Rock to pay one hundred dollars, most of his capital, to join their train. And there was no advantage in complaining.

Indeed, from the start he had feigned sympathy for their sect—he knew they would be more welcoming of a potential convert than of some mere infidel wage laborer. His *charade* (or *camouflage*, as he conceived it) was that of a lay friar passing one season in a monastery, seeking enlightenment but without orders and not permitted—*grâce à Dieu*—to sing in the choir.

He no longer sought out Priscilla for conversation, since he had learned from her all she knew concerning Benjamin Knowles. Rather, he spent each of his idle, dark winter hours contemplating the moments of that ultimate encounter. He considered himself intimately acquainted with Knowles by now—members of his own family aside, on what person had he ever lavished more thought? And so the justice exacted must be accordingly intimate and correct . . .

He also avoided Priscilla because she unnerved him. Was it the elfin eyes? Was it such dovish innocence in what he knew to be a whore's body? Or was it because she reminded him of his unfulfilled obligation to Pinkerton, who had given him so much of his own trust and Prime's money to find her? That still rankled like a bad toothache. But at least Monsieur Pinkerton, Drumont reassured himself, would never learn of his duplicity—that he had traveled and then lived alongside Priscilla and Billy Whipple for months and never proffered Prime's deal to them, made no attempt to entice or force the girl to return to New York . . .

Yes, encounters with the girl—why, even thinking about her—made Drumont pensive and nervous, and no possible good could come from that.

⇥ ▸•◂ ⇤

61

February 9, 1849
. . .
the American River Valley, California

*D*UFF HAD WALKED east for an hour at a quick pace, close enough to the river to hear its soothing roar. But when he reached the notch in the hills where the stream widened, he had not finished his rosary, so he did not turn around and retrace his steps to Ashbyville, as usual. The sky had cleared. He would give Polly and Ben some more time alone. So he kept walking north, into the woods, as he finished the prayer.

He hiked for hours. He passed through a long, dim canyon and finally into the next valley, beautifully honeyed with late-afternoon light. *I shall not want.*

The temperature was warm, maybe 60 degrees. *He maketh me to lie down in green pastures.* Duff stopped at the edge of a grove of oak and pine high on the hillside and lay down, looking left into the sun, creation's ultimate and essential blaze, destroying and creating at every instant, a ball the size of a million flaming earths. In his view, the sun was God's perfect achievement—not this wet, mucky, complicated earth, teeming and festering with too much life.

With no river running through it, this valley was much drier than Ashbyville's. He had not eaten since breakfast. A jackrabbit raced past and Duff suddenly imagined himself as Christ in the desert, fasting alone in the wilderness of Judea with the beasts. Then he remembered that it was there that Satan had appeared to Jesus to tempt him . . . Duff recited the Lord's Prayer and crossed himself.

As the blazing orange touched the western horizon, Duff whispered "Amen" and glanced up into the boughs of the nearest pine tree. He saw some kind of mistletoe momentarily taking on the sunset hues. Or so he thought at first.

No; it was the *butterflies.*

He stood. *The monarchs,* hundreds, thousands, tens of thousands, resting and waiting on every branch of every pine he could see, the way they had covered the slope of the Mexican volcano two winters ago. He had been *led* to this valley, another of the monarchs' winter roosts, by God.

With his head cocked all the way back, he twirled around in wonderment, looking up. *Delivering me from evil, leading me not into temptation. Though I walk in the valley of darkness, I fear no evil, for you are with me, you are with me* . . . Duff dizzied himself with his whirling, knocked his shin against a rock, and stumbled forward, scraping his face hard against a stump as he fell to the ground.

"Hallelujah," he cried out loud. With his right hand he felt twigs and needles and pinecones caught in his hair, like a crown of thorns. He touched his wet left cheek and then looked at his dripping red fingers. "This is my blood," he said breathlessly, and made the sign of the cross again, "shed for the forgiveness of sins. Hallelujah."

"Sir? *Hallelujah?*" called a female voice.

Duff, ecstatic, looked up into the sky, hoping to see an angel.

"Hallelujah . . . the name of you?" the voice asked again.

Now he turned and saw the Indian woman speaking to him.

She was perhaps thirty, and stood with a younger woman behind a large rock a few yards away. In their arms each held a conical basket like those Jack and Badger used to wash gold, but these baskets were filled with acorns.

The younger woman touched her left cheek and nodded toward Duff. "Ow," she said.

Duff stood up, smiling. He pointed to his wound and said, "*Ow,* yes."

Each of the women had three short straight scars on her chin, and two more fine scars running from the corners of her mouth toward her cheekbone, like a child's drawing of a smile. The younger one talked quickly and quietly to the older, and as she spoke she pointed out the rough oval scar on his right cheek, the new gash on his face from which blood still dripped, and, most curiously, the spots of blood with which they had just watched him ritually daub himself—one on his forehead and three more in a row across the top of his buckskin jacket.

Maidu boys, when they became men, painted their faces and went into the mountains to listen for the lessons of the *kakeni,* the animal spirits. But these women had never seen any of the *sakini*—the "ghosts," as they called white people—decorate himself with paint or scar his skin like a real person, like an Indian. The girl wondered if he might be a trapper affiliated with one of the foreign tribes who lived way up north or east of the mountains, a so-called French Indian. But her aunt said she had never seen a Paiute or Klamath or any other Indian scarred like this boy, with a red-hot knife on the cheek . . . and decorated with *real blood* instead of red paint, on his clothing as well as his head. This was nothing she knew. Maybe he had eaten jimsonweed, the young one said, and was suffering delusions. No, replied the other, he was probably drunk, or simple.

Duff took their curious and wary chatter as concern for him and his injuries. They were like the women of Jerusalem on the road to Calvary, and like Jesus he wanted to reassure them. He took out his leather purse, which he held up in front of him. "You may have my money," he said. "Do not worry about me." They said nothing. Jack had told him that most of the Indians knew Spanish better than English. "No se preocupe de mí," he said, and shook his purse. "Mi oro está para usted."

He is offering gold?

"Soy bueno. Soy su amigo."

This confused and bloody young white man is saying he is good? the older woman said to her niece. *That he is our friend?* Both women smiled. *He is a sweet boy,* the girl said to her aunt, and proposed that they lead him to the pond to wash his wound, and that she chew some leaves of a certain herb to make a salve for his cut . . .

"Le traeré a las aguas," she said to him, pointing at his cheek. *I will take you to the waters . . .* "Para lavar la sangre." *To wash the blood.*

He crossed himself again. *She leadeth me beside the still waters. She restoreth my soul.* "Mi nombre es *Duff.* Soy *Duff.*"

The whites' bizarre *f* sound the women always found amusing, the way they'd found the soldier chief Frémont's name funny when they'd first heard it. "Usted es Duh-*vuh*," the younger one repeated with a giggle. "Duh-*vuh.*"

February 10 and 11, 1849

. . .

Ashbyville

DUFF HAD NOT returned to Ashbyville Friday night. Skaggs reminded Polly that her brother had stayed in the woods after dark in the past, and that at this point he could feed himself for days on berries and mushrooms.

But when Duff had still not returned by Saturday noon, Ben walked to Jack's camp and two others nearby; he had not been seen. Ben and Polly and Skaggs then spent the remainder of Saturday walking in widening semicircles around the edges of Ashbyville, calling out his name. It was another warm day, but Polly was not reassured.

On Saturday night it rained. Polly cried, apologized to Ben for stinting on sympathy for the deaths in his family, and then cried some more.

Sunday morning she lay on their bed in the cabin, fully dressed, eyes closed, wide awake, hands folded over her stomach, praying for Duff's safe return. She wondered whether the Sabbath would give more power or less to her prayer, or if it mattered at all. If Duff did not return by midday, they had agreed, Skaggs would ride to Old Dry Diggings to post word of his disappearance, and Ben and Polly would walk together to search the other side of the hills to the north.

Outside in Ashbyville's "piazza"—the rough benches surrounding the star-shaped stone fire pit—burning logs hissed and popped as the two men read, wrote, nibbled dried beef, and occasionally chatted about fathers and brothers and the various bulletins of civilization.

"To tell the truth, I am surprised at the ache I feel," Ben said, "but he was a lovable monster, my father. And he certainly lived the very life he wished to live."

"The last time I visited home," Skaggs recalled, "I asked mine if we might carve 'Happy at Long Last' on his stone when he passed. He thought that for once his jackanapes son was being sincere, and tears came to his eyes."

On the fat redwood stump between them, beneath a river stone, lay the stack of new *Alta Californias*, thoroughly perused, crinkled, and folded into thick quartos and octavos.

They had already discussed the newspapers' accounts of the counter-revolutions that were retaking power across Europe as swiftly and in-eluctably as the revolutions had grabbed it away. The democrats had been defeated now in Milan, Budapest, Berlin, and Vienna as well as Paris and Prague. The social quakes and blazes whose beginnings Ben witnessed last February—not even a whole year ago, he marveled—were already stilled, quenched, dead, gone.

Ben was writing a letter. Skaggs was deep into his new book—*Eureka*, the freshly published edition of Edgar Allan Poe's astronomy lecture from last February. Now and then he sighed or shook his head and then read a passage aloud, all but shouting *Eureka* each time. " 'He who from the top of Aetna casts his eyes leisurely around'—*Aetna*, the man writes!" Skaggs said, pointing up toward his half-finished observatory. "From Aetna he is 'affected chiefly by the extent and diversity of the scene. Only by a rapid whirling on his heel could he hope to comprehend the panorama in the sub-limity of its oneness.' Is that not a lovely idea? Is that not how I have at-tempted to live my life? A rapid whirling panorama!"

And this oneness that Poe imagined, Skaggs explained to Ben, was quite literal at the creation of the universe—a primordial particle which exploded outward in a trillion trillion pieces, flying in every direction and filling the vastness of empty space with matter. Every speck of the universe—"you, me, Polly, Duff, the gold, the guano, biscuits, guns, New York, New Hamp-shire, Saturn, its moons, *everything*"—unfolded from that single, infinitely dense particle eons ago. "And furthermore," he said excitedly, "as a result of the magnetic attraction of every atom of matter to every other atom of mat-ter—"

"I understand gravity, Skaggs."

"Well, Poe theorizes that gravity must finally pull *all* of the matter back *together*, like a steel spring or a sheet of rubber stretched tight, and all of it, *snap*, returning to that original, all-consuming, all-containing speck." He made a tight fist and held it in front of his face. "Creation . . . annihilation," he said, slowly opening and closing his hand.

"Your man Poe sounds like Duff Lucking."

"He suggests that all of it—the universe, and time itself—is *not* infinite, but rather a kind of . . . *blossoming* . . ." Skaggs opened and closed his fist again. "And withering."

"Perhaps the flower of the universe continues to bloom and die and bloom again."

"Yes! Perhaps it does. Is that not an awesome picture of existence?"

Ben nodded, and returned to composing his reply to his brother Philip. In order to rekindle his sense of offense, he reread Philip's second letter.

"I now have the unhappy duty to inform you," Philip had written, "that *another* of our clan has been snatched from us—my beloved and angelic Tryphena is now an angel in *fact*, having succumbed to the Bengalis' horrendous plague." He had gone on to describe in detail his initial lack of alarm at her symptoms—at her stomach cramps ("a most frequent female complaint"), at her damp skin and diarrhea (which had afflicted Tryphena for a few weeks, he recounted, as a result of his withdrawal of her opium supply). He'd thought of the cholera only when she'd vomited all over the breakfast table at Great Chislington Manor "on the first day of hunting season. Tryphena faded and left us the next day—*among the very first* to be stricken by what is becoming an epidemic," he'd added, in a kind of boast. "In the mere weeks since, many thousands more have been snatched away from the Thames and across the Styx by this Asiatic fiend." Surely he'd filched that last fragment of bad poetry directly from the *Times*.

"Miss Winslow has been particularly attentive and kind to me in this time of need. Lord and Lady Brightstone also attended the funeral, which pleased me greatly," Philip continued,

and they seem to have recovered from the tragic madness concerning Lloyd's unnecessary and ridiculous voyage thanks to the French. (Even on his deathbed, Father asked that you be informed of this latest news.)

In fact, Ben had known nothing until now about the discovery of Lloyd Ashby's misplaced remains—his father's own letter on the subject of Ashby, written just before he'd taken ill, had arrived at Sullivan Street after Ben left the city. Ben found his brother's choice of words—"ridiculous"—callous and glib even for Philip.

Precisely why & how he wound up in Shanghai, of all places, I do not understand still, though I suppose the disorder in France was frightful. It was one of our Foreign Office laddies, by the way, who finally discovered him packed and hidden in a back room somewhere in the French concession—tattered and rank and nearly unrecognizable, as one might imagine. Lord Brightstone arranged to have him shipped home aboard a clipper bound for London round the Horn.

And why had Philip waited "weeks" to inform Ben of Tryphena's death? Because he was primarily writing to his brother in America not for reasons of sentiment, but of commerce.

After desecrating the memories of his late wife and Ben's late friend, Philip had gotten to the point. "Captain Owen of the barque *Caroline* informed us that you and your companions have arrived safely in California to establish a mining business." Philip and some business associates in China had a scheme to "round up and transport" thousands of "tractable young Chinamen" to California to work as "two-guinea-a-month contract labourers in the gold mines." And they wished to engage Ben to act as managing agent for this enterprise in San Francisco.

Furthermore, Philip said, "the Jardine Matheson fellows in Hong Kong"—employees of his late wife's family's firm—wanted Ben's help in "opening a new market" among "the natives & half-breed Spaniards in California and other Western territories, who seem as likely as the Celestials in this connection." That is, Philip and his associates wondered if they might profitably sell Bengal opium to Indians and Mexicans in America, as they had done for years to the Chinese in China, where they had bred several million addicts. "Imagine, if you will," Philip had written, "opium clippers carrying chests from Calcutta to San Francisco—from the Indians of India directly to your red Indians."

Philip had intended this last line as a stroke of wit. But the satire of Ben's brief reply would escape Philip entirely:

My dear brother,

I was most interested to receive yours of September last. I shall always remember Tryphena fondly. However, your remarkable and ~~farcical far-fetched~~ farsighted plan to export Bengali opium and Chinese slaves to California seems premature, given the primitive state of our mines at present, and the great industry of our local Indians and Mexicans at finding gold on their own account—a spirit of industry which a regular opium habit would, I suspect, countervail if not destroy. Therefore I must ~~regretfully regrettably respectfully~~ decline your offer of employment.

Please give my most affectionate regards to our sister.

Yours,
Benjamin

Rereading his letter, Ben decided to add a postscript that he knew would give Philip conniptions of envy and disapproval.

P.S.
Our own modest gold mining enterprise, employing four unskilled laborers, has in only four months turned a profit of more than £1,000 (and winter is said to be the least productive season). We call our little settlement Ashbyville—should the opportunity arise, you might inform Lord and Lady Brightstone of this commemoration. Finally, brother, I wish to ask you the favor of subscribing a £10 donation on my behalf to my friend Frederick Engels, to be sent in care of Ermen & Engels in Manchester.

Ben held the paper in front of his lips and blew on the wet ink. The letter from Engels in Geneva had been an urgent request for donations to support the democratic newspaper he was publishing in Cologne, "a small but essential barricade" against the resurgent oppressors in Prussia and beyond. Engels had just heard of the rush to California for gold, which he admitted in his note to Ben was "a confounding fact, not provided for in our *Manifesto*—that is to say, the creation of large new markets out of *nothing*."

"Do you know Newton's Third Law of Motion?" Ben suddenly asked Skaggs.

"I believe I do—pendulums, billiard balls, the kick of a shotgun . . ."

"Yes, but I've just realized now that the Third Law explains the *political* events of this last year as well. It explains Europe. 'For every action, there is an equal and opposite reaction.' You see? A season of revolution, a season of counter-revolution. Hope running ahead of itself, then the despots reasserting themselves with equal force. The monarchs run off, then they return. Blossoming, withering, just as—" He suddenly stopped, and stared.

Skaggs was so startled he bobbled and tossed his book to the ground. Ben gripped his pen like a dagger.

An Indian stood at the doorway of the cabin Skaggs and Duff shared. He had a deer's face placed in front of his own, a stole of knotted rabbit-skin strips over his shoulders, and a white paste smeared on his neck. His hands and wrists were bloody. He held a bow and arrow. Ben, thinking he was about to attack Polly, or perhaps already had, stood to grab a log from the fire and charge, battling him to the death if necessary.

"*Hallo* there," Skaggs shouted.

Suddenly Polly rushed outside, her feet bare, her eyes wet. The Indian was no Indian but Duff, dressed in a Maidu costume.

He removed the mask and in a rush of words, as animated as they had ever seen him, recounted his last forty-eight hours. After he lost his way, he discovered a flock of butterflies roosting in a stand of pines, and then he'd fallen and cut his face, but two Maidu women had appeared. The beautiful young one, Yauka, had placed a warm green poultice from her mouth on his cheek, and then they'd taken him to their village, Hembem, which consisted of a dozen conical huts—huts called *hu*, he said, made from slabs of bark with beds of pine needles, like the miniature forest cottages Polly and he had built in the Clove Valley for the imaginary gnomes. Only thirty of the Indians currently lived at the village, mainly women and children and the very old.

Most of the men and many of the women were off at the mines. And nine others from their village, Duff said, including Yauka's fiancé, had been killed three years ago in a massacre of one hundred Indians by Kit Carson and Frémont's soldiers and their gang of Indian hirelings from the east.

"The place was magical," he gushed. "It was the *Peaceful Valley*, just like in my book *Old Hicks, the Guide*—'graceful creatures shut out, by their steep hills in this enchanting recess.' "

Skaggs snorted.

"I envy you your adventure, Duff," said Ben.

"Are you hungry?" Polly asked.

"No! Before we left for the hunt this morning there was a feast—acorn soup and acorn bread and fried deer tongue . . . And crickets. I ate a cricket."

"This is hunting attire, then," said Ben as he touched the rabbit fur on Duff's shoulders.

"I impersonated a deer to draw in other deer. And it worked! We killed two bucks. That is, we drove one over a cliff, the other Bayam and Kumisi killed, with arrows." He held up his bloody hands. "Bayam is Yauka's younger brother, and Kumisi is a cousin. In return for my gold, they gave me the costume, the bow, and these as well." From the ground behind him he picked up a small red blanket woven with zigzag black stripes.

"The bow and arrows are a gift for you, Ben." Ben had told Duff about his boyhood love of archery. "The blanket, the *bayeta*, is for you, Polly. The moccasins are yours, Skaggs."

Ben rubbed the Indian cloth between his fingers like the textile manufacturer he used to be. It reminded him of the red baize Knowles & Company had produced in Manchester. (In fact, this very blanket had started six years ago as Knowles & Company baize, dyed red with imported Mexican cochineal, then exported from Manchester to Bilbao, and then from Spain to Mexico, where a Navajo Indian in Sonora had unraveled the cloth and rewove the threads into this *bayeta*. The Navajo had traded several blankets to a Mexican for *aguardiente,* and the Mexican, now mining in California, had in turn traded this one to a Maidu for a pinch of gold.)

Rolled up in the blanket were twelve arrows. Ben took one and fingered its sharp, carved stone head. Shooting at targets in England, he had fired arrows with small, soft brass points. Polly went to fetch the bottle of benzoic acid and a sticking plaster for Duff's wound.

"I gave them the two ounces I had with me," Duff confessed, a little bashfully. "Yauka told me that I am a *llano.*"

"You understand the Indians' lingo now?" asked Skaggs.

"*Llano* is Spanish," Duff said. "It means level ground, but . . . about a person it means steady and humble and trustworthy." He blushed. He was smiling.

"Ah, right," said Skaggs, recalling something from his visit to North Fork Dry Diggings, "your *Spanish.* At the saloon on Friday I was speaking with a Mexican gentleman whose English was better than serviceable—a gold-hungry Mexican *judge,* up from the city of Hermosillo. After a few mescals he got into a tussle with one of the Americans about the war— about the Irish deserters who switched sides and fought for the Mexicans. St. Patrick's Battalion?"

Duff wanted to disappear. The truth was catching up. He clasped his hands in front of him, and watched Ben pull the bowstring. He thought of Jesus's words at the Last Supper: *One of you will betray me.*

"Judge Suárez made the mistake of *toasting* the Irish renegades, but he called them by a Spanish name . . ."

"Los San Patricios . . ."

"No, no, he called them the 'Legión de Extranjeros.' And I recalled that evening last spring, the night of the victory parades on Broadway, when I played my practical joke, poking my walking stick into your back, pretending I was an armed Mexican. Do you remember?"

"Yeah."

". . . And I believe something like *la Legión de Extranjeros* was a phrase you whispered to me that night . . ."

Duff thought perhaps he should simply turn and bolt, run back into the woods to Yauka's *hu* and never come back.

"... 'The Legion of Foreigners' was Judge Suárez's translation."

"Uh-huh."

"And so I fail to understand why you spoke *that* phrase to me in New York . . ."

"It was a Mexican phrase, during the war."

"Rain," said Ben, holding his palm out to feel the drops, and Skaggs felt one, and both men raced to the benches to collect their papers. Polly hurried Duff inside to receive his antiseptic and bandage.

62

late February 1849

. . .

Ashbyville

HE RAINS OF February made it impossible to mine more than two or three days in a week.

Duff had finished helping build the observatory (which he sometimes called the chapel), so he spent his days of leisure at the Indians' village, huddled in Yauka's *hu*. He watched her grind acorns, taught her and her brother English, and learned about the Maidus' ceremonial fasting and ingestion of *toloache*, jimson root tea, which they believed enabled them to communicate with spirits. It sounded to Duff like a Lenten first communion, in which receiving the Holy Eucharist *actually* connected one with God. He had stopped cutting his hair, and started parting it in the middle. And at any appearance of the sun, Polly noticed, he turned his face skyward to brown his skin.

Skaggs read astronomy books, and now awaited the arrival of the telescope itself from New York, and the dome from Mexico.

Ben had his new private diversion as well. Polly had painted four concentric circles on the back of one of his thick white work shirts, which they wrapped around two feet of scrap lumber. She used charcoal for the outside ring, blue and red tempera for the next two, and for the bull's-eye she mixed gold dust into a spoonful of collodion, the clear chemical jelly Skaggs used to coat daguerreotype plates.

He took up archery with the same single-mindedness he had applied as a boy, but now with the muscles of a grown man. For an hour at least twice every day, at dawn and before dusk, Ben shot half a round—seventy-two arrows. On days when the rain made it impossible to work, he would shoot two or three rounds. They had mounted the target on the huge oak at the western end of the camp, forty yards beyond the tents, so that even in downpours he could stay dry by shooting from just inside the canvas, then run to pull his arrows from the target and replace them in his quiver—Skaggs's spyglass case. After a week he had hit the bull's-eye so often that it needed regilding, and the following week Polly resorted to yellow tempera instead.

Ben had become an archer again. The biceps of his right arm bulged, and his three string fingers were callused. He thought about trying to kill a rabbit or turkey.

Polly felt she had drawn every inch of Ashbyville twice, and had acquired no new pastime. She started to admit to herself that she missed crowded sidewalks. She missed furtive glances at strangers and wondering who they were and where they lived and what they thought. She missed the theater, and music. She missed shopping. She missed the sunlight and shadow on fine big stone buildings, and the sound of church bells. She missed the society of women. She missed the city's sense of endless permutation and infinite possibility.

One night during a long silence at supper, she looked around at her compatriots. She was very fortunate, she knew, and very fond of all of them, but the quiet meandering and murk of ordinary life in Ashbyville had grown somewhat tiresome. Skaggs had been right. She *was* spoiled. She sighed.

"You are bored, my dear," he suddenly announced, "and boredom becomes boring for those in proximity to it."

"*Skaggs,*" Ben snapped.

"I am simply—"

"Timothy is not wrong," Polly said, "I have been a terrible mope. Forgive me."

"And allow me," Skaggs replied, "to propose a miracle cure."

February 28, 1849

· · ·

San Francisco

THUS POLLY AND Ben and Skaggs found themselves one morning a week later making their way slowly along San Francisco's plaza, from the Excelsior Restaurant toward the wharf. All three were bathed in hot water, dressed in well-laundered clothing, full of good food—poached eggs! *fresh* sausage! corn cakes with *maple syrup!*—cooked by strangers and served on china. Ben and Skaggs had not worn neckties nor Polly a dress since they were last here, the day they had landed in California. Ben had shaved for the first time since Christmas, and Polly had perfumed herself with lavender and rose. Walking on springy twelve-foot-long timbers suspended a few inches above the muddy slough of the street was like a game to them, not a chore, they were all of them so pleased to be in a city. Every so often, blue sky showed itself and the sun shone.

Since November the winter weather had pushed thousands of miners out of the Sierras and into San Francisco for days or weeks at a time. The quiet, nearly deserted town of last fall was now filled with several thousands of people, every second one of them shouting. Three men no older than twenty, one a brown-skinned, blue-eyed Kanacker from the Sandwich Islands, stood together in the mud singing "Buffalo Gals," in celebration of . . . who knew what? On the next block, a hatless bald man in a new suit and bare feet sat on the windowsill of a new house, giggling and wiping away tears as he held a six-ounce nugget in front of his face.

It reminded Ben of Paris the day after the monarchy dissolved. It reminded Polly of the Bowery on a Saturday night in the spring. Skaggs thought of his father's dreadful damnation of cities with an air of the permanent carnival. He wished his father could see this.

But it was not all a spree, and that is what made it unlike anything any of them had seen. If San Francisco was loose and sybaritic, it was also a kind of go-aheadish Yankee paradise. Those men not gallivanting were hard at work calculating, bargaining, weighing, selling, hauling, and building with an intensity equal to that of the holidaymakers around them—"like a Shaker with a week left to live," Skaggs said about a grunting carpenter with a sledge in one hand, an awl in the other, a ruler in his pocket, and a screwdriver between his teeth. Everywhere the air smelled of milled pine. A city was arising—instantly, all around them, even as they walked through it. Twenty-three houses would be finished by the end of the day, and twenty-six others started the next.

"It is as if they are all in some great contest," Polly remarked.

"Not 'as if' they are in a contest," Ben replied. "They *are* in one."

The seeds of a permanent and substantial place—a wharf, tenscore houses and stores, even a school—had been planted a few years earlier, when Yerba Buena was just another Mexican port, before the gold. So now it was a bona fide town, not a camp, despite the hundreds of tents pitched everywhere. The temporary structures were plainly annexes, transitory shelters for people and mules and cargo while a true city was being assembled. New settlements back in the hills had comical names, like Second Garrote and Growlersburg and Rough and Ready, because their inhabitants understood that all the shanties and lean-tos might be abandoned next month and vanish next year, as soon as the ground was denuded of gold. But San Francisco—for all its makeshifty, brabbling, brangling rudeness—was already filled with a great pride in its own existence.

They passed the new post office—where a line of customers snaked around the block—and approached the pier at the water end of Clay Street, where several hundred others had already gathered to watch a celebrated ship put into port. They moved to the edge of the crowd, most of whom gave Polly a glance or two on account of her gender, a third glance on account of her race, and still another for her face and figure. A white woman! A pretty young white woman in fashionable silks! At some of the men who frankly stared, Ben stared back, and Skaggs actually scowled until they smiled or looked away.

A large ship had passed through the Golden Gate into the bay. Ben, seeing its canvas unfurled, cocked his head and listened. He heard no thunder of six hundred horsepower from across the water. The engines had given out. The brand-new SS *California*, the first vessel of the Pacific Mail Steamship Company, would come inside the kelp under sail, not steam, her pair of thirty-foot side wheels mere ornaments.

Ben and Skaggs had seen this ship before, in the Manhattan dark between midnight and dawn, from above, hours before its launch, looking down last spring from a rooftop at the shipyard in Avenue D where it was built.

The three of them watched the streams of passengers scramble off the gangway—four hundred people from a vessel built to carry two hundred, men (and six women) from the States as well as South America, every one of them fevering for gold. Ben and Skaggs and Polly felt like California old-timers.

They had timed their trip to San Francisco to coincide with the ship's arrival not as sightseers, however, but to collect a certain cargo.

No one stopped them as they made their way into the hold, for the crew of the *California* was already deserting, despite the remarkable wages they had been offered to stay on.

Polly was the first to spot the crate.

"My God!" Skaggs cried. "Dear, dull, cautious Jonah actually *did* it! Bless you, Jonah!" He looked around. "A crowbar."

"Perhaps first we ought to get it ashore—"

"*No*, we must jimmy it *now*."

He found a chisel and began to attack the lid. They had never seen him so determined. When they finally pried open the box, Skaggs cleared away the wood shavings inside like a ravenous man digging for food, then stopped short. He was breathing heavily. He stroked his prize softly, slowly. It was a tapered mahogany tube the color of toast and as smooth as butter, ten feet long and half a foot in diameter at its wide end. The brass fittings at the eye-piece shone like . . . gold. The telescope had arrived.

"Good Lord. Have you ever in your lives seen a more beautiful thing?"

"It is very handsome," Ben agreed.

"Why, it is *perfection*."

"We are pleased for you, Skaggs," said Polly.

"My God," he said, looking up, as if he had surprised himself by winning a dare, "I shall be an astronomer."

Skaggs had his treasure.

the American River Valley

DUFF WAS BEGINNING to see that his life had a scheme imposed from above. Why, for instance, had he taken up Sam Houston as his boyhood hero? Now he knew why: because Senator Houston had run off to the frontier as a young man to join an Indian tribe, to take an Indian name and an Indian wife.

He spent every hour he could at Hembem, hiking over the hills to it in the afternoon and returning for his next appointed workday only at dawn. He no longer washed with soap, since Yauka found the smell unpleasant—instead, he used a certain onion to cleanse himself. He trimmed his beard with a glowing hot stick. And with an obsidian splinter he had cut the tops of his hands—a line and two tiny circles on each—and rubbed the cuts with burnt nutmeg to darken the scars.

He wore moccasins all the time, laced up over his ankles like half boots. He no longer chewed tobacco, but smoked it in a wooden pipe. He played tunes on a four-holed elderwood flute. On his trips to and from the village, he stopped to gather chervil and lamb's lettuce and the first tender shoots of columbine and larkspur.

While Polly and the others were in San Francisco, Yauka surprised Duff by giving him a special necklace she had strung. That night as they lay together he started counting its wooden beads.

"¿Porque estas contando?" she had asked him.

". . . twenty-three, twenty-four, momentito, twenty-five, twenty-six . . ."

And when he'd finished counting—". . . one hundred sixty-two, one hundred sixty-three, *one hundred sixty-four,* my Lord, *one hundred sixty-five*"—he sat up and made the sign of the cross. The necklace Yauka had made happened to be a perfect rosary, one bead for each of one hundred and fifty Hail Marys, another for each of the fifteen Our Fathers.

San Francisco

SAN FRANCISCO WORKED wonders on their moods. Seeing a busy harbor and being among houses and hubbub again—"*just* enough civilization," as Skaggs called it—made all three of them merrier than they had been in a while.

As soon as the *California* disgorged its passengers, San Francisco's population had increased by a fifth. And the very horde made Ben and Polly taste their sweet luck. Every man Polly saw seemed underripe or overripe or in any case overwrought, which made her appreciate the sober, faithful, slightly Whiggish Englishman she had—Ben was a *llano,* as Duff put it. And for Ben, the sight of the same mob of men, all lonely and longing and panting (the true state of males everywhere, but permitted such brazen expression only here), reminded him of his own exceptional good fortune in finding and then refinding Polly. They were both lucky as any miner yelling about a nugget as big as a cannonball.

Just before they left their room at the St. Francis Hotel to meet Skaggs for a walk through the plaza and an expedition to the beach before dinner, he grabbed her and kissed her on the lips. "*You* are my great bonanza," he said, which made her laugh. Perhaps he had been cured of his Whiggishness.

The largest and liveliest saloon in San Francisco was the El Dorado, a canvas cube so packed with men most of the day and night that its milling crowd extended permanently out into the streets. There were as many men sharing bottles and betting in the mud of Washington and Kearny streets—

on the roll of a die, the flip of a coin, the speed of a bug across a puddle, the number of teeth in a randomly chosen stranger's mouth—as there were inside the tent.

A new El Dorado, its two stories already framed and half joined, was under construction next door. And on the opposite side of the tent, just down Kearny Street, was another big half-finished saloon and hotel, the Parker House, and next to it another, the Bella Union. Even now, after sundown, dozens of carpenters were cutting and nailing, working by the light of candles and lamps scattered high and low inside all three of the open timber superstructures. The unmuffled roar of a thousand boozy voices in the tent of the El Dorado, punctuated by solos—cries of pleasure or anger, yelps of triumph or defeat at the gaming tables, occasionally even a few bars of some song—was mingled with the racket of fifty saws and hammers.

Ben and Polly and Skaggs stood on a warehouse dock across Washington Street, surveying the scene.

"The music of our new American democracy," Skaggs said, "ugly and beautiful both, unaware that it is either."

They had seen but three females tonight—two they recognized from the *California* gangway, and one of the two women who worked in the El Dorado as card dealers. Polly's thoughts inevitably turned to one of her former professions. *Where,* she wondered, *are the brothels?* Her curiosity made her slightly anxious.

"And Young America," Ben added. "I have seen hardly a man older than . . . well, Skaggs, than you."

They watched as one of the oldest and most distinguished-looking fellows politely edged his way to a clearing in the mob, placed his hands on his knees, and vomited, then vomited again, stood upright, nodded politely to his several onlookers, replaced his hat, and walked back to his dice game. The men standing near his puddle of spew took not even one step away.

Barely half the crowd had buttoned collars, and all of the hats—lumpy felt slouches with enormous brims, glazed leather caps with no brims at all—were those of drovers and butchers. Not that there weren't fops. One man wore a coonskin with the tail dyed a bright blue, and others had decorative beards—tied into pigtails, braided into pretzels, festooned with feathers. In lieu of cravats, some of the men had big red or orange bandannas wrapped around their necks. A couple wore good coats and waistcoats over red flannel undershirts. Another wore a huge silver necklace. Several of the Mexicans had velvet tunics and baggy trousers that hung so low at the waist that the white tops of their drawers and an inch of their belly flesh showed. Two young men from Ohio whose only Spanish was *vamoose* and *desperado* and *fiesta* were draped in woolen serapes striped blue and pink and yellow. Mexicans chatted and gambled and laughed and argued with Yankees, Peruvians with Frenchmen, Virginians with Polynesians.

"Jiminy cricket," came a shout from the left, "I'll be *blowed* if it ain't my old boy Tim *Skaggs!*" A grinning young man in stiff, dirty jeans and knee-high boots was stomping through the slop up Kearny, obviously drunk. He climbed up to join them on the warehouse dock.

"Noah," said the boy as he stuck out his hand, "from back in Illinois?" a little chagrined at Skaggs's failure to recognize him.

Noah James was Billy Herndon's nephew from Springfield, whom Skaggs would see loitering around his uncle's law office. He occasionally provided bits of unflattering gossip about Lincoln to Skaggs in exchange for drinks of whiskey. When Skaggs had seen him last, before the boy had hired on as a teamster with his neighbor George Donner's train of emigrants for California, he'd been a fourteen-year-old debauchee in the making.

The boy's woozy good humor returned when Skaggs introduced him to the lady and English gentleman as "the celebrated Mr. James, one of the bold young survivors of the celebrated Donner party." Noah informed them he had "given up prospecting for the wintertime, at least," since he was now paid a couple of ounces a week by Mr. McCabe, the owner of the El Dorado, simply to "hobnob with the customers."

"Why is that?" Polly asked. "Why does he pay you?"

"Because I *survived*—proved I'm *lucky*." He winked his left eye, but his right one half shut along with it. "And Mr. McCabe says I give gamblers the idea they can be lucky too, so they gamble more."

"It is the same reason," Skaggs said, "prizefighters operate saloons on the Bowery—because Noah is a *celebrity*. Drunkards (and, for that matter, the muddled in general) are reassured by proximity to the well-known."

"A 'celebrity'?" Noah repeated happily. "A celebrity! Strap my hide and call me Charlie, that's a new one on me, Tim. You still a scribbler?" Almost no one in California considered "miner" his official occupation, although it was the way nine out of ten earned a living.

"Mr. Skaggs is an astronomical photographer," Ben said.

James, having no idea what that meant, ignored it, and suggested to Skaggs that he would be happy to "introduce you to Kemble." Edward Kemble was a former New Yorker, he said, now editor and publisher of the

Alta California. "He mustered out of Frémont's army spring before last, around the same time I nicked in here—*finally,* you know, after my misfortune," he added with a smirk. "Him and I are the same age, just about."

"I think you must be confused, Noah," Skaggs replied.

"No, sir—Kemble turned twenty November last, and I'm nineteen now."

"And he owns the newspaper?"

"They call this a country where the youth prospers best." The boy winked again. "Say, do you rich miners care to buy me dinner? I could eat a damned horse I'm so hungry! I could eat the tail off a *rat.*"

They looked at him agape. He seemed oblivious to the fact that his fame derived from having spent Christmas of 1846 and New Year's of 1847 at a cannibal feast.

Finally Ben broke the silence. "We have dined already, thank you." That was a fib. "We are off now to go beachcombing." He held up his lantern and two small baskets.

"OK, then, but while you're in town, if any—*hey,* damn, there's McCabe already," said Noah. He pointed at a man in a striped suit and high hat parting the crowd as he made his way into the glow of the El Dorado. "With the Countess McCready."

The countess was on McCabe's arm. She wore a glossy pleated purple silk dress with a bodice that barely clung to her shoulders. To Polly it looked vulgar—she had never been one for décolletage—but fashionable. Indeed, she wondered if it might be a new *1849* style. She wondered too how the countess had come to be among the dozen white women in San Francisco. And then she learned the answer.

Noah leaned close to Skaggs, as if he were going to whisper a secret. But instead he confided in a shout. "They say that the Countess McCready's girls, when they arrive—white girls, French girls—will charge *twenty ounces* a man. *Twenty.*" He grinned and shook his head. "I better get on in the crib now or he'll dock me." He jumped off the platform with a loud squish. "I'll be seeing you, Tim, and miss, and Mr. John Bull, sir."

They watched him trudge away, arms flying, mud up to his shins.

"Nasty little skellum," said Skaggs. He was enjoying this visit to the city, but at that moment he realized, to his everlasting surprise, that he was not a bit tempted to live in San Francisco. He would be happy to visit regularly, but for now he was through with his urban existence. A life of solitude in his little cabin on the river among the pines and redwoods and deer had become a happy prospect, as long as newspapers and books and the odd *aguardiente* with a convivial stranger were no more than a few hours' drive away. He was an astronomer now.

The sound of the city faded as the three continued their constitutional along the waterfront, crossed California Street, passed a neat bed of mint, and finally stepped onto the sandy shore itself at Yerba Buena Cove, continuing toward the tent neighborhood called Happy Valley. The tide was low. Ben lit the lantern and took out Duff's jackknife, and with Skaggs began to examine certain boulders.

While the men worked and talked, Polly wandered along the beach by herself, staying just a foot or two from the surf's edge, looking out at the hundred reflected editions of the moon on the waves. Relieved of Ben's shaming presence and of any obligation to listen or talk, she surrendered to her uninvited thoughts.

Twenty ounces. On their very best days at the placers these days, the four of them, working tediously from seven to four, washed out twelve or thirteen ounces, and on most days no more than ten. Polly was never very skilled at multiplication, and like everyone else she had abandoned the habit of converting ounces to their dollar equivalents. But now, gazing over San Francisco Bay in the darkness, she worked out that twenty ounces was worth . . . three hundred dollars in cash. In New York City, there had been rumors of $20 Gramercy Park strumpets, but the $10 Polly earned in Mercer Street was the top price any woman could ordinarily demand. *Three hundred for a fuck!*

And so while Ben and Skaggs carefully scraped and picked at the rocks up the beach, she imagined how such an occupation might be conducted in California. It was only an idle conjecture, she assured herself, just to satisfy her curiosity—"a purely speculative computation," as Ben called his elaborate penciled sums concerning the new flume he proposed to build at Ashbyville. She figured that $300, one customer each day, would amount to . . . $2,000 a week, and thus . . . $8,000 a month. Life in San Francisco was expensive, but one could still live comfortably for a month on $500. Leaving a profit of . . . *$7,500.* A very rich man's annual income for a woman working an hour or two each day for one month each year. Such a woman might live, for instance, in a large house built of redwood, say, on a high hill with a garden overlooking the ocean . . . down the coast past San Jose, for instance, which was said to be warmer and much drier . . . and then decamp to the city for that mere one month of unrespectable work each winter. Or she might, if she wished, designate a part of her large income as capital to underwrite a theater in which professional productions of Shake-speare and Molière and Dickens might be mounted in California for the first time, together with premieres by new playwrights such as Mr. Benjamin Knowles of London and Mr. Timothy Skaggs, the New York novelist . . .

"Polly?" Ben called. "I believe we are finished."

She felt her face and neck flush, and turned to rejoin the men.

The two baskets were each half filled with a particular species of barna-cle. Skaggs delightedly summarized for Polly the science he had learned from Ben's correspondence with "his scientific pornographer friend"—that barnacles possessed, in relation to their size, the longest penises of any crea-ture on earth, "long enough to extend *over* six of his adjacent fellows in order to inseminate the distant object of his hermaphroditic affections. And an individual may copulate *ten times* in a day."

Ben held the lantern near the baskets and handed Polly the drawings he had received from England. She peered at each.

"My God," Skaggs said as he saw her face in the light, "my little venereal lecture has caused Polly Lucking to *blush!*"

"You are mistaken about that, my vain friend," she replied evenly, and after a minute of scrutinizing the creatures, Polly agreed that, yes, each type seemed to match its respective pen-and-ink depiction. Before they returned to Ashbyville, Ben would pack up the barnacles and ship them to Professor Darwin at Down House in Kent.

63

March 11, 1849

. . .

Coloma, California

*T*HE SACRAMENTO WAS flooded to twice its width of the week before. Spring was arriving.

After disembarking at the Embarcadero—in SACRAMENTO CITY, as the Sutters' large new municipal signs grandly declared the empty grid of streets and thirty cabins-to-be—they boarded the new stage line that ran for fifty miles along the Coloma road. Skaggs rode on top of the coach with his telescope all the way into Coloma.

They found the New York Hotel, and Polly retired directly to the room. To be outdoors on a Sunday in a camp town was, for any woman, to draw a crowd. Ben and Skaggs strolled. They waited for almost an hour at a tiny tent to see, as its sign promised, EXTRA-ORDINARY SPECTACLES FROM PARIS. In the queue they chatted with a German portrait painter who had just arrived in California, and agreed to meet him later, with Polly, for dinner. Inside the tent they paid a French Canadian a pinch of dust to peer inside a wooden chest for one minute at five candlelit photographs mounted on each side of a pentagonal plinth. The pictures were indeed extraordinary. An absolutely naked black woman reclined on a couch, staring dreamily at the camera, legs spread wide, one hand wedged lazily behind her head, the other resting on her crotch with its forefinger pointing at her pudendum. An absolutely naked white woman seated upright on a bed, in profile, one foot on the mattress and the other on the floor, her face turned away but her large, pretty left breast and pubic fur both fully exposed. Notre-Dame Cathedral and the river Seine, an astounding 150-degree panorama made with a newfangled camera using a rotating lens and a semicylindrical plate. And two views from a rooftop of a half mile of the barricaded Rue Saint-Maur in the Faubourg du Temple neighborhood of Paris—the first picture made last June 25, on the final Sunday of the red radicals' uprising, and the second on the next day, after the army and Garde Mobile had pushed through the barricades and slaughtered the insurgents. During his night in the streets of Paris last year, Ben Knowles had made his way around rubble and fires on those very blocks.

THE MAIN SALOON of their hotel had been hired that night for a ball. Two fiddlers and a trumpeter were playing polkas and mazurkas, and at least a hundred miners were in attendance. As Polly and Ben and Skaggs prepared to leave for dinner, they glanced inside—and it was not the Chopin that made them pause to watch from the shadows. A score of the men on the floor wore dresses, and had stuffed the bodices to overflowing. Some had rouged their faces and tinted their lips.

"On this occasion," Ben said softly, "one does understand the utility of corsets."

Polly wrinkled her nose in reply. A moment later, she pointed out that among every dancing couple in which both partners were dressed in customary shirts and trousers, the trousers of one had a small square of canvas stitched onto the hip.

"*Designated girls,*" Skaggs said. "The patch betokens femininity, yet without the expense and bother of a gown and cotton bosoms."

The dancers with the patches were just as likely as those without to be bearded. The visitors from Ashbyville silently wondered for how many of these men the charade extended beyond the dance floor.

Finally Polly tugged on Ben's arm to go to dinner.

"We were informed earlier by the chatter in the street," Skaggs told Polly as they stepped into the night, "that it is now certainly all *over.*"

"What is over?" she asked.

"The gold," Ben explained. "The easy gold is finished, they say. The northern mines all 'petering out.' "

"If the good old days have indeed ended," Skaggs said, nodding in the direction of the river and Sutter's Mill, "they numbered precisely . . . four hundred. And I am not fazed." He was happy in California. The sooner the gold was gone, perhaps, the better.

"But that was the same talk in San Francisco the first day we arrived," said Polly. "Do you not remember? 'All dug out along the South Fork, every damned ounce.' 'This is the end of it.' Well, I say, look around us." Coloma's Main Street was filled with spiffy miners chattering and sauntering. "I'd wager most of these have a few ounces in their pockets. Look at them."

"Look at *him*, do you mean?" Skaggs asked of a man a few yards to their right. "That is an 1849 miner for you."

The man stood in the shadows of an alley at the side of the hotel with his face turned away from the street, crying and shaking. He was simply the latest evidence for Skaggs's new view of California brainsickness. One Saturday some weeks earlier, a downpour had forced him to remain at Old Dry Diggings overnight. And as enthusiastically dissipated as he had been for much of the preceding two decades, as familiar as he was with every sort of saloon and dive from Hanover, New Hampshire, to Cluj-Napoca in Transylvania, he had been shocked by the scope and extremity of the drunkenness in the camp that night. He had seen nobody—not one man—who was unquestionably sober. By nine o'clock, several score men lay scattered and motionless in the dirt and grass, as if some bloodless massacre had occurred, and before midnight the count of unconscious bodies was over a hundred. And he could not sleep for the noise that arose from the tents until dawn— whinnies, whimpers, howls, croaks, groans (of agony more than ecstasy), and the unending sobs of hundreds of boys and men. Such an experience might have amused Skaggs in the past, but instead it had rattled him.

"Men predisposed to melancholy," Ben said after they had passed the man weeping in the alley, "will be just as sad in El Dorado as they were in New York or Hartford or Leeds. But here they may bawl openly, in the streets. Which I count as progress."

"The gold is not gone," Polly said. "I don't believe it."

Up ahead, Skaggs spotted their new German acquaintance, the painter, and asked Ben how to say *"It's dinnertime, you Prussian bastard"* in German.

late March and early April 1849

. . .

Ashbyville and Sacramento City

WHEN YAUKA AGREED to marry Duff, Polly and the others immediately accepted his proposed new arrangement. Each week from now on, he would sleep at Ashbyville one night, and work the placers for all the daylight hours during the day before and after, in return for only a half share of gold.

For the first time since the war, he seemed to be at peace.

He brought Yauka to Ashbyville to introduce them to her, and although the communications were halting, with Duff serving as interpreter, she seemed sweet and bright and soft as the spring.

"Where do you wish to hold the ceremony," Polly asked Duff and his fiancée, "and when?"

Duff did not translate the question into Spanish for Yauka. "They do not hold wedding ceremonies," he explained to his sister. He had asked for Yauka's hand, she had consented; he would give some gold to her brother and mother, who would make a separate bed for the couple. And then the marriage would be a fact.

"Your type of freethinkers," Skaggs said, "eh, Polly?"

In fact, she found herself disappointed that there would be no wedding. And Yauka's stories of disease at Hembem and the other Maidu villages troubled her. Polly worried that the rigors of her brother's new life—eating crickets and worms, drinking herbal liquors, going half naked half the year—would make him vulnerable to peculiar Indian illnesses. Yauka's earliest memories, she told them, were of the days and days one spring spent harvesting hundreds of pink canchalagua flowers. The blossoms were supposed to be an antidote to fever and chills, but the year Yauka turned three, she said, *la plaga*, the malaria epidemic, took away her father and three siblings and half her cousins and aunts and uncles. And during the last two years, she said, outbreaks of flux and fever and pox had returned. Indeed, Yauka's cousin Kumisi had been feverish lately.

SKAGGS HAD SUGGESTED several medicines Duff should lay up for the people of Hembem, and it was that errand that took Duff one day early in April down the American River to Sutter's Fort. It was a work of mercy in the name of Jesus Christ to please his Lord God and Savior, as Bishop Hughes had commanded him to perform a year ago. The morning after he arrived in Sacramento City, dressed in leggings and a serape made from a mountain lion skin, he spent twenty-seven ounces on his medical supply. And he ate lunch at a saloon on the Embarcadero jammed with coughing, sneezing, hand-shaking, jovially unclean newcomers all crawling with germs from two dozen different pestilential ports of call.

As he was leaving town that afternoon, he came upon a crowd listening to a speech by a man standing on the back of a wagon. The fellow had a southern accent. He was campaigning to be elected as a Democratic delegate to California's first constitutional convention, and he said he had always fought for the rights of the downtrodden. Duff liked the sound of that. His name was Peter Burnett, and he had served as a judge and legislator in the Oregon Territory before coming south for the gold last fall. Before that he had been a lawyer, and despite his own Roman Catholicism had defended the Mormons' founder, Joseph Smith, against trumped-up charges of arson and treason in Missouri. Duff liked the sound of all that, too.

"But, gentlemen, my deep-seated passions, and my long struggle for the liberty of *every* man from *every* nation on earth," he said, "are not those of a fanatic." In Oregon, he said, they had outlawed slavery, but they had also passed a law that "forbade the emigration of free Negroes and mulattos into our virgin country . . ."

Duff did not much like the sound of Oregon's Territorial Exclusionary Act.

"And as for the race of beings who teem in their nakedness and dig in the dirt of *this* beautiful land, I am afraid we are faced, my California friends, with two choices. Either we shall indulge their savagery and permit them to usurp the land and water and gold—or we must wage a sort of war, a war of extermination that shall continue until the Indian race dies out, as extinct as the dodo."

In Duff's valise, among the medicines, was his Colt's revolver. This man Burnett deserved to die. Duff crossed himself. He wondered how close he would have to get to be sure of a lethal shot. He would need to load the chamber and edge his way to the front of the crowd. He could do it.

But if he killed Burnett, he would immediately be captured and hanged. Yauka and her people would never receive the life-giving elixirs and pills in his bag. And he imagined how the fact of his Indian costume might provoke revenge against the Maidu. He would let the villain live.

As he rode Jenny Lind east past Sutter's Fort, he spotted thirty gaunt and tattered packers making camp on the riverbank. They were pitiful. A few, he saw, were Indians. He approached one of the company, a white man standing at some distance from the tents, smoking a pipe and staring at the river. The fellow's eyes looked fatigued and forlorn, like a soldier's after a battle.

When Duff introduced himself, the man said he was a geologist from Baltimore, and complimented his English.

"Some of our men are Indians, too, from back east," he said, nodding toward the camp.

Duff was flattered. Did this Baltimore geologist truly believe that Duff Lucking could be an Indian's name? And that California Indians, even halfbreed *cholos*, had blond hair?

"Where have you traveled from, then?" he asked the man.

The man looked down, shook his head, and sighed. "More or less straight from hell," he said. They had set out in October from St. Louis on a private expedition to find a southern route to San Francisco. But they had become lost and then snowbound in the Rockies for a month. A third of the men and all the mules had died. In January they had finally reached the settlement of Taos. "We rested awhile there at Kit Carson's rancho, praise God, before we marched on across the desert and up to here." He shook his head again and puffed on his pipe.

Duff wanted to make the sign of the cross. "At Kit Carson's? The *real* Kit Carson?"

"Yes, of course, 'the real' Carson. He's the colonel's dearest pal." He cocked his chin toward the tents. "Frémont and he more or less *founded* this country here together, don't you know."

Duff was astounded. This fresh camp was John Charles Frémont's. He was speaking to one of Frémont's men. Frémont himself—the archvillain responsible for the murders of Yauka's kin and one hundred of her neighbors by Kit Carson and his gang in 1846—was within hailing distance, a stone's throw away. A Colt's shot away.

"Yes," Duff said, "I do know. Well, welcome to California."

April 11, 1849
. . .
Ashbyville

T HEY HAD NEVER dammed and diverted Generosity Creek or built the Supremely Long Thomas. Others elsewhere built flumes with great success, however, and Ben read enviously in the *Alta California* of the great aqueduct that drained a rich flat by guiding water in a wooden flume *suspended above* a stream. He recalled that Duff had been in the Company of Sappers, Miners, and Pontoniers—trained by the army in Mexico to rip holes in the ground with canisters of black powder. So when he heard about the new, laborious mining practice of "coyoting"—searching for gold by digging thirty feet deep, then digging secondary holes perpendicular to the main burrow—he proposed that they blast into the bedrock buried along the river in Ashbyville to expose new veins.

Duff had already used powder to level the top of Mount Aetna for the observatory. But Polly repeated her arguments about despoiling the land, and Duff himself was torn. He was exhilarated by the prospect of unleashing pure explosive energy—he had reveled in detonating the charges for Skaggs, bombs that maimed and killed no one and destroyed nothing but rock. But the green and eager California spring and his months learning Maidu ways made him agree with his sister that blasting for profit would amount to a kind of war against the earth. And Skaggs worried that repeated explosions might disturb the telescope's delicate mount.

"But was it not *you*, Duff," Ben had said crossly at the end of the community's final meeting on the subject, "who suggested that with a good fire pumper and hose we might wash away promising hillsides at the rate of one hundred fifty gallons per minute?"

Duff shrugged. He hated disappointing anyone.

"We are old-school, I am afraid," Skaggs replied, "and you are now more American than the native-born Americans."

Ben knew that Ashbyville would not be a lasting enterprise if it failed to grow, and that it could not grow if they failed to innovate. His thoughts returned to his talk with Professor Darwin the year before. The professor had suggested that as any creature developed in the womb, as an embryo, at each successive stage of development it resembled each of its ancient ancestors in turn. Ben saw that the same principle applied to the birth of the new California. Mining had already passed through all of its embryonic stages, from swirling pie pans and scratching at rocks with knives and forks to big rockers to dams and flumes, to deep tunnels and broad pits and man-made floods designed to remove any acre of soil daring to hide a vein. Centuries of industrial progress had been recapitulated in a year's time. And soon, Ben knew, mining in California would achieve the form and scale of the present century—flumes four yards wide and a mile long, steam turbines and railway tracks and great machines grinding and washing a ton of dirt and rock each afternoon.

There were still fortunes to be made in California. But now luck had become occasional and scarce, like luck in most places at most times. The true-life tales of gold in hollow trees and hidden beneath dead bears were rarer. Most of the easiest color *had* been taken. The beginning of the end was nigh, for the Gold Rush had begun. In Ashbyville and the rest of the mining districts they had almost no inkling of its magnitude. But at the moment tens of thousands of gold hunters in hundreds of ships—and now, with spring, thousands of wagons as well—were racing for California.

Although the mercury trick had given Ashbyville a longer run than other diggings, even their output was in decline, despite the sunnier season.

Yet Ben had Polly, thank heavens. Hadn't he? She was all that he required. Wasn't she? They lacked the official bonds of matrimony. But what of it?

Alas, however, today of all days she had abandoned him, off since dawn to the German painter's tent at North Fork Dry Diggings, the damned fulsome fawner, playing his artist's model again.

She would return tonight to their bed. Wouldn't she? And perhaps, he thought, if not tonight, then some night soon, tranquilized by a balmy spring breeze and birdsong, she might consent to grant him the other gift for which he longed. Ben wanted a child.

At Ben's age Archibald Knowles already had his firstling, although that child was the notoriously colicky Philip. Philip was in Ben's thoughts because the monthly mail from the east had arrived the day before with a letter from London.

Philip—*Sir* Philip—had written Ben to announce his engagement "to marry Lydia at the beginning of spring at St. George's Church, with Hanover Square to be cleared of ordinary traffic owing to the good offices of Lord Palmerston."

So: weeks after the unexpected death of Philip's wife, the grieving widower had become engaged to remarry.

And he was marrying his brother's former fiancée.

And *now,* Ben Knowles knew as he chewed on this bitter new information, Lydia Winslow was already Lady Knowles of Grafton Street. He was certain that nothing had ever pleased her more. *Lady Knowles:* the title his mother had died too soon to assume.

Ben released the bowstring and let the arrow fly toward the painted circles on his old, shredded shirt. He hit his 102nd bull's-eye of the day. To give himself a new challenge lately, he had been postponing his final rounds until dusk and beyond. He could strike bull's-eyes even in moonlight.

Duff walked up from the placer, having put in one of his exceptionally long days of labor. "How many have—"

"One hundred two," Ben said.

"Really? Out of—"

"One hundred forty-one." Ben was in an ill humor.

If only a telegraph wire had been laid across the seabed of the Atlantic from the Old World to the New and across the American desert all the way to San Francisco—if only a dozen more years had already passed—then Ben would have had the *latest* news of his brother and new sister-in-law. And his spirits on that evening in California would have been lifted by the guilty pleasure of schadenfreude.

He would have known that Sir Philip and Lady Knowles had disembarked the previous afternoon at Gibraltar, the first port on their honeymoon trip through the Mediterranean to Malta and the Nile. Philip had gone for an hour to the governor's residence for a bit of gin and Foreign Office business. Then, walking back to his hotel after dark, he'd found the town's Main Street intolerable—the rabble of Italian sailors and blobber-lipped Africans and superior Jews was simply too much. He took a detour. As he turned down a side street called Bomb Lane, a trollop—an Irish convict, transported to Gibraltar a decade earlier—had approached and proposed that he pay half a crown to have his way with her. He did not slow his gait, but on principle informed the woman that she was "not worth sixpence, and an absolute disgrace to the United Kingdom." "An' *I* won't touch that itty cock o' yours for a *guinea*, ya mincing sod," she replied. He turned back and slapped her face. She screamed, whereupon a hulking Spaniard appeared and clubbed Philip to the pavement with an Allsops ale bottle. He awoke with two little Barbary apes crouched beside him, lapping up the mixture of ale and blood, and staggered back to the governor's house, where he passed out. A physician had told Lady Knowles that Sir Philip must not be moved—his lacerations were superficial, but the concussion was a serious matter.

However, Ben knew none of this, and would have no idea of his brother's fate until the news reached London and followed him across the Atlantic to New York, down to the isthmus and up the Pacific coast to California. And even with gold hunters' ships blowing out of northeastern ports two and three a day bound for San Francisco, that letter would not arrive until summer.

As the light dimmed on the Middle Fork of the American River, Ben felt none of spring's hopefulness. He was angry with his brother, angry with the woman he himself had declined to marry, and angry with the woman who now declined to marry him. His final arrow hit the bull's-eye.

"A hundred and *seven*, and one left to shoot," Duff said. "*Wow.*" In Ben's previous best round of 144 he had shot 101 bull's-eyes. Duff quickly made the sign of the cross, as he now did twenty times a day—following any remark that seemed blasphemous, prideful, greedy, envious, angry, lustful, gluttonous, or slothful. Or otherwise unsettling.

Ben offered the bow to Duff.

"Will you shoot?" he asked.

Duff shook his head. "Bayam and Kumisi say the twilight is a trickster. They say you really want to shoot only when the shadow of the arrow stuck in the ground is no more than twice as long as the bow."

The sun was now behind the hills. Ben got a whiskey bottle from the tent and they took the path around and up Mount Aetna—the summit was only forty feet high, but reaching it required a real climb.

Skaggs came up each clear evening at around five to pull back the tarpaulin, make adjustments to the mount in daylight, read his *Scientific American*s and *Sidereal Messenger*s, and watch the magnified Venus. After "coming down to earth," as he called it, to join the others for supper, he would return to the observatory until midnight to stare at the moon and planets and stars, scribbling notes by lamplight. He had the past week made two lunar daguerreotypes, experiments to test the new iron collar that fastened his camera's lens to the eyepiece of his telescope.

He heard the others coming up the rock.

"I have read here just now," he shouted out before they had entered the building, "that the new observatory in Cambridge—Cambridge, *Massachusetts*—is fixed atop blocks of granite twenty feet wide and fifty-five feet high—half sunk underground. Our foundation, sirs, is *at least* the equal of Harvard's." Skaggs knew, however, that the telescope at Harvard, the so-called Great Refractor—such puffery!—was fifteen inches in diameter, three times as large as his. "Welcome." He spotted the unopened bottle in Ben's hand. "We are drinking tonight, I see, as well as observing the wonders of the universe."

A rail encircled the top of the little house, a circle within a square awaiting its great dome top. Until now, Ben had not seen the big iron bearings installed. He reached up to the rail and rolled one.

Duff crossed himself and looked away. The iron balls looked to him like one of the exploding shells that had flown from the navy's 68-pounder, raining death on the innocent people of Vera Cruz. He picked up a daguerreotype from Skaggs's bench. "This is the moon?" he asked.

It was. The plate showed a spectral white oblong smudge, unrecognizable as the moon. The clock drive, when it arrived, would nudge the telescope smoothly across the sky so that any heavenly object would remain in sharp focus.

"Once we have the clock," Skaggs said, "the craters will be as clear as the pockmarks on my face."

"And do you think you can make good pictures of the stars as well?" Duff asked. He brought his fingers to his chest, but refrained from making the cross.

"We shall see."

"If you are able to photograph the stars, and the sun, you should be 'the Daguerreian of Fire' once again, more brilliant than ever." Now Duff crossed himself: pride.

Skaggs smiled. It had been a year since he had thought of that moniker, meant to promote his specialty of New York blazes and firemen. "If so," he said, gesturing toward the telescope, "all thanks shall be due to the brilliant *Germans*." The lenses of the camera and telescope were made in Munich, and the clock-driven mount invented by a Bavarian.

"To hell with your goddamned Germans," said Ben.

Duff crossed himself.

Ben uncorked the whiskey and swigged it. "I thought the telescope was *French*."

"Aha," said Skaggs, remembering that Polly had been all day with the unctuous German painter they had met in Coloma, "indeed it is, French, quite right." He lit the lamp. *She was a trollop when you met her, sir,* he did not say, *so it should not entirely surprise you if, God forbid, she were to revert to that earlier condition.*

"Don't be jealous, Ben," Duff pleaded. It was nearly seven o'clock. "Shall we cook the salmon? We can keep Polly's warm."

Ben drank some more whiskey and handed the bottle to Skaggs, who also took another slug, and another. Neither made any movement to descend to camp.

"Now, the *French*," Ben said, "the French are the race to whom we are indebted. Voltaire. Daguerre. My cousin's husband."

"Nepotist," Skaggs snapped.

"I am in earnest now—it is the French inventing the new ways to live and think."

"*Terrible* new ways," Skaggs said as he lit his cigar. "It is your French contriving to make over love as a science, meddling with ovaries and menstruation in order to tell us when we may copulate 'safely.' And it was a *French* quack," he continued, "who contrived the cruel, stupid notion he called 'nymphomania' in order to define ordinary, unfettered female passions as illness."

Ben took another big gulp.

Duff, appalled by this turn in the conversation, tried pushing it back in a more seemly direction. "The French want liberty, and risk their lives to gain it, again and again."

"*Yes,*" Ben said with the zeal of drink, "the *revolutions*. It is always the French struggling to lead mankind toward liberty and equality."

Skaggs did not reply immediately. He stared at the red tip of his cigar and blew smoke up toward the night sky. "What have their revolutions produced apart from death?" he said finally. "The French are the great engineers of modern killing. The flintlock. The guillotine. This hideously accurate new rifle bullet, their minié ball. Heating cannon shot to maximize the suffering . . ."

Duff's scar stung, and he made the sign of the cross.

"But, Skaggs, honestly," Ben said, "you know it was the French whose assistance allowed the American Revolution to succeed."

"And your own very hero, Jefferson," Duff added, "loved the French."

But Skaggs whiskeyed was not about to stop being contrary, even on the subject of his dearest Founding Father. "Jefferson held some incorrect opinions," he said. "Nor do I mean the slaves. Or not *only* do I mean his slaves. I mean his view of the Indians. 'The same world would scarcely do for *them* and *us*,' he said. Oh, Duff, Jefferson would have happily murdered your girl and all her people. Stand and sigh and make your popish gestures all you wish, boy, but it's the plain truth! 'I leave it to you,' he told his general, 'to decide if the end should be the Indians' extermination, or their removal."

Duff was already out the door.

And Ben, wallowing in his own dark slough, vaguely and silently recalled a relevant foretelling by a certain Frenchman. *I believe the Indian nations of North America are doomed to perish,* Tocqueville had written, *and that whenever the European shall be established on the shores of the Pacific Ocean, that race of men will have ceased to exist.*

"We are sots," Skaggs said. "And I'm a mean and sour sot. Back to temperance on the morrow."

A minute later, they heard Duff shouting from below. They listened. He was hailing someone. Ben arose and ran.

Skaggs heard the jingling bells of approaching oxen and wagon wheels. Polly had returned. "Ode to joy," he said to himself with a large smile, "under the starry firmament."

April 13, 1849

SKAGGS HAD HIRED a teamster to truck his purchase from Sacramento City to Ashbyville, and asked him to stop in Coloma on his way back to fetch Polly at the painter's tent. It took all four residents plus Jack and Badger and the teamster the following day and most of the next to unload the wagon and finish the job. They used a crane, pulleys, chains, windlass, lever, and winch, powered by Jenny Lind and the oxen, to raise the two tons of Mexican wood and metal into place on the top of Mount Aetna.

Under the midday California sun the twelve-foot copper dome shone so brightly that when they looked at it they couldn't stop smiling. Skaggs was abashed by its splendor. Ben said the observatory now looked like a Byzantine church, which pleased Duff. It was a small wonder of their world nearly finished at last.

After their celebratory dinner, with Skaggs blissfully ensconced as a watcher of the sky and Duff hiking north to Hembem, Polly turned to Ben. The breezes off the river tousled her hair just as they had on their first evening alone together a year before.

"I have a rather large proposal to make," she said. "More than one proposal, actually."

Part

FIVE

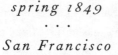

spring 1849
· · ·
San Francisco

EN'S TASTE FOR speed made him avid for reading histories. Books about the past compressed time, allowing one to whisk through centuries in a few hours. (Even in *Decline and Fall,* Ben had once calculated, Mr. Gibbon reduced each of his 1,500 years to a mere thousand words—every fortnight of the Roman Empire distilled to a single sentence.) He decided that Skaggs had been exactly right about 1848. Even as it was occurring it seemed like an account in a history book, bright and quick. And in California, the new year was unfolding in similarly dramatic, implausible fashion.

As the temperatures warmed and skies cleared, three ships reached the Golden Gate on some days. At busy moments they had to await their turns to sail into the harbor. Hurry and rapacity were in the very air. *More, faster, more, faster.* At the end of April, a clipper arrived from New York around the Horn after only 125 days. The fastest on record! But almost immediately thereafter another ship arrived from Philadelphia in 113 days. The *new* fastest! And another company of New Yorkers managed to sail and paddle and steam to Panama and up to San Francisco in just *44 days.*

Every day, more hundreds of fortune hunters hustled into California and made for the Sierras, a thousand and then two thousand invaders each week by land and sea—most of them seasick or sunstruck and unsuited to the tasks ahead, but all feeling lucky to have finished their journeys alive, and giddy about putting icy winter and civilization behind them, about gliding into sunshiny California, about the outrageous liberties of San Francisco, and giddy too, of course, about the gold, the gold, the gold.

Almost every vessel that brought them, however, became useless the moment it dropped anchor and its crew got a glimpse of the rapture: they came, they saw, they vanished. Their ships, 300-ton barks and 200-ton brigs as well as little 80-ton schooners, were simply left to rot in the water like discarded wrappings in the gutter.

For those just arriving, San Francisco inspired panic. All the abandoned ships and nervous crowds increased the frenzy to get to the mines with pans and shovels and quack devices (Signor d'Alvear's Goldometer, three dollars apiece) as quickly as possible, before the magic finished and the gold was gone. Ships could be wasted, but not *time*.

However, when Polly returned to San Francisco in the summer—Ben, of course, had agreed to both her proposals—the sight of all those forsaken ships would not inspire her to race back to the mines but rather to sit quietly near the wharf and *look*, with pen in hand. She would try to depict on paper this queer, accidental, floating ghost city. She would draw in the style, as best as she could recall it, of the Italian artist from the book of etchings in Washington that had frightened and delighted her as a girl. Ben would sit close to her, holding her ink bottle, and he would remember the Italian's name— Giovanni Piranesi—that she had not been able to recall.

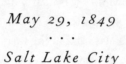
May 29, 1849

. . .

Salt Lake City

HE HARD LEATHER tip flew and reached its victim and cracked and retreated, all in an instant—and seven feet away, a little burst of pink and green confetti fluttered to the grass. On a warm afternoon in Salt Lake Valley, the bloom of yet another lady's slipper had been targeted and struck. Each time, he had the feeling that the flower was *surprised* to disintegrate. The feeling pleased him. The designated enemies today were not the yellows or the purples or the pure whites, but the pinks and reds, any flower blossom with even a blush. It was an arbitrary choice, of course, like the rules in any game. That's what distinguished games from real life.

Around him in the meadow was a thirty-yard swath of elegant destruction, the beheaded stalks of two hundred wild daisies and clover and lady's slippers like a vanquished and surprised-looking mob. His own long shadow loomed over them like a giant.

He had practiced for a hundred hours with the whip, maybe longer, and he was adept, more accurate than he had ever been in Algeria, when he had been paid and ordered to wield one. Perhaps, he thought, his skill here was proof of the virtue of amateurism. Or perhaps it was because he had never liked whipping human flesh, not even African flesh. His problem wasn't so much the pain and bloodshed. Rather, he was uncomfortable with the ambiguity of any assault not meant to end in death: when was one *finished* whipping a man? Twenty lashes, thirty, forty—it was arbitrary, a game.

He wiped the sweat from his brow and turned away from the botanical detritus toward the big boulders, the sandstone ridge, the desert, the setting sun, California. The March rains had been extremely heavy, which was supposed to mean that the snows in the High Sierra passes would be deep through April and beyond, according to his bunkmates who'd come from California last year. But now May was nearly over. The time had come to go west and finish the chase. He was to receive his final month's pay packet on Friday, the first of June. They said that the fort of Captain Sutter, the Swiss *patron* of northern California, was five weeks' ride from Salt Lake.

He smiled. Knowles would be surprised, an unsuspecting red flower in his sunny field on the frontier.

"Mr. Drumont, hallo."

He was startled.

The *girl,* the damned girl he had been dispatched by the good Mr. Pinkerton to capture and return. Why had she come out here to the tall grass to haunt and bother him? Just when his way ahead seemed clear, she appeared, like a specter, and reminded him of his negligence and failure.

"I was strolling to the springs," she said.

When they all finally reached San Francisco, he would contrive to put her aboard a ship and return her to New York. He would do his duty.

"We have not seen you for some time," she said as she came closer.

Her husband was off in Cottonwood Canyon repairing some passing stranger's wagon axle, she explained. He had worked every night this week to serve the travelers who had begun pouring in by way of Fort Bridger and Fort Laramie, all bound for the gold region. The mechanics and artisans and gardeners of Salt Lake City, he said cheerfully, would have a good year supplying the gold hunters.

"The leaders say it is another blessing from God." She shrugged, then smiled. "But it seems that you, Mr. Drumont, may have too *much* company on your expedition to California. The trail west will be like a city thoroughfare, they say."

"Yes?" He did not really understand.

"The first mails are leaving the square for San Francisco tomorrow."

"Yes, yes." Drumont knew that a Mormon post wagon was about to roll west. What of it? He despised small talk.

"I shall write Miss Lucking tonight, and tell her that while *I* will not see her this season, Ben's friend Mr. Drumont will join them soon. I shall let them know of your impending arrival."

No. This he understood. *No.*

She continued to smile, thinking of her friend and San Francisco, and let herself chatter on, like the fourteen-year-old she was, in the violet twilight. "I will send a letter to Polly. And also write my father in New York, so the old scamp knows where his married daughter has wound up."

This he understood nearly as well. He understood, anyway, that Pinkerton would learn from Mr. Christmas of Drumont's duplicity and failure. And that Knowles would be forewarned of his avenger's arrival. A trap was closing. Drumont felt desperate.

"*No,* to your father *we* will post your letter in San Francisco with *our* hand, no? And if we, you and Billy and I, leave from here in this week, perhaps Saturday—you can be ready in this time—then you will be with Polly yourself in July, you *see* her, *talk* with her. So this letter to post *now* to her has no sense to do, you understand?"

Priscilla's smile had turned rueful, apologetic. She sighed. "I was afraid that I had not made myself clear before."

"No, yes, you tell me before—you are to be now a Saint. I do understand this."

"But *we* will remain *here,* for good, in this valley. Billy and I have decided against seeking our fortunes at the mines, Mr. Drumont. We won't be traveling on to California with you, not at all. We are remaining *here.*" She pointed at the ground.

No. *No.* "No! I give you *money* to go away from Billy, and give money to him also. *Hundreds* of dollars. If you return to Mr. Prime. He want you in New York very, very hard."

Priscilla was too astonished to be frightened. How did Drumont know of Samuel Prime? Why had he said nothing before? Return to New York? "*What?*"

"To be the *maîtresse* of Prime. To have rich things, good dress, to . . . lie with him more when he wish."

Without another word, she turned to walk back to town.

He grabbed her wrist. "I tell Billy," he said, "and all the others too that you are the slut and the whore from the street."

This moment had been enacted before, last spring, in the alley off Mercer Street, and she had submitted then to Fatty Freeborn's nasty fuck in order to keep Polly's brothel life a secret. But now she had nothing to fear, and no one to protect.

She looked him in the eyes. "Billy knows. I have told him of all my past wretchedness." Her face formed the hint of a smile. "You cannot hurt me, Mr. Drumont." She was calm.

And then she shivered, and felt gooseflesh spread up her neck, even though the temperature was almost 80. One of her hunches was descending, the first since they'd left the States in the fall. Perhaps, she thought in that instant, the sensations were beginning again because Salt Lake City had grown so big, that the visions did indeed depend on some . . . urban ether. The image forming in her mind was not the usual muddy, moky swirl but strangely clear and sharp and jet black. The goose bumps swept down her arms and chest like a wind riffling grass.

She understood her premonition only at the moment his fist struck her face. And her last, fleeting thought was pity for dear Billy.

Drumont needed to finish the deed quickly, before she awoke, before she was missed, before his regular hour of return to the bachelors' barrack. She was light as a child. He was behind the boulders in no time, and at the ravine twenty paces later. He could not simply flee; he wanted the wages he was owed; if he ran, they would come after him. The coup de grâce had to come from a single blow to make it appear plausible, a rock of the right size slammed once with just the right force on her temple, so that it seemed as if her head had hit the limestone after an accidental tumble down the steep escarpment above the springs.

Priscilla was dead before the sky was dark over Zion.

68

June 19, 1849

· · ·

New York City

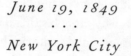

*I*N JUNE THE city was as hot and stinking as any foul August, an early "heat wave," as the newspapers called it. Some people believed the swelter made the disease extra deadly, the infection more virulent. Or perhaps the haze and sweat simply united the island's whole half million into one awful, sticky, democratic mass, reminding each one constantly that somewhere in New York somebody, a new case, was cramping and retching and blasting quarts and gallons of thin, fishy soup out both quivering ends. Yesterday the grocer's strapping son might die, this afternoon the laundress will fall to the floor with spasms, tomorrow the downstairs neighbor's baby, or maybe oneself. And this accompanying epidemic of dread had a kind of demonic, self-fulfilling function: the mental disquiet, everyone believed, made the body more vulnerable to the disease.

It was the June of the cholera. One hundred every day were dying now, Samuel Prime had read in the morning's *Tribune,* maybe more—and in the western cities it was twice as bad. No one seemed to have any very good idea when the plague might run its course.

He and his family were safer on Long Island, the scientific gentlemen and doctors believed, than in the miasma of the city, inhaling the same air exhaled by the wretched. So they had decamped to their refuge, as almost everyone in their circle had done. The lawns and gardens of Hurlgate, ten times as big as the Park, were separated from the pestilence and dying of

Manhattan by a few hundred yards of water. Yet his proximity to the rushing East River itself seemed to have an antiseptic effect, as if the waters were scrubbing the edge of New York as well as keeping the city quarantined from the Primes. The well-to-do were by no means immune, of course: he knew people in Bond Street and the Fifth Avenue who had died, and today the papers carried the news of former President Polk's death from cholera—albeit in Nashville, in the dirty South.

Prime's desire for cleanliness was no fetish, as school friends used to tease ("Sanitary Sam, Sanitary Sam"), and this contagion had surely proved his prudence correct. It was why, from his first intimacies with the other sex, he had insisted on *young* women, and as the city had grown filthier and more crowded, younger still. The youngest were the cleanest, he believed, not only less likely to fester with the French pox and other infections too horrid to contemplate, but cleaner in every way—freer from dirt, from moral impurity, from all the sluttery and snares of the world. Putting one's nakedness atop an older whore, he imagined, would be like using another man's handkerchief. Now, the girl . . . the pale fugitive girl—*heavens:* he was ashamed that for a moment the name of his secret youngest child's mother slipped his mind—now, *Priscilla Christmas* had been spick-and-span.

Because thousands of gentlemen had lately fled the city, or at least its unwholesome precincts, the parlor houses of New York were empty too. And so proper orgasms by the tens of thousands were denied and dammed, a collective stoppage that, like the unusual heat, exacerbated in some small way the terror and pessimism besetting the city.

He still indulged his taste for *passion*—of the animal kind lately only with Mrs. Prime, to whom he had always attended once a month without fail—and of the nobler romantic kind, too, in his quest to find and redeem his bastard offspring, wherever the child had been taken. He had so far spent $545, according to the ledger in front of him. His longing and his search last year for the girl had been a wild whimsy. But his new plan, Prime pleased himself thinking, was an act of atonement, the right thing to do.

Last autumn, Pinkerton had reported, their Frenchman had tracked Priscilla Christmas to a Mormon camp on the very frontier, where she had planned to marry some fellow rambler. The Frenchman had proceeded to follow them west. Prime wondered if she had given birth on the trail, at a campfire, perhaps with some Indian midwife. And had she gone all the way west to scratch for gold in the ground, like a ragpicker combing through the trash? California gold was a perfect whore's dream, he thought as he gazed out his window at the river—fortune without merit or industry. Two clerks from Prime's firm, one of them a senior man, had sailed for California, and a third was about to go. The newspaper said that a ship of gold hunters now left New York every second day, each with dozens of men aboard; such delirium! On the other hand, fortune had smiled on all the Argonauts who had already sailed—by leaving New York, they had escaped this plague.

It would be convenient if Priscilla Christmas and his child were living near San Francisco, as the detectives believed, for his man could easily bundle the infant aboard one of the returning gold-seekers' ships for the trip back to New York.

Prime had already contrived a respectable story, a fiction that Mrs. Prime not only believed but which had inspired in her a new tenderness toward him. The child, he had told her (and would tell his friends if and when it arrived), was the orphan of one of the family's former charity tenants, Miss Lucking, who had apparently died in California. Prime planned to keep the child away from the filth and temptations of the city at Hurlgate, perhaps in the cottage the Luckings had occupied during their year here.

"Mr. Prime, sir?" It was Otis, his steward, out of breath. "You wanted to know about the flatboat to Randall's? I seen the one coming upriver just now. If you wanted to look. And there's another *big* trip of hogs you can see too, sir, all the coppers running them north."

Prime followed him quickly across the lawn to the water's edge, asked Otis to have one of the kitchen girls bring him a lemonade. He sat down in the shade of a big elm and aimed his spyglass at Manhattan.

A hundred and fifty policemen, a fifth of the force, were spending the day as swineherds, as another troop would do tomorrow, and so on, for days to come. They had been ordered to round up and drive away all of New York's freely ranging street pigs, to chase them past Manhattanville and Bloomingdale and the other suburban villages to an exile in the woods and empty wastes beyond, at the northern end of the island. Like the unclean poor, and the local population of dogs, which bounty-hunting boys all over the city were at that moment clubbing to death for two bits apiece, the swine were among the creatures suspected of causing the cholera.

With his telescope Prime could make out the pigs—a thousand? two thousand?—as a frantic stream of pink and brown gushing ahead of the police.

He adjusted his aim downward, to the river channel, and found a steamboat and, at the end of a chain behind it, the cholera barge. Its deck was covered with bodies—two layers, he saw as he studied the scene through his glass. He counted by twos, and estimated two hundred in all. It looked like a cargo of mummies, but mummies hastily prepared. The white canvas sheets wrapped around each body flapped in the wind. He watched the barge dock at Randall's Island, upriver, where the corpses would be carried to an acre of upturned earth, dug by boys from the adjacent House of Refuge.

My child may be a whoreson, Prime thought, *but at least it shall have a chance at a healthy life.*

Even with the spyglass he could no longer see much of interest at such a distance. He could not, for instance, see the diligent, hungry army of rats swimming across the river from Manhattan to Randall's Island for their latest feast.

And whenever my youngest child perishes, it shall have a respectable burial, in a casket, with a stone.

But, of course, unbeknownst to Samuel Prime, his child was now a fiction. Priscilla Christmas had had an abortion more than a year before, when the fetus was barely two months along. Prime's inch-long spawn had been tossed out by Dr. Solis's nurse among the tons of New York garbage that morning, and promptly became another morsel in the gutter luncheon of one of the pigs now scudding out of the city.

69

July 5, 1849

· · ·

Sacramento City

*U*NLIKE MANY OF the Americans in California, the postmaster at Sacramento City was able to distinguish among foreign accents. Although the stranger had attempted to explain that he was seeking information, not any mail, the postmaster was searching his boxes that held letters from abroad.

"May I wish you a happy Independence Day, sir, your first as a citizen of a *free republic* of France."

Yesterday had been the Americans' national day, Drumont knew. He had arrived in the country one year ago. Such a long journey. "Yes, yes, thank you."

"And may I ask if you are bound for the Gallic camp up on the Yuba, sir? Where your countrymen have pioneered?" The postmaster was also one of the very few Californians who still scrupled to call strangers "sir," or to wear a necktie. He was also a busybody.

Drumont indulged the bureaucrat's small talk as a necessity, in order to obtain the information he needed. And get it he finally did: Mr. Knowles and his company, the postmaster informed him, lived at a place they called Ashbyville, their *petite communauté socialiste* on the Middle Fork of the American River, beyond Ford's Bar.

"And although our U.S. postal service from San Francisco does not commence *officially* until next month, in return for small extra sums we have been happy to handle the mail for men at all the camps within fifty miles or so. Mr. Skaggs, who was quite a celebrated author in New York—did you know?—has begun to receive an absolute *flood* of papers from the States— a *déluge*, as they would say in France, yes? *Look.*" He picked up an armful of Skaggs's latest magazines. "*Dozens* on every mail boat . . ." He started to enumerate the titles: "*The Knickerbocker, The Literary World, The Flag of Our Union . . .*"

When Drumont offered to deliver the mail to Ashbyville himself, the prattling fool drew him a map.

Drumont finally left the post office—he badly wanted a real dinner, a good night's sleep, and a box of fresh cartridges for his pistol—but before he was two steps out the door, the postmaster yelled out to him.

"Eureka! Eureka!" He was holding up a letter. "My lucky cubbyhole! Of course, I had presumed your correspondents would be writing from *France*—but *here*, 'Mr. Gabriel Drumont,' is one for you from Chicago, by way of Panama and San Francisco."

Drumont was shocked—impressed as well as ashamed. How on earth had he been found? No one knew where he was. Pinkerton was a true genius, if not all-knowing, then a grand master of intuition, America's young Vidocq. And now he surely considered Drumont a thief and a liar. He probably had written to the police or the American army in California. Drumont feared he might be apprehended before he had a chance to find Knowles. He had seen troops as he rode into Sacramento City.

"An epistle from . . . a loved one?" the postmaster asked as he watched Drumont tear at the envelope and breathlessly read, hurry-scurry—and then stop, and give him a long, hard look.

"I cannot understand this good. You speak this to me?"

Not a day passed that the postmaster wasn't asked to read a letter aloud. He was delighted.

" '. . . *I trust this letter finds you well after your long journey* . . .

" '. . . *in addition to our work on behalf of the aforementioned gentleman, I wish you also to investigate a certain Mr. Duff Lucking, an army traitor who is implicated in an arson in New York.*'

"Mr. Lucking! My *goodness!*

" '*I have reason to believe that Lucking may have gone to California to hunt for escaped slaves instead of gold* . . .

" '. . . *money to cover your passage to New York with the child (should the infant be recovered), and your expenses in California, a draft for two hundred dollars in Mr. P——'s name shall be available to you at the Exchange and Deposit Office at the Parker House, in Kearny Street . . .' "*

Drumont was grinning. *"Incroyable,"* he said. Such a stroke of good fortune. *"Bizarre."*

THE POSTMASTER, for all his presumptuous familiarity with other people's business, was unaware that Mr. Knowles and Miss Lucking had left their mining camp on the summer solstice to reside in San Francisco, and that Mr. Lucking now lived with his digger wife somewhere back in the hills. That is, he did not know enough to tell his rugged, fervent inquisitor that Ashbyville's full-time population had lately shrunk to one, the author and astronomer Mr. Skaggs, in whom the fellow from Paris had no interest whatsoever.

Ashbyville was not officially defunct. At their last community meeting, they had voted to declare the collective mining enterprise—as distinct from "the Mount Aetna Observatory, T. Skaggs, founder & director"—in a state of "suspended animation." When they'd pulled the treasury out of its hole that same afternoon to divide it up, it had looked somewhat unimpressive. That was in part because Skaggs had already withdrawn some of his share to pay for the observatory dome. The rest of their eight months' accumulated profit—every ounce of remaining dust, every speck, fleck, flake, and plinker, packed tight inside the redwood chest—was the size of a large loaf of bread. However, the loaf weighed forty-nine pounds, and it was worth $13,000. In New York or London, each share would have provided a comfortable living for years.

Ben and Polly had said they might "rerusticate" one day, when their thirsts for the civilization and chaos of the city were slaked, but no one, including they themselves, quite believed it. Skaggs would continue to work the placers (with Duff's help) two days a week, just enough to pay for the essentials—food, brandy, soap, lamp oil, daguerreotype plates, chemicals, books, magazines. When Priscilla and Billy arrived, Polly had said, the community would spring back to life, and they could take the cabin she and Ben abandoned. Ashbyville had not dissolved, but its heyday was over.

AS THAT SUMMER began, the heyday of California was either ending or beginning, depending upon where one looked. An era of acute uncertainty had begun. In the north, June of '49 seemed like the fantastic summer of '48 all over again. On the North Fork of the American River, someone pulled a forty-ounce nugget from the sludge—and then, days later, someone else a twenty-five-*pound* chunk. And up on the Yuba's North Fork, two brothers found nuggets scattered on the bank in piles like stones on a beach, half-pounders here, two-pounders there, and yet *another* twenty-five-pounder . . .

The excitement was an echo of last year's, but everything else had changed. During 1848, luck had shone on everyone. Not only had there been more gold in the ground and fewer people looking for it, but all of the men (and the several women) at the mines in '48 had managed to get there fortuitously—they happened to live in Oregon or Mexico or California already, or their regiment happened to muster out in San Diego or Los Angeles or Monterey, or they happened to be racing from New York to the frontier on quests for utopia and adventure and true love.

Each of these new "forty-niners," on the other hand, had made a large and risky investment. Each had abandoned his family and friends and job and familiar surroundings on a bet, persuaded by mere stories in newspapers, equipped with no special advantage, nothing but a *longing* for good luck. And so each of the bonanza stories in 1849 filled the hearts of ten times as many lonely greenhorns with envy and desperate desire, inciting them to dig and wash more and more dirt faster and faster, hoping that they, dear God, might be among the fewer and fewer lucky ones. The Eden of 1848 was disappearing. Economic life was returning to normal. The losers and middling survivors would once again vastly outnumber the winners, as they always had.

WHEN BEN AND Polly stopped in Coloma and Sacramento City on their way out of the gold district, the new mood had been palpable. It reminded Ben of the roundelay game called the Sea During a Storm that Lydia had loved to play at London dancing parties. Each round ended when the music stopped unexpectedly, one girl left the dance, the men all scrambled to find new partners, and the man left alone was expelled from the game. Ben had hated the artificial scarcity and panic of the game. He was happy that in California, he and his dance partner were retiring from the party early.

On the day they'd spent in Sacramento City waiting for Duff to join them directly from Hembem, the temperature had reached 91 degrees. In scarcely four months since their previous visit, the population of the city had grown tenfold.

"My Lord, it is like the summer in New York," Ben had said as they'd walked down the crowded Embarcadero. "We need a parasol and Panama hats."

"Except that in New York as well as Panama," Polly had said, "one never quite—" She had stopped short, struck dumb by the sign in front of a half-finished building. The interior walls were being made of sails stripped from abandoned ships, and at the back of the large main room they could see cargo chests pushed and nailed together to make a platform—a stage, in fact. THE EAGLE THEATER COMPANY, the outside sign had read, FIRST STAGE IN CALIFORNIA—OPENING FALL, TICKETS $3 & $5.

She'd looked at Ben, suddenly fascinated by a new prospect.

"Perhaps I should act as your representative and ask them," he'd said.

"What is my question?"

"Have they cast their first plays, and what are the principal female roles?"

She shook her head. "I should like to know the costs of *erecting* such a place," she'd said. "And whether there are plans afoot for a theater in San Francisco."

Ben and Polly had decided to use their capital and some of Duff's, a little more than $8,000 in all, to set themselves up in San Francisco as entrepreneurs of some kind—and to parcel out to each employee small bits of the enterprise as well as a wage. Once they'd become certain that Skaggs was determined to remain in the countryside and pursue his astronomy, they'd dropped their notion of starting a magazine, *The Illustrated California News*, to be printed on the *Alta California*'s new steam press. Lately they had discussed becoming book publishers instead, or manufacturers of Knowles's Waterproof Boots—knee-high mining boots to be made of rubber. The idea of operating a theater had not yet been broached. That day, Ben enjoyed imagining how the news—the proprietor of a *theater* in *California*—would appall his brother and titillate his London friends. He was delighted to consider it.

He was delighted to consider almost any new venture, no matter how capricious or improbable, ever since Polly's return from the German painter's tent. That night she had offered to marry, if he "still wished it." And so on a clear and cool Saturday evening in May, Skaggs's new Mexican friend, Judge Suárez, had presided over a wedding ceremony atop Mount Aetna, inside the observatory, with the new dome open to the blazing western sky. All of Ashbyville—as well as Yauka, Jack, and Badger—had been in attendance.

Two months later, as they stood in the heat of Sacramento City watching the Eagle Theater take shape before them, Ben had grasped his wife's sweaty hand in his. "We shall become impresarios, do you think?"

"Perhaps so. If they're getting three dollars for a *cheap* seat."

"Or rather, the great theatrical impresaria and her trusty aide-de-camp?"

She'd smiled and performed a small, quick bow.

—⇢•⇠—

70

June 30 and July 1, 1849

. . .

San Francisco

HEIR FIRST FULL day as residents of San Francisco was the last day of June, a Saturday. They spent the morning and most of the afternoon, accompanied by Duff, inspecting the city with a real estate broker. They had not heard prices denominated in dollars for a year. The real estate man showed them an empty store on the plaza—only six *varas* wide, sixteen and a half feet—that he'd rented out the day before for $2,000 a month. The new Parker House, he said, brought in rents of more than $10,000 a month from the hotel, the gambling saloon, and the bank, which meant that it would earn back its cost of construction by the end of July, its third month of existence.

He showed them a small adobe warehouse some blocks up toward Little Chile, as he called the South American neighborhood, that might be bargained away for as little as $1,500, or rented for $300 a month. Duff said it looked reasonably well built, and that finishing it as a theater or publishing house or waterproof-boot factory was a matter of only a few weeks' work.

At the end of the day, Ben and Polly and Duff retired to the wharf to watch the sunset and relax. They sat on an empty chest that had carried bags of filberts and jars of Worcestershire sauce fourteen thousand miles from New York. It was one of hundreds of boxes scattered along the wharf, broken and discarded. The cargoes—sperm candles, packs of playing cards, claw hatchets, gilt buttons, blue flannel shirts and denim pants, hinges, quilts, bathtubs, carbines, Russian hemp rope, Milanese steel, French wine, English linseed oil, Irish linen, Havana cigars—had been scooped out like fruit and taken away to sell, the boxes left behind like rinds on the docks where the stevedores had chanced to drop them.

Polly scratched at her sheet with a new nib, first drawing each of the nearest ships, whose names they could read—the *Panama*, the *Ringleader*, the *Radiant*, the *Metropolis*, and the *Phantom*, with their fluttering ropes and rolled-up sails—and then fragments of the others ranked behind for almost a mile, a riot of verticals and horizontals in layer upon layer, foremasts and mizzenmasts and bowsprits and jibbooms. They were nearly all empty of men, and bobbed together on the high tide. It was a great American ruin, another *instant* ruin, sad and funny, unprecedented and amazing.

While Polly drew, Ben counted. "I believe there are one hundred eighty-seven," he said. "More than in the Invincible Armada." England's defeat of the Spanish Armada had been Ben's favorite military history as a boy.

"And look there," Ben said to Duff, pointing in the opposite direction, toward Signal Hill. "A big ship of the line."

Duff turned to look, and he shuddered. The two rows of open gunports along the hull—a dozen black squares on each lower deck—formed a 200-foot-long jack-o'-lantern's grin. *Yea,* he said to himself as he touched his forehead and then his heart, *though I walk through the valley of the shadow of death*—he touched each shoulder—*I will fear no evil: for thou art with me.* The ship was the USS *Ohio.* Duff had seen it two years earlier in the Gulf of Mexico, firing broadsides from those 42-pounders onto Vera Cruz.

"Very big," he said, turning his back on it and then excusing himself to go shopping before the stores closed.

Although Skaggs had warned Duff away from patent medicines ("brandy and cocaine by the quarter pint at ten times the fair price"), the coughs and fevers and rashes among his new people at Hembem persisted, and Duff had faith only in pharmaceutical cures manufactured in the States. Indeed, he and Yauka believed that his arrival in their valley had been fated. The Indians had started to call him *nuestro médico,* "our doctor" in Spanish, and even *sakíni yomi,* the "white medicine man" in Maidu. So in addition to advising Polly and Ben about crooked joists and plumb walls and water-soaked eaves, he had come to buy more medicines in San Francisco, where they were cheaper. And hopeful-looking remedies such as Trask's Magnetic Ointment were not even available in Sacramento City. Duff spent an hour filling his valise with little bottles and tins and boxes.

Duff's appearance—deeply tanned but clean-shaven, blond hair falling to his shoulders, hatless except for a cap of twine netting from which a top-knot poked out like a pony's tail, necklace of wooden beads, doeskin serape, moccasins, the four brown bars and two dots scarred neatly across the tops of his hands—was strange even for San Francisco. But for all the curious looks he attracted, he believed that his costume and coiffure made an excellent disguise. Surely no one there who might have known him in Mexico—not the officers who'd sentenced him nor the men who'd whipped and branded him, not even his fellow soldiers—would recognize him in his transfigured state.

IT WAS DARK by the time he rejoined his sister and brother-in-law in the saloon at their hotel.

"Did you find *all* of your medicines?" Polly whispered. She had told him that a few doses of Blue Mass and laudanum might alleviate the anxieties that seemed to overcome him in cities.

He nodded. And as soon as she glanced away he crossed himself, for he hadn't bought either of the drugs she'd suggested.

A pair of miners had just introduced themselves to Ben—an Australian fresh off a brig from Adelaide ("three months of vomiting and revomiting, aye?") and a blustery red-haired lawyer from Boston named Shepley who already had 117 ounces, he said, mined in three months near Volcano. But his placers were cleaned out, and he was looking for somewhere new.

"*Ashbyville?*" repeated Shepley, who wore a red bandanna and a mustache waxed to resemble two letters *S* pushed end to end. "Of course—the famous *lady* of the Middle Fork. The Brook Farmers! Mr. and Mrs. Knowles," he explained to the Australian, "have established a peculiar camp on the American River sometime since, socialism in the hills, if I understand correctly." He smiled. "May I ask how many have joined you?"

What Polly took as mere condescension or political antagonism, however, was salaciousness. Unbeknownst to all of Ashbyville's citizens except Skaggs, miners elsewhere referred to the camp as Assville and Middle Fuck.

"We have had a membership large enough, sir," Polly replied, "to take well-nigh seventy *pounds* of color from our little stretch of the American."

Duff very quickly crossed himself twice—to atone for their greed and her pride. The strangers wondered if he was feebleminded, or suffered spasms in his right arm. His attire inclined them toward the former.

"A successful and contented lot up there, are you?" said the grinning Bostonian.

"We have been indeed, very pleased," Ben said, "and for that matter, we might have taken another seventy pounds had we wished."

The fellow furrowed his brow and made a puffing noise. "If you had *wished?*" he asked.

"Yes," Ben answered calmly. "Our particular terrain lent itself to the construction of a long flume, and together with our use of quicksilver to recover gold which would otherwise—"

"Ben," said Duff, swatting his arm and then crossing himself twice—anger, greed—with the same hand. "The *patent.*" Their application to Washington was still pending.

"Our productivity," Ben finished, using a word none of his listeners had heard before, "was exceptional, as a result both of our technical innovations *and* our unusual spirit of cooperation."

Shepley now looked serious, and intrigued.

"Well," said the Australian, raising his glass of porter, "share and share alike. To Ashbyville, then, aye?"

Duff crossed himself once more.

"You have spoken of Ashbyville in the past tense," Shepley said. "May I ask why?"

THREE NEW DRINKING establishments opened for business that Saturday in San Francisco, which was unremarkable in 1849, although the twiddle-twaddle around the plaza had it that those three licenses were the 1,999th, 2,000th, and 2,001st issued by the city fathers. Given the week's favorite estimate of the population—11,000—that implied nearly one saloon for every five permanent residents. Of course, *permanence* was a fluid concept in California.

A group of four singers outside Dennison's Exchange were improvising an ode to this latest civic achievement, sung to the tune of "O, Susanna." "San Francisco, *oh,* one for every five,/To booze upon the plaza is the ideal life for me . . ."

Ben and Polly and Duff, having finished dinner, passed them on their way into Dennison's. The lead man in the quartet, catching sight of Polly, invented a new verse. "Oh my goddess, *oh,* we're lonely as can be/If you loved us we'd surely die from apoplexy." The singers laughed.

Polly ignored them. Duff hated them. As Ben paid the admission fees he nodded good-naturedly. "A fair try, boys, even if it does not *quite* scan."

Polly and Ben had wanted to have a look at Dennison's—as well as the Parker House, the El Dorado, and the Bella Union, all clustered within fifty yards of one another around the intersection of Washington and Kearny streets—because the big hotels and gambling halls were what currently passed for theaters in San Francisco.

The interior of the first floor was both splendid and rustic. Three of the walls were plain pine boards painted bright yellow and dark red in alternating vertical stripes, so that the whole room appeared to vibrate, and the fourth wall was simply a hanging canvas curtain, a rough patchwork of four topsails. The windows had no draperies, but from the ceiling trusses hung a dozen banners embroidered with the mottoes and nicknames of states (EMPIRE, HOG & HOMINY, WOLVERINES, LAND OF STEADY HABITS) and epigrammatic fragments (NEVER FADING BLISS and FREEDOM & DESIRE). Six big pink glass chandeliers also hung from the ceiling, each holding a hundred candles.

Hundreds of men were packed tight around the buckskin-covered gaming tables. Twenty drinkers at one end of the main liquor bar were transfixed by the narrow six-foot-tall glass tube mounted in the shadows behind the bartenders. Inside the tube, sparks moved rapidly in a spiral pattern up and down and around the glass, the effect produced by an electrical charge from a generator cranked by an Indian boy crouching on the floor.

One of the bartenders, the spinner of the fortune wheel, and two of the card dealers were women who looked like (and had been) schoolteachers in the States, but with the slightly wry, incredulous expressions of women earning this week what they had made all last year as teachers. Each of them sized up Polly with a quick look—and vice versa—as she walked with Ben and Duff to a table. Here and there were other women, seven among the whole crowd, each accompanied by a man (or two or three) and all dressed and painted in the overscrumptious fashion of their profession.

Duff stared at one of the whores, a Creole wearing a bodice cut lower than any he had ever seen in his life. His scar had not stung for months. In the woods, at Hembem, it never stung. Now he imagined its fire spreading up and encircling his right eye. "I tell you that anyone who looks at a woman lustfully," he whispered as he crossed himself, "has already committed adultery with her in his heart. If your right eye causes you to sin, gouge it out and throw it away."

The canvas back wall was tied open to catch the breezes, but the room was still hot, and many of the men were cooling themselves with ladies' fans. Polly gave hers to her brother to hold in his right hand and disguise his signs of the cross. At the twenty-one table a few paces away, an elated, red-cheeked boy of twelve was betting five dollars on each hand. Every time he won, several miners leaned over to tap his head for luck. He wore overalls in a gaudy floral print.

Duff's lips barely moved, and his murmur was inaudible over the noise. "Let the children come to me, do not prevent them, for the kingdom of God belongs to such as these."

The boy made Polly think of Priscilla. She wondered if California might suit her—might suit her too well, she worried, glancing at one of the doxies at the faro table. *Twenty ounces a man. Lord.* Would Polly ever manage to conquer her lust for money? She thought of the verse from the Sermon on the Mount that her mother had quoted so often, about the sin of sheer desire, of lusts in one's heart. *Twenty ounces every day, or twice or three times in a day if one wished.* But perhaps the figure had been an exaggeration.

For his part, Dennison's reminded Ben of the loud, sodden gambling sprees in the London clubs, which he had never much enjoyed. Those long nights had reeked of this very mixture of tobacco and liquor, glee and looming melancholy, energy and torpor, captivity and liberty. The atmosphere was gay to the point of mania, a strenuous pleasure-taking. The differences, of course, were the absence of women and the conformity of dress in the parlors of Pall Mall. There was also the democracy of San Francisco: *anyone* could plunge into this melee if he had a couple of pinches of dust or a friend with a bit extra. There was even a colored man drinking at the bar. (Ben was unaware of the house policy concerning Negroes—they got a free drink the first time they came but were told firmly never to return.)

A brass gong was struck loudly, followed by four beats of a bass drum, then the gong again, more drumbeats, and the gong a final time. The volume of the general gabble diminished, although not the gamesters' cries variously blaming and thanking the dice or the cards or God. A man about Ben's age wearing a white jacket had climbed onto a low scaffold in the corner and began addressing the crowd in a theatrical shout.

"Welcome and good evening, *kind* gents—*and* good ladies." His English accent had been diluted almost to American. He joshed about being "a San Franciscan from the old days," since he had arrived from the States "nearly two months ago." And he said that he had been "recently over in police court—where I *sang*, I did." A good many of the crowd laughed and hooted. In fact, a week earlier he really had performed songs and humorous imitations at the little courthouse across the plaza for two hundred people who had paid three dollars apiece—a performance already legendary as the city's first professional theatrical event. "And tonight, for a fraction of the cost, you shall be subjected—that is, *treated*—to a few ditties sung by the one, the only, the formerly British and only very slightly annoying Mr. Stephen C. Massett. Later I shall offer up my rendition of Colonel Frémont teaching Spanish to President Taylor . . ."

"Stephen Massett!" Polly said. They had never met, but she knew the name. He had performed roles as an actor in New York, and Skaggs had known him in Buffalo a decade earlier.

"Apparently only Duff and I," Ben said, "lack acquaintances and old friends in our new city."

Duff crossed himself—this time not to atone for any sin, but to amplify his constant prayer that God keep his path clear of acquaintances from the army.

". . . first tonight you shall hear a song, hot off the presses and arrived in the mails this week, a ballad from the beloved Hutchinson Family . . ." Duff and Polly exchanged a smile. The trumpeter and guitarist began to play. "It is entitled 'Ho! For California,' " Massett said, which provoked curiosity and excitement in the room. Even the gamblers looked up from their cards and dice and wheels.

> *"We've formed our band and we're all well mann'd*
> *To journey afar to the promised land,*
> *Where the golden ore is rich in store,*
> *On the banks of the Sacramento shore.*
>
> *"Then,* ho, *brothers* ho!
> *To California go.*
> *There's plenty of gold in the world we're told,*
> *On the banks of the Sacramento.*
>
> *"Heigh-o, and away we go,*
> *Digging up the gold in Francisco."*

At the end of the first verse, practically everyone in the hall—shocked, flattered, elated—was not only listening but giggling, humming, clapping, and stomping in time to the music. Men rushed from the street to the door to see what had provoked such an uproar.

"As we explore that distant shore,
We'll fill our pockets with the shining ore . . ."

The crowd hollered. Some men punched their fists in the air. One fellow sprinkled gold dust on the grinning, upturned face of a friend.

"And how 'twill sound, as the word goes round,
Of our picking up gold by the do{en pound."

At this line, almost all five hundred stood and yelled hurrahs. Massett performed a little jig on his platform, waiting two bars before he continued.

"Oh! the land we'll save, for the bold and brave
Have determined there never shall breathe a slave . . .
Let foes recoil, for the sons of toil
Shall make California God's Free Soil.

"Then, ho! Brothers, ho!
To California go.
No slave shall toil on God's Free Soil,
On the banks of the Sacramento . . ."

A good fraction of the crowd applauded the antislavery sentiment, albeit with less enthusiasm than the celebration of easy wealth. At the bar, the Negro acknowledged a few friendly glasses raised in his direction.

"Heigh-o, and away we go,
Chanting our songs of Freedom—oh!"

When the performance finished, Ben introduced himself to Massett as a pal of Timothy Skaggs's and brought him over to their table to discuss the idea of starting a theater. Massett complimented Polly on her performance a few years back as the merchant's ingenue daughter in *Fashion* ("so nicely unaffected"), and Duff on his authentic Indian look. He told them that nothing in New York had changed since they left—Chanfrau had celebrated his

250th performance as the heroic Mose Humphreys onstage, and was about to "get even richer in yet another sequel, if you can imagine." Massett smiled. "The new one is *Mose in California*—I swear it."

Ben saw Polly catch the nub of a new plan. He was excited simply watching her think.

"I knew Frank," Duff said in a monotone, sounding neither proud nor envious. "We ran with the same machine." He stared into a middle distance as he parsed this news.

"Well," Polly said, "should we not get up a production of *Mose in California* here, at a theater? Look at this audience! Look at how your California gold song stirred them up! Imagine *three acts* of Mose at the mines!"

Massett agreed that the play would cause a sensation, and sell thousands of tickets at three or five dollars apiece. "The trick would be finding a real b'hoy to play Mose." He turned to her brother, which startled Duff. "Do you also happen to be a veteran, Mr. Lucking—?"

"*Yes.*"

"—of the New York theaters? Yes?"

"*No*, no, I never acted. I do not act."

Ben and Polly talked some more with their new acquaintance about the kinds of shows that might succeed in California, and Massett mentioned that he too had seen the Hutchinsons perform in the Park last year during the Springtime of the Peoples.

"Have you heard the latest news about little Abby Hutchinson?" Massett asked.

He had retrieved Duff's full attention.

"A fellow *just* out from New York told me that our sweet young fighter for freedom and justice has married, and married well—a member of the stock exchange."

Duff's face fell. He was bereft, horrified. "Abby, she . . . she married a . . . *Wall Street* man? A *banker*?"

"Virtue may be its own reward," Massett said, "but in Miss Hutchinson's case, apparently an income of ten thousand dollars is also welcome." He spotted someone he knew at the door, and waved.

They turned to see an extravagantly dressed woman accompanied by two Indian girls with waists corseted and faces powdered white. Ben and Polly recognized the older woman as the brothelkeeper who had been pointed out to them in February by the Donner party boy—the countess.

Now Duff could barely breathe, and he found himself silently reciting

Genesis 18. *The cry of Sodom and Gomorrah is great, and their sin is very grievous* . . .

"Do you know Irene?" Massett asked.

Husband and wife shook their heads.

"A very saucy and enterprising lady from New Orleans, Mrs. McCready is."

Duff, dressed as an Indian, looked at Mrs. McCready's Indian girls, dressed as white harlots, and wanted to cry. *If I find in Sodom fifty righteous within the city, then I will spare all the place for their sakes* . . .

EARLY THE NEXT morning, Duff took his bags to Polly and Ben's room at the St. Francis. It already looked more like a home than their cabin at Ashbyville ever had. Polly had put out vases of morning glories and yellow monkey flowers and spread the Navajo *bayeta* on the end of the bed. Ben had tacked up Polly's pen-and-ink picture of the jammed harbor next to the window containing the same view, and hung the Maidu bow and his makeshift quiver over the sconce by the door. Books neatly lined the top of the bureau. Duff was happy for Polly and Ben, embruced them both, and kissed his sister goodbye.

He walked with his satchels the half mile to Vallejo Street, practically the suburbs. The Church of St. Francis of Assisi was a shed with a rough cross nailed to the front gable. The contest to organize churches was as fervid as the one to finish saloons and brothels—the Presbyterians had just beaten the Catholics, but the Catholics had celebrated their first Mass, well ahead of the first Congregationalist and Baptist services, and three months before the Jews would celebrate their first Yom Kippur. Apart from counseling Polly and Ben on carpentry and buying supplies for Hembem, attending Mass had been Duff's reason for this visit to San Francisco.

The priest, a visiting French Canadian, spoke English. During his reading, Duff had the distinct feeling that Saint Matthew himself was speaking to *him,* and confirming that his new life with Yauka and her people in the woods was righteous and holy: "Ye cannot serve God *and* mammon . . . Behold the fowls of the air: for they sow not, neither do they reap, nor gather into barns; yet your heavenly Father feedeth them . . . Consider the lilies of the field, how they grow; they toil not, neither do they spin . . . Take therefore no thought for the morrow: for the morrow shall take thought for the things of itself . . . *Verbum Domini.*"

It *was* the word of God. And it was nearly indistinguishable from what

Yauka and Bayam and Kumisi and the other Maidu said about money and wisdom and birds and flowers and the folly of worrying. *"Deo gratias,"* Duff said as sincerely as he had ever given thanks. In his mind, Catholic teaching and the Indians' philosophy became one that morning. When he sipped the blood of Christ from the cup, he imagined it was the *toloache,* the jimson root tea they drank from a stone chalice in order to commune with animal spirits, and then suddenly he realized—why had it not occurred to him before?—that the *toloache* might permit him to communicate directly with the Lord as well. It seemed so simple to him now, clear and bright as the deep blue July sky as he strode from the church.

"Ragged little doghole, ain't it?"

It was a fellow his age, in the costume of a b'hoy—red flannel shirt, tight pants, thick boots—who had kneeled next to him for communion. Duff shrugged and kept walking.

"I can say so, pard, because I helped build it myself in '47. *Army* work." He put out his hand. "Otis Waterman. I like your mountain-man costume."

Duff crossed himself, put down a bag, and shook Waterman's hand. "Hallo."

"Colonel Stevenson's Seventh New York Volunteers, retired. I'm a clerk now, in a land sales office. And," he added very proudly, "an officer of the Society of Regulators—the old *Hounds,* you know." Duff had seen their headquarters just south of the plaza, a tent they called Tammany Hall. It was filled with idlers spitting and drinking and cursing too loudly while they played with knives. It was, Duff saw, San Francisco's version of New York's Spartan Association, thugs posing as an urban militia. Fatty Freeborn had been a Spartan.

"I work placers," Duff said. "At Ashbyville."

"Did you know," asked Waterman, "that it says *D* on your skin there? I noticed it when we were receivin' communion. That's a *D.*"

At last it had happened: the coded scar on his right cheek, the army brand that meant DESERTER, had been deciphered.

Duff stared at his accuser. Waterman wore no jacket and was apparently unarmed. Duff's pistol was in one of his bags. What did this foul b'hoy mean to do? And why was he *smiling?*

Waterman touched the Maidu tattoo on the top of Duff's right hand, a bar and two dots in a row just above the knuckles. "In the telegraph alphabet, that there, *dah-dit-dit,* is a *D.* I was an apprentice operator for a year at Magnetic Telegraph, just before the war."

71

July 6, 1849
. . .
Ashbyville

E HAD SOLD Badger a few ounces of mercury when the boy came to visit; he had given directions to a score of new miners heading east down the Middle Fork; he had made a friend of an army lieutenant come to map the gold district for Washington; and yesterday an impertinent Boston twerp named Shepley had appeared to inspect the bit of Ashbyville that Ben and Polly had apparently offered to sell him for forty-five ounces. Yet except for those few minutes or odd hour here and there, Skaggs had spent the previous two weeks alone. And he'd found the experience entirely and shockingly agreeable. He did miss his conversations with Ben and his playful cuffing of "the Lucking kids," as he still thought of Polly and poor Duff. But after twenty years of incessant companionship and chatter, he felt as if he'd been freed from a cramped cage in which he had been a performing dog.

Instead of turning every twitch of his brain into some hasty squib that he tossed at anyone within shouting distance, he rediscovered the pleasures of writing out his thoughts—about the "large but trifling cost" of his $2,812.50 observatory in the woods; about "the twenty-seven-year-old rays of starlight" he was attempting to capture on a daguerreotype plate, and the Capricornid meteor showers that "entertained and inspired" him night after night, like "a camp meeting but the way such a spectacle *ought* to be—beautifully real and entirely benign brimstone from the heavens, with no Christian sermons at all"; about Duff's "flibbertigibbety swings between all-happy bliss and relapses of the deep dark blues"; about California as "a crucible for the very best and worst in our reckless American character"; and about his plans to take a photograph, in color, of the next transit of Venus across the face of the sun, as an old man in 1882.

And two days earlier—on the Fourth of July, for the first time in his life a day without explosions or speeches—he had rewritten and finally finished in one sitting his essay about the modern perception of time. He'd been inspired by a definition he'd happened across in his dictionary between *relapse* and *relax: "relativity, n.: a thing not absolute or existing by itself."* From that germ, he'd written, he had "concluded or, rather, intuited" that the recent miracles of breakneck speed had "simply begun to *unblind* us to the essential *relativity* of *all* perceptions and *all* measurements." And this morning he had decided to stitch together all of his new writing into a real book, "a history and philosophical memoir" called *Wonderstruck: The World in a Freak, or, A Former Cynic's Chronicle of Our Fantastic Modern Times.* Perhaps Ben and Polly's publishing house would make it their first title.

And he had taken to dressing outlandishly, because it amused him, and because there was no need to dress otherwise. On this particular Friday he had pulled on one of Ben's shredded archery-target shirts and Polly's billowy blue silk pants, which extended only to his knees and which he left unbuttoned. (She had taken none of her refashioned trousers and overalls to San Francisco, having decided that as long as her gender was outnumbered a hundred to one, she did not wish to invite *extra* attention from men in the streets.)

Skaggs found the long midsummer days paradisiacal—a few hours writing, a few hours digging and washing, an hour fishing or hunting turkeys with Ben's English shotgun, an hour walking, an hour eating, an hour napping, a few hours rereading old numbers of *Scientific American* and *The Literary World,* and on clear, balmy nights (six out of seven), a final few hours on Mount Aetna gazing up through his lenses into the brilliant night. It was heaven.

"I hear you approaching, paleface!" he shouted out to Duff, who had just climbed to the top of Mount Aetna. "By now I should have loaded my musket and taken aim."

When Duff appeared at the open door of the observatory, Skaggs was there to give him a hug. The man wearing blue silk short pants and a target on his back hugged the browned white boy wearing only a leather breech-cloth and moccasins. Skaggs was not in the habit of hugging Duff, but he was about to raise a fraught subject.

He needed to lance the great boil, to hear the confession.

"Welcome home."

Duff saw the pallet on the floor. "You have brought up your bed."

"One hot night I dozed off, and when I awoke, the breezes through the open dome were delicious. A perfect place to sleep, perchance to dream."

Duff handed him the latest editions of the *Alta California,* now published thrice weekly, and apprised him of Ben and Polly's latest San Francisco plans.

As he spoke, Skaggs saw now that the scar did indeed resemble a *D.*

"Have you taken your 'hundred-million-million-mile portrait' yet?" Duff asked.

Skaggs intended to make his first stellar daguerreotype of Vega, a million times as distant as the sun.

"Oh, until the *damned* clock drive arrives, it's simply no use attempting it."

"Because the star moves across the sky, like the moon."

"No, because our little ball of water and rock moves across the sky."

"The Maidu say that *everything* was water until a turtle asked God to make the sun and stars and land and all the rest."

"So does your Bible say the same. Except, I believe, for the part about the turtle. 'And the spirit of God moved upon the face of the waters, and God said, "Let there be light," and there was light.' "

Duff's eyes shone. "Yes. *Yes.*"

"Are you hungry?" Skaggs asked. "I still have three good eggs."

"I must go. It's late, and at dawn the *kaui-tson* starts." Each July, the Maidu began burning acres of dried grasses, both to fertilize the ground and to roast unlucky grasshoppers, which they harvested from the ashes for food.

"Ah, the great annual burning," Skaggs said, declining tonight to make his "tasty crispy cricket corpses" joke, or to tell Duff again that the difference between crickets and grasshoppers is that the latter "have their ears in their crotch." Instead he glanced up through the open dome. "The moon is full, and you know the way back home like a wolf to his den. At least stay with a lonely old white man for a few more minutes to talk."

And so they sat down together on the bench.

"Have you stayed put here since we left you?" Duff asked.

"I took Jenny Lind to get the mail and buy sugar and barley and eggs—and for a splurge, a tin can of *oysters*."

Duff inhaled sharply, as if to speak.

"Do *not* ask how many ounces I paid," Skaggs said. He paused. "I received a letter from New Hampshire, from brother Jonah." He touched the envelope on his desk.

"Another already? That must cheer you."

"And surprise me. Jonah Skaggs would never invest forty cents on postage unless he was very keen to tell me something." He paused again. "And my friend Taylor at the *Tribune* has written as well. It seems Greeley has dispatched him *here*—to chronicle this, us, all of it, California, better late than never. So after Bayard arrives, I shall have another chum in the neighborhood.

"And speaking of new company, while I was out at Auburn I spent two lovely hours with a fine fellow who's camped up on Bear Creek . . ."

"*Auburn?*" The only Auburn that Duff knew was the prison in New York, the place he had imagined as his Calvary. "What do you mean, 'at Auburn'?"

"Uh-huh—the boys at North Fork Dry Diggings have decided to change the name of the camp—henceforth it shall be Auburn. A civilized, townish, post-gold-fever name, I suppose."

Duff wanted the subject to change. "Tell me about the miner you met. Your new friend?"

"Not a miner at all—a surveyor and mapmaker, actually, from Massachusetts. Mr. George Derby. A very witty Yankee, here to draw a proper map of El Dorado for the government. For the army. And he understands *these* machines"—he waved at the telescope—"at least as well as I do."

"For the army?"

"An officer in the Topographical Engineers, *Lieutenant* Derby, West Point. In fact, he sailed from New York for Mexico the same time as you left, in '46, and fought at Vera Cruz as well . . ."

Yea, the shadow of death, fear no evil.

". . . wounded at Cerro Gordo, he said, in the great final charge against the Mexicans. Now, Duff, you were at Cerro Gordo, if I recall correctly."

An army officer. A West Point mate of his own despised Lieutenant McClellan. An engineer. At Vera Cruz—and hit at Cerro Gordo. Perhaps it was one of his own shots that had struck him. This lieutenant might well recall the name Duff Lucking.

"I was there."

Duff felt once again as if he were being hunted and haunted and pricked and probed and tested.

And this time, for once, he was not imagining it. Skaggs was determined to unburden him of his secrets.

"I should like to invite Lieutenant Derby here for dinner one day. You shall meet him yourself."

Duff stood. "I don't need to know him. It has gotten very late. I need to go."

Skaggs stood and, facing his friend—his rescuer—put his hands on his shoulders. He wanted to hug the boy again. "I know what happened in Mexico, Duff. I had begun to put two and two together some time ago, but—but now I know your mystery."

Verily, I say unto you, that one of you shall betray me.

"My brother is a lawyer with the firm of Pierce & Minot in Concord—with Frank Pierce, *General* Pierce." He glanced toward the letter from New Hampshire. "General Pierce informed Jonah of your"—*treason*—"reversals, and your months with the St. Patrick's Battalion, and your capture, and your trial. And your"—*mortification, lashing, branding*—"punishment." Now he strained to avoid any glance at the big red scar—the *D*, for deserter—on Duff's cheek. "I know all of it, Duff."

Shadow, death, fear, evil.

Skaggs tightened his grip. "You need not suffer any more torment over this, boy, or intrigue to keep it a secret. It is the past. It is unhappy history. You are a moral man, Duff, and you are plainly no coward. Whatever was your rationale for"—*deserting*—"forsaking the army at Vera Cruz and joining the Mexicans, well, I have no doubt whatsoever your decision was wholehearted, and excruciating, and irresistible."

Streams of tears were running down Duff's cheeks. "Do my mother and father know?" He saw the flicker of confusion and fear in Skaggs's eyes. "I mean my sister—Polly and Ben."

"I am no snitch. I leave it to you to tell them what you will. For now, you have my love and forgiveness."

Duff ripped himself from Skaggs's embrace. *"No, no, no.* You are no priest. I don't require your forgiveness. *God* can forgive me, God *has* forgiven me."

"I know, I know."

Duff started to sob.

He was now under the impression that Skaggs knew all of his secrets.

"I did it for them, you know, for those wretched, unarmed Mexicans we were slaughtering. *Slaughtering.* We bombed their *churches*! Worse than slaughter, because the burned and blasted lived on, my God, for hours and hours in that dust and heat, crying and bleeding, bugs all over them. Women and children, oh, the children—two *babies.* A lieutenant ordered me not to waste my rounds and powder on the dying, on 'ordinary Mexicans,' he said, but I, I had to disobey. I had no choice. Did I?" He was not really asking the question of Skaggs. "They moaned and suffered so terribly. I shot the first one, a man, and the woman on the ground next to him thanked me as I re-loaded, maybe his wife, maybe not, *Gracias, señor,* and then I shot her, and then reloaded, and then the next. Then I found the others. Point-blank, every one in that block. The most of them thanked me if they could speak. Point-blank, so it was painless. For them. Afterward I was covered in blood. I was soaked red. If the lieutenant had seen me then, he would have known, he would've checked my powder and counted my balls and then ordered a court-martial. So I was good as dead already. I did it all for them, those poor Mexicans, only for them. It did *me* no good at all."

He took a deep breath and now looked straight at Skaggs to address him directly.

"It is a relief to me that you know everything, Timothy. But you must understand that I burned the distillery because of the swill milk—because of the babies they murdered, such as Grace and William, may they rest in peace." He crossed himself. "And the brothel in Mercer Street, to free the women imprisoned there, to end the degeneracy. It was the same too with Freeborn's shack—to punish him for the horrors he visited on poor Priscilla Christmas. And the sugarhouse burned, well, that was to repay the Primes, and it was on behalf, too, what was it . . . for the proletarianites, all the workingmen enslaved by the bankers who own such places.

"The blazes were *all* for *others'* sakes, you know—once for *you*, Timo-thy, for you as well. Do you remember the winter you became so very angry at Greeley and his paper? Their punishment was on *your* behalf."

Skaggs realized immediately what he was saying: four years before, the night of a terrible blizzard in New York, the *Tribune*'s building had caught fire and burned down.

"I cut old man Prime for Polly," Duff continued, in the tone one might use to say *I went to Stockton to buy a horse.* "And Freeborn for Priscilla." He made the sign of the cross. "I never *enjoyed* doing a bit of it."

Skaggs was speechless. Two minutes before he'd meant only for Duff to admit what he had done in Mexico, to begin clearing his tortured mind and get on with his life. Skaggs had asked for a confession, and intended to give absolution. He had been a friend and uncle to the boy, had instructed and employed him, and thought he'd known the dark, cold undercurrents beneath the sincerity and loyalty and conscientious pluck. But now he saw an abyss.

Duff Lucking was cracked.

But . . . was he suffering awful, demonic *delusions?* Did he only imagine that he had set the *Tribune* and the distillery and the brothel afire, and that the suicide of Nathaniel Prime was his doing? Or was he truly an arsonist and a murderer? Skaggs now recalled the bakery fire that had happened to destroy Mrs. Stanhope's parlor house just before they left the city, and Fatty Freeborn's letter confessing suicide and arson conveniently delivered to the *Herald,* which in this light looked implausible.

Skaggs had decided to a fair certainty that his friend was not merely cracked but a monster.

"You do understand, Skaggs, do you not? *I am a soldier.* I believe I have always been a soldier—and soldiers must be ready to take lives. We don't wish to do it, but sometimes we must, in the name of justice and honor, and even for mercy's sake."

Skaggs was at a loss. Should he shriek? Embrace him? Inform him of his insanity? Question him further about his crimes, ask that he enumerate each arson and murder? Give him a brandy dosed with fluoric acid, or use Ben's shotgun to dispatch him, for his own good and the safety of the world? Tell him to retreat into the Sierras with his Indians and never return?

"It is late, Duff. You must go home."

As he stood at the edge of the rock watching Duff walk in the bright moonlight along the river bend below—Piccadilly, they had called that path—Skaggs wished he could erase him from his thoughts forever.

Instead he poured himself a cup of brandy, cried, then finished the pint and fell asleep.

HE WAS AWAKENED after midnight by a pounding and a shout from down below, at the cabins.

He walked outside in his archery-target shirt and drawers and called down. "*Duff?* What is it? What do you want?" No reply came. What fresh madness was this? He would go down and find out why the wretch had re-

turned. Perhaps what he had said before was temporary insanity, a hallucination produced by too much prayer and Indian holy juice, and he had come
back now to recant and declare his mental soundness. Skaggs returned to the
observatory to put on his shoes and specs so that he could make the climb
down. But as he stepped toward the door, a human figure blocked the light.

"*Duff,* " he said with a start, but in the part of his mind that operated
faster than his tongue, he knew even as he spoke that it was not Duff.

"*Sit,* " said the man. "Sit down and make your hands open, up above
your head. I have the gun."

When the man stepped inside and out of the way of the moon, Skaggs
could see the pistol. It was cocked, the hammer pulled back like a lizard's
open mouth. He raised his hands, turned, and walked to the bench to sit.

"You have the big circles on the shirt. For *les flèches* . . . *comment est-il
dit*—the bow and arrows?"

"Yes, I do."

"And you are Doof Lucking."

"No, sir, I am not Duff Lucking."

"You *lie* to me, eh, Lucking?"

"No, sir." Why was a *Frenchman* looking for Duff?

"Yes, you lie because you are the *criminal,* eh? Un *déserteur,* yes? And
you set fires to New York, I know this, and you come to California not to
find the gold, no, but to catch the Negro slave for money, yes? Yes? I know
all these truth."

This Frenchman did know an astonishing amount about Duff. But *catch
the Negro?* "I am not Duff Lucking. And since you, sir, are so knowledge-
able, you must know that Mr. Lucking is a *young* man, only twenty-two. I am
certainly not twenty-two, as you can see."

The Frenchman said nothing for a moment. "*Allumez*—fire the candle."
Skaggs obeyed. Drumont stepped closer, still pointing his pistol at him.

"Then you are . . . Skaggs. The *journaliste,* the *photographe,* the *auteur.*
Yes? *Astronome* also," he said, indicating the telescope, "this I do not know
before."

"Yes. I am Timothy Skaggs. And may I ask your name, sir?"

"Sergeant Gabriel Drumont. I have your mails from the Sacramento
City . . ."

With his left hand he pulled a thick wad of pages from his pocket and
threw them toward Skaggs. A dozen *Knickerbocker*s and *Literary World*s
and *Flag of Our Union*s fluttered to the floor. (The two latest issues of *The*

Flag of Our Union each contained a new work by Poe—one a tale about the discovery of a technique for turning lead into gold and the resulting ruination of California, the other a poem, "Eldorado," concerning a knight's quest for gold that leads to a meeting with Death.)

"Your revolution magazines, eh?"

Skaggs wanted to smile. The revolutionist *Knickerbocker*! How was it that abusive policemen and soldiers of every nation were abusive in precisely the same stupid, surly fashion?

"No, monsieur, literary magazines. *Patriotic* magazines."

"Now: Where is the address of Benjamin Knowles? It is Knowles I want. He is my reason to come here."

Suddenly Skaggs understood. This Drumont was not after Duff, or him. How many times had he heard Ben retell the story of his apprehension in Paris, the penguin, the shots, the fallen soldier, the murder of Ashby, his escape, the pursuit all night through the streets, his encounter at the hotel, the chase through the Thames Tunnel . . . Skaggs had always assumed a certain amount of exaggeration, even from Ben. But here was the French sergeant, come all the way to California to find him.

"I am afraid," Skaggs said with some relief, "that Ben and Mrs. Knowles have—"

To arrest *him.*

"—have gone to S—"

No, to kill *him, of course.*

"—to Sonoma. They are living now in the town of *Sonoma,* to the west, toward the sea."

"Sonoma? Not San Francisco?"

"No, *Sonoma,*" Skaggs repeated, "perhaps thirty miles *north* of San Francisco. You can ride there straight across the Sacramento Valley. You might reach it in . . . a week?"

Skaggs was pleased with himself. If the Frenchman went to Sonoma, Skaggs would have time to reach San Francisco and warn Ben, to save him . . .

Drumont looked long and hard at Skaggs's face, the candlelight reflecting off his eyeglasses. He could sense the dissembling, smell the trickery. And he had already encountered the two Indians on the road earlier tonight. Jack and Badger had told him that Knowles and the woman were living in San Francisco. Now Drumont was certain they had told the truth.

"You lie to me, monsieur," he said.

. . .

TWO HOURS LATER, Duff did return to Ashbyville. He had walked home to Hembem and then turned around and run all the way back.

"*Skaggs!*" he shouted from the base of Mount Aetna. "*Skaggs, get up!*"

He could see the flickering candlelight in the observatory. "*Please,* I need you to come with me—Yauka is *very ill.*"

As soon as he had seen her gray face and glassy raccoon eyes by the firelight, before she'd turned away to puke, he'd known that she was sick. He'd felt her pulse racing. He'd brought her water and she'd begged for more.

"I *believe* it may be the *cholera,*" he called out. His diagnosis was correct. "Skaggs!" Duff had all the medicine he needed, but Yauka's condition seemed so acute that he needed Skaggs to *inject* her with the ammonia and calomel and laudanum, perhaps to bleed her, whatever was required to save her life. "*Skaggs?*"

WHEN DUFF SAW the empty brandy bottle lying on the desk near the candle and Skaggs sprawled, face down, magazines scattered around him, he thought he understood what had happened. More than once, Duff had seen him passed out on the floor of his apartment in New York.

"Oh, *Skaggs,*" he groaned.

He set the bench upright, and the brandy bottle, and collected the magazines and papers in a stack that he put on the desk. He took the candle from the desk and crouched down to awaken Skaggs.

In the candlelight he saw the wet patch of hair and dark pool on the floor near his neck.

And then he turned him over and saw the hole in his face.

He carried Skaggs's body to the bed and removed his bloodied eyeglasses.

Down in the tent he found the bottles of naphtha and the quarter hogshead of lamp oil and climbed carefully back up Mount Aetna. He made the sign of the cross over Skaggs. With drops of the oil he anointed his eyes and ears and nose and lips, and his hands and feet, and then recited the Lord's Prayer.

". . . Look not on our sins, but on the faith of your church, and grant us the peace and unity of your kingdom where you live for ever and ever. Amen. Bless you, Timothy Skaggs."

He kissed his cheek, then stood and blew out the candle. First he emptied both bottles of naphtha over Skaggs's body, drenching him, and then poured the oil in widening circles on the floor, and splashed the walls.

He stepped outside, crossed himself once again, lit a match, and dropped it in the pool at the doorsill. By the time he reached the path at the back of the rock, the observatory was ablaze.

The Maidu burned the houses of the dead, and then never again mentioned their names. From the piazza Duff looked up at the flames and smoke pouring out of the half-open dome on the west wind. Copper, he had learned in the army, melted at a much lower temperature than iron. He could see the tip of the telescope pointed northeast, toward the High Sierras—in fact, toward the star Vega. The Maidu believed, as Duff understood it, that death released the soul along the path of the sun to the Milky Way and then to heaven.

"It is *all* fire," he said aloud, meaning the blaze up on the rock and the sun and the stars. He thought of his father's maxim, *Destruction and creation are the cycle of life.* He tried to recall Skaggs's Latin motto about flames and light and trickery, but he could not remember it.

Cave ignis fatuus: Beware the fictitious fire.

EIGHT OF THE *hu*s in Hembem had been burned since the beginning of the year. Their occupants had died of dysentery and malaria and pneumonia and consumption and all the principal fevers—typhoid and scarlet, puerperal and nervous, lung and brain—but none had succumbed to the cholera. Yauka was the first, although she would not be the last.

When Duff returned again to the village before dawn, her brother Bayam handed him a mourning necklace to wear over his rosary, and a red-hot fagot to singe his hair to stubble—mourning length.

In a single dreadful night, Duff had lost his best friend and his wife. And what made the pain worse was his arrival at their sides too late—*just* too late—to save them or succor them or wish them farewell. As he breathed the sulfur stink of his own burning hair, he decided he was not being punished by God for his misdeeds. To the contrary, he believed that Satan's own agents on earth had killed Skaggs and, somehow, Yauka as well. *No torture could be more painful than this,* he thought as the day broke.

But the truth, if he had known it, would have been unendurable. Somewhere in his vocabulary journal was the word *bacteria.* Duff had picked up the cholera bacterium three months before at the restaurant in Sacramento City; he had carried the new contagion deep into the California backwoods; he had infected Yauka and the others who would soon retch and wither and die of the cholera at Hembem.

. . .

A DAY LATER—the sixth Sunday after Pentecost—he walked back to the Middle Fork, stopping at Jack and Badger's camp to tell them of the deaths of Skaggs and Yauka.

"A stranger pass two nights since," Jack told him. "A soldier, from Vuh-rance. He know your name, Duh-vuh, and Skaggs and Pully. He know Pen most. He travel twelve month, across all America."

Duff had an inkling. "What was this Frenchman's name?"

Jack did not recall, but Badger thought he did. "Dro-mont?" he said. "Or Tree-mont?"

Frémont. Was the killer Frémont himself? Frémont had just traveled across America on his failed expedition. Or perhaps the boy misremembered, and the assassin was one of Frémont's men, an advance guard returning to finish off the Maidu as well as their white allies. Duff recalled the politician Burnett's promise in the street in Sacramento City, that they would wage a war of extermination against the Indian.

So the war was under way.

He took out his Colt's and told Jack and Badger to "beware, beware." They did not know the word. "Ten mucho cuidado," Duff said. *Be very careful.*

AS HE CAME around the bend of Piccadilly approaching Ashbyville, he saw a donkey tied to one of the pines. It was not Jenny Lind. After a few more steps he saw a man near the river at one of their old placers. Duff hid behind an oak and watched. The man was squatting, and poking into the ground with a long knife. After a while the fellow walked up from the bank and, still holding his knife, started to explore—looking into the cabins and the tents, disappearing for a minute up the back trail they'd called Broadway.

Duff cocked his revolver and crept from tree to tree into camp. Finally he rested the barrel on the stub of a pine branch, aimed, and spoke. *"Trespasser."*

"Ho, *what?* Who is that?" The man spun around and, seeing Duff and his gun, raised his hands.

Duff saw now that it was the smirking man from the saloon at the hotel in San Francisco, the slick Boston braggart with his 117 ounces from Volcano. "Why are you here?"

"I am Ronald Shepley," he said, "here to see about purchasing a claim from Mr. and Mrs. Knowles."

"*Liar.*" If Polly and Ben were selling claims, there would have been a meeting about it. Ashbyville was a democracy.

"I've spoken with Mr. Skaggs. I have a letter . . ." He started to reach into his pocket.

"*Stop.*" Duff stepped from behind the pine, careful to keep his aim as he stepped toward Shepley.

Shepley recognized him now, despite the short hair. "You're the brother, the brother of Mrs. Knowles. Look here, sir, you misunderstand, I have come—"

"*Shut up.*"

Duff stopped walking and gripped the gun with both hands in front of his chest, the tip of the barrel two feet from Shepley's face. If he allowed him to live, that would surely count as a great work of mercy in the name of Jesus Christ to please the Lord God and Savior.

"Who sent you here? Why were you rummaging back there on the trail?" The hole where they had buried their gold was behind the cabins where the trail into the hills began—at the foot of Broadway. This dastard murdered Skaggs, Duff now suspected, and returned in daylight to rob them. "I saw you snooping back there in Broadway. Why?"

"*Broadway?*" he said. "I am only here about a deal of business, sir, and I don't know 'Broadway' from *Tremont* Street, if—"

"*What* did you say?" Duff had heard *Frémont's Street*.

"I *said* I am here about your gold."

The scoundrel had admitted it: he had meant to steal their cache.

"You killed Skaggs up in his observatory, didn't you?"

"*What?*" Shepley glanced up at the blackened ruin on the rock. "Oh no, no, sir, your friend died in that blaze? Good *Lord*. Now I understand your agitation—you've been *attacked*. Do you know," he said, looking up at Mount Aetna again, "I had wondered, I wondered if one of the diggers had done that. The *Indians* . . . sometimes they burn their *own* houses, as I understand it, for no good reason at all. Crazy damned *pyromani*—"

Duff pulled the trigger, and Shepley flew back into the grass. He was dead before the echo ended.

Duff stepped forward and looked down at his face. Around the bloody hole in his cheek was a circle of charred, smoking flesh, and around that a larger ring of soot that covered most of his face. It looked like one of Ben's archery targets in miniature, the circles red, black, gray, and pink instead of yellow, red, blue, and black.

It was horrendous. *My God, I am heartily sorry for having offended thee* . . . He had not fired a gun since the shooting gallery at Barnum's. . . . *because thou art all good and worthy of all love, and because sin displeases thee.* He had never fired the Colt's. *Pardon me through the merits of the passion and death of Jesus Christ, thy Divine Son.* He laid the pistol down next to Shepley's body. *I purpose by the help of thy holy grace never more to offend thee and to do penance* . . . He would never fire it again. *Amen.*

Before he took Jenny Lind and left Ashbyville for the last time, he packed up all of his belongings that remained there, including the black powder and fuse.

72

❖

July 14, 1849

· · ·

San Francisco

*D*RUMONT REGRETTED SHOOTING the astronomer. But had he any choice? The man would have warned his friend, and that would have been intolerable. Monsieur Skaggs was a casualty of war. And his fib had made it easier to pull the trigger. Americans, Drumont had come to think, were very poor liars.

After spending nearly his last dollar on the boat passage downriver, he had fretted that Prime's two hundred dollars would not be awaiting him at the bank, or that the bank would be closed for business on a Saturday—but his luck continued to hold, Pinkerton had been true to his word, his purse was full once again, and Benjamin Knowles was all but dead. As soon as he had finished, Drumont would post a letter to Chicago informing his employers of his discovery that both Miss Christmas and the child were, alas, deceased. And with the two hundred dollars—did he not deserve it, really, in any event, after all that he had endured?—he would steel himself to make one final goddamned ocean voyage, and ship out for good to *les Caraïbes françaises.*

Or perhaps, he thought, he might become a gold millionaire himself. San Francisco seemed to Drumont not like an American city. Its spirit was too loose, and with the sun and blue sea and pretty hills and adobe buildings seemed altogether *méditerranéen.* Perhaps he would stay.

He glanced at the receipt the bank clerk had handed him, and noticed the date: the fourteenth of July. He had not carried a calendar out of Salt Lake City. And now he decided this was a fine portent: it was the sixtieth anniversary of the storming of the Bastille, the disorderly beginning of the true revolution, which had been the disorderly but necessary preamble to Napoleon and the empire.

Once he had determined that Knowles was not a guest at the Parker House, Drumont took a room there, then skulked quickly from hotel to hotel asking quietly if he was in residence. At the fifth place he inquired, catty-corner across the plaza, the young American at the desk was delighted to tell him that, yes indeed, Mr. and Mrs. Knowles were guests of the St. Francis.

"They are over in Sausalito for the day today," the fellow said, "but I expect them back late tonight on the last ferry."

"It arrives at what hour?"

"By nine, ordinarily."

"And if I wish after to make a gift to them later, from, uh . . . from a different city, to their room in the hotel, it is the room number . . . ?"

"Forty-seven, sir, but all you need to write is 'Knowles, St. Francis, San Francisco,' and we'll get it right to them."

Drumont returned to his own hotel. He would wait in his room until the end of the day to finish his work. The darkness would make escape easier. And he had always imagined their final encounter occurring at night, like their first.

He sat on his bed and drank from a bottle of wine as he flipped through Inspector Vidocq's *Mémoires* one last time, rereading the great man's descriptions of lockpicking and of his greatest successes—in particular the apprehension in a Paris street of the confidence man Champaix, whom he had ordered to *stop in the name of the law*, even though Vidocq was at that late date a private detective.

At eight o'clock Drumont cleaned his gun and loaded the chambers with new linen cartridges.

At quarter past eight he examined himself in the mirror as he dressed by the light of the setting sun. When Knowles had first seen him in Paris, Drumont had been shaved and barbered normally. At the time of their encounter in London, his hair had been bristles and he'd worn a mustache. Now Drumont had a full beard and long, shaggy hair, like most men in San Francisco.

At eight-twenty he returned to the St. Francis, and by half past eight he was in position, standing beside a locked door inside a large, moonlit room on the fourth floor of the hotel, number 47, holding his cocked Baby Dragoon, waiting, listening to his own breaths. The room smelled of lavender and morning glory.

It was nearly ten when Ben returned to the hotel.

"Good evening, sir," said the white-haired Mexican who manned the St. Francis's desk in the evenings. He handed Ben a letter from London and the key to his room. "Should we expect Señora Knowles soon?"

"Well, Luis, that is a question I cannot answer with any certainty. I left her some time ago down at Hainey's barbershop. She was initiating Mr. Hainey into the mysteries of *ladies'* coiffures, by lamplight, so . . . for all I know, Mrs. Knowles may not return until midnight."

"The most beautiful lady in San Francisco," Luis replied with a smile, "has certain obligations to her thousand admirers. And for her we have the second key whenever she appears." As Ben turned toward the stairs, Luis remembered "Ah, sir—a friend of yours was here earlier, and very eager to see you. A handsome gentleman of the Old World, the same as you, sir."

Old World? Ben wondered if it had been Stephen Massett, or the German painter from Coloma, or perhaps Luis meant Ronald Shepley's mining partner, the Australian . . . "What is the gentleman's name?"

"He would not give it—he told me he had traveled 'halfway round the earth' to find you here, and wanted to surprise you. I have probably told you too much." Luis smiled.

Halfway round the earth . . . Ben had a wild thought: Could it be his cousin's husband, the Count de Tocqueville, dismayed and disappointed by the revolution and counter-revolution in France, returning to explore the new America? Or—might it be?—his brother Philip, come personally to oversee the importation of Chinese laborers and Indian opium through San Francisco? America and California had inured Ben to the occurrence of the incredible and impossible.

"And where is this gentleman now, Luis?"

Luis shook his head and shrugged. "I cannot say, sir. He did tell me he craved a glass of good French wine. He arrived in San Francisco only today."

"Thank you, Luis."

Ben read the letter from London as he climbed the three flights.

It was from his sister Isabel. And it was shocking. It filled him with grief and shame and delight, a bewildering mixture of all three. The old dream-like giddiness overtook him as he reached the fourth floor—floating above the earth, a balloonist without a balloon, his flight not quite under his own command but powered, in some obscure way, by his very astonishment and vertigo.

He tried to imagine what Polly's reaction would be to this news from England.

He unlocked the door and lit a match. During the second or two of phosphorescent flash he sensed something awry in the room, the balance of light and shadow slightly different.

But he had turned right to light the candle on the sconce and Drumont was on his left, behind the open door, so when the whispered command came—

"*Stop*, Knowles, in the *name* of the *law*."

—Ben was startled, and dropped his burning match to the floor.

"I have the *gun*."

When Drumont slammed the door shut with his free hand, the breeze extinguished the flame of the match on the floor.

"Fermez—eh . . . boulonnez la porte, ah, the *door, lock* the door."

Drumont was so excited that his English was in retreat.

Ben did as he was told, unthinkingly. He was confused. "Monsieur le Comte?"

There was no reply. And even in the dark, Ben realized that the intruder was not, of course, Tocqueville. *Eager to find you . . . the Old World . . . halfway round the earth . . . would not give his name . . . wanted to surprise you. I have the gun.* The truth was even more incredible.

Drumont, his eyes long since accustomed to the dark, stepped carefully into the center of the room, keeping his pistol aimed as he took his place a few paces behind Ben. During their three previous encounters Knowles had surprised and humiliated him.

"Make the hands above the head."

Drumont took a deep breath of profound satisfaction. *La fin. Nous sommes finis.* "We finish," he said. "Killer of French boys. Killer of la France."

The man is perfectly mad, Ben thought.

He was too far from the window to leap, and would likely die in the fall anyway. The knife he had brought from Ashbyville was packed away. Then he remembered one of his brother-in-law's tedious disquisitions on lunacy—how making ordinary conversation, Roger Warfield had said, could soothe madmen. It was ridiculous, but he would try, for the extra minute it might give him.

"Hallo, sir. I understand that you are extremely angry with me. But I do not understand what you think I have done. I have killed no French boys, I—"

"*Liar! Liar!*"

Drumont nearly pulled the trigger, but he did not wish to finish in anger. He was a soldier. This was to be an execution. Nor did he want his moment of triumph, delayed so long, to pass so quickly.

Ben expected the pistol to fire. *Roger was unfortunately mistaken* would be his last living thought.

"Who is *dead* in the Rue du Helder on the twenty-three of février, eh? My *boy*, mon petit frère, my brother Michel, I bring him out of la Corse, from la Corse to Paris like I am his *father*. And he is *dead* in Paris. Because of *you*. Because of your revolution. By my pistol, but you make his death." He took another breath to regain his dignity, "Now you, Knowles. By my pistol *and* I make the death of you."

From la Corse, Ben thought, as in Dumas's *Les Frères corses:* this fellow and the soldier he accidentally shot were brothers, from *Corsica*—literally Corsican brothers. *If only Ashby could hear this* would be Ben's last living thought.

"I am sorry to learn that he died. Very sorry indeed. May your brother rest in peace."

Ben's eyes had adjusted to the dark. He saw Drumont nod.

"And I am no revolutionary," he continued, "I assure you of that. My late friend and I were simply . . . walking around Paris that night, sightseeing."

"Your 'late friend'?"

"The man with me, who died . . . Whom—whom you killed." At least his last living thought would be dignified.

"*I? I* kill? Liar! I kill no man from you. The friend he run to go with the radicaux, et alors . . . he escape to them . . . I fire, ma balle ne l'a *pas* frappé . . ."

While the lunatic was making his unintelligible French excuses for murdering Ashby, Ben remembered his fondest souvenir from Ashbyville, which hung now an arm's length away on the wall, near the door. During their two weeks in the city he had come to see it as a mere decoration . . .

"And *you*," Drumont was saying, "you carry the *bombe* of the girl, the

radical, the friend Marie. And *you* are cinquante mètres from the other radicaux in the boulevard when they charge to the battalion of the army. When
my pistol fire—*you* make this fire—the army hear this, et ils ont mis le feu
pour se défendre. They fire to *defend*! The *error* of *my* gun was the *cause* of
the revolution—the error made by *you*." He sighed deeply. "C'est énorme,"
he said, "c'est *énorme* . . ."

Ben had nothing more to say. The man was insane. And there was no escaping.

They both heard the iron latch shake and jiggle. Drumont, alarmed,
leapt back to his original hiding place, on the far side of the door from Ben.

And as the door opened, blocking the Frenchman, Ben turned and
reached with both hands toward the wall.

In one second he had grabbed the bow off the sconce where it hung.

In two he had nocked an arrow.

In three he had drawn it to his cheek.

And the instant the Frenchman kicked the door shut, Ben released the
string and let the arrow fly, inches in front of Polly's face, and then hurled
himself onto her to drive her down, out of harm's way.

Drumont's pistol had fired once, and did not fall from his hand as he fell
backward. He lay on his back, on the floor.

Ben was unhurt. And when Polly sat up and discovered why her husband
had tackled her to the floor, she found that all of her injuries—a sore shoulder, a very sore haunch, a sprained hand—were the result of his tackle.

The assassin was still. The arrow, traveling several times as fast as a railroad locomotive, had entered his left eye, enfiladed his brain, and pierced the
back of his skull. Only its last few feathered inches poked out from his face.

Ben removed the smoking revolver from his grip and picked up the bow
and quiver.

When they left the room, they encountered a single curious person, the
man who occupied the adjacent room, standing in the hallway, staring.

"I thought I heard a shot," he said.

"We were ambushed. By a lunatic. But we are both all right. And he's
dead."

"Well, congratulations," the man said, "you're lucky," and with that returned to his room and shut the door.

They would go and tell Luis what had happened, and ask him to notify
the proper authorities—whoever those were, since San Francisco still had
no police force.

As they walked downstairs, Ben told Polly the main news in his sister's letter. During Philip and Lydia's honeymoon in Gibraltar in April, he had been badly beaten in the street ("by an insurgent of some sort, evidently") and had died a day later of a cerebral hemorrhage.

"Oh, *Ben*, good Lord, how *awful*. How terrible! What a terrible year for your poor family."

He said nothing more as they walked down the last flight to the lobby. He decided that to explain at that particular moment the various ramifications of his brother's death—*I am no longer a younger son, I am now Sir Benjamin Knowles, Philip's widow is the Dowager Lady Knowles, and now you, Polly, are the Lady Knowles*—would be inappropriate.

"Ah, Mr. *Knowles*," said Luis delightedly when he saw them, "I was about to send a boy up for you—the gentleman has returned, your amusing friend."

"He was not my *friend*, Luis. He was . . . my great enemy. And he is dead."

Luis was perplexed—Mr. Knowles was carrying a pistol and Indian archery gear, and he appeared to be serious and shaken, not drunk or joking. "No, Mr. Knowles, no, no—I spoke with the gentleman not five minutes ago—he is just there, in the small saloon, sir, awaiting you. With joy."

Given what had already occurred, Ben was willing to entertain any dreadful possibility. Perhaps there was an accomplice—the third soldier from that night in Paris. He instructed Polly to wait with Luis while he went to confront the mysterious stranger who claimed to be his friend. He cocked the Frenchman's pistol.

BEFORE HE HAD stepped into the saloon, Ben spotted him.

He was sitting with a glass of red wine and a book, a candle pulled close to illuminate the pages. He still wore a beard, and his hair was quite long and knotted into a queue, like a gentleman of their grandparents' day—no, like a Chinaman. He wore a collarless pink silk robe brocaded with blue clouds. For an instant Ben thought it was Skaggs playing a prank.

As he approached he saw the red cap lying on the table beside the candle, the *bonnet rouge* purchased last February in Paris from the clarinetist's child for two francs.

He now felt himself flying and swooping through the very heavens, among stars and comets, in sight of a true miracle.

"*Christ Almighty,*" he shouted, "how can this *be?*"

Other patrons turned to stare.

Lloyd Ashby smiled and stood.

"Look at this rough and shaggy mountain man," he said, "Hawkeye himself, with gun drawn *and* Chingachgook's bow and arrows."

They embraced furiously, exclaiming and laughing.

"You did not die!" cried Ben.

Only as the words left his mouth did he realize that the denials of the man he had just killed upstairs—*I kill no man from you, the friend*—had been the truth. "But you never returned to the Ile Saint-Louis, I waited all night and day, your friends believed you were dead, we *all* did."

"The crappo bastard fired at me, but I plunged into the back of the mob running away, running east, and escaped by the hair of my chinny-chin-chin. Notwithstanding the *tragic* misinformation you supplied to my grieving parents—and the dead Jewish bloke you shipped across the Channel to Cadogan Place."

"He—he wore a waistcoat like yours."

It took the two of them some time to sort out exactly what had happened in the Rue du Helder and during the chaotic days afterward.

Juliet, Ashby's mistress, had been a close associate of some of the leading red republicans—and had actually stored a small cask of black powder in her apartments. Given that the success of the revolution was highly dubious on that first night, and with the Garde Municipale pursuing him, Ashby and the "rather panicky and operatic" Juliet had decided to leave the country and embark on their Oriental journey *immediately.* "And our folly was prudent, as things turned out," Ashby said, "for if we had been in Paris in *June,* she doubtless would have died on a barricade, and probably her silly English lover along with her. On the other hand, she would have been deprived of the opportunity to leave me for the French consul in Shanghai."

Ashby had written his parents from Constantinople, en route to China, so it was not until summer that they'd learned he was alive—and only this past winter in Shanghai had *he* learned that they and all of London had for several months believed him dead.

"I wrote to you in New York," Ashby said—but by then, of course, Ben had gone missing on his trip across America in pursuit of Polly. As Ashby had been about to board his China clipper bound for London, "a Foreign Office fellow" informed him that Benjamin Knowles was now living in San Francisco.

And thus there was Lloyd Ashby, in the drinking saloon of the St. Francis Hotel, stopping in America for a visit with his old friend on his way home to England.

Ben informed him that their French sergeant—a true Corsican brother on a vendetta that had taken him to London and then all the way to California—was at that moment lying dead upstairs with an arrow in his head.

"He says that those two shots in the street in Paris," Ben continued, "his brother's shot and his shot at you, running, were the provocation that caused the troops at the ministry to panic and fire on the mob. He insisted that *we* therefore caused the massacre, that *we* were therefore responsible for everything that followed. *Everything*. Inadvertently. Accidentally."

They stared at each other, speechless, unsure whether to believe it—that their bumbling lark was the spark that had ignited the first of fifty revolutions—and unsure whether to be appalled or proud or simply astounded. *It is enormous*, Ben thought, *enormous . . .*

"Hallo . . . ?"

"*Polly,*" Ben shouted as she approached them, and then in his dither forgot her married name: "Miss Mary Ann Lucking, allow me to introduce you to my great friend—Mr. Lloyd Ashby."

Polly's mouth fell open, and Ashby bowed.

73

late July 1849

. . .

Ashbyville

IT WAS ANOTHER week before they learned of Skaggs's death, and the burning of his observatory, and the killing of the miner Shepley at their camp. Why had the Frenchman murdered Skaggs and Shepley? This Gabriel Drumont was a monster, a destroyer beyond understanding.

"You may think me awful," Polly told Ben, "but it makes me *glad* that you killed him."

They worried for Duff, and wondered where he had gone. When they'd returned to the gold district and Ashbyville—accompanied by Ashby—Jack had told them he last saw Duff on "the day with all the deaths." Duff had told Jack he was going off with the donkey to live by himself and "put things right again."

Polly painted a message for her brother on the door of one of the cabins in blue tempera, giving the address of the house she and Ben had rented in San Francisco and letting him know that Skaggs's remains would be in a grave at New Helvetia Cemetery, near Sutter's Fort.

DUFF DID CREEP back into Ashbyville one last time, and found the camp occupied by squatters, a group of miners newly arrived over the Sierras from Kentucky. They had renamed it Burnt Rock.

74

August 16, 1849
. . .
San Francisco

*T*WO HUNDRED PACKERS and wagoneers were crossing the mountains from the east every day. And hordes continued to arrive by sea. During just the fortnight Ben and Polly and Ashby were gone to bury Skaggs, five thousand new Californians had been deposited in San Francisco by another fifty-one ships, twenty-two of which remained anchored in the harbor as additions to the ghost armada. There were pilings for two new wharves, and another had been extended a hundred feet into the bay. On every block a building had been finished or a new one begun. Where the "Tammany Hall" tent headquarters of the b'hoys' gang had stood was now a vacant lot, and half of the Tammany Hall toughs had been convicted of riot and murder and would be sent to prison as soon as a prison could be rigged up. A police force had been organized and the first mayor elected. But Stephen Massett assured them that—so far—he had heard of no firm plans to start a theater or a book publishing firm.

THE EVENING WAS very warm. Ben stood outside in Clay Street, waiting, watching the regular plaza hullabaloo, which tended to reach its first peak now, at sunset. He and Polly and Ashby were to meet at seven and then walk together to a restaurant run by Peruvians in a tent, to have a supper of crispy roast rodent called *cuy*. Polly had spent the afternoon with Massett in Washington Street, interviewing several young men who might be turned from

miners and laborers into stage players for a production of *Mose in California*. And Ashby was off painting in the Chinese district—he had undertaken
a portrait of a launderer's two children in exchange for the chance to practice his rudimentary Cantonese.

On the edge of the plaza twenty yards north of where he stood, a handsome fellow with curly hair and a loud voice was exciting a crowd near the
offices of the new mayor and city council. He was a military adventurer, but
he was not recruiting soldiers. He was a politician, but he was not seeking
votes. He was John Charles Frémont, the most famous man in California, in
his reckless blowhard's fashion now making an announcement that he was
also among the luckiest. Ben could see men pressing in to look at the rocks
in his hands—fist-sized pieces of quartz veined and encrusted with gold.
The rocks came from his Rancho de las Mariposas in the south, he said. A
few years back, before the discovery at Sutter's Mill, Frémont had bought
the tract of land—"twice as big as New York Island," Ben heard him say,
"and now twice as *rich*"—for seven cents an acre.

Ben glanced to his left. Polly was walking toward him quickly from
Dupont Street. The sun setting behind her made her radiant, with a golden
nimbus, like some enchanted princess. She wore a dress of turquoise silk that
exposed her shoulders, and the hem of her skirt had a fringe of dirt. She held
her folded parasol in both hands.

"Good evening, my love. Did you find your Mose?"

She grimaced and shook her head. "What show are *you* watching?" she
asked.

"Colonel Frémont, in person, up from the San Joaquin with stories of his
new mother lode."

"Really?" She looked over at Frémont. "He is so young, so much
younger than I imagined."

"Skaggs would be pleased to hear it. He mentioned once that he and Frémont were precisely the same age."

She squeezed his hand and kissed his cheek. And then he, feeling the
speed of life's passage and breathing in her lavender, put both hands on her
waist and kissed her directly on her sweet cherry lips right there in
Portsmouth Square.

"*Unhand* that fair kicky-wicky, Sir Benjamin—you're in *Dai Fou*, man,
not Sodom or Gomorrah!" It was Ashby, prancing toward them. From the
moment Ashby had discovered that the local Chinese called San Francisco
Dai Fou, or "big city," he had followed suit. In London, he had regularly

created a stir with this sort of loud, theatrical remark in public. But here no one gave him even a glance. "Knowles, you are a low, mindless lewdster."

How strange. This scene already happened. Eighteen months before, Ben had been waiting in a gay, foreign, venturesome city at sunset for Lloyd Ashby to meet him at a certain corner (where the Rue des Martyrs intersected the Boulevard des Martyrs). A pretty girl in a soiled silk dress (looking like a prostitute or an actress) had walked quickly toward him from his left down an alley, carrying a stick, and spoken to him—and then Ashby had appeared across the street on his right, shouting and teasing about lechery . . .

"How strange," Ben said.

Polly touched his hand. "Are you quite all right?" She wondered if he had been stricken by the heat, or a new pang of grief over Skaggs, whom his old friend resembled so.

"Shall we sit down before we walk," Ashby asked, "and have a cup of something cold?"

"No, no, I am fine. But what has just happened here, our rendezvous, Polly's arrival first from over there, then you from that direction, her parasol, the dress, even the words of your jest, Ashby, I—it was a repetition of the first minutes of our night together in Paris, do you remember? A virtual *recital*. It was uncanny."

"A refrain," Ashby said, then clasped his hands in front of him like a priest. " 'The thing that hath been,' " he said in a reverent drone, " 'it is that which shall be; and that which is done is that which shall be done: and there is no new thing under the sun.' " He dropped his hands. "You do not suppose, do you, that as in Paris last February, the noisy fellow over there"—he pointed at Frémont and his crowd—"is electrifying this rabble to take up arms and overthrow the . . . *ah,* there's the rub with your uncanny recurrence, is it not? For what tyranny exists here that one would wish to overthrow?"

"The tyranny of the male sex, perhaps," Polly suggested.

"Or of gold," said Ben as they walked past Frémont toward Little Chile. "The hunger for it."

"The wise heathens of China," Ashby said, "believe that the cause of *all* suffering is desire. Perhaps, Knowles, you are a Buddhist. Perhaps your flash of insight, of your life repeating, was a Buddhist revelation." He explained that the Buddhists believe that the world and the universe have been destroyed and remade over and over again. "Everything repeats, perpetually."

Skaggs had once joked that Ben was a devotee of the Buddha, he recalled now.

Polly had never heard of Buddhism, and she was fascinated. "Over how long a period does this supposed recurrence of events take place?" she asked Ashby. "How long is the cycle?"

"Longer than eighteen months, I am afraid. A bit more than a thousand million years, by way of four stages—creation, another stage, then another, then destruction, creation once again, and so on."

"I wonder," she said after a while, making slow loops with her forefinger, "if it is best imagined as a *circle,* round and round exactly the same each thousand million years . . . or rather a *spiral,* where nature and mankind changes and improves a little each time. Inches upward." Polly considered this. "I hope it is an upward spiral."

They walked the rest of the way in silence.

Ben thought of Skaggs again, and their conversation last winter in Ashbyville about the planets and stars springing open like a blossom, then shrinking and dying from gravity's pull, then reblossoming, on and on forever.

And Ashby—his recitation of Scripture, his talk of cycles of destruction and creation—had reminded Polly, of course, of her missing little brother.

late 1849 and 1850

. . .

northern California

*D*UFF WAS ON an extended retreat, roaming the beaches and woods and cliffs in solitude, mourning Yauka, reciting the rosary and Act of Contrition. He feasted on seeds and insects and wild fruits, catalogued the fragrances of nature in his journal, followed monarchs every which way through the sunlight and ferns to wherever they happened to lead him, slept on beds of moss beside giant sequoias. His remaining share of the Ashbyville gold, eight pounds strapped under Jenny Lind's saddle, could sustain him for a long, long time, perhaps forever.

At a store in Bodega, on one of his rare visits to a town or camp to buy supplies, he'd heard men talking of John C. Frémont, and the rich lode he had discovered in the San Joaquin Valley. Duff had turned away and pretended to examine barrels of corn, praying for strength to keep his promise to God—*Avenge not myself, vengeance is the Lord's, forgive those who trespass against us*—and made the sign of the cross. Then he'd heard one of the men say that Frémont's ranch was at the head of Mariposas Creek, the Rancho de las Mariposas. The creek of the *butterflies*. The ranch of the *butterflies*. Duff took this as a message from the Lord, and prayed for some understanding of its meaning, and crossed himself again as he stared into an open cask of Chinese oolong tea.

When the weather turned cool, Duff built himself a small *hu*, and an adjacent stall for Jenny Lind. After the rainy season began he spoke to no one but the donkey for two months. Finally, one day in December, he returned to Bodega. As he was paying for his pounds of dried beef and beans and flour and salt he read a story in an *Alta California* on the counter. Peter Burnett, the man he had heard making the speech in the street in Sacramento City urging the extermination of California's Indians, had been elected the first governor of the territory. And John Charles Frémont had been elected to the U.S. Senate.

Duff wanted to keep his promise to God. He did not want to kill any more villains. But his rage burned.

San Francisco

TWO DAYS BEFORE Christmas of 1849, Duff crept into the city. He attended Sunday Mass at St. Francis of Assisi, and just before midnight he found the address. He stared for a long time in the darkness.

He could not bring himself to knock at the door. They were surely asleep. And besides, what if Timothy had told Polly about all of Duff's lies and dark deeds? If so, Duff could not bear for her to see him. She might *say* she still loved him, but he knew that only God could forgive such sins as his.

He was pleased to see the house where she and Ben lived, however, to smell the flowers on the alder trees growing in their little front yard and the piñon smoke coming from their chimney.

It also relieved him that their house was a full mile west of downtown, safely away from the wicked, dangerous hurly-burly around the plaza.

What's more, a stiff wind was blowing from the west that night.

AROUND SIX O'CLOCK in the morning, a fire started in Dennison's Exchange, on the corner of the plaza. Dennison's was the only San Francisco gambling hell Duff had ever visited, the night with Polly and Ben when they heard the Hutchinsons' song about California and learned that Abby Hutchinson had married a Wall Street man, and seen the Maidu whores.

The fire spread quickly back through the block, with the west wind, toward the water. By dawn on the morning of the day before Christmas, fifty buildings between Kearny and the wharves—brothels, saloons, banks— were ablaze. *The Lord rained upon Sodom and upon Gomorrah brimstone and fire from the Lord out of heaven.*

· · ·

THREE WEEKS LATER, a small earthquake struck San Francisco. On the same day, the city's first dramatic production premiered at a new theater in Washington Street. Its author, James Sheridan Knowles (an Irishman and no relation), was also the author of *The Hunchback and the Dumb Belle,* the comedy Polly considered one of her New York stage triumphs. The play that was produced in San Francisco had been mounted in London originally, years before, at Covent Garden. In fact, it was the first play Ben had ever attended, and he remembered it fondly. It was called *The Wife.*

A NEW SALOON and gambling hall was built almost immediately on the ashes of Dennison's after the Christmas Eve fire, but on the following fourth of May, during its first weeks of operation, the new place caught fire and started a blaze that burned once again through the same block, this time destroying several times as many brothels and saloons and banks. . . . *brimstone and fire from the Lord out of heaven. And he overthrew those cities . . .* They were rebuilt. In June, a third great third fire destroyed 125 buildings.

They were all rebuilt. Three more big fires burned downtown San Francisco that year. But all those hundreds of buildings, too, were rebuilt, and more after those, which burned again, and were rebuilt.

Cambridge, Massachusetts

ON A SUMMER night nearly a year to the day after Timothy Skaggs died, a photographer and an astronomer used the Great Refractor at Harvard to take the first stellar photograph using a telescope. It required an exposure of one hundred seconds. The star was Vega.

ACKNOWLEDGMENTS

——➤•◄——

SUZANNE GLUCK IS the perfect agent, and her colleague Erin Malone a delight.

At Random House, Peter Olson and Ann Godoff believed in this book when it was just an idea; Gina Centrello kept the faith; and Jennifer Hershey—with the cheerful, unfailing assistance of Laura Ford—not only believed in it but made the actual thing much better, single-handedly disproving the notion that book editors no longer edit. The copy editing by Amy Robbins and Steve Messina was intelligent and scrupulous far beyond the call of duty. And the designers Gabrielle Bordwin, Robbin Schiff, and Stephanie Huntwork made the book look perfect. Thanks to them all.

Tom Dyja and Michael Jackson each provided important bits of research, and I am indebted to the work of many dozens of authors and scholars. Three online reference resources were indispensable every day: Making of America, the library of hundreds of nineteenth-century books and periodicals assembled and digitized by Cornell University and the University of Michigan; Noah Webster's 1828 *American Dictionary of the English Language*, maintained by a company called Christian Technologies; and Douglas Harper's amazing Online Etymology Dictionary.

Martin Pedersen enthusiastically published early portions of chapters 2 and 26 in *Metropolis*. Joanne Gruber's editorial suggestions and corrections were brilliant and invaluable. Susanna Moore and Alessandra Stanley were acute, generous readers as well—and Alessandra, along with Susan Horton and Eric Rayman, helped me get the French right.

And thank heavens for Anne Kreamer, who is essential.

KURT ANDERSEN is the author of the novel *Turn of the Century* and *The Real Thing*, a collection of essays. He writes for *New York* magazine, of which he was previously editor in chief, and has written columns for *The New Yorker* and *Time* as well. He was also a co-founder and editor of *Spy* and hosts the public radio program *Studio 360*. Andersen lives with his wife and daughters in New York City.

ABOUT THE TYPE

This book is set in Fournier, a typeface named for
Pierre Simon Fournier, the youngest son of a French
printing family. He started out engraving woodblocks
and large capitals, then moved on to fonts of type. In
1736 he began his own foundry and made several important contributions in the field of type design; he is
said to have cut 147 alphabets of his own creation.
Fournier is probably best remembered as the designer
of St. Augustine Ordinaire, a face that served as the
model for Monotype's Fournier, which was released
in 1925.